PRAIRIE FIRE

Other Books by Dan Armstrong

Taming the Dragon
Puddle of Love
Chain of Souls
The Open Secret
The Eyes of Archimedes I
The Siege of Syracuse
The Eyes of Archimedes II
The Death of Marcellus
The Eyes of Archimedes III
Zama
Cornelia: First Woman of Rome
Blake College
The Jewel Case
Sir Gawain and the Green Knight
Quicksand
Princeton Charlie's got the Blues
Stella: The Mushroom Girl from Outer Space

PRAIRIE FIRE

An American Tragedy

A Novel

Dan Armstrong

To Bill,
Live, love,
Struggle!
Dan
9/13/2025

Mud City Press
Eugene, Oregon

Prairie Fire

Published by
Mud City Press
http://www.mudcitypress.com
Eugene, Oregon

Acknowledgement is made to the following publishers for permission to quote from song lyrics:

ISBN 978-0-9830045-1-6

Printed in the United States

To Judith

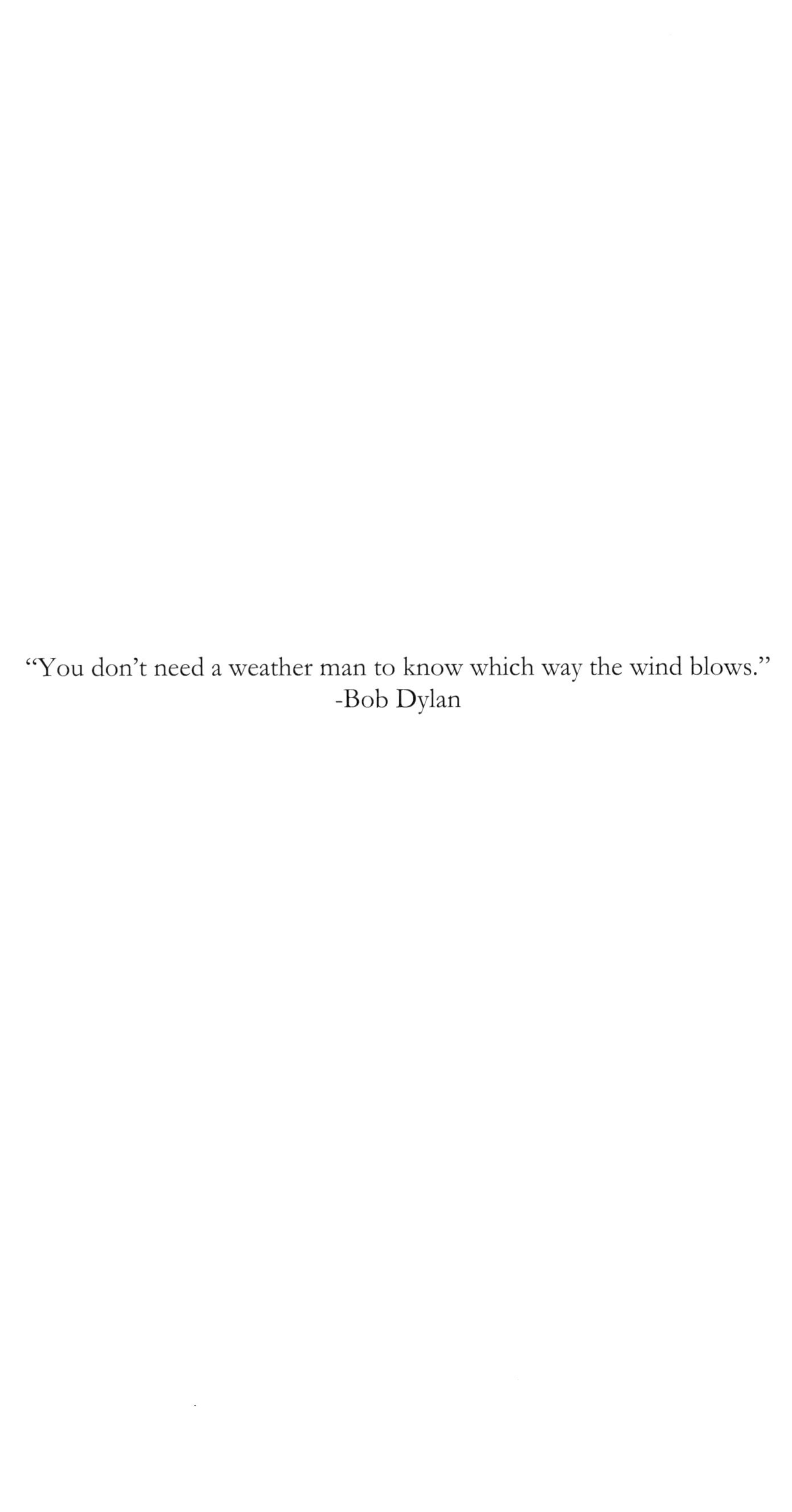

"You don't need a weather man to know which way the wind blows."
-Bob Dylan

PROLOGUE

There was something weighing on Nathaniel Cromwell as he went to bed the night of June 21st. There was something weighing on all the farmers across America's heartland as spring turned to summer and the winter wheat ripened for harvest. The American farm community had been up against it many times in the past one hundred years, but well into the third millennium, things seemed different, more urgent. Talk at dinner tables across the Midwest during the middle of June grew tough and caustic—or gave in to glum silence.

The farmers were frustrated for a whole lot of reasons, from subsidy politics to the skyrocketing price of petroleum products to recent fluctuations in the grain market. *Fluctuations, hell, out and out manipulation is what a lot of folks were saying!* One way or the other, all agreed. Things had been pinching in pretty hard on the small guy of late. The cost of farming, human and financial, didn't quite seem worth it anymore.

Nathaniel Cromwell knew the story as well as anyone. Although he'd spent sixteen years in the Army, he was a third-generation farmer and for the past ten years had raised wheat and feed-grade corn on the Kansas farm he'd grown up on. After a long day of work, the retired Colonel went to bed early on the twenty-first of June with all the same questions in his head that his neighbors had, figuring good times and bad times were like the weather—they came and they went. But he woke from a restless sleep that night just before two a.m. with light filtering into the room like it was daybreak. He rolled out of bed rubbing his eyes and crossed the room to the window. He pushed aside the curtains to the sight of flames flaring all across the western horizon as far as he could see.

Cromwell pulled on his jeans and boots half asleep, stumbled down the hallway, denied what he was thinking, and shouted out to his son in full alarm. "Will, get up! Quick! There's a fire at Tom's place."

His mother Mary appeared in the doorway to her room in a worn flannel nightgown. "What's going on, Nate?" Her tone suggested she already knew.

Cromwell was punching numbers into the kitchen phone. "Big fire at Foster's, Ma." He glared at the receiver. "And their phone's out of order! Call 911. Tell Will to follow me in his jeep. I'm outta here."

Cromwell burst out the back door and into his pickup. Nothing but a cloud of dust down a half-mile of driveway, he slid into a left climbing through gears like surges of adrenaline headed south on Route 6. He drove like he didn't know what was going on, but he knew. In his gut he knew.

Three miles down the road, he spotted two pickups pulled off at the edge of a scorched and smoldering wheat field. He recognized his neighbors right away. Horace Thompson hung on to a CB mike stretched out the window of his Ford. James Peabody, the county grange rep, knelt on one knee like he always did, a fist to his chin. Standing beside him was Tom Foster's wife Jenny, her shoulders slumped down around her waist. All three of them were staring west, hypnotized by the wall of fire lighting up the Kansas night like midday.

They turned in unison as Cromwell's truck skidded to a stop beside them. He leaned out the window. "Where's the containment going to be?" He saw the tears on Jenny's cheeks before she bowed her head.

James Peabody stood slowly. "It's all been contained, Nate. Down the length of Route 6 to 405. The wind will take it to the Little Muddy. No stopping it now. Every bit of Tom's wheat gone."

"Some of it not two weeks from harvest," deadpanned Horace Thompson.

Cromwell glared at the racing flames and braiding pillars of smoke. "How'd it happen?"

Jenny lifted her head. "Tom lit it, Nate."

The soldier turned farmer lifted his chin slightly and frowned a deep inward frown. He'd been feeling Tom's attitude going sour all spring.

"Must have been planning it for a week or more." Jenny's voice sounded small and wounded, like she was apologizing. "Took every drop of gasoline and diesel we had."

"Where is he now?"

"That's the worst of it, Nate." Horace grimaced farmer's joy and turned to face the flames again. "Tom's out there in the middle of it. I had him on the citizen band a moment ago."

Cromwell dropped his head and muttered a low thoroughly disgusted curse. He looked up at Jenny. Her eyes, pooling with tears, flashed with the reflection of the flames. He reached over and flipped on his CB. "What channel is he on?"

"Good luck," said Peabody putting an arm around Jenny. "We just spent twenty minutes arguing with him. He's got his mind set firm as a fence post."

"What channel, damn it?"

"Thirteen."

Cromwell keyed the mike. "Breaker one-three, breaker one-three. Tom. This is Cromwell. Talk to me. *Now!* Over."

The CB buzzed and squawked. A voice broke through the crackle of static. "The war's just begun, Nate. Clean and load your rifle."

"What are you talking about, Tom? Get your ass out of there."

"Just wait," came sizzling back.

"Come on, Tom, you're talking crazy."

Static. Then. "Too late now, Nate."

"NO! Drive out, Tom. Don't be a fool. Blow right through those flames."

"Sorry, Nate. Sorry, Jenny. Speculators ain't makin' a dime off me." The static jumped tenfold…"Not a dime"…swelled to a sharp shriek…then went dead.

Will's metallic blue jeep rumbled down Route 6 from the north and pulled to a stop alongside the cluster of pickups as Cromwell slammed down the CB mike. His eyes swung wildly around the group, held a moment on his mother staring at him from the jeep's passenger seat as though she could see right through him and into the future, then he turned and fixed a long hard stare at the wall of fire burning west like all hell let loose on the prairie.

PART I

GRAIN AND GASOLINE

"When all the various factors for growing grain and raising livestock are included, petrochemical fertilizers, pesticides, herbicides, enriched feed, farm equipment fuel, product transportation, and plastic packaging, the average American family effectively puts more petroleum products in their belly each year than they put in the tank of their car."

-Forest Mahan, President of the National Grange.

CHAPTER 1

"Linda, your piece this morning." *The New York Financial Times* Washington Bureau Chief Frederick Manning waited for his prize columnist's eyes to meet his. "I almost didn't run it."

Linda Bennett knew this was coming. "New York?"

Manning nodded.

They were in a tiny café off "M" street in Georgetown, tucked in a quiet back corner, just done with lunch on Thursday afternoon. Linda looked down at her cup of coffee then up at her boss and mentor. There was no one in the business she liked or respected more than Frederick Manning. He was almost sixty. Under six-foot. Attractive if you looked at him long enough. Sensual if you were patient enough to feel it. Exceptionally thoughtful. Poised. Considerate. Kind in every way. But he was old school when it came to running the paper, and he could be blunt.

"Bernstein claims you used the second paragraph in a column last week—and in another two weeks before that. I know that's an exaggeration, but the point is, he wants you to find another issue."

Only Manning could have said this to Linda without setting her off. They had talked about her columns many times before. She trusted his opinion and valued his respect. Still her emotions were rising. She took a sip of coffee and breathed in the aroma of Viennese roast to gather herself.

"Tell me, Frederick, what do *you* think is going on with this pipeline security legislation?"

Manning's look said he wasn't there to the debate the subject. Linda knew that.

"Humor me," she said as serious as she could be.

He lifted his eyes to the ceiling, almost comically so. "I think it's straight up, Linda. The higher the price of petroleum, the more dear it becomes, the more it becomes a terrorist target. As you've said in your column, half the world's remaining petroleum will pass through that pipeline." He shrugged as though there could be no other conclusion. "It needs protection."

"It's more than that, Frederick. Look at the history. The reapportionment of Iraq. The destabilization of Iran. The two-faced policy with Saudi Arabia. The military presence throughout the Middle East steadily creeping across Central Asia. Someone's got an agenda—and this damn pipeline's at the center of it."

"We've been through this before, Linda."

"But this is what I'm hearing, damn it." The words hung between them. She hadn't wanted to curse.

Manning looked at her, his blue eyes as soft as his voice. "Any chance your sources have an agenda too?"

Her sources were the one sore issue between them. She took a deep breath and let it out. "I want to stick with it."

"Don't."

"I want what I write to matter. This legislation is absolute..." She caught herself this time.

Manning had an easy smile that worked counterpoint to his knowing eyes. He smiled now. "Your column matters only as much as it works," he replied. "If you overdo it, it turns people off. Your influence goes only as far as your audience will take it. Use a lighter touch and listen to your editors. We don't need a column every week on the oil industry."

Linda would have told anyone else to stick it. Instead she backed off. "I hear what you're saying, Frederick, and I also accept that in many ways you're right." She paused, uncertain how to proceed. "But I've become a different person since my father died. Maybe it's just that I still have stuff to work out or I'm angry or something, but whatever it is, I'm more determined than ever to take on some of these issues that everyone else is so willing to ignore."

Manning smiled, a gentle, wan smile, letting her go on because she needed to.

"My father was changing in an elemental way in the year before he had the heart attack. I don't know what he was working on for the Agency—he didn't bring that home, but in the months before his death, our discussions focused more and more on the management of natural resources, particularly how petroleum depletion would affect the global economy. The price of everything, he'd say, is based on petroleum. *What happens when we run out?* He asked me this many times, in many different ways, like he was egging me on—*what happens when we run out?*"

Frederick's eyes reminded her that they had talked this one over before too. "The market allocates resources best," he said. "Petroleum should be no different. We'll transition smoothly into other energy sources."

"But that's not what we're seeing. Petroleum *is* different. Price elasticity doesn't apply. Increasing scarcity is prompting greater profit taking. Instead of conserving the stuff, we're hurrying to an end. The positioning of U.S. Armed Forces in foreign oil regions is symptomatic of something larger, something that's been obvious for years, yet something no one in the mainstream wants to talk about."

Frederick liked Linda a lot. It was a testament to who he was and his real human qualities that he had allowed Linda this moment to make her point when his message was not about content but good journalistic sense and pace. He spoke now as a friend. "I know this last year has been difficult for you, Linda. I've seen it. But the column is not the place to struggle through emotions. What I'm saying to you is out of concern and a lot of experience. You're pushing too hard. For my sake, for your sake, give it a break. Find a new bone to worry."

Linda took a breath. *The Times* was not essential to her career. Over a hundred other newspapers nationwide carried her column "The Global Report." She could work anywhere. Frederick knew that. Instead of pointing this out, she said, "Okay," confident she knew things that would get this issue right where it deserved to be—front page, above the fold.

CHAPTER 2

Jonathan Mayfield skittered stop-and-go like a hustling midfielder through the Friday mayhem of London's Futures and Options Exchange (FOX). Dancing at a run through this grand electronic bazaar, winding around the trading pits and packs of jabbering brokers, Mayfield shot periodic glances to the banks of overhead monitors, glowing with green encryptions like mission control for the world of trade. Copper here, pork bellies there, rice, wheat, soybeans, coffee beans, crude oil, bonds, exchange rates, securities contracts, commodities and financial instruments of all varieties were bought and sold a hundred times over in the flash of his eyes.

The twenty-six-year-old Mayfield was a natural born commodities trader, but he didn't work the floor anymore. He'd done his time in the pits, doing the day to day buying and selling, fighting and scrambling for every quarter-point of margin. He was an analyst now. He worked for Linton International and spent most of his time on the third floor of the FOX logged onto Linton's mainframe—determined to make a name for himself—maybe today!

In the last six months, he'd perfected his own customized version of the infamous *Provide* software, allowing him to interface with markets all over the globe, giving him the largest private commodities and financial market database in the world. And now it had become his most important tool. He ran scenarios on it. He'd input imaginary variables—sets of commodities, timetables, quantities of money, harvest dates, shipping routes, weather dynamics—and run them out years in advance, looking for insights into this market or that. And this morning he'd struck gold!

A little bit hipster, a lot computer nerd, Jonathan was tall and thin, almost gaunt, with a shaggy mop of dark hair and a bleached blonde chop-pad below his lower lip. Today as he hustled through the FOX, he wore a black suit, a white shirt, but no tie.

He nodded to the FOX doorman as he approached the exit. The man smiled and opened the door, offering a tip of his gold-braided cap as Jonathan hit the gray streets of London, headed at a walking run through a light mist to the Linton Executive Building twenty blocks away.

Although excited and quite anxious, Jonathan tried to stay within his normal hacker/slacker self when he entered the building, nodding and saying a soft hello to fellow employees as he hurried through the lobby to the elevator. He fretted and shuffled all the way to the twentieth floor, edging up close to the elevator door in anticipation of its opening. Then he was there, standing in Linton's swanky executive suite reception lounge. A moment later, he entered his boss's office about to deliver what he hoped would be the most important pitch of his short career.

"Sit down, please, Jonathan," said Linton's CFO Louis Hampton, after an energetic handshake and a swell of his usual businessman's vitality. "Now, what's this proposal you're so eager to show me?" You mentioned something about grain on the phone."

"I think I've spotted a turn in the market, sir," said Jonathan sitting down across from Hampton.

The CFO's left brow lifted ever so slightly.

"This morning," continued Jonathan, "I ran an analysis of grain shipments since 2005, looking for fluctuations in the yearly patterns. As expected, there was a slow but gradual rise with each passing year." He edged up in his seat. "But beginning the second week of May of this year through the end of October, there's a notable jump in the number of grain freighters leased for transport in the eastern portion of the Indian Ocean, around the tip of Malaysia, and into the South China Sea."

Hampton's eyes narrowed with gathering interest. "Go on."

Jonathan withdrew a written proposal from inside his jacket and placed it on Hampton's desk. "It's more than freighters, sir. Grain elevator leases are maximized in almost all the Pacific Rim ports across this same period of time. It looks like something quite substantial."

Hampton, conservative in manner and dress, picked up the proposal and thumbed through a few pages, then peered thoughtfully at the young man across the desk with two silver rings piercing his right brow. "What do you think it is?"

"I have nothing for certain, sir." Jonathan hesitated a moment. "But it has all the earmarks of a huge orchestrated buy."

Hampton sat back in his chair. He used the pen to scratch idly at his thick brush moustache. "How much grain is involved?"

"Upward of twenty percent of total world exports." This was Jonathan's most conservative estimate. He didn't want to overdo it.

Hampton's demeanor had changed very subtly since Jonathan sat down. Wheels were turning in his head. Much like Jonathan, Hampton had men above him he wanted to impress. "That's billions of dollars, Jonathan."

"That's the problem, Mr. Hampton. I've run through the financial flows over and over. There's nothing to tie into the buy."

"No clue who's doing it?"

"The elevator leasing is so evenly spread around the Pacific Rim it's impossible to tell what's going on."

"What are the harvest projections for Asia?"

"They won't be out for another six weeks. There's nothing pertinent in the Asian press—no alarms, no warnings. The only evidence of anything is the upswing in freighter and elevator leases. Somebody is taking a huge gamble—or knows something no one else does."

"But you see an opportunity regardless?"

"That's what brought me in here, Mr. Hampton. Whether it's a market play or just a growing middle class in Asia, I'd say grain is a great buy right now."

"Very interesting, Jonathan." He held the proposal in his left hand. "Let me read through this over the weekend. You get back to the computer. Rerun your programs. Double-check, triple-check everything. Work out a buying plan. Get me something more by Monday."

"Yes, sir." Jonathan stood to leave, thrilled by the excitement he sensed in his boss.

Hampton stopped him. "Who knows about this, Jonathan?"

"Only the two of us, sir."

"Keep it that way."

Jonathan exited the office and walked across the reception area to the elevator. Once inside and the door closed, he balled his right hand into a fist and gave it a hard celebratory pump. "*Yes!*"

Meanwhile, in the executive office, Hampton punched three numbers into the secure phone on his desk. It was a direct line to Linton's mother company, Canada's Andreas Grain. When the secretary in Toronto answered, Hampton went straight to the top. "Curtis LaPalme, please."

CHAPTER 3

Seated in the dining room of the historic Nelson Mansion in Newport, Rhode Island, three major players in the prestigious Council of American Policy and their hostess watched the hired help clear the table. The casual talk during the meal was about to give way to the reason they had dined together on this Saturday evening.

Atossa Andreas-Nelson lived alone in her grand Newport mansion and sat at the head of the table, wearing an all-black, high-collared, long-sleeved dress. Her ebony hair was pulled into a tight bun at the back of her head. A black net pinned to her hair veiled her face. She was fifty-seven years old and sole heiress to Canada's Andreas Grain. Her brother-in-law Frank Nelson, President of American Bank and Chairman of the board of Merit Oil, sat opposite her at the other end of the table. To her right was the wheelchair bound Secretary of Defense Lawrence Fitzgerald. To her left sat the inveterate Wall Street lawyer John A. McClay. All three men wore dark conservative suits.

Two tall antique candelabras at either end of the table provided the only light in the vast dining room, shrinking the sense of space to two hovering halos above an expanse of white linen tablecloth. The fragrance of roasted garlic from their dinner of steamed prawns, fresh pasta, and chanterelle mushrooms still held in the room. A Filipino steward entered the dining room with three glasses of liquor on a silver service. The steward circuited the table, ducking into the candlelight, placing an aperitif before each of the men. The young man passed behind Atossa, who didn't drink, and left the room. As the swinging door to the kitchen hushed shut, John McClay turned to Atossa, then Frank Nelson.

"The House will pass our bill next week. It will clear the Senate the week after that." Well into his seventies, McClay had spent thirty years as general counsel to the American oil industry and in the last year had guided lobbying strategy for the Trans-Eurasian Security Act (TES), a piece of legislation designed to provide American military protection for what would eventually be twelve thousand miles of oil pipeline sprawled across Central Asia like the tentacles of an octopus. "The only real uncertainty," McClay paused for emphasis, "is in the White House."

Portly, pear-shaped Frank Nelson, sitting back from the table with a snifter of cognac in his hand, turned to the Secretary of Defense. "Fitz, what chance does our little piece of legislation stand with Kenaghy?" Frank leaned forward over the table with a presiding gravity that seemed to sag off his face in multiple chins and baggy jowls. "He wouldn't think of vetoing it, would he?"

Fitzgerald had done all the ground work for the Eurasian pipeline as Secretary of State for the previous administration. It was as much his baby as Frank's. The handsome but frail *Skull and Bones* Yalie took a studied sip from his cordial of anisette and peered over his half-glasses to the firm eyes of John McClay. They'd had this conversation the day before with the Foreign Policy Advisory Board. He lingered over the sweet licorice perfume of his drink, then lowered it to the table with a disturbing precision. "Kenaghy is entirely unpredictable at this point, Frank. As far as I'm concerned, he's a loose cannon. Ever since I leveled with him on the deeper intentions of our foreign policy last fall, he's become harder and harder to talk to. I don't know what he'll do any more." The fingers of his right hand remained on the stem of his cordial. He twisted it one way, then the other as he spoke. "He just doesn't seem to understand that TES is essential to our long-range economic positioning."

McClay turned to Atossa, attentive behind her veil. "I'll talk to the President, Ms. Andreas," McClay said evenly. "Given some time, he'll listen to me."

"Given some time," groaned Frank sitting up straight. "We've been working on this for twenty years. We can't allow some idealistic Democrat to start dragging his feet now. Apparently, he has no idea what this is really about. It seems impossible that he's become something we have to deal with."

Atossa stared at her brother-in-law from behind her veil. Although she agreed with all he'd said, she thought he was an arrogant ass. She'd married Frank's older brother, Millhouse Nelson, in the 1990s, effectively merging her own significant grain holdings with the Nelson family's American Bank and Merit Petroleum. Millhouse had died two years ago. Atossa, still wearing mourning black, and Frank now shared control of Andreas-Nelson Enterprises and one of the largest pools of ancestral capital on the planet. There may be no true royalty in the United States, but if there was ever a queen of the world, it was Atossa. "Are you finished, Frank?" she posited with a coldness that made even the old boardroom warrior John McClay shudder.

Frank turned to Atossa with a vacuous smile then took a sip of his cognac. Atossa ignored him and directed a question at McClay. "What will we do if Kenaghy uses his veto?"

McClay was private influence incarnate and all business. "Either we'll override it or move him out of office next election and wait until the administration change to try TES again. It's a delay, but I don't see any other way without undue public theatrics."

Frank compressed his lips to keep from cursing at the lawyer's measured analysis. The Secretary of Defense agreed with McClay. "It's a shame we didn't see this side of Kenaghy four years ago. This last year has been one legislative nightmare after another." He shook his head and spoke softly and downward, as to his after dinner drink. "Why is it so difficult for these elected officials coming to Washington for the first time to accept the fact that they're stepping onto a moving train, not into their own chauffeured limousine?"

"He's a damn fool if you ask me," slammed Frank. "I'm sick of these delays. With a cap on terrorist interruptions, we could go double-time with construction. If we have TES by July, there's still a chance we could have our pipeline completed by winter."

McClay was firm. "Let me talk to Kenaghy." He lifted his B&B and took a sip. "And if he won't see it our way, his term is over in eight months. We'll be fine."

"For Christ's sake, John, that adds another year. I don't want to wait. If he doesn't listen to you, put pressure on him. Tell him we'll impeach him."

McClay lifted his head indignantly. His eyes swung to Fitzgerald who understood entirely. None of the Big Money was pleased with what they'd endured with the latest American President, but rash action was not the answer. A thick silence held. Atossa suddenly rose from the table. "Gentlemen," she said, "please excuse me." All of them bid her good night. She turned and walked away from the table.

An hour later, Atossa paced back and forth anxiously in her bedroom on the third floor. She'd changed from her black dress to a white silk dressing gown. The distant thud of helicopter rotors brought her distracted pace to a stop. She moved over to the window and peered between the drapes to look out into the night. She watched the Merit Oil helicopter lift off the pad east of the house with her two dinner guests and her brother-in-law. She was glad they were gone and immediately began to relax.

Atossa did not enjoy gatherings like the one tonight. Except for the occasional dinner party, Atossa sought little external society and insulated herself from the world in the Nelson Mansion as though it was a mysterious twenty-first century castle. Yes, she thrived on the power of her position, and she felt very strongly about her smooth-running family grain business, but the oil industry was always ensnared in politics and controversy and caused an excess of emotional duress that she didn't need.

She turned away from the window and strode across the room to her full-length mirror. Despite her age, she had maintained her physique through a grueling regime of daily exercise, physical therapy, hormones, and careful eating habits. She opened her robe and let it drop to the floor. She wore nothing beneath. The product of luxurious beauty spas and the world's best cosmetic surgeons, her body resembled that of an athletic thirty-five-year-old woman. She pulled the pins from her bun and shook her hair out around her shoulders. Excessive care, expensive conditioners, and regular dyeing kept it black and lustrous. She studied herself in the mirror, running her hands along the outside of her fine firm thighs and up across her lightly muscled belly, on up to her surgically perfect breasts, massaging them until the nipples stood up.

In contrast to the supple wonder of her body, however, her face was a horror. Half Venezuelan and half Canadian, Atossa had possessed a dark exotic beauty earlier in her life, uncommonly so as a child. Her Venezuelan father fed his massive ego by showing her off to his friends like a thoroughbred racehorse to watch trot around the track. She had loved the attention then and that need for a stage presence became the core of her being. So much so, that early into her thirties, she began to doctor every little imperfection in her face.

Too many face lifts, too many chin tucks, too many Botox injections worked against the natural life and resiliency of her skin. In the last few years, her looks had taken a drastic plunge. The over-worked skin resembled taut, bleached parchment—so thin and stretched her physiognomy appeared etched onto a skull. Grotesque without makeup, merely ugly with it, for almost two years now, since the death of

Millhouse, she wore a veil in public—ostensibly out of grief, but more and more out of a twisted and painful self-consciousness.

Such were the extremes of her looks, her face and her body, the contradiction of it screamed back at her now from the mirror, and she abruptly turned away from the mirror with a curse.

The walls of Atossa's bedchamber were draped all around with thick crimson velvet. The ceiling was high and peaked with a wide skylight angled to the east. A divining table sat below it with a deck of Tarot cards stacked in the center. Atossa crossed the room to the table. Standing beside it, she stared up through the skylight to the stars and a large waxing moon. She thought for a moment about President James Kenaghy. She clenched her left fist and cursed his name and wished him dead—as though the thought of it could make it so. Then she forgot all about Kenaghy and the pipeline nonsense. Her thoughts swung back to her face. The name of a cosmetic surgeon, Dr. Nina Colleen, repeated over and over in her mind.

Dr. Colleen was all the rage of late because of a new skin grafting technique, her so-called *face transplant.* A recent magazine article had described the horribly difficult procedure, initially only used in extreme cases of disfigurement. The face of a just deceased youth was lifted in one piece and fitted to the face of a burn victim or now, for the first time, aging Hollywood stars. For the last week, it was all Atossa could think about. Grain, oil, money be damned. What she really wanted was a face to match her body.

With this idea centered in her mind, Atossa placed a hand on her deck of Tarot cards. She cut to the middle of the deck and turned over the card on the top. *Two of cups.*

"The union of Artemis and Aphrodite," she hushed to herself, then muttered, mocking and sarcastic, "Love for me? Ha!"

But Atossa quickly lost her bravado and fell maudlin. "Could I know love again?" she wondered aloud. Memories of those rare moments in her life of deep but fleeting infatuations ran through her mind, followed by a vivid image of her late husband. She looked up through the skylight into the clear night sky, knowing she'd never have another relationship like the one she'd had with Millhouse. She spoke as if beseeching whatever furies she believed in. "No, it's not love this card portends," she said with rising hope, "but the union of my face with new skin."

Impulsively she reached again for her Tarot cards and reshuffled the deck. Focusing again on the work of Dr. Nina Colleen and the prospect of a new face, she cut deep into the pile and turned the top card. She glared at the card in her hand. "What kind of joke does the Tarot play on me tonight?"

She stalked back to her mirror and stood before it. She stared at the physical contradiction of herself in reflection. She leaned up close to the mirror surface and ran the edge of the Tarot card across her cheek. There was hardly a wrinkle or a crease on her face, but the skin shone like burn scars, not youth. It was uglier than age. It was a mask with vanity screaming out from behind. "Could anyone really love this?" she asked in a soft disheartened hiss. "Could anyone really care about me?"

Atossa crossed the room to stand beneath the skylight again. She gazed up at the moon, and for a moment, just stood there, basking naked in the moonlight, contemplating this great hole in her life. She had a son with Millhouse. Nineteen-year-old Edmund. She loved him as any mother would her son, but it was not returned. Edmund was aloof and distant. *What could you expect from a spoiled teenager?* And then there was Alise, her thirty-two-year-old daughter from her first marriage. Alise had been such sweet child. There had been a deep unblemished love between them for a while. But of late, that relationship had become strained. Alise had grown critical of her mother and her obsessive ways. Maybe that meant she cared, thought Atossa, shaking her head sadly, knowing that if there was any love left in her life, it existed in the difficult tension between Alise and herself.

Atossa veiled her face and pressed a button on the side of the table, then in disdain for her moment of emotion, sailed the Tarot card in her hand out across the room. A soft knock tapped on a door hidden behind the crimson drapes, as the two of cups—the two of hearts in an ordinary deck—fluttered to a landing, face up on her bed. "Come in, Fredrico," she commanded. A young dark-skinned man parted the drapes and entered the room, wearing nothing but a red thong.

CHAPTER 4

Whenever a new politician comes to Washington, one of his or her first epiphanies is the ponderous inertia of the so-called Washington Consensus and the gradual understanding that opinion in the nation's capital is slow to change. The new man or woman might have great and wondrous ideas for the country, but the foundation of American governance has been built upon a long tradition dating back to the moguls of the nineteenth century. Powerful banking and aggressive industry are considered part of the government contract. As President James Kenaghy entered his fourth year in office, he began to question this tradition, and it had become a major concern to some very influential people in Washington.

Early on in his career as a two-term Governor of Massachusetts, James Kenaghy had been tagged as a left of center Democrat. To get the presidential nomination, however, he'd toned down his message and made many compromises within his party and to big money donors in the business sector. By the time he entered the White House, he seemed just another centrist politician with a modest progressive leaning. Tall and angular with small intense, brown eyes and a thick shock of rapidly graying, brown hair, Kenaghy won people over with his disarmingly open demeanor and clear common sense. When he told stories, he could ease into a convincing Maine drawl and be quite humorous. But beneath this façade of casual charm, he was a complex man with a stubborn intellectual side and a lot more courage than many in the Washington establishment initially realized.

Kenaghy's first two years in office had been reasonably productive, but Congress went Republican in the midterm elections. Things slowed down, and his legislative efforts struggled. The truth is nobody could have done much at that time. It was a period of recovery in the United States, and partisan politics wore heavily on the nation.

Then late in his third year, Kenaghy had a day of awakening in the Oval Office, prompted by the dressing down he'd received from his Secretary of Defense Lawrence Fitzgerald. It amounted to the syndicate of big oil, defense contractors, the tech industry, and Pentagon brass reaffirming the chain of command. It triggered something in Kenaghy. In retrospect some might call it spine, but the American aristocracy labeled it belligerence. And since the New Year, he was looking more like the outspoken governor most thought had been left back in Massachusetts. Washington was displeased and wanted him gone.

A few minutes past noon on a Sunday in April, President James Kenaghy stood awkwardly at a podium that was a too short for his height before a small gathering in the basement of the West Wing of the White House. A ceremony to present a posthumous Intelligence Star to Dr. Arthur Rivenhouse, a career CIA officer and, in his final years, the deputy director, was coming to an end. The Star, as an inscribed plaque, was being awarded for Rivenhouse's career. The plaque would be presented to his family but would hang in the lobby of CIA headquarters in Langley, Virginia.

Because most of what Arthur Rivenhouse had done to distinguish himself remained protected by top-level secrecy clearances, the ceremony included no cameras, no tape recorders, and no press coverage. The gathering was limited to a handful of intelligence people, several high ranking government officials, and two members of the family. Across the front row of chairs sat Kenaghy's National Security Advisor Don Reed, Chairman of the Senate Armed Forces Committee Senator Raymond Blount of South Dakota, Rivenhouse's widow Marianne, and his thirty-one-year-old daughter, *The New York Financial Times* columnist, Linda Bennett. Standing behind and to the left of President Kenaghy was the current CIA Director Admiral Harry Wendover. And standing at the very back of the small auditorium, off to one side, was the Wall Street lawyer and oil industry lobbyist John A. McClay, dressed immaculately in a navy-blue suit, a pale blue shirt with a white collar, and a red-striped tie.

"It's a shame," said Kenaghy bringing the memorial statement to a close, "that a man like Arthur Rivenhouse will never be widely recognized for what he contributed to the United States. Those of us in this room, we knew Arthur, but he was never known publicly. He's been gone a year now, and to the people of this great nation, it is as though a true American hero never existed. Within the intelligence community, however, Arthur Rivenhouse will be forever remembered as the perfect silent patriot, deftly walking the fine line between being a good man and being a good spook."

This last line got crooked smiles from a couple of intelligence officers at the back of the room, but for Linda Bennett it hit home. Although her father had been an economist and did his work for the intelligence community in an office, not out in the field with a cover, he had often jokingly referred to himself as a spook, and in this emotional setting, Linda couldn't help thinking that her father was now literally a *spook* and that in some way or another, if only as a deep personal memory, his spirit, his ghost, was there with her now.

"I don't believe our country has ever known more trying times than this first portion of the twenty-first century," continued the President, his eyes meeting momentarily with John McClay's in the back corner. "The tragedy of September 11th, 2001 changed the lives of Americans forever, but it turned the intelligence world upside down and inside out. Arthur Rivenhouse made his career in this difficult period, fighting an invisible army of terrorists and subversives. He was as instrumental as any man alive for maintaining a sense of security in the land of the free and the home of the brave."

Kenaghy spoke the words someone at Central Intelligence had written for him with feeling and conviction, but the entire time his thoughts were elsewhere. He knew the heavy-hitting lawyer John McClay was not there for the ceremony and would want to talk to him afterward. It would be an unpleasant confrontation for the first term President, and he would avoid it if possible.

"Arthur Rivenhouse's wife and daughter are here today," announced Kenaghy, "I would like to present this plaque to them." DCI Wendover handed Kenaghy the plaque. "The Intelligence Star is considered by some to be the second highest award this country can give. I feel that the Intelligence Star for a career is even better than that." Kenaghy turned his eyes to Linda Bennett Rivenhouse. She used her mother's maiden name professionally for reasons related to her late father's position in the intelligence community. "Ms. Rivenhouse, would you please accept this award for your father."

Linda rose and stepped forward to take the plaque. There was light applause.

The award surely meant more to Linda than anyone else. She'd had an excellent relationship with her father and had deliberately followed his footsteps into the Washington arena. She'd graduated from Smith in economics, received a master's in journalism at Columbia, then gone to the School of International Affairs at Princeton for a doctorate. The past three years she'd written her column for *The Financial Times*. At thirty years of age, she was single, a shade under five-foot five, and as attractive a brunette as she was intelligent.

When she shook the hand of the President, whom she'd met once before, he spoke to her with sincerity. "Linda, I did know your father. He truly was a credit to the intelligence community." He handed her the plaque. "I wish we had a few more like him."

Linda could only say a trembling, "Thank you." Even though her father's heart attack had been more than a year ago, she missed him badly, and the moment suddenly became overwhelmingly emotional. Everyone in the room stood to applaud as she took the award. Wiping away tears, Linda managed a weak smile then held the plaque out to show her mother.

While others came forward to pay their respects to the family, John McClay, as expected, eased around the back of the group and approached Kenaghy as he was leaving. McClay offered a smile and extended his hand, "How are you, Mr. President?" He was smooth, polite, and full of intention.

Kenaghy took McClay's hand like he was reaching into dark waters. "Fair to middlin'," said the President with the folksy restraint of a New Englander.

"Do you have a few minutes? Allow me to walk you up to the Oval Office."

Kenaghy nodded. He might be the President of the United States, but he'd gradually learned that John McClay carried even more influence in Washington than he did. When Kenaghy had first been elected, his friends and advisors directed him to McClay for assistance setting up his cabinet. He'd spent a rainy afternoon at McClay's townhouse in Georgetown, running through names and learning some of the critical dos and don'ts of the Washington establishment. It had been an eye-opening experience for Kenaghy. McClay had been warm, generous, and matter of fact with his advice to the new president. But there had been something quietly forceful in the old lawyer, and it surprised the stubborn Yankee in Kenaghy how easily he'd gone along with several of McClay's suggestions—including his biggest mistake, placing the hawk Lawrence Fitzgerald in the most powerful position in his cabinet. That meeting foreshadowed the entire presidential indoctrination process and the difficult times to come.

During the two and a half months between election and inauguration, when he lived at the Blair House in Washington receiving twice daily briefings, and through the entirety of his first year in the White House, Kenaghy had been impressed with the efficiency and diligence of the career staff people and bureaucrats who were the unchanging bottom of American governance. During this time, he was gradually initiated to the state secrets and the subtle chain of command that made the system work for the power players in the background—the captains of industry, their bankers, their lawyers, their lobbyists—the private power behind the public power. Men like McClay.

Kenaghy was no stranger to politics. The attention and embrace of Washington politics had a way of making a man feel important, and he understood that deals had to be made, compromises accepted. Add to this, the sometimes-treacherous confidences of the intelligence community, and the whole process made the Massachusetts Governor what he had always disdained, an insider—an accomplice to the system that was already up and running when he arrived. But with all this said, tense politics can become personal, and Kenaghy had grown to dislike McClay.

As the two men walked and separated themselves from those who had attended the ceremony, the lawyer talked, rambling at bit at first, but gradually working toward his reason for singling out the President. "James, the Trans-Eurasian Security Act is going to be on your desk in less than ten days. It will get two-thirds of the House and a solid majority in the Senate. But there is concern about your position on this bill."

They came to a stop in front of the elevator. Neither man reached for the *up* button right away. Kenaghy had already thought long and hard on this one. The politics of the Eurasian pipeline project had been at the outer layers of the foreign policy onion long before his election. The situation was complicated by the ethnic complexity of the region and the thick threads of Russian Mafia that remained through all that had changed in what was once the Soviet Union. But it wasn't until Kenaghy was actually in office, during his third major CIA briefing, that he began to understand *how* important this project was to certain parties in the United States. He was told that a hand in Eurasian oil production was integral to American economics and national security. This was reasonable enough to the new President, but the language the intelligence men used to explain this and the sense of how much of it was already determined alarmed him. When he queried them about the details, he immediately understood they thought his questions were naïve and almost humorous. This angered him. But James Kenaghy was a subtle man. He kept his indignation to himself.

He felt something of that now, and he wanted to lash out at the staid old lawyer, because of late he'd gotten fed up with the institutional presumption of national security as it related to the oil industry and the Pentagon's priority over domestic budgetary needs. Instead, however, he stuck to the game. "I'd thought to ask Congress to tack on a rider or two," he said, looking straight ahead at the elevator doors.

McClay turned to Kenaghy, a bit surprised at his answer, but especially irked by Kenaghy's offhand tone.

"Yes," said Kenaghy, now reaching for the *up* button. "Those little matters of taxing currency trading and eliminating offshore tax shelters would be the perfect source of revenue for pipeline protection." Kenaghy had pushed for both of these issues earlier in his term with no success.

McClay felt the sneer in Kenaghy's voice, but he let it go, determined to stick to business. "I don't understand, Mr. President."

Kenaghy faced McClay, looking down on the short stout man. "I just don't believe the American people should pick up the bill for the oil industry." The elevator doors opened, and the President stepped in.

McClay followed. "This is not about the oil industry. It's about stabilizing Central Asia and securing energy for this country for the next fifty years."

"Maybe so, but it's also about the give and take of big business." Kenaghy pressed the button for the ground floor and turned to McClay. "Wouldn't it be much more appropriate for industry to give up its post office boxes in the Cayman Islands and take on the full share of their tax responsibility? My guess is it would more than pay for the surveillance system and the military presence that's being asked for."

This was Kengahy's new combative side, and McClay hadn't seen it up close until now. "It doesn't work that way, Mr. President." The tone was that of a reprimand.

"Then, yes, Mr. McClay, there should be concern about your bill." The elevator began to ascend.

McClay tensed but softened his voice. "James, you must know that the most important industrialists in the country have sponsored this bill. These are the same people whose contributions put you in office. Their businesses and their capital are the true backbone of this nation."

"I thought the backbone of the United States was the American people." Kenaghy's sarcasm was heavy. He was simply tired of being pushed around.

McClay got this fully and bristled. "The American people will profit from the success of this pipeline."

"Not nearly as much as the oil industry."

"Let me give you a little economics lesson, Mr. Kenaghy." McClay's ire was rising. It spiked in his voice like a lecturing parent. "The value of the dollar used to be based on a gold standard. Many years ago, Richard Nixon took the dollar off gold and floated it on the international market—effectively floating it in petroleum. Let's call it the black gold standard—petro-dollars. In a word, *oil* is the go in the American economy and has been for a hundred years. Control of oil is the foundation of the American dollar."

"Doesn't the Middle East have as much or more control than we do?"

"No. Not at all—because our position is backed by the world's strongest military. There is no control anywhere without that. And because of it, the American dollar is the foundation of the world economy. Our success is the world's success and our people's success. This is the most profound economic equation of our time."

"Not equal tax responsibility?"

The elevator door opened, and Kenaghy stepped out. McClay was furious. "Those riders would be a huge mistake, Mr. Kenaghy." The elevator began to close halfway through McClay's threat. He stopped the doors with his hand and exited, confronting the President in the hall. "The next election is only six months away." The sarcasm was McClay's this time. "You would be wise to rethink your strategy on this legislation." Then looking around, he noticed the security people and other White House staff in the hall going about their duties.

"Then how about a veto, John?" replied Kenaghy loud enough for anyone to hear.

McClay stood there with his mouth open as the President turned and walked away.

CHAPTER 5

Back in the White House basement, as the last few well-wishers were trailing out of the closed ceremony, a CIA officer by the name of Bob Richards, who'd been sitting in the back row, sidled up to Linda Bennett while she waited for her mother to finish talking to Admiral Wendover.

"It's an important award, Linda," said Richards. A youthful and handsome forty-two, he looked every bit Ivy League CIA.

Linda smiled uncomfortably. Richards was from the generation that followed her father's, and as far as she was concerned, he represented everything that was bad about post 9/11 intelligence work.

"Even if Kenaghy was the man who presented it," he added as though it might be humorous.

Linda tried to be polite. "Please, Mr. Richards, not today."

"Come on, Linda. You can call me Bob." He paused to cast a quick glance around the room. "You have a minute? I have something from Langley for you."

Linda took a deep breath. Her father's position at CIA had garnered a few difficult contacts for her. Richards was the worst, but he was always where the story was and hard to ignore. He put his briefcase on a chair and opened it. He took out a thick manila envelope and handed it to Linda like it was nothing. "Some reading. Might inspire your next few columns?"

"I'll look at it," she said curtly, really very unhappy to have been approached like this in the White House on this day. "I'd best be moving along. I'd like to spend the rest of the afternoon with my mother."

Richards gave her an unwanted hug, dropping his left hand to the curve at the top of her hip in the process, totally infuriating her, then walked away. As Linda stood there trying to collect herself, a friend of her father's, Charlie Patio, touched her on the shoulder from behind. His smile overlaid the sadness that, to Linda, always seemed to be in the eyes of the older intelligence officers.

"Good to see you, Linda." He gave her a real hug.

"And you too, Charlie. It's been a while."

"I'm about to get out. Six more months."

"You're never out, Charlie. Once a spook always a spook."

This timeworn line got a little smile from him, but he became serious. "What did Richards say to you?"

"Nothing of importance. He gave me something to read."

Charlie came up close to her and lowered his voice. "Be careful with those people, Linda."

"Yeah, I know." She looked down at the floor. Charlie touched her arm, and she lifted her eyes.

Charlie caught them full on. "Catch me for a cup of coffee sometime." His tone suggested something more than the words. "You know my number."

"Yes. I'd like that."

As Charlie walked away, Linda took a seat in one of the auditorium chairs. Still upset by Richards' gall, she half-heartedly opened the envelope he'd given her and pulled out the sheaf of papers. *The Implications of Climate Change on World Food Supplies* was printed across the title page. She thumbed through a few pages. It was an agricultural report on grain production. She returned the papers to the envelope and went to save her mother from Admiral Wendover.

It was one of those stunning spring afternoons in Washington, D.C. when the cherry trees were in full bloom. Linda took her mother from the suffocating undercurrents of the White House basement out into the fresh air. They walked briskly down Seventeenth Street past the Washington Monument, then slowed to stroll and talk beneath the rows of cherry trees along the south edge of the reflecting pool. The ceremony had been a formality; nonetheless, it stirred things in both of them, particularly Marianne.

Within their little family of three, Marianne was the one who had felt the most angst about her husband's profession. Arthur loved intelligence work. Linda was fascinated by it, and Marianne found it personally oppressive. Although she rarely said a word about it, the secrets, the secrecy, and the silence underlying everything within their home worked against her, a steady, emotional wearing away.

"Do you still enjoy working in Washington, Linda?" Marianne had asked her daughter this question in various forms many times in the last year. Each time it took Linda longer to answer. "I think it started to get to Arthur toward the end."

They walked twenty or thirty yards to the hum of the weekend tourist traffic before Linda responded. "Mom, I like it here. Enjoy might not be the right word. But, for better or worse, Washington is unique. I can't imagine not having the perspective it allows, that feeling of being at the center of the world, the center of the action." She peered up into the pink and white cherry blossoms overhead, suppressing the frustration these kinds of questions caused in her. "You get addicted to it. You get addicted to being in the know."

Marianne smiled sadly. "Your father said almost the exact same thing to me once." They walked on a little farther. The air was full of the fragrance of the blossoms.

"I noticed Bob Richards with you today. I didn't know you still had connections with the Agency."

"They just give me stuff to read," said Linda, continuing to walk along, knowing that beneath her mother's question was the real message.

"Couldn't that compromise your column?"

"Mom, you know how this works. It's just the subject they want in the discussion. Yay or nay, they don't even care what I write. Just open the argument. It's nothing." But it wasn't. Linda was as conflicted about her sources as was her mother. Frederick Manning called it a deal with the devil. Her father called it *everything.*

"Then why do you do it?"

"It gets me a security clearance," said Linda, hearing the years of ache in her mother's voice.

"How much does that matter, Linda?" Again, the same message behind her questions—*get out, get out, get out.*

"It's like being in a secret club. It makes me an insider. I can know things others can't."

Marianne nodded. "Are you afraid to say *no* to them?"

Linda looked off for a moment, out toward the honking, stinking traffic. "No," she said, fighting the whole thing, frustrated with her mother and her own tangled feelings. "I'm hoping if I hang around long enough, maybe one day I can get into Dad's papers. I'd like to know what he was working on at the end."

Another question appeared in her mother's face, but it fell away blank.

Linda answered it anyway. "Something was changing in him, Mom. Something in his work was bothering him. I could feel it."

Marianne's face remained blank. They walked on without talking, both thinking of Arthur. He had only been fifty-nine. His death was unexpected and sudden. It still hurt. Even worse, there were some questions that hadn't been asked. Linda had been too emotionally wrought at the time to pursue them. Of late, she'd gotten curious. Maybe she was imagining things. Maybe she was just determined to make it all worse by digging at the scab. But seeing Charlie Patio and the things he'd said had been a prompt. She definitely wanted to talk to him.

When they reached the east end of the reflecting pool, Marianne broke the spell. "Do you expect to stay with *The Times*, Linda?"

"Of course, Mom. I've made it. I'm one of the respected voices in this city. My column is read around the world. It's possible I'll be invited to join the Council on American Policy next year. Many people work a lifetime to achieve what I already have."

They were standing still. The Lincoln Memorial was at their back. The Washington Monument stood directly before them at the opposite end of the long narrow reflecting pool. There was a light breeze. The monument's image wavered slightly on the water's surface. Pink petals floated here and there like tiny boats on a mirror. It was as beautiful a setting as there was in the nation's capital. Mother turned to daughter. "Does that mean you have no interest in raising a family?"

Linda stared at the surface of the pool. "Do you know how many times you've asked me that?"

"Any men in your life at all?"

"Men take time, Mom. I'm into solitaire right now."

"Do you ever talk to Pete?"

"Not really," said Linda softly, fighting the anger these questions brewed in her, knowing her mother only wanted her to have a real life—not the reclusive life she had. Trailing off Linda added, "Occasionally I get an email."

Neither of them spoke again for several minutes.

Then Marianne asked again. She would never let go of this. "Is it really worth it, Linda? All the late nights and the pressure."

Linda was staring off at the five-hundred-foot obelisk, bold against the azure sky and white cumulous clouds. She turned to face her mother's sad beseeching eyes. Mother and daughter peered into each other. Linda said what worried her mother most. "I'm like Dad, Mom. I like the work. I like the pressure."

CHAPTER 6

While the masters of the universe were moving pieces around on a chessboard in Washington, out in America's Heartland three men in faded blue jeans, worn work shirts, and baseball caps had gathered at the one fence post all three of their farms had in common, and in the laconic farmer drawl were discussing the most important thing on the face of the Earth—topsoil. It was a slow Sunday afternoon, twelve days into April, pretty much smack dab in the center of Kansas, not too far from the ninety-eighth meridian. The winter growing season had been good, and the wheat was less than three months from harvest. There was reason to be satisfied, but the talk was subdued.

Nathaniel Cromwell was one of these three men. He sat on the fence with his boot heels hooked on the bottom rail. Tom Foster, who'd be dead in ten weeks, leaned heavily on the shared fence post, and gray-bearded James Peabody hunkered down on one knee facing the other two. Cromwell was forty-nine-years-old. Peabody was sixty-two. Foster wouldn't make fifty-one. They were all good friends and had met at this location many times over the years to scratch their heads and work through the problems of running their mid-size family farms—something that seemed to be getting harder and harder with each passing year.

Tom Foster was having the most difficult time of the three. His cap pulled down tight on his head, and so lean he needed to crack a beer to keep his jeans on his hips, he spat on the ground. "This farmin's barely worth it," he said as serious as three thousand acres to plow and harvest. He drew a tin of Copenhagen out of his back pocket and pried off the lid with his thumbnail. Off to the south, the uneven hum of a tractor rumbled in the distance. "Might as well try plantin' seed in this here snoose," he said, pinching a load between a yellowed forefinger and thumb. He stuffed the smokeless tobacco into his cheek, so his left eye squeezed shut and the right one widened. He used his palm to wipe a little brown drool off his lip and fixed a combative pop-eyed glare at his friend and grange rep James Peabody.

Peabody reached down and scooped up a handful of dirt at the edge of his property. Fighting the cloudless midday glare, he squinted up at his two neighbors through black-rimmed glasses. "This soil," he said, letting it sift like sand through his fingers, "is a lot like Tom here." He allowed a tight grin, then flicked his hand, tossing away the rest of the soil. "Stressed and worn out. Nothing but dead dry dirt and petrochemicals. This ain't farmin' anymore, it's chemistry." Peabody was the smallest of the men. The intellectual and the optimist. He wore his hair long in a scraggly ponytail and kept the loose ends out of his face with a red, sweat-stained St. Louis Cardinals' ballcap.

"You know, there is another way to go about this farmin' business," he drawled, looking up at his friends again, a little twinkle in his eyes. Peabody had gone to Kansas State, graduated with a degree in agronomy. He'd experienced the seventies like every college kid did back then. Campus politics, marijuana, the Grateful Dead. But he'd followed his dad and settled into forty years of farming.

"Shit-o-dear," moaned Foster. "Not more of that grange hall agricultural science crap." He spit again, as if in reaction to what Peabody was about to tell them. Tom was fond of saying his education had been at the farmers' school of hard knocks.

Cromwell enjoyed these two men, even ornery old Tom. He'd grown up on this farmland just like they had. But he'd gone off to West Point. While Foster and Peabody stayed home to farm, Nate had a career in the military and attained the rank of Colonel before coming back to farm with his aging father. "Easy there, Tom," he advised playfully, "maybe we ought to be listenin' to our book-reading friend."

"That'll be the day, Nate," spat Tom. "I've been farmin' beside this hippie my whole life. He does a lot of talkin'. But when it comes plantin' time, I never seen him do nothin' different than me."

"Now there's where you're wrong, Tom." Peabody absently picked up another handful of soil. "I have a couple experimental fields you've never seen. Might be about time." He grinned like he knew something the other two didn't.

Tom muttered. "More no-till farming malarkey."

Peabody shook his head. "Give it a chance, Tom."

Nate lifted his faded green cap with the Caterpillar logo on it by the bill and scratched the top of his head like he was trying to bring back a memory. "Seems to me my dad talked no-till every now and then."

"Never did any though," said Tom. "I'm sure of that."

"Come on, boys. Take a little walk with me." Peabody stood up, tossing away the dirt in his hand. "I got a field I've been meanin' to show you two."

Tom sucked at his snuff and spat. "I got work to do."

Nate let out a little chuckle and dropped down off the fence. Not so tall as square, he looked kind of dangerous the way his thick arms hung half-cocked at his sides. But his face gave him away. Clear blue eyes the color of the sky and a farmer's slow easy smile. Even laid over eight years of worse-than-hell Special Forces combat experience, Nate glowed with a cowboy confidence and country boy honesty. There was something else though. An unnamable element. Something immediately felt, but indescribable in parts and pieces, which gave wonderful force and fire to anything Nate said or did.

"Let's go, Tom," he said, no push, no pull, and stubborn Tom Foster mumbled something, then bent down and slipped between the fence rails with all the grunts and groans of a working man fighting the process of aging.

Peabody led his two neighbors down the fence line between his farm and Nate's about a hundred yards. A big old crow sat on one of the fence posts watching them approach. It squawked and flew off as the men took a right between a couple of empty plots ready for corn.

Peabody kept talking. "I know neither of you pays much attention to what goes on at the grange. But if you ever get the notion, Nate—check it out. It's way too late for me to worry about Tom here."

"You got that right," grumbled Tom, dragging along behind Nate, barely within earshot.

"Look at the website," pushed Peabody. "The National President, a fellow by the name of Forest Mahan, writes a weekly column. Gets into some interesting stuff."

"Like makin' farmin' pay," sneered cheery Tom Foster.

"Like fighting erosion. Cutting down on our dependency on chemicals. Even some ways to get more mileage out of our water."

"Water, now there's my problem in a word," said Nate. "Seems like I'm pumping more water every year just to get the same results."

"It's gettin' hotter all across the U.S., Nate. It's this climate change thing they've been talking about for so long. I'm planting my corn almost three weeks ahead of when my daddy used to."

"Climate change, my ass," called out Tom from behind. "No way to know that kind of stuff—unless you been around ten thousand years. We've just had a long spell of warm weather."

Peabody kept walking, talking over his shoulder. "One way or another, Nate, the moisture content of this soil's been on a steady decline for quite some time. This Mahan, he's my brother-in-law's neighbor in Missouri, hardly spends any time at the grange office in Washington. Runs everything out of his home, so he can keep at the farm. He's been tracking moisture content for thirty years. Says it's down by half—less than fifteen percent right now."

"He makin' any money?"

"Hell, Tom, as far as I can tell, he's the most successful farmer I know. Grows six or seven different crops, raises livestock, even does a fair bit of organic farming." Peabody took another right turn, along a row of chest high winter wheat.

"Right here, fellas." He stopped at the edge of a large plot, clearly segregated from the other fields. He put his hands on his hips and stood back, belly foremost, like a proud father. "Now how's this wheat look to you boys?"

Nate responded first. "Well, James, doesn't really look that much different than what I'm growing."

"Yeah," followed Tom, "except this is the damn trashiest field I ever took a look at. When's the last time you cleaned up the stubble, ran a disk through here?"

"Reach down and try some of that soil."

Nate knelt down, pushed the organic matter away from the base of the thick green stalks, and dug his fingers into the dirt. "Seems quite moist," he said over his shoulder as he scooped up a handful. Tom came up close, and Peabody leaned in between them as Nate, still on one knee, prodded the fresh, dark dirt with his forefinger.

"Nothin' like that dead dirt I showed you out there by the fence post. Right? By not tilling, you leave the microorganisms that enable much of the plant biochemistry in the soil, leaving it healthier and alive."

Tom looked skeptical. Nate sniffed the dirt in his hand and slipped back within himself. Being in the fields, smelling the ripe wheat, smelling the soil, it was totally different than being in the military and the life he used to live—before the discharge…

A U.S. Army special operations MH-47E helicopter weaves its way through the Hindu Kush Mountain Range, over the Afghanistan border north of the Kyber Pass into the White Mountains, and some of the most austere country in the world. The big black helicopter left Peshwar, Pakistan at nineteen hundred hours, disappearing into the Eurasian night with a crew of three and a payload of seven, their destination an Al Qaeda cave fortress ten miles to the northeast of Tora Bora.

Lieutenant Colonel Nathaniel Cromwell, U.S. Army Special Forces, kneels between the pilot and copilot, looking over his shoulder into the shadowy bowels of the big chopper. Someone strikes a match and lights a cigarette, briefly illuminating the glistening faces of his people, six battle-tested "irregulars," as he calls them, a hand-picked mix of Army Rangers and local intelligence. The 400-mile round trip into the mountains and back at this time of year is dangerous enough due to the weather and the dark of night, but add their mission, and all you got from this group was dead silence or gallows humor.

Colonel Cromwell turns back to the instrument panel in front of him. In the center, a direct feed from a reconnaissance satellite two hundred miles overhead glows green on the pilot's integrated avionics monitor. A little red dot on the satellite map tracks their position relative to the ground. They've been in the air more than two hours now, and when the sweet smell of freshly lit tobacco makes its way to the cockpit, Cromwell breathes it in as welcome relief to the prevailing metallic staleness of grease and diesel.

"Check it out, Colonel," calls out the copilot over the blistering rotor noise, handing Cromwell a set of ANVIS-7 night vision binoculars. "You've been down there, sir," continues the young man, "what do you make of those dark spots on the east side of that canyon? Those the caves we're looking for?"

Cromwell lifts the binoculars to his eyes and focuses on the canyon wall. He'd been down there alright. Spent a year and a half in these mountains as an in-field advisor to the Hezbi-i Islami guerillas. He'd seen them do things to prisoners he still couldn't talk about. As far as he was concerned, no one would ever rout those brutal sons-a-bitches out of this rock quarry.

The savage Pushtan tribes had controlled these highlands for a thousand years. The English tried to take them out for fifty years in the 1800s. Even armed one set of tribes to combat another, only succeeding in arming them all. A century later, the Russians could do no better. Long ago it was smooth barreled rifles, then German-made carbines, now it was hand-held missiles from China, Kalashnikov AK-47s from Russia, and all sorts of wonderful electronic shit delivered through Pakistan's

Inter-Service Intelligence as a gift from the CIA. Fuck, for all they knew, they'd be shot out of the air by ordinance made in the good old USA before they even entered the warren of caves and Al Qaeda hideouts they were looking for. Three MH-47Es had already met that fate before winter hit, but for the first time in this strange damn war, they had a real lead. If it wasn't the Big Daddy, it was one of his chieftains.

"That's my take, Lieutenant," growls Cromwell, lowering the binoculars. "Get this thing down low and slip in as close as you dare."

The pilot grins at Cromwell. "Your boys got snowboards, Colonel." He pushes forward on the joystick and the chopper dives straight down. "We'll just drop you out of mid-air and you can shred on in." He yanks the stick to the left. The chopper swings sideways, prompting groans and curses from the people in the rear, then sways within feet of the ravine wall.

"FUCK THIS ROLLER COASTER!" screams from the rear.

Cromwell grips at the seats on either side of him, holding himself upright, looking from the ground to the screen and back.

"Zoom that thing in again, LT," he calls out getting more and more into the hunt. "Is it possible to see something the size of a man?"

The copilot bangs at the keys and triples resolution. Three dark hollows are aligned along the east wall of the canyon just as intelligence described. "At night, I doubt it, sir. We've been watching this location for eight days and haven't spotted anything conclusive yet—shadows and weather make this a hard place to see from outer space."

"Yeah, yeah, don't matter, I guess. This is where we're supposed to be. Any closer and they'll know we're here. Set her down, cowboy," he says to the pilot, then to the copilot. "Map it, Lieutenant."

"Gotcha, Captain Kirk." The pilot pulls back on the stick, and the chopper heals over to the left in a sharp, sudden turn.

"There goes lunch!" comes screaming up from the back.

"Easy back there, Rusty. This carnival ride's just gettin' good," throws back Cromwell, grinning through clenched teeth. Yeah, he thought he had some guts until he'd fought with those Pushtan tribesmen. Man, they had that Jihad thing going for 'em. They go into battle thinking there's no better way to die than for Allah. Couldn't believe he'd come back for a second try in these godforsaken mountains. Probably be digging out some of the same guerillas he fought with ten years ago. There was more than a little irony here if you had the cynicism to dredge it up. Best not to think about it. Best not to think at all…

Nate let the soil fall through his hand. He poked two fingers into the base of a nearby wheat stalk, then pulled it out clear to the roots. He studied it up close and breathed in the thick scent. He dug a finger into the stringy fibers and picked out a worm. "Plant looks just as healthy as this red wiggler, James, roots, soil, and all."

Tom Foster pinched off a wheat tassel and twirled it between his fingers. "Nice and full here too, Jimmy. What's so special except that you forgot to weed this plot?"

"Them weeds and debris slow evaporation, Tom. Hell, Mahan says a season of no-till's worth two inches of soaking rain." Peabody grinned. "I haven't taken a plow to this field in five years. Water it half as much as the others. Cut way down on herbicides and pesticides. Don't use much fertilizer at all. I let the bacteria and microorganisms do all the work. Got about a quarter the hours into this acre as I would with conventional cultivation."

"Bullshit, Peabody. What kind of crap you tryin' to sell us? What's the yield been?"

"Look for yourself, Tom. Started slow enough, but each year the yield's been a little better. This year. You can see it. Equal to any other acre I got out here—for a lot less money and lots less work."

Nate looked up from his kneeling position, worm still twisting in his fingers. "What's your secret?"

"Four, five years of a different kind of soil management." Peabody knelt beside his friend and watched him put the worm back into the ground. "I harvested my last crop of conventionally cultivated wheat in this field five years ago. I left all the stubble and residue in the field. Planted corn right into it with a chisel plow. Once the shoots began to appear, I threw on some heavy doses of herbicide. Later on, I sprayed the field with Furdan for the insects. I double-cropped every year. Starting with two years of corn, then alternated with soybeans, barley, and then this here wheat. No secret. Just been following a formula. You can get all this off the grange website."

"But you're using lots of chemicals?"

"Only at first, Nate. Smart crop rotation is everything. The soil gets healthier every year, so I need less chemicals. The plants get stronger and can fight off the weeds and the insects too. It's not that much different than what the Amish do in Pennsylvania. And they got some of the most beautiful farms in the world."

"And the downside is?"

"It took all those five years to get going, Tom. And a shit-load of chemicals early on. This is my first competitive harvest. I couldn't have done this to my whole farm all at once. I would've had too many years of low return. There's no quick or cheap changeover from conventional to no-till. It takes time and money."

"Great," groaned Tom. "Meaning if you're running as close to the edge as most of us, you'll never have the chance to make the switch."

Peabody shrugged. "Hey, at least there's a way. And what I did here isn't really the best way for farming in Kansas. Ridge-till is what Mahan preaches. It's not no-till but reduced till. In any case, it's conserving the soil."

"A new farming guru, eh?" Tom just didn't want to hear about change.

"Ain't new, Tom. You know as well as I do, conservation tillage's been around longer than you or I. Mahan's just another farmer. Did some research and took some chances. Last five years he's been remaking the grange as well. Says the farmer's best friend is another farmer. Why not get together a little bit? Tighten up the community."

"Shit-o-dear, Peabody, you sound like some kind of evangelist. I got to get back to my failing farm before you break out a Bible or something." Contentious and pissed-off as he always was, Tom turned away abruptly and stomped out of the field.

Nate looked at Peabody and shook his head. "Nobody's going to change how Tom Foster does things." Then he smiled. "Interesting stuff though, James. Thanks for the lecture. I don't know if I'm quite ready for all this, but I'd have to be a fool not looking into it a bit more."

"Well, I'm not that far ahead of you, Nate. I did a little experimenting with a couple acres here and there. I have close to three thousand more of the industrial style. I'm not sure what I'm going to do with it—but I am preachin' it. Appreciate your listenin'."

"Not a problem," said Nate, turning to watch his old buddy Tom pass out of sight at the edge of the field. "And regardless of how Tom moans about it," he looked back at Peabody, "we've all got a decent wheat crop this year. I figure I can still make a nickel—but not if I don't get my ass back to work. As you say, corn's going in earlier every year."

CHAPTER 7

Jonathan Mayfield sat in one of the two chairs in front of Louis Hampton's desk. It was nine-fifteen Monday morning. He'd just given Hampton his proposal. He was both excited and nervous as Hampton turned the pages and scanned the report, quickly working his way to the back and the most important numbers.

Jonathan had spent the entire weekend preparing a buying strategy. What was happening was much more substantial than he'd first imagined. Over a three-month period nearly a third of the world's exportable grain would be stored in elevators in Bangkok, Jakarta, Singapore, Manila, Saigon, Da Nang, and forty smaller cities around the Pacific Rim. Going back thirty years, never had more than six percent been stored in these ports at one time. Somebody was up to something.

And if it was what Jonathan envisioned, it would be the largest grain buy he'd ever heard of—over a hundred million tons—even more outrageous in impact than when the Hunt brothers tried to corner the soybean market in the late 1970s. That had been a horrible fiasco and had ended with an unsolved murder. But no one could corner the grain market. It was too big, too massive—and yet, with the kind of insight Jonathan now had, smart buying by Linton International would put them in a position of tremendous, almost immoral, market leverage. If he wasn't mistaken, this proposal, this buying schedule, was going to knock the socks off his boss and be a red-letter day for his career.

Hampton folded over the last page, laid the proposal on his desk, and sat back in his chair with his arms crossed. "This is very nice, Mayfield." His tone hinted of displeasure.

Jonathan couldn't believe it. "Thank you, sir." He cleared his throat in an effort to disguise his dismay. "Implementation should begin immediately."

Hampton just stared at him.

"Of course," continued Jonathan, fumbling to find himself, "it will be necessary to keep a close eye on the grain market. Everything is based on a buying pattern to fill those freighters and elevators—and that hasn't begun yet."

Hampton maintained his stare.

Jonathan squirmed beneath his boss's heavy eye. "Is there something wrong, Mr. Hampton?"

Hampton uncrossed his arms. "I thought we had something a bit bigger than this, Mayfield," he said with genuine disappointment, as much for his own expectations as in Jonathan's buying scheme. "This is a decent little proposal. But I must say your earlier description led me to believe we had a much more significant play in the works. Something really hot. Not this conservative little buy and sell schedule." Hampton placed his hands on the desk and leaned forward into Jonathan's pierced face and punctured confidence. "I think you can do better than this, Jonathan. *Much better.*"

Jonathan shifted in his seat. "That is true," he confessed. "It's possible to take a larger piece of the market, Mr. Hampton, but," he sighed, "it's the grain market, sir. Our presence will affect prices worldwide, and, well, the low end of the market depends on grain to survive. I felt it would be better for all involved to be moderate. Bigger might be better, but more obvious. There could be adverse publicity if we make too much of an impact on the market. That was the idea behind my plan. Just like our mystery buyers in the Pacific Rim, I have tried to spread our buy so evenly around the world and with so many traders that Linton's presence would be completely invisible. That's—that's what's so beautiful about it. We can make a lot of money and not be held accountable when the price of grain doubles—which, in my opinion, will happen before the first of June."

Hampton lowered his eyes and slowly dragged his index finger down the proposal's cover page. "How often," he asked, lifting his eyes, doubling his intensity, "does a commodities trader get the kind of opportunity your projection forecasts? Once, twice in a lifetime? Our business is about profit, not social conscience. My guess is we could double or triple your buying increments and still remain safely beneath the shadow of this other operator."

Jonathan's right hand went to his mouth. He squeezed his lower lip between his forefinger and thumb.

Hampton smiled aggressively, man to boy. "Jonathan, you know computers inside out. And you have as good a mind for the market as anyone. But you are young, and there are some difficult lessons that are not trends or gigabytes. I know you will get over this little moment of compassion." Deeper motives angled across Hampton's brow. "Linton has many large and important clients. We owe it to those clients to make as much on their investments as we possibly can. We really do." He lifted the proposal from his desk. "I want you to go back to your office. And I want you to revise this. I want you to crank it up and wind it out so tight it stinks of money. I want you to think like a business man, not Mother Teresa."

Jonathan nodded uneasily and stood. "I will do my best, sir," was all he could make himself say walking backwards out the door.

"Tomorrow," said Hampton with a big overdone smile. "Same time."

Jonathan rode the elevator down to the ground floor in abject silence. He felt both pressured and stupid. Head down, he exited the building into another gray London morning and headed dejectedly back to the FOX. A few blocks from the Linton Executive Building, a black Mercedes limousine with tinted windows pulled up along the sidewalk ahead of Jonathan. The rear door opened, and an older woman with a scarf over her head struggled painfully out of the car. The woman was just clear of the door when she dropped her purse. Jonathan, who'd lifted his head long enough to watch this happen, took two quick steps to retrieve the woman's purse. As soon as he bent down, two strong hands from inside the Mercedes took hold of his shoulders and, with an assist from the woman behind, yanked him off the street into the car. Jonathan was thrown to the floor as the door slammed shut, and the big black vehicle accelerated away from the curb into the morning traffic.

Inside the limo, two sets of hands pinned Jonathan down. He twisted around, flailing at the air, knocking the hair off the supposed woman—noting she was an Asian man—just as a chemical soaked cloth pressed into his face and his consciousness dissolved.

CHAPTER 8

Atossa Andreas positioned herself in the rectangle of sunlight beneath the skylight in her bedchamber. She turned and faced Dr. Nina Colleen, then lifted the veil covering her face. "Surely you can improve on this, Doctor?"

It was Monday. Atossa had Dr. Colleen flown in from Atlanta that morning in one of Merit Oil's many private jets. They'd had a cup of tea in the dining room while the veiled Atossa ran through the history of her facial work and Dr. Colleen explained the skin transplant procedure. Then they adjourned to the bedroom for privacy and the doctor's first glimpse of Atossa's face. She'd seen much worse in her work with burn victims, but none as bad where the expectations would be so high. She came up close and ran her forefinger across Atossa's forehead, then down her cheek. She stepped back and looked at the damaged skin from several angles.

Atossa grew impatient. "I want new skin. I don't care what it costs. I can make you the most sought after cosmetic surgeon in the world."

Dr. Colleen only nodded. She was not an attractive woman. Past forty and plump, she wore thick, owly glasses, and her hair was a dingy blonde, cut short with little style. "Of course, you know, Ms. Andreas, I am not restoring your face. You will not look like you used to. Or like the donor. It will be an entirely new face that I will sculpt out of the transplanted skin and your muscles beneath."

Atossa had thought about this aspect of the surgery more than any other. And it did give her pause. What would it be like to see a stranger in her own mirror? But more disturbing than that, it would stress her most delicate relationship. The transplant, especially a completely new face, would not sit well with her daughter Alise. Not at all. "Yes, Doctor, I am aware of that."

"What about the rest of your body, Ms. Andreas?"

"Take a look for yourself." Atossa began unbuttoning her blouse. "I'm open to whatever improvement you can offer." She opened her blouse and slipped it off her shoulders. She wore no bra. "I don't mind admitting it, Dr. Colleen. I'm a very vain woman. But I have the money to afford it." She laid her blouse on the bed and undid her skirt at the hip. She stepped out of her skirt, kicked off her shoes, and shimmied out of her bikini underwear. With a disarming lack of modesty, Atossa displayed her perfect body with a slow pirouette, turning her head so she wouldn't lose eye contact with the doctor, the way she used to do it for her father's friends as a girl.

"You look quite good for a woman in her fifties, Ms. Andreas," said Dr. Colleen coolly. "Who did your derriere?"

"Dennis Wagner. And hours and hours on the Stairmaster. He redid my breasts too. There's no implant. They've just been cut and tucked."

"Any work on the labia?"

Atossa looked down at herself. "Is it obvious?"

The juxtaposition of Atossa's beautiful body and the sleek slate of her face was striking to Dr. Colleen. She ignored Atossa's question and pondered making the face to fit the body. "The entire face and neck, Ms. Andreas?"

"Yes." Dr. Colleen's distance irritated Atossa, but she knew charm was not what she needed out of this woman.

"There are many unknowns with this kind of procedure, Ms. Andreas."

"I could look no worse, Doctor."

Nina took a deep breath. She only did this high end cosmetic work so she could attend to burn victims at a lower cost. "You will have to come to my office in Atlanta. We will do a computer model of your bone structure. There will be skin tests and some blood work."

"I can be there tomorrow." Atossa strode back and forth before Dr. Colleen, her excitement and anxiety mounting with every moment.

"I will need a no-fault release."

"Fine. Can it be done and healed by July first?" Atossa's annual masquerade bash was always on the Fourth of July. It was her one big social moment of the year and the only time she opened the Newport mansion to the rest of the world.

"There are too many variables for such a promise, Ms. Andreas. We must first find the proper donor. Not only a young woman who will die in the proper timeframe, but a woman whose face is similar in shape and color to yours. And then there is the problem of skin compatibility. You will be taking immunosuppressants for the rest of your life. Even after the surgery has healed, there could be several months of adjusting drug levels to prevent the skin's rejection."

Atossa again strode back and forth across the room. She stopped directly in front of Dr. Colleen, hands on her hips, legs apart. "But if things proceed well," she couldn't accept anything but what she wanted, "is July first a possibility? I'll double your fee."

Nina Colleen had witnessed this kind of attitude too many times to react in any but a professional way. "The money cannot help what I can't control. If everything goes well, July first is possible, but not guaranteed."

Atossa smiled in spite of herself. "Then let's do it!"

Nina nodded without emotion. "Be at my office at noon tomorrow. We'll sign the papers and do the preliminary work up."

"I'll be there."

An hour later, with Dr. Colleen on her way back to Atlanta, Atossa assumed her position on her throne, a gilded Victorian high-back, situated at the north end of the massive formal living room in the historic mansion. The house was originally built in France at the turn of the eighteenth century and had been shipped piece by piece to Newport in 1891 by Frank Nelson's great-great grandfather, the oil magnate, Robert Nelson. The ceilings were arched with massive wooden buttresses and seemingly supported by faux columns along the east and west walls. Every piece of furniture was an antique. Original art by Monet, Cezanne, and Seurat decorated the walls. A three-hundred-year-old, twenty-by-thirty Bukara covered the floor. Though overwhelming and pretentious, it was a beautiful room in a magnificent house.

Frank Nelson slouched on the divan to Atossa's right, wearing a gray suit, the coat unbuttoned and open. An after-lunch bourbon and water sat on the glass coffee table before him. Atossa had herbal tea. They awaited the arrival of Andreas Grain's CEO, Curtis LaPalme. He'd called over the weekend requesting an audience for this afternoon. He'd said it was urgent.

"So McClay couldn't get through to that ass, Kenaghy?" Atossa's hair was knotted in a tight bun on top of her head. She wore a conservative black suit buttoned high at the neck. The ever-present black veil covered her face.

"He even had the nerve to suggest adding a rider containing his offshore banking legislation," whined Frank, sitting up and reaching for his drink.

Atossa squeezed her left hand into a tight fist. "I'd like to have Kenaghy's balls in my hand right now," she hissed in a whisper.

"And crush them like peanuts and spread them on bread for lunch, eh, Atossa." Frank straightened himself on the sofa and tittered nervously at his own ugly remark. Even veiled, Atossa's glare made him extremely uncomfortable.

Atossa didn't smile. Her makeup and Botox injections barely allowed it. But she wasn't amused either. "I don't like the way Kenaghy thinks," she said, taking a sip of her tea. "I don't like the way he looks." Behind the veil today, the once lovely heiress was hardly more than a drawing room Darth Vader, a pair of cold black pearls embedded in a plaster mask of her old self. "I don't even like the way he talks," she added. "Thank the devil, our congressmen and senators need those offshore accounts as much as we do."

"You know what I've always said?" Frank belched under his breath. He had chronic dyspepsia, aggravated by the presence of Atossa. "Sovereign currency be damned. Make it all plastic."

"Don't be an ass, Frank. People would hate it. No real money to handle and pass around. No coins to jingle in their pocket. No bills to count. People like something they can touch and feel." Atossa held her cup in both hands. She looked down at her veiled reflection on the surface of the tea and tried to imagine herself with a different face.

"Think about it though," continued Frank. "One card worldwide. No more cash. No more exchange rates. All plastic. All electronic. Everything neatly recorded by computer. A single international market standard. Think how much easier it would make things." Frank's blue eyes went wide with this vision he'd been pushing at Atossa ever since his brother's death.

"Where's our advantage, Frank?" she asked, not really caring, her mind stuck on her meeting with Nina Colleen, and behind that the eventual confrontation the transplant would cause with Alise.

"Not only would we own most of the money, Atossa, but we would also be in charge of its creation. We would make money coming and going with every credit card transaction. The black market would disappear. The drug and weapons trade could be monitored. Nations would eventually disappear entirely. The world would be run by the clean, clear laws of banking and commerce." He grinned ugly as only a banker could.

"It already is, Frank," stated Atossa with derision, lifting her eyes and distantly appraising her brother-in-law's financially aroused state. As far as she was concerned, these money and numbers men were all eunuchs. Frank was merely the head eunuch. That he even had a penis, let alone one that got hard, seemed absurd. "Who are we going to get to replace Kenaghy?" she asked, distractedly roiling the fingers of her left hand. "Surely not that Spencer Thomas?"

"Well, it's either Thomas or Carlson," Frank answered. "They're the only ones making any kind of show in the primaries. I like Carlson, myself."

"Samuel Carlson." Atossa said his name aloud. "He's a stiff shirt."

"What do you expect? He's a Wall Street man. He wants status quo. And he knows money." Frank licked his lips at the mention of it. "All that's really important is that he doesn't get in the way of the pipeline project."

"That's the biggest thing you've ever put together, isn't it Frank?"

Before Frank could answer, there was a knock on the black lacquered, double doors at the far end of the room. Atossa reached for the button on the side of her chair. The lock buzzed and a Filipino steward in a white jacket and black slacks pushed open the doors and announced Curtis LaPalme.

LaPalme strode the length of the room to where Atossa and Frank were seated. He was a handsome forty-eight-year-old Canadian with dark eyes and black hair, long and swept off his forehead, streaked fashionably with gray. He'd just flown in from the corporate offices in Toronto and, in spite of the travel, was crisply dressed in a black suit, white shirt, and printed yellow silk tie.

"Hello, Curtis," offered Atossa as he approached.

"Ms. Andreas, as always a pleasure to see you." He gave her an abbreviated bow, then nodded to Frank. "Hello, Frank."

"I'm anxious to hear what more you've got on this grain move, Curtis." said Frank. "Do you need something to drink?"

"Blended whiskey on the rocks would be excellent." The steward still standing at the double doors exited from the room. "Let's just say we have a plan." He spoke with a slight French-Canadian accent.

"Please, Curtis, sit down," said Atossa evenly. The sharpness in her voice had vanished. She'd known LaPalme a long time and liked him. "Bring me up to speed."

LaPalme took a seat, and almost immediately the steward was at his side, placing a drink on the coffee table. LaPalme raised his drink to Atossa and Frank then took a sip. He peered over his shoulder waiting for the servant to leave. When the doors closed with a click, he stood, drink in hand, and began to speak.

"An analyst from one of our affiliate trading offices in London, Linton International, predicts there will be a major grain shortfall in Asia this summer."

Atossa's eyes angled to Frank's. Atossa reigned supreme over the grain portion of their empire, but she always requested that Frank be present at any of her business meetings as a financial advisor. Their eyes connected for the briefest moment.

"I got a call last Friday from Linton's investment manager Louis Hampton, one of our most trusted commodities strategists. According to his report, it seems that a consortium of buyers around the Pacific Rim is maneuvering to leverage the grain market when the shortage occurs." LaPalme was arguably the most influential non-family member in the Andreas-Nelson Empire. He'd begun as an international grain buyer for Andreas in his early twenties. He worked his way up through the company and now held the top position in the grain portion of the Andreas-Nelson conglomerate. His opinion was as highly regarded as his loyalty to the company and the family. He was one of the few executives Atossa allowed any kind of familiarity—such as this visit to her home.

"Do we know who is behind this consortium, Curtis?" asked Atossa, her curiosity beginning to push the face transplant to the back of her thoughts.

"We don't." He paused to take a sip from his drink. "They're using multiple buyers, shippers, and storage elevators in such a way as to be all but invisible—until the moment they begin to buy—which could be any day."

Atossa took a sip of her tea. "Didn't the Russians do something like that in the early seventies, Curtis?"

"Not to the extent that these buyers are."

"Really?"

"They'll nearly corner the Asian market in the three most important months of the grain calendar." He took a deep drink from his glass.

"That we know about this now, however, before their buy has begun, amounts to completely legal insider market knowledge. Good research and analysis paying off."

"So how does this work for us?" asked Frank.

LaPalme's eyes narrowed. "Imagine having advanced information on the Soviet buy in the seventies. What if you'd known the price of wheat would spike in less than two months? That's the urgency of this visit. There's a great opportunity for Andreas Grain to go very long with this right now. We have the storage and the transportation capacity to increase our holdings one hundred percent in the next few weeks without any risk—and the likelihood of tremendous advantage by the end of May."

Atossa gave Frank a look, then asked the question. "Any chance the buyer could be one of our competitors?"

"It's possible, Atossa, but highly unlikely. It would be foolish disregard for our many roundtable agreements."

"But surely we must have a way to discover who it is?" she asked. "I mean, we do have means other than market analysis."

"Well, yes. That's why I gave Frank the heads up Friday night. His intelligence connections may be of help. Perhaps he already knows something I don't."

"Not yet," lied Frank, leaning forward to place his drink back on the table. "Who else knows about this?"

Again, LaPalme looked over his shoulder at the double doors. "Only Hampton and the analyst who discovered it. Whoever is doing your investigation, and, of course, whoever or whatever is behind it."

Frank absently pulled at his excess of chin. "What can you tell me about the analyst?"

"The man's name is Jonathan Mayfield. He's worked at Linton for three years. Very young, very talented, and totally loyal. This is his first real breakthrough."

"In other words, Curtis," said Atossa, "we have a situation where we can take advantage of someone else's market manipulation."

"That's right, Ms. Andreas. And if the buying is done properly, our long position would appear to be incidental."

"Properly?"

"That's where Hampton's boy Mayfield comes in. He gave Hampton the draft for a buying strategy this morning. With little or no risk, we can buy in the shadow of this other consortium. We always have holdover stores of grain. Of late we've kept that at a minimum, but even an extra fifty million tons would not stand out with what we've had in surplus over the last ten years. Depending on how that grain is bought and stored, we might even be able to double that amount without its being noticed."

Atossa looked to Frank then turned to LaPalme. "Nothing to risk?"

"Even better than that. In the event of a world grain shortage and a doubling of prices—which is what the analyst predicts, we dump our stocks and drive the price of grain down. From the outside, it will look like we're the good guys because we have the reserves on hand to save the world. Meanwhile, we would pick up tremendous profits with our timely buy now, sell later."

"I like it," grinned Frank.

"There's more work to be done. Apparently, this Mayfield is still finalizing his proposal. It should be in tomorrow. We would also like to know who or what is behind this consortium. But since we have little at stake—some extra grain to store—it's not essential to know anything more than we already do." He paused in his distracted pacing to take a sip of his drink. "Should I assume Andreas Grain wants to move ahead on this?"

Atossa turned to Frank. He nodded an affirmative.

Atossa faced LaPalme. "Yes, Curtis."

That night Atossa stood beneath the wide skylight in her bedchamber. The sky was clear, and the stars stood out like gems sparkling in the fabric of time. Mars was visible. As was Venus. The moon was full and bright. Atossa took it all in. Slowly breathing in. Slowly breathing out. She had enjoyed LaPalme's enthusiasm this afternoon. Grain deals were much more exciting than the oil business. She still enjoyed the thrill of playing a stacked deck against the other grain companies. But the trip to Atlanta the next day and the prospect of the face transplant pushed this other business out of her mind.

Atossa stared up into the stars from the depths of her twisted soul and knew that more than anything ever before she wanted this new face. And the opportunity to reveal it for the first time at her grand Fourth of July masquerade ball. It would be like beginning a new life—starting at the very top. She looked down at the Tarot cards on the table where they always were. With a sweep of her left hand, she spread the deck out across the table face down. With her right, she selected a card and turned it over. *The Tower.*

The image on the card was a tower tipping over with flames at its base and people running away from it. It was symbolic of major personal change or revolution. It portended something difficult and important. Not necessarily bad, but likely to involve turmoil. Atossa frowned at this. She strode over to her mirror and pressed her face up near the surface. Eye on eye, she looked into herself trying to know her future. Unexpectedly the image of a grain elevator flashed across the cinema of her mind, several of them toppling over with grain spilling out on the ground and bursting into flames. She turned away from the mirror, wanting to deny what she'd seen.

There was a light tap at the hidden bedchamber door. She was in no mood for play.

"Go away, Fredrico," she commanded.

CHAPTER 9

Monday evening, Mary Cromwell stood at the kitchen sink and looked out the window at her son. Nate and Tom Foster were standing in the driveway next to Tom's pickup. The sun was low in a clear sky, and the men's shadows stretched across the gravel like long black planks. They'd been there a while, and Mary hoped to politely get Nate in for dinner without inviting Tom. Sure, Tom was an old friend. She'd known him ever since she and Nate's dad William left Illinois as newlyweds and bought the farm next to the Foster's. He just wasn't her favorite neighbor.

Tom was a good man and a hard-working farmer. But he was just too dour and cynical to have sitting around the dinner table providing the dark side of everything you talked about from the price of wheat to rhubarb pie. Tonight, she just didn't want to hear it. It was half-past six now. She'd been waiting almost twenty minutes, hoping Tom would just leave on his own and go home.

Mary peered out at the expanse of Kansas farmland that had been her home for almost fifty years. The driveway came in from the west, off Route 6, into the wide gravel turnaround where Tom and Nate were talking. The yard, as they called it, was boxed in on three sides by two barns, one big, one small, a fifty-foot tall, corrugated steel silo for corn, and their robin's egg blue, single-story house with white trim.

The small barn was for storage, seed, hay, fertilizer. The big barn was the workshop and all-around maintenance building. It had a classic gambrel roof and a huge aluminum sliding door so you could drive a combine right in. A fair-sized dent in the white enameled aluminum reminded Mary of little Will's first try behind the wheel of a tractor. She shook her head and allowed a smile. Behind the barn were two hog pens and a farrowing house. From her position at the sink, Mary could see the corner of the electric blue tarp Nate had tacked on the farrowing house roof during the rain last month. Things were never quite entirely fixed on a farm.

Mary was pretty dang proud of her son. She still couldn't believe he was back on the farm, even though it had been close to ten years. Something about Nate made her well up with emotion whenever she thought about him. She was getting that feeling now. Maybe that happened to all mothers when they thought about their children. It just seemed Nate had gotten such a dirty deal with all that military-political stuff. One moment he was a national hero. A Medal of Honor winner on the cover of *Time Magazine*. Then he was being ridiculed for speaking out against what was so clearly wrong. The U.S. Army being mixed up in the Afghan heroin trade. There was some horse pucky about helping fund the resistance to the Taliban and a lot of other shadowy excuses. She didn't understand a lot of it, but in the end, as Nate said, no matter what color they were painted, Army vehicles were being used to transport raw opium. If he'd turned his head, he'd probably be a general by now.

Mary couldn't quite reconcile the man out there in the yard. Her son. And the soldier she knew he'd been. And what his career in the Special Forces suggested was inside him. Clark Kent in work boots and blue jeans, that's how she thought of him. Yep, Nate was a farmer now. Incongruous as it could sometimes seem. God, just thinking about it made her soul ache. She shook her head again and used the back of her hand to wipe away a tear. Better off here in Kansas planting corn than playing globo-cop in East Ba-jesus, she thought.

Fighting the wind, swaying side to side like an anxious elephant, the big chopper hovers over a flat canyon ridge. One by one, in wild flurries of sand, snow, and bitter cold, Cromwell and his people rappel from the MH-47E. Their equipment is thrown out after them. Then the ugly beast shoots straight up and is gone, to be back before daybreak to this very spot—saved in the chopper's silicon brain.

"I don't know about you Eskimos, but I feel a lot safer out here in these nasty-ass mountains then bouncing around in that roto-gyro." This is Major Jerry Rust. One of three in the group that like Cromwell has been in the Afghanistan highlands before.

No one else says a word as they gather up the gear and look around at hell frozen over. Cromwell slings an MP-5 over his shoulder and draws a five-inch by five-inch wafer from his pocket—could be a woman's compact for the way it pops open in his hand. It's an electronic map, programmed off the computer in the helicopter and attached to a GPS. It marks the location of the Al Qaeda caves and tracks their progress as a red dot on a green grid. The whole god damn mission is based on the fact that no human should be up here this time of year. Even the guerillas are buried deep in their caves, holding out for winter to pass.

Cromwell initializes their drop point on the map, aligns the terrain with the compass, and visually sets a mark on the black horizon to direct their march. He looks around at his charges. Wrapped up in gray, white, and black winter camo and wearing night vision goggles, they might as well be a unit on the planet Mars for the way they look.

"Alright," he screams into the howling wind. "Let's check it off one last time."

All the gear is on their backs, and they line up in front of Cromwell in the dark. He calls them out one by one at the top of his lungs.

"Rust."

"Aye-aye, Colonel." Also yelling to make himself heard over the wind, Major Jerry Rust is the tallest one in the group at a lean six-three, with black hair and small penetrating brown eyes. With his mouth covered by a full beard, he could easily pass for a local. Rust is wise-ass and testy on the surface, but deep down possibly the most dependable soldier Cromwell has ever known—and a superb marksman. His first tour, straight out of ROTC, was in northern Iraq with the Kurdish guerillas in 1993. Cromwell was his C.O.

"Electronics?" bellows Cromwell.

Rust is communications and demolition. "Without them we're just another snowflake in this goddamn blizzard," he bawls out.

"Priestly."

"Yes, sir." Lieutenant Paul Priestly is the intelligence officer and the second youngest person in the group at twenty-five. A light-skinned black man, he's a West Point graduate in economics, was strong safety on the Black Knights football team, and like all the others has grown a beard. This is his first Special Forces tour. Cromwell took him on a recommendation from General Harrison Newbury, the West Point commandant.

"Weather gear?"

"Check."

"Davenport."

"Yes, sir." Captain Lena Davenport is the crew's other demolitions officer. A graduate of MIT in chemistry, she got her masters in plastic explosives at the Army War College and rose to the forefront of her division for her work in Bosnia. Clever, capable, and imaginative with explosives, she's a redhead with freckles, but today her skin is brown, and she wears a false mustache and beard. Volatile as dynamite, but

with a long fuse, Lena, five-three, one hundred and twenty pounds, looks younger than her thirty years—when she's not wearing the beard!

"Got the black bag?"

Behind her beard she grins, then at full volume, "With enough plastic to bring the Grand Canyon to the Himalayas, sir."

"Masoud." Lt. Colonel Faud Masoud is on loan from the Pakistani ISI. He's thirty-six-years-old, thin, and bearded. He's been trained as an assassin, is particularly adroit with a knife, and knows every dialect between India and Syria. As a teenager, he fought with the Mujaheddin guerillas against the Soviets in these same mountains.

"Rocket launcher?" hollers Cromwell.

"Yes, sir," calls out Masoud.

"Alvorretti?"

"Sir." Sergeant Charles "Canary" Alvorretti sings it out. He's the only enlisted man in the group, worked his way from boot camp to sergeant in five years. Twenty-three-years-old, five-six, one hundred and eighty pounds, he's all muscle, half Italian, half Irish, and as handsome as the Devil himself. He has a soft spot for Opera and is here for one reason—he's as fearless as the Muslim guerillas.

"Provisions?"

"Right here, Colonel."

"Jast?"

"Aye, sir." Tenzing Jast is a Sherpa from Nepal, and the oldest member of the group at forty-eight. A tiny brown man with a perpetual smile framed by a thin mustache and long countable chin hairs, Jast met Cromwell on the India-Pakistan border four years earlier on a reconnaissance mission to the edge of China. He's here for his incredible capacities as a mountain climber and as a good luck charm. Rust has nicknamed him the Tibetan Leprechaun.

"Emergency cold weather tents?"

Goggles down around his neck, a colorful Nepalese woolen cap with tasseled earflaps on his head, Jast breaks into a wide grin of fine bitter winter wrinkles. "Aye, aye, sir." His tiny black eyes twinkle through the creases with a snowy ranges' mystery that brings a glow to Cromwell every time he looks at the man.

Cromwell appraises them all again, pulling them in close to minimize the yelling. "This is either a wild goose chase or the most dangerous mission I've ever been part of. There's every chance we'll find nothing but bats and vipers in these caves, and it's just as likely none of us will get out of here alive. I told you this before we left. I'm telling you again—just to keep you on your toes. If we're captured, we'll be tortured." He looks straight at Lena. "Or worse."

"No telling what kind of evil red hair means to these Islamic freaks," sneers Rust.

Lena lifts a single finger within her mittened hand. Masoud turns to Rust. Whatever is in his eyes is hidden behind his ANVIS goggles.

Cromwell pushes through the tension. "According to what we've been told, this is one of the largest remaining Al Qaeda strongholds in the area. There are three cave entrances inside the east wall of this canyon—roughly three miles south of here. There are two more openings, presumably back doors, somewhere on this side of this ridge. If we've got it right, this will be a beehive of terrorist activity with miles of caves and tunnels, containing electric generators, communication systems, weapon storage, maybe several hundred of their best men, and maybe, just maybe, the man himself. Getting into something like this is our whole reason for being in Afghanistan." He looks at his watch. Twenty-two hundred hours. "It'll be light in eight hours. Let's get on with it. We'll verify the main entrance first." He approaches Masoud standing at one end of the group.

"This make any sense to you." He shows him the electronic map.

Masoud nods.

"Okay, folks, let's go." The group shoulders their packs and automatic rifles and trudges off in the snow, Masoud and Jast in the lead.

When Mary finally gave in, the sun sat just above the plain, and the sky had gathered an orange cast that stretched out overhead like spilled watercolors. The Border Collie, Peg, lay in the dust in front of the big barn licking at the stump of her back left leg, and one of the three farm cats lounged on the roof of Tom's fire engine red GMC club cab pickup—with Tom there beside it, one foot up on the custom, pebbled chrome running boards, jawing at Nate.

She pushed through the screen door and headed out to where the men were talking. Tom saw her coming and tipped his ball cap. Nate's crooked smile meant he knew what she wanted and all the other Tom Foster implications.

"Evenin' Tom, haven't seen you in almost a whole day." If it wasn't Tom here, it was Nate at Foster's helping with this chore or that.

"Evenin' Mary," drawled Tom. "Think you'd better keep a close eye on this boy of yours," he said, tugging down on the bill of his cap to shade his eyes from the ember glowing on the horizon. "He's been listenin' to that crank neighbor of ours, James Peabody."

Nate presented a tight grin and looked at the ground.

Mary passed a hand through her bobbed white hair. "Now what's wrong with Jim, Tom?" She was thin with a face of tight, fine wrinkles and bright blue eyes, clearly a beaut when she was younger and looking pretty good now at seventy-one. Today she was wearing a faded blue plaid, gingham housedress with a collar, buttons to the waist, and a matching cloth belt.

"He's got all these fancy ideas about farmin' without a plow." Tom sluiced saliva through the snuff in his gums. "Ever hear anything more ridiculous in your life?" A stream of amber fluid lit by the low angle of the sun squirted from his mouth like a streak of flame.

"Come on, Tom," prodded Nate. "All I said is there might be something to conservation tillage."

"Conservation tillage. You mean no-tillage," sneered Tom. "Some folks always lookin' for a shortcut. But there ain't none on a farm."

Mary wagged her head. "I don't know what you're talkin' about, Tom. But I do know Jim's a pretty smart man." She gave Nate a little wink.

"Well, you've got Nate's Army pension comin' in every month. Maybe you ain't quite so up against it as some of the rest of us." He spat again and squinted off to the west toward his farm. "I been doin' this all my life. My dad and his dad too. Ain't no secret to farmin'." He sounded angrier than he should be.

"You've got to be doing alright, Tom," Mary replied. "We've all had a real decent winter."

Tom grimaced and kicked at the gravel.

"Not the way he tells it, Ma. Life's a bitch, then you die." Nate grinned.

Most of the time Tom could muster a little dry humor out of all the dirt and dust, but he wasn't laughing today. "Mary," he said, turning a dark eye at her. "Farmin' never did pay. Probably never will. But it really makes me sick to hear all this nonsense about no-till and this organic crap. Like maybe that'll make money where the old way don't. Ain't got nothing to do with farming and everything to do with them grain dealers and goddamn middlemen."

Mary didn't know how to respond. Nate rolled his eyes. Let it go, he was telling her. She did, and suddenly they all fell silent.

Nate broke the spell. "Hey, I'm getting hungry. I better scoot the cook back into the kitchen or else it'll be nightfall before we eat."

"Yeah," said Tom. He opened the door to his pickup and spat once more before climbing in. The cat leapt off the truck when he cranked up the big engine.

Nate put an arm around his mother's shoulder. They watched Tom's GMC motor around the yard and out the driveway, leaving a trail of exhaust and the smell of spent diesel. When he turned left on Route 6 and cut across the setting sun, now a deepening blood red, Mary turned to Nate.

"Things that bad for Tom?"

"I'm not sure what he's up against." Nate rubbed a thumb across the blonde stubble beneath his chin. "He's right, though. You take away that money the government sends me every month, and we'd probably be a little more concerned about how close to the edge this farm really runs. You know, if I had the courage to work it out, I'd bet we're making less than three bucks an hour for every little thing we do to keep things going."

Mary persisted. "Should we be worried about Tom and Jenny?"

"Tom's fine. You know the deal. Farmers just aren't real comfortable with optimism."

"Aren't real comfortable with optimism?" she chuckled. "Now there's shining the brightest light on the dark side."

Nate laughed. "Let's get inside. It's been almost seven hours since lunch. I'm hungry."

"Yes, sir." She snapped off a salute. Then she laughed. "That's what brought me out here in the first place. It's time to eat!"

"Shit," Nate suddenly exclaimed. "I was headed to the farrowing house to check on the old sow when Tom drove up. Let me see if she's feeding the little ones, and I'll be right in."

Mary Cromwell watched her son dash across the yard and disappear behind the big barn. As much as she loved having him here, something elemental in her son had changed when he'd traded in his uniform for dungarees. He'd spent two years trying to get that illicit business in Afghanistan in front of the right people. Doing everything by the book. Writing up report after report. Being ushered up the entire chain of command. Right to the Secretary of the Army. Then just when he thought he'd finally gotten the audience he needed. The meeting was canceled. Word from above stopped the inquiry.

That hit him hard. He decided to break rank, go public. That led to the discharge and two more years fighting the system, touring the country, talking at universities, interviews on the radio and television—followed by a surge of negative publicity and another mug shot on the cover of *Time Magazine*. They gave him the full whistleblower treatment. It ruined his marriage. Ruined his life. Couldn't blame Catherine for getting out, taking the boy and all.

All this did thing something to Nate, not something you'd notice if you didn't know him real well, but he'd changed. He ended up back here on the farm, helping his old dad grow corn and wheat. Seemed like Nate poured his frustration into the hard work those first few years. Then William died, and it was just her and Nate for a long while—until little Will came to live with his dad. That made her smile. Thinking of the day Nate returned from Milwaukee with Will and all his stuff. Seemed like the years had flown by since then. It'll be sad to see the boy go off to college in the fall. Thank God, he'd chosen Stanford over West Point.

The screen door creaked as Mary entered the house. She shook her head and pushed away another tear. "Will," she called forcing the emotion out of her voice. "Dinner's on the table."

"Bout time, Grandma," came back from down the hall.

Mary Cromwell shook her head at it all one more time.

CHAPTER 10

Outside the town of Saravena, Colombia, a phone rang on a cluttered desk in a partition office in the dusty Cano Limon Construction Company warehouse. The phone rang two more times before an employee came into the little office to pick it up.

"Yeah?"

"I want to speak to Rust."

"Who does?"

"This is Michael Stewart at Hamilton Heavy up here in California. I want to talk to Jerry Rust. I was told I could reach him at this number?"

"You got me," said Jerry, looking back through the doorway into a warehouse full of oil pipeline and earth moving equipment. He still had a beard, but his hair was a little longer than when he was in the army, and it was sprinkled with gray. "What's up?" Cano Limon Construction was a subsidiary of Hamilton.

"Got the word?"

Jerry muttered the password. "FARC this."

"Jerry, Richards wants you packing up and heading off to Lake Balkhash immediately. Go to the Bogota office. Tickets and all the information you'll need will be there."

"Great," deadpanned Jerry.

"You'll love it," said the voice on the other end.

"*Chupame*," said Jerry and he hung-up.

He wandered back through the vast warehouse and out the big sliding door. It was a hot and humid Tuesday afternoon. He pulled a red bandana from the back pocket of his jeans and wiped his forehead. He kind of liked it here in Colombia. He had no desire to go to Kazakhstan. Afghanistan, Pakistan, Uzbekistan, he'd had enough of the 'stans long ago.

One of the local kids came into the clearing around the warehouse from a path that led into the surrounding jungle. The slender youth might have been eighteen, with brown skin and black hair. A thin adolescent mustache greased his upper lip. He wore red bell bottom pants that were too short, battered black cowboy boots, and a stained white, v-neck, t-shirt.

"*Que pasa, hombre*?" said the boy, chewing on a leaf and strolling up to Jerry like he was an old buddy.

"*Mierda,*" said Jerry sullenly.

The boy frowned and spat the leaf from his mouth. "What's the matter, Jerry?" He pronounced it, Harry.

"I'm being sent to the middle of nowhere."

"*Que lastima*," said the boy, coming up close.

"Yeah, what a shame."

The youth entered the warehouse and climbed into the driver's seat of one of the bulldozers parked inside. Jerry watched him pushing and pulling at the levers, pretending he was moving dirt. Suddenly the boy stopped playing. "You will not be here to help us, Harry? Do you think we can do these things we do on our own?"

Jerry directed his eyes to the warehouse's concrete slab floor. "Forget about that stuff."

"But that was our great fun." The boy pulled a green leaf from his pocket and put it in his mouth.

Jerry lifted his eyes to the youth. "Get out of here."

This response surprised the youth. His brow furrowed. "You are kidding?"

"No. Get out of here. Now. Scram. Forget about me and get rid of those coca leaves."

The boy climbed off the big yellow earthmover. He stopped in front of Jerry on his way out of the warehouse. He spit the coca leaf in his mouth on the floor, then dipped his hand into his trousers and withdrew a handful of the small green leaves. "You must be going somewhere very bad to be so angry at me."

"That's right," said Jerry, taking the leaves from the boy, then watching him run off into the jungle. Jerry walked back into the warehouse, entered the partition office, and closed the door behind him. He pulled a roll of Tums from his pocket and pinched one off the top. He popped the tablet in his mouth and chased it with a handful of coca leaves.

PART II

CONTROL OF THE MARKETS

"As Rockefeller and Standard oil in the 19th century had become bigger than the industrial states of the union, halfway through the 20th century, the giant oil companies had become larger and richer than most national governments. They had romped across the world ahead of most other multinational corporations, and way ahead of any effective international authority or regulation. For some observers, this simply meant that they were the forerunners of world government."

-Anthony Sampson, *The Seven Sisters.*

CHAPTER 11

Thursday, June 18 The New York Financial Times

THE GLOBAL REPORT
By Linda Bennett

Unfortunately, the popular conception of climate change doesn't elaborate an essential facet of the warming trend. It's not just that average global temperatures move upward a few degrees—what difference is 53 degrees from 56 degrees? The increase in temperature means less water resides on the Earth's surface and more resides in the atmosphere. The effect of this isn't more rain, but more extreme dynamics in the weather—that is, a higher frequency of torrential events. Localized episodes of extreme cold, extreme heat, hurricanes, tornadoes, heavy snows, and drought will be more prevalent as weather systems become more volatile and less predictable. This goes a long way to explaining the world's recent grain market upheaval.

An unusually mild winter in the Subcontinent and East Asia initiated the chain of events. The snowpack across the Himalayas diminished by thirty percent. A dry spring added to the problem. Many large rivers in the region never completely filled their beds, and irrigation systems became impossible to maintain. While farmers in North America currently enjoy a fine growing season, across India northeast through China and Korea, the Asian grain belt is suffering through a severe water shortage. Harvest projections are down twenty to twenty-five percent in several critical grain producing countries. A shortfall of one hundred and fifty millions tons is predicted in China alone. The world grain market exploded when all of this became evident last month. Prices doubled then tripled, pricing many Third World countries out of the market entirely.

As we all know, the United Nations stepped in at this point and requested that the world's reserve grain stocks be used to ease market pressures and allay fears of famine. Reserve stocks were reduced from 350 million tons to less than fifty million during a

> three-week grain dump. By last week, grain prices were very close to normal, and the panic was over. In the aftermath, it has been said that the grain crisis was contained through good management in the private sector—and that the free market had responded admirably to a major test...

There was a loud knock on the door. Jonathan Mayfield put down last week's newspaper and sat up on his cot as the door opened. A well-groomed and pleasant looking, middle-aged Asian man in a tailored blue sharkskin suit entered the room. Behind him, outside the doorway, stood two much larger and eminently more threatening Asian men, also in suits. Jonathan stood as the man came forward extending his hand and speaking in perfect English. "Good morning, Mr. Mayfield. How are you today?"

Jonathan did not take the man's hand. He was both suspicious and puzzled. He had been in this windowless, eight by ten cinder block room for more than two months now. He didn't remember arriving there and only dimly recalled being dragged off the streets of London into a black limousine and drugged. He awoke with no idea where he was, lying on a cot in this room—empty except for a closet shower and toilet, a stack of paperback books, a pitcher of water, a glass, and a bowl of rice. All he really knew was that he'd been kidnapped and indefinitely imprisoned. Three times a day, there would be two loud knocks. The door would open. An Asian kitchen worker, accompanied by these same two Asian thugs, would put a tray of fresh food and water on the floor and shut the door. At these times, the Asian men would say nothing, completely ignoring Jonathan's questions about what was going on and where he was.

A week ago, things changed for the better. A chair and desk were added to the room, and the meals vastly improved. Rice wine came with dinner, and *The Asian Tribune* and *The New York Financial Times* came in the morning with an English-style breakfast of eggs, toast, and tea. But he still received no information from those who came and went. Now for the first time, he was being spoken to and it caught him completely by surprise—and it showed. As much suffering from ten weeks of solitary confinement as confusion, Jonathan could only stammer a weak, "What's going on?"

The Asian man retracted his hand from the cowering Englishman. "I'm sorry, Mr. Mayfield. I must apologize for the treatment you have received. It had to be this way."

Jonathan did not trust the kind words and backed away from the man. From the beginning, he had feared for his life. He'd been kidnapped because he'd stumbled on someone's plan to manipulate the market, and they were very unhappy that he had. In the weeks of confinement, he had dreamed up an infinite number of paranoid scenarios—including his torture and eventual death—and he wondered if that was why these men were there now. They'd upgraded his provisions this week as one last grace before they killed him. "What do you want from me?" Jonathan asked hesitantly.

"Please, Mr. Mayfield," continued the Asian man, coming closer to Jonathan, drawing the other two men into the room. "You have nothing to fear."

Strained by the long period of solitude and anxiety, Jonathan simply didn't believe what he was being told. He backed up against the wall, his eyes on the two men in the background.

The Asian man turned to his escorts and motioned for them to wait outside. He took another step toward Jonathan. "My name is Parker Chen. I work for the Development Bank of Asia," he said, then with a polite smile added, "I've come to offer you employment."

Jonathan looked at the man in total dismay. "Do you always court potential employees in this manner?"

"Only in special situations, Mr. Mayfield. Only in very special situations."

"Special situations?" said Jonathan in disbelief. "I've spent the last two months in constant fear, assuming all along I would be killed."

"That was something we considered. At first, we thought you might be an intelligence operative. But after much deliberation and the passage of ten weeks without anyone coming to your rescue, it was concluded you might be worth more to us alive than dead." This was said with so little emotion Jonathan knew it was both chilling and true.

"Are you saying this is an offer I can't refuse?"

"No, not at all. In two weeks' time, you will be given the choice of accepting employment with DBA or a plane ticket back to London." He reached inside his jacket and took out a white envelope. "Enclosed is a contract. Read it carefully. It's open to negotiation."

"Two weeks? I appreciate your giving me so much time to consider your offer." His sarcasm was heavy as he took the envelope from Parker Chen. "But I've already made up my mind."

Chen shrugged. "You would be wise to read this contract first, Mr. Mayfield."

"What's your interest in me?"

"I think you already know." The man turned to leave.

"Please." Jonathan stopped the man halfway out the door. "Can you at least tell me where I am?"

"Singapore, Mr. Mayfield."

"And what of my family? What do they know?"

Chen considered this for a moment. "You have been missing a long time, Jonathan. They probably think you are dead."

Then the man was gone, the door closed and locked behind him. Jonathan stood there thinking of his mother and father. Finally, he just shook his head and reached for the newspaper he'd been reading. He ran his finger down the newsprint to where he'd left off:

> …it has been said that the grain crisis was contained through good management in the private sector—and that the free market responded admirably to a major test. But there is room for cynicism here. It used to be that grain reserves were held by the governments of the large grain producing nations, primarily the United States. Since the Farm Freedom Act in 2009, however, when many farm subsidies were curtailed in the U.S., all large reserves of grain have been managed by private interests. Meaning the Farm Freedom Act could not have better positioned the large grain companies for a grain shortage.
>
> While seven large international grain distributors contributed to the UN's emergency request, most of the grain came from the three grain giants—Carlyle Distributors, International Harvest, and Andreas Grain—with Andreas having the largest reserves on hand by far, over one hundred and fifty million tons—nearly half of what was needed. These three companies were hailed by international food organizations and government leaders as saviors for their timely answer to the grain shortage. But these large companies also made huge profits from the sell-off. Be certain America's family farmers didn't miss this; they didn't make a dime.
>
> One important question arises from all this: Is it really a free market when only the industry giants have the wherewithal to take advantage of major market shifts?

Of course, thought Jonathan, Linton International was a subsidiary of Andreas Grain. The grain giant's perfectly timed long position had been based on his analysis of the market in April. His idea had been every bit what he'd thought it would be. That's why Chen wanted to hire him. He'd made a great call.

CHAPTER 12

It happened more or less spontaneously. Better than a thousand farmers from all over the Midwest showed up for Tom Foster's funeral on June 25th. Forest Mahan from the National Grange was there, and a lot of other important farm folk were there too. It was a somber affair though. Times were hard on farmers and didn't appear to be getting any better. When people got together afterward, talking more farm politics than mourning, Nathaniel Cromwell ambled back to his farm and disappeared into the big barn to repair equipment and think.

Nate crawled under his Alis-Chalmers combine and appraised the knuckle-barking, head-banging job of replacing the bolts that held the main pulley drive in place. He'd noticed it last fall. One of the bolt heads had been sheared off, and he hadn't taken the time to check the others. With harvest around the corner, there was no better time to check this than now. He began by cleaning the dirt and grease away from the big red beast's guts, revealing that three of the six bolts that held the drive in place were badly worn. A few more passes through the field, and who knows, the drive might have dropped out completely. He wondered if only by Tom's dying had he gotten to this dirty job before that happened.

Lying flat on his back on a mechanic's creeper, covered in grease and field muck knocked loose from the combine's innards, Nate used a grinder to buzz the heads off the three worn bolts. Then he wedged a cold chisel up against the first of these bolts and slammed awkwardly at the chisel with a ball peen hammer. The damn thing didn't budge. He slammed all out at the bitch, ten, fifteen times, then lay back on the creeper and let the ache in his shoulders subside. He twisted his body around, adjusted his placement of the chisel, and as he arched back for another whack at the stubborn bolt, he heard men's voices. He cursed under his breath and turned on his side. All he could see from beneath the combine were two sets of legs entering the barn through the big sliding door. He wasn't feeling too sociable. Something in him just wanted to stay under the combine. He stared upward through the dirt crusted gears and oil smeared machinery, gathering attitude.

"Nate." It was James Peabody. "Come on out of there before that monster swallows you whole. I've got someone here who wants to talk to you."

Nate grimaced. He didn't want to see anyone right now, not even his neighbor. "Well, if it ain't that miracle working mechanic down there at McDougald's, I don't have much time for talk."

Despite the growling words, he used the combine undercarriage to pull the creeper and himself out from beneath. When he got to his feet, his green Caterpillar cap was turned sideways, and dirt and sludge streaked his face. He held the ball peen hammer in his right hand and the cold chisel in his left. Thin trails of blood ran down his fingers from busted knuckles on both hands. In his mechanic's overalls with the sleeves ripped off at the shoulders and his arms pumped up from slamming the hammer, he could have passed for the village smithy.

Peabody stepped forward with a man Nate recognized from the funeral. The tight, creased skin around his eyes said he was just another sunbaked farmer, but the pressed slacks and checked shirt suggested he might be a seed salesman. "This is National Grange President Forest Mahan, Nate. Forest, this is Colonel Nathaniel Cromwell." There was a sure pride in Peabody's voice as he introduced his famous neighbor—the renegade hero.

Mahan was Peabody's age, but he had black hair, no gray at all, cut across his forehead in bangs and long around some rather large ears. His green eyes sparkled, and he smiled as he extended his hand. "It's a tremendous pleasure, Colonel Cromwell, and an honor."

Nate put his hammer aside and pulled a faded, red rag from his overalls. He wiped his hands of grease and blood then stuffed the rag and cold chisel in his back pocket. "Nate's just fine, Mr. Mahan," he said, taking the man's hand. "Jim's had nothing but praise for your work at the grange," he added, pushing himself to be sociable.

Mahan accepted the compliment with a little nod, never breaking eye contact.

"Forest came all the way from Springfield to pay his respects to the Foster family," said Peabody. "And talk to you, if he could."

Nate didn't react one way or the other. He was interested in meeting the Grange President. Peabody had been talking him up for months now. Seemed like a decent man. But today, he just wasn't too excited about anything.

The three men stood beneath the high arching roof of the huge barn for untold moments. The smell of fresh-cut hay, laced with the fragrance of sharp, sweet diesel, seemed to thicken with the growing awkwardness.

Mahan spoke up. "It looks like you might be busy here, Nate." He was looking Cromwell straight in the eye. He wasn't very tall and possessed a curious elfin quality. "But there's a little stir brewing among us farmers. Not unrelated to the actions of Tom Foster this week and those other two field burnings earlier in the month."

Nate cast a glance at the floor like *why you telling me this?*

"You got more than a minute?" asked Mahan.

Nate lifted his cap by the bill and brushed a hand through his close-cropped hair, scratched at his left sideburn, then replaced the cap straight on his head, knowing he'd already said he was busy.

"It's important, Nate," prodded Peabody.

"Alright," he said, giving the combine a sad look. "Maybe some coffee will help me get this bad boy fixed." He turned and headed into the depths of the vast barn. Mahan looked at Peabody. Peabody nodded and they followed Cromwell around a tractor and some empty fifty-five gallon drums to a closed-in office against the back wall. It was a cozy little room with a wood stove, a beat-up armchair, and a straight-back chair at a desk piled with dirt-stained papers. An electric coffeepot sat on a vegetable crate in the corner next to a wash basin and two open seed bags. A faded John Deere calendar from 2010 hung on an angle from a nail over the desk. Peg, the old Border Collie, came limping out of the corner on three legs, wagging her tail.

"Hey there, old girl," said Peabody reaching down to scratch the dog behind the ear.

"Need a cup, Forest. I know James is off the stuff."

"Please."

Nate poured three cups of coffee and handed them around as Peabody took the desk chair and Mahan settled into the soft armchair. Nate grabbed a five-gallon bucket from the corner and sat down facing the other two men. Peg lay down at Peabody's feet on the dirty old rag rug in the center of the room.

Mahan took a sip from his cup. "Not bad for barn coffee."

Nate took a sip himself. "Taught Peg here how to make it." He allowed a little grin then looked off absently at the floor.

Peabody leaned forward, elbows on his knees. "There's talk of a farmers' strike, Nate." He said this in a whispering hush, but with excitement, rubbing his hands together. "Got goin' quite heavy after the funeral today."

Nate turned skeptical eyes from the floor to his neighbor.

"Believing in ourselves is half the problem, Colonel," said Mahan. His voice was soft and easy, but the conviction behind it was strong and sure. "Grain farmers from western Pennsylvania to eastern Washington are fed up. A lot of them took that winter cash-forward price to finance their crops this spring. Didn't seem so bad then, especially since there's no more government PIK certificates and interest rates are up. You know what's happened since, and like your neighbor Tom Foster, we've got plenty of farmers saying they'd just as soon burn it as give it up to some middleman."

Mahan took another sip of coffee. "The last two weeks, my phone lines have been buzzing off the hook. I've been at the grange five years now, never seen anything like it. Strike talk is real." He might not be a seed salesman, but he did have a pitch. "I've called a national meeting for next Saturday night at the big grange hall in Pratt. Every state grange will be represented. A good bunch of our county reps will be there too—and surely plenty of interested farmers. Whatever we do, it's got to happen soon. Harvest is already underway in the south. And all our assets are in the field."

Nate looked up slowly from his cup of coffee. "Why are you here telling me this face to face when my county rep could do it just as well?"

Mahan looked at Peabody then back to Cromwell. "We need a leader."

Nate took a deep breath and exhaled, "Shit, I'm no union boss."

"Nate," said Peabody, leaning closer to his friend and neighbor. "No way it can work if we don't have at least seventy-five percent participation. No way it can work if we don't have someone at the top every farmer knows and respects—hell, honors—the way they do you."

Nate removed his hat again, ran a hand over his bristles, laid his cap on the back of his head, and folded his arms. "I don't think so, fellas."

Mahan picked it up a notch. "Colonel, we've got a soil crisis ripping through the center of this nation. We're washing thousands of tons of soil and fertilizer through the Mississippi watershed every day. We've generated a huge dead spot in the Gulf of Mexico with the excess of nitrate wastes. If we don't act right away to change the way we farm, we risk destroying the biggest garden on the planet. This little market tiff is the perfect catalyst for getting things going."

Nate shook his head. "You don't need me to tell people that."

"There's more to it," said Peabody. "We're split down the middle."

"State militias are getting popular again," followed Mahan. "A good portion of the farmers are connected to them. Their agendas are a little more extreme. The rest of us are just trying to keep on farming. We aren't interested in an all-out fight with the government or burning more fields. That's just nonsense as far as I'm concerned. That's why we came to you. You might be the only person in the world the ordinary farmer trusts who can get these others to come along too. We have to get unified. We need a single focused voice."

Nate made no response.

"All I want you to do is think about it," continued Mahan. "Come to Pratt next Saturday night. See what we've got going. Just your being there would be huge. Think about it. Two million family farmers in the U.S. About a quarter of them are raising grain—most of them just scratching by on small farms or leased land. Of the 350 million tons of grain we grow in this country each year, people on our side are growing nearly half of it. Throw in soybeans and we surely have enough influence to pressure the market. Folks are screaming for action." Mahan caught himself. He bowed his head then looked up. "I'm not a radical, Colonel. I'm a farmer, tend to be conservative as anyone—vote Republican like most of us across the Sun Belt. But we're getting stiffed. Stiffed bad. We didn't even get a sniff of those twelve dollars a bushel wheat prices last month. Heaven knows the little guy could have used a little help like that."

"Think of Tom, Nate. Think of those two other farmers down south."

"Yeah, old Tom figured that Asian shortage was his ticket out of the hole," said Nate wistfully, reaching down to pick a piece of loose straw from the rug. He studied it with a frown and stuck it between the little gap in his front teeth. "Farmers tried organizing a couple times before, right?"

"Wheat farmers in Kansas got together in the 1920s to demand $3.00 a bushel. Dairy farmers did that milk dump a few years back," said Peabody

"American Agriculture Movement had a thousand tractors parked out front of Congress in 1979 to protest Jimmy Carter's grain embargo," added Mahan.

"Don't recall any of it working too well."

"They weren't organized like we could be, Colonel."

"Nationwide is what we're talkin," pitched in Peabody.

"We've got computers today. They're in every grange hall—and most of the farmers got'm too. We can communicate all at once. It's the age of information. Farmers can take advantage of it just like anyone else."

Nate drew the straw from his mouth and stirred his coffee with it. "Forest, I appreciate your coming here. I appreciate that you and James have such a high opinion of me. And I understand the problem. It isn't any different than what ate at my dad here in Kansas and maybe my granddad in Illinois. I guess I'd even burn my damn fields if that's what had to be done. But leading this thing. No, that's not for me. I've had enough trouble in my life. I came back to this farm to get away from anything with even a whiff of politics. All I want now is an honest life. Raise a kid and some corn. Stick my hands into the earth. I don't know, maybe it sounds like I'm running away. But I did my thing. And it bit me in the ass."

Peabody hung his head. Mahan just looked straight at Cromwell. "James told me you'd be a long shot. I came over here today anyway. Maybe just to meet someone face to face I've admired from afar. But please think about it. Just come to Pratt. Just be there. That alone would help."

Nate pursed his lips and made no other response.

Mahan stood up. Peabody did the same. They walked out leaving Nate alone with Peg—and his thoughts, starting with the memory of Tom Foster's voice coming through the CB three days ago, then working back to his years in the Special Forces, specifically that operation in the winter of 2002 that won him the big medal and all the damn attention…

Even at double time, their progress across the rough and icy Afghan terrain is slow and cautious. Tenzing Jast ventures ahead scouting, waits for them, then goes out point again. For two hours, they advance in this manner until Tenzing tops the eastside of a stone-strewn ridge overlooking a deep canyon. He raises his goggles and waits for Cromwell to climb to his side. "I think we are there. Yes?"

Cromwell smiles beneath his goggles and nods. He withdraws the electronic map from his breast pocket, lifts his goggles, and pops open the map. He studies the map for a moment, then raises a set of night vision binoculars to his eyes and scans the canyon floor two hundred feet below. It runs mostly north-south then cuts southeast limiting how far down the canyon he can see. He lowers the binoculars and checks the electronic map again. "If I'm not mistaken, Tenzing, the openings to the caves are just beyond the turn in the canyon, possibly right below that promontory." He points southward to a high point on the canyon's east rim.

By this time, the others are clustering up from behind. Masoud moves up close to look at the map. He knows this area as well as anyone in the group. Cromwell hands him the binoculars.

Masoud takes a look. "Yes, this is it."

Cromwell glances at his watch. It's a few minutes after midnight. He allows everyone a chance to appraise the situation and rest momentarily, then he turns to Rust. "What's your take, Rusty?"

"If this is the place, there must be lookouts somewhere." He looks down into the canyon then off to the high point on the ridge. "Best view point is up there."

"I wish we had some idea what kind of electronic reconnaissance they have up here. As far we know, they've been watching us since we dropped out of the chopper."

Rust nods. "Yeah, too damn quiet out here for me. We might as well be cowboys in Indian country."

Captain Davenport joins the group. She lifts her goggles. In the darkness, Cromwell can only see the glint of her eyes. "You okay, Lena?"

"Excited," is all she says.

Paul Priestly and Canary Alvoretti are in the huddle now. All the goggles are up. Cromwell scans his personnel. "From this moment on, we assume we can be seen—so battle ready at all times." He looks at Rust. "You and the leprechaun take wide angles around the back of that promontory—carry only your rifles and the black band radio. The rest of us will take the gear and set up a temporary base of operations about two hundred yards south of here on this back slope."

Rust grimaces. "Hope the fuck the CIA didn't loan them any of these black bands."

"Just get going. We're short on time."

Cromwell watches his old combat partner and Tenzing hustle upward toward the highest point on the canyon rim, then split up and circle around the promontory from two sides. The others gather up their gear and push ahead across the back of the ridge.

They find a protected nook in the rocks and begin stashing their gear. The green light on Cromwell's black band radio flashes. He puts it to his ear. "What'd ya see?"

"We're right on target, Boss. Two large wide-mouthed caves. One smaller one. Just like we've been told. Looks like a road leading up the canyon from the south. Saw two guerillas step out for a smoke. The leprechaun raced off to get a closer look."

"I'm coming up. Stay put."

"See ya."

Cromwell turns to the others. "Masoud, go on up there with Jerry. I'll be right behind. Lena, assemble your demolition gear. Paul, Canary, set this place up. Go through the firearms. Then get something out for us to eat. We have a long night ahead."

Masoud is already there with Rust when Cromwell bellies up to the canyon rim alongside them. It's just as they've been told. A narrow canyon, running north by southeast and three cave openings.

Rust points off to the left. "See down there? Just below that black streak on the canyon wall?"

Cromwell scans the wall with the night vision binoculars.

"Keep looking. It's moving now. That's our leprechaun."

"Man, I wish he'd waited."

"You know how he is."

"What do you think, Masoud?"

He's been looking through night binoculars also. "There's clear evidence of traffic coming in and out of those caves, but I don't see a single lookout."

"Maybe they figure it's just too shitty cold."

Rust looks out at the night. "No one in their right mind would come up here this time of year." The other two men ignore the implication. Rust points into the dark. "Hey, I think our boy is on his way back."

Cromwell uses the binoculars to watch Tenzing pulling himself across the canyon wall like Spiderman. He lowers the glasses. "Maybe he's seen something."

It isn't long before Tenzing is back. He kneels beside Cromwell, grinning. "Ten, twelve men sitting inside the mouth of the biggest cave. Some smoking cigarettes. Rifles across their laps. Talking."

"See any lookouts?"

"Two high on the opposite wall of the canyon. Impossible to see from here. Two more on this wall, right below us."

Cromwell takes a deep breath. "Okay. Let's go down to the others and get something to eat. Rusty, you bring Davenport up here and do your demolition setup along the top of this ridge. Tenzing, after you get something to eat, take Canary and look for the back doors to these caves. My guess is they're farther south along the back of this ridge. You've got two hours max."

"Faster alone, Colonel," says Tenzing. "I don't need food. I can go now."

Cromwell looks off to the south, then turns back to his men. "Okay, fine. Go."

Masoud, Rust, and Cromwell watch Tenzing crawl off across the treacherous rocks.

"Got to hand it to you, Boss," says Rust. "You really know how to handle your men."

"I knew what Jast was like when I picked him, Rusty. And he knows me. He's not a soldier, and he's out here risking his life for chicken feed—literally, knowing the way they live in his village. When you get out here, in a situation like this, either you trust your people and their judgment or you don't bring them at all. The way I see it, within the parameters of the mission, everyone's on his own. Even you, Major."

Nate looked up from his seat on the five-gallon bucket. His son Will was standing outside the door to the office. "You okay, Dad?" he asked, coming into the room.

"Oh yeah."

Will was taller than Nate, but teenage lean with his mother's brown hair and his grandmother's gray eyes. He sat down in the straight-back chair across from his father. He held a manila envelope in his hand. "Who was that man with Mr. Peabody?"

"A friend from the grange." Nate smiled. The absolute best thing about getting out of the military was these last few years with Will, working together on the farm, being a real dad. "What's up?"

"More college scholarship forms. They've got some questions about our income that I'm not quite sure about." Will pulled a sheet of paper from the envelope and handed it to his father.

Nate read through the form, wondering what the proposed strike would do to his income.

"Dad, do you think it's worth it? All this money to go to Stanford? I might not get this scholarship."

Something of the moment was tugging at Nate. The talk with Mahan and Peabody had pinched in at him more than he wanted to admit. And then Will coming in here like he knew there might be some tough times ahead. Maybe he'd heard some of the talk at Tom's funeral. Nate looked up from the forms, his eyes almost tearing for how he felt about his son and how lucky he really was.

"I could go to a cheaper school, Dad."

"Naw, it's worth it, Will." It wasn't the money so much as losing the best hand on the farm for nine months a year. "We'll do whatever it takes. Stanford's a good school."

"It's a great school." Mary stood in the office doorway wearing her only black dress. "What's goin' on back here? Seems like a whole lot of people comin' and goin'."

Nate almost laughed. "Whole lot of people, Ma? Two."

"Usually we got none," she said.

With sunlight from the open barn door at her back, Nate couldn't see her face, but he heard everything he needed to know in her voice. Apparently nobody missed the talk at Tom's funeral. Least of all Mary. Something was in the wind, and everybody knew it.

CHAPTER 13

Linda Bennett received a phone call from Bob Richards asking her to come out to Langley for a talk. She wasn't too happy about the idea or none too proud of her connection with the man, but the material he'd given her in April had become her new bone, and she couldn't help wondering what part of the skeleton would be next. She walked into Richards' office at a quarter to eight on Friday morning, and things immediately heated up.

"You're not telling me the whole story, Bob. I can smell it." Linda leaned forward and put her hands down flat on the CIA department chief's desk. "Why are you *really* asking me to go to Kansas City?"

Richards gave her a gratuitous smirk. "You know, you're really very sexy when you're angry."

She pressed in closer ignoring the bullshit. "What is this job, Bob? CIA doesn't do the militia."

"Need to know, Bennett. That's all I've got to tell you." Richards stood up to meet her at eye level and grinned. "That is, unless you'd consider dinner tonight."

Since her father's death, Richards had been pushing his luck with Linda. One game after another. But she'd come prepared today. Instead of exploding into the riot act, Linda stood back from the desk and offered him a coy smile. She took hold of her skirt at the hem and lifted it slowly. Just as his eyes began to bug out, she reached up between her legs to a thigh holster, withdrew a CIA-issue pancake twenty-two, and leveled it at him. Richards fell back in his chair like she'd stuck a silver dildo in his face. "I'll dine alone tonight, thank you."

"How the hell did you get that through security?"

"I told the guard I was going to use it on you."

He glared at her with a tight, thin-lipped anger.

"Be straight with me, Bob, and I'll be straight with you. Now what's really going on? ATF, FBI, even the Homeland Security people, I could see them getting into this militia stuff. But why CIA? And why me?"

Richards eyed the gun and eased out a sullen, "It's a national security issue, Ms. Bennett. That's how we qualify. Put that gun away and I'll tell you what I can."

Linda sat down and put the twenty-two in her purse.

"We're concerned about those three instances of farmers burning their wheat—especially this last one with the suicide." Richards drew a sheet of paper from a file on his desk and handed it across to her. "It's become part of the militia chatter."

Linda read the one page report and looked up at Richards. "Is this that crazy militia general out in Montana who keeps pushing for secession? Vincent Hayes. Isn't that this name? No one takes this stuff seriously."

"Hayes commands the largest state militia in the U.S. He's worth watching. But there's more to it than that. Recall an ex-Special Forces Colonel by the name of Cromwell?"

"The Medal of Honor winner who spoke out about drugs in Afghanistan?"

"That's our boy. A real American hero. And a quiet little farmer the past ten years."

"He's mixed up with the militia?"

"We're not sure. But if he were we'd be uneasy. There's talk about the farmers organizing. His name has come up. And with the recent grain market shake-up and the depletion of world's reserves, America's harvest is this winter's bread."

Linda knew the story all too well, but this was the first she'd heard about a connection between the farmers and the militia. It sounded a little far-fetched. "National security, really?"

"Ever stop to think what would happen to the stock market if Montana seceded? Then Idaho? Or if half the world's exportable grain goes up in flames when there are no backup reserves? I want to know what's happening out there."

"Who thinks this besides you?"

Richards ignored her skepticism. "Do some interviews. Talk to some militia people. Talk to some farmers. Get their reactions to the field burning."

"I can write this any way I like?"

"Just get their side of the story. Tell it straight. Write a couple more pieces before you go. More of what you've been doing. Nothing too heavy. We just want them talking to you when you get there."

"What's the bigger picture?"

"Colonel Nathaniel Cromwell. I want you to track him down and interview him. The concern is that he has the kind of reputation, charisma, mystique, if you will, to get something serious going. Farmers are individuals by nature—not easily organized. But this guy could do it. He's one of them. He isn't really the militia type. But he's a war hero with some downhome pull. Check him out."

"I might have done a leak or three for you guys, but I don't want to play mole. What if I say *no*?"

Richards shrugged. "Just go out there and mix with the locals."

"You're nuts. The farmers won't burn their crops. It's suicide."

Richards just grinned at her. "Cromwell. Check him out. I just gave you a lead on a great story. Now I want yours. How'd you get that gun in the building?"

"I didn't. I stopped in Rita Thayer's office on the way down the hall. I borrowed the gun and holster from her. Girls against jerks united."

Richards laughed at what wasn't meant as humor.

"I owned up, Bob. Now what's the rest of the story on this trip to Kansas City?"

Richards turned in his seat and looked out the window at the lush forest behind the CIA complex.

"Bob. All I've gotten from you is very standard shit. You gave me that report on grain over two months ago—a month before the grain market blitz. What else is going on here? It's not some ex-Colonel in Kansas playing soldier with a hoe."

Richards continued to stare out the window. He spoke without looking at her. "Write the columns, Linda. Allison will give you the paper work on the way out. Kansas City—let's say, in three weeks. Maybe sooner. I'll keep you posted."

Linda didn't much care for Bob Richards or the way he talked to her or she to him, but he did have the inside poop. And in Washington, you're either *in* or you're *out*. For better or worse, in Frederick Manning's terms, this was the devil she'd decided to shake hands with. Linda stood and strode out the door, putting just enough purpose in her hips to let Richards know she knew where his eyes would be. *Eat your heart out, asshole.*

CHAPTER 14

When Dr. Nina Colleen entered Atossa Andreas's bedchamber, she immediately asked the attending nurse to leave. Across the room, Atossa sat on the edge of her bed, a mask of gauze hiding her anxiety. Her black hair was pulled back in a bun. Only her eyes, her lips, and the edges of her nostrils were visible beneath the facial bandages. Eight weeks earlier, Dr. Colleen had performed a radical single-piece skin transplant on Atossa's face and neck. The procedure lasted eight hours. Atossa spent a week in the hospital. Two nurses had attended to her the last seven weeks at her Newport home, and Dr. Colleen made weekly visits. Today, Atossa would see her new face for the first time.

"How are you, Ms. Andreas?" said Dr. Colleen advancing to Atossa's bedside. Her manner was, as usual, subdued and aloof.

"I'm not sure," said Atossa, a powerful woman in a vulnerable position, doing her best to contain the horrible nervousness she now felt. The rest of her life, it seemed, held in the balance of the next few minutes.

Dr. Colleen placed her black bag on the bed and opened it. "This shouldn't hurt. There should be no tug on your skin at all." She had replaced the bandages weekly. She knew the results of the surgery, but Atossa had not been allowed a mirror.

Atossa sat as still as stone while Dr. Colleen took a pair of surgical scissors and did some preliminary snipping, delicately pulling back the edges of the gauze. "Your skin will not be entirely healed, Ms. Andreas. As I said before, there will be some discoloration and a few minor blemishes. But after today, there won't be bandages on your face." She lifted the gauze from the left side of Atossa's face. Another snip and the right side fell away. "In the next little while, we will be watching your body's acceptance of the new skin." Dr. Colleen removed a few last remnants of the bandages and placed them in a medical waste bag, then stepped back. Without a word, she viewed Atossa from several angles, appraising her work like a self-critical artist. Finally, she came up close to Atossa and touched her cheek with her index finger. "Can you feel that, Ms. Andreas?"

"Yes," said Atossa, moving her face as little as possible to say the word.

The doctor touched her in the center of the forehead. "That?"

"Yes."

She touched her chin. "That?"

"Yes."

Dr. Colleen stepped back. "Blink your eyes."

Atossa did as requested.

"Flair your nostrils."

Atossa followed her instructions.

"Furrow your brow."

Atossa very slowly lifted her brow.

"Smile, Atossa."

Atossa's mouth curled upward very slightly at the edges.

"No, Atossa. Smile!"

Atossa still fought it. Dr. Colleen came closer and lifted the hand mirror from the bedside table. "Look at yourself, Atossa. It's a wonderful success."

Atossa's hand shook as she took the mirror. She hesitantly lifted it to eye level. It shocked her at first. Her face was different. So much so it would be difficult for a close friend or even her daughter to recognize her. But as she turned the mirror from side to side and saw past the discolorations and the incredible change, she began to realize that she had been granted her miracle—a face to go with her body. A real smile spread across her face. "Nina, you are fantastic. It—no, I look fabulous."

"Give it another week. The patchiness of color will fade." She ran her finger along Atossa's hairline. "The shadow lines of my incisions will never completely vanish, but the lightest makeup will hide them from anyone but your cosmetic surgeon."

Atossa put the hand mirror down and stood slowly. Her legs nearly buckled as she cautiously crossed the room and dared to present herself to the full-length mirror that she spoke to more than any human. She contained her gasp. Yes, there were still some blemishes where the old skin met the new, and some darkness around her eyes, but that was nothing compared to the luster and fit of her new skin. The results surpassed anything Atossa could have realistically anticipated. "Oh, my

God, Dr. Colleen. Oh, my God. Is that really me? Has someone painted the portrait of a young woman on my mirror? Or is that really me?"

Dr. Colleen showed little reaction as she watched Atossa caught in the spell of her mirror. When she turned from her reflection to hug Dr. Colleen, the doctor accepted the embrace but provided only the slightest warmth in return as Atossa openly wept on her shoulder.

When Atossa released Dr. Colleen, she was at a loss for what to do with the moisture on her face. Confused and embarrassed, "Can I wipe these tears away?" she asked.

Dr. Colleen finally smiled. "Yes, Ms. Andreas, your face is stable. You can even wash it with soap and warm water. But don't use makeup or creams until the last of the blemishes are healed. Sterile powder only if you absolutely must. We still need to monitor the acceptance of the new skin. It will be months or longer before we can consider the transplant a full success."

"Oh yes, of course," said Atossa. Then she stopped. "My party is next weekend. Will these marks be gone by then?" she asked, thinking how much she wanted to show herself off before her guests.

"Eight days? Perhaps."

"You marvelous woman, you have done it." Atossa spun around the room in her excitement, returning to her mirror for another look. "You have done the impossible." She turned abruptly from the mirror to face Dr. Colleen. "I am a powerful and wealthy woman, Dr. Colleen. I can give you anything you want. I will build you the most modern and technically advanced burn victim clinic in the world—wherever you like."

"In time, Ms. Andreas," said the ever-guarded Nina Colleen, "in time."

This same Friday afternoon, Atossa's brother-in-law Frank Nelson was finishing lunch at the *University Club* in New York with four of the principal players in the Eurasian pipeline complex. President Kenaghy, as promised, had sent the Trans-Eurasian Security Act back to Congress unsigned. This had caused quite a stir in Washington, and during the last few weeks, a strategy for rewriting TES was gradually being hammered out. A recent flurry of bombings at pipeline construction sites in Kazakhstan had added urgency to the security debate and prompted Frank to call this meeting for finalizing the new TES package.

Five men sat around a table for six in a private, oak-paneled room at the back of the club. Secretary of Defense Lawrence Fitzgerald, sitting in his wheelchair at one end of the table, presided over the gathering, which, along with Frank Nelson, included Chairman of the Joint Chiefs of Staff General Austin Sinclair, Senator Raymond Blount, and a Russian oligarch and central banker Viktor Ivanov. Although all of these men were pushing for the same thing, each one had his own motives for promoting protection of the pipeline. For Fitzgerald, everything related to the grand chess game, long-term strategic global positioning.

"As far as I can tell," said the Secretary of Defense, "Kenaghy is going to do everything he can in the last few months of his term to prevent the passage of TES no matter what form we agree on. With Congress rejecting his offshore banking restrictions, I think he's purely into spiteful stalling."

"And with that kind of message coming from the White House," said Frank at the other end of the table. He thought unabashedly in terms of barrels of petroleum per day. "It seems the extremists have decided it's open season on our pipeline."

"Which in turn has pushed our numbers up in Congress and the latest public opinion polls," continued Fitzgerald, glancing around the table, then looking straight at General Sinclair sitting to his left. "We want to up the ante in the TES package to two divisions. We think the situation is that bad, and we want the support of the Joint Chiefs on this."

Sinclair was tall, handsome, and in great physical shape at fifty-four years of age. In a Brooks Brothers suit, instead of his uniform, he looked more like the successful CEO of some mega-corporation than a military officer. He sat back in his chair with the air of a man very comfortable with who and what he was. "As you know, gentlemen," he said, "there is reluctance in certain corridors of the Pentagon to sending our boys all over the world to act as police." He looked at Frank Nelson, then Senator Blount. "I need a few assurances before I take anything to the Joint Chiefs." This meant a larger piece of the next year's budget for the military. "But I'm wondering, why do you expect the President to consider this version of TES after refusing the other?"

Frank deferred to Senator Blount on his right. The heavy set, white-haired South Dakotan was positioning for Senate Majority Leader. Pushing TES through would go a long way toward achieving this. He spoke with the gravity of thirty-one years in the Senate, most of them working on defense spending. "It's simple, General. With the increased terrorist activity of the last month, the Senate will go over two thirds majority on the second round of voting—the House already has, meaning Kenaghy really has no choice. We can override a veto."

Sinclair nodded.

"But we'd like to avoid that," said Fitzgerald. "If we can enlist the support of Mr. Ivanov, I'm thinking we could force Kenaghy's hand." The Defense Secretary turned to the Russian banker. "First of all, I would like Mr. Ivanov to remind Kazakhstan's president that the diplomatic promises we made during the previous administration are still intact. Our full military assistance is available for just the kinds of problems we're having with the pipeline now." Fitzgerald sat slightly tipped to one side, leaning on the arm of his wheelchair. His words were aimed at Sinclair as well as Ivanov. "But nothing could be a stronger deterrent to these terrorists' actions than the long-term presence of American forces. An all-purpose military base makes a lot of sense right now, and I believe a personal request for this by President Mendelev to President Kenaghy would be hard for him to deny—especially if the Joint Chiefs and the rest of the National Security Council are all ready to go with it."

Sinclair responded with the crisp positivism that was his trademark. "The Pentagon always prefers military bases to the temporary deployment of riot squads."

Ivanov, a thin pencil of a man, already knew how Kazakhstan President Nursultan Mendelev would receive this proposal. He glanced over at Frank Nelson. These two men were the real drivers of the deal. Two bankers working through back channels to get all the right people into the right positions at the right times with the right amount of money.

Educated at Yale, apprenticed on Wall Street, Ivanov spoke with only the slightest accent. "I can get that request from President Mendelev, if you can assure me that he will not be embarrassed by a refusal from President Kenaghy." He said this knowing from private talks with Frank and Fitzgerald that despite all that had already been said at the table today, there could be no assurances about President Kenaghy's response.

"With both houses of Congress on board, the President is effectively out of the loop," said Senator Blount. "Kenaghy would be a fool to get in the way, Mr. Ivanov."

"But some say he is a fool," said Ivanov, his eyes again sliding to Frank's.

"Tell your president, Kenaghy is on the way out," replied Fitzgerald. "His response means nothing to the big picture."

Ivanov sat back, thinking of the great quantities of oil money that would have to pass through his bank, not the particulars of the arrangement. The moment held while eyes flashed around the table in anticipation of what the Russian would say. Ivanov leaned forward slowly, as though he hadn't known exactly what his answer would be long before the meeting took place. "Fine. I'll see what I can do."

Frank Nelson raised his drink. "Then we have it."

The ensuing silence meant no one objected. Ivanov raised his drink to Frank. "I leave for Kazakhstan tonight. I will speak to President Mendelev in person tomorrow."

While the others raised their drinks, Frank's eyes connected with Fitzgerald's. One important fact was never mentioned in the discussion, something only Frank and Fitzgerald were privy to. The Kazakh oil fields were considerably richer than previously projected, particularly one deposit beneath Lake Balkhash. Estimates made in the late nineties projected ten billion barrels. That was ample enough. But when the pipeline engineers arrived last year and began to use western oil money to upgrade the infrastructure of the entire Kazakh oil industry, Frank, concerned that the earlier projections had been inflated, as they usually were, asked for new estimates using absolute top-of-the-line, state-of-the-art technology. Those estimates had come in considerably higher three months ago. So high, in fact, Frank asked them to be done again. They were confirmed earlier this week. The Balkhash deposit compared to the legendary Ghawar deposit in Saudi Arabia, meaning it was one of the two or three largest oil fields ever discovered. Pipeline protection was only a secondary concern to Frank now. He wanted an American military base in Kazakhstan to secure the big puddle of petroleum beneath Lake Balkhash. Neither he nor Fitzgerald planned to make this known to the Kazakhs until after the base was already in place.

CHAPTER 15

There was reason for the people of Kazakhstan to love their President Nursultan Mendelev. In his twenty-seven years as political leader of this vast Russian state that stretched from the Caspian Sea to the western border of China, the "Sultan of Kazakh" had turned the nation's tremendous economic potential in petroleum, natural gas, and coal into an immediate reality. To the chagrin of some important people in Moscow, he had used Kazakhstan's enormous natural endowment as a lure for billions of dollars of foreign investment. In particular, the investments of Essex Petroleum and Merit Oil changed the Kazakh capital city, Astana, into Eurasia's model for progress. These two oil companies paid for and built a modern sewage system and an international airport for Astana. Essex and Merit were also responsible for ten new schools, a museum, and a symphony hall in what was once a provincial farming town on the southern bank of the Ishim River. Kazakhstan oil production was currently at an all-time high of three million barrels a day, but, hopefully, in the next year or so, there would be thousand miles of Kazakh pipeline pulsing petroleum at twice that rate to countries all over the world. As Mendelev would say repeatedly, the best is yet to come.

There was also plenty of reason for the people of Kazakhstan to hate President Mendelev. He had ascended to power through a ruthless purge of all his opponents. The so-called elections that occurred every six years had always shown eighty percent or better support for a man who was really no more than a legitimized mafia thug, rising to power through the aegis of Kazakhstan's black market drug syndicate. Although his mother was of Islamic ancestry, as was nearly half of Kazakhstan's population, he had led a steady racial attack on the Islamic peoples under the auspices of what he called the "Anti-Terrorism Economic Priority." He was making Kazakhstan a safe place for western investment, and the results were plain for all to see. Astana was Eurasia's jewel.

Today, President Mendelev sat in his private dining room at the Aqmola Bistro, eating lunch with his right-hand man, banker-ambassador Viktor Ivanov, just back from the United States. The President had a fabulous new palace in Astana, yet he preferred to do his most important political business in this well-fortified restaurant on the banks of the Ishim. Aqmola meant "White Grave" in Kazakh. It seemed an appropriate name for the place where Mendelev had some of his most powerful political adversaries gunned down.

All pretense aside, Mendelev was a gangster. An enormous man of over three hundred pounds with little or no discernable neck, he settled into his chair this afternoon like a tuskless walrus in a suit. Done with the meal, he belched under his breath and pushed aside his empty plate. "So, Viktor," he asked, speaking Russian in a gruff, hoarse voice, "these Amerikans want a huge new military base in Kazakhstan?"

Ivanov had not eaten. He stood across the table, hunched over a demitasse of coffee balanced on a saucer in his right hand. Tall and angular, he was the stork to his walrus boss. "That is their latest request."

"I do not mind if Amerikan soldiers are here protecting our nice pipeline project—even if they are here forever. But I do not mind only if there is something in it for me." Mendelev's eyes were large and blood shot and cast a ruthless kind of telepathy at their target. He peered at Ivanov now like he were entering his mind and transporting himself back to the lunch Ivanov had attended the day before in New York. "So, what do they offer this time?"

"Stock options are available in the new Kazakh subsidiary of Hamilton Heavy Construction," said the banker, more than aware of the President's powerful gaze and explosive temperament.

"Is this another of our friend Mr. Richards' constructs?" asked Mendelev, wallowing in his chair like Jabba the Hut and commanding the same kind of threatening majesty.

Ivanov nodded to the huge brutal man. "He will take three billion of our tenge in exchange for ten million American dollars in stock options."

Mendelev's lips, thick and feminine, compressed with computations in his head. "Is Richards aware that we know Hamilton will profit more than we will by the laundering of our dirty tenge?"

"I think Mr. Richards believes we are quite ignorant in Kazakhstan." Ivanov raised the tiny cup of coffee from its saucer and took a sip. "But the upside is worth such a foolish image of ourselves. These stock options will grow twenty times in value when the pipeline is fully up and running."

Mendelev smiled, a wide leering smile above triple tiers of chin, also upturned in happy crescents. "The Amerikans will believe they own our country when they have big new military base here. But I think of it as a statement to Moscow of our independence, plus a new modern army of my own, paid for and managed by the U.S."

"Nursultan, the stock options are one form of payment, but the spring was too dry this year. We could use some wheat and corn. A little relief for the people wouldn't hurt. Our friend Richards might be able to get us a deal on grain with our tenge."

"What I'd like more is a nuclear weapon on top of a missile." Mendelev meditated on this idea. Under great international pressure, Kazakhstan had dismantled its nuclear arsenal shortly after the collapse of the Soviet Union.

Ivanov began to pace back and forth along the edge of the table. "Grain is a more sensible request."

There was a knock. A security guard opened the door and stuck his head in. "Mazhit Kulekeyev, President."

Mendelev nodded.

A small, round, agitated man with wire rim glasses and a completely bald head entered. The security guard came in with him and stayed.

"Mr. Kulekeyev," said Mendelev, "how nice to see you today."

"President, the honor is mine." Kulekeyev, like all who gained audience with the volatile Kazakh President, experienced it with a certain trepidation.

"What can you tell me about the progress at Kaztransoil?"

"The news is of more bombings, Mr. Mendelev," said the Kazakhstan Pipeline Coordinator.

Mendelev frowned. "Who does this?"

"It is the same. Local extremists. But we fear they're being organized by someone from out of our country. Perhaps an American leftist."

Mendelev clasped his big hands together and set them into a thick rolling motion. "That is easy enough. Find him and kill him."

The pipeline coordinator heard this like a threat against his own life. "Anything else?"

"Yes, President," the little man said cautiously. "I find it curious that the drilling in the Tengiz, Kashagan, and Karachaganak oil fields is progressing so slowly. We feel Kashagan is our top priority, and yet the Americans concentrate on the pipeline and obscure technical data."

Mendelev sat back in his chair. He pinched the excess of skin beneath his chin between his forefinger and thumb and held it. His big fluid eyes slid to Ivanov, then back to Kulekeyev. Neither of them could tell if this was the preliminary for an outburst of anger or thoughtful comment. "Let them do what they will, Mazhit. Just watch them closely." He twisted the flab of skin between his fingers, left then right. "But I am sure they know what they are doing. They own the oil market." He winked at Ivanov. "Besides, what is there to lose? We get our share for nothing." Then he laughed, a series of rough barking sounds.

CHAPTER 16

Some two hundred and fifty miles west of Lake Balkhash, just outside the small copper refining town of Zhezkaghan, a beat-up 1965 VW microbus, hand-painted dark green, putted south through the night on one of the two paved roads that crossed the central Kazakh steppe region. Behind the wheel and driving without lights was ex-Army Special Forces Light Colonel Jerry Rust. With his long shaggy hair bound by a red bandana, a thick beard, and those tiny dark eyes, Rust looked more like a speed freak when he smiled and showed his teeth than the environmental activist his Kazakh acquaintances thought he was. He glanced into the rearview mirror. Five young Islamic men passed around a bota bag of fermented mare's milk in the back of the van, gathering courage for tonight's operation. A sixth man, Rasheed sat beside Rust in the passenger's seat.

Although the pay was exceptional, Rust didn't like working with the Muslims and hadn't wanted to come back to Central Asia. He took heart in knowing he would be out of this godforsaken place and headed back to his home in Chicago by the weekend.

He declined when the bota bag made it up front and Rasheed offered him a swallow. He preferred good old American whiskey to the "crap" the young radicals drank to steady their nerves.

One of the first things Jerry Rust had done on arriving in Kazakhstan two months ago was to climb the thirteen-thousand-foot peak of Zailiysky Alatau. The pristine southeast wilderness area of Kazakhstan had opened up in the last few years to tourism. It had an international reputation for world-class hiking and rock climbing, and Jerry felt like checking it out, just to get away for a couple of days before settling into his new cover.

Standing atop Zailiysky Alatau that day, looking northeast over the stunning glacial ravines and green valleys, spreading out flat into the infinite Asian steppe, Jerry could just make out the distant glint of Lake

Balkhash, lying low in the distance, as though it had puddled up in the center of the Earth's largest land mass. If he looked closely using binoculars, he could see a string of oil rigs along the edge of the lake and farther off the pipeline threading in from the west. Another three hundred miles and it would reach the Chinese border headed for Beijing. One day this would be the longest stretch of oil pipeline in the world.

Jerry didn't know that the Lake Balkhash oil field was quietly being called the greatest prize in all of Russia, but he'd seen the oil industry from this end before. There was no doubt in his mind that this was big, big money. Petroleum for Asia. Fuel for another four hundred million cars. Five, ten years' worth—and another 50 billion tons of carbon particulates exhausted into the atmosphere.

Jerry knew the situation as well as anyone, declining reserves, greenhouse gases. Humankind would be faced with some difficult decisions in the near future. But he wasn't one to think about the future. He had a biker's mentality for risk and got paid for it. He walked out of the mountains that afternoon with a backpack and a tent and hitchhiked to Zhezkaghan. He worked his way into the street life, then the radical underground, gradually infiltrating the extremist cell his sources told him was there.

Jerry took a quick glance over his shoulder and barked out somcthing in Kazakh to his passengers. The young men put away the bota bag and came to complete attention. Rust pulled from the road and drove several hundred yards into the wayside scrub brush. When he stopped, all of them piled out of the van. Not a word was said. Entirely businesslike, they clustered beside the van, passing out equipment—four shovels, two bolt cutters, several large sheets of brown canvas, and fifty pounds of explosive with all the necessary triggers, timing devices, and fuses. They all knew the routine. All carried pistols. All dressed in black.

With everything unloaded, they pulled stocking caps over their heads and covered the van with branches from the brush. Single file, Rasheed in the lead, Rust at the back, they scrambled through the margin of thick vegetation another hundred yards to the pipeline's defoliated perimeter. They crouched at the edge of the undergrowth appraising the scene. On the other side of the perimeter, a ten-foot chain link fence followed both sides of the buried pipeline as far as they could see. Lights were mounted on the fence at twenty-yard intervals. On a nod from Rust, two of the young Muslims dashed across the perimeter to the fence. Using the bolt cutters, they opened a hole large enough for a man to pass through.

Just as one of the fence cutters stood to wave to the others, the droning approach of an airplane coming from the west broke the night quiet. The men at the fence lay down and pulled a piece of brown canvas over themselves and their tools. The five in the scrub brush crouched deeper into the undergrowth and watched the American-built Skymaster pass overhead as part of the regular pipeline patrol. When the plane was safely in the distance, the five men in the shrubs hurried across the perimeter to the hole in the fence. Experience taught them they had thirty minutes before the Skymaster would be back. Three of them spread out down the length of buried pipeline several hundred yards as lookouts for guards on foot. The other three, under Jerry's supervision, began digging down to the buried pipeline.

The pipeline had been laid recently and the dirt was relatively loose. They made good progress before the drone of the plane began to beat again in the east. Rust, Rasheed, and the two other diggers dove into the hole and pulled the canvas over themselves. The lookouts laid flat on the ground beneath their tarps.

Jerry had taught them the entire procedure. He could almost laugh at the absurdity of it. The image of a snake biting its own tail kept coming to mind. But the long and the short of it was Jerry's experience in Afghanistan and the Special Forces made him an invaluable asset. Unlike Nathaniel Cromwell, Jerry had taken advantage of his inside track with the system instead of fighting it. He'd been contracted out of the Army as a covert intelligence operative—more accurately, in this instance, an *agent provocateur*. He'd assembled this band of youths, none older than twenty-one-year-old Rasheed, into a crack demolitions unit. This was their seventh terrorist foray in three weeks.

With the plane now disappearing into the western sky, they were back at it full speed, hoping to be done before another pass. One of the shovel blades clanked on hard steel, and soon after, a space beside the pipe was prepared for the bomb. Rust jumped into the hole alongside Rasheed to assist in rigging the explosives and setting the timer. When all was complete, Rasheed stood up and gave one short whistle. With Rasheed's help, Rust laid the canvas over the hole as the lookouts came running down the fence line from both directions. One by one, all seven of them slipped through the fence and raced across the perimeter.

Then it was an all-out scramble through the undergrowth and scrub brush to the van. Rust got behind the wheel as the others pulled away the brush and loaded the equipment. They were ten miles away, again running without lights, when the explosion lit up the night. Rust never looked back, but the young Muslims cheered, squeezing their faces up against the windows, just able to see the glistening gusher of oil spraying hundreds of feet upward into the starry night.

After a moment, Rasheed turned to Rust. "Jerry, we bomb the pipeline because we want the project to fail. Perhaps all we do is make the construction more expensive. But I don't understand what this means to you. All of this spilled oil is a horrible insult against your treasured Earth. Isn't this exactly what you want to prevent?"

Driving without lights was incredibly difficult on these dark Central Asian roads, and Rust didn't divert his eyes when he answered. "We aren't so concerned about the oil stain on the ground or the waste," he said. "As long as this oil isn't burned and doesn't add to the carbon already in the atmosphere, the act is worth the risk." He turned his eyes from the dark road to Rasheed beside him. "It's the warming of the planet that will be the death of us all." Then he grinned, showing his teeth, before turning his attention back to the road.

Rasheed laughed. "And you Americans think *we're* crazy."

CHAPTER 17

President James Kenaghy was a smart man. He knew Washington was a tough town, a gossipy place all about power and ambition. Rumors were political tools. Leaks were a method of communication. And things got done through the successful manipulation of bureaucratic infighting. With each day in office, he got better at these tactics. But he overplayed his hand when he sent the first version of the Trans-Eurasian Security Act back to Congress at the end of April without his signature. All need for political subtlety vanished. The White House became a target. His Secretary of State resigned, and the full current of the town's consensus turned against him.

Don Reed, his National Security Advisor and temporary fill-in for the yet to be replaced Secretary of State, reaffirmed this to the President several times in the simplest possible terms when it became clear that TES would be rewritten for a second go. He said it again Monday morning in the Oval Office. "Time to give up on this one, Jim."

Kenaghy didn't respond.

Reed was the President's closest advisor. They had known each other as undergraduates at Dartmouth. The President had lured him out of Harvard's Kennedy School of Government with the opportunity to manage policy firsthand. But Reed had a hard time of it. He didn't like gun slinging with the media, and he'd begun to second-guess the President. "You're simply fighting a losing battle," he stated flatly.

Across the office, the President's Chief of Staff Cameron Phillips nodded in agreement with Reed. This was the administration's inner circle. Or what remained of it.

Kenaghy sat in his chair, pushed away from the desk, one leg crossed over the other. Reed occupied one of the cane-back chairs in front of the President's desk, and Phillips leaned against the fireplace. They were going through the President's Daily Brief in preparation for the day. It was six-twenty-five. The morning smelled of freshly brewed coffee and conflict.

"I'm with the consensus on this one, Jim," repeated Reed. "Give them their military base."

Kenaghy turned away from Reed to the window. Holding his coffee cup with both hands, he peered out into the bleak dawn of what would surely be—in more ways than one—a hot day in Washington. The State Department had received a cable from Kazakhstan Sunday afternoon with President Nursultan Mendelev's request for increased American military assistance. The Foreign Policy Advisory Group met late Sunday night. Two of its members would bring the group's finding to the White House in the next few minutes. There was little doubt what they would say.

"It's time to compromise on this bill," continued Reed. "Show these people that you're still flexible. That you can be worked with. It's the only way you're going to get any give on your domestic agenda."

Phillips watched the other two men. It wasn't the first time he'd been witness to their arguments. He was an up-and-coming thirty-seven-year-old black man. He'd been with Kenagy during his eight years in Massachusetts, ran his presidential campaign, and stayed through the entirety of the current stormy administration. He owed much of what he'd achieved to the President. "You know, Mr. President," said Phillips softly, "Don's got a point."

Kenaghy continued to stare out the window.

"God damn it, Jim," cursed Reed, standing and shaking the brief in his hand, "you can't just hole up in here and fight these madmen. They will win. Your pride is getting in the way of your reason." Reed didn't like what he'd seen in the White House over the past six months. He equated Kenaghy's bullheaded stand to political suicide, and it embarrassed him to be part of it. "Recent events verify that there is a real threat out there. No matter what you think of the oil industry's deeper motives, we have to show a strong hand to these terrorists. We have to."

Kenaghy turned his swivel chair to face Reed. There was sadness in his eyes and in his voice. "I know what you think of this, Don. I know this isn't what you signed on for. I didn't plan things this way. But I've seen too much. I have no intention of changing my position."

The President hadn't fully understood whom he'd challenged until after he'd vetoed TES. Yes, he knew he was fighting the post-atomic bomb national security power structure, a tremendous force centralized in the military and industrial sectors, but he didn't understand its extent, how much it was already in control, its long-range goals, nor its maliciousness—until he stood up to them.

The experience of the recent Democratic Convention had been the real eye-opener for Kenaghy and also for Reed. As the incumbent, the President's nomination should have been automatic. A celebration. Yet Kenaghy had to battle tooth and nail for it. Several of the keynote speakers criticized his policies and inefficiency. It was an insult. It didn't bode well for November.

"More important than the action of terrorists half way around the globe," said Kenaghy with increasing emotion, "is what's going on right here. The balance of power is leaning fully to the right. Congress is compromised. The Justice Department is compromised. The Supreme Court is compromised. And I'm compromised—while Wall Street and the Pentagon call the blasted shots. The military isn't being asked to defend the nation. It's being used to prop up a deeply corrupt global economic system. That's not what the founding fathers had in mind. That's why the Constitution gives me the powers I'm currently using. Futile or not, someone, sometime has to stand up to these goons. And it's going to be me! I refuse to send American troops abroad when the social security system is rupturing, when Medicare is radically underfunded, and when nearly every state government is working at a deficit. I will not abide by the policy of world domination when it's not in the true interests of the people of this country, much less the rest of the world."

"Mr. President, Jim, my dear friend," Reed twisted and turned, gestured and grimaced, trying with all his might to present his case as reasoned logic, "you're blowing this out of proportion. No one's talking about world domination. TES is about securing an important international energy source against renegade extremists. It's good for us, and it's good for the world. This week's polls show these recent bombings have pumped pipeline security approval up close to sixty percent—disapproval has dwindled to thirty-seven. Jim, while you still have a constituency, while you still have a few senators with you, let go of this Pentagon paranoia, grant them this concession."

"Congress is likely to override anyway, sir," offered the usually supportive and fiercely loyal Chief of Staff Phillips.

"That's right, Jim. Your resistance will amount to nothing more than a stubborn show for the media to play on. Out of pure common sense. Let this one go."

Kenaghy bowed his head. He truly loved Don Reed, a man he'd known over thirty years. He fully understood that he was asking his friend to take the same dangerous leap he was taking. *And it was frightening!* After some of the phone calls he'd received from senators and lobbyists in the first few days after he'd sent TES back to Congress seven weeks ago, he'd actually feared for his life. But he soon realized that was a foolish concern. They were already halfway to un-electing him in five months. He was a lame duck before his time. Besides, he'd become so thoroughly insulated from the public, the opposition wasn't even afraid of what he might say. The media acted as a censor. His public appearances were all taped and network orchestrated if not entirely controlled. Even the secret service seemed like a fence to keep him in, not protect him. The only place he could vocalize his dissent was here in the Oval Office or to his wife in bed—that is, until last night, when even Marjorie told him to buck up or she was leaving.

Incredibly, despite his determined political stand, very few knew how hard he was fighting the establishment. To the outside world, it appeared he was still toeing the line—a company man—when in fact he was really a dissident imprisoned within the White House. The President lifted his head and faced his friend. The stress he was under was evident in his eyes. "We send two divisions to Kazakhstan, Don. Then it will be a division to Uzbekistan. Then another to Tajikistan."

"I don't think so, Jim."

"Christ, Don, don't you get it? That's what they're after. Fitzgerald practically rammed it down my throat one morning. A commanding military position in Central Asia. Absolute control of the world's petroleum resources. It's all part of their grand chess game. Damn it, if they really want it, they can pay for it. I gave them a compromise. And a fair one. Cut the offshore tax hijinks."

Reed shook his head and sighed. "Maybe fair, but in the existing scheme of things, impossible."

"In the existing scheme of things?" Kenaghy looked to the ceiling as though expecting some higher power to intercede. The intercom on his desk spoke instead of God. "Mr. President, General Sinclair and Mr. Houseman are here for the six-thirty meeting."

Kenaghy fell rapidly back to earth. He made eye contact with his security advisor. "You ready for this?"

"Yes. I'm fine, Jim."

"Cameron, I think you'd be better off out of this one."

The Chief of Staff exited through a side door. A moment later, two of the establishment's heaviest hitters entered the Oval Office with the report from the Foreign Policy Advisory Group. No one expected this meeting to go smoothly. Chairman of the Joint Chiefs of Staff General Austin Sinclair, in full uniform today, was a tough, single-minded man, but he was reasonable and would be respectful of his Commander-in-Chief. The stocky Director of Homeland Security Paul Houseman, a McClay protégé Kenagy should never have put in his cabinet, was a different story entirely. A former Los Angeles patrolman who'd worked his way up to Police Chief and later became CEO of Thackenhut Security, Houseman had learned his manners on the street with a billy club. Now he had one of the most important jobs in the nation and was presently pushing Congress to privatize the National Guard—recently renamed the Homeland Guard. His disdain for Kenaghy filled the room like foul body odor the moment he walked in.

The tension in the legendary office cranked up ten more notches as stiff formalities were passed around, and the President offered the men seats in the arrangement of chairs before the fireplace. Houseman was seated directly across from Kenaghy, but he was up on his feet immediately, the first one to speak—and as always with emotion and passion.

"They think we're going soft, Mr. President. We should've had a division over there two months ago." With eleven years at Homeland Security, Houseman was an institution, considered too entrenched to change and impossible to fire. "Somebody's got to pull the trigger on this." The words were accusatory enough, but his tone was worse.

Reed took offense. "Mr. Houseman, is that your opinion or the finding of the Foreign Policy Advisory Group?"

"Good God, Reed, where have you been?" Houseman had a taunting edge to him, always challenging and aggressive. "It's the opinion of the entire United States Congress, the foreign policy establishment, and every other goddamn person in this country. I don't know why we even bothered to meet last night. There is only one answer to Mendelev's request. A resounding *yes*."

"Thank you for your thoughts, Mr. Houseman," said Kenaghy. He turned to Sinclair. "General, anything to add?"

Sinclair answered in his implicitly positive way of stating things. "It was unanimous last night, Mr. President. Let's put a military base in Kazakhstan." He handed Kenaghy the finding that had been written up after the policy meeting. "Boots can be on the ground before the end of next week, sir."

Kenaghy took the report and read the first paragraph, then handed it to Don Reed. Houseman hadn't liked the way Kenaghy brushed him off. He watched the exchange of paperwork like he'd eaten a bowl of razor blades for breakfast, and they were just reaching his lower intestine. "I get the feeling, Mr. President, that you're not taking this very seriously. We're talking wholesale terrorist action against American economic interests. There have been nearly thirty hits against the pipeline in the last year. Eight in Kazakhstan this month alone. This represents a definitive breech in our national security—a veritable act of war." He was standing right in front of the President, too close. "I'm here to demand you act on this and act properly."

Kenaghy stood up. He towered over the stout, pushy Houseman. "You feel that I'm not taking this seriously, Mr. Houseman? You demand that I act properly?" The two men stared at each other with a thick physical imminence.

Reed spoke up. "We put troops in Kazakhstan now, gentlemen. And it's Tajikistan next month. Uzbekistan the month after that. Suddenly we have four full divisions over there. The President is firm in his stand against limiting American troops in the independent Russian states."

"Independent states? Christ, man, this is the perfect wedge to squeeze in between Moscow and eastern Russia." Houseman spun away from the President and stomped off across the room, red with heat, muttering under his breath, loud enough for all to hear, "Missing this opportunity is grounds for impeachment."

Kenaghy knew all about Houseman's bullying methods. He was determined to be above them. "Mr. Houseman, your opinion is duly noted." The calm in his voice only provoked the Homeland Security Director more.

General Sinclair spoke up. "Mr. President, with all due respect, there is much evidence to suggest that the petroleum reserves in Kazakhstan are some of the most important outside the Arabian Peninsula. We can't allow ourselves to be soft on this position. It's immensely important to show President Mendelev and the other Russian leaders that we are behind them. And if this leads to putting more American troops in the arena, it's for the best. In ten years," his emotion was beginning to outrun his containment, "that oil will be the most important strategic military resource on the planet. I'll lay my stars on it. And with China right there and Mendelev asking for our help, this is an open invitation to gain a critical foothold in Central Asia."

The National Security Advisor was standing now also. He was watching Kenaghy and Houseman. They were squared off menacingly over the presidential emblem woven into the office's blue carpet. "Thank you, General," said Reed hurriedly. "And thank you, Mr. Houseman. The President and I will take what you have told us under advisement."

The tense moment held. No one moved. Then suddenly Houseman turned and stalked out of the office. Sinclair took three steps toward the door then stopped. "Mr. President, please excuse Mr. Houseman's emotion. I understand you have your own priorities and that there are political compromises you are offering in exchange for pipeline protection. I make no claim to understanding your deeper purposes. But as a military man, the logic is clear, sir. If we could string a few military bases along that pipeline, all the way across the Caucasus, we'd be in a position to redraw the map of Asia. This could be our country's greatest opportunity since the Louisiana Purchase."

Kenaghy took a deep breath. "Thank you, General."

Sinclair fired off a crisp salute and strode out of the office.

Reed ran his hand over his forehead and up across what remained of his thinning hair. "Christ, James, for a second there I expected you to haul off and deck Houseman."

Kenaghy didn't respond to the comment. His emotions were boiling. His nerves as taut as mainlined caffeine. He walked away from Reed over to the window behind his desk. The sun was above the buildings to the east. The traffic was heavy on Constitution Avenue. He wondered if he had the political leverage to get rid of Houseman.

"You know, Jim," said Reed, still intent on reaching his boss with reasoned compromise, "there's a chance these men are right. Perhaps there will be a time when we'll want a strong military position in Central Asia."

Barely able to contain all that he was feeling, Kenaghy spoke without facing his old friend. "Think about what you're saying, Don. You're falling for the logic of madmen. What does the United States really stand for? What exactly is the central aim of our foreign policy?" He turned now into Reed's blank response. "Is it military might? Is it economic advantage by force? Is it bully and plunder? If that's the case, these men are right, and I don't belong in this office. But if this nation stands for freedom and democracy and giving other nations the opportunity to make their own choices, then they are just plain wrong."

"But the world has changed, Jim. Terrorist threat has thrown all of our ideals up for grabs. We've entered into a different kind of realpolitik. Petroleum is a big part of it."

"Realpolitik, my ass!" Kenaghy slammed his fist on his desk so hard everything on it but the phone lifted into the air. "What's that? Carry a big stick and smash everything that moves. Not as long as I'm in charge."

CHAPTER 18

It was Wednesday morning, July first. Linda Bennett had just taken a table in a little coffee shop off Pennsylvania Avenue. She sat by a window with a latte and looked out at the seven o'clock traffic, knowing she'd be out in it before too long. Right on time, Charlie Patio sauntered in and made eye contact. He got a cup of house blend, black, and sat down across from her.

"Thanks for coming, Charlie."

"My pleasure." He took a glance out the window at the morning ordeal. It was hard not to. Like a mechanical river stop-and-going by, it attracted the eye. He faced Linda with a sardonic smile and shook his head. "Crazy world, eh?"

Linda had known Charlie since she was fifteen and trusted him like an uncle. She'd called him the night before asking to meet this morning. They hacked it back and forth a bit, then Charlie just stopped talking and stared at her. "Okay, what's bugging you, Linda?"

"Richards." Behind her on the counter a coffee steamer hissed and gurgled.

Patio took a sip from his cup.

"What do I need to know about him, Charlie?"

Patio looked down at his hands wrapped around his cup. "I think I already gave you my advice about Richards."

"I know that."

"Just so you heard me," he said.

"All my columns, all this stuff about the farmers in the Midwest and the commodities market, it started with him."

Patio nodded. "I figured."

"Where's it coming from? What's his larger purpose?"

"And you've asked him?"

"All I get is this concern about Colonel Cromwell. Does that make any sense?"

Patio looked out the window again. Whatever he was thinking about was what Linda wanted to know. She let him be. After a minute, he spoke. "If you weren't your father's daughter, if you didn't have the same good instincts he did, I'd tell you for a third time to stay clear of Richards." He took another sip of java and looked over his shoulder. A woman with a purse and a laptop entered the little shop.

"The last few years your father focused on money flows. The Agency has always monitored the movement of large sums of money, legal and illegal. Money laundering, drug deals, weapons deals, same old stuff. There is probably no better way to understand the world than to watch the shadow side of the financial district. Rarely do we do anything about it. Mostly we just watch." He paused, blanking his stare out the window. His reluctance to talk was palpable.

"I don't know anything about farmers organizing or Colonel Cromwell, but if Richards has anything to do with it, black money is where it starts and ends. The saying has always been *follow the money*, but Richards follows the black money—where it's coming from and where it's going, and how operations might redirect it. Press a little on this bank. Crack down on this illegal operation. Help another one, perhaps. We've seen it in one form or another for years. Use black money to help the good guys win. It's legit, I suppose—if it's in the interests of the U.S." He took a sip of coffee.

"About a trillion dollars is laundered annually, Linda. That's almost two percent of the World GNP. Insert that trillion, here and there, where it's needed, or where U.S. economic or political interests need it, and it fills in the gaps, makes things work. It's not new, but it's bigger and more important since 9/11. Black money is where it's at, Linda. Your dad watched it. The operations boys use it."

"And that's what Richards is about?"

Patio nodded.

"Can I ask you one more question, Charlie?"

He gave her a wry smile. "No."

"Are these guys bad? Or is that just me?"

Patio looked her square in the eye. "I've already answered that one."

"Yeah," she said with a little drum of her fingers, watching him take another slug of coffee. "One more last question?"

He looked out at the sluggish river of cars like he was ignoring her, but she saw the flicker of a smile reflected in the window.

"Any way to get to my dad's files?"

He squared around in his seat. "You leave first," he said like he hadn't even heard her question.

She smiled into his stone wall and stood up. "Thanks, Charlie. Really."

"Be careful."

Linda left the coffee shop not really sure what she'd found out. She had hoped Charlie would be a little more specific. The only real clue Charlie had given her was Richards' connection to money laundering. Mostly what he'd told her was to stay out of it. That meant not even going to Kansas City. She knew that was good advice. With Richards it was likely she would be used in ways she would never fully know or understand. Still Linda was just hardheaded enough to think that she could play the game to her advantage anyway.

PART III

INDEPENDENCE DAY

"Grain is the currency of currencies."
-N.I. Lenin.

CHAPTER 19

Farmers from all over the Midwest flowed into the vast grange hall in Pratt, Kansas, a hundred miles west of Wichita. The building was little more than a giant warehouse, ten thousand square feet of open space and a bunch of folding chairs. But on this Fourth of July evening, the place was full to overflowing. They stood in the aisles and sat in the windowsills, with more lined-up outside trying to get in. They wore t-shirts and jeans, ball caps and cowboy hats, militia uniforms and camo. A good number of women were there, a contingency of hippies, a scattering of Blacks and Hispanics, and reps from every grange in the nation, representing all fifty states. Something big was afoot, and it was clear to everyone there.

Lost in the nation's Independence Day fanfare, the meeting was as close to secret as they could make it. Like the highland clans coming to the lodge to talk family matters, you couldn't get in without being known by another farmer. Outside the giant stick-framed meeting hall, armed farmers were posted all around, worried the FBI would show up or the ATF or the Homeland Guard or, worse yet, the press. These folks wanted none of it. This was the first serious attempt in fifty years to unify the farmers of America in a stand against an agricultural system that was as old and antiquated as the buggered-up version of democracy that was supposedly running the country.

The meeting had been set for seven-thirty, but it had taken an extra hour to get everyone in, settled and seated, all the howdy-dos passed around. And the place just kept buzzing until Forest Mahan stepped up to the podium, a huge American Flag hanging on the wall behind him. He tapped on the microphone to make sure it was on, and the hubbub gradually subsided. With six thousand Missouri acres of ready-to-harvest wheat and three thousand more of corn three months behind that, Mahan was as well-off and successful as any farmer there. But in his mind, things were out of hand, and it was time to speak out. He leaned up to the mike.

"Most of you who know me realize rabble-rousing isn't my usual way," he began in a loud Missouri drawl. "I'm just a farmer like all of you. And I'm not that pleased about being here. I'd just as soon be back in Missouri getting things ready for harvest. But I'll say it in clear, clean English, I don't like what this country is doing to its farmers or its land, and it's been going on for too damn long. We're up against the wall like never before, and it's a grand day to declare our independence! Right now! Tonight!"

A loud cheer and many whoops and hollers exploded from the anxious and angry crowd. Somebody in the back lit off a pack of firecrackers.

"For years now," Mahan bellowed over the noise, bringing quiet again to the hall. "As long as I can remember, we've been paying folks to lobby for us in Washington, trying to get our grievances heard. We sent groups to testify in Congress. We elected all the people we thought were farm friendly. We've followed all the federal guidelines and chased government checks to the point we were spending more time reading and filling out forms than we did in the field. Yet things have only gone from bad to worse, leaving us with only two choices. We can bend over and take it like we have for a hundred and fifty years, or we can do what American farmers haven't been able to do since Oliver Kelley first set up the grange in 1870—that is, organize."

The place erupted again.

"The system as it stands is controlled by the grain dealers, seed companies, and fertilizer manufacturers. It's backed and maintained by the bankers. And corrupted by the speculators. The government sits back and greases our backsides with just enough tax incentives and phony-baloney subsidies to make all these other monkeyshines seem fine and dandy. But in the end, we're caught in a paper chase, not making smart agricultural decisions. And it just doesn't add up. We all know this. We've known it a long time. Little farmers, big farmers, each year we sell more of our crop before we plant it, just so we have the money to buy the seeds, chemicals, and machinery we need to get to harvest. We're so habituated to this system we hardly think about it. It's just the way it's always been. But it's back-ass-wards. And plum wrong. The American farmer has become little more than an indentured servant to the merchant class. What happened this spring in the grain market is sure proof of that. Somebody made a pretty penny off that little bump in the road. And it sure as hell wasn't the guy growing the grain."

Nathaniel Cromwell was out in the crowd, leaning against the wall, thumbs hitched in his hip pockets, wearing a faded, red Kansas State sweatshirt with the sleeves torn off and a green Caterpillar ball cap. His two neighbors, James Peabody and Horace Thompson, sat in chairs at the end of the row where Nate stood. They'd driven the hundred and twenty miles to Pratt in Jim's pickup and were there for the same reason as all the other farmers and grange reps.

"We've mortgaged ourselves to a system we all know stinks to high heaven," continued Mahan, "just for the privilege to dig our asses into the dirt for one more sun-blasted year. Just for the privilege to go a little deeper in debt and bring ourselves another missed loan payment closer to being an employee at a convenience store or making that dreaded move into the city to trade in our overalls for a coat and tie. One missed payment closer to losing the land our parents farmed, and their parents, and their parents. And all we've done is work the land harder and harder to make it through each winter—at the cost of our land. We've irrigated so much the aquifers are running dry. We've used fertilizers and pesticides so much the soil burns our hands. We've been sold a bunch of malarky about engineered seeds, hoping to get another bushel per acre, with the only result being lowering the price of that bushel and losing ownership of our seeds."

A chorus of *right ons* and *amens* sounded from the crowd. The place had a dangerously rowdy feel to it. Like a bunch of country boys ready to play football or just plain drink and brawl. A silo full of hayseed and chaff waiting for a spark!

Even Cromwell got caught up in it. Forest Mahan made good sense. Since that day he'd stopped by to talk, Nate had gradually come to learn a lot more about the President of the National Grange. Although the man had asked Nate to get involved in something he didn't want anything to do with, Mahan had presented his offer in a very decent and thoughtful manner. He hadn't pressed too hard. He hadn't gotten pushy.

Mahan was not your usual farmer. He was part literary man, part naturalist, and part activist—with a little bit of Tenzing Jast's snowy ranges wisdom sprinkled in for good measure. His five years at the head of the National Grange had been groundbreaking. That he called this meeting fit the natural progression of his efforts. Family farming was in trouble, and Mahan believed that revitalizing the grange was one way to get at the problem.

"Eight years ago, they began cutting back on price supports and opening American agriculture to the free market. It was supposed to be our salvation. Well look what happened! It ain't no free market when three giant companies have the capital and storage capacity to control the price of grain through a shortage like we saw last month. Those distributors got a premium price for last year's leftovers. Surely a price that would have made any farmer's year worth the sweat and tears. Pay off the bank, buy some new machinery, lay a few acres fallow, maybe make a dime or two for all the time put in each day. But we didn't even get a whiff of that price! Instead, we'll fall short on our bank payments, sell off a piece of machinery below book to feed our families through the winter, and plant every inch of our farm next year with the hope that this spring's price will be there when we've got to start the whole damn process over again. All I can say to you right now is don't bet on it."

Coarse curses were shouted throughout the crowd. Threats against the agricultural combine. Threats against the government. Threats against President Kenaghy. A man stood up on his chair in the center of the hall, held up a box of Corn Flakes breakfast cereal, and yelled, "The guy who printed this box made more money off it than the farmer who grew the corn inside."

More *right-ons* and *you-got-that-rights* chorused from the crowd.

Horace Thompson and James Peabody had their eyes on Cromwell. Ever since Tom Foster's death, he'd been pretty quiet. He didn't say a word the entire two-hour drive to Pratt. Now he was showing a little life, clearly taking in the energy and emotion of the crowd and the speaker.

"The whole horrible truth, fellas, is we ain't got word one to say about the way the system works. No matter how we vote, the politicians go about business as usual, keeping the big boys happy—while we remain slaves to the seed dealers, the industrial farms, and the petrochemicals. They say if you want to keep up with the industry use this new pesticide. So we use it. They say if you want to keep up with the industry inject this into your cattle. So we inject it. If they say add more fertilizer per acre, we add it. If they say grow corn for ethanol, no matter how much waste or subsidy bullshit is involved, we grow it! They've got us so strapped into the way we farm and the way we sell our product that we can't win for losing. Farming used to be a labor intensive operation.

Now it's all capital. I'm a farmer not a financier. Sure seems like a damn sin to me.

"We all know the guy who tried to go another way. Conservation tillage or organic farming. Lay off the fertilizer. Lay off the chemicals. Reinvest in the land and soil, instead of borrowing against its future. New crops. Alternative techniques. All sorts of things that might make our farms better in the long run—maybe even more profitable. Some of those guys make it, but not many. The change over takes too long. It's too costly. And time is running out. The land is gullied and raw. Abandoned fields everywhere you look. Nothing but bindweed and puckerbrush. Hell, for every bushel of crop we produce, two bushels of topsoil wash away. They used to say a good farmer's land got richer every year he farmed. When he left it to his children, it was better than when he'd gotten it from his parents. How many of us can say that now?"

An ugly murmur of disgrace and regret echoed from one farmer to the next. Horace and James shook their heads. Like everyone else, they knew they burned their soil with fertilizer, then it was blown or washed away by the wind and rain. Some four hundred million tons of topsoil washed down the Mississippi every year. It was a sin against the land and the code of farming—and it came from the fact that every year they were in competition against the combine—agribusiness and their huge industrial farms.

Nate imagined his father looking down on them from Heaven or some such place, nodding his head, knowing, as probably many generations of farmers had known, things would eventually come to this. After his discharge from the Army, Nate had come back to Kansas to take over at the farm for his ailing father. The war hero had focused all his bitterness and frustration into the land. He had gradually turned himself around and become a real farmer. And now, much like in the military, he found himself being pushed up against something that was just plain wrong.

"The question we've got to answer today is what are we going to do about it?" demanded Mahan at full volume. His eyes found Nate leaning up against the wall. Every farmer in the grange knew who Nate was, what he'd done. "Every man for himself. Try to struggle through to next year. Or go over the top. Burn your crop and yourself with it, holding a single finger in the air to the capitalists who own this country, own our land, and own us. Or do we get together and stand against the tide? Start working together. Form a farmers' union. See if we can't find a way to make farming a respectable and profitable way of life. Some might say that's an impossible dream. That family farming is a way of the past. I say they're wrong."

Mahan was getting worked up, and he took a moment to catch his breath. "We've got something big going for us right now," he said lowering his voice. "The grain reserves are used up. Meaning what we have in the field in wheat and corn represents a sizeable portion of what's available worldwide. Until that grain is harvested and hauled off to the man we promised it to five months ago, we've got some serious leverage in the situation. How best to make use of that leverage is what we've got to figure out tonight—right now. And mostly it's just us working together. Without that, we might as well go home and refinance the house and the property. Forget the kids' college education. Forget it all. Sell the land for a loss, buy a tie, some black oxfords, and move to stinking Chicago."

Fuck Chicago came back from five or six voices in the crowd.

"Sometimes I think the politicians forget how important we farmers are. The world's breadbasket is right here in the middle of these United States on up into Canada. But not only do we feed ourselves and the world, this grain is also our national security. It's our annual meal ticket to the economy of the world. Between grain and oil, this world turns round. Got to eat and got to drive them gasoline rigs. The Arabs have a big puddle of tar, and we farmers got breakfast, lunch, and dinner for the hungry of the world. For a long time, the problem was we grew too much for our own good. The government had to buy our surplus just so we'd stay on the farm. Well, if that Asian shortage means what I think it does, it's telling us that the population of this here planet is catching up with grain production. Maybe things will change for the better in the next five years for us farmers—if we're still on our farms to take advantage!"

"Thank God for the second amendment," called out a man in camo in the back.

"Out of my cold dead hands," screamed someone else.

Mahan pushed on. "Everything Congress does these days is to prompt business. Financiers run the show. The unions are gone. The family farm is disappearing. If we don't act now, as a group, in another few years there won't be enough of us left to impact the market. We'll be an anachronism. A side bar. So right now, I say we've got grain. I say we've got power. And if we use it right, we can change the system."

Mahan paused long enough to let this settle in and gather his audience, then he called out, "So, what are we going to do?"

A man in a straw cowboy hat with a feather stuck in its rattlesnake hat band stood up and shouted, "Burn the fields from the Ohio Valley to the Rockies. FUCK'M. ALL."

Almost half the group let out with cowboy hollers.

Forest Mahan surveyed the crowd with a grimace. This time when his eyes met Nate's, he let them hold a moment before he spoke. "Yeah, that's one answer, boys. Burn the fields. And fuck'm all. If we can't make a dime, why should they? But what do we do then? Where do we go from the fire? Into the frying pan!"

Fuck'm chorused again out of the crowd.

"Alright, I hear your frustration. But if we burn the fields, we cook our own goose. As long as the grain is in the field, we've got something to work with. Something to bargain with. Maybe we give them until harvest to cut us a new deal. Forgive the loans. Or cut the interest rate. Maybe we ask for low-interest loans to change over to no-till or maybe organic if you feel that way. Anything to save the soil.

"We're not being greedy," he stated flatly. "We just want to feel like we're not goin' backwards. So, whatever we do with our grain, we have to gain something. We can't just cut ourselves out of the deal by burning our cards. You all know what I'm saying. So tell me? What are we going to do about it?"

A tall man with a red beard, in fatigues and a soft olive green military cap, stood up in the center of the hall. It was Major General Vincent Hayes. The head of the Montana Militia, known for being as radical as any militia group in the country. "I have a way out of this mess," he announced with a loud, stentorian bravado.

Vincent Hayes was the latest evolution of the radical right that had taken over large parts of Montana and Idaho in the 1980s and 90s. A mixture of fundamentalist Christians, gun-toting survivalists, white supremacists, and anti-government militia types, the area became a very frightening place to mainstream America back then. But Hayes, a successful cattle rancher, brought a new libertarianism to the region. Concerned about peaking oil production and surviving the social havoc it could cause, he'd reinvigorated the militia movement. He didn't talk religion and wasn't a racist. He just hated government graft and believed in the Bill of Rights and states' rights. This clear and simple message won him a lot of influence and, thankfully, cut heavily into the power of the swastika-waving nut cases—not that he wasn't extreme. He'd had several run-ins with the federal authorities over firearms and repeatedly pushed initiatives for Montana's secession from the Union. If he lived in any other part of the country, he'd be in jail, but out in Montana where his individualistic style was admired, he had political clout, and the local government left him alone.

In the farm community, the opinion on Hayes was split. Either he was a blowhard militia freak or a courageous new-age patriot. Like many there at the grange that night, Forest Mahan wasn't entirely sold on Hayes. But he knew the militia was a force among the farmers, and they needed to have their say. He stepped to the side of the podium and leaned over to the microphone. "Well, come on up here, General. Tell us what you have in mind."

Both Horace and James looked over at Nate as the Major General made his way to the front of the hall. Nate rolled his eyes and almost grinned. That Hayes was all suited up with stars on his shoulders and big black combat boots, looking quite a bit like the reincarnation of Fidel Castro, was really too much for Cromwell.

Hayes nodded to Mahan, stepped up to the podium, and adjusted the microphone. "I'm here representing the Montana Militia and, unofficially, all the militia organizations in the United States." A cheer rose from about a third of those in the hall. "And a good portion of us are farmers." This got another cheer.

"The Grange President here has pretty much described the farming situation. But I think he might have been a little easy on those boys in Washington." Hayes' eyes were a blazing green. He ran them over his audience, even held momentarily on Nathaniel Cromwell out there in the crowd.

"Up in Montana, we have a stronger take on what's been going on in the United States. As far as we're concerned, there was a coup in this country in November of 1963. I won't bore you with the specifics of the oil depletion allowance, the intelligence community joining hands with the underworld, or what was behind 9/11. But the way I see it, some fifty years ago this country was taken away from the people and given over to a tight syndicate of bankers, defense contractors, big oil, and the Pentagon. Eisenhower's military industrial complex, if you will. I know a lot of you out there are starting to roll your eyes, thinking, oh no, pretty soon he'll be telling us about aliens and Roswell, New Mexico. No need to go that far. If you do the research, it's not way-out conspiracy theory.

It's the coalescence of big money. Like the gradual buying up of small farms by the megalith industrial farms, the government has been victim to a steady and powerful corporate takeover."

The calls of *right on* and *you got that right* boiled out again across the crowd.

"Plain and simple, the government's been bought out. The system is polluted with money and corrupt up to its ears. The whole damn government's on the dole. And that's the way it's been for a long time. Those hot shots in Washington have lost touch with real folks like us who tend the land or raise livestock."

Hayes let this message hold and allowed the crowd to murmur and hum.

"If you want an answer, I've got one for you," he continued, quieting the place like he held some secret they just couldn't wait to hear. "We take back our country. We own this land. It's ours. We don't need Washington to run our lives. And we tell them that. We decentralize government in a big way. We secede from the union! As many states as dare!"

A good portion of the meeting hall erupted with this. Hooting and howling. Standing and stomping. Another few strings of firecrackers went off. Like the call to war always has for Americans, this was the spark amid the chaff.

Although less than half the crowd was up and yelling, the numbers were enough to make it seem like the whole place was rocking. Those who stayed in their seats, however, were unsettled by this raucous reaction to Hayes. It was exactly what Mahan had feared. Horace Thompson and Jame Peabody, still seated, turned to their famous neighbor. He was staring at the floor.

CHAPTER 20

The Nelson Mansion in Newport was lit up like Disneyland. Fireworks rocketed into the sky from every corner of the property. Rolls Royces, Mercedes, Lincolns, Cadillacs, limousines rolled one after another around the horseshoe driveway, picking up or dropping off some of the most influential and richest people in the world. Movie stars, artists, European royalty, diplomats, politicians, central bankers, scientists, ranking military officers, famous athletes, but above all the Great Gatsbian magnates of business filled the guest list tonight. It was Atossa Andreas-Nelson's grand Fourth of July gala. Always a masquerade. And the only time the elite got a glimpse of what Atossa might be like behind her austere image as matriarch of Andreas Grain.

Atossa stood before her mirror in a horrible state of agitation. Dressed as a mermaid, she was absolutely stunning. An elaborate, very tight, jewel-scaled dress split high up her thigh and spread out behind her in a shimmering fishtail. From three inches below her navel up, the costume was sheer, a long-sleeved diaphanous nothing that accentuated and supported her cosmetically sculpted figure. Her hair, freed from its prim bun and re-dyed the color of red wine, hung to her waist. And with her new face, a face that bore only the slightest resemblance to her old self, she looked like she was thirty—maybe twenty-nine—hardly older than her daughter!

Her new youth and beauty intoxicated her. Never had she dared so revealing a costume at her masquerade. There was every chance she would be the most ravishing woman attending the party tonight—except for one remaining blemish from the skin transplant. The small patch of red lines, like a star of broken blood vessels in the center of her left cheek, would be nothing to cover with makeup, but Dr. Colleen had been emphatic, no creams, no cover-ups, until the entire skin surface had stabilized. Looking as good as she did, Atossa desperately wanted to present her new face tonight, yet because of this one small blemish, she resolved she must wear a mask.

Filled with anxiety, she turned abruptly from the mirror and paced back and forth across the room. Soon she must make her entrance to the party. Last year's party had been a bore. It seemed some vague memorial event to Millhouse Nelson. Yes, she had loved her husband and missed him greatly this very moment. But all anyone could talk about a year ago was Millhouse. This year's party had to make up for the last. And the success of the surgery was just that! Except for the disturbing little detail that she had to wear a mask.

As always, the Tarot cards sat in the center of her divining table. She sidled up to the table and cut the cards. Holding the top third of the deck in her hand, she said aloud, "If I have cut to the Priestess card, I will chance makeup tonight." She turned her wrist to look at the card. It was the nine of pentacles—prosperity and solitude. "I've enough of that," she muttered.

Atossa appeared without announcement at the top of the staircase that wound down from the second floor and fanned out on the main floor of the Newport mansion's grand hall. Even wearing a white porcelain mask, everyone knew who it was as soon as she appeared. She lingered for a moment then slowly descended. Because of the way she'd let her hair fall around her shoulders, partly covering her breasts, it wasn't until she reached the bottom of the stairs that the sheer and revealing nature of her costume became apparent to the crowd. She circulated into the throng like a snake, her scaled-tail sidewinding behind, dragging along with it the stares of jealous older women who wished they had the gall, daring, and body to dress as Atossa had tonight.

The mansion was decorated like Versailles for the party. Gilded mirrors replaced the artwork on every wall. All the antique furniture was put away so eighteenth century French reproductions could be put in its place. There was a stage at one end of the vast, two-story grand hall for the rock band *Blood Money,* due to play at ten. Across the floor, opposite the stage, a mermaid fountain sculpted in ice rose up out of a punch bowl the size of a satellite dish. Banquet tables spread with food from all over the world ran along the walls. What would soon be the dance floor swarmed with wealthy and famous guests. Some wore black tie or high fashion or patriotic stars and stripes. Others wore exquisite and imaginative costumes of all variety, culture, and cost. The place gushed with the show of money. Pearls, rubies, diamonds, and sapphires glistened throughout the crowd like rumors on the society page—yet every one of these was true!

Since her husband's death, Atossa had gradually withdrawn from the social world. Her mansion became a sanctuary, where she kept to herself, secreted away with her harem of boys and her portending habit. But tonight, she'd had a drink or two, and she was coming out of her cave. A deep-sea creature allowed for the evening to breathe among the land animals. She serpentined up behind Frank Nelson, who was dressed all too appropriately as Tweedle-dee in short pants and suspenders. His drunkard brother, Dave, was Tweedle-dum, mingling somewhere with the guests.

Atossa playfully spun the propeller on Frank's red, white, and blue beanie to get his attention. On seeing who it was, Frank's party smile suddenly became all business. He leaned close to her and whispered. "Atossa, we must talk. It's the question of Kenaghy's replacement. I'm going to test the waters with Sam Carlson's name later tonight at the Trillionaire's Club."

It was all Frank could get in before Curtis LaPalme, dressed as a hockey player, approached them. "May I intrude?" he asked. Not having witnessed Atossa's entrance, he didn't know who was behind the white mask. She merely nodded, and LaPalme, a well-known ladies man, gave her his most charming smile. He took Atossa's hand and ran his eyes like fingers over her stunning costume. "Could this lovely creature be your date, Frank?"

Frank made a face. He thought nothing of Atossa's attire. He knew her too well and had seen her in situations radically more revealing. "Curtis LaPalme," said Frank stiffly, "this is our hostess, my sister-in-law, Atossa Andreas."

LaPalme suddenly straightened. "Ms. Andreas, you look absolutely stunning tonight."

Even with her face covered, Atossa felt a new confidence, as though she held a powerful secret. "It's a party, Curtis," she said, casually pushing her hair over her left shoulder, revealing even more of what was already quite daring. "Call me Atossa. And I must congratulate you on that wondrous grain buy. This is the first time I've seen you since that afternoon you came by with the proposal. How are you?"

LaPalme was awe struck. This woman he'd never once thought of in a sexual way was turning him on. "Well, I'm fine, Ms., uh, Atossa, and thank you."

Atossa stepped in closer, clearly feeling LaPalme's confusion and enjoying it. "What do you make of those field burnings last month?"

"It's nonsense, Atossa," said LaPalme, trying not to stare. "It's to be ignored."

"Yes, it seems quite ludicrous to me also," she said, watching LaPalme's eyes from behind her mask.

He turned to Frank out of self-consciousness. "So, you've found our missing grain analyst?"

Frank looked around assessing those within hearing range. "That's right. We've located him—just recently—in Singapore."

"Does he know that we acted on his market valuation?" LaPalme kept looking from Frank to Atossa. All he could see of her face were the dark eyes behind her ceramic mask.

"There's been no direct contact with him." Frank seemed reluctant to talk.

"What's going on?"

Frank looked around at the crowd uneasily. "I can't say."

LaPalme seemed perturbed by this response. "Are you concerned he might reveal why we were so well prepared for the grain shortage?"

"Is there a problem, Curtis?" asked Atossa, catching the tone in LaPalme's voice.

Frank frowned. "No, not at all."

"Then we know who the buyer was?" asked LaPalme, pressing into what Frank was hiding.

"Curtis, this is not the right time. I'll have to get back to you on this." Frank's eyes seemed to fasten on a face in the crowd.

Atossa glanced from one man to the other, suddenly bored with their talk. "Catch me later, Frank." She turned into the crowd and disappeared.

LaPalme faced Frank. "God, that's quite a costume she has on."

Frank's thoughts were elsewhere. "I didn't notice," he said distractedly.

Atossa wound through the crowd looking for her daughter Alise. For all Atossa's power and influence, she always felt somewhat disarmed in the company of her oldest child—because she cared so much about what her daughter thought of her. Tonight, the situation was heightened.

Atossa had not told her about the face transplant. The secret that made her so playful with LaPalme would have a more complex effect on Alise. Like a teenager hiding a new tattoo from her mother, Atossa wanted both to hide and flaunt her secret.

Atossa spotted Alise in a plain white evening dress, standing with her husband Richard in the far corner of the room beneath a potted palm tree. All around the palm's base were horn-shaped baskets overflowing with cut and whole tropical fruit. Atossa crossed the room with a rising heartbeat, knowing the attire she'd worn unabashedly to create envy in her friends would bring bristles from Alise. At the last moment, she quickly rearranged her hair, unsuccessfully trying to cover her all but bare breasts, and approached the young couple from out of the crowd. "Good evening, Alise."

"Mother?" Alise was dark like Atossa, and pretty, but too thin. She looked her mother up and down with a frightened kind of revulsion. "I didn't know that was *you*."

"Hello, Richard." Atossa offered her son-in-law, who wore a tux, an outstretched hand.

"Hello, Ms. Andreas," he said, always intimidated by his mother-in-law, but even more so now by the way she was dressed. He kissed the back of her hand.

"Mother, what in the world made you dress like that?"

Atossa cringed behind her mask, imagining what her daughter might say about her new face. "It's a masquerade, Alise. It gives everyone, even me, a chance to break code."

"Richard, stop starring at my mother's boobs."

"I wasn't. It's the whole effect of the costume. It's, it's…wow."

"Thank you, Richard," said Atossa.

Alise gave her mother the once over one more time. "Why the show, Mother?" Her tone cut Atossa like a sheet of paper.

"Can't I have fun? Can't I get out and kick up my heels one day a year?"

Before Alise could reply, Richard blurted out, "Is that Derek Davis over there?"

"My, he's handsome whoever he is," said Atossa, following her daughter's and son-in-law's eyes to the tall black man dressed as a genie crossing the ballroom floor.

The man seemed to have had heard Atossa's remark. He turned and immediately advanced to the trio beneath the palm tree. He paid no attention to Alise or Richard, but with palpable assurance addressed Atossa.

"I couldn't help noticing your costume, Ms. Mermaid," said Davis with a smile as dazzling as his legendary basketball skills. He wore an electric blue turban, white silk Arabian pantaloons tied with a red sash at the waist, and a shimmering gold sequined vest with no shirt beneath. With his Adonis physique, bare muscled arms, and glistening black skin, he was the only person at the party to command as much attention as Atossa.

"Nor I your costume," returned Atossa, running her eyes all over him, as so many had her. "You must be some kind of athlete," she continued, reaching out to take his hand, "judging by your height and," she spread his fingers out with both of her hands, "the size of these wonderful hands."

Davis was tickled she didn't know who he was. "I ride thoroughbreds," he said with a wink that caught Atossa entirely off-guard—and had Alise shuddering and pulling Richard away by the hand.

Atossa might have slapped him for the wink, but Davis had captured her with his flashing brown eyes, his beautiful smile, and, of course, his body. For a moment, she didn't know what to say and, surprisingly, was feeling self-conscious. She crossed her arms over her bosom, and Davis dared to laugh at her sudden concern.

"Ms. Mermaid," he said, looking down on her from his six and a half feet. "I am Derek Davis. Crown prince of the hardwood. You must tell me who you are." He reached out with both hands and deliberately took hold of hers, so he could open her arms and reveal what she covered. "And my, to wear a dress such as this, you must be very bold." The touch of his hands on hers and the obviousness of his ravishing eyes so turned Atossa on her nipples hardened and stood up high. "Or very cold?" His grin was so assuredly wicked, she blushed at her arousal and turned away, rushing off into the crowd.

Davis called out after her, but she was gone. She was so completely struck by this man, not to mention embarrassed, she disappeared altogether from the party and ran back to the safety of her bedroom.

Not far from the live palm tree, watching this exchange, stood a silent couple dressed exquisitely in embroidered gold silk as a Chinese Emperor and his consort. They were, in fact, both Chinese. The man was of inestimable age, at least forty, maybe seventy. The woman, petite, extremely beautiful and delicate, was very young, perhaps in her teens. On her right hand, she wore a gold glove, embroidered with a small red blossom.

In a sense they were not in costume. Zhao He was one of the most powerful men in the People's Republic of China. To the outside world, to those at this party, he was a vastly successful electronics manufacturer. The largest in Asia. More importantly though, in China, he was the head of a very old and influential Chinese kongsi, a close-knit business clan or extended family of finance and industry—not unlike the mafia.

Beside him was his daughter Xian He. This was her first trip to the United States and part of her grooming for the day she would take her father's place as head of the kongsi. This rare excursion from their home in the mountains of Southern China was the exception of exceptions, and Xian's eyes filled with the temptations of the western world.

Xian and her father remained at the party for three hours, not eating any of the food, not having a drink, hardly moving from the spot they occupied, and speaking only to a few others at the party, mostly bankers. When they left, it was as an emperor and his consort. Quiet. Formal. Sedate. They climbed into the black Mercedes limousine Zhao had rented, and as soon as the door was shut, Zhao slapped Xian in the face.

She made no outcry.

"That was for the way you were watching the western men. I will not have it." That was all he said, and they drove back to their hotel, stayed the night, and left for Singapore the next morning.

CHAPTER 21

The grange hall was boiling over. While some remained in their seats dismayed, others shouted for secession. Field burning. Armed revolution. Civil war! General Hayes surveyed the pandemonium with grim pleasure and backed away from the podium.

Forest Mahan remained off to one side, watching the unsettling mix of insanity and consternation, uncertain what to do next. Through the riot of the crowd, he saw Cromwell, leaning up against the wall, eyes downward. Mahan kept his eyes on Nate until the retired Colonel looked up. Right at him. The talk they'd had in the barn ten days earlier sparked between them in the flash of their eyes.

Nate felt it like an alarm sounding. Too much of what Hayes said was true. The balance of power in the United States had been corrupted by huge pools of capital. He'd known that a long time. He'd seen it up close and personal. But civil war? He couldn't even say the words to himself without a certain exasperation and sinking in his stomach, followed by memory after memory of that year he'd spoken out against the opium connection he'd seen in Afghanistan, the lies against him, the smearing of his name, his life, his family.

And here he was on the spot again. He saw this before him as clear as day. He was being called from the plow to save the country he had loved all his life—yet that had also betrayed him. The farmers had real grievances that went back several generations. A stand of some sort was needed. Mahan's opening speech had convinced him of that. But secession? Armed revolution? No. That's why they needed him. He was the man, maybe the only man on the face of the Earth, with the internal and external wherewithal to unify the movement. He took a deep breath, knowing full well should he step forward now, it would chew him up and spit him out in the end. It had happened before. It would happen again. Politics of this sort was unrelenting. His mother and son would be drawn in whether they wanted to or not. He tried to deny what he was thinking. He tried to deny the clarion call, but one question kept coming back to him: *What better cause for a farm boy than the health of the land?*

Nate leaned over to Peabody and whispered, "From this moment on, I'm a target. Watch my back." Then he strode out of the howling crowd up to the podium like the cowboy he was. Mahan stepped up to adjust the mike.

The place went dead quiet.

Square of shoulder, burnt by the sun from daily toil, tried and true in the bloody fields of battle and the amber fields of grain, the soldier turned farmer stood there behind the podium a moment and scratched the side of his head so his baseball cap rose up and down. Playing the country boy, Nate panned the whole shit-kicking crowd, then drawled matter of fact like, "Maybe it's about time us farmers formed a union. Put us together a little strike."

The place went nuts.

A young man in camo with a shaved head and a homemade swastika tattoo on his forearm, sitting close to the podium, jumped up in his enthusiasm, clicked his heels together, and gave Nate a straight-armed Nazi salute. Nate took one step around the podium and cold cocked him right back into his seat. For a second time the place went dead quiet. Nate sneered into the faces all around him. There wasn't a black or a Hispanic in the first ten rows.

He snatched the microphone from the podium. "If anybody thinks they've come to some kind of neo-Nazi cross burning, if anybody thinks this is about hating Jews or blacks or prejudice of any kind, I suggest you leave right now. Because that's not what this is about. We hold these truths to be self-evident. If nothing else, get that straight." He paused and made sure everyone did.

Holding the microphone in his right hand, he stepped up close to the audience and lowered his voice. "A good deal of what General Hayes said is true. This thing capitalism. This economic system that some think defines our democracy is out of control. Flawed by the simple fact that money generates more money. The rich get richer, and the farmer goes another dollar in debt. But we can't change capitalism or pull down the corporate machine or break the hold the wealthy have on Congress by any quick and easy means—even by seceding. That's more than we can reasonably expect.

"So, for now, to have any real chance at all, we need focus. We must concentrate all our energy on one thing. Organizing ourselves with the intent of getting a fair price for our product. Nothing more. Then maybe, from there, we'll have the influence to work little by little on some of these other problems. But we won't get it all at once. Even going out there and burning our crops won't get us out of the hole we're in now." There was some mumbling in the group, some restless movement, but no one left their seat. No one shouted him down.

"As I look out at all of you now, I can see you are both angry and scared. Just as I am. Angry for the way you've been treated. Scared for your livelihood and your family. Because, like Mahan and Hayes have both said, we're sitting here talking about standing up to the government. And it isn't a pleasant thing to think about. Secession? I don't think it needs to come to that. Burning fields? That's pushing it too. I'm hoping we can just give a strong show of unity, reveal the real power of the farming community, and maybe through due process get some changes made. Because we do have one huge thing going for us—it's all that grain we've grown. I figure Mahan has that right. That grain is our hostage. We hold on to it until we get what we want or in the extreme we turn it under—even burn it if need be. But we have to hope it doesn't come to that. And until then, we've got to stay together—regardless of what our individual feelings might be.

"Yeah, I know a lot of you are all set to pick up a rifle and maybe a torch. I see you out there in your multi-colors. And believe me, I've been watching this militia thing spreading out across our country the last few years. I've seen the newsreels, read the magazine articles, and listened to the interviews. The right to bear arms, the right to form a militia is part of our constitution. But I think it's important to be very cautious about any kind of armed stand against the government. Our position is one where we have a lot to gain but also a lot to lose. Take my word for it, no one wins in war." Nate scanned the crowd, dotted here and there with men in militia uniforms, eventually focusing on Major General Hayes glaring hard right back at him.

"Let's put aside our differences for now and concentrate on what we have in common," he said straight into Hayes' glare. "We don't have time to argue. We must begin smack dab right now to have any chance at all. And don't get me wrong about this militia thing. I might not be gung-ho about uniforms since I got discharged, but there is a time and place for what you bring to the situation. Because once word gets out that we're going to offer the grain industry and the government an ultimatum, we're going to have the Homeland Guard, maybe even the

U.S. Army, in our fields. And you boys are our only line of defense. Until then, until we know what kind of response we're going to get, we can't be split between radical and conservative. We can't be split between no-till and organic. We can't be split between white and brown or black or red or yellow. We must be one."

Nate stopped to feel out his audience. "Now I'm a wonderin'," he began again, falling back into his farmer's drawl. "If what I'm sayin' rings true to you all? And if I was willin', me being someone everyone knows and trusts to some extent, what would you think, for the sake of not wastin' the energy of further debate—what would you think about me takin' over this thing?"

The crowd held silent for a few moments, then there was murmuring and talk. A few voices in the back began to chant, "Nate, Nate, Nate." It began to pick up, steadily, "Nate, Nate, Nate," until the entire place was rocking and rolling with it, feet stomping, fist shaking, "Nate, Nate, Nate."

Throughout this display, Nate was staring straight at Hayes. Hayes might have been the only man in the place sitting still and quiet. His eyes still on Hayes, Nate raised both of his hands, palms open, to calm the place. It took some time but quiet came.

"I assume that little demonstration means you're all with me on this." The place broke into laughter then slowly fell quiet again.

"Okay," Nate grinned. "Listen up. This thing begins now. The farmers' union is settled, but we have a few things that we'll have to work out in the next week or so. We'll have to come up with a statement and a platform to circulate through the various grange halls, underlining the fact that we're preparing for a strike. Not a war. And once we get the wording right and make sure we have the necessary support, we stop paying our bills to the seed and fertilizer dealers. Stop paying our credit cards and our bank loans. Pay the little guys, the local store owner, the hometown mechanic, and trade among ourselves. Keep the community together. And then we'll make every preparation we can for two things: harvesting our fields on time or, if we have no other choice, if we have to, turning them under or even burning them. If it turns out that some crops are lost, those losses will be shared by the group—that is, if anyone comes out of this thing with a dollar or two—it's shared. We're in this together or not at all. And if you aren't, say so. I need no excuses. I need no explanations. It ain't with us or against us. It's simply with us or not."

He paused and took a breath, realizing the importance of what he'd just said and that it had begun—just as suddenly and as unexpectedly as war. "If I thought we could maintain secrecy I would say so. But I know it's impossible. More likely than not, there are journalists among us now. I expect news of this meeting will be in the papers tomorrow or the next day. That said, from now on, all communication is based on a need to know. Just go about your business. If you want updates or help, go to your local grange. There will be betrayals and there will be traitors. But it doesn't matter. It just doesn't matter. We will do what we have to do no matter what. We are a labor union, not a political party, not a covert action, and remember we're talking strike—not war. Everything we do will be more or less legal—until it can't be."

Cromwell paused, measuring his audience, then looked straight at the militia leader.

"If he'll take the job, I'm going to ask General Hayes to be my second in command and in charge of organizing the militia throughout the Heartland—I think that's thirty-seven states. He's already put a lot of energy into this, and I accept that he's trustworthy and efficient." Hayes' eyes acknowledged nothing. "Forest Mahan will be our union president. He'll coordinate our actions through the National Grange. He'll be our liaison to the government and the industry."

He paused again measuring the response. "I'll be the media man. The recognized commodity. The face on the box of Wheaties. And the strategist. I will coordinate with Hayes and Mahan. Give us a few days and we'll have a platform. We'll send it out through the grange and ask for your feedback.

"Now remember, first things first, I want each and every one of you to go home, talk to your family and neighbors, and get ready—your family, your farm, and your community in that order. You militia people report as soon as possible to your commanding officers—and forget the uniforms. Blue jeans and t-shirts are the ultimate camouflage for what we've got ahead. If you're not in the militia and want to be, find your local battalion. For the rest of you, remain on your farm. Again, along with preparation for harvest, consider the logistics of field burning—firebreaks, getting the machinery in, your livestock contained, and warning non-farmers in the vicinity. Those of you who have extra time and energy, the best thing to do is help your community organize. Each township must be tight as a drum. Think as a family, as a unit that can survive without help from the outside world. Maintain a survivalist attitude—food, water, gasoline, sanitation, guns. And again, trust the grange." He paused and grinned a moment. "Now get the hell out of here, all of you. We've got work to do."

The place exploded with applause, screams, hoots, and hollers. Then they slowly milled out of the building to the chant of *Nate, Nate, Nate.* There were doubts and confusion as to what to do and where exactly things were headed, but one thing they all held in common, almost to a person, was a certainty that the right man was in charge.

CHAPTER 22

It was twenty-five minutes before midnight, and while the party was in full swing downstairs, Atossa sat at her divining table in her mermaid costume, a veil replacing her porcelain mask. Beside her stood Stephen, a tall, lean blonde boy of eighteen, wearing nothing and shaved clean except for his head. A single candle on the table provided a dim hovering light. Forty-nine yarrow sticks were spread out in front of Atossa in bundles of threes, fours, and eights. Her copy of the *I Ching* lay open to an analysis of the seventh hexagram. With her right hand, she wrote with a quill pen in a diary that tracked her entire history of *I Ching* consultations. With her left hand, she cradled the young man's testicles, rolling them gently between her fingers.

After leaving the party, she had hurried up to her bedchamber, seeking the comfort of the Taoist oracle. During the course of a day, Atossa might cut at random into her deck of Tarot cards for an immediate measuring of the moment. But rarely did she use the Tarot for a full reading. She preferred the Chinese *Book of Changes* for more deliberate and in-depth insights, as she did now. Although her mind was still on her encounter with the basketball star Derek Davis, she had asked the *I Ching* a more general question about her grain company. The field burnings troubled her more than she let on.

The oracle answered with the hexagram *Shuh:* earth above water. *In the middle of the earth is water,* said the Book of Changes, *the image of the Army. Thus the superior person increases his masses by generosity toward the people.* Atossa dwelled upon the meaning of these lines as one might dwell upon his or her image in a mirror. There was no doubt in her mind that Andreas Grain had done something good for the world by being prepared to help in a time of shortage. Yes, this was clearly her generosity to the people.

Ground water, continued the Chinese Oracle, *is invisibly present within the earth. In the same way the military power of the people is invisibly present in the masses. When danger threatens, every peasant becomes a soldier; when the war ends, he goes back to the plow. He who is generous toward the people wins their love, and a people living under a mild rule become strong and powerful.* This is exactly how Atossa felt about herself and Andreas Grain. Her company was the number one grain distributor in the world, both in total revenues and, now that they had responded to the crisis with such timeliness, world respect. For the moment, her concerns were dismissed by this positive reading.

Money, power, and the overwhelming success of her grain business, these conceits were but a temporary balm for Atossa's deeper personal anxiety. Ever since the death of her husband Millhouse, loneliness had undermined the pleasure of her material wealth. Although their sexual relationship was never more than an aside to the marriage, there had been trust and a real love. She had always been able to confide in Millhouse, and he in her. That had been extremely important to both of them. But she no longer had that vital companionship. And she longed for a close friendship with her daughter or, impossibly, a lover. As it was, these boys she hired rarely touched her. They were only necessary as part of her portending habit, black magic accessories, if you will.

She turned away from the *I Ching* text and observed the young man standing quietly beside her. It was his first night with her. He accepted the restless embrace of her left hand with obvious pleasure. Atossa studied his body. Despite its beauty and youth, her mind returned to the handsome black man she had just met.

Atossa impulsively reached across the table for the Tarot deck. Using her right hand only, she shuffled and cut her Tarot deck into three piles, then stacked them on top of each other. The entire time she kneaded Stephen's balls with her left hand, believing a more powerful form of divination could be milked from his arousal, his orgone spark. Her mind focused on Derek Davis, she turned over the top card.

The image on the card stopped her cold. It was the Tower again, collapsing and burning. It struck her powerfully. And with visions. For a second time, she saw grain elevators toppling over—all in a line like dominos. But now with people running around them, carrying pitchforks and guns. An army of farmers assembling out of a field of wheat. It was all vivid and clear. She stood and pushed Stephen away, striding into a distracted pace.

Atossa stalked back and forth across the room several times, then suddenly stopped. Stephen stood beside the divining table, staring at her, uncertain what to do. "Leave," she commanded, knowing she had seen vividly into the future, as it so rarely ever came to her. "I will call you if I need you."

Stephen turned and crossed the room to the curtained wall. Atossa watched his bare hindquarters without thought. When Stephen had pulled aside the heavy curtains and exited, Atossa removed her veil and strode back to her divining table and stared down at the one card that was face up. The image of toppling grain elevators ran through her head over and over until she simply erupted and upended the table. The yarrow sticks, her diary, the Book of Changes, the cards, the candle went flying in all directions across the floor. She stormed once again into a furious pace, back and forth, snaking her long fishtail behind, finally halting beneath the skylight. She glared up into the night sky at the moon. For a moment, she just stood there, her jeweled costume glistening in the moonlight. "If there is to be an uprising, I will smother it," she pronounced, stomping down on the still burning candle on the floor.

A knock on her bedroom door broke her ugly muse. The knock sounded again. Atossa tried to ignore it.

"Atossa! Please, this is Frank," came from the other side of the door. "I must talk to you."

Atossa didn't move. The only person she wanted to talk to was Derek Davis. He had played with her, made her feel powerless and insecure. She hated it. And she loved it. He'd teased her. He'd laughed at her. And frightened her. She'd felt his fierce assuredness, and she wanted more of it.

"Atossa, please. I must talk to you tonight. Now, if possible."

"Go away."

"Atossa, it's business."

She reached over to the edge of the upturned table and pressed a button. A buzzer sounded at the clasp to her bedroom door. Frank opened the door and took two steps into the shadowy moonlit room.

He hadn't noticed the nature of Atossa's sudden departure, but he knew she'd left the party early. "Thank you, Atossa," intoned Frank to the dark figure across the room.

Atossa hardly acknowledged Frank. Her mood was as obvious as the table on its side and the cards and yarrow sticks scattered on the floor. Frank pushed through it. "I have spoken with several of our friends this evening. I have probed them on strategies to deal with Kenaghy. Almost universally, they believe we should move quickly on finding his successor. If we cut his financial support from the business community and continue further media attack, Kenaghy will have no chance in November."

Atossa nodded perceptibly. She was thinking about Derek Davis. His touch. His look. His gall.

"Before the end of the party, there will be a little gathering. I want to pass around the name of Samuel Carlson. I think he's our best bet." Frank paced back and forth before Atossa, getting more excited as he spoke. "What do think, Atossa? Can you go with Carlson?"

She watched his arousal with grim displeasure.

He stopped his pacing and looked right at her. It was too dark to see her face or her searing eyes. "I know we can get him past Kenaghy."

Atossa's left hand restlessly kneaded the air.

"The convention is next week," Frank continued. "By my count, there is no consensus as yet. Thompson and Carlson split the primaries. But we can't let our candidate look weak. Whomever we choose, the convention reaction must be strong. It must look good on television. I like Carlson."

Atossa heard nothing of what Frank said. She was fixated on the black man dressed as a genie. She spoke abruptly. "Is that all, Frank?"

Frank frowned. "Well, what do you think?"

"I could give a damn, Frank. Please leave me alone. You have my support."

Frank smiled. "Good," he said and walked out.

As soon as Atossa heard the door shut, she went over to her mirror and turned on the light above it. She stroked her breasts beneath the gauze of her costume until the nipples stood up straight—nearly half an inch. She just stared at them in the mirror trying to determine how obvious it was. Very. Something of it turned her on, thinking that the handsome Davis had seen her in such a state of arousal. She moved up closer to the mirror and inspected the red threaded blemish on her cheek. How it vexed her. Just a little powder and a touch of makeup, she thought, and the porcelain mask would not be necessary.

CHAPTER 23

As the last few farmers drifted out of the Pratt Grange Hall, five men remained. James Peabody and Horace Thompson waited by the door. Forest Mahan leaned against the back wall next to the American flag. Nathaniel Cromwell stood at the podium, and a grim Vincent Hayes sat in the center of a sea of empty chairs. A confrontation was unavoidable as far as Peabody and Thompson were concerned. They looked at each other and left the building. Mahan stayed only a moment longer. He wanted to talk to Cromwell, but he also knew that Hayes and Cromwell had some things to sort out before anything else could happen. He spoke across the room, "Nate, I'll talk with you in a bit," and walked out.

Nate waded through the rows of folding chairs toward Hayes. Hayes didn't move. Nate straddled a chair backwards and sat down right in front of him. He leaned forward so his thick forearms rested on the back of the chair. The two men sat there, eye to eye, for expanding seconds.

Hayes was an extremely proud man. He was five years older than Cromwell, several inches taller and leaner. Except for two tours in the Marines, one during Desert Storm, he'd spent almost his entire life on the plains of Montana running a huge cattle ranch. With his olive-green cap pulled low on his forehead and the thick, untrimmed red beard covering most of his face, Hayes' expression was concentrated in his eyes.

Nate knew very little about Hayes, except what he could judge from the man's physical bearing, the words he'd spoken earlier in the evening, and that his backing was absolutely essential to getting anywhere with the farmers' strike. Nate's approach to men and life and conflict was always the same. Straight on. He dropped his eyes to the floor for a moment, then looked up at Hayes, noting that the militia general had a little silver Christian cross pinned to his shirt collar.

"Well, General, I say anything that didn't work for you?"

Hayes pursed his lips. His eyes moved perceptibly across Nate's face. "Colonel Cromwell, I am as aware of your career as anyone. Not only your war record, but also your effort to stand up against your superiors. I know you have personally experienced both the power and corruption of our government. You must surely understand the deep distrust of Washington within the militia movement. Some of us doubt that working with the system can produce positive results because the system is so corrupt. We feel that the democracy has been sold out. And that secession is the only way to show our distaste and frustration." He paused, looking Nate in the eyes. "But as you said, Colonel, our best chance against these bastards is together. We, the militia, will try it your way until otherwise disposed. Personally, I am honored to serve under you."

Hayes' words surprised Nate. He'd expected a fight. Nate tipped back his ball cap and nodded his deep pleasure and appreciation. Both men stood and clasped hands.

"We have a tough assignment, Hayes. Your responsibilities will be of the utmost importance. To what extent is the militia organized?"

"Very well," said Hayes. "One of the tasks I have taken on in Montana is to coordinate with the other militias in the United States. I would say we are as close to a unit as could be hoped for at this time."

Nate nodded. "We have you and the grange. Other than that, we're just a bunch of farmers spread out across the Great Plains. Mobile phones, internet connections, antique CBs, and a focus of purpose hold us together." He paused. "I want each state militia to coordinate with their grange. Can that work?"

"Yes, sir."

"And I trust you are in agreement with my comments about race, color, and creed."

"The militia went through a lot of soul searching after the Oklahoma City bombing, Colonel." Hayes looked Cromwell straight in the eye, not a waver, not a blink. "I think you'll discover the militia is more interested in preserving the Bill of Rights than denying it."

Cromwell nodded. "That's the only way it can be."

Forest Mahan, standing outside the entrance to the grange hall, watched the meeting of the two men. When he saw them shake hands and begin talking, he reentered the building and walked slowly to where they now were. He reached the two men at this last exchange.

"Thanks for standing up tonight and taking charge, Nate," said Mahan, extending his hand to the man he knew only through their talk the week before, *Time Magazine* covers, and television interviews.

"I wasn't too much of a blowhard?" Nate grinned.

"Don't see as you had much choice."

"Maybe not, Forest. Thank you for having the courage to get this first meeting underway. Do you two know each other?"

"Only from tonight," said Mahan, reaching out to take Hayes' hand.

"So much for formalities then," continued Nate. "I was just telling the general that each state militia unit will need to work in conjunction with its grange."

Mahan had always distrusted the militia movement, but he understood the choices were few and far between. "Sounds good to me."

"One thing we should all be aware of is leaks. We must assume that the militia and possibly the grange have been infiltrated. FBI, ATF, who knows what else? Does that sound like a fair assumption to you, General?"

Hayes nodded. "And I doubt there's anything we can do about it."

"So, we proceed as though everything we do is known. Even what we say between the three of us." He looked each of the two men in the eye and went on. "In the next twenty-four hours, Forest, I want you to verify internet communication with all the granges."

"It already exists."

"Good. Keep the lines open. Get each grange to organize its farmers. Have them deliver the same message I told the people here tonight. Prepare their families, farms, and communities. And set up some kind of relief fund. In cash and commodities. No banks. This is all in family until the end. I also need all the information you have on the crops. How much. Where. Harvest dates. Names of important farmers. I'll be at your place tomorrow, late afternoon, and we'll prepare a statement to the industry, the government, and the media, so the whole damn nation knows out front what we are about."

"Gotcha."

Nate turned to Hayes. "General, can you be at Forest's farm in Missouri tomorrow afternoon?

Hayes' eyes remained in contact with Nate's the entire time. "Yes, sir."

"Any questions, gentlemen?"

"Think we've got a chance with this, Nate?" asked Mahan.

Nate took a deep breath. "We won't know unless we try. Hayes?"

"The militia will be ready, Colonel."

Nate opened up into a genuine smile. "Shit, Vincent, you scare me. Seems like your people have been waiting a long time for this. Just keep in mind, until otherwise announced, no burning, no gunfire. All we're trying to do is get a little respect for us dirt diggers."

"We'll be right and ready, sir."

"So will I, Nate."

"Then we'll talk again tomorrow. Forest's place is outside Springfield. My neighbor Jim Peabody can tell me how to get there. I'll leave it to you two to get directions straight. I have to get back home and prepare my family for this."

Nate headed double-time across the dirt parking lot to Peabody's pickup. Farmers filled the area, milling around, lighting fireworks, and bullshitting. The young man he decked earlier in the meeting suddenly came at him out of the crowd.

Nate braced himself. "What's on your mind, son?"

The youth handed him a newsletter. "Here's something I think you should read." His voice was flat and without emotion.

Nate took the newsletter calling itself *The New Patriot* in rippling red, white, and blue ink and read enough to realize it was white supremacist propaganda. "No thanks," he said, holding the newsletter out to the young man.

The youth just stared at him, refusing to take it back.

"You ever know a black man?" asked Nate. "You ever know a Jew?"

"Wouldn't want to."

Nate frowned. "You haven't had any real experience with life, son. You've probably lived your entire life out here in the lily-white Midwest. You haven't fought in the trenches with men of all colors around you. You haven't seen a black man die beside you. You haven't had an Asian save your life. You haven't seen stacks and stacks of the dead. We all die the same."

"You sound like some kind of liberal."

Nate shook his head. There was something strangely detached about this young man—in his voice, in his eyes. "You on drugs, son?"

The youth spat on the ground.

Nate crumpled up the newsletter and got up close to the boy's face. "Where you from? Who gave you these?"

The kid didn't even seem to hear the question. Nate wanted to grab the boy and shake him out of his trance. But he didn't. Someone had probably done too much of that already.

"Look, son. We're trying to do something good here. Get rid of this trash." He flipped the wadded up paper at the youth who caught it. "Find a positive way to contribute or just get out of the way."

"Yeah, sure," the youth sneered.

Arms at his side, Nate squeezed his hands into fists and turned away, hoping he wouldn't get a bullet in the back.

James and Horace were in the pickup. Nate climbed in without a word, and they hit the road. No one said anything for ten or fifteen minutes. Peabody broke the spell.

"Kind of figured you were gonna pull something like that, Nate."

Nate looked across the cab at his neighbor and nodded. Another ten minutes passed before anything more was said. This time it was Nate.

"I'm going to need some help, guys. I'm discovering real fast that trust is going to be tough to find out here."

"That militia general give you some trouble in there?" asked Thompson.

"No, not at all. He surprised me quite a bit. He might be our best ally in this thing."

"Really?"

"We'll find out soon enough. Once we announce the strike and put our demands on the table, we'll know what we're up against. That will be the test. Then we'll know if the farmers and the militia can act as one."

"What's your gut feeling, Nate?" asked Peabody.

"Some difficult times ahead."

It's nearly oh-two hundred hours in the Afghan morning. The moon is disappearing behind the ridge they're encamped on. Rust and Davenport are back from the ridge overlooking the three main cave entrances, where they planted explosive packages all along the upper rim of the canyon. Everyone has eaten. All is ready—explosives, rocket launchers, grenades, spelunking gear. But Tenzing Jast is not back yet.

Cromwell keeps staring off to the south along the back of the ridge expecting to see Tenzing. He has yet to voice his anxiety, but everyone is feeling it. Even Rust is smart enough to leave Cromwell alone now. All of them are getting edgy with the approach of zero hour with too many uncertainties ahead. They understand that they are about to drop themselves into a deep black hole from which there is every likelihood they will never return—and time is their least expendable resource.

All of a sudden Canary sings out. "That him?"

Rust reaches for his MP-5. Cromwell for his night vision binoculars. "Easy, Rusty."

Jerry lowers his rifle, and they all hold their collective breath, watching the little man scramble over the snowy rock and rubble, wondering what news he'll bring.

The seemingly tireless Sherpa enters camp with his ever-present smile. "That good, huh, Tenzing," mutters Rust.

"I found the back entrance, Colonel. Not so far from here. I would never have found it except for the guards."

"You weren't seen?"

"No, Colonel, no. The three men at entrance were more concerned about staying warm than being lookouts."

"Tell me more."

"Thirty minutes from here—maybe longer with gear. One large opening, one small. I cannot say for certain they lead to the caves on the other side, but the location is where we were told."

"Can we get to the guards without them seeing us?"

Tenzing nods, black eyes twinkling. "I think so. They sit back within the entrance out of the wind."

Cromwell nods and scratches his bearded chin. "Rusty, Priestly, Alvoretti, sit on the front door with the rocket launcher and some grenades. Don't do a damn thing unless I call you on the black band or they start coming out. In the dark, hidden in these cliffs, the three of you should be able to hold off an army. And if not, Rusty use those charges you and Lena set up—but only after all else is complete or failed. And be aware of the lookouts on the east side of the canyon."

Although he's talking calmly, hurry-up is behind his every word. He looks at Davenport. "Tenzing is taking you, Masoud, and me to the back door. And we're going in. If we don't find our way to the main chamber or chambers, we're coming back out to try something else. If this back entrance is the right one, I want to appraise what they've got going before we collapse the place. If all goes perfectly, we plant our explosives and get the hell out. We'll give you guys," he looks at Rust, Alvoretti, and Priestly, "the heads up on the black band when we're done, then all of us will high tail it out of here before we bring the mountain down. If things get crazy or you don't hear from us, it's back to the pickup spot by oh-six hundred. Here take this." He hands Rust the GPS device. "With Masoud and Tenzing, we'll find our way. If we don't show, you're on your own. Do whatever it takes to save your skin. If we get caught, they'll be swarming out of those caves to see who else is with us. If you haven't heard from us at that point, blow the charges."

Everyone grabs only what gear is absolutely necessary, and they split into two groups. Tenzing leads Cromwell, Davenport, and Masoud south across the face of the ridge, all of them carrying silenced automatic hand guns instead of their rifles.

It's oh-two-thirty when Cromwell's group gets sight of the back entrance. A stiff wind is blowing from the south, and it's getting colder by the second. Cromwell and Masoud remove their packs. Tenzing and Davenport stay put, hunkered down with their gear in the rocks. Cromwell motions to Masoud and they move in on the cave. When they are close enough to see the guards as more than shadows—there are four not three, sitting side by side, smoking cigarettes, and talking as though they're at the bazaar in Kabul. Cromwell draws his nine-millimeter Beretta and Masoud his assassin's knife.

Cromwell's approach is straight on. Masoud circles over the top of the cave. Because of the dark and the increasing wind, which is pushing the guards deeper into the cave entrance, Cromwell and Masoud get within a few yards without being seen or heard. It's too easy. Cromwell peeks out from behind the edge of the opening. Starting left to right—tishhh, tishhh, tishhh, tishhh—he puts bullets in the guards' foreheads before they can distinguish the silencer's sound from the wind. Masoud drops down into the entrance as Cromwell steps out into the open. Masoud checks the bodies, then quickly peeks into the cave. Seeing nothing, he ventures in—then comes back out. "Could be a long way, Colonel."

Cromwell takes a look. "It's what it is." Then he climbs out of the recess in the rocks and waves to Lena and Tenzing to join them.

CHAPTER 24

As was the tradition at Atossa's masquerade party, a last dance at midnight signaled the formal ending of the night's festivities. Of course, many would stay later. There would be drinks and private gatherings for hours afterward. But the last dance was the ceremonial climax of the Gatsbian ball. The band would stop playing. The dance floor would clear. Atossa would be escorted to the middle of the room. The music would begin again, and Atossa and her partner would begin the last dance, always a waltz.

Since the first party twenty-one years ago, until his death, Atossa's husband Millhouse had been her partner for this final dance. Last year, her then eighteen-year-old son, Edmund, had led her to the center of the dance floor. Tonight Edmund had not attended, probably to avoid this moment. Atossa had missed too much of the party to know this, but with the witching hour drawing near, her daughter Alise was all too aware of it.

"Richard?" Alise drew her husband close to shout over the rock'n'roll that had begun at ten. "Have you seen my step-brother this evening?"

"No, I haven't," Richard answered, looking around the crowd. "I don't think he's here."

"Who's going to dance with my mother?"

Richard gave her a blank look.

"It may have to be you."

"Alise, no."

"Who then? Certainly not Frank. He' such a twerp. The way she's dressed tonight she needs someone that at least looks the part—not Tweedle-dee."

"The way she's dressed tonight, Alise, I'd be scared to get that close to your mother. Where is she, anyway?"

"I haven't seen her since we left her with the basketball player." Alise took Richard by the hand and began moving through the crowd. "What was his name?"

"Derek Davis. How could you forget *his* name?"

"Where is Mother?" Alise continued as they wound through the crowd. "You and I might have to open the last dance."

Richard rolled his eyes then looked at his wristwatch. "Christ, Alise, it's midnight now!" As soon as he said it, the music stopped.

"I don't believe it," Alise continued in her anxiety, "for the first time ever, I'm actually hoping my mother shows up!"

With the sudden silence of the band, those who were dancing moved off the floor, creating a silent ring of onlookers in expectation of the ceremonial last dance. When nothing happened right away and the floor remained empty, a murmur of talk spread through the crowd. Even the famous rock band began to stalk about the stage with their guitars, looking at each other, wondering whether they should begin the waltz or delay things with more rock'n'roll.

Alise surveyed the crowd, knew what was called for, and took Richard by the hand. As they reached the edge of the dance floor, the buzz of conversation stopped, and all eyes turned to the grand staircase. Atossa stood on the top step. For the second time that evening she began her slow descent. She still wore her fantastic mermaid costume and the ceramic mask, but she had discarded the diaphanous top. Only her long glossy hair covered her bare breasts, and that fleetingly, as she descended one step at a time.

All present, especially the older women, watched in growing awe and distaste as Atossa proceeded down the stairs. Yes, the wealthy and famous people who attended Atossa's party paid her a reluctant homage, but this startling entrance had them back on their heels, muttering to one another. And no one was more shocked than Alise. Her mouth open, her left hand squeezing her husband's right, she whispered weakly, "Is that really my mother, Richard? Please, tell me it's not."

When Atossa reached the bottom of the stairs, all fell silent. The partygoers at the base of the staircase parted, and the fish-tailed queen passed through to the center of the ballroom floor.

With Atossa's son Edmund nowhere to be seen, Frank began to fidget in anticipation that he would have to dance with Atossa. Curtis LaPalme caught Frank's eye, apparently thinking the same thing, while

Alise tugged at Richard's sleeve, hoping he would dance with her brazenly unclad mother.

Even amid this tense and unsure moment, Atossa, in her daring attire, shimmering burgundy hair, and hidden face, was arguably the most alluring woman at the ball. There were younger women and prettier women, but the provocative mystery of her mask, her fine surgically sculpted body so openly on display, and the serpentine flow of her dazzling mermaid tail captured the rapt attention of every man and woman there. She was like black fire, too hot to ignore, too cold to approach.

For lingering moments, the party suspended on this high wire, with no one daring to join Atossa on the dance floor. Alise, feeling deeply for her mother, could not bear to watch another pendulous second. "Richard, you must. You must save Mother." She pushed at her husband, but he stood firm. "Please, Richard, please," pleaded Alise on the verge of tears for the embarrassment she felt for her mother.

Then, just as Richard took a hesitant step forward, the ring of people opened across the way. Someone had rubbed the magic lantern and the genie had appeared. Derek Davis, the wondrous basketball player, tall, black, bare-chested, and perfectly attired to dance with a mermaid, strode to the center of the floor. He knelt on one knee before Atossa, looked upward over her bare torso, smiled slyly into the dark eyes peering out from behind the porcelain mask, and offered her his hand.

Blood Money took the cue. At the moment Atossa accepted Davis' hand and drew him gracefully up from one knee, the band began an elaborate electric version of Franz Liszt's *Mephisto Waltz*. Davis put his free hand on Atossa's waist, and the dazzling couple danced. And they danced beautifully. From one end of the ballroom to the other, the magnificent and bizarre couple glided and twirled to the haunting gypsy melodies of Liszt's famous waltz, played on a solid body electric violin and backed by *Blood Money's* virtuoso guitarist. The crowd was stunned and enchanted. No other couple dared set foot on the floor for fear of breaking the magic of the evening.

For the first minute, neither of the dancers spoke. Atossa hovered between ecstasy and penetrating horror. Here was the romance. The high-flying exhilaration of her grandest dreams. Enacted before those whom she wished most to impress. It was too good to be true, and she feared breaking the spell with a single word. At the same time, Davis kept looking downward at Atossa's mask, wondering exactly who it was he held in his arms. Finally, leaning down to her ear, he whispered. "Who are you, mermaid? From that entrance, my guess is you're the hostess of this fairy tale?"

Atossa remained silent.

"I very much like the change you made in your costume," continued Davis. "I like a forward woman." He lifted his right hand from Atossa's waist and pushed her hair back over her left shoulder, exposing her breast. He gave her a suggestive smile, then pulled her in close so her breast pressed against his bare chest.

Atossa lifted her eyes into his boldness that was enhanced all the more by the eyes of an audience.

"Could this house really be yours?" Davis used his left hand to push her hair over her right shoulder, increasing the contact of their skin.

Atossa still didn't answer, as all around them, one by one, other couples began to join them on the floor.

"Are you going say anything, mermaid? Or don't mermaids talk?"

Atossa's heart was pounding so furiously, she wondered if Davis could hear it. But her silence was doing to him what his beauty was doing to her. He was charmed and captivated by this woman he knew must be fabulously wealthy and powerful.

"I don't want the evening to end with this dance," said Davis with obvious intent.

Neither did Atossa, but she knew that it must. This was all that there could be. This dance. This moment. And then the end. The floor was full. Dancers swirled around them. She looked up sadly into his eyes.

Even with the mask, he could read her answer in the expression of her eyes. "Then I must know your name. How else will I see you again?"

Suddenly they both stopped, and she bowed her head.

"You must answer. I must see you again."

Atossa hesitantly lifted her head. "I am Atossa Andreas-Nelson."

Davis, three years retired, had come with Terry Linsdorf, the owner of his old basketball team and a multibillionaire computer magnate. Davis knew little of this level of society. The name Andreas-Nelson meant nothing to him, though he clearly understood there was plenty of money behind it. "I want you tonight, Atossa," he said, with the voice of a man who gets what he wants when he wants it, to a woman who gets what she wants when she wants it.

"That's impossible. Leave your phone number and I will call you."

"No, Atossa. Tonight," he pressed, glowing with lust and smiling his beautiful smile.

"If you wish to know me, it must be on my terms and my terms only. Please, our evening is over now. Escort me to the staircase, and when you leave, give your phone number to the doorman."

Davis stared at her blank white mask. No one spoke to him like this. And yet such was the authority in Atossa's voice, he obeyed and offered her his arm. With the dancers opening the floor before them, he walked her to the base of the staircase. She ascended three stairs, so they stood face to face, both of them head and shoulders above the crowd. Incredibly Davis was as uneasy as she was. "You must at least remove your mask," he said, "or you will never hear from me again."

Atossa knew this was as daring and romantic a scene as she could possibly imagine. It struck her with the same magic and meaning she'd felt when her father paraded her before his friends. She dramatically bowed her head, allowing Derek Davis to lift the porcelain mask from her face. She had powdered the blemish. It hadn't fully covered, so she'd dared a touch of something more opaque. Glowing now, in the wonder of the moment, she was a beautiful young woman again.

Davis was awe struck. He took her hand and kissed the back of it. She turned and ascended the stairs. Davis watched her all the way, fascinated by her trailing tail and remarkable form. When she reached the top stair, she turned and looked out at the sea of guests, first catching Davis' dazzled gaze, then Alise's wide eyes, staring up at her, aghast at her mother's secret and scandalous transformation. Atossa blew a kiss to Davis then rushed down the hall, wanting to get back to her room to wash her new face as soon as she could.

CHAPTER 25

Linda Bennett was up late on the Fourth of July, playing solitaire at the kitchen table in her nightgown, puzzling over ideas for her next column and trying to decide whether she should go to Kansas City. *Some social life*, she thought, putting a black nine on a red ten, *Saturday night and I'm home playing cards and trying to work*. It was almost funny for all the times she'd assured her mother that this was what she wanted—a serious career. The all-work-and-no-play approach to life could get her down at times, but her connection to Richards made it all worse. She had secrets. They cut hard at honesty when you tried to get to know someone. A real love life was basically impossible when you couldn't tell the whole truth and nothing but the truth. She wondered if her father had thought about that when he opened these possibilities to her. She knew her mother had. Linda closed her eyes, took a deep breath, and pushed the negative out of her mind.

The phone in her office rang. Linda looked at the clock. Twelve-twenty. She stood up awkwardly, jarring the table and knocking half the playing cards onto the floor. The phone rang for a third time as she read the caller ID. She cursed under her breath and picked up the receiver anyway.

"It's late, Bob," she said with clear irritation, noticing she'd stepped on a card in the kitchen, and it had stuck to the bottom of her foot.

"I want you in Kansas City as soon as possible."

She pulled the card off her foot. It was the two of hearts. "I'm set to go in two weeks."

"The farmers are forming a union. Cromwell has taken the leadership. They're preparing a strike as we speak. How about tomorrow?"

"Impossible."

"The militia's involved."

Linda idly turned the card over in her hand, trying to imagine what all this meant, knowing it was important, but not trusting Richards as far as she could throw him. Charlie Patio's warnings rang in her ear. "Just interviews?"

"Yes, I want you to interview Cromwell."

"I need at least a week to complete obligations here."

"Kansas City by Wednesday. And get two more columns out before you leave."

"Am I a mole, Bob? What's going on?"

"I want to see your pieces before you turn them in to your editor."

"Give me a break—and I can't make Wednesday. Next Monday, perhaps."

"Then Thursday—five days from now."

"I can't, damn it. I'm not even sure I want to go." She slammed the phone down in disgust. But for all her theatrics, she knew it was a good story—regardless of how she'd gotten it. A farmers' strike? Even after following the story for three months, it seemed unlikely. But the focus Richards was putting on Cromwell was curious, she thought, staring at the two of hearts in her hand. She'd done plenty of research on Cromwell since his name had first come up. His face on the cover of *Time Magazine*—the first time, as a hero—appeared vividly in her mind's eye. It was clearly powerful stuff. That Richards had her onto this from the beginning made it all the more intriguing. Still, she wasn't going to jump when he said jump. She did have other commitments. The TES thing was heating up again, and she wanted to be in Washington for the second round of congressional debates. Kansas City would have to wait.

CHAPTER 26

Just before midnight central time, James Peabody wheeled his big Chevy around the yard at the Cromwell farm and came to a stop. Nate climbed out of the pickup and said goodnight to his friends. He entered the house and immediately noticed the light in his bedroom.

"How'd it go, Nate?" asked Mary as soon as he entered the room. She sat in the chair next to his bed with her reading glasses on and a book in her lap.

"Oh, about as expected, Ma," he said, somewhat surprised she'd stayed up for him.

"And how's that, Colonel?" There was a hint of irritation in her voice.

"We've got ourselves a little union."

"Farmers don't unionize," she said grim and serious. "How do you fit in?"

Nate should have known this was coming. "Well, you know me. I just hung off to the side."

She didn't smile. "When are you leaving?"

"As soon as I can get you and Will set up with what we have to do here. Hope to be on the road by noon tomorrow."

"Where are you going?"

"Mom, ease up. This is something I'm going to do."

"Farmin' and politics don't mix, Nate."

"I'm going to Springfield to meet with the President of the National Grange."

"Why you?"

"Because I am who I am. We need to talk out the strategy for a strike."

"Strike? Damn, Nate." She wasn't one to curse, but she did. She shook her head dejectedly. "Are there going to be more fires?"

Nate sat down on the bed across from his mother and peered into her sad, angry eyes. "We're asking the industry to give us a better return on this year's harvest. If they don't respond, I'm afraid we've got to do something. Strike is one option. Fire might be part of it. That's what you and Will have to do here. Get the fields ready to burn—if and when the time comes."

Mary gave him a sour look and closed her book. "We'll talk about it in the morning. I've got to get some sleep." She got up and walked out of the room.

Cromwell knew every farmer in the country would be facing a very similar test. Telling their family about the strike. It was harder than facing the feds. No one would be too happy about a strike. It felt too much like war, he thought, too much like war…

Masoud led the way into the larger of the two cave entrances, followed by Tenzing Jast, Lena Davenport, and then Cromwell. All of them have stripped off their winter camo and changed into guerilla disguises. They aren't using lights. Instead, they're wearing night vision goggles, and the green cast they produce is especially eerie in the tunnels.

At first, they are able to stand, but the farther in they go, the smaller and tighter the tunnel becomes. Soon they are crawling, dragging their packs behind. The closeness and the thick dank smell are overwhelming—none of them are talking. When they encounter a fork in the tunnel, Masoud stops and turns back to the group. "We must make a choice," he whispers.

"Does one tunnel seem more used than the other?"

Masoud turns on a flashlight and inspects the area. "Not clearly, Colonel." He flicks out the light.

"Take the right branch. I'll mark the ceiling."

In five minutes, they are in a small chamber with another choice to make. Again, they take the right-hand tunnel and Cromwell marks the ceiling. The tunnel curls to the right. After five minutes of crawling, they are in another small chamber with two more choices. When they all gather in the chamber, Masoud asks again, "To the right?"

Cromwell looks at the chamber ceiling and sees his mark. "We were just here. We've completed a circle."

The imposing dimension and complexity of the caves strikes them all with a thick claustrophobic dread.

"They have deliberately dug these side routes to create a maze," says Masoud.

Cromwell looks at his timepiece uneasily and acknowledges this with a grim nod. He points to the right-hand tunnel. "That's how we got here."

Tenzing suddenly scoots away from the wall to his left. "Colonel," he says, pointing toward a cutout at the base of the wall. All heads follow his eyes. Masoud points the flashlight and illuminates a large mountain viper coiled in its nest. It hisses and flicks its tongue at them. All around it are ten, twenty, thirty little ones, winding and twisting over each other.

Masoud nods at the danger. "Bad bite. Even the little ones. They're attracted to these warm ventilated caves."

They all push away from the back wall. Cromwell looks at Davenport. Even in the dim green of the goggles, he can see sweat beading on her forehead. "Lena, you okay?"

She nods.

"Let me know," says Cromwell. "The rest of you. Same thing."

No one says a word as they backtrack on hands and knees to the original fork. Masoud is there first. He notes Cromwell's mark on the ceiling. To the left is the direction out, to the right—a light suddenly flashes far down the tunnel. "Back, quick. Quiet," he hushes.

All of them push back into the chamber, knowing the mama viper is on edge. From the entrance, Masoud watches the light flash down the tunnel, coming closer and closer, until he has to back all the way into the chamber. Behind him, Cromwell, Lena, and Jast are already in as deep as they dare, more uneasy about the snakes than the approaching guerillas.

Masoud watches two men pass the intersection. He whispers back over his shoulder. "They will find the dead guards. I must go after them."

Cromwell hesitates only a moment. "I'm behind you."

Masoud is already off at a triple-time crawl.

Cromwell looks at Lena and Tenzing, "Follow me up to the intersection and wait."

"Gladly," whispers Lena, glancing over her shoulder to the cutout in the wall.

By the time Cromwell reaches the first intersection, there is just enough light ahead to see Masoud scooting after the two guerillas. Masoud, knife clenched between his teeth, grabs the leg of the man ahead of him. The surprise is too much. In a heartbeat, Masoud has slit his throat. And is off again, after the other one.

The lead guerilla calls back to his partner. There is no response. The man hesitates and calls back again, turning the light on Masoud who lunges at him knife first. This man is more prepared and takes a wound in the forearm fending off Masoud's blade. His flashlight falls and goes out. Suddenly all is dark.

Scrambling on hands and knees as fast as he can, Cromwell climbs over Masoud's first victim, as the two men ahead of him grapple in the confines of the tunnel. He pulls his gun but can't ascertain which man is Masoud. Suddenly the wrestling stops. Cromwell levels his gun waiting for the winner to declare. The man on the bottom worms out from beneath the other. Cromwell discerns the face of Masoud in green outline. It's a frigid, emotionless mask. Cromwell lowers his gun. Masoud crawls forward. "Let's go, Colonel. The clock is running."

CHAPTER 27

Long after the party had wound down, about three o'clock in the morning of July fifth, Frank Nelson invited several of the party guests to the Nelson Mansion's basement game room for a private gathering to discuss Republican presidential strategy. This was his big moment. And as far as he was concerned, the real reason for this party in the middle of an election-year summer.

Frank's group included all the principles in the Eurasian pipeline project plus a well-considered selection of some of the world's most important corporate players. The three largest oil companies, two major grain distributors, two giant defense contractors, seven interlocking international banks, Wall Street, the Pentagon, the Senate, the tech industry, and the President's cabinet, all were represented. In effect, this international gathering, whose money was mostly banked in London and New York, formed a fair-sized Gibraltar of the global economy. Their network of operations impacted over forty percent of the global net product. Six of the conglomerates, including Andreas-Nelson, had a net worth over a trillion dollars. Thus the little cardboard sign, hand-printed in green crayon, that Frank's brother Dave had hung over the game room doorway: *The Trillionaires' Club.*

Although the ceiling was only eight feet high, the game room was quite spacious and plush. Paneled in dark mahogany, the east wall was an open bar with Dave the acting bartender. The rest of the room was situated around a twenty-by-thirty putting green with three holes and a fair amount of topological contour. Tables and chairs were arranged around the green's apron, creating the ultimate indoor nineteenth hole.

The atmosphere and conversation were superficially casual, but the intent was serious. There was no note taking. No tape recorders. To an outside observer, it wouldn't be evident that this gathering would have more to do with who would be the next President of the United States than either national convention or the election itself. In dollars and cents, this was the establishment. The industrial/technical/financial consensus of politics in the West. And Frank was as excited as he ever got in anticipation of naming the man he most wanted to replace the present disaster in the White House.

"You know, Frank, some of us don't really care which man takes the office," said Elizabeth Devereaux of France's International Harvest. She was dressed as Marie Antoinette and shared a table with Lawrence Fitzgerald. "This Kenaghy seems a bit unpredictable, but all that's really important is keeping the economy of the United States stable and growing. The rest of the civilized world can ride along with that."

Frank squatted on the putting green, using his putter to line up a shot. "It's really a bit more complicated than that, Elizabeth. Kenaghy has proven to be a waste of time and a royal pain in the ass."

"Especially in Central Asia," said Fitzgerald. "It's essential to our long-range plans to keep the Independent Russian States independent. The best way to do that is to work with them financially one by one. Should they unite or rejoin with Moscow, they are very likely to manage their natural gas and petroleum resources on their own."

"But they won't do that," said Frank, now standing over his ball, ready to putt. "All of us, the bankers and the oil people anyway, have invested a lot of money in these Central Asian states. And as we all know, money is a greater lure than old political ties." He looked down at his ball, drew his putter back, and knocked it three feet past the hole.

"Need another drink there, Frank?" quipped Dave behind the bar.

Frank gave him the finger.

Stodgy Rosalind Davis of Essex Petroleum sat with Emily Dunn of Dunn Chemicals at a table a few feet from Elizabeth Devereaux and the Secretary of Defense. In this gathering, only Rosalind along with Frank, John McClay, Fitzgerald, and Lyman Goodrich of Hamilton Heavy Construction knew the big secret about the Lake Balkhash oil field. Rosalind spoke up. "So back to the point in question, Frank. We need protection for the pipeline project, and this damn Kenaghy of yours is really botching our game."

"Please, Rosalind, don't refer to Kenaghy as mine," said Frank, watching Thomas Hartzel of Lockwell-McDougald Aerospace Industries preparing to putt. "Carlson's my man."

Hartzel, in a tuxedo, as was his brother Warren, tapped the ball in from four feet. "That's a hundred dollar putt, Frank!" he exclaimed, walking over to him and giving the propeller on his beanie a spin.

Dave Nelson opened a fresh bottle of bourbon and walked the length of the bar to pour a shot in General Sinclair's glass. The General, wearing camo, stood next to John McClay at the dark end of the bar. "I spent Monday morning with the President," said Sinclair, advancing to the center of the green, drink in hand, a black beret tilted rakishly on his head. He wasn't wearing any medals, just four stars on each shoulder and a sidearm on his hip. "You all know the outcome of that meeting. A dead end in the Oval Office and more delays. What's next, Uncle Sam?"

"A head count for an override, General." Senator Blount, wearing a red, white, and blue top hat and white chin whiskers, put his glass on the bar to be refilled. "Then it's on to the Republican Convention. And I'm with Frank. I like Carlson."

It was Benjamin Gutzka's putt. His company, Comtel, was arguably the most advanced electronics and communications outfit in the world. It was the leading edge in surveillance and guidance technology and, in many ways, the real heart and soul of the modern military.

"Ten bucks says you miss that one, Ben," challenged Frank.

Gutzka, dressed as a geek, a slide ruler on his hip and a plastic pocket protector in his shirt's breast pocket, looked up from his twenty-foot bender at Frank, then back at his line. "You're on." He stepped up to the ball, took two quick peeks at the hole, a slow back swing, and gave it a roll.

"Not a chance," cried out Dave behind the bar. The ball stopped eight feet short of the cup.

McClay stepped out of the shadows, as always immaculately dressed, tonight in a navy-blue pinstriped suit. "Sam Carlson's at the top of the Economics Roundtable's list. He's from the Street. We can't go wrong with him."

"I like Carlson too," followed Gutzka.

"Might be nice to get a few divisions in the old Soviet Union, right General?" said Dave, getting a little loose. "Right up close to the Chinese border?"

Sinclair gave him a look. Then smiled. "If we were playing chess, Dave, with Earth as the big prize, I'd say we'd be one move from checkmate."

Rosalind Davis nodded to Elizabeth Devereaux at the table beside her. "Sam Carlson? That could be."

Dave threw down what remained of his drink. "Carlson's a faggot," he chortled. "And he doesn't know a damn thing about oil or foreign policy."

Frank took a deep breath and rolled his eyes.

"Is that true, Frank?" asked Warren Hartzel. "Is Carlson vulnerable?"

"All bankers are faggots," laughed Dave, falling all over the bar. "Look at Frank!" He burst into hysterics.

"Ignore him, Warren. Carlson might be a little weak on foreign policy, but..."

"I can take care of that," interjected Fitzgerald.

Thomas and Warren Hartzel exchanged a glance. "What's in the man's closet?" asked Thomas. "We can't present this man, then have something untoward come out. It would be a dangerous opening for this fool Kenaghy."

"He's not a homosexual, Tom. My brother's drunk. Sam's a straight-ass banker like me. We don't need sex." Frank laughed uneasily. "When we get horny, we play with our money." He turned from the two brothers to watch Dave refilling his own glass.

Lyman Goodrich stood against the west wall opposite the bar. Hamilton Heavy Construction did infrastructure all over the world and was the leading contractor on the pipeline project. His men had made the latest Lake Balkhash estimates. "How's this Carlson going to look to the Christian right?" he asked.

"Like any banker, he's multi-denominational," chirped Dave with a chuckle. "He's got fives, tens, twenties..."

"Including Jewish?" This was Edwin Zillari of England's Dawson Pharmaceuticals. He was Jewish. And he wasn't laughing at any of Dave's attempts at humor.

"Including Jewish," said Frank. "He may be a southerner, but he's a banker first. He speaks with dollars and sense. And as for Israel, he knows that's our rock in the Middle East."

Warren Hartzel turned to Rosalind Davis beside him. "Our autonomous fifty-first state."

Zillari overheard the comment and ignored it.

Sinclair selected a putter and a ball from a rack on the wall. He dropped the ball on the green. "Carlson's fine with me—as long as the man realizes the importance of maintaining America's military supremacy."

"Here, here," seconded Gutzka.

Emily Dunn got up and walked out. Dave watched his brother watching Emily's exit. "Don't worry, Frank. Silence is an affirmative from Emily," he grinned. "The faggot's a go."

"Shut up, Dave." Frank scowled at his brother. "Sam Carlson's not queer. He's true blue Wall Street. Status Quo. Just what we need."

One by one, Frank made eye contact around the room, starting with Rosalind Davis—she nodded ever so slightly, Lyman Goodrich—he merely met Frank's glance, Elizabeth Devereaux—she lifted her drink and took a sip, the Hartzel's—two thumbs up, and Edwin Zillari—no response at all. Benjamin Gutzka watched each reaction, while Sinclair stood over his ball and took aim at the hole farthest away.

"The convention's next week," said Frank, very pleased with himself. His eyes ran to McClay, then Fitzgerald and Goodrich. "I like Sam Carlson's chances."

Sinclair gave his putter a swing. All watched as the ball followed a long slow arch for eighteen feet then plunked into the cup. He got light applause. A statement of consensus. Sinclair returned his putter to the rack and walked out of the room.

"Now there's the guy to keep an eye on," popped Dave, before tossing down the last of his most recent drink.

Frank walked over to his brother. "No, you're the guy I need to keep an eye on." He flicked Dave's spinner and headed toward the door.

Senator Blount moved up alongside Frank as he exited the room. "Got any thoughts on our friend Mr. Houseman and his little move to privatize Homeland Security?" he asked as they walked along.

"Well," said Frank, "Paul's a little overbearing, but I like privatization. Rings of free markets and efficiency to me."

The Senator nodded. "You know, he wants to take all the intel with him?"

"He's got it already, doesn't he?"

Blount grimaced. "That's all the personal stuff, email, bank accounts, eavesdropping access. A lot of power, Frank."

Frank stopped. "This some kind of warning, Ray?"

"Just want you to think about it. Likely to be a close vote in Congress. And I've got some doubts."

PART IV

UPRISING IN THE HEARTLAND

"We have heard of many roads to salvation. We have heard that economic development will save us, solar heating will save us, technology, the return of Jesus Christ who will restore the heaven and the earth, the promulgation of land reform, the recycling of materials, the establishment of capitalism, communism, socialism, fascism, Muslimism, vegetarianism, trilateralism, and even the birth of a new Aquarian Age, we have been told, will save us. But the principle of soil says if humans cannot maintain the planet's topsoil, they cannot live here."

-William Kötke, *The Final Empire*

CHAPTER 28

It had been a tense morning. Nate stood by the back door at one end of the kitchen, and the two most important people in his life sat across the room at the kitchen table. Lunch was over. The smell of cooked bacon for BLTs hung in the room like ozone after a storm. The empty plates were still on the table. Will's eyes were on his dad. Mary stared down at her coffee cup.

Mary understood the farmers' dilemma all too well, but she didn't want Nate to be part of the union leadership. And she'd told him so many times already that morning. It all felt too much like war. And she hated politics. But mostly it was just her not wanting to see her son hurt again—in any way. "When will we hear from you?" The inevitable sounded in her voice for the first time all morning.

"I'll call you tonight."

"And you can't tell me when you'll be back?" Her tone made Will wince.

"Too much I don't quite know yet, Ma. I'll have the cell phone." Nate looked at Will. "You know what you need to do. The firebreaks. Help your grandmother organize some food and drinking water. Stock up on gasoline and diesel. Stay in close touch with Horace and James. You can do everything, right?"

"Of course, Dad."

Will grinned in a way that reminded Nate of his ex-wife. He still had to talk to her about the money for Stanford. "Keep the rifles ready."

"Yeah, I know." This was all kind of thrilling to Will, but Grandma was on edge.

Mary took a sip of coffee and with a stiff deliberateness put her cup back onto its saucer. "We in any danger here, Nate?"

This was Nate's biggest concern. He could barely even think about it. "If the industry doesn't respond to our initial request," he answered, "I'm not sure where we're headed. In any event, strike or whatever, the same people who forced me out of the Army might give me a call—and there could be some pressure. If things get really crazy, they might come here. I'm not sure." He looked at his son and his mother as through a broken window. "Maybe all you should do is get this place ready and leave. Stay with Horace and Sarah."

"I don't want to leave my own house."

Nate looked down at the floor. "I'll be back in a couple of days."

Mary stared at Nate. As far as she was concerned agribusiness would love to push all the farmers off the land. Let'm strike. Let'm burn their fields. Let'm all go belly up. Then some hotshot would come in and buy up all the prime farmland cheap. Turn the entire Heartland into one big industrial farm. "You better get out of here, Nathaniel Cromwell. 'Cause if I think any harder on this…" She didn't finish her sentence. She just got up from the table and walked out.

Will looked at his dad. "We'll be fine."

Cromwell tried to smile. "Yeah." He turned away before the tears in his eyes began to show and quickly stepped out the back door.

Nate kicked at the gravel as he crossed the yard. The sun was high overhead and already pushing temperatures past ninety. Another record setting summer pressed on. He opened the pickup door and slid into the oven of the cab. He quickly rolled down the windows, then stared out at the vast expanse of ripening wheat. There was nothing more beautiful to a farmer—except delivering it to market.

How fucked was this, he thought, sitting there in the cab, trying not to think about it. He wiped the tears from his cheeks with the back of his hand. He'd given the best years of his life fighting for a government he'd steadily lost faith in. His heart ached for this almost as badly as it did knowing his participation in the union put his mother and his son at risk. A farmers' strike? Christ, what chance did they have? Maybe it was just a way of life that's time was passing. No, he couldn't convince himself of that. America's farmland was an asset of immeasurable importance. And it was best farmed by the families that owned the land. What was the damn line? *Government for the people and by the people.* It wasn't happening that way anymore. Yeah, he could barely admit it to himself, but somebody needed to shake things up good. He looked out the windshield into the wide blue Kansas sky. "Who better than I?" he said softly, closing his eyes, thinking of his mother and son. "Who better than I?"

Deep within the Al Qaeda caves, Masoud turns back to Cromwell and the others. "There's light up ahead and possibly an exit from these hand-dug tunnels. Stay here and I'll check."

Cromwell nods as Masoud scoots ahead. From behind, Cromwell can see Masoud's figure as a silhouette exiting into a lit chamber. After a few seconds, Masoud is motioning for them to advance.

Cromwell hustles Lena and Tenzing through the last of the tunnel, and they come out in a large natural cavern lit weakly by a single electric light bulb. They glance around the chamber. There are three exits—the hand-dug tunnel they just crawled out of, a wide natural crease in the cavern that is no more than three feet high, and a man-made enlargement of a second natural passageway that is tall enough to stand in. Masoud traces the electric wire leading from the light bulb across the ceiling and into the largest passageway.

"This is surely the way to the main cavern, Colonel, but we'll soon encounter more Al Qaeda."

Cromwell appraises their appearance. In the dim light, they might pass as Islamic guerillas, but that depends on how many men are here and how well they know each other. They cannot assume that they will blend in. Masoud, yes, but the rest of them, Lena particularly, hard to say. "Masoud, you take the lead well in advance. We'll be behind." Cromwell looks to Lena. "I want you to start planning your system with this chamber as our exit point."

"Yes, sir."

Masoud follows the electric wire running along the ceiling. It's only twenty yards before Masoud stops and waits for Cromwell to reach him, then Lena and Tenzing. Farther down the passage are brighter lights and the sound of activity. "Could be the main cavern is just ahead, Colonel."

"Lena and Tenzing, stay here."

Masoud and Cromwell hurry ahead. It's obvious they are coming to something big. They crawl the last few yards, finding themselves on a ledge overlooking a vast, well-lit cavern a quarter the size of a domed football stadium. The ledge they are on extends the length of the north wall and is about seventy feet above the cavern floor. The area below is partitioned like a manufacturing plant with different operations going on in each section. Three or four hundred men are spread across this veritable underground city.

Cromwell looks at Masoud lying beside him, withdraws his binoculars, and begins surveying the cavern, trying to decipher the multitude of activities taking place. At the same time, Masoud, also with binoculars, traces along the ledge, on the lookout for others coming their way.

After thirty seconds, Cromwell lowers his binoculars, clearly what he's seen has him thinking. "Masoud, I'm getting Lena."

Masoud lowers his binoculars. "I think this ledge is only used as access to the back exit, Colonel. We should have some time to ourselves up here, but it's hard to say how long."

"I'll be quick."

And he is. With Tenzing left behind to watch their back, Cromwell and Lena crawl up beside Masoud on the ledge. Cromwell hands Lena his binoculars and takes her on a tour of what he's seen. "Verify, if you can, what I think I've seen down there."

Lena focuses the binoculars and begins a systematic scan of the entire place.

"On that far wall to our left, I see munitions assembly. Loading and packing black powder into a variety of shells."

"Damn, Colonel, are those two Soviet T-55s parked down there?" Her attention lingers on two tanks on the cavern floor.

"Yep, and in those plastic tents to their right," he continues in a whisper. "Are those computers? Some kind of communications system?"

"I think that's right, Colonel. It's hard to see through the plastic."

"Then to the left. That other plastic tent. What do you make of that?"

"I may be wrong, Colonel, but it looks like a chemical lab. Fairly sophisticated too."

"Agreed. Remember these folks have some pretty heavy funding. What about farther to the left? In the cordoned off section against the back wall. Masoud, you check this too. More chemical work. Could they be refining opium?"

"Yes, Colonel, I see it that way," says Masoud.

"And off in that far corner, it looks like a series of gasoline powered generators, and what's that—a ventilation system, sir?"

"Right, Lena. So, how do we take this place out? Give it some thought." He looks at his watch again and frowns, then withdraws a camera. "Maybe they can figure this stuff out back home if I bring them some photos."

After a moment, Lena gives the binoculars back to Cromwell. "It's a little bigger than we'd imagined, Colonel, but I think I've got it figured out." She shimmies away from the ledge toward the wall and gets to her knees where she's left her equipment. She counts out ten packages of C4 plastic explosive, then delves into the electronic timing devices.

By this time, Cromwell is using a telescopic lens to take photos. When he zeroes in on the heroin processing lab, he focuses on the faces of two of the workers. Incredibly, he recognizes one of them from his previous Afghan visits. He snaps the shot. A few more and he's done. He stuffs the camera in a pocket and taps Masoud on the shoulder. "You stay with Lena."

As he gets to his haunches, there is a muffled cry from within the tunnel where Tenzing has been guarding their back. In two steps, Cromwell is full speed into the passage. Two guerillas have Tenzing pinned to the ground. One of the guerillas glances up. Cromwell greets him with a boot toe to the face. He uses his fist to crack the jaw of the second, then pulls Tenzing to his feet. A spin. A kick. And his right hand is on the throat of the first of the assailants. His windpipe is crushed and nearly ripped out. A knife glints in the gray light. The other man lunges at Cromwell.

*Even as quickly as Masoud has followed, he is only in time to see Cromwell pull his nine-millimeter and—*tish*—put a bullet in the man's head. For the first time since they left Peshwar, Cromwell sees something close to a smile on Masoud's face.*

"What happened, Tenzing?" whispers Cromwell.

"A man came out of this side passage. I thought I could surprise him in the dark with my knife until the second man appeared." He looked downward. "I am sorry, Colonel, I nearly ruined things."

"You okay?"

"I'm okay."

"Masoud, you and Tenzing go back to the tunnel and wait. Drag these fellas with you and hide them somewhere." He looks at his watch again. "Five minutes, then we're out of here. I'll get Lena."

Lena is still at work, assembling things as fast as she can. Cromwell kneels beside her, looking down the length of the ledge, checking the time, hoping to hell no one comes their way. He turns to Lena. "What's that?"

Lena looks up momentarily with eyes big as silver dollars. "I'm going to run charges all along this ledge, but I also want to get some explosives out there in the middle of the cavern, so I'm using a small charge to launch these larger ones. When the electronic timer goes off, half of everything I brought goes out there. If I can't bring down the mountain, I'm surely going to stop operations in here—then there's no telling what happens if their shit ignites."

Cromwell breaks into a smile at her language. "Okay, sister, get with it."

"Two hours from now. Go boom."

Cromwell checks his watch and nods, then watches her hands bounce from one connection to another. "Each one," she says, eyes down on her work, "has its own timer in case any single one should fail or be found." She buries her little black box launcher and its load in a pile of loose rocks and dirt against the wall. Then grabs her five assembled packages of plastic and starts scooting down the wall, carefully burying them every five yards.

Then she's running back toward Cromwell, full speed, bent down close to the wall.

"Let's go, Colonel!"

Masoud and Tenzing are waiting at the exit as Cromwell and Lena reach the chamber. "Masoud, take the lead. Then you, Lena. I'll be at the rear."

One by one, they enter the tunnel and begin the long crawl out. Twenty minutes of knee busting hustle, just past the viper's chamber, they encounter the two bodies Masoud had left behind in the tunnel. As a precaution, Cromwell drags them back to the intersection and pushes them into the chamber with the snakes. He does this by himself and falls several yards behind the others.

Soon the others are at the end of the hand-dug tunnel. Masoud is the first one out. As he steps into the cavern entrance, he is grabbed from either side by Al Qaeda guerillas and thrown to the ground. Lena and Tenzing are so anxious to get out of the close confines of the tunnel, they don't notice and are also grabbed upon exiting by eight awaiting guerillas.

Cromwell, yards behind, hears the foreign voices at the end of the tunnel and suddenly stops. A light flashes down the tunnel. Instinctively he rolls sideways into an irregularity in the wall. The light does not catch him. He draws his nine-millimeter Beretta, reloads it, and, leading with his weapon outstretched, worms his way forward.

CHAPTER 29

Jonathan Mayfield stretched out on the bed and stared at the ceiling of his cinder block cell. He had a decision to make. A note that accompanied today's breakfast told him Parker Chen would be there to confer at ten. It was one day short of two weeks since Chen had offered him the job at the Development Bank of Asia. The conditions of his imprisonment in Singapore had steadily improved in that time. Better meals. Cable television. A comfortable chair. French wine with dinner. Even additional clothing, including a tailored suit. But these things meant little to him compared to going home.

Jonathan's decision should have been an easy one. A plane ticket back to London was the obvious choice. But Jonathan wasn't the obvious person. He'd read over the contract Mr. Chen had left with him. They understood his talents. It was a very generous one-month offer to be a computer consultant with an option for a full year. Although the money was a temptation, London was where he wanted to work and live. But Jonathan's curiosity hung him up. He wanted to know how the Asian grain buy had been orchestrated—and by whom. The Development Bank of Asia surely had a hand in it.

Jonathan had not entirely made up his mind when there was a knock on his cell door. He sat up as the door opened. It was Parker Chen. Behind him were the ever-present, square-shouldered Asian thugs. "Hello, Mr. Mayfield," said the well-dressed Chen with a modest bow and an easy smile. "I trust you have come to a decision on our offer of employment."

"Well, actually, Mr. Chen, you said two weeks and you're a day early," said Jonathan as he stood. He was wearing the suit he had been given, but not the tie. "I'm still thinking."

"Very funny, Mr. Mayfield." Chen's smile persisted. "What is your decision?"

"How soon can I leave for London?"

Chen's smile disappeared. "Today, if you like."

"Today would be good."

Chen turned to the men behind him and said something in Mandarin. One of them walked away. Chen faced Jonathan. "We will have a car ready in a moment. Is there anything here that you want to take with you? Your old clothing perhaps?"

"No, only what I'm wearing."

"Then, Mr. Mayfield, we can leave immediately."

"You mean, Mr. Chen, you have a ticket already?"

"Yes."

Jonathan did not believe what was happening. This was too easy. "May I see it?"

"Of course." Chen reached into his suit jacket and retrieved a thick white envelope like the one the contract had been in. He handed it to Jonathan.

Jonathan opened the envelope. And, yes, there was a Northwest Orient Airlines ticket inside with his name on it. Singapore to Bombay to Frankfurt to Heathrow. Sixteen hours of travel. The envelope also included a passport and ten thousand Singapore dollars. "Excellent, Mr. Chen. I'm ready to leave."

With that, Chen led Jonathan out of the cell with the remaining thug trailing after them. The threesome followed two narrow hallways to a stairwell. They climbed up a flight of stairs and entered a large kitchen where an Asian cook was pushing small sizzling pieces of pork around on a flat open grill. They filed through the kitchen out a back door into a service alley.

It was the first time Jonathan had been outside in months. From the thick oily smell of frying meat into the bright sunshine and fresh air felt like a psychological dip in the ocean. Jonathan took it all in while checking out the neighborhood. He'd been in the basement of a very large and ornate home amid many other large homes in an upper class Singapore suburb.

A black Lexus limousine with dark tinted windows came rolling down the cement paved alley. It stopped in front of Mr. Chen. The thug opened the door. Mr. Chen deferred to Jonathan. Still wary and wondering if he was being taken off to be murdered, Jonathan slid into the limo. Mr. Chen climbed in next to him. The thug closed the car door and took the front passenger's seat. The other thug was behind the wheel. He put the car in gear, and soon they were motoring through downtown Singapore.

For five minutes no one said a word. Jonathan simply didn't believe what was happening. For all he knew, they could be taking him to a warehouse to be hacked into little pieces. He wanted to jump from the car and dash into the crowded streets every time the limo stopped for a traffic light. He had the ticket. He had some cash. He could get himself to the airport.

But he couldn't bring himself to do it, and he just stared out at the tropical city of Singapore until he saw a sign along the road for the airport. They really were letting him go.

"Mr. Chen," said Jonathan, "you have held me in a room for three months. Now you are sending me home. I don't get it."

"Would you prefer that we'd killed you?" Chen was blasé. The thug in the forward passenger's seat turned around.

"No. Of course not. But I felt I couldn't seriously consider DBA employment until I knew if you were actually sincere in your offer to let me go home." The limo pulled off the freeway onto a ramp to the airport. "And it seems you were. Give me an hour to negotiate with the management, and I might change my mind."

Chen smiled. "I like your style, Mr. Mayfield."

Jonathan laughed out of nervous relief.

Chen said something in Mandarin to the driver then continued to Jonathan. "We are turning around and going straight to the corporate offices. I think it's time you met your prospective boss."

"And who is that?"

"He is the number one man at DBA Pacific Rim. His name is Parker Chen."

Jonathan smiled. "Then let's not waste any time, Mr. Chen. Perhaps you can answer some of the questions you wouldn't earlier?"

Chen tilted his head inquisitively.

"This was all about the grain market, right?"

Chen nodded.

"So why, after keeping me imprisoned for so long, am I suddenly free?"

"We wanted you out of the way for a while, Mr. Mayfield. The grain buy is over. Our gambit worked perfectly. No longer do we care what you say or do."

"So, I was kidnapped in order to keep me quiet until the deal was done."

"That's correct. As I said, early on there was some talk of killing you, but I requested you be left in my custody."

"Because you thought eventually you could make use of me?"

"Again correct, Mr. Mayfield. I was very impressed when I was told someone had anticipated the grain buy."

Jonathan smiled. "I have seen nothing in the papers or on television to explain the buy—other than the harvest shortfall. What else can you tell me?"

Chen looked forward as though appraising the traffic, then turned to Jonathan. "All I'm at liberty to say is that a wealthy man bought the grain to avert widespread famine in China. It was an act of mercy."

"He made no profit at all?"

"I didn't say that. He simply secured the market."

"A single buyer? That's billions of dollars?"

Chen again titled his head slightly.

"So how did they know? The harvest reports weren't out yet—by a month or more."

Chen smiled knowingly. "I have said too much. But, perhaps, if you accept the job I am offering, and your work is good, which I'm sure it will be, it may be that my client would like to meet you. Then you might learn more. You see, I think there is quite a bit of mutual respect at play here."

"And should I take this job, I will be entirely on my own when I'm not at work?"

"You'll have money, and you'll have freedom. I will secure a room for you this afternoon at the Singapore Hilton. You can do whatever you like. All that will bind you are the great business opportunities that will open before you."

Jonathan nodded slowly and said, somewhat sarcastically, "What more could I ask?"

CHAPTER 30

The meeting at the grange hall Saturday night didn't get a lot of attention from the media Sunday morning. The newspaper in Pratt had it on the front page. So did *The Wichita Eagle*. But the farther the publication was from the center of the country, the farther the story drifted back into the second half of section A. *The Chicago Tribune* gave it five inches on A12. *The Denver Post* had two inches on A23. None of the big newspapers on the east coast or the west coast mentioned it, and it didn't appear on network or cable TV at all—while Atossa's party got fifteen seconds on CNN.

In other words, the grange hall meeting was pretty much a non-event as far as most of the country was concerned. So, while the greater part of the nation was ignoring the farmers as they had for far too long, the farmers were pulling things together. Less than twenty hours after the grange hall meeting Saturday night, Nathaniel Cromwell and Vincent Hayes were headed to a meeting at Mahan's farm in Springfield, Missouri. This would be the real launching of the movement—the nuts and bolts of forming and running the union. They had to come up with a platform and a strategy for the strike. In a sense, it would be a reenactment of what went on the night before, three different and powerful personalities agreeing to act as one.

A few miles outside Springfield, Missouri, Nate dropped his Dodge Power Wagon into second and turned in Mahan's driveway. White rail fence traced along both sides of the long, paved driveway all the way to the house. Lush green lawn spread out beyond the fencing on both sides. The driveway ended with paved turnaround wide enough for a semi-truck. At the far end, a flagstone walkway led to a beautifully maintained, red brick, ranch-style home. To the east were fields of corn and alfalfa running off to the horizon. Behind the residence stretched hundreds of acres of ripe, ready to harvest winter wheat. To the west was an apple orchard and an open pasture, divided up for horses, cattle, and sheep. It was a fabulous looking farm by any standard.

Cromwell had rethought the previous night many times during the five-hour drive from Kansas. He'd been impressed by Forest Mahan. He'd gotten a good sense of the man the day he came by with James Peabody, but his opening speech at the grange hall and this beautiful farm proved beyond all doubt what Forest was about. He wasn't even close to going under this year or next, and yet he had decided to put himself on the line for those who were in trouble.

Two pickups and a metallic blue Toyota Prius were parked straight in at the walkway to the house. Nate pulled in beside the Toyota, climbed out, and strode up to the front porch. On either side of the door were decorative panels inset with frosted glass—a sheaf of wheat was etched on the panel to the left, a stalk of corn on the panel to the right. He pushed the doorbell. Chimes rang inside. A moment later, he heard the approach of footsteps.

A small, round woman with a white halo of cotton candy hair and bright blue eyes opened the door. "I'll bet dinner tonight you're Colonel Cromwell. I'm Forest's wife, Louise. Come on in." Her smile was all country welcome. "General Hayes is already here. Forest's got his paper work on the dining room table."

Cromwell removed his Caterpillar cap and held it with both hands at his waist as he stepped through the doorway into a hardwood-floored foyer. To the left was a spacious living room with Ethan Allen furniture, wall-to-wall carpeting, and tasteful reproductions on the walls. To the right was the dining room. Nate followed Mrs. Mahan in.

Forest stood next to General Hayes on the back side of the dinner table, opened up with four leaves to accommodate the stacks of maps, lists, and multi-colored graphics. Both Mahan and Hayes looked up as Cromwell entered. Mahan broke into a wide, excited smile. Hayes, dressed in officer's camo, masked by his dark red beard, acknowledged Cromwell with his eyes.

"Welcome to strike headquarters, Colonel." Forest stepped from around the table, extending his hand. "Need some coffee?" There was enough charge in his voice to suggest he'd been at Mr. Coffee on the sideboard a good part of the day.

"Not right away, Forest, thanks anyway." Cromwell took Mahan's hand and glanced at the paperwork spread out on the table. "How are you, General Hayes?" he asked, purposely using Hayes' rank, knowing this cold, dark man was the individual whose trust and confidence he needed most.

"Quite well, Colonel," he said crisply, reaching out to shake Cromwell's hand.

Cromwell could feel the tension in Hayes right up through the clasp of their hands. He knew this in men, especially hard-edged military types who weren't quite ready to lay their egos aside. He pushed past it. "So Forest, looks like you've been at it since we spoke last night." Cromwell lifted one of the multi-colored computer printouts and took a closer look.

Forest beamed. "More like all last month," he said, stepping up to the table, flashing his eyes over his work. "Let me run through what I've got here, Nate. I already started with General Hayes." The coffee chattered behind his every word. "But I'm sure he won't mind if I backtrack a bit."

Hayes nodded, clearly containing himself, and not as awe struck by Cromwell as was the fully animated Mahan.

"First are these maps of the United States. I have a separate one for corn, winter wheat, spring wheat, rice—which isn't much of a factor—and soybeans—which aren't grain but figure heavily in the market. The maps are color-coded for the approximate times of the year each crop is harvested." The phone rang in the back of the house. Forest looked up from the papers. The phone didn't ring again. "That's the fax. I've been getting reports all day from the various county granges—evaluations of their crops, what kind of participation we can expect from their farmers, all sorts of ideas. The response is hugely positive." He smiled enthusiastically. "But back to these maps."

He pointed to the winter wheat map. "See this yellow strip through Southern California, Arizona, most of Texas, Mississippi, Alabama, and Georgia. Pretty much all of that was harvested by the second week of June. Now just above that," he ran his finger over the red portion of the map. "The lower half of Oklahoma, Kentucky, Virginia, the Carolinas, southern Missouri—this is all ready to go. The wheat you saw driving in. I could harvest it tomorrow."

Cromwell looked at Hayes and allowed a little grin for Mahan's exuberance. Hayes had relaxed enough to show the same in his eyes. Mahan just kept going. "You see this blue portion? Kansas and northern Oklahoma, Illinois, Nebraska. The big wheat states. As you know, Nate, you boys are still a week or so away from combines." He picked up another few maps. "I've got this same kind of information for the corn and soybeans which harvest in early fall."

"So it's not an all or nothing proposition," said Cromwell. "We can literally bargain with each part of the harvest as it comes due."

"Exactly. It gives us some flexibility."

"Incredible work, Forest."

He nodded. "Most of the maps came right off the USDA website. Some of this other stuff is strictly out of the National Grange files." Mahan's eyes twinkled with natural born magic. "This set of statistics here, for instance," he lifted a handful of spreadsheets, "tells us the acreage and yield we can expect in each state, county by county, crop by crop." He pointed to another stack of papers. "This here's the breakdown I'm getting from the granges—names of farmers, what they grow by acreage, last year's yield, phone number, email address if they have one, and if they are willing to participate in the strike. I'm telling you, Nate. It's happening out there. These farmers have been waiting for an opportunity to get heard, like I said last night, for a hundred and fifty years. Your dad, my dad, and their dads too! Sure you don't want some coffee? Either of you?"

Cromwell chuckled. "Hell, Forest, I think I'd better if I'm gonna keep up with you. Sure, pour me some of that joe."

Mahan laughed out loud, and even the stiff Militia General allowed a smile. "Yes, I'll have some too, Forest."

"Got any information on silos," asked Nate as Forest filled two cups with coffee.

"You mean, farmer-owned?"

"Yeah, seems like whatever we can store ourselves, without turning it over to rented elevator space or to the dealers, is just that much more grain we can hold as collateral." Cromwell made eye contact with both men. "I'd be interested to know the total quantity we can store on our own." He looked at Hayes. "With unhappy distributors and creditors wondering where their grain is, your boys, General, might end up guarding silos."

"No problem, Colonel," replied Hayes. "Like Forest here, I've been doing my homework. I've been in touch with all the major militia groups in the United States in the last twenty-four hours. We've set up an encrypted website that allows us to communicate through the internet with something approaching secrecy. All units are on standby—armed and prepared for fire management—or silo guard, if necessary. Total militia count is 65,000 men and women. Prepared to act as a single force or separately county by county. They will respond like a traditional military operation. I'm the commanding officer."

Cromwell nodded.

"And I take orders from you, Colonel." Hayes saluted

Cromwell returned the salute involuntarily, almost laughing at the insanity of this thing that had burst open on him in the last twenty-four hours. "Now all we have to do is sit down and come up with a strike statement and a strategy." He took a sip of coffee and looked at Mahan. "My guess, Forest, is you've already got that worked out."

"You better believe it, Colonel. I've been thinking about this all my life," said the grange president buzzing as much on pure inspiration as caffeine. "Our first priority is the market. With those prices we saw last month, some of the big dealers will make three hundred percent profit off the grain we sold them cash advance. That's criminal with the situation of the average American farmer. So, our first demand is addressed to the industry. We want a cut from the windfall profits they made off the Asian grain shortage. We'll ask for a dollar kickback on every bushel of corn and wheat sold in advance last winter—two on each bushel of soybeans. That means, right away, a sizeable check for every farmer."

"That's a long shot," said Cromwell with Hayes nodding alongside him.

"Perhaps, but it gets everybody on board right away, because we're asking for something every farmer can relate to—more on the bushel and immediate cash."

"You'd better be ready to burn some wheat," warned Hayes.

"I don't think so," said Mahan, getting more excited with every exchange. "As far as I'm concerned, they owe it to us. Our steady production has been the foundation of global food supplies for well over a century. If we work together, we can get whatever we want."

"And you really figure we can run farming like a union?"

"The farmer worldwide is the lowest paid worker on the planet. It gets worse when you look at the details." Mahan picked up a sheet of paper from his mountain of it. "Look at this graph. The farmer got a dollar and a half for a bushel of corn in 1950. And two for a bushel of wheat. Sixty-five years later, the price of both have almost tripled—which sounds okay."

"Until you figure in that everything else is up twenty-five times," said Hayes.

"Exactly. The loaf of bread that cost twenty cents in 1950 is over five bucks today. Gasoline is even worse."

Hayes nodded. "Meaning you're getting about an eighth of what your father got for that same bushel of corn."

"That's right. With chemicals and irrigation, we're growing more crop per acre. Fine. But the net effect is higher production costs and scorched land." Forest paused to look at his audience of two. "In the long run, guys, I'm pushing for a change in the way we farm. We can't compete against agribusiness and the industrial farms. Capital intensive we lose. I say we drop out of the heavy fertilizing and pesticides. Get out of the monoculture approach to farming. We work ourselves into our own niche—conservation tillage, organic farming, specialized produce, diversified crops, even permaculture in some cases. Unfortunately, the average farmer is hooked on the chemicals, and it's expensive to change over. That's where we need some government support. We're asking for a five-year, low-interest government loan, or preferably a grant, for farmers making the transition to conservation tillage or organic. It's a straight-ahead push for saving the soil. We'd be doing the whole nation a service and be growing cleaner, better food to boot."

"You're dreaming," said Hayes.

Cromwell wasn't so sure either. "In other words, Forest, you want us farmers to become environmentalists?"

"And why not?" demanded Mahan. "It's the only way to preserve the garden of the Heartland. Thirty years ago farmers would sneer at this. But today, with the aquifers pumped dry, our topsoil filling up the Mississippi delta, and the planet warming as we speak, the time is ripe for a change."

"Are the farmers ready for this, Forest?"

"With the state of the Heartland today, Colonel, if you aren't part of the solution, you're part of the problem. And those who are undecided will join in because of the provision for a cash kickback in demand one. I'll send our statement out to the granges tonight, and we'll find out right away what kind of backing we have. With the feedback I've been getting the last few years, my guess is it will be good. Farmers need to preserve the land, not kill it."

Mahan gave the two men a fiery look. "Here read this." He opened a manila file folder on the sideboard and took out two copies of the strike statement he'd already prepared. He handed each man a copy. It was a detailed critique of the present state of agriculture in the United States and a long-range alternative agricultural program for the future. It was as much an environmental impact statement as it was a new philosophy for farming America.

There had been a steady maturation of American farmers' environmental awareness during the years of Forest Mahan's tenure as National Grange President. The farmers were slowly realizing that they weren't just farming as individuals. They were collectively gardening a critical portion of the planet. Humans were a global entity. The way they lived, and farmed, affected the biosphere. Obvious changes in the climate—impacting soil moisture and planting times—made this impossible for farmers to ignore. In the United States, the wheat belt was moving northward. The same was true for corn and soybeans. Even sugar maples in New England were steadily migrating into Canada. Growing patterns were changing, and the way the Earth was farmed had to change with them. Farmers needed to see themselves as stewards of the global garden. The over-fertilizing. The pesticides. The excessive pumping of the aquifers. The monoculture philosophy. All were taking their toll on the land. Passing your farmland down to your child in better shape than you received it, enriching the soil as you farmed, could be done in a way that also helped clean the water and the air, while also growing better produce. Even forest management was included in Mahan's farming program. This was huge. It involved a complete overhaul of the existing system.

Mahan's statement proposed creating a national farmers' bank, run by farmers for farmers, with interest rates set at one or one and a half percent, just enough to cover the cost of running the operation. It recommended building large arrays of strategically located community grain elevators. Grain storage was a constant shell game for the farmer. Never enough. Logistics and capital invariably worked against the little guy. The statement also detailed a plan for tax incentives for community supported agriculture and community seed banks, and included a relocalization strategy to minimize fuel costs by cutting the distances for shipping and selling produce. The choice was whether to constrain the market and kill speculation—which would never fly. Or, if it was truly going to be an equitable market, give the same storage and banking opportunities to the family farmer that the distributor enjoyed.

These same issues had raged for over one hundred and fifty years. The farmers take the risks, and the middlemen reap the profits. It seemed far-fetched, but Mahan's plan was a conjoining of the nation's farming community. It was Orville Kelley's grange organization, plus a little of A.C. Townley's Nonpartisan League of the 1920s, a little of Edward Faulkner's no-till primer *The Plowman's Folly,* and a touch of Masanobu Fukuoka's *One Straw Revolution*—all hooked up to the internet. If the farmers could work together with storage, buying cooperatives, banking, and as a political coalition, they had a chance.

And there was more than farming strategy to the Forest Mahan Phenomenon. With a unique collection of personal qualities, foremost intellect and sensitivity, Mahan, from his position as National Grange President, had managed to strengthen the links between the many diverse groups within the farming community. For instance, the conservation tillage people and the organic farmers agreed heartily on the need to steward the soil but argued viciously over the use of chemicals. Mahan wrote his grange articles deliberately to both sides, emphasizing the common ground and looking forward to the day when the principles of each philosophy could lend something to the other.

Mahan's rational approach to farming, the real common sense in everything he said and did, swelled out of his being. Although he never mentioned anything about Christ or religion on his grange webpage, the clarity of his words, his positivism, his general reverence for living things, his overall respect for people and their beliefs made him a favorite among Christians and non-Christians alike. The pragmatic gravity he brought to farming translated as sacredness to some and plain good thinking to others. All of this was critical in his positioning for farmer unification.

Cromwell finished reading the statement and looked up at Mahan. "This is more than I bargained for, Forest. But I can't argue with it. You're absolutely right. We've got to change the way we farm." He turned to Hayes who had also just finished the document. "Ain't gonna be easy, pardner."

"Damn near impossible, Colonel," said Hayes. For the first time, there was a sense of connection between Hayes and Cromwell. But Hayes wasn't sold. "We refuse to deliver on our cash-advanced harvest, and the buyers get an injunction against us from the government. The government demands we harvest and deliver. And if we don't, they send in the Homeland Guard and arrest us. I don't see this working."

"They can't put a million farmers in jail," said Mahan digging in his heels. "If we work together, they have to bargain with us. It's a strike. We're a union."

"A farmers' union," Cromwell said softly. "So how do we start?"

Mahan snapped his fingers. "Pratt, Kansas last night!" His eyes sparkled. "The next step is getting this statement approved by our constituents. With our computer network, I can have a response from each and every grange in two days or less."

"Really? Two days?"

"They're ready and waiting for this. It can happen. Once it's approved, we send the statement to the government and the industry. Tell them we want another dollar on a bushel."

"That's a lot of wasted time, Forest," said Hayes right into Mahan's enthusiasm. "I say we act right away. A show of unity and daring. We burn a million acres just to get their attention."

"No, no," said Mahan emphatically, shaking his head. "We have to present the statement before we do anything. The industry and the government must have a chance to respond. Besides, a large portion of the farmers who are behind the strike are against burning. We need to make an offer before we do anything stupid."

"With the proposal you've just laid out, Forest, they'll laugh at us. They'll flat out call us fools. We have to show them we're serious right off the bat if you want a serious response."

"No," slammed Mahan. "To be taken seriously, we have to go about this in the accepted fashion."

"Accepted fashion?" Hayes looked up at the ceiling. "How long have we been going at that already?"

"Hold on, guys," said Cromwell. He was dead set against burning, but too much of what Hayes was saying rang true. He edged up to the table and turned through some of the papers. "We can go both ways." Hayes and Mahan looked at him. "We send the statement out to the granges for response immediately. We give it two days to filter through the system from state grange to county to farmer. As soon as we know we've got the support we need, we inform the industry, the government, and the media of our existence. No threat of fire or secession. No mention of a strike. Just an announcement of our new union and our platform. We make absolutely sure they know we have grievances that need to be addressed. Then, if we're attracting any attention at all, if there is any kind of positive response, we sit down with the industry and talk it out."

Mahan nodded. Hayes' eyes had grown hard. Cromwell looked right at him. "At the same time, as quietly as possible, we make every preparation for a big burn. If the response to our union is, as Hayes suggests, a big corporate laugh, we'll be ready. We light a match and hit it fast."

Cromwell laid one of Mahan's color-coded maps on the table and pointed to the red strip across the middle. "Without any warning, we burn, say 500,000 acres right across here." He ran his finger through Oklahoma, Missouri, Arkansas, Kentucky, Virginia, and North Carolina. "To get their attention, as Hayes says, with a show of unity and daring. Then we announce the strike and submit our demands—with the threat to burn another couple hundred grand if we don't get some priority."

Mahan wasn't ready for this. "But, Nate, shouldn't we start with something less drastic than fire? Stop paying bills or stage a march on Washington before we start burning our bridges?"

"You're dreaming," tossed out Hayes.

"Forest, I don't want to do any field burning at all. I don't want to put any one at risk. But if it's clear right away we won't be taken seriously, we have to act immediately. The harvest timing demands it. Besides, they won't be expecting any kind of action from us until we've announced the strike. But that gives them a chance to prepare. The guard can be readied. They'll hit our farmers with propaganda. They'll try fear tactics. They'll begin undermining us before we've even started. I think Hayes is right. If we don't get a positive reading right away, we hit them out of the blue. And we start getting ready for that now."

"God, Nate, are you sure about that?"

"No, I'm not sure. But I look at this strike in the same way I do a battle where the odds are stacked against me. Surprise and preparedness are everything."

"I like it, Colonel," said Hayes.

"It frightens me."

"And it should, Forest, it should," replied Cromwell. "But like you said, the farmers of this nation are ready like they've never been before. If we don't act now, we'll never get the chance again."

Mahan took a deep breath and sighed.

"Now of course," continued Cromwell, "we can't do this until we've talked to the farmers that own fields ready to harvest. And we've got to be able to tell them if there is a burn early and a settlement afterward, that we will cover their losses, and that all the other farmers will be behind them when the Homeland Guard shows up, and that we will be sending them people to help prepare their land and control the burn."

"We're ready," said Hayes.

"I don't know," muttered Mahan.

"Forest, your fields will be on the line right away. As one of the successful farmers and head of the grange, you must be ready and willing."

Mahan wasn't. "I've done a lot of talking to a lot of farmers. I know they're screaming for help. But I don't know about this burning thing."

"We must show them we mean business."

"I can have men ready tomorrow."

Cromwell turned to Hayes. "Once we do this. Once the surprise is over," he said with increasing force. "It's going to get a lot harder. So, we've got to get the first one right. Total control of the fire. Total control of your men."

"How can we guarantee we can pay these farmers back?" Mahan was still fighting it.

"It's all or nothing, Forest. This first burn is just a skirmish, and the long term fix is the war."

"But do we stand any chance of winning this way? Won't the burning bring public opinion down on us?"

"You asked me last night. Do we have a chance? This is it. We have to have some guts. It's a total risk. But go through the numbers. I thought about this driving here. Wheat, the first harvest, is the least important of our assets. Second harvest is corn. That's a lot of acreage, but the margin is low. The key is the soybeans. That's our real money crop and where we have our greatest leverage in the world market. Even if we fail with corn and wheat, if the numbers are right with the beans, we can still cover our losses and do no worse than if we did nothing at all."

Mahan put a hand beneath his chin, rolled some numbers through his head. "Damn, Nate, you might be right."

"You came over to my place last week and asked me to help you out. You said you needed someone who could bridge the differences between men like Hayes here and men like yourself. That's what I'm doing. Hayes revised his position last night. It's your turn now. But most of all, you have to trust me. It isn't going to be easy. And giving your crops up in our first act of defiance is critical for bringing in the others. The little farmers will be easy. It's the bigger ones, like you, who will make us or break us."

Mahan nodded reluctantly, thinking about all that was about to break open like a dozen eggs on the hen house floor.

Cromwell turned to Hayes. "Now, again, General, once those fields start burning—if it comes to that—it's going to look a lot like your civil war. But it ain't. It's nothing more than dairy farmers spilling milk. Remember. It's all about control. This is a strike, not armed revolution."

Hayes grimaced a nod.

"Okay, Nate, I'm with you," said Mahan in a tone that belied the words, thumbing through his list of wheat farmers in southern Missouri, Oklahoma, Arkansas, and Kentucky. "But I better get on the horn and see how many of these boys are willing to take the plunge. We had a lot of words last night—now we need commitment."

"Then let's get this statement out as soon as possible. The first thing we have to know is if we have support. Then we need to find some sacrificial farms. In three, four days we have to be pulling things together—one way or another."

Cromwell looked at Hayes. "General, can you get through to the militias in these states in the next few days?" Again, he ran his finger over the red portion of the map. "Prepare them for what we need to do? Get some of them cutting firebreaks by tomorrow?"

"Yes, absolutely." For the first time all day, Hayes' green eyes were on fire. He wanted this kind of challenge, this kind of action. "As soon as we're done here, I'll start driving. If I have a couple, three days, I can personally visit militias in all these states. I'll have them ready."

"Forest, you have my cell phone number. Do you have General Hayes'?"

"I do."

"As soon as you have significant acreage, get a hold of Hayes and me. Don't say anything that gives us away. Just a *yes* or a *no*. Then we'll meet back here Wednesday or Thursday at the latest."

"Nothing more than that for secrecy, Colonel?"

"It is what it is. We don't have secure lines. We're working by phone, text messages, and email. Once the state granges start putting out the word, farmers all over the country will be talking. But you know what—

NSA always picks up a lot of chatter and loose talk. Those spooks are so overloaded with concerns for Islamic radicals and drug dealing wackos we're not even on their radar. Besides they can't sort through all the stuff they pick up as it is—let alone fast enough to act on anything that will affect us. It'll take them six months to get tuned in to us farmers babbling about our day-to-day troubles. By then, the damn strike will be over." Cromwell laughed at the thought of it.

"Of course, we'll impress our people about the need for secrecy," he continued, "and we'll use as much cloak and dagger as possible. We'll promote the use of CB radios instead of cell phones. And use word of mouth for anything critical—like plans for burning. We've got so many folks out there on our side, if necessary, we could relay information by networks of cars and drivers—like the pony express. And always, always face to face between the three of us for anything important. We'll go low tech. And sure, some of it will get out—but I have this sneaky feeling it won't be taken seriously. Even as word got out about our meeting last night, the media didn't pick it up. There was nothing on TV. That's what this first move is about. I just don't believe anyone expects us to do anything. Yes, we must be ready for state or federal resistance—Homeland Guard, state police, the Army, who knows? And, if by some chance, we get a decent response from the industry right away, we can sit down and talk. There's no loss in being prepared. Because if we get our demands thrown back in our face, as Hayes suggests, we'll need this first free shot to get the kind of attention we want."

Except for a seven o'clock dinner break provided by Louise, the three men worked late into the night, sending out the union platform by computer and answering questions by phone. Step by step, grange by grange, farmer by farmer, it was happening. Bottom line, in three days' time, big decisions would have to be made.

CHAPTER 31

Atossa roused slowly Monday morning. She'd had a horrible night of sleep filled with restlessness and recurring angst about Derek Davis. The party had been a tremendous success. Or more accurately, as the feedback filtered in from friends and associates, Atossa had been a tremendous success instilling awe and envy in all the women whose jealousies mattered most to her. All the speculation about her veil covering a rapidly withering face was shattered. Now the questions circulating among the power elite were much more flattering. How could she look so good? How could she look so young? Did you see her dancing with Derek Davis? But for all the success of her masquerade ball, more importantly, her heart had been stolen by the brash, handsome Davis.

Atossa climbed out of bed and looked at the piece of paper on her bedside table with Davis' phone number on it. Did she dare call him? And if so, she wondered, when would be the exact perfect time? In a day? In a week? The mere thought of him brought a warm visceral rush, followed by wave after fearful wave of anxiety.

Atossa slipped on her white silk dressing gown and crossed the room to her mirror for her first-thing-each-morning appraisal of her face, specifically the blemish on her cheek. The flashing light on her bedside intercom stopped her.

"Yes?"

"Excuse me, Ms. Andreas." It was Nancy Waters, her personal secretary. "Frank Nelson is on the phone."

"Tell him I'm not up yet."

"He says it's important," came back hesitantly over the speaker.

Atossa growled with displeasure. "Fine, Nancy. Put him on."

The intercom light went from flashing to *on*. "What is it, Frank?" she snapped.

"We're getting some negative blowback on our grain position last month."

"So what?" She turned the light on over her mirror as she spoke and leaned up close to inspect her face.

"There's chatter about a farmers' strike. They want a percentage of what they're calling the industry's *windfall profits* from the Asian grain shortage."

The blemish on her cheek had grown during the night. "That's why you called?" she said in building irritation.

"Yes, Atossa. I can't imagine anything coming of this. No one else does either. But you might check Linda Bennett's column in *The New York Financial Times* this morning. Her analysis is worth reading. A large percentage of the world's available grain is still in the field—and much of it is owned by these same farmers."

Atossa wasn't listening. She was barely six inches from the mirror surface, running a finger over her face, checking every detail. The spot on her cheek was slightly upraised. "Fuck them," she screamed in despair for her face.

"Just thought you might be interested."

"Well, I'm not," she snarled. "Good-bye." She took another look in the mirror. "Nancy," she called out to the open room.

"Yes, Ms. Andreas," came back from the speaker.

"Get Dr. Colleen on the phone immediately."

CHAPTER 32

Nathaniel Cromwell and Vincent Hayes remained at Mahan Farms Sunday night, sleeping in bunk beds in a back bedroom. They were up early Monday, and Louise cooked them a breakfast of eggs, bacon, and pancakes. Forest never went to bed. He stayed on the computer all night and joined Cromwell and Hayes at the breakfast table to brief them on the early returns. "Nary a dissenting response," he boasted. "And look what I just pulled off *The New York Financial Times* website." Forest laid a copy of Linda Bennett's Monday column between them on the table. A portion of it was highlighted in yellow:

> Three hundred million acres of prime farmland stretch across the center of the United States. From Pennsylvania in the east to California in the west, from Texas in the south to Minnesota and the Dakotas in the north, America is a veritable garden of eatin', a breadbasket that feeds the entire nation and significant portions of the rest of the world. Grains of all kinds, rye, barley, sorghum, oats, wheat, and especially corn grow easily and in vast abundance. For over a hundred years now, this great national endowment has been the Gibraltar of the U.S. economy. And while this wonderful natural resource steadily produces tens of billions of dollars' worth of grain annually, deep in the midst of these amber fields, a vital concern for the health and maintenance of the land has spread among the farmers. Just as the pioneers cut across the grassland prairie with John Deere's moldboard plows in the latter half of the nineteenth century, frustration and discontent now tear through the farm families of America's Heartland in the twenty-first. The land is eroding. The farms are burning out and so are the farmers.

"Who is this writer?" asked Cromwell.

"Same one who called attention to the positioning of the big distributors at the time of the grain dump," said Forest. "I've been checking her column regularly for the last month."

"And judging by that thumbnail beside the column, she ain't too bad looking either," said Louise, coming over to the table and topping off the coffee cups.

Cromwell laughed. "Yeah, but you know those photos are always about ten years out of date."

"I've read her column a few times," said Hayes gruffly. "I like her stuff on the oil industry and that she dares to write about peak oil, but I still don't trust her. Anything out of that paper is just more capitalist spin."

"Well, maybe General," said Louise, "but it seems to me, we can use whatever help we can get."

After the meal, Hayes drove off to visit militia posts in Oklahoma, Arkansas, Missouri, Kentucky, and the Carolinas. Cromwell told Mahan he'd be available on his cell phone and climbed into his battered blue Dodge. He didn't go directly back home. He went northeast on Interstate 44 headed to St. Louis and points north.

Not long after Cromwell left Mahan's farm in Missouri, he passed a sign on 44 that marked the old Mason-Dixon Line. Was it possible that America was on the verge of another civil war? God, he hoped not. He'd do everything humanly possible to avoid it. Could it really come down to burning the fields? Again, he hoped not. But he was afraid Hayes was right about the response they would get. No one really gave a damn about the farmers.

Cromwell's thoughts wandered to Robert E. Lee. Lee had always been one of Nate's favorite military heroes. In his days at West Point, Cromwell, like many cadets, became fascinated by military strategy and history, and Lee's feats of courage and tactical daring during the Mexican War were legendary. But Cromwell's admiration for Lee had also instilled him with a strong sense of honor and dedication to duty. It was this accursed sense of honor that had pushed him to question the drug traffic coming out of Afghanistan—and it had changed his life forever.

Now as he drove, Nate couldn't help comparing his current position to that of Lee's. They were both West Point graduates and highly decorated officers, but Nate was no fan of the rebel cause and disdained Lee's ownership of slaves and his stand against abolition. Where was the honor in that? Standing up for the farm community was far different than supporting secession and the institution of slavery.

Nate had always thought of modern secession movements as nonsense. And he still did, but with a deep uneasiness. There could be a strike, and if Hayes' assessment was right, it might be necessary to make some show of field burning. But he could not sit easily with anything akin to civil war.

An hour later, Cromwell pulled his pickup into a gas station north of St. Louis on Interstate 55. While he was having the tank filled, he went into the convenience store and bought ten of the popular ten dollar cell phones with prepaid accounts—often referred to as disposable phones. Cromwell had his own cell phone, but for this particular call, he wanted to go a different way. He knew there were people the intelligence community never let go of. Doubtless he was one of those people. Once he'd blown the whistle on the Afghan heroin connection, an indelible red star had been attached to his electronic file. And despite what he'd said to Mahan and Hayes the day before about NSA surveillance, he'd decided it was best to assume his every word was heard and traceable—no matter where he was.

He punched a number into one of the new cell phones and listened to it ring at the other end, hoping to hell he wouldn't get the recorded message he'd gotten when he'd tried this number before. It rang three, four times. No recorder? One more ring…

"Hello? What do you want?" Cromwell recognized Jerry Rust's voice right away.

"Don't say anything."

"Who is this?"

"You know who it is." Cromwell paused. Jerry's silence was an affirmative. "You in Chicago?"

"Yeah."

"I'm headed your way. Corner of South LaSalle and West Jackson. Directly across from the front doors of the Chicago Board of Trade. Seven-thirty tonight. Just a *yes* or *no*. Can you do it?"

"Yeah. Sure."

Cromwell hung up.

After paying for his gas, as he walked across the lot to his rig, he casually dropped the cell phone he'd just used into the back of another pickup at the pumps. Every phone contained a GPS system that was activated by the first call. If anyone had traced his call to Jerry Rust, that cell phone would, at least temporarily, put them on a track that had nothing to do with him.

Cromwell continued north on Interstate 55 to Chicago. For a short time, 55 followed the Mississippi River. Periodically along this stretch, Cromwell noted grain depots where train tracks and Mississippi barge traffic merged. He was struck by how many giant grain elevators there were. These huge arrays of contiguous concrete cylinders were capable of holding millions of pounds of wheat or corn. Some were locally owned. Some were owned by coops. Others sported the logos of the world's largest grain buyers, International Harvest, Andreas Grain, Carlyle Distributors. There were hundreds of these elevators throughout the Midwest, holding some huge portion of America's grain. He wondered if in the coming weeks these silos would have heightened security and armed guards. It could come to that. He could imagine things becoming very bad. Train loads of grain being derailed, gasoline tankers hijacked off the freeways, or these elevators becoming strategic targets. He hoped to hell these extremes would never come to pass.

Farther north into Illinois, he passed through some prime corn and soybean country. The plants were maturing beautifully, full and green. Seeing these lush fields, two months from harvest, full of potential, reconfirmed how deeply he didn't want to be doing this. He wanted to be home working on his farm. Even worse, he'd left his mother and son alone. Although he'd dug himself into farm work for ten long years, and for all practical purposes disappeared into the Heartland, as with his call to Rust, the paranoia just never went away. Now like a prairie dog he'd come up out of his burrow, and there was every likelihood this would make a lot of people in some very influential places uneasy. That was why he was headed to Chicago. If he was going to become a public figure, he was going to need some backup. Jerry Rust's name had immediately come to mind.

Cromwell can hear the guerillas screaming at Masoud. He knows some of the dialects. They are threatening Masoud, demanding he tell them what he is doing there. A gunshot rings out. Lena screams. There is a slap. He can't lie there listening to his people being brutalized. He crawls ahead, his Beretta leading the way. There is another slap. Masoud curses. Another gun shot. And a cry. He hears what he interprets as "red hair."

Boiling with anger and anxiety, he continues forward, hoping they won't shine the light into the cave again. In any case, the explosives are planted. That's the mission's top priority. After that, they are all expendable at some logistical level.

He is less than ten feet from the entrance. There is another slap. Lena is sobbing. The guerillas are laughing. Something about her "other" red hair!

Cromwell worms ahead fully prepared to die. With his night vision goggles, he sorts out the action of eleven people in the shadowy light at the cave entrance. Six of the men are holding his three people. Two others are standing before Lena. Her headdress and beard are off. One man runs his hand through her short red hair. The other unbuckles her belt. He rips her pants down to her knees and when all attention is on Lena's bare groin, Cromwell aims his Beretta and catches six guerillas with killing shots to the head. He hits another in the shoulder and kills him with a second shot. The eighth guerilla turns to run, and Cromwell takes him down with a shot to the back of the head.

Lena falls to the ground in tears. Masoud, shot in both knees, is crumpled on the ground. Tenzing is the only one standing, fear in his black eyes and no grin.

Cromwell climbs from the tunnel. He turns over the guerillas one by one with his boot, making certain they are all dead. He helps Lena to her feet. He looks her in the eye as she cinches up her pants. "You okay?"

She wipes away the tears and composes herself. "Yes, sir."

Cromwell kneels beside Masoud. His knees are a shattered mess of blood and bone, but the Pakistani is as cool in agony as he was in killing. He looks at Cromwell. "They were lookouts from the eastside of the fortress on their way back. They discovered the other bodies just minutes before we crawled out. I'm certain no one else knows of we're here."

Cromwell nods, wondering how the hell they'll get Masoud across the back of the ridge and out of harm's way before the explosives go off. Forty-five minutes have passed. They have an hour and a quarter until the explosives blow, two and a quarter to meet the helicopter—barely enough time to make the pickup even without Masoud.

Masoud reads his mind. "You must leave me, Colonel. There is no time."

Cromwell knows Masoud well enough to know he means it. Also that it is a necessity. He doesn't waste time thinking about it. "You have a gun?" His meaning is clear.

"In that pile over there." His eyes target the pile of weapons stripped from Lena, Tenzing, and himself.

Cromwell retrieves Masoud's pistol. Their eyes meet as Cromwell hands him the weapon. It's all business. Nothing is said.

Cromwell takes a deep breath. "Lena, Tenzing, gather it up. We have to go. Fast as possible."

Lena looks at Masoud. She doesn't want to believe what they have to do. But she offers no argument. The three of them climb from the cave entrance with their equipment. Cromwell turns to Masoud as the last one out. He salutes Masoud. Masoud returns the salute. A short distance from the cave entrance, Cromwell tries the black band.

"Rust, you out there?"

"Yeah, Boss."

"We're out. Headed back to camp. Anything to report?"

"It's fucking cold."

"What else?"

"We're the only fools out tonight, Colonel. We've seen next to nothing on this front."

"Good." He looks at his watch. "Set the timers for oh-five-hundred and meet us at the camp."

Cromwell puts away the radio. "Lead the way, Tenzing."

Lena speaks up. "You know, Colonel. There's no telling what's going to happen to this ridge when that plastic goes up."

"I know. We could use an extra half-hour."

"Or more."

"Full speed ahead. Let's go."

They make it back to the camp in thirty-five minutes. Rust, Priestly, and Alvoretti are waiting.

"Where's Masoud?" asks Canary.

"Must have decided to stay with the other diaper heads," cracks Rust.

"Keep that shit to yourself," snaps Cromwell. "Grab the gear and let's get going. We've got about forty minutes to get as far from here as possible. Move it."

No one says a word, and suddenly it's nothing but asses and elbows.

The time flies. They're all exhausted and fighting it, even Tenzing. Lena is clearly past her limits, but she, more than any of the others, knows the potential of her work. She can't help but look at her watch. "Less than a minute, Colonel."

The entire group stops and turns to look. The canyon ridge where they first spotted the caves is just a shadow against the night sky—maybe a mile away.

As anxious as anyone for the success of the mission, Lena looks again at her watch. "It's time."

Nothing happens. They exchange looks. "Don't tell me we have to go back?" quips Rust.

Then there is vibration beneath their feet. "That's it. The charges on the ridge should go now!" As Lena says the words, the exterior explosives blow—one, two, three, four—like howitzer rounds.

"I wonder if that's it? I was expecting something more," says Lena to Cromwell and Priestly beside him. Before either of them can respond, a thick muffled roar and its following shock wave knocks them all on their butts. A wide tongue of flame licks up over the edge of the canyon lighting up the sky. The ridge they have just crossed begins to break up. Collapsing earth and rock run at them like surf on the beach. It's happening too quickly to react. They all sit there frozen, expecting the ground to drop out from beneath them—when it suddenly stops. Maybe two hundred yards short of where they are.

Rust sums it up. "Who's got the TP?"

Lena turns to Cromwell. "Colonel, I think we triggered their munitions."

"And who knows what else," adds Canary.

Cromwell smiles. "Nice work, Captain."

"Yes, sir," she grins.

"Now let's get our asses out of here before any more of this place collapses or the explosion draws more rats. Move it! We've got little more than an hour to reach the pickup spot, and it's two hours away."

CHAPTER 33

Linda Bennett had written her column for Monday morning on Sunday afternoon. It was essentially a propaganda piece. She had decided to go to Kansas City, but only after the second version of TES went through Congress. In preparation for the trip, and after learning about the grange hall meeting from Richards, she'd taken his advice and given the farmers some positive ink. She wasn't entirely on board with their position. She thought unionizing was futile. But the farmers were right on one account. The market didn't work for them. Above and beyond anything to do with Richards, however, Linda had written the piece because it was good, controversial material that deserved attention, not because she believed so strongly in the movement. Monday morning, she filed a second more aggressive column to be published in the Wednesday *Times*.

The New York Financial Times managing editor David Bernstein flew into Washington from New York Monday afternoon. He had business with several people in the Washington Bureau, but the real impetus behind his trip was Linda Bennett. He'd read her latest submission that morning and didn't like it. Upon arriving at the *Times* building, he headed straight to Frederick Manning's office and commandeered his desk. Twenty minutes later, he called Linda in. *Somebody had to set this wayward columnist straight.*

When Linda entered the office, Manning sat off in one corner and Bernstein was at Manning's desk. Bernstein's jacket was off, his tie loosened, and his sleeves rolled up. He stood as Linda approached the desk. He held a hard copy of her Wednesday's column in one hand and a half-smoked, unlit cigar in the other. "Ms. Bennett," he said flatly, "I'm calling off your trip to Kansas City."

Bernstein was a superlative editor. Linda had come to *The Times* because she wanted to work with the best—and that was Bernstein. He was overbearing, brilliant, and large—over six feet tall, close to two hundred and eighty pounds—with a big head, huge cow eyes, thick firm lips, and wide nostrils bristling with hair. When he really, really wanted to make a point, he would talk so slowly and with such force and sentiment, you could not doubt its accuracy or truth.

"These people do not need this kind of encouragement," he stated smugly, slapping the piece on the desk and pinning it there with a fat forefinger. "Speculation about populist revolution has no place in a financial newspaper."

Linda wanted Bernstein's respect, but his tone was as a man to a child. That he didn't know Linda's trip to Kansas City was CIA prompted, and Manning did, made the discussion all the more awkward.

"It's a good story, Mr. Bernstein."

"No, Ms. Bennett," he said, posturing with his stogy, wafting the wet bitter odor into her face. "The family farm situation is a sad story. Farmers are a vanishing breed. Talk of a strike is absurd. This field burning is nonsense. It's a bad story. Publicizing it is a bad idea. I want you to find a new topic."

"You said the same thing about my columns on the pipeline in Central Asia, Mr. Bernstein. I'm sorry if on occasion you don't like what I write, but it is my syndicated column. I want to go to Kansas City. And I want to interview these people. Maybe it will never come to a strike. But in my mind, the story of the American farmer and the land is an important story. I want to tell it."

"The land," said Bernstein sarcastically, turning to Manning. "The farmer becomes environmentalist. Is that what this is about?"

"David," replied Manning. "I'm with Linda. It is a good story, even if the economics of family farming is a losing proposition."

"She may want to tell this story, Frederick, but I want some objectivity." He jammed the cigar into the side of his mouth and frowned petulantly. "I don't like it when a journalist starts sounding like an activist."

This was a low blow. The objectivity comment and the third person reference. Linda managed to contain herself. "At the end of the day, Mr. Bernstein, you call the shots at *The Times*. I accept that. And there is no other paper where I would rather base my column." Her eyes met momentarily with Manning's. "But I suggest you trust your bureau chief."

Bernstein glared at her as though that was all he needed to do to turn her into mush. But Linda was no easy ticket. "I'll write the columns that inspire me," she said. "You print the ones you like." Then she turned and walked out.

All the way back to her office, Linda wondered if she'd blown it, imagining what Bernstein must have said to Manning after she'd left. If he had wanted to fire her, she would have heard it halfway down the hall.

To hell with Bernstein anyway.

Badly distracted, Linda sat down at her computer not noticing the FedEx overnight delivery on her desk until she'd put her fingers on the keyboard. Still buzzing from Bernstein, she opened the package without much thought. The cardboard envelope contained two computer disks and no cover letter. She looked at the return address on the envelope and didn't recognize it.

She put one of the disks into her computer, checked it for viruses, then opened up one of the electronic folders. It contained scores of email files. She clicked on one. It was an email written by her father ten years earlier. She tried another and another. More of the same. It was all there. Her father's complete email history from thirty-one years with the CIA. She looked at the return label again. Just a street address. No name. But it came to her in a flash. She said it aloud. "Thanks, Charlie."

Charlie Patio had done her a tremendous and risky favor.

CHAPTER 34

When Cromwell reached south Chicago, it was after seven. Fifteen minutes later, he'd found a parking place on South Wacker Drive. He was early so he took the time to compose a letter to Lena Davenport in California. He had some ideas concerning strike backup strategies he wanted Lena to think about. Feeling snail mail at this point was more secure than a cell phone, he sealed up the letter and dropped it in a mail box as he hustled the three blocks down West Jackson to his appointed meeting.

It was still light out, and he spotted Rust from a block away walking toward him. He hadn't seen him in over ten years. He'd shaved and picked up some gray. Cromwell walked right up to him before Rust recognized him in his green Caterpillar cap and blue jeans.

"Boss! What's up?" Cromwell couldn't stop him. The taller man took him in a bear hug, then stood back to look at his war buddy. "Don't look too bad for an old fart? What's with all the cloak and dagger?"

Nate couldn't deny the good seeing Rusty inspired. "Let's find a place to sit down and have something to eat."

"Sure, Bossman, whatever you want. Why this end of town?"

Cromwell looked across the street to the massive building that housed the Chicago Board of Trade. "It's symbolic, Rusty. You'll get it after we talk. Tell me about you as we walk. Then we'll get to my stuff."

Rust looked at him. "You don't want to know about me. That damn political stuff they put you through left me with a bad attitude about too many things. I'm a professional cynic now."

"Then you haven't changed," laughed Cromwell. "You still married?"

"Fuck no. Something about that Special Forces stuff infected my being. Ordinary life doesn't sit too well with me. Jane got the kids and the house. And, believe it, I'm working as a fireman. Seem to be addicted to emergency." He grinned. "They send me all over the world to start fires."

"How much free time you have?"

"Enough. I just got back from two months on the job."

Cromwell laughed. "You look good."

"Lean, mean, fighting machine as they used to say." Rust stopped and pointed down South LaSalle. "There's a brew pub down this way. They'll have something if you're not too picky."

"I've been driving for eight hours. I'll eat whatever they've got."

They found a booth in the back corner of a dark little tavern off Main Street. A TV behind the bar had the White Sox game on. Most of the patrons were men, drinking out the end of the day and jawing about the action on the tube. The place stunk of stale cigarettes and spilt beer, plus a whiff of well-used urinals and toilet pucks anytime someone went in or out of the men's restroom. It wasn't exactly a high-class place, but it was about perfect for what Cromwell had in mind—and the food wasn't half bad.

They had eaten and were well into a second pint when old times ran up to the immediate. Cromwell went through the events of the last two weeks, starting with Tom Foster burning his wheat and working his way into the details of the farmers' union.

The look on Rust's face was a half-cocked question. "So why are you here talking to me? I don't know shit about this farming stuff. I mean, I followed your story, and it's great to see you, but why me?"

Nate took a long swallow of beer and grinned at his old buddy. "Because I trust you more than anyone in my life but my mom."

Rust guffawed. "That's a mistake."

"If we strike, it's going to be a bitch. Farmers have never been able to organize. The big guys—agribusiness, the elevator owners, the millers—they hold all the cards, and as much as I don't want to admit it, a strike is about as likely to succeed as my attempts to get the Afghan connection into the public eye twelve years ago."

"But didn't you say you have all this wheat and corn you can use for leverage?"

"It's a long shot, Rusty, and the logistics are more than difficult. The more I thought about it as I drove up here this afternoon, the crazier it seemed. But we have to try something." Despite the doubts, Nate had made his mind up. "The system is steadily taking the farming away from the farmer. Maybe it's progress. But, boy, to me it's criminal. Like I said, we have all these militia folks on our side. I think they just want to play war. And these conservative farmers. They just want to do what they've always done. Maybe I'm still steamed by the way I got treated back in the day. Maybe I just want to get back into the fray. In any case, I'm in it up to my elbows now."

Cromwell leaned over the table. "But even if this union thing goes down the drain and our whole effort is a failure, it's going to scare the shit out of some big concerns. The government isn't going to like it, but the conglomerates that sell and ship the grain are going to hate it. It's like an uprising of the slaves." He stopped for a moment and stared at the surface of his beer. Something happened on the TV and several men at the bar cheered. He lifted his eyes. "In the next week, I'm going to know if we'll be negotiating or fighting strike breakers. It could get ugly and there's a lot at stake. I'm here talking to you just in case things go sour. If that happens, two things come to mind. One is that I become a target—if I'm not already—and I need a bodyguard."

Rust laughed. "Sergeant Rock needs a body guard. Okay." He laughed again. "It would be an honor. What's two?"

"Two is a backup plan. Something tells me, if we have any chance at all, I'd better have a few back doors set up. Apart from all that I might do with the farmers' union and with the militia, I might need some black ops that nobody knows about but me."

Rust lifted his head like a dog catching a scent. "What are you thinking?"

Cromwell leaned back and crossed his arms. "I have a few ideas." His eyes firmed up and an image of the grain elevators up and down the length of the Mississippi River rolled across his mind. "Nothing worth talking about until I see what goes down in the next week or ten days. Can I count on you, anytime I call, no questions asked beyond what you already know?"

Rust sat back and grinned a wide, toothy grin. His little eyes creased into slits. "You don't really trust me, do you?"

Cromwell looked down at the table. For a moment all you could hear was the ballgame's grainy whisper in the background. He lifted his eyes. "Need to know is something we worked with all our lives, Rusty. Right now. There's no need for you to know anything beyond what I've told you. Standard operating procedures are standard because they work."

Rust shook his head at the nonsense of it all. His grin straightened out into seriousness. "Sure, Boss." He said it softly. The bathroom door to their left opened and closed. "I'm yours."

"Can you take two months off from firefighting?"

"I've got child support payments."

"If I help with that, how long can you get by?"

"As long as you need."

Cromwell nodded. "Get everything straight with your employer. Your ex. Whatever. And clear up some time—just in case."

Rust nodded.

"The next little while is going to be telling. I'll call you when I know more. And all communication is considered unsecured unless it's like this, face to face."

Rust sat back in his seat, lifted his arms up, and put his hands behind his head. "I like it, Colonel." A huge smile expanded across his face and into his eyes. "Just like old times. I like it."

"I figured, Rusty." Cromwell looked to the door. "You leave first. I'll pay the tab."

Rust nodded. "Dig it." He stood up. They shook hands, and he walked out. Cromwell went up to the bar, watched a half inning of the game, paid the bill, and left.

CHAPTER 35

James Kenaghy stood beside his desk and stared down at the latest draft of the rewritten Trans-Eurasian Security Act. It would undergo a variety of changes as it passed through the House and the Senate before a final version would come back to him for signing in a week or two. It had been on his desk since Monday, and he had yet to read it. Also on his desk was a copy of Monday's *New York Financial Times* open to Linda Bennett's column. He'd read it three times since yesterday. In his hand was a single sheet of paper. It was Don Reed's resignation. He'd read it ten times in the last hour. The National Security Advisor was the third member of his cabinet to resign in the last six months. All *his* people. All the compromise appointees were hanging tough—and so would he.

The intercom broke the Oval Office's silence. "Cameron Phillips is here, Mr. President."

"Don's gone," said Kenaghy as soon as Phillips came through the door. He handed his chief of staff the letter. "I think I'm beginning to know how Richard Nixon felt."

Phillips read quickly through the letter. He'd thought many of the same things Don Reed had written. His sympathy for Reed felt like betrayal—until he saw TES on Kenaghy's desk. It hadn't moved since he'd first put it there. His stomach tightened at the thought of the stalling that was ahead. It was part of the reason Reed was gone.

Kenaghy stalked to the other side of the office, still mulling over Don Reed's resignation. "What the fuck," he muttered to himself. "I'm not even going to appoint a replacement. We'll go without a National Security Advisor."

Phillips eyed Kenaghy across the room. "What about Secretary of State?"

Kenaghy turned around wildly and glared at Phillips. "Who needs one? That goddamn Paul Houseman seems to be running foreign policy."

The language and anger caught Phillips off-guard. He stood there watching the President—now sullenly staring out the window. For the first time in eleven years, he wondered about the emotional state of a man he'd never seen waver. For the first time in three and a half years, he had serious doubts the President would be re-elected. *God*, he thought, *I've got to do everything I can to get this man through the end of the term with some grace.*

Kenaghy turned away from the window. "What do you make of this?" He lifted *The Times* off his desk and handed it to Phillips. "This is Arthur Rivenhouse's daughter."

Phillips hadn't seen it. He read the first few lines. He looked up. "Several of the senators and congresspersons got letters today from the state granges. Something about a farmers' union and some grievances. I don't know the situation well enough yet."

"Neither do I. I called Dean Dutz at Agriculture a little while ago. He mentioned this union thing also. Said it's nonsense. Ignore them and they'll go away."

Along with the new version of TES, thought Phillips, looking again to the stack of paper on the President's desk. "Did you read TES yet?" he asked like he didn't already know the answer.

Kenaghy ignored the question. "Finish that article. I don't know if Linda Bennett has it right, but I thought we handled the Asian grain shortage pretty well."

Cameron pushed through the eight-hundred-word commentary. "Wow, fairly incendiary for *The Times.* You know this is not your constituency. The Sun Belt states all went Republican."

Kenaghy nodded. "Can't say I've ever spent much time thinking about the plight of the family farmer." He lifted his hand to his chin. "You ever hear of Colonel Nathaniel Cromwell? Dutz says he's mixed up with this farm thing."

"The name rings a bell. Didn't he win a Medal of Honor?"

"Then returned it. I met him once. He was speaking at Boston University about the role of the CIA and the U.S. Army in heroin trafficking. Impressive man. Seems odd that he would suddenly show up leading a farmers' union. Can you get me some more on this?"

Phillips was staring at the big print on the desk, *Trans-Eurasian Security Act*, wondering how he could get the President's attention on more pressing matters. "I'll see what I can find. Anything more?"

Kenaghy wasn't listening. He was staring out the window again.

"Anything more, sir?" He said it a little louder.

Kenaghy didn't divert his gaze. "No, that's all, Cameron. I just can't believe Don's resigned. I wonder who's next," he continued dreamily.

Phillips took a deep breath.

CHAPTER 36

Nathaniel Cromwell drove all night from Chicago and arrived at his farm just before sunrise Tuesday. He smelled the coffee as soon as he opened the back door. His mother sat at the kitchen table, having her second cup. Nate hadn't called since he'd left Mahan's, and his sudden arrival got a cold response.

Nate went straight to the coffeepot and poured himself a large mug. He got the cream from the refrigerator and sat down at the table across from his mother. *The Wichita Eagle* lay in the middle of the table open to page four. The headline read: US FARMERS FORMING UNION. He poured a little cream in his mug and stirred it in, his eyes moving from Mary, to the article, to his coffee.

"Go ahead, read it," she finally said. "I already have." Her tone said it all.

"That bad?" He pulled the paper over to his side of the table.

"What are you going to do, Nate?" Her question echoed with deeper suggestions about their farm, his son, and her doubts.

"I'm part of it, Ma. It may be futile, but it's necessary. Something I'm doing as much for the two million family farmers in the U.S. today, as for Dad, as for Granddad and Grandma, as for all the pioneers who homesteaded this wild country into the most productive farmland in the world." His eyes dropped down to the paper in front of him. He read the article's subtitle: *Farmers seek government intervention for their management shortcomings.* He lifted his eyes and continued. "I feel more committed to this movement than I did to the Army when I was sworn in at West Point." He read another couple lines into the article and looked up.

"I made a pledge the other night to lead the union. I made a pledge in front of maybe three thousand desperate men and women. And yet, I made that pledge without first asking you or Will, full knowing that it would impact your lives just as much as mine. It might even have put your lives in jeopardy. Perhaps I should have talked this over with both of you before I committed to the farming community." He lowered his eyes again, this time closing them as he spoke. "I don't feel I need your permission, but I do want your support."

Mary stared at him hard. "I already gave you my opinion. Farming and politics don't mix."

Nate's cell phone rang. He stood to take the phone off his belt. It was Mahan. His eyes were still on his mother. She stood and walked over to the kitchen counter.

"Yeah, Forest, I'm getting my first look at today's paper now."

"Not good. Not good at all," said Mahan. "I've been on the internet checking some of the east coast papers. If they mention us at all, it's with ridicule. You don't even want to know what they think of us farmers forming a union. Hayes was right."

"What kind of response are you getting from the granges?"

"That's a different story. Total support. Some suggestions for changes in our platform. Mostly minor. But it's happening. When can you get back here? Hayes arrives in twenty-four hours. And you know what he'll be pushing for."

Cromwell was listening but looking straight at his mother's back. "Just a minute, Forest." He covered the receiver but didn't even get a chance to ask.

His mother faced him, then shook her head like he was a kid skipping school. "Christ-all-mighty, Nate, there is no way in the world I would make you go back on your pledge to those poor farmers." She put her hands on her hips. "You have to know that after fifty years of eating Kansas dust I'm just as much a part of this land as anyone. I don't like what you're doing, and I don't think you have a snowball's chance in hell, but to tell you the damn truth, as much as I hate saying it, I doubt there's a better man to do the job than you. Do what has to be done and let's get on with it."

Cromwell removed his hand from the receiver. "I'll be there tomorrow by noon."

"Then I won't waste any more time on the phone. We both have things to do, and strategy is best discussed in person. Thanks."

Nate put the phone back in its holster and went over to his mother. He put his hands on her shoulders and leaned over her. He hated it that she'd been swearing. He kissed her on the forehead. The moment stilled with a peculiar clarity. He sensed a need to doubly imprint this instant in his memory. When he straightened up, Will was standing in the kitchen doorway. He was just out of bed, wearing only his boxer shorts.

"How'd it go, Dad?"

"I guess that depends on your point of view, Will."

"What do you mean?"

"The newspapers think we're a bunch of fools."

"Does that really matter?"

He looked at Mary, then back to his son. "It's not a good start, Will. It's important to have the ordinary people behind us, and as long as the media portrays us badly, the average American might never truly understand how difficult our situation really is or what we're doing."

"Can't we expect the working class of the United States to be with us, Dad? I mean, aren't we really facing the same situation they are?"

Mary spoke up. "One would expect that, Will, but the truth is farmers are generally thought of as something separate. A class of people unto themselves. I think that's part of the reason we've had so much trouble all along. We're perceived as different."

"But we're not."

"No, I think we are," she said. "And that's going to be more and more evident as the next few weeks unfold."

"Are we going to burn our fields, Dad?"

Nate heard a hint of the romance of it in his son's voice. It made him sad. His mother looked at him. She felt the same thing in the boy. It passed between them. The meeting tomorrow in Missouri would be all about the use of fire. "Could be, Will. Could be."

Although cold and thoroughly exhausted, Cromwell pushes his team over the rough terrain and snow, trying to beat daylight for their rendezvous with the chopper. Thanks to Cromwell's global positioning map and Tenzing's instincts, they are right on target for the pick-up, but late. The slightest crease of orange peeks over the horizon in the east. Every minute of delay at this point increases their jeopardy and the helicopter's. Priestly spots the chopper first—the silhouette of a dragonfly coming out of the southeast.

"Hallelujah," exclaims Cromwell, "let's get this gig headed home." Cromwell turns on the black band. "This is A-one-red-bandit. Can you read me?"

"Loud and clear. We've been hanging out here a bit waiting for you, Colonel. Coming right in."

"Fantastic. Over and out."

The group has piled their gear up and is watching the MC-47E coming in against the dawn. It has dropped down from several thousand feet to a few hundred, when out of the north, a small rocket cuts across the sky headed for the chopper—missing high. The black whirlybird reacts with an explosive upward lift, pulling off to the south and out of range.

"What the fuck was that?" comes out of the black band, as Cromwell and the others grab their weapons and fan out in a semi-circle facing north.

Cromwell queries the chopper. "Have a reading on their position?"

"Roger. I caught a peek just before we took the elevator. There's something in a culvert, due north of you about half a mile. I think that was one of those damn hand-held Chinese rocket launchers. I doubt they know you're there and just spotted us coming in."

Cromwell looks out in that direction. Because of a slight rise in the terrain, the culvert is below his line of vision. "Can you see anything else?"

"No, Colonel, that's all we've got. But judging from their position, I don't think we can get an angle on them with our machine guns—or into you without risk of taking one of their rockets."

"Yeah," says Cromwell, running through the scenarios in his head.

"Even worse, Colonel. Because you were a little late, we only have enough fuel to hang here for about another thirty minutes and still get back home."

"We'll get them."

"Do it quick, Colonel, or you might have another night on the rock."

"Got it. I'm handing this radio over to a Captain Davenport. She'll be our base. Try to draw some fire so we can locate them."

"Yes, sir."

Cromwell quickly briefs the others. He gives Lena the black band and tells Tenzing he's to stay with the gear. Priestly, Alvoretti, and Rust, along with himself, are going in from four angles. "As far as we know, they don't know we're here. The chopper is going to keep their eyes in the sky, and if we ain't fast, we're here another day."

"Well, that's some huge incentive," mutters Rust.

"Yeah. Now let's advance just far enough to see what's below this rise to the north. Rusty take the left flank, Priestly the right. Alvoretti, you've got the rocket launcher. You and I split will the difference up the center. Once we've spotted their hole, we pinch them down with our rifles, so Canary gets a chance to drop a rocket on them."

The four men belly up across the top of the snow-covered ridge in increasing daylight. They look down on a culvert that runs east to west. The helicopter takes one low pass over the culvert and lets go with a hundred rounds from its starboard guns.

A rocket shoots out of a naturally formed bunker of boulders on the far side of the culvert, almost directly across from Rust's position on the left. Again, it misses as the chopper passes over the backside of the culvert and out of the guerillas' view. The chopper swings around immediately, taking another pass from the front, throwing out rounds. Another rocket and automatic rifle fire explode out of the culvert, but the chopper is out of range.

Cromwell's men use the exchange of fire to dive into the culvert, adjusting their positions so they triangulate the bunker. They are within a hundred yards and closing, working through rocks and snow drifts.

When the helicopter takes a third pass, even higher this time, two guerillas stand in the bunker opening and flail hopelessly at the chopper with their AK-47s. Rust, Cromwell, and Priestly stand and rattle their MP-5s into the bunker. Both guerillas are hit. Alvoretti rises up with the rocket launcher on his shoulder. A gunshot rings out from the rocks twenty yards east of the bunker. It hits Canary, opening like a rose bud in the chest. He staggers under the weight of the launcher, steadies himself, even as another bullet hits him, and puts a rocket right in the bunker, then collapses on the ground.

Priestly is the closest to Alvoretti. Cromwell and Rust spray the sniper's location with fire for cover. Priestly rushes to the downed sergeant. Cromwell and Rust push forward, rifles at the ready, circling in from two sides on the sniper's location, ever conscious of the smoldering bunker.

Priestly rises up to call out to Cromwell. "Canary's dead, Colonel." And the sniper fires again. A bullet catches Priestly in the shoulder, knocking him to the ground. Rust notes the exact location of the sniper, sees the barrel of his rifle move, and puts a bullet where the shooter should be.

Cromwell and Rust hold quiet. Then move forward on the sniper's blind. Rust takes a grenade off his belt. He and Cromwell edge closer. Still all quiet. They are less than twenty-five yards away. Rust yanks the pin with his teeth and lobs the grenade at the sniper's location. He and Cromwell hit the dirt. The explosion rocks the ground and showers the men with debris. When they stand, Cromwell nods to Rust.

Rust moves up to check the sniper. Cromwell dashes down to Priestly. He's badly wounded but alive. With help, he manages to stand.

Rust is with them in seconds. "The bunker is history, Boss, and so is the sniper."

"Good." Cromwell looks to Priestly. "Can you make it back?" Priestly nods. "Rusty and I will get Alvoretti. Get going."

Ten minutes later, Cromwell and Rust drop Alvoretti beside the gear. Lena offers the black band to Cromwell. "They're waiting for orders, sir."

He takes the radio. "Okay, you guys, we got 'em. How's the time?"

"None to spare. We're coming in. Sorry about those hits, Colonel. What's the read?"

"One badly hurt. The other needs a body bag. Hurry up, get down here. I think we woke up every nasty in these hills."

"Yes, sir."

With the rotors thwacking at the air, they load Priestly in the chopper's side door fighting the heavy blow-down. Canary goes into a body bag. The equipment is next. Lena follows that. Then, just as Tenzing grabs hold of the chopper's doorframe to pull himself in, five guerillas top the rise to the west. Three open fire. Two steady a rocket launcher.

"Christ, get in," screams Rust. Several quick punctures appear in the MC-47E's skin—and Tenzing's jacket! He falls half in, half out of the chopper. Rust pushes Tenzing in as the anxious pilot accelerates the rotors for liftoff. Cromwell dives to the ground, rifle outstretched and sprays the western horizon with lead. Three of the five guerillas go down. Rust is already aboard. The chopper is lifting off as Cromwell scrambles to his feet and races to the rising beast. Another six guerillas top the rise. Cromwell takes Rust's hand and scrabbles in as the chopper jerks straight up and banks left. A rocket passes just beneath them, then they are out of range.

Inside the chopper is turmoil. Priestly is sitting up, leaning against the bulkhead, his shoulder bleeding badly. Lena kneels beside Tenzing lying on the chopper deck. She looks at Cromwell. "Jast is dead, Colonel."

"Fuck," snarls Cromwell, "there must have been scores of them out there. Fifteen minutes sooner we beat daylight." He crawls through the equipment to the little leprechaun. His dark eyes are still open—but without the spark of eternity. Cromwell uses two fingers to close Jast's eyes. He looks around at the others, then stares out the side window at the Afghan dawn.

"Easy, Boss, we did what we had to."

Cromwell doesn't respond, continuing to stare out at the rising sun. After a few minutes, he realizes they are flying north. "Hey, pilot! Where we headed?" he growls. "Pakistan's the other direction."

The copilot turns around. "Change of plans, sir. We're headed to Uzbekistan."

"Little city over the border, Colonel," says the pilot. "Kurban Tube."

"Why the change?" asks Rust.

"Beats me. I just follow orders."

Cromwell shakes his head and turns his attention to Priestly.

"Paul, you okay."

He forces a, "Yes, sir," through gritted teeth.

"Lena?"

"Fine, sir."

"Rusty?"

"When do we get to do it again?"

CHAPTER 37

While Tuesday was dawning in Kansas, it was winding down in Singapore. Jonathan Mayfield had accepted the one-month contract with the Development Bank of Asia and had a room at the Singapore Hilton. After a long day of giving seminars to the bank's computer technicians in preparation for a major streamlining of DBA's entire Southeast Asian network, Jonathan was now parked at the bar in the Hilton lounge, sipping a Guinness, thinking about the call he'd made earlier to his parents in London, explaining his "trip to Asia." It was almost as crazy as the story he'd used to explain why he'd gotten his brow pierced. He smiled to himself remembering that one.

"Do you mind if I join you?" A long-haired, bearded man with round wire-rimmed glasses sat down beside Jonathan at the bar. The lounge was elevated four steps and off to the right as you entered the lobby. A Filipino trio with a five-piece band did a Supremes act on a little stage in the corner.

"No, go right ahead," said Jonathan after the man had already made the presumption.

"Aussie or Limey?" asked the man. He might have been thirty-five, wore a white linen sports coat, faded, battle-worn blue jeans, and a red t-shirt displaying the face of an Indian chief, with the words *AMERICAN HOLOCAST* printed below in white block letters.

"I'm from London," replied Jonathan. He was not an outgoing individual, but he'd had two pints of Guinness and was feeling quite good after a hard day of work. "You must be an American."

The man grinned easily. "Like stink on shit." He surveyed the bar's stock of liquor, then called out to the Asian bartender, waving a piece of blue paper currency, "A shot of Cuervo 1800." He turned to appraise what Jonathan was drinking and added, "Make that two."

Jonathan didn't really want any hard liquor, but the two shot glasses arrived with two slices of lemon and a shaker of salt before he'd come up with a polite way to say no.

"The name's Dan," said the man, sticking out his hand. "Ever do tequila?" he asked, directing his eyes to the shot glasses and lemons.

"Jonathan," he said, giving Dan's hand a shake. "Never have." He lifted the shot glass and passed it beneath his nose. The fragrance was nothing like scotch, more like medicine or something synthetic. He took a small sip of the Mexican alcohol. His eyes flashed with its bite.

"Don't work that way, Jonathan," chuckled the hippie. "First this." He licked the back of his hand and sprinkled salt on the wet spot. "Then this!" He licked the salt, threw down the shot of tequila, and bit into the lemon. He shook his head, blinked his eyes, and exclaimed, "Tah-kee-la!" like they did in the fifties rock'n'roll instrumental by the same name. "Try that!"

Jonathan had his doubts, but he'd just been released from three months of confinement. *Why not break out a bit?* So he did just as the American had. Licked his hand. Tossed down the tequila, and bit into the lemon. He gasped at the taste, licked his lips, then grimaced. "Bloody strong."

Dan waved his empty shot glass at the bartender. "Two more. And a couple Tsing-dao chasers."

"That's not necessary, Dan."

"Hey, man." The American hippie waved him off. "I'm just glad to find another freak in this crazy place. What do you think of Singapore?"

"Not quite sure yet," said Jonathan, suddenly realizing that small talk would lead to difficult questions. "I really haven't seen much more than this hotel."

Dan looked over toward the faux-Supremes. They were dancing in line, singing *Stop in the Name of Love.* Each time they reached the refrain, they abruptly stopped dancing and held up a hand like a traffic cop. "On the upside, Jonathan, everything is a cheap imitation of American." The bartender arrived with two more shots of Cuervo, two slices of lemon, two Chinese beers, and two glasses. "On the downside, the poor are poorer and the corruption deeper. It's the same way throughout Southeast Asia. It's the armpit of the world." The bartender gave Dan a funny look as he filled the glasses with beer. Dan grinned it off and selected a few bills from his wallet and put twenty Singapore dollars on the bar.

"So, you know this part of the world?"

Dan licked the back of his hand and salted it. "Been trying to figure it out the past eighteen months." He took a little sip from his beer. "Thailand, Burma, Cambodia, Vietnam, now here. Pretty little women with straight black hair. Slick businessmen in shiny suits, silk ties, and big black cars. The appearance of money everywhere." He nodded toward a table of just such men drinking and talking. By western standards, they looked like hoods with their cigarettes and greased back hair. "It's a very strict place though. Quasi-fascist, if you ask me." He licked, swilled, and bit into the lemon—again using the oldies refrain as an exclamation, "Tah-kee-la."

Jonathan glanced with reluctance at the glass in front of him, licked his hand and salted it. He hurriedly bit the lemon, licked the salt, and tossed down the tequila, losing some out the side of his mouth. "Agghhhh!" He squeezed his eyes shut, struggling with the taste. "Do Americans like this?"

Dan laughed, lifting his beer. "When they do it in the right order. Have a taste of beer."

Jonathan did just that—noticing a slight sway in the room as he tipped back the glass. "My," he said, placing the beer carefully on the bar. "I can feel it already."

"Another?"

"No, I think that was enough for me." Jonathan gave him a wide smile, feeling the buzz.

"What brings you here, Jonathan?" asked Dan, grinning at his work on the young Englishman.

Jonathan hesitated a moment, then spouted it out. "Just took a job at the Development Bank of Asia."

"Really? You don't look like a banker."

Jonathan was feeling pretty good all of a sudden. He watched the Filipino Supremes in their short, tight, gold lamé dresses. He thought they were quite entertaining. "I do computers," he said, turning to the American. "How about you?"

Dan looked across the lounge to the brightly lit lobby. Although it was nearly eleven, people were still climbing out of taxis and pushing through the big glass doors, assisted by redcaps carrying their luggage. He turned back to Jonathan, sizing him up, seemingly determining how to answer this last question. "I'm here doing research." There was a hint of brag in the way he said it.

Jonathan gave him a quizzical look, knowing he could have said much the same.

"I'm using you as my cover," said Dan.

Jonathan's facial expression was a question.

"In the restaurant." Dan nodded in the direction of the hotel restaurant across the lobby—also elevated four steps. It was mostly empty. "The farthest table. The Chinese man in the white suit and longish silver hair. Sitting with three other Chinese."

Jonathan saw the man. "Yes."

"He's my subject of research tonight."

"You're watching him?"

Dan nodded.

"Can I ask why?" The tequila was funny, thought Jonathan. He was definitely tipsy but in a kind of clear-headed way.

Dan took another sip from his beer. "I'm a freelance journalist. I'm working on a story."

"You must want me to ask what it's about?" Jonathan was being much more forward than he normally would and it felt good.

"Guerilla economics."

This caused Jonathan to smile. "And that is?"

"Black market money flows." Dan looked off toward the restaurant and the Chinese man with silver hair. "I came here to write a book on the heroin trade. I think it plays a larger part in world economics than is generally admitted." He took another swallow of beer. "It's become more than I expected."

Jonathan nodded. "I don't know anything about the black market, but I know something about economics." Dan's eyes were on the man in the restaurant. "Asia is gradually becoming an integral part of the big picture."

Dan grinned. "That's an understatement. It's the Chinese, Jonathan."

"Well, yes, of course, since the Olympics. China is the big piece."

"No, that's not what I said. It's the Chinese. That's what I'm writing about." He looked around the bar, appraising those within earshot. "I'm not really trying to put this out until the book is done, but it's also not often I run into someone I think will understand."

"Try me," said Jonathan, not really too certain where the American was headed.

Dan leaned close to Jonathan and lowered the volume of his voice, so that Jonathan had to lean over to hear. "Hundreds of years ago, the Chinese merchant class began migrating south out of China. Now, everywhere you go throughout Southeast Asia, it's the Chinese who oversee and direct commerce. Thailand, Burma, Malaysia, Indonesia, Singapore, Vietnam, the Philippines—in all of these countries, the business infrastructure is generations deep in Chinese. Everything important—banking, real estate, transportation, prostitution, drugs, guns, the police, even the military in some cases—all are managed by expatriate Chinese."

"I've never heard that."

"There are these old Chinese merchant families called kongsi. They're like business corporations tied by blood. There are five major ones. They control most of the money and most of the economic policy, legal and illegal, throughout this area." Dan paused to finish off his glass of beer. He raised it in the air to get the bartender's attention.

"In the 1940s, as the Communist Party began to assume control of mainland China, huge sums of merchant class money moved out of China into this network referred to as Overseas Chinese. Their financial grip on the Pacific Rim, from Singapore to Shanghai around to Seattle and San Francisco, is extensive."

The bartender put two bottles of Tsing-dao on the bar. Jonathan waved off the bartender. No, he didn't need another. Dan picked up his first bottle of beer. He eyed the remains, then lifted it over his head, draining it into his mouth. He put down the bottle and wiped his lips with the back of his hand.

"After the death of Mao, gradually, since the eighties, more and more since the turn of the millennium, this Overseas Chinese money has begun a cautious return to mainland China. Although the government still claims to be communist, capitalism is at work, building industry and infrastructure for the new China. It's been these expatriate Chinese who have funded the vast development of China over the last thirty, forty years. And the key to doing business around the rim is knowing which Chinese control which concessions and whose palm to grease if you want to be part of it." He refilled his glass from the second bottle. "Know what I'm sayin'?"

"Yes, I suppose. But I thought you were interested in the heroin trade?"

"That's where I started. But I soon discovered there was no separating the heroin trade from the kongsis that control it. The Chinese are natural born bureaucrats and bean counters. They are so good, in fact, these other Asian countries have simply handed their books over to them. It's so pervasive, it's incredible. And when it comes to the black market—drugs, women, guns. They make it happen. Payoffs to government officials, to the police. Everywhere." Dan took a slug of beer and shrugged. "I guess it's really no different than politics anywhere. It's just that here in Asia, it's the Chinese that are the glue that keeps the system together."

Jonathan found this more interesting than his American friend could possibly know. "So, who's this man in the restaurant?"

Dan's eyes turned in that direction. "Zhao He. He's an extremely successful computer manufacturer and the number one man in the Teochui Kongsi. The kongsi at the top of the heroin pyramid." Dan stiffened. "Don't turn around, but there's a group of Chinese men entering the hotel at this moment."

"I can see them in the mirror," said Jonathan.

"This is what I've been waiting for." Dan reached into the breast pocket of his linen jacket. Whatever he pulled out, he palmed in such a way that it was hidden. "Lean to your left, Jonathan. That's perfect." Dan lifted his right hand like he was adjusting his glasses and used a mini-camera to snap three pictures just as Zhao He stood from his table and shook hands with the first of the Chinese entering the restaurant from the lobby. Then the little camera was back in his breast pocket, and Dan was lifting his beer to take another sip. Jonathan noticed that Dan's hand shook when he reached for the glass.

"Thanks," said Dan.

"Catching that meeting was why you were here tonight?"

Dan nodded. "Photographing those two men together."

Jonathan lifted his glass and finished his beer. "Isn't this story of yours a bit dangerous?"

Dan nodded again. "Totally. I want to get out of this hellhole as soon as I can. I'd like to be back in the States, putting my book together in two months or less."

Jonathan smiled. "I'm impressed."

"Don't be. There's too much more to this I haven't told you." Dan winked, stood, lifted his glass, and drained what remained. "Thanks for the cover and the conversation, bro, but I'm out of this popcorn stand."

"Thanks for the introduction to tequila."

"My pleasure." Dan took a pen from his pocket and wrote a phone number and an address on his napkin. "Call me if you want to try it again sometime." He handed Jonathan the napkin. "Ta, ta." Dan offered him a flat palm. Jonathan grinned and gave him five, then watched the hippie weave through the lounge, past the Supremes, and out the back door.

Jonathan sat there a few minutes, pondering what Dan had said about the kongsi, wondering if in some way this could play into the grain market. But he was tired and way too tipsy. He needed to go to bed.

As he stood to leave, he noticed a computer disk on the floor beneath the stool Dan had been sitting on. He picked up the disk. It had a paper label that said *file one* and *file two.* Jonathan fished the napkin from his pocket and compared the writing. They were similar. Maybe the disk had fallen from Dan's pocket when he'd gotten his camera out or maybe the pen. He'd call him tomorrow and check.

CHAPTER 38

Nathaniel Cromwell spent the rest of Tuesday cutting firebreaks at his farm with Will, then got up early Wednesday to drive to Missouri. The temperature was just reaching an even one hundred degrees when he arrived at Mahan Farms shortly after noon. General Hayes was already there.

Nate, Hayes, and Mahan immediately retired to the office at the back of the house. They needed to make a decision about the union's next move. Forest began the meeting by reading an editorial from *The Washington Post* written by the Secretary of Agriculture Dean Dutz.

"There is no doubt that the position of the small farmer is a difficult one, but it cannot be considered a situation so extreme as to merit welfare. The government has maintained farming subsidies for years to keep the farmers in the field. Now that these subsidies are being phased out to open the market, the farmers either make it on their own or they don't make it at all. Neither the government nor commercial grain dealers should be expected to bail them out as they have in the past. The real point of contention is whether small farms should exist at all. There were 30 million family farms in the United States in the 1920s. Today there are less than 2 million. It's something called economic transition. Maybe it's time the family farmer just accepted this, packed up, moved into the city, and left farming to the more efficient methods of the large industrial farms." Forest stopped reading and spoke directly to Hayes and Cromwell. "That might be one of the worst, but it pretty much sums up the reaction in the east—when they react to us at all."

General Hayes was not the I-told-you-so type, but nonetheless, he crossed his arms and sat back rather smugly, allowing a lingering moment of silence, before he threw in his two cents. "This is the same philosophy that runs through our entire government. The big guy does it best. If he's successful, his profits trickle down upon us peons. Sounds more like a golden shower to me. No doubt about it. The big boys would be just as happy to see us all go away."

"Maybe we should review our demands," said Mahan. "Maybe we're asking for too much."

"Maybe we should just forget the whole thing, Forest. Take our harvest to market and take our whipping like good boys."

Mahan grimaced at Hayes' sarcasm. "I just can't believe we should rise up and start burning our fields. There must be a step in between."

"They aren't going to take us seriously until we do something serious. I've been to ten of the largest militia outfits across the harvest belt. They're ready to go." Hayes turned to Cromwell. "What do you say, Colonel?"

Nate wasn't all that excited about field burning either. But damn, they hadn't even gotten support in the Midwest papers. Oh, there were a few positive commentaries here and there. Some of the very small farm community newspapers offered full support, but the bigger Midwestern papers barely touched the story. When they did, their opinions reflected their ownership, and the ownership was not local. They were syndicates, subsidiaries of multifaceted conglomerates, publishers interlocked with banking interests, diversified into chemical companies, agribusiness, and who knows what else. "Forest," asked Nate, "what kind of response have we gotten from the farms that have wheat ready to go?"

Mahan sighed. "They're still coming in, Nate. Many of the Christian communities are adamant against destroying their crops, but plenty of others are willing to make a statement. Given another couple days, we might have your five hundred thousand acres."

"Vincent, can you get men digging firebreaks by tomorrow?"

"It's already begun, sir." His eyes were alight with the prospect.

Nate paused momentarily to look around Forest's study. A big framed map of the United States hung on one wall. A visual reminder of how much of the country was cropland. Two walls were top to bottom bookshelves. Quite a lot of history books. Quite a lot of American history. Just scanning the titles ran Nate through the trials and tribulations of maintaining a democracy for 250 years. The fourth wall was the window behind Forest's desk. It looked out on acres and acres of ripe winter wheat—wheat that would be part of the first burn. "What about our storage capacity, Forest? What's the report on empty silos?"

"It's a tradeoff, Nate," said Mahan. "There's space, but everyone's got a different plan for how they want to use it."

"What about storage space further north? Couldn't we harvest part of what we want to burn and ship it north for storage? Then when we burn the fields, it looks like more devastation than it is. We don't burn the whole bridge, just the railings."

"Come on, Colonel, what little could be stored won't make much difference compared to the message we'll be sending."

"No, I think every bushel counts, General. If the field burning makes the statement we hope it does, we might not have to set more fires. In that case, what we store now can go to market later."

"It's possible, Nate," said Mahan. "But I want a definitive response from Congress or the industry before we do anything. I think we've got to give ourselves that chance. And if things are still as negative as they are now—fine. We make the show of fire."

"We already have a definitive response, Forest," stated Hayes, standing up, irritated at Mahan's reluctance. "Dean Dutz's commentary says all we need to know. More calls, more letters. That's just a waste of time."

"Damn it, Vincent, it's not. Unity is our only chance. We're talking about the Bible Belt, and a lot of those people are truly terrified of field burning. They think it's a mortal sin to waste the grain."

"No, Forest," said Nate. "We went through this same argument the other day. Like Hayes says, we've gotten their response and their message is clear. Besides, the wheat won't wait. It's already more than a week past harvest. I don't like it any more than you do, but it's time to act. We need some respect, and we need it now." Mahan had no answer to this. "General, when can you have the fields ready?"

"Friday. Saturday at the latest."

Mahan shook his head sadly.

Cromwell looked him in the eye. "Here's the deal, Forest. We'll be set to burn by the weekend. That gives you four days to come up with something positive enough to stop us. Try the phones, try another push of letters and emails. Do whatever you can. But no mention of strike. No mention of fire. Just go at it straight. If you get something substantive by Sunday—and I mean really solid, we hold off. If not, we hit it. All at once. Shotgun start. Day break Monday."

"If we press, we could do it Saturday, Colonel. Why not? Time is everything."

"No. We want a weekday. We want a market reaction. This is a media event. We want prime time TV Monday morning. Besides we'll be better prepared. And it will give us a chance to harvest some of the wheat and get it stored."

Mahan still didn't like it. It showed all over his face.

Cromwell asked him point blank. "Can you do this, Forest?"

Mahan bowed his head and softly said, "Yes."

"And you, General?"

"The fire crew awaits your command."

Forest lifted his head and looked at Nate. "You know what all this means, right?"

Nate nodded. "We've agreed to take on the government." He looked over at Hayes.

"And if things get rough and either of you need a place to go," said the militia general, crossing the room to the big map on the wall. "This is where you can find me." He put his forefinger on a spot in the foothills of the south Montana Rockies and looked right at Nate. "Tumble Mountain. Password—*Yellowtail*."

Nate repeated the location and the password. Forest merely frowned at the prospect and turned sad eyes toward the window and his ready to harvest wheat.

The day is breaking on a ragged land that time forgot. Long sharp shadows shear across the jagged peaks of the White Mountains like black knives as the sun gradually lights the crystalline February morning. Wisps of clouds trail out across the horizon in the distance. Below is the Uzbekistan border.

Fifteen minutes later, the chopper with Cromwell and his depleted crew is settling down in a wide blacktop construction yard in the tiny border town of Kurban Tube. The yard is fenced in with ten-foot high chain link, topped with coils of razor wire. It contains three large corrugated steel warehouses, numbered 1, 2, and 3. There's a sign on warehouse 1 that reads Hamilton Heavy Construction.

An ambulance is waiting. The medics rush up to the black helicopter as soon as the hatch opens. After a few furious moments beneath the thwacking rotors, Paul Priestly comes out on a stretcher, straight into the ambulance, followed by two body bags. Lena Davenport is out next to ride with Priestly to the hospital. Rust leaps to the pavement, stretching his arms, followed by Cromwell. They are both appraising the surroundings when two men in dark suits come out of the nearest warehouse. They walk right up to Cromwell and introduce themselves.

"Turner Grayson, Colonel," says the first man, extending his hand.

"Howard James," says the other as Cromwell shakes the first man's hand, then the second's.

"What can I do for you, gentlemen?" Cromwell gives a little look to Rust standing beside him. "And why were we brought here?"

Grayson returns a gratuitous smile. "Debriefing, Colonel." He pulls a billfold from his breast pocket. With a flick of his wrist, he opens it, revealing a CIA identification card, and just as quickly flicks it closed. "Standard stuff."

Cromwell nods. "Lead the way." He motions to Rust to follow.

Grayson's eyes swing to Rust. "Just you, Colonel."

"Rusty, make sure they give proper attention to Jast and Alvoretti. I'll be right back."

"They can get cleaned up and have something to eat in number 3."

Cromwell gives Grayson a look. "They're the ones in body bags."

Grayson lowers his eyes.

"But I'm not," says Rust. "I'll have some of that grub."

Cromwell follows Grayson and James into warehouse 1. The large warehouse is partitioned into many small offices. Each one with a computer and a man at the keyboard. Going deeper into the building, they pass a bank of monitors showing satellite images of Afghanistan, Pakistan, Iran, Turkey, Israel, Lebanon, Syria, and Iraq. At the back of the building, Cromwell is led into a glass-enclosed office. They take seats around a table and begin the debriefing. It's all standard and lasts an hour.

As they are wrapping things up, there's a knock on the office door. A man enters and spreads a stack of photos out on the table. They're the digital shots Cromwell took while in the cave. Cromwell picks up a photo. It's of one of the underground labs and has been enlarged and enhanced.

"Nice work, Colonel," says Grayson looking over the photos.

"Almost looks like I knew what I was doing," Cromwell replies, selecting a second shot of the same lab. "This opium processing?"

"That's how we see it," answers James, looking at the sheet of paper that describes the analysis of each shot.

Cromwell points to a figure working in the lab. "Can we get a zoom on this man's face?"

Grayson and James exchange a look. James nods. "Yeah, I'm sure they're in the system by now." He goes over to the terminal in the corner and starts punching at the keyboard.

Grayson hands Cromwell a photo. "Look at this one, Colonel."

It's an aerial view of a crater. "I didn't take this one."

"A satellite did. That's what your people did to that cave complex."

Cromwell nodded, thinking that Lena had done her job well.

James calls from the terminal. "Here you go, Colonel."

Cromwell ambles over to the terminal. The entire screen is a man's face. Cromwell shakes his head. "Jesus Christ," is all he says.

"What is it, Colonel?" Grayson looks at the image on the screen.

"I recognize that man. He was working with you guys last time I was in Afghanistan. Any way to find out who this is?" There is some irritation in his voice.

Grayson and James exchange another look. James goes at the keyboard again. Grayson walks away from the terminal and leans over the photos on the table. Cromwell watches the windows coming and going on the screen. After a few minutes, James turns to him. "Nothing."

"Then print that enlargement of the face. I'd like a copy for myself."

Cromwell leaves warehouse 1 with the picture folded up in his pocket and heads over to number 3 to shower and eat. Inside are a cafeteria, a small lounge, and a locker room. Rust is in the lounge, stretched out on a couch with an open beer can sitting on his belly.

"I'm not completely sure I'm in with these CIA boys, Rusty," says Cromwell. "I photographed a guy in that cave who I thought worked for us." He shakes his head in exasperation. "How many sides to this war can there be?"

Rust had already showered and eaten. He'd also been debriefed while Nate was in the other warehouse. "As many as they can imagine, Boss."

Cromwell and Rust were friends. Good friends and combat buddies. But they were different. Cromwell was an idealist—all honor and duty. Rust was a cold hard cynic.

"Well, I don't like being lied to," said Cromwell. "Those boys weren't straight with me just now. I don't really the fuck know what we just blew up." He grimaced at the thought of it. "As far as I can tell, we got three men killed knocking out a terrorist cell we created. This stuff makes me sick."

"Hey. We're mercenaries, Boss. You just gotta accept it."

Cromwell scowled. "When I go out there with men on the line, I want to know exactly what I'm fighting for and why."

"It's all done with smoke and mirrors, Boss. No way to know what's real."

Cromwell stared at his friend. He couldn't disagree more. But he kept it to himself and headed off to take a shower.

CHAPTER 39

Atossa Andreas flew to Atlanta to see Dr. Colleen on Thursday morning. She walked into the doctor's office and launched into a bitter diatribe about the spidery red star on her cheek. "I've even gone back to wearing a veil," she stated as though it were some kind of threat.

Dr. Colleen was not easily intimidated. She took ten skin samples and analyzed them under high magnification. It was clear very quickly that Atossa had used more than sterile powder on her face. When she returned from the lab to speak with Atossa in her office, her unvarnished manner was a direct confrontation. "Ms. Andreas, you used makeup on the transplanted skin."

Atossa was seated, her veil removed. She straightened up and bristled as much at Nina's tone as the accuracy of the accusation. "That's not true."

Nina stared at her. "Do you think a lie will make it go away?"

"It was a light cover—not makeup at all—just a dab. It was on no longer than fifteen minutes." Atossa did not like being put on the spot. "It was nothing!" she exclaimed with an invoking tone of her own.

"It was absolutely contrary to my instructions, Ms. Andreas." Nina advanced to the side of her desk. "You invested a great deal of money in a delicate cosmetic transplant then turned around and sabotaged the entire procedure. Now you come to me complaining. How do you think I should respond to that kind of behavior?"

Atossa puffed up with indignation. Only her daughter Alise could get away with speaking to her like this. She abruptly stood, all set to give voice to her rage, when her emotions overtook her. She burst into tears and slumped back into her chair, covering her face and sobbing, humiliated, frustrated, and embarrassed.

Witness to the horrible ravages of fire on young children, this meant nothing to Nina Colleen. She turned away from Atossa's display and sat down at her desk to review her skin analysis and write a note to herself.

When Atossa realized she was being ignored, she peeked through her hands at the cool Dr. Colleen. She quickly gathered herself, angry at her breakdown. "What can be done, Doctor?'

Nina put down her pen. "I will give you a deep cleansing lotion. I will have an assistant show you how to use it before you leave. It may stop further eruption."

"And what of this blemish?"

"I'll try some steroid injections."

"Then I haven't ruined the transplant completely?" Her mind sailed off thinking of Derek Davis and the call she'd been putting off. "What kind of time frame are we talking?"

"A day at a time, Ms. Andreas."

When Atossa returned from Atlanta and entered her home in Newport, she was immediately informed that Alise had driven out from Boston and was in the living room. Atossa's day had been hard enough already, but now it was about to get worse. She had dreaded this confrontation with her daughter from the moment she had first decided to have the transplant. The expression she'd seen on Alise's face the night of the party had verified that anxiety. In all the world, she cared not one jot what anyone thought of her vanity—anyone other than Alise.

Atossa accepted the inevitable. She removed the veil she had worn for the trip and pushed through the doors to the living room. Alise was standing across the room, looking at one of the Monets. She abruptly turned to face her mother. Her expression was one of disdain and something bordering on repugnance. Atossa pretended she felt nothing of what that look inflicted on her.

"Hello, Alise," she said, advancing into the room. "I didn't know you were coming today. What a rare treat."

Alise just stared at her mother. The situation was a double reversal. Atossa was usually the forthright, critical one. Alise the soft spoken, unassuming one. "Is that really you?" asked Alise with a tone intended to cut.

"Isn't it amazing what they can do—isn't it?"

"Oh God, Mother. Can't you just accept getting older?"

"But why? Why accept something that you can put off?"

Alise came up closer, staring at her mother's new face.

"It's a complete transplant, Alise. All new skin." Atossa forced herself to smile. "It's not such a horrible thing. I feel so much better about myself. Can't you allow me that?"

Alise shook her head in disbelief. "But you don't even look like the same person. Doesn't that bother you?"

"It takes some getting used to. But it's so much nicer than the way it was."

"You mean the way all the other surgeries left you? With no chance to age gracefully." Alise came up closer still, as curious as she was disturbed. "What's that mark on your cheek?"

"Oh, it's nothing. There's a long process of adjusting the immunosuppressants. We're still working that out." Atossa tried to push through it, crossing the room to her chair. "So, what brought you here today?"

"What do you think?" Alise continued to stare at her mother. "After that incredible scene you created at the party, I had to know if that was really you." She sighed. "And now that I've been here, I know that it wasn't. It was some other thing speaking with your voice. I guess my real mother has long since been replaced by transplants, silicone injections, and circuit boards."

"Oh, Alise, don't be silly. It's the same me inside."

"Whoever that is," replied Alise with a fragile emotional edge in her voice. She turned suddenly and ran from the room.

Atossa had put up a good front, but she was devastated. The surgery that made her feel so good about herself could not have had a worse effect on the one person who mattered most. Why did it have to be this way? She bowed her head and cried in desperation for the second time that day.

CHAPTER 40

Linda Bennett started reading her father's email chronology Monday evening right after getting it from Charlie Patio. Each night as the week progressed, she'd settle into bed with her laptop and advance through it one email at a time. By the second night, she had become more interested in reading this chronology than doing any of the other things she was working on.

Most of her work day of late was spent running around Washington, trying to follow the progress of the new version of TES. Because Congress would be taking a six-week break at the end of the month, she expected the bill to move rapidly through both the House and the Senate. Everything she was hearing suggested that a finalized version would be on the President's desk for signature in the next ten days or so.

Linda also needed to prepare to go to Kansas City. Her feelings about this trip remained mixed, partly because of its connection to Richards and partly because she really considered Washington her journalistic arena. She wanted to put it off until August when the summer session of Congress ended, but Richards was pushing her to go much sooner than that—because, as he kept telling her, "Every day counts." So, while Linda played one end against the other by day, at night her father's email was telling a story she couldn't get enough of. It was basically the inside of her father's head through thirty hard fought years in Central Intelligence.

Wednesday night she stayed up until three before she was able to put the chronology down. Thursday night was more of the same. At eight-thirty, she turned on the TV to watch the last night of the Republican Presidential Convention in Phoenix, hit the mute, and stretched out on the couch. With a few pillows propped up behind her and a glass of pinot noir on the coffee table, she popped open her laptop and, between glances at the political craziness on TV, read one email after another, happy as a clam.

About an hour into her reading, Linda came upon a memo her father had written in August two years back and emailed to all the CIA department heads. It discussed petroleum depletion in language that was far stronger than what she would ever have expected from her father:

> *I've spent the last month reviewing all that the Agency has written on world petroleum reserves. It's clear that we are rapidly approaching a point where the reserves will effectively be exhausted. Once production peaks, which could be sooner than currently forecast, the entire global economy will be forced into a vast overhaul. By my evaluation of the situation, we should already have begun the changeover to alternative energy sources, even though the market has not yet given us that signal with dollar signs. I have to believe that the thinking man plans ahead better than the greedy market. Because of this, I see an American economic policy that is not credibly positioning itself for this inevitability. It seems that petroleum has been the bull's eye at the center of our foreign policy and military strategy for so long we're losing track of our purpose. We just watched ourselves stumble all over the Middle East. Now it seems we're going to do the same thing in Central Asia. Why do we continue to deny what we've known for so long? If we are really a working intelligence service, we have to act with intelligence.*

Although her father had never out and out said this to her, just led her on, he was expressing the same conclusion Linda had come to on her own: The free hand of the market was not the best way to distribute the world's most critical resources. Even more, it reinforced everything she was writing about the Trans-Eurasian Security Act.

In the past few months, particularly after her conversation with Frederick Manning in April, Linda had ached for the opportunity to talk to her father about just these questions. She had learned much more about the petroleum situation in the year since his death and had longed to bounce her ideas off his sound reasoning. But now she had what she wanted, verification of all that she feared, written by the man she trusted more than anyone else.

Linda sat there on the couch, laptop on her knees, and looked around the room, half expecting to see her father in ethereal form, sitting in the armchair or standing in the doorway, a real spook come to visit his daughter. But there was no ethereal form in Linda's room that night, only the electronic presence of her father's thoughts, messages sent to her on a different kind of ether. She forced a smile as she pondered this and wiped away the single tear that rolled down her cheek.

CHAPTER 41

Fifty-five stories above the streets of Phoenix, in the living room of his penthouse apartment atop the America Bank Building, Frank Nelson was discussing variations of this same theme with Lawrence Fitzgerald. For the moment, Frank held a drink in one hand and stared out the window at the city. The flatland lights stretched out as far as he could see in all directions. To the south was the America West Convention Center, where the Republican gathering was taking place. In a very short time, the Grand Old Party would name their presidential candidate for the upcoming election.

Frank took a sip from his Manhattan then turned to face the oversized television screen on the opposite wall. The TV cameras panned the screaming crowd, the placards, the imitation straw hats with red, white, and blue hat bands, the American flags, the sea of political insanity. He cursed under his breath at the stupidity of it all. *Like they're the ones making important decisions.*

Across the room, sitting in his wheelchair, also with a drink in his hand, was Fitzgerald. He repeated what he'd just said to Frank.

"The key to all politics in Central Asia is the black market. You know it's true, Frank. We've been through this before. It's the same thing now. Mendelev is a crook, no more than a gang boss."

"In other words, the pipeline project is little more than a giant money laundering service for half the Russian Mafia." Frank shook his head.

"Lake Balkhash, Frank. You know what it's worth."

Frank smiled at the mention of it. "You're right."

Two knocks sounded on the door.

Both men stopped talking. A single knock followed. Frank nodded to Fitzgerald, then went to the door and opened it. Lyman Goodrich of Hamilton Heavy Construction entered. "Hello, Frank." They didn't shake hands. He spotted Fitzgerald. "Evening, Fitz."

Fitzgerald lifted his drink in Goodrich's direction. Goodrich was a tall, heavy set man, a few years younger than Frank. He headed directly to the bar like it was his own. The penthouse was huge, six bedrooms, four baths, everything in excess. The real power brokers had been coming and going from there all week. None of them bothered stopping by the convention center. Who needed the hysteria? This was mission control.

Goodrich poured himself a shot of scotch on the rocks. He took a sip and peered at the big screen. "It's not over yet?"

Frank glanced out the window at the expanse of city lights, then back to his company. "Carlson will get the nomination in the next few minutes. Shortly afterward, we'll get his acceptance speech. I'm curious to hear him speak in the spotlight."

"Then I guess we're celebrating tonight."

"In a manner of speaking," said Fitzgerald.

Frank stepped away from the window, closer to the others. "The celebration will be when Carlson defeats Kenaghy."

Two knocks sounded on the door. Then a single one. Frank gave a knowing look to Fitz and Goodrich. He went to the door. It was Emily Dunn. If there was a second most powerful woman in the world, she entered the penthouse now. Over seventy, matronly, white hair, subdued, the exact opposite of Atossa, Emily Dunn was American royalty all the way back to the 1820s. Banking, railroads, and, of course, petrochemicals, Dunn Chemical was one of the big five transnationals and sat on vast sums of ancestral money.

"Glad you could make it, Emily," said Frank.

She acknowledged the other two men. "Hello Lawrence, Lyman."

"Could I get you a sparkling water, Emily," continued Frank, escorting her into the room and offering her a chair.

"Please," she said sitting down, seemingly weary, though she'd only come from one floor below and a large suite of her own.

"I hear your boy Mathers is in line for VP, Emily," said Goodrich.

Frank handed her a glass of sparkling water. "Yes, that's why I'm here. To watch the acceptance speech with Frank." She sipped from her glass. "But I'll be losing a good CEO. I wish he were the one running for President. This Carlson is a nice man, but I don't really know him."

"It'll be fine, Emily," comforted Frank.

"Maybe so," she answered, "but the oil pipeline has become so complicated and controversial this past year. I'll just be glad when it's over."

"Don't worry, Emily. It will be fine," said Fitzgerald, continuing with reassurance for the aged matriarch.

She looked at Fitz with one eye squinted. At one time or another, he'd been on the board of directors for all three companies represented there tonight. "I hope you're right."

"It's only money to you, Emily. To me," said Fitz, "the prize is control of Eurasia—with the nice little bonus of the most important resource in the world."

"So give me some help here, Frank, how big is this new field?" With her man Pete Mathers being tabbed for VP, the owner of Dunn Chemicals had gained inclusion to the inner circle—those who knew about the significance of Lake Balkhash.

Frank stroked his chin with a gratuitous pleasure. "Upper end, one hundred billion barrels. Lower end, fifty billion."

"How does that compare to the Saudis'?"

Frank smiled. "Enough to make OPEC sweat."

"And what does this do to peak production estimates?"

Frank looked to Fitz then Goodrich "It pushes it back two maybe three, four years."

"Is that all?"

"At a hundred million barrels a day, Emily, it goes fast," said Fitzgerald. "One thing we've known all along is there isn't an infinite amount of petroleum, but I expect we'll make several more big finds before it's over."

"Definitely," said Goodrich. "My guess is we've got serious offshore fields on both sides of the U.S., plus several others off Africa."

"How does that impact global warming projections?"

Frank looked at Fitz. Fitz deferred with a nod. "It's not really a worry, Emily," said Frank.

Fitzgerald coughed.

"Alright," continued Frank. "It's difficult to figure. But, hell, in ten or twenty years we'll be weaning ourselves off the petroleum. The age of oil will have passed. We'll take our profits and put them into water rights, clean energy research, and rare earth metals. Ten years after the conversion, the atmosphere will be halfway to cleaning itself."

"I'm glad I won't be around that long. I don't like this. I never have."

"Emily," comforted Goodrich, giving the positive spin another twirl. "The Earth is as resilient as you are. We've been on this track for almost fifty years. It's perfectly predictable and really nothing more than good business when you look at it. The oil was here. We used it. It enabled us to sophisticate our technology. When it's gone, we'll have climbed above it. The pipeline to Beijing is just the final piece."

A loud crowd reaction at the convention drew everyone's attention to the big screen. They'd just announced Samuel Carlson as the Republican nominee. The four of them stared at the screen as the convention center rocked for minutes on end. Then the man was at the podium. Carlson's wife and two sons were with him. Off to the left stood Pete Mathers.

Carlson lifted his arms to quiet the crowd. "Thank you," he said, raising his hands again for quiet. "Thank you." He looked to his wife and Mathers, all of them smiling. "Thank you," he exclaimed again as the cheers finally began to diminish. "Thank you all. Thank you for your support and your hard work. Thank you for putting me up here with a chance to be President of the United States…"

Frank the king-maker grinned as he watched. *Thank you, Frank*, said a little voice inside his head. *Thank you, Frank, for putting me up here.*

Back in Newport in the sanctuary of her bedchamber, Atossa, still distraught from Alise's visit earlier in the day, had just watched the very same tumultuous nomination scene. It disgusted her more than it did Frank. She waved her hand, and the flat screen television ascended into the ceiling of her bedroom. "Carlson," she muttered to herself. "How wonderful."

Wearing a silk robe, Atossa strode over to her divining table. Wednesday's *New York Financial Times* lay on the table open to Linda Bennett's column. Atossa looked down at the newspaper and reread Linda's opening:

> There's a fire in the Heartland. A metaphoric fire burning out of control from the banks of the Old Muddy to the Flat Irons. And it's not just that three farmers burned their crops. It's not just isolated frustration. It's symptomatic of a more general and far-reaching malaise. It's a symbolic statement. It's a primal scream. It's reveille.
>
> *Wake up America! Pay heed!*

> I've seen it in the papers. I've heard it on TV. Nobody gives the farmers the slightest chance of success in standing up to the industry. But I think it's wise to go through the numbers. Because of the shortfall in the Asian grain harvest, the world's reserve stocks have fallen below fifty million tons for the first time in seventy-five years. The grain that will get the world through to the next harvest is in the ground and maturing in North America. The world will need every kernel of this grain to get through the winter without humanitarian disaster. Close to half of this grain is held by family farmers—farmers now calling themselves a union. My advice is to keep a close eye on your Corn Pops. By December, you may be hoarding your nickels and dimes to pay for breakfast cereal.

"Symbolic statement, my ass," sneered Atossa, wadding the paper up into a tight ball. She threw it across the room and watched it bounce across the floor. She stood staring at the wad of newspaper for several minutes, then, determined to push all the politics and farmer bullshit out of her mind, pushed the button on the side of the table.

A moment later, there was a knock on the door hidden behind the curtained north wall. She dropped her veil over her face. "Come in, Russell," she said.

The curtains parted. A tall black man, possibly thirty years of age, wearing electric blue bikini briefs, entered the room. Atossa motioned for him to come closer as she sat down at her table. The handsome, muscular man took the appropriate position beside her. Atossa looked him up and down, then putting her forefingers into his briefs at either side of his hips, slipped the thin nothings down past his knees. He stepped the rest of the way out of them. His body was shaved, except for his head.

As was her way, Atossa took her deck of Tarot cards in her right hand and the black man's testicles in her left. Shuffling the cards with one hand and rolling the man's balls with the other, she imagined she was fondling the basketball star Derek Davis. In how many days, she asked the Tarot, would this fantasy, in fact, be real. Using only her right hand, she put the deck of cards on the table and cut to the middle. She drew the top card from the remaining half. It was the six of cups. A grim smile crept across her veiled face. "Resolution in love," she said aloud. "Six days."

She closed her eyes in an effort to transport her mind to that future moment. Her right hand took hold of Russell's penis. With both hands, she worked at the man's genitals for several minutes. When the man arched up on his toes, nearing climax, Atossa's fantasy began to run from her, and she found herself thinking again of Alise. Trying to refocus on Davis, she opened her eyes to watch the thick jets of jism spurt into the air, then drool down the penis shaft onto her hand. But when she closed her eyes again to imagine the towering basketball star and his wondrous smile, she saw, instead, hauntingly, toppling grain elevators and kernels of corn spilling on the ground.

PART V

A SINGLE SPARK

"When God gave Noah the rainbow sign,
He said it won't be water, be fire next time."
-traditional folksong

CHAPTER 42

By Saturday afternoon, July 11th, the farm union's next move was obvious. With only a handful of exceptions, the congresspersons and senators of the thirty-seven states with the largest populations of family farmers responded in like manner to Forest Mahan's last ditch phone call and email barrage. The legislators understood the complaints. They were even somewhat sympathetic, but there was absolutely no way they could support any kind of cash kickback for the farmers in this calendar year. They would do what they could to address the farmers' problems after the presidential election when the new Congress convened in January. In other words, the farmers, as usual, were being given the brush-off.

Mahan had spoken directly to Secretary of Agriculture Dean Dutz. He chuckled when Mahan introduced himself as the head of the Nonpartisan Farmers' Alliance. When Forest asked him about the article he'd written in *The Washington Post*, Dutz became indignant. That was the last straw. The fire crews were immediately mobilized.

With the help of the militia, almost four hundred thousand acres of ripe winter wheat were prepared for Monday morning. Incredibly, and in as quiet a way as possible, significant portions of the fields to be burned were also harvested Saturday and Sunday night. When local silo space filled up, wheat was trucked—pickups, campers, big farm rigs, anything on wheels—to available silos in the north. Sunday afternoon, Mahan supervised making a videotaped strike statement read by Nathaniel Cromwell. Ten copies would be distributed to television stations throughout the Midwest once the fires were underway.

If there was any doubt about the strength of this latest attempt to unify the farmers, that doubt would soon be gone. Monday morning, seven Eastern Time, fire crews from North Carolina to the Colorado state line would put torches to the wheat fields. By noon, two million tons of wheat, most of which had already been sold to dealers or elevator owners, would be whole grain toast. Another one million tons would have been harvested and secretly stored as security against greater loss.

No one thought the farmers were capable of this kind of action. The few incidents earlier in the summer when individual farmers had burned their fields were considered freaks, instances where a farmer had so badly managed his operation that he or she was just throwing in the towel. Besides, what could a smattering of small-time farmers do against the agricultural combine?

Stars were still visible in the sky to the west. Just the faintest hint of orange creased the wide flat horizon to the east. It was early Monday morning. Nathaniel Cromwell stood on the north bank of the Cimarron River a little southwest of Stillwater, Oklahoma, some two hundred miles south of his farm in Kansas. Out before him stretched ten thousand acres of hard red winter wheat. It was dry and brittle, ready to harvest.

The owner of this wheat and one of the largest family farms in Oklahoma was Barry Elms. He knelt on his left knee beside Cromwell, chewing on the sweet end of a wheat straw, looking out over his farm, bordered on the west edge by the natural fire break of the Cimarron River. Next to Elms was a short wooden staff with one end tarred, stuck in a two-gallon galvanized bucket and smelling heavily of petroleum.

Elms looked up at Cromwell. Even though it was hours before the real heat of the Oklahoma day, beads of sweat stood out below the hatband of Barry's black Stetson. He drew the straw from his mouth. "How much longer, Nate?" His voice was thick and slow with accent.

Nate lifted his arm to look at the illuminated dial of his wristwatch. Elms was a farmer he'd gotten to know in the years since his return to the farm. He'd been instrumental in unifying the farmers of Oklahoma. He had as much at stake as any farmer in the union. Without the support of men like Elms, the strike was impossible. "Less than four minutes," replied Nate.

Elms stroked his cheek down to his neck with his right hand. "I don't know what my daddy would think about this, but I bet Granddad would be right here with us if he could."

Nate nodded, knowing exactly what Elms meant. Elms was ten years older than Nate. He'd taken over control of his family's farm in the Willie Nelson "Farm Aid" era. His father's generation had gotten caught up in the "better yields through chemistry" approach to farming. Those had been some of the Heartland's best years. The generation before that had experienced the Oklahoma dust bowl, the depression, and several failed attempts to unify. Both Barry's and Nate's grandfathers had known real trouble—trouble that FDR tried to solve by regulating the farming industry.

The Agricultural Adjustment Act of 1933 created price supports for farm produce. The Commodity Exchange Act of 1936 set trader requirements to crack down on market schemes and manipulation. In the years since, the federal government had entered more and more into the control of the commodities market, establishing a whole array of farm subsidy programs to stabilize prices and make farming a more predictable business.

Unfortunately, these changes had a hard time keeping up with market expansion. In 1974, Congress passed the Commodity Futures Trading Act that increased federal control, but also opened the futures market to government bonds, treasury notes, and eventually all variety of mortgages and financial instruments. As late as 1977, the commodities market was primarily for agricultural trading. Ten years later, prompted by the advance of computers, it had become something wholly other, with financial contracts trading at three times that of agricultural contracts. In other words, the money changers and middlemen had won. The family farmers' long slide downward accelerated from that point on.

A minute or two had passed without anything being said. Nate spoke as much to himself as Elms. "Always quiet this time of day."

"Yeah," said Elms. "I like to be out in the barn about this time each morning."

"Wish I was today."

"None too excited about this, are you, Nate?"

"Not at all." Nate stared off to the southeast and the outline of the Ouachita Mountains. It reminded him of a morning on the southern plains of Afghanistan looking north to Kandahar. "Just as soon be back there in Central Asia fighting the Taliban as being here about to ignite a confrontation with our own government."

"Sad ain't it."

"Worse than that, Barry. Worse than that."

The two men became silent, both seemingly intent on the subtle changes of color off to the east. Another two minutes passed in silence. Nate's cell phone rang. Elms rose up. The phone rang again, a little louder as Cromwell pulled it off his belt. His eyes met Elms' before pushing the *talk* button. They both knew what this call was.

Cromwell put the phone to his ear. "Yeah."

"Not a breath in the air, Colonel." It was Hayes. "Perfect conditions."

Cromwell's eyes drifted off to his left and the dark, slow moving Cimarron, then to Elms. Elms merely nodded and lifted the tarred staff from the bucket. Men in the distant fields were watching them with field glasses, waiting for a signal. "Still here too, Vincent. I call it a go."

"Yes, sir," came from the other end.

Cromwell punched in Mahan's number. "We're on, Forest."

"Okay," was all Forest said. But it was with palpable sadness. When Mahan signed off, Cromwell's eyes met Elms'.

Barry drew a red plastic butane lighter from the hip pocket of his blue jeans, released the safety, and flicked the Bic. He applied the little flame to the stick. It burst into a fiery torch. He lifted the torch over his head and waved it back and forth three times. Five similar torches appeared like tiny butane lighters in the distance.

Cromwell watched Elms walk along the edge of the wheat field and, at imprecise intervals, light the wheat grass heavy with thick golden tassels. In the distance, the same thing was happening all along the northeastern edge of Elms' huge farm. Cromwell imagined Mahan lighting up his wheat in Missouri, Hayes signaling for more of the same in North Carolina, and others he didn't know following suit in Arkansas, Tennessee, and Virginia, starting fires across a fifteen-hundred-mile-long, two-hundred-mile-wide belt of the southern United States. As he watched the flames travel rapidly through the field directly in front of him and those further off, building quickly, bringing light to the day faster than the slow turn of the Earth around the sun, he wondered how this might look from above—that is, if NASA or the NSA were watching from a satellite—what would they be thinking?

For the first time all day, Cromwell smiled. Oh, maybe it wasn't really a smile. Maybe it was just a sneering grin. In spite of all the horror he truly felt for what he'd just set in motion, he did feel that what the farmers were doing was right—or at least justified. But this little flicker of a grin didn't last long. His expression turned to flat awe as the flames leapt into the sky. Elms had stepped back from the wheat and was standing beside him. Tears began to run from Cromwell's eyes. He was thinking of Tom Foster. He was thinking of the tragedy of the whole damn thing and why it even had to come to this in the first place.

CHAPTER 43

News of the fire traveled as fast as the fire itself. Visually it was overwhelming. Towering columns of flames and billowing smoke could be seen virtually from anywhere across a patchwork swath of farmland from Oklahoma to Virginia. Local radio stations had it on the air by 7:30. Videotaping TV crews were broadcasting from trucks before eight. CNN had it there on everyone's television by 8:15 with ten reporters scattered across the fifteen hundred miles of fires. The other big news stations weren't far behind. The impact was like the World Trade Center incident of September 11th. It took several hours to get the story straight—primarily that it was a political demonstration and not an act of terrorism. There was never any real danger throughout the six-hour burn. Local fire departments and police departments across the south were made up of farmers and farmers' relatives. With few exceptions, they simply joined the strike crews and became part of the safety net around the fires. Handfuls of farm buildings got burned by accident. A few farm animals and a lot of rodents were caught in it, but all in all, the protest was met with strong support in the rural communities. In the rest of the nation, the non-farming community was shocked and horrified at the danger and waste. On Wall Street, the Dow began a steady tumble in reaction to climbing grain prices.

President Kenaghy had been told earlier in the week by the FBI that there was on-going internet chatter about a farmers' strike and talk of field burning. There had been the three isolated fires at the time of Tom Foster's suicide and the recent grange-organized flood of letters to Congress, but the general response from the intelligence community was that there was no way the farmers could come together in a strong enough alliance to do anything substantial. That the grange had recently become a player in these communications only added to the skepticism—the National Grange was considered about as dangerous as the 4-H.

President Kenaghy received a call from Cameron Phillips at seven-forty-five notifying him of the fires. He got a call right after that from the Head of the Secret Service, Jason Toms, informing him of heightened security measures for the White House. They were blocking off traffic inside the rectangle formed by Constitution Avenue, Eighteenth Street, Twelfth Street, and Farragut North. Two swat teams would be deployed on the White House grounds. The President downplayed the security risks, but Toms would have none of it. No chances would be taken.

Kenaghy was eating breakfast and watching CNN in the private study off the Oval Office when Cameron Phillips came in.

"Didn't think they had it in them," said Phillips, shaking his head at the images on the television.

The President swallowed his last mouthful of cold corn flakes. A fresh cup of coffee steamed on his desk. "Every state grange representative called his congresspersons and senators last Thursday, Cameron, asking for help and advice. They voiced specific requests, and many of their grievances are valid. Got to give them credit. They were pretty much ignored last week, but they've got our attention now."

"No doubt about that, Mr. President," said Phillips, handing Kenaghy a document. "We just got this on Dean Dutz's fax machine. It's a strike statement."

Kenaghy read quickly through the first page then hit the button on his intercom. "I want the Secretary of Agriculture at the White House as soon as possible." He sat back then reached forward to push the button again. "The Labor Secretary too, please, Amy." He paused to think. "And Norma Whitlock." He picked up a piece of whole wheat toast from his breakfast tray and settled back in his chair. He started to take a bite then stopped to stare a moment at the buttered piece of bread.

Wall Street, Congress, and the media had teamed up against him all year. No matter what he said or did, it didn't seem to get out to the people in the right way. He'd spoken out against the latest push to privatize the Social Security Administration. He'd proposed key banking legislation, attacking critical corporate tax shelters. He'd pushed for regulation of the energy industry monster. He'd lobbied for increased education spending and larger medical benefits for the elderly. All the right stuff. Still, he was pictured as a nut, not a savior of the people. And now, six months left into what all forecast to be his last term, he saw something in the prairie fires that might save him.

He had watched the farmers' situation from a distance and with little interest his entire career. Like most he'd accepted that the small farmer was a dying breed and no longer a political force of any kind. But now, as he read through the visionary platform drawn up by Forest Mahan, and intermittently glanced up at the images on the television, he wondered if this farmers' strike might not be exactly what he needed to get an angle on the corporate octopus. Hell, even if it meant his political demise, he thought in this vivid moment of epiphany, what did he have to lose? He took a bite of the toast and chewed it thoroughly.

"You know, Cameron," he said, swallowing, "all along we've been the sort of liberals who paid half-hearted allegiance to the environmental movement. Lip service, no more."

Cameron stood beside him intent on the television screen.

"Not once did we connect the environment with the farming industry." Cameron nodded, still watching the screen. "Not once. And yet, who would make better stewards of this country's natural abundance than the farmers?"

Phillips turned to Kenaghy. "What are you trying to say, sir?"

Kenaghy smiled in a way he hadn't in many months. It was a wry, crooked little smile. "I'm not sure yet, Cameron. I'm not sure." He looked at the piece of toast in his hand with one bite gone, then back to his chief of staff. "What happens if we take the farmers' side in this strike?"

Phillips' face was a blank. "I've no idea."

"Let's check it out. No statement leaves this office until we've done a little research."

CHAPTER 44

Atossa pressed up close to the surface of her mirror. She'd just awakened, and the first thing she'd done was slip into her silk robe and check her face. It had been four days since her visit to Dr. Colleen. The cleansing had stopped the growth of the blemish on her cheek, and today, for the first time, she could see evidence that the steroid injections were working. The spidery red spot was still quite visible, but no longer upraised and clearly healing. Within her shell of anxiety, she was pleased.

If she followed the advice of the Tarot and the six of cups she'd drawn Thursday night, she should call Derek Davis on Wednesday. Two days from now. She didn't want to call him until the blemish was completely gone, but today she'd seen enough improvement in her face to think a Wednesday call might still be in the cards.

Her intercom began to blink. "Yes, Nancy."

"Frank Nelson is on the line."

"It's too early for business."

Atossa's attention returned to the mirror. She opened her robe. God, she really did look good. Like a young woman. Maybe that was it. Alise was simply jealous.

Nancy's voice spoke again. "Frank says turn on CNN."

Atossa cursed under her breath. Probably more fucking politics. The damn convention and that dullard Carlson.

"He says it's urgent, Ms. Andreas."

"Fine, Nancy. I have the message."

Atossa strode to the center of the room and waved her hand. The 55-inch television screen descended from the ceiling. She clapped her hands. It snapped on. "Seven-four-four," she said aloud. The tuner scanned to CNN.

America Burns! blazed across the bottom of the screen in red letters of flame. Aerial footage of the fires raged behind their number one news anchor Mike "the most trusted man in America" Edwards, as he told the story and spoke to authoritative faces in two other video windows.

Atossa watched for only a few seconds before calling out, "Nancy, get Frank on the line!"

A moment later, Frank's voice spoke was in her bedchamber. "I thought this might interest you, Atossa."

"What's going on, Frank?" When she got upset about business, all her anxiety targeted Frank. It was his job to make the business world operate properly—for her. "The damn farmers are burning their wheat!"

"No," corrected Frank, who got some strange pleasure from answering to Atossa's whim. "They're burning our wheat, Atossa. We bought it five months ago."

"How do we stop them?" she demanded to the air, getting agitated when she wasn't supposed to be getting agitated—for the sake of her new face.

"They have strike demands. It's a reaction to the May market."

"What?"

"I told you before. They want a dollar more per bushel. We received some letters from the National Grange about this last week. It's nonsense."

"Have you spoken to LaPalme?"

"He's in a plane headed to Phoenix now."

"Who started this?"

"It's complicated, Atossa. There's a lot we don't know. Watch the news. I'll get back to you after I've spoken to LaPalme."

"Good-bye," she snapped, glaring at the screen of flames. She felt her muscles growing taut throughout her body. Her cheek began to tingle. The collage of videotaped images and squawking talking heads only further fueled her tension. She slapped her hands together, cutting off the TV, and stalked to her divining table.

Only two things could soothe her now, Tarot cards and warm testicles rolling like the planets in her palm.

CHAPTER 45

Linda Bennett was at the kitchen table with her laptop, trying to squeeze in a little time reading her father's emails before going into work—when her cell phone rang. It rang twice more before she picked it up and read the caller ID. She shook her head and touched the screen. "What's up, Bob?"

"Turn on CNN right away," said Richards. "The isolated field burning has become a firestorm."

Linda went into the living room and found the remote. Richards continued to talk as she pressed the button and the image filled the screen. Cromwell was part of it. So was the militia. A strike statement had been faxed to the Department of Agriculture at the same time the fires began. A copy was already headed her way via email.

"I want you in Kansas City tomorrow," pushed Richards. "And write something about today's fires before you leave."

Linda held the receiver out at arm's length and stared at it. Instead of telling him that she didn't, in fact, work for him, she calmly said, "Send me an airline confirmation by this afternoon."

"Done."

Linda skipped her usual four-mile run, opened her email, and read the strike statement. Then, like nearly everyone else in the United States, she hunkered down before the television without moving for two hours, watching the crisis unfold and listening to the analysis. The footage of the flames was mesmerizing. Up close. From helicopters. In satellite pictures. It seemed that the imagery of her commentaries had come to life right there on the tube. It was powerful and frightening. The farmers were right, she kept saying to herself in disbelief. Maybe their position was untenable, but they were right.

Linda wished her father was still alive so she could ask him what he thought about the farmers' actions and the CIA's involvement. As usual that futile wish came with a flood of emotion. She took a deep breath, closed her eyes, and told herself that her father was always there with her. Then, with all the calm rationale she could muster, she asked his invisible presence for an assessment of the situation.

Good intelligence is always about the big picture was something Linda had heard her father say a hundred times, if not more. He had a little riddle he often repeated to instruct her on this: *What is God?* Gee-Oh-Dee. Guns, oil, and drugs. Those were the real strategic commodities.

Guns were obvious. Guns were for war, security, black market negotiation, and intimidation.

Oil was obvious too. Steady and predictable petroleum production had been the backbone of world economic growth since World War II. Automobiles, electric power plants, plastics, fertilizers, pesticides, herbicides, explosives, everything from energy production to agriculture to transportation to war depended on fossil fuels. Oil was the economy. Linda was already deep into that.

And drugs? Drugs were invisible money and like guns useful for universal barter. Charlie Patio's comments were apt. The sale of black market drugs accounted for two percent of the world gross product. That was big. Surpassing a trillion dollars in unaccountable cash. Great for buying black market weapons, running illicit wars, even invisibly pumping up Wall Street market valuations—giving the economic flywheel a helpful little push. *Or perhaps for playing the commodities market!*

Linda pondered the possibilities for some time, then the spook she was now sharing her life with came up with another angle on the situation: *Was grain about to become one of those critical strategic commodities?* Cereal grains—rice, corn, wheat, oats, barley, millet, sorghum—provided half the world's edible calories. If you included what was fed to livestock and used in aquaculture, more than half of what the world ate originated in fields of grain. Grain had always been important, but there had always been a surplus. In the fifties and sixties, the United States gave wheat and corn away as aid to developing countries. What if that was changing? How did that impact the old population, arable land, clean water equation? How many people can the Earth feed sustainably? That was right at the heart of the grain report Richards had given her back in April—and led back to the reason he was sending her to Kansas City in the first place—with no reserves, the current grain crop was a key part of national security.

After a moment, Linda just shook her head and turned her attention to the fires raging on her television screen. Regardless of what she did or didn't know, even if it was Richards who'd put her onto this, it was a prime journalistic opportunity. TES be damned. America was burning. *Kansas City, here I come.*

CHAPTER 46

The Secretary of Agriculture Dean Dutz filled an armchair to the right of the President's desk with his indomitable bulk. Prim and proper Labor Secretary Clifford Pierce sat in one of the office's cane-backs in front of the desk. Secretary of the Interior Norma Whitlock, a tall attractive black woman, was on the left in another cane-back, and Chief of Staff Cameron Phillips, now the President's closest confidant, paced back and forth behind them too agitated to sit. The embattled President lay back in his chair, hand to his chin, pushed away from the desk, and gazed out the window.

An hour had passed since James Kenaghy had learned of the fires raging through the south and the resulting instabilities in the commodities market and the stock exchange. It was fifteen minutes since cabinet members and building tensions had invaded the Oval Office. The meeting so far had been little more than competing opinions thrown back and forth at varying levels of semi-polite hostility. Part of the problem was that too many of the administration's cabinet positions had been filled as political favors. Homeland Security Director Paul Houseman was the worst. Pierce and Dutz were merely lesser evils. Whitlock was one of Kenaghy's silent victories. She was hardly a *Green*, but by establishment standards she was an environmentalist.

Kenaghy had called this meeting for two reasons. The obvious one was to solve the problem. The farmers were burning their fields and something had to be done. The other reason was to find out what was at stake politically in the farmers' strike. His presidency was slipping away, and he wondered if there weren't some way to use the situation to regain traction. He appraised the soldiers posted across the back edge of the Rose Garden then slowly turned from the window and faced the frown of Dean Dutz. "What if we tell the industry the government will split the cost of the cash kickbacks with them?"

Indignant and angry, Dutz's blood pressure climbed ten more millimeters of mercury at the mere mention of appeasing the farmers. "It's not the way it's done, Mr. President." It was all he could do to mind his manners when he started going hypertensive. "They sold that grain five months ago at the going price. It was their decision. No one forced them to do it. Now, just because the market spiked in May, they seem to think they've been cheated. That's nonsense. It's no different than selling shares of General Motors in February then watching them double in value in June. You can't demand a cut." Dutz heaved with suppressed emotion. "Farmers have been selling their crops in advance since the beginning of time. They've had wins and they've had losses. It's ludicrous for them to think they can change that now because of events beyond anyone's control in Asia."

Kenaghy ignored the flat presumption in Dutz's words. "And there's no chance that the system is wrong or backwards, as the strike document suggests?"

"Mr. President, the government has been bending over backwards since the 1930s with subsidies, farm loan programs, all sorts of generous legislation, just so the small farmer could make it from harvest to harvest. What's backwards is these farmers expecting someone to pick up the tab at the end of the year when they've proven once again that they don't know how to manage their own businesses."

"Don't you think you're being a little harsh, Mr. Secretary?" Norma Whitlock had found Mahan's proposal incredibly provocative. "It might be that asking for a kickback on this year's crop is inappropriate by some standards, but as I read the second part of this demand, this man Mahan makes a lot of good sense when he addresses the health of the land." The forest, not farming, had always been Whitlock's pet project. That Mahan included forest management in his statement really impressed her. "All these subsidies and programs you mention, yes, they have artificially supported small farmers, but they have also dictated how they farm—and amount to corporate welfare for agribusiness whose farming practices are degrading huge portions of Midwest farmland."

"Ms. Whitlock, you're missing the point," Dutz blustered. "This country is about making a profit when you're in business. Yes, there's an economy of scale that puts the family farmer at a disadvantage, but plenty of these small farmers can make it. The ones that don't, don't belong. That's the genius of capitalism. That's what the system is about, weeding out the weak and inefficient."

"At the cost of the long term health of the land? I don't think so, Mr. Dutz."

"Wait a minute," interrupted the Labor Secretary. "We're giving these people too much credit by even discussing their demands. There is no official farm union. They have no authority to call a national strike, and no authority to make demands on the grain industry. In my opinion, this field burning is a criminal act—hardly an organized labor strike. They're destroying something that isn't theirs anymore. We should just go out and arrest these farmers, harvest their fields, and give the grain to those they've sold it to. The whole thing is impudence."

Whitlock laughed at this. "Yes, Mr. Pierce, we should go out and arrest a million farmers. That's a great idea," she said sarcastically. "That's how a democracy should always respond to collective bargaining. Government-assisted strike breaking."

Pierce pretended not to hear her. Cameron Phillips stepped between them. "Mr. Dutz, do the farmers really have any leverage with what they have in their fields?" He'd read Linda Bennett's Wednesday column. "What if they burned it all? Where does that put us?"

Kenaghy sat up with Phillips' question and turned his eyes to the Agriculture Secretary.

Dutz ran a thick hand over his forehead and into his oily black hair. "It's a bluff, Phillips. I don't have any solid figures yet, but I got some estimates in before I came over here." He pulled a wrinkled white handkerchief from his suitcoat breast pocket and wiped his mouth. "Family farmers, let's say those with under ten thousand acres, could have as much as 130 million tons of grain, maybe a little more than that, in their fields right now. That's about a third of our annual total. If they refuse to bring that to market, most of which was sold to dealers cash advance many months ago, the independent dealers that are short and don't have reserves of their own will be at the mercy of the market. Many will go under. The big grain companies are in a better position. Many run their own farms and keep huge reserves. But because they responded to the Asian shortage and basically saved the world with their reserve stocks, they'll be stressed more than usual." He removed his thick-framed glasses and mopped his brow. "In any other year, this would be nothing. Right now, even the largest distributors will feel the pinch."

"But not much of one considering the profits they made in May," snapped Whitlock.

Dutz continued as though he hadn't heard her. "In the long run, however," Dutz adjusted his black rim glasses with a haughty dispassion, "whether the farmers know it or not, they will effectively crash their own farms and trim out some of the weaker independent grain dealers." Dutz knew several of his constituents could live with that. "It doesn't make sense for the farmers any way you look at it."

"I think there's more to it than that, Mr. Dutz," said Phillips. "If you didn't notice, not only is wheat up this afternoon, but the Dow is down. That 130 million tons of grain expands into tens of billions of dollars trailing through the economy, quite a bit of it as lost export income. That translates into further negatives for our balance of trade. Not to mention how the Dow will react should these fires continue. I say we press the industry a little harder—because in the long run, it's cheaper and better economics to give the farmers their cut than completely eliminating their grain from the equation. It's just not that much money for the trouble this strike could cause."

"And worldwide, Mr. Secretary," added Whitlock, "with increasing prices due to the burning, whole nations will be priced out of the grain market."

"Don't we have a population problem?" deadpanned Dutz.

Whitlock stood up. "I beg your pardon, Mr. Dutz."

Suddenly the Oval Office doors flew open. Paul Houseman, the Homeland Security Director, stood in the doorway huffing and puffing. Two secret service men stood behind him at a loss for what to do with him. "Why wasn't I included in this secret meeting?" he stormed as he barged in. "This field burning is a blatant act of terrorism. The Homeland Guard should be out there now."

Kenaghy waved his hand at the secret service men. "Please, take this man out of here. He can make an appointment if he wants to talk to me."

The men stepped up beside Houseman. He brusquely pushed them away.

"I'm with Houseman," exclaimed Pierce. "We commandeer the fields and harvest them. It's clear the farmers don't know what they're doing."

"It's far worse than that," followed Houseman, "they're goddamn terrorists!"

The security officers looked to the President, uncertain what to do.

"The grain has been sold," snapped Dutz. "The farmers have no right to burn it. Houseman's right. This isn't a labor strike. It's a national security emergency. That makes it terrorism."

Norma Whitlock backed away from the group in dismay. Cameron Phillips shook his head and noticed for the first time this morning that the TES draft still sat on the President's desk unmoved. The final version would be voted on in the Senate next week.

Kenaghy stood. He'd had enough. "Alright, gentlemen. Ms. Whitlock. I have your opinions. Thank you. And Mr. Houseman, you're done with this administration. I'd like you to write me your resignation."

Houseman sneered at the men on either side of him then snarled, "Kenaghy, you're the one that's done." He spun on his heels and stomped out, ignoring the security men entirely. Dutz struggled up out of his chair and waddled out as though he'd been insulted. Pierce followed Dutz. Norma Whitlock looked helplessly at Cameron Phillips then the President.

"Norma, I'll talk to you later," said Kenaghy softly.

"Should I go too, Jim?" asked Phillips when the door closed behind the Secretary of the Interior.

"No," said Kenaghy, staring out the window, hands on the sill. "We have to figure out what to do with this."

"What do you mean?"

Kenaghy faced Phillips. "We're going to turn this thing around."

"Politically?"

"Precisely," said Kenaghy. "And I think I'd like to talk to Linda Bennett."

"The journalist?"

"That's right. I'd like to talk to her as soon as possible."

CHAPTER 47

Singapore time ran thirteen hours ahead of that in Washington, D.C. When Jonathan Mayfield opened the door to his room at the Singapore Hilton on Tuesday morning at seven o'clock to get the newspaper, the headlines on *The Singapore Times* read UNITED STATES UP IN FLAMES in big red letters. He picked up the paper, turned back into his room, and fell deeply into the story, then went to his new laptop and logged onto the internet. He ran through four different news services, several world newspapers, and a whole array of commodities markets. Grain prices were up all around the world—wheat by thirty percent.

After the initial adrenaline surge of the news, Jonathan sat down with the pot of coffee he'd ordered from room service. He'd been working at the Development Bank of Asia for a week. The prep work of employee seminars and training was nearly over. In another day or so, he'd be into the bank's computer network, doing basic streamlining. It was not his favorite kind of work, and so far he had gained little or no insight into the grain buy. He doubted he would stay more than the one month he'd signed on for. He was, however, curious to see how news of the farmers' strike would be received at the bank, particularly by Parker Chen.

As he sat there, sipping his way through his third cup of coffee, he noticed the computer disk he'd left on the coffee table. It was the one he'd found on the floor of the lounge the night he met Dan the Hippie. He'd resisted putting it in his computer to check it out, believing he should talk to Dan before he got too nosey. He'd tried to reach Dan by phone several times since finding the disk. A recorder had answered the phone the first few times he'd called, but he didn't leave a message. Three days ago, he called and left a message with his room number at the Hilton. When he hadn't heard back in two days, he tried again last night. No one answered the phone, but the recorder didn't come on either. The phone just rang and rang.

Jonathan still had an hour before he was due in at work. He reached for the phone and punched in Dan's number. Instead of a phone ringing without answer, he got a *please check your listing—this number has been disconnected.* He hung up the phone and stared at the disk, then the piece of napkin Dan had written his phone number and address on. The address was 7426 Orchid, apartment twenty-six. He didn't really know the city, and the street name meant nothing to him. Hell, he thought, he'd made an honest effort.

He snagged the disk off the coffee table and stuck it in his laptop. Jonathan knew scores of tricks for getting into the files of protected disks, but he didn't need them. The disk was on a standard format. It opened instantly and contained only the two files written on the disk label—*file one* and *file two.* They were both text files, and Jonathan's word processor converted them into documents with the stroke of a function key. In both cases there were long lists of names and addresses. Several thousand entries in each file. There was no further explanation of the material. But because of the things the American journalist had said that night, there was one obvious explanation for these lists if the disk was actually Dan's.

Dan had spoken of the Chinese Kongsi, clans of Chinese who worked together as family corporations or business networks. Perhaps each file was a kongsi. Jonathan remembered the particular kongsi of Dan's interest, the Teochui. He also remembered the name of the man Dan was there to photograph that night—Zhao He. And sure enough, Zhao He, with an address in Singapore and in China, was the first name on the list in *file one.* The Teochui Kongsi, according to Dan, played a large role in the Southeast Asian heroin business. This disk, thought Jonathan, must be valuable to someone. It might, for that matter, be something that was dangerous to have. But no one knew that he had it, except possibly Dan, if he'd listened to the message on his phone. This caused Jonathan to think again. What if someone else had listened to the recording? Could he be traced by the message he'd left? He'd included his room number, but only referred to himself as the man in the Hilton lounge. Amid a tremor of paranoia, Jonathan decided a room change was in order.

Jonathan continued reading through the list in *file one* looking for another name. Halfway through, he found it—Parker Chen of the Development Bank of Asia. He closed up his computer, went down to the main desk, and requested a new room, adding that should anyone call the old room, neither his name nor his new room number should be mentioned.

CHAPTER 48

After watching the initial burn at the Elms farm, Nathaniel Cromwell drove east along the fire line, across Oklahoma into Arkansas—some four hundred miles. He made several short stops on the way, checking the progress of the fires, the morale of the farmers, and the organization of the militia. Over the course of the day, he spoke with as many as fifty farmers and six or seven militia battalion leaders. What he saw in the people uplifted him. Their smiles, their energy, their spirit. They'd been down a long time, and most, it seemed, were happy to be doing something about their situation, knowing there were no guarantees, just enthused to be doing something.

That evening, Nate was invited to dinner by the Morningdale family in Bytheville, Arkansas. After the meal, just before six, he and Tom Morningdale, his wife Eve, their four children, and two other farm families squeezed into the Morningdale's little living room and huddled around the television in anticipation of the broadcast of Cromwell's video-statement filmed the day before at Mahan's home. Running through sixteen different news broadcasts coming in on the satellite dish, one thing was certain, they'd stirred things up good. The whole country was talking about the farmers' strike and the field burning. As extreme as setting the fires had been, it was exactly what the movement needed to get some attention. It made great TV and scared the shit out of the city folk, who really had no idea what the farmers might be upset about. Unfortunately, the TV commentators, especially on the major networks, were highly critical of the farmers and skeptical to the point of sarcasm concerning any hope for the strike's success.

At six o'clock, Tom used the television remote to tune into the local station, WCTV, for the evening news. The whole room went silent as the headline film collage focused on the strike and the fire, opening with a close-up of Cromwell, followed by footage of the fires, and a long shot of Capitol Hill. A male voice spoke over the collage. "The Nonpartisan

Farmers' Alliance, the farm group claiming responsibility for the fires, delivered a videotaped strike statement to ten large television stations in the Midwest this afternoon. WCTV received a copy of the videotape from our affiliate in Little Rock shortly after five o'clock this evening. We will air the farmers' statement after the break."

Reminiscent of the video clips of Osama Bin Laden shown after the World Trade Center tragedy, the station flashed a video bite of Cromwell speaking to the camera from the center of a field of wheat, then broke for a commercial. Everyone in the little living room cheered. Congratulations were passed around in celebration that the tape was actually being taken seriously and would be televised.

Following three commercials, the local news team appeared on the screen. The woman newscaster thumbnailed the story. The Nonpartisan Farmers' Alliance was calling for a nation-wide farmers' strike. They claimed responsibility for the fires and intended them as a symbolic statement of farmer unity.

The male newscaster segued from there, reporting that the Farmers' Alliance had faxed a written document to the Secretary of Agriculture that morning to present to Congress. It contained a strike statement and a list of demands. This same document had been sent to the corporate offices of the grain industry leaders and would also be printed in most U.S. newspapers the next morning. Then he introduced the video, stating with clear intrigue, that speaking for the Farmers' Alliance was the heavily decorated and controversial Medal of Honor winner, retired Colonel Nathaniel Cromwell.

The newscast then cut to the video statement. The camera centered on Cromwell's face with Forest Mahan's fields of sweet winter wheat in the background. Tom pumped the volume up three increments as Cromwell began by introducing himself and the alliance.

"I speak for about one and a half million farmers here in the United States. Some five hundred thousand of those farmers grow grain or soybeans. This morning, we burned approximately four hundred thousand acres of ripe, ready to harvest winter wheat as a demonstration of our unity and the seriousness of our position. We did this with great regret and sorrow and would like to offer an apology, on behalf of all the farmers involved, to the people of the United States. This is not to say we consider what we did wrong or a mistake. We simply want it known that we are aware of the vast impact of our actions and are concerned about any fear we might have caused in the populace with the field burning. It was properly managed and completely contained. We are also concerned about the excess of particulates and carbon dioxide we added to an already polluted atmosphere and the related waste of food. There are far too many people starving in the world for us not to take what we did with considerable forethought and apprehension. Despite the appearance of a great prairie fire on television, we burned less than one percent of the grain harvest. It was intended, as I said, primarily as a demonstration of farmer unity and the grave seriousness of our predicament."

Linda Bennett had gone into work that afternoon and was there into the evening trying to finish one more column before leaving the next day for Kansas City—when Frederick Manning stuck his head in her office. "Linda, quick, there's something on television you need to see." The video hadn't reached the eastern television stations in time for the six o'clock news and was being released now at seven o'clock as a special news bulletin.

Linda saved her work on her computer and followed Manning to the office television room. Ten or twelve of *The Times'* reporters and management were standing around the television rapt on the screen. Cromwell was already well into his statement.

"This morning, we delivered a written document to the executive branch of the government and the leaders of the grain industry, stating our position and our demands. You will have a chance to read it for yourself in tomorrow's newspapers. In short, it stated that we, the Nonpartisan Farmers' Alliance, are on strike and want to make sure that the public, as well as the government and the grain industry, understand what it is we're asking for and why. If those demands are not met or acknowledged in such a way that we can anticipate solutions to our grievances, we will continue to burn portions of the grain crop as it comes due to harvest. Although this will increase the cost of bread throughout the world, our target is not the people who eat the bread, but the grain market and those who use the market to control grain prices and the way we farm. In our estimation, we have enough grain in our fields right now to use the market in the same way that it has been used against us for well over one hundred years."

Linda nodded to herself as she watched and listened. This man Cromwell presented himself quite well. He seemed very real and genuine compared to the newscasters and politicians that usually dominate the televised news media. He projected, even over television, something of honesty, simplicity, and strength. In his words and manner, he was making something that was so frightening to see on TV seem fair and reasonable. She smiled at how good a job he was doing.

In Newport, Rhode Island, Atossa Andreas was lying in her bed staring at the television. Frank had just called, prompting her to quickly turn on the news. Propped up on three big pillows, she kneaded her left hand and frowned at the face on the screen telling her what was wrong with her business.

"We are asking for two things," continued Cromwell. "The first might be difficult to understand for those who are not familiar with the way commodities like wheat are bought and sold. This is not the time or place to explain that to you now. It's in our strike document. For simplification, I will only say that for many years the middlemen—the dealers, distributors, and elevator owners—have made increasingly greater profits by leveraging the market in ways that are not easily available to the family farmer. Capital advantage has worked heavily against the smaller farms for decades, but even more so in the last few years—and to an unconscionable degree this spring because of a huge shortfall in the Asian grain harvest. Our first demand is to the industry. We are asking for a nominal share of the profits they made off the Asian grain shortage. I will not get into all the numbers here, again they are in the document, but the so-called free market provided excessive profits for the grain dealers, upwards to three hundred percent on the cash-forward winter grain prices many farmers used to finance their crop. Our demand is for another dollar per bushel on last winter's cash-forward sales of wheat and corn and two dollars per bushel on advance sales of soybeans. Even with these cash outlays, the industry will make twice their normal profit on this year's grain harvest."

Atossa cursed out loud, "Bullshit!"

"Our second demand is to the United States government. It asks for a complete review of farming in the United States. The old standard of maximum production through chemicals and irrigation does not pertain anymore. Monoculture on the farms and in the forests cuts at the very vitality of all living things. Not only are we diminishing genetic heritage and the variety of life on Earth, but we are also gradually burning out the center of the nation with fertilizers, pesticides, and poor topsoil management. America's cropland, our nation's greatest natural endowment, is slowly being destroyed by the same forces that are eroding the environment of the entire planet."

Back at *The Times* Washington Bureau office, Frederick and Linda stood side by side, staring at the tube as Cromwell came to the end of the statement.

"That's our message," said the retired Colonel. "I want all of you to consider what I've just said and what is written in our strike statement. Then I want you to write or call your congressperson or senator and tell them what you think about our position—yea or nay. In the balance are the environmental health of our nation's farmland and the livelihood of the family farmer—backbone of this country for the last hundred and fifty years. Thank you."

When the video ended, Linda just stood there lost in thought, paying no attention to the talking heads that came on to comment on Cromwell's performance. Frederick touched her lightly on the shoulder. "Well, Linda, there's your man. What do you think?"

She turned and looked into her boss' face. "I'm afraid the farmers are misguided by believing they can get any kind of kickback from the industry on this year's crop, but there's quite a bit of truth to what the Colonel just said about the state of the farmland."

Frederick smiled like he was looking into her mind. "But what about the man himself, Cromwell? What did you think of him?"

"He was good. Kind of down home for what I imagined, but he was good. His presentation was strong."

Frederick nodded. "The farmers' stand may be tenuous, but I agree, the Colonel had a real presence. It will be curious to find out what urban Americans think about this twenty-first century John Wayne."

"No kidding. I sure hope I get a chance to interview him."

"So do I," said Manning. "Could be some powerful stuff."

The video was broadcast throughout the United States. In nearly every case, the commentators that followed Cromwell's statement were highly critical of both the burning and the strike demands. To the chagrin of the crowd in the Morningdale's living room, these analysts seemed to be making light of something that meant everything to them.

The major networks' standard follow-up to Cromwell's statement was a taped interview with Robert Prescott, President of the American Farm Bureau Association. The AFBA was a government farm support organization, but it was also heavily sponsored by agribusiness. Prescott's comments were the harshest of all the speakers. He had early access to the statement that had been faxed to the Secretary of Agriculture. His critique of Forest Mahan's new vision for the family farmer was especially cutting. He went through Forest's suggestions one by one, tearing them apart.

"Many of these so-called new farming techniques," said Prescott, "really amount to nothing more than erasing years of advances in farming technology. In the last fifty years, we have doubled and re-doubled productivity per acre. The use of high-grade petrochemical fertilizers and genetically engineered seeds are part of this and are essential to America's answering the food demands of the world. As to concerns about nitrate runoff in the Mississippi, it's an environmentalist scare tactic. Yes, there is evidence of hyponia, or a dead zone, in the Gulf of Mexico. But it's small and contained. The benefits in production are more than worth the modest trade-off."

Tom stood up and turned off the set. "Christ," he exclaimed. "The Voice of Agriculture! What a bunch of crap. The AFBA is nothing more than a mouthpiece for big Ag. And, damn it, just because of his suit and tie and television credibility, most of America is going to think this guy knows what he's talking about."

"Voice of Agriculture, is that what they call it, Tom?" asked Nate.

"Incredible, isn't it?"

"Nothing but big business providing us with ignorance," followed one of Tom's neighbors. "We might be into this strike for the long haul, boys."

About nine-thirty that night, Nate called his mother from Bytheville. "Well, what'd ya think, Ma?"

"I don't know, Nate," answered Mary. "I'm not so sure anyone but us farmers have the slightest idea what this strike is about."

"Yeah, the newscasters' so-called expert commentary certainly didn't help. But don't worry, Ma. The people throughout the rural areas are with us. The burning went as smoothly as could possibly be imagined. No arrests. No shootings. Lots of support from the local communities. We'll have our statement in the newspapers tomorrow. That should help people understand our purpose a little better."

"When will we see you? That is, other than on TV."

"I meet with Mahan tomorrow. We'll review what went down today. That could take a while. But from there, it's straight back home. Hopefully by midnight.

"And how long are you going to stay here?"

"An hour or so. Long enough to get my laundry done."

"And who might be doin' that for you?'

Nate laughed. "Don't fret, girl. You have to believe we're doing something good. I wish you could've seen the faces of the farmers I saw today."

"I'll bet. All black and covered with soot. How's the militia working out?"

"Good. I mean it. Worst thing we had today were some livestock casualties and a barn or three that caught fire. All in all, it was what we wanted."

"But will it get us anywhere?"

"We'll see, Ma. Is Will there?"

"Right next to me."

"Let me talk to him."

Nate heard the phone change hands, then Will's voice. "How are you, Dad? You looked great on TV."

"I'm fine, Will. Thanks. How's work progressing on the farm?"

"By lunch tomorrow, I'll have plowed a firebreak around most of our largest fields. We've got plenty of water and gasoline."

"Good."

"I also checked in with Mr. Peabody and Horace Thompson. It's getting exciting around here."

"Well, be smart—and ready for anything." Nate turned up the intensity in his voice. "I mean anything, Will. Understand?"

"Yes, sir. Loud and clear."

"Okay, like I told Grandma, I'll be there late tomorrow night."

"Be careful, Dad."

"You keep a close eye on your grandmother."

"Don't worry."

Nate hung up the phone and immediately began to worry about his son and mother. He wished he were already back in Kansas.

CHAPTER 49

Atossa Andreas had grown up in the grain business. The farmers' problems were nothing new to her. Cromwell's plea touched her like a dirty street urchin's hand. As soon as the statement ended, she called Frank at his Phoenix penthouse apartment.

"Frank, I just saw that damn Army Colonel on the news." The television was still on behind her, hissing with the white noise of commentary. "I didn't like it. I didn't like it at all."

Frank stood before a window, drink in hand, looking out upon the glistening Phoenix night. "Easy, Atossa. Remember, when you have as many angles on the market as we do, there's no situation we can't turn to our advantage."

"Explain that," she demanded, feeling the tension building in her, fearing it was working against the healing of her face.

"The worst case scenario is further grain shortages—which will include climbing prices. Thanks to our little spring buying gambit, we are in a better position than any of our competitors. Everyone is short—except us. Meaning more profits. And should the farmers foolishly burn all their grain, come winter, my guess is there will be a great opportunity to invest in some cheap farmland."

"You sound too confident, Frank." Atossa picked her deck of Tarot cards off the table. "Have you spoken with LaPalme?"

"Yes, he's here with me right now."

"I want him in on this."

"Fine. I've got the speaker on…now."

"Curtis?"

"Yes, Ms. Andreas."

"What does this strike mean to Andreas Grain?" Her eyes strayed to the television screen as she spoke. The TV analysts were going at it in a four-window debate.

"At this point, very little. Only a very small portion of the winter wheat crop has been destroyed. The television broadcasts made it seem much worse than it really was."

"But what's their point?"

"They feel a portion of those profits we made this spring belong to them."

"To hell with them. The market is always a gamble."

"That's part of their grievance," continued LaPalme. "Included in their strike statement is a request for a review of the market."

"Could that be a problem for us?"

"The market review is a joke," said Frank.

"What about that analyst from Linton? Could he be a problem?" Atossa was pacing furiously back and forth, looking at the television screen and shuffling the deck of Tarot cards in her hands.

"We didn't do anything illegal, Ms. Andreas." The voice was LaPalme's.

"But wouldn't our buying schedule look bad in an investigation if this analyst came forward?"

"Don't worry, Atossa," said Frank. "We've got a man in Singapore watching Mayfield's every move—even giving him direction."

"You mean more smoke and mirrors? That doesn't help my uneasiness about this market review. What else, Curtis?"

"I'm with Frank, Ms. Andreas. Our position is the strongest among all the big grain distributors, but I am a little concerned about soybeans—if the strike stretches out into the fall."

"That will never happen," snapped Atossa. "It can't. Right, Frank? We have every important official in the business in our pocket."

"Except Kenaghy."

"What can he do?'

"Probably nothing. Rumors coming to me from Washington, however, say he's playing this one very close to the vest. No comment yet."

"Who cares about his comments?" Atossa paused to stare across the room at her reflection in the mirror. "I don't want to hear any more. It's just a bunch of farmers. We can handle this. We don't pay Congress for nothing. Get back to me tomorrow with some good news. Good-bye."

Atossa stared at the television screen and the continuing replay of the day's fires. "Burn it all, you dumb hicks. What do I care?" She clapped her hands and the screen flashed off and ascended into the ceiling, then she stalked over to her mirror.

She ran her index finger over her cheek and across the spidery red blemish. "God, I think it's getting worse," she gasped, throwing her deck of cards across the room. She clenched and unclenched her left hand, glaring at the cards on the floor, some face down, some face up. For no reason, her eyes fastened on the one card that unsettled her most—*The Tower*—face up beneath her divining table. The images of collapsing grain elevators and farmers destroying their crops were no longer in her head, they were on network TV. "THIS CAN'T BE," she screamed.

CHAPTER 50

Linda Bennett got a call late Monday night from President Kenaghy's press secretary Wayne Stevens. The President had learned of her trip to the Midwest and was requesting an opportunity to speak with her before she left. Both honored and surprised, she accepted an eight o'clock appointment at the Oval Office. Afterward, she would catch an eleven-fifteen flight from Ronald Reagan Airport to Kansas City.

After a night of little sleep, Linda caught a taxi to the White House from her Georgetown apartment just after seven. Coming up the visitor's driveway, going through the first check point, she noted the soldiers posted around the grounds and spotted several men with automatic rifles on the White House roof. On the way into the building to the reception room, she passed through two sets of metal detectors and was patted down before being escorted to a waiting area in the West Wing.

Linda sat there almost fifteen minutes, watching the various couriers and attendants scurrying up and down the halls. She'd met Kenaghy twice before, both briefly in ceremonial situations. Once with her father at a formal gathering at the White House in Kenaghy's first year and earlier this year at the posthumous award ceremony in April. Knowing the pressure the administration was under, she couldn't help feeling bemused by the ironic setting of this third meeting.

The exterior of the White House was protected like a fortress, yet the real threats to the President were political insiders, not intruders from the outside. The old saying *just because I'm paranoid doesn't mean it's not true* had become the Kenaghy inner circle's operational mindset. The White House workforce had become like a medieval royal court, so full of eyes and ears, tapes, taps, and video cameras that all was conducted as though for eavesdroppers. A once respected and well-intentioned American governor was slowly becoming a very nervous and edgy individual. The Washington power brokers had him on the ropes. If a stubborn

Congress didn't get the message across, if dwindling corporate campaign donations didn't make the situation patently obvious, if the media didn't broadcast it loud and clear, the steady bleed of leaks and innuendoes out of the White House, the steady loss of loyalty within, *did.* The Presidency was in trouble, thought Linda, and here she was sitting right in the middle of the storm.

The President's aide appeared and escorted Linda into the Oval Office at two minutes after eight. The President stood from his desk. "Mr. President," said the aide, "the journalist from *The New York Financial Times*, Ms. Linda Bennett."

Kenaghy advanced and took Linda's right hand in both of his. "Ms. Bennett, I hope you don't mind my asking to see you with so little notice." At close range, his eyes revealed sentiment, intelligence, and strain.

"Sir, it would be an honor any time you wished to see me."

He smiled—one of his front teeth overlapped the other. Then he waved off his aide, and Linda was suddenly alone with the President of the United States. She took a seat in one of the cane-back chairs, and he stood behind his desk.

"You're probably wondering why I've asked to see you." He didn't give her a chance to respond. "You must be aware, that of late, I have become little more than an embattled public official—and am extremely unpopular among some very powerful factions in this country." He paced behind his desk as he spoke. "Trust has become a difficult thing for me to find in Washington." He looked around the room with an expression that Linda interpreted as disdain for whoever might be eavesdropping on him at that very moment.

Clearly distraught and agitated, he came from behind his desk and sat on the front edge. "I wanted to talk to you this morning because of things you have written in your column in recent weeks."

"Regarding the situation with the family farmers?"

"Yes. After the statement made yesterday by the Farmers' Alliance, I'm not sure that's the kind of editorial this country needs right now." He looked directly into her eyes, probing. "If I'm not mistaken, Ms. Bennett, you're on your way to Kansas City today to do a series of interviews on this *prairie fire* as you have called it. I want you to be careful. I can't tell you what to write. But I want you to be careful. As an expert in the commodities market, you must realize that burning the wheat is dangerous to our economy. And with world grain stocks already low, it's likely to take food off the tables of large parts of the Third World."

"Yes, sir, I'm aware of the graveness of the situation." She felt like she was getting lectured.

Kenaghy rose from the edge of the desk and wandered back behind it again. "What's happening in the Midwest is not that surprising. As you've said in your commentaries, there are some very serious questions to be asked about the direction of our democracy. They apply directly to the farmers' grievances—how do the little people fit into corporate America? In recent months, I have tried to address some of the inequities of big business and have discovered considerable resistance in Congress. I'm afraid the farmers' demands have little or no chance of being fulfilled, and the burning of their fields is a foolish mistake."

Linda nodded.

"When you write about this farmers' strike, when you are out there talking to the farmers, try to make them understand what they are up against."

"Yes, sir." She tried to catch his eyes. "You probably haven't read my column in today's paper."

"No, I haven't had a chance."

"I compare the grain industry to the petroleum industry, sir. Both commodities rely heavily on middlemen for storage, refining, and transportation. Both are absolute necessities. And both are managed with large strategic reserves that are used to control market prices in times of emergency. Above and beyond OPEC, a handful of western oil refiners work in concert to control production and manage gasoline prices. The same is true in the grain industry—though it's not as well known. Three large distributors control eighty-five percent of the grain market. And to their credit, much like the oil refiners, they have done a credible job stabilizing the market. But in no way are either of these commodities sold in a free market as advertised. The farmers have a legitimate beef."

The President nodded.

"There is also increased concern and growing documentation that both of these commodities are beyond their days of gluts and are headed to days of shortages. That is, increasing demand against geophysical limitations. I've always believed in a free market, but the world is changing, and I'm beginning to understand that certain, strategic commodities—like grain and oil—need to be subject to government management. I'd call it a stand for reason against market ideology. I think that's what this strike is pointing to."

Kenaghy nodded again. "Do you think the farmers have any chance of getting what they demand?"

"No. I believe the farmers are right. I believe the system needs an overhaul—both in the market and the field. But I also believe that this should have been addressed thirty years ago. And it's probably too late now."

The President nodded thoughtfully, then gazed absently out the window, almost like he wasn't really interested in what she was saying. He turned away from the window and his eyes met hers. They were hard and penetrating with something soft and understanding behind. "You must know it's very unusual for a President to call a journalist into his office for this kind of conversation. It's because of the impact of the fires yesterday and because I knew your father somewhat and respected him highly. I simply wanted to talk to you personally. I want you to be very careful with the incendiary language." He put his right hand in the pocket of his suit jacket and came back around to the front of the desk.

"Yes, sir," she said, facing him, thinking all this rather strange.

The President extended his hand directly from his coat pocket. "Good day, Ms. Bennett," he said stiffly. As she stood and took his hand, he looked her in the eye and pushed a folded piece of paper into her palm, then turned away.

The door to the Oval Office opened from the outside, and the same aide who led her in, escorted her out.

Linda took a taxi directly to Reagan Airport for her flight to Kansas City. All through the drive and the early part of the flight, she struggled to make sense of the strange meeting she'd just had. Not until she was somewhere over Tennessee and could actually see blackened fields below, did she summon the nerve to retrieve the President's note from her valise. It was handwritten in small neat print on White House stationery:

> *Ms. Bennett,*
>
> *I hope you will forgive me for this form of communication and anything I might have said to you in my office. As you know, the office of the President of the United States is an embattled one. There are too few in Washington who I can trust, and at this*

moment, because I have so little choice, I am reaching out to you. I would like you to act as a special emissary for me. If this is a mistake, then it is already too late…

Your editorial today was beautiful. More than anything else, this country needed a strong statement about the value of our grain supply and how we manage it. Although I am certainly against the field burning, I do believe the farmers' demands are justified.

As I understand it, you are going to be interviewing farmers, militia organizations, grange officials, and, I presume, Col. Nathaniel Cromwell. If you do reach Col. Cromwell or Grange President Forest Mahan, I want you to assure them personally, that regardless of what the media has to say about me or how they interpret what I say, short of violence, I am fully behind the farmers in their efforts.

Unfortunately, because of legislation I have recently tried to block and my present political straits, this may not account for much, and the outcome of the strike might already be out of my hands. Still, I want the farmers to know that I do want to talk to them. Political tact might make it impossible for me to do this through ordinary channels. But I do seek contact with them, and I do have an offer to make; however, it must be done behind closed doors. This is the message I am entrusting you to relay. I want to talk to them, but only if it can be done in strict secrecy.

If you can, use this note to arrange such a meeting. Should you need to contact me, go through my press secretary Wayne Stevens as though you were pursuing your ordinary business—make no mention of your purpose. No one other than yourself knows of this note or my intentions.

Sincerely,
President James Kenaghy

CHAPTER 51

Nathaniel Cromwell was up early with the Morningdale family. He got the special treatment at breakfast—fresh eggs, bacon, homemade bread, everything straight off the farm except the Colombian coffee. Then he was on the road again headed to Mahan's farm.

Nate drove northwest from Blytheville through a hundred miles of still smoldering farmland. The expanse of burnt wheat fields and charred outbuildings looked more like battlefields than farms now. His stomach tightened with memories of other such blackened landscapes he'd seen in other countries and the ugly possibilities that lay ahead for the U.S. He grimly continued up over the Ozark Escarpment into the hills of southern Missouri before rolling out of the Ozarks and picking up Interstate 44 to Springfield.

Nate arrived at Forest Mahan's farm just before lunch. He dropped down a gear as he drove along the west side of Mahan's property. What had once been one of the most beautiful farms he had ever seen was scarred by scorched black fields, stretching out as far as he could see where Forest's ripe winter wheat had been two days earlier. He dropped down another gear and turned into the driveway.

Nate pulled in alongside several other pickups. He hopped out of his Power Wagon and strode up to the front porch. Before he could knock, Louise Mahan opened the door. "Come on in, Colonel, you're just in time for lunch."

"How are things going, Louise?" he asked, entering the foyer. Looking through the dining room, he could see several women working in the kitchen.

"Busy." She glanced back to the kitchen. "Forest's back in the office with some of the local farmers, trying to sort through all the information that's coming in. Go on back there. You know where it is."

"Yeah, thanks. I'll do that."

"Lunch in about ten minutes."

Nate stopped in the doorway to Mahan's office. Four men were there including Forest. In his blue jeans, work boots, t-shirt, and Caterpillar ball cap, turned a tad off center, Nate could have been any farmer, but as soon as the others saw him, all the bustle in the room suddenly stilled. Forest was at the keyboard of his computer. "Nate! Been expecting you." He glanced around at the others. "Like you to meet a few of the local boys. We've been trying to figure out what really went down yesterday."

The three other men, dressed more or less like Cromwell, clearly farmers, from thirty-five to fifty years old, stepped forward eager to shake the hand of the war hero.

"What ya got so far, Forest?"

"I've heard from almost every farmer on the initial burn list. A handful didn't go through with it, and we got some grief from a few of the stronger Christian communities. Other than that, it was pretty much what we expected." Forest pushed a couple pieces of paper around on his desk. "Also starting to get some reports from the north on the storage situation. It seems we got close to a third of what was in those fields harvested at the last minute."

Cromwell looked down at Forest's desk then up into his eyes. "If we have to burn again, what kind of storage do we have?"

"If we have to burn again." Forest shook his head at the thought of it. "We're talking twice the acreage. Up to a million acres. It'll take every barn and makeshift lean-to to get a third of that stored."

One of the other men spoke up. "What about getting building crews going, Forest?" He was one of the younger men, tall and thin, three days of dark stubble on his face. "If there's some time before we burn again, couldn't we throw up some stick buildings to serve as temporary storage?"

Forest nodded. "Could be? What do you think, Nate?"

"Yes, definitely, yes. Especially if we can get them close to the fields in question. The less trucking we have to do the better."

"Good. Let's do it," said Forest. "Jim, can you get some crews together? I'll give you some locations and phone numbers after lunch."

"Sure. Now that my fields are burnt, I'm itchin' to help somebody else."

"What have we heard from the industry, Forest?"

"Not a word directly. Read some comments in *The Washington Post* this morning. Mostly ridicule. They aren't giving us much credibility."

"Maybe a million-acre burn will get us some," said Nate. Out the window behind Forest's desk were black and barren wheat fields, a solemn backdrop to everything that was said. "What will it take? A week to get that together?"

"Something like that."

"What about the government? Heard from Washington?"

"I've gotten some calls from our usual friends in Congress—mostly telling me the field burning is a big mistake and that we should wait until the new Congress. The Secretary of Labor Pierce backs the industry. Said the Nonpartisan Farmers' Alliance has yet to file papers and has no official status as a union. Homeland Security put the country on Orange Alert—called us terrorists. Dutz at Agriculture is saying our portion of the harvest is too small for any kind of market leverage."

"That's an outright lie," said one of the local farmers. A grim man, looking stressed and worn out.

Forest agreed. "That's part of the battle. Propaganda."

"And there's been nothing out of the White House?"

"Generally, presidents tend to stay out of labor disputes as long as they can," said the third of the locals, the oldest one.

"Hell with Kenaghy," said the grim man angrily. "He's on his way out anyway. Along with this Orange Alert bullshit, they're calling us traitors. It's an insult."

"I'd like to see Kenaghy name a federal negotiator," said Forest. "Minimally we need to get a dialogue going."

"Then no respect is still the message?"

"I'd say so, Nate," sighed Forest.

"Okay then, full speed ahead on preparing fields. Where's Hayes?"

"He's way out ahead of us. Near your neck of the woods in Kansas now, cutting firebreaks and organizing harvest for fields likely to be in the next burn." Forest paused. "As a matter of fact, I've got a big truck here for him. If we can get your pickup in the back, maybe you could drive it to Hayes on your way home."

"Sure. I'd like the chance to talk to him anyway."

"Got some early returns on your television appearance," said Forest with a smile.

"Movie contract, I hope." This got a chuckle out of two of the other men.

"Better than that. Two reputable polls say we've got a lot more support from the populace than expected. I don't know what you saw yesterday, but I got the feeling the entire rural community was behind us. Not just the farmers. It was real positive."

Nate nodded. "Yeah, I saw the same thing."

"I also got some positive feedback from two big environmental groups. They're pulling for us. It's important to get their backing. I think this country's more ready for change than anyone in Washington, D.C. is prepared to admit."

"It's too bad though," said Nate, "if it's going to take another burn to get them moving."

"Another burn or two," said the man who'd offered to build storage bins.

CHAPTER 52

Linda Bennett deplaned at the Kansas City International Airport feeling like a different woman than when she'd boarded. She couldn't help thinking she'd unintentionally become a double-agent, somewhat at crossed purposes. And it made her unusually self-conscious as she followed the overhead signs to the baggage claim. What was she really doing here? Working as a mole for Bob Richards, an emissary for the President, or, as she had always assumed, a free agent of the fourth estate.

The baggage was slow arriving to the carrousel. During the wait, Linda became aware of a face in the crowd—a man in a phone booth adjacent to the baggage claim—who had also been a passenger on her flight. At first, she dismissed the man's flashing eyes as an admiring glance, but the second time, it bothered her more than usual, and she began to wonder if she was being watched. She made no obvious sign of concern but kept an eye on the man in every way she could without looking at him directly—window reflections, her makeup mirror, abrupt turns of her head. Throughout her wait, he remained on the phone.

When her bags finally arrived, instead of going directly out to the front of the airport to wave down a taxi, Linda headed to the terminal's main concourse. She found a small sandwich shop and bought a container of yogurt, then sat down at a table in the concourse. As she dabbed at the yogurt with a little white plastic spoon, she spotted the man again. Damn, if she didn't have a tail! It had to be the visit with the President. She knew the CIA didn't trust Kenaghy—apparently, they didn't trust her either. And it wasn't just this one man. As she sat there, seemingly lost to a cup of strawberry yogurt, haphazardly gazing about with each spoonful, she noticed the telltale body language of a second man, clearly watching her as he read a newspaper.

After Linda finished the yogurt, she found an airport newsstand and purchased a pack of yellow post-its, then veered off to the ladies' room.

She found a seat in an open stall and composed two post-it notes. Upon exiting the restroom, she quickly relocated the two tails. One hadn't moved and was still reading the newspaper. The other was some distance away, window shopping in front of one of the airport bookstores.

Linda set off at a fast pace for the most crowded part of the concourse and the entry to a long, two-story escalator. As she stepped onto the escalator, she looked into the reflection of an overhead sign—both men were following. When she reached the top of the escalator, the first of man was stepping onto the moving stairway and the other was several yards behind. Linda paused at the top of the escalator, as if in a moment of indecision, until the second man had committed to the moving stairs and the other was half way up, then she abruptly turned and got on the escalator going down. When she reached the first tail, going up as she went down, he turned his back to her. With the lightest possible touch, she stuck one of the post-its on his back. Farther down the escalator, she passed the second tail and, in much the same way, posted a note on the back of his jacket. Once off the escalator, she beelined for the car rental.

Short of climbing over the escalator railing, the two tails reversed field as soon as they could and rushed off after Linda. The one farthest behind spotted the note on the back of the other. He entered into a full sprint to see what it said. In black magic marker was written *I work for the CIA*. He tapped the other man on the shoulder. "Hey, buddy, you're slip is showing."

"What?"

The man took the post-it off the others back and handed it to him.

"Fuck, where'd this come from?" the man snarled. Then he saw there was a message on the back. *You're doing a horrible job of following me. Lay off!*

By this time, there were several travelers standing nearby chuckling at the two men. The first tail suddenly reached out and pulled the post-it off the other man's back. His said *I work for the FBI.*

"Christ! What is this?"

In the meantime, Linda went right through the car rental and out the other side, hailed a taxi, and was off.

A few minutes before three that afternoon, Linda entered the office of Elizabeth White, Editor-in-Chief of *The Kansas City Kansan*. Conservative and a bit matronly, Ms. White was considered one of the top women editors in the country and had turned *The Kansan* into the Midwest's most respected newspaper. Frederick Manning had arranged this meeting with Ms. White so Linda could use *The Kansan* offices as a base of operations during her time in the Midwest. White didn't know who Linda's father was or any of the other related CIA connections.

The two high-powered women immediately began to grate on each other, starting with the appraising look Ms. White gave Linda as she stepped through the door. "Ms. Bennett, I've been anxious to meet you ever since Frederick's call last week." Despite the kind words, her tone was puffy and condescending, as though Linda was just a little too pretty and stylish for her taste. "Even more so since reading the piece in *The Times* this morning. Please sit down."

Tired and stressed from a complex day, Linda fought her first impression of the older woman and sat down with a polite smile. "I hope that's a compliment, Ms. White. I've gotten a wide variety of responses to that piece." She thought of the President saying he hadn't read it, then his reversal in the private note.

"That doesn't surprise me. It's a controversial piece." White offered Linda a contained smile. "All things considered, I thought the piece was excellently written."

All things considered! "*The Times* probably sent me to the Midwest hoping I'd stay," said Linda choking down the affront.

"We have plenty of editorial writers right now," replied White with a straight face, stretching it out into an awkward silence before she continued. "Let me offer you this one insight, Ms. Bennett. Writing about what's going on out here in the Heartland from Washington is one thing, but really knowing the people is another. We're different out here. I do think you're brave for supporting the farmers, but it's more complex than you can possibly know. Farming is not so romantic up close. I've lived out here and written about these people all my life, and I still can't say I completely grasp what this field burning thing means or what they expect to gain."

Linda could barely believe how she was being talked to, but she deflected it as diplomatically as possible. "I'm sure what you're saying is correct, Ms. White. I don't have the experience in the Midwest you do. To tell you the truth, I'm a little nervous about this assignment, and I'm entirely open to your insights."

"What kind of pieces do you have in mind?"

"I'm looking at five in-depth interviews. I want to talk to at least two of the farm families that burned their fields yesterday. And I want to talk to someone from the militia. I also want to talk to the Grange President, Forest Mahan, and, if possible, Nathaniel Cromwell. Mostly I want to write about the strike from the farmers' side."

"Just be careful you don't stir them up with any fancy language. We don't need sensationalism right now. We need reason."

Linda's hackles rose again, but she held on. "These pieces will be going to *The Times* as political commentary. They'll also be published in many other newspapers that carry my syndicated column. I'd like you to consider them for *The Kansan*."

"I'm the final line of defense here," White said smugly. "Get a piece by me and it's in."

"I think I already knew that." Linda had to laugh to herself. Here was this righteous Midwest editor pronouncing authority, when earlier today she'd become confidant to the President of the United States.

White stood. "Let me show you your work space and introduce you to a few key people." She led the way down a hallway. "Then you're on your own."

Thank God.

CHAPTER 53

Jonathan Mayfield was on to something in Singapore. He had printed out the two files of names and addresses that were on the disk he'd found in the Hilton lounge. In the next two days, while going about his system design work for the Development Bank of Asia, he ran spot checks on nearly a hundred of the names. All of them had DBA accounts and a high percentage of them lived in cities where Jonathan had found grain elevator leases maximized.

By the afternoon of the second day, Jonathan believed he knew how the Asian grain buy had occurred so quietly. The Teochui Kongsi had used their huge, closeknit network, spread literally throughout the Pacific Rim and the Malaysian Peninsula, to organize thousands of superficially unrelated small buyers to accumulate over a hundred million bushels of grain. It was as simple as that.

Jonathan found this very exciting and dearly wanted to talk about this with Dan the Hippie. But how could he get a hold of him? Was he even in Singapore? He thought about trying the phone number one more time then decided he didn't want to call from his office phone. When the work day ended, he found a pay phone on the street. Feeling more and more like a secret agent, he punched in the number off the napkin Dan had given him. Again, he got the disconnected message. He looked down at the address and thought what the hell. He stepped out to the curb and flagged down a taxi. He slid into the back seat of a late model Ford and gave the driver the address.

It was located on the far west side of the city, and it took them almost an hour through rush hour traffic to get there. The building was a flat-roofed, three-story apartment complex in a neat but rundown neighborhood. Jonathan asked the driver to park two blocks down the street and wait for him as he went to check the apartment.

Jonathan appraised the place as he approached. The building was not so old, as poorly built and in need of paint and repair. The stairs were external, and an exterior walkway ran across the two upper levels of the building. Number twenty-six would be on the second floor.

After quick a glance around, Jonathan decided to risk a closer look. Several barefoot brown children ran down the stairs as he went up. A mother screamed at a child. Dogs barked from behind the building. Cars honked in the distance.

When Jonathan reached the top of the first flight of stairs, he looked left then right to determine which way the numbers ran. He walked past twenty-four. Then twenty-five. The door was open. An older Asian couple peered out at him from a shadowy interior as he passed. The door to twenty-six was closed and the window curtains pulled. With some trepidation, he knocked on the door. There was no answer. When there was no answer to a second louder knock, he tried the doorknob. It was unlocked. He pushed the door open partway. "Anyone here?"

Again, there was no response. He stepped into what appeared to be a vacant apartment. "Anyone here?" he tried again, half-expecting to find a body on the floor. He moved farther into the apartment and peeked into the little kitchen. There were dirty plates and chopsticks in the kitchen sink. There was no furniture at all, only a thin mattress folded over in the corner of the bedroom. There was a phone jack next to the mattress. But no phone. And, thankfully, no dead body.

Satisfied that either Dan no longer lived at this address or never had, Jonathan exited from the apartment and closed the door. When he passed number twenty-five on his way out, the door was closed. He knocked on the door. No one answered. He knocked again. He was about to leave when the door opened just enough for a gray-haired Asian man to stick his head out.

"Did an American live next to you?" Jonathan asked in English.

The man shook his head as though he didn't understand.

Jonathan tried hand signals. He pointed to the apartment. Then used his hands to describe a man with a beard and long hair. The old man just stared at him as though he was crazy. The man turned and said something in Mandarin to the woman Jonathan assumed was his wife. The woman came to the door. From behind the man, she looked at Jonathan like he was some kind of curiosity. He tried the sign language with her. She raised a camera and snapped his picture as he was trying to demonstrate long hair and a beard. Then the door abruptly shut, leaving Jonathan at a loss. He descended the stairs and returned to the cab, wondering what had happened to the American journalist.

CHAPTER 54

The New York Financial Times leased a furnished one-bedroom apartment for Linda Bennett's two-week stay in Kansas City. She rented a car after her introduction to Elizabeth White and drove straight to the apartment. Her appraisal of the place started with the bathroom. It was just what the doctor ordered. It had a wide vanity, a shower, and an over-sized tub with Jacuzzi jets. Linda immediately filled the tub and stripped off her clothes. She slipped into the water, anticipating a long leisurely bath. As tired as she was, she just wanted to close her eyes and relax, but her brain wouldn't let go and her eyes kept flashing open. The meeting with the President and the note he had given her had unsettled her. That this trip had been inspired by Richards was bad enough, but now she had a message to deliver that was more important than the columns she was supposed to write. Where would she start? In the least obvious way possible. Tomorrow morning, she'd find a farmer to interview and see if she could get that done without being followed.

After the bath, Linda put on her bathrobe and made some orange spice herbal tea. It was four-thirty. She snuggled into the king size bed with all four pillows propped up behind her and opened her laptop. The last few days had been busier than usual, and it had been two days since she'd made any progress in her father's email chronology.

Very soon after she began, in an email from September two years back, she found a reference to a white paper entitled *Implications of Climate Change on World Food Supplies.* Presumably this was an earlier version of the same report Richards had given her in the White House basement. From the way her father referred to the paper, it seemed that something in the last chapter was very controversial and troubling, and he wanted it discussed in a general meeting of CIA department heads. The subject of this white paper appeared in his email three times in the next month—mostly pushing for discussion of the paper's conclusion.

In an email dated November 12 with the subject line of *Population Recession,* Linda found the following passage:

> *I can't believe this is the course a democratic society would choose to follow. If trends in population, pollution, and the depletion of natural resources point to an economic collapse so severe that our analysts forecast a thirty percent human die-off, the challenge is to alter these trends, not try to maximize profits off the situation, not to use the system of capitalism as a guillotine. This paper recommends using free market forces to make all the tough decisions about who lives and who dies as the global economy seeks equilibrium with reduced resources. The rich will inherit the Earth. Isn't that what this is really saying? A financial survival of the fittest. Let's take our marbles and run. Control the water, control the grain, control the petroleum, and cut back on people! Starting at the bottom! This is the social elite saying they'd rather trim the world population than cut back on their lifestyle. Don't believe for one minute that this kind of arrogance can be achieved without costly repercussions.*

Here it was again! The same topic her father had been talking to her about in the year before his heart attack—global resource management—but with implications far graver than anything he'd ever described. It pointed to the same kind of global positioning strategy Linda saw behind the Trans-Eurasian Security Act. But clearly petroleum was only one piece in the natural resource puzzle. The recent grain crisis in Asia revealed another. What if there had been no reserves? The market would have determined who got food and who didn't. Linda wasn't entirely unaware of such scenarios. She'd read many doomsday forecasts with just this prediction, but they all read like B-grade science fiction. Now here it was in her father's own writing. Verification of the basic Malthusian premise—the Earth can only support so many people—but with a critical new twist—western capitalism was positioning for it, instead of trying to avert it.

CHAPTER 55

The rift that had grown between the President and the nation's most influential power brokers was not as obvious to the outside world as it was in the halls of Congress or to political insiders. James Kenaghy still maintained some appeal to his Democratic constituents and fought only moderately elevated levels of disquiet in the Republican base. Yes, the President's numbers had fallen during the second half of his first term, but the real measure of his Presidency was the disdain coming from the biggest players in Washington. And this had been strictly backroom knowledge until his first veto of TES. Then Washington's displeasure began to leak into the social gatherings and gossip pages of the nation's capital. The average American might still consider President Kenaghy the most powerful political figure in the world, but connected Washingtonians did not.

The First Lady, Marjorie Pickett Kenaghy, tended to stay out of politics in public. She truly loved Washington society, the big balls, the formal dinners, the fund raisers for children's causes, the opportunities to get dressed up and be in the limelight, but she was not controversial and watched what she said. In private, however, she did express her opinions, political and otherwise, to her husband. And in the last two months, especially as James' disfavor began to cut into their social calendar, Marjorie had become quite critical.

Tuesday night, the day following the farmers' first burn, James and Marjorie had no social engagements and no guests. They ate dinner alone together in the White House. The meal passed in a tense silence through the salad, main course, and dessert. But after the decaffeinated coffee was served and the couple faced each other across the expanse of antique White House linen, Marjorie wanted some questions answered.

"What are you going to do about these farmers, James?" she asked one sip into her coffee.

Kenaghy didn't answer right away. He had a plan. He'd set it in motion earlier that day with the note he passed to Linda Bennett. But he had no intention of talking about it until he'd gotten a better feel for what was or was not happening. "I'm playing it by ear," he said offhandedly, pushing away from the table with his coffee cup and crossing one leg over the other.

"What have your advisers suggested?"

Kenaghy was not in the mood to talk about this. "Mostly they're telling me the farmers are making a mistake. That a strike is complete nonsense."

"I would agree with that—don't you?" There was doubt in her voice.

"I haven't completely decided."

"What do you mean? Isn't it completely obvious?"

He just looked at her.

"What's holding you back? These people are burning what is clearly an important American asset. It can't continue."

Kenaghy was on edge enough. He didn't need this from his wife. "All I'm saying, Marjorie, is that I'm still thinking about it. These farmers aren't entirely wrong." He turned away from her and looked across the room absently.

"Is this going to be like the TES thing? Where you just get bullheaded and take on what is so clearly a losing position? Are you deliberately throwing everything away?" The shrew was building in her voice. "I don't get it, James. I don't like the looks I'm getting these days when we go out. Don't be a fool on this one, too."

Kenaghy thought for a moment. He could either tell her to shut up, or he could tell her his fears about military policy being hijacked by large corporate interests. He could tell her about his plan to appease the farmers, bring them into his camp, and make a wild run at a second term—which everyone now felt was impossible—or he could say nothing. He turned to face his wife, then looked down at the cup of coffee he held in his lap.

"So?" demanded Marjorie. "What's going on? You can't just sit there. This is my life too. You might want to be a failed President, but I don't want to be a failed First Lady. This is my presidency as much as it is yours."

He hated this kind of talk. Below the edge of the table, his free hand tightened into a fist. "I'd like to give it a few more days before I make any decisions," he said.

"Why? How could things change? More fires? More criticism in the press? The attacks on you are also attacks on me. I'm not as thick-skinned as you. I take it personally and—and it hurts." Suddenly she was crying.

Kenaghy didn't know what to say. She was being very stupid right now. But she wasn't a stupid woman. It was the stress and the pressure. It could drive anyone nuts. "Trust me, Marjorie," he said, getting up from the table and going over to her. "I know what I'm doing." He put a hand on her shoulder. She looked up at him with wet, red eyes.

"I don't think you do," she snapped. "I don't understand you at all anymore." She stood and hurried out of the room. "I need a break from Washington. I'm going up to Boston to see my mother."

"Marjorie," he called after her. "You don't need to do that."

"I can get a plane tonight." She was out in the hallway.

He raised his voice. "Please don't." She didn't respond.

The President stood there in the dining room alone. He forgave her. None of this was easy. He knew that. In six more months, either they'd be gone from Washington and the pressure would be off, or he would have turned things around, and she would know for a fact that he did know what he was doing.

CHAPTER 56

It looked like an invasion from another planet. Cresting the hill in the truck he'd brought from Missouri, Nathaniel Cromwell could see the headlights of ten huge combines plowing through the fields at midnight, reaping wide swaths in the ripe winter wheat like giant mechanical insects. This kind of night harvest was nothing new to farmers. Come harvest time, they often put in twenty-hour days behind the wheel of a combine, sealed into an air-conditioned cab, surrounded by a cloud of dust and chaff, as they mowed through the wheat or corn, reaping and threshing all at once.

Tonight, however, they would not harvest the fields completely. The drivers were cutting less than half of what was there, reaping alternate rows or sometimes, when they got bored, making designs or writing messages. The idea was to leave enough wheat in the field so it didn't appear to be harvested but would burn with the appropriate display of defiance.

This was the kind of effort that could make Nate smile. The organization, the teamwork, everyone pitching in to get the job done. That was one thing the farmers had in spades. Workers unified by purpose. And Nate did smile as he plunged down the dirt road beside the fields and keyed the CB mike. "Breaker one-one," he shouted over the roar of the engine, "this is Pacman. I'm in the truck on the southwest corner of the swale. Over."

The citizen band cackled and buzzed. "Got ya, Pacman. Perfect timing. We can use that truck right away." It was Hayes. "Stay put. I'm headed your way. Over and out."

Nate pulled the truck to a stop at the corner of the field and watched as one of the combines altered its course, coming straight at him. He climbed out of the cab as the huge Case International 2160 ground to a halt at the edge of the field.

The combine was the size of a city bus with tires as tall as a man and a big tilted, floor-to-ceiling windshield. Nate could see Hayes at the wheel through the swath cut in the dust and dirt by the wiper blade. Nate reached the big red beast just as Hayes kicked open the door and jumped down to the ground. For the first time, Hayes wasn't in uniform, instead wearing jeans, a sweaty t-shirt, work boots, a busted up ball cap, and the heavy fragrance of fresh cut wheat and diesel.

"Nice to see you in camo, General," said Nate with a crooked grin, sticking out his hand.

"Yeah, even got a little bear grease on." Hayes took off his hat and wiped his dirt streaked face with a faded red machinist's rag. "Damn, this is some kind of work. I haven't got the hours behind one of these monsters you real farmers do." He took Cromwell's hand with a firm grip. "How are you, Colonel?" Something like warmth came from the usually icy militia officer.

"I'll tell you after I get back to my farm," said Nate, noticing that the little silver cross he'd seen on Hayes' collar before was now pinned to his cap. "Other than that, I can't complain."

The two men stood beside the combine's twenty-foot wide, paddle wheel header and made eye contact through the glare of the rig's headlights. "Your men did a nice job yesterday," said Nate. The distant growl of field machinery denied the quiet of the heartland night.

"Thank you, sir," returned Hayes. There was a crisp military sense to their exchange, but more than that, a mutual respect.

"Mahan says he could have another million acres available if we have to do it again. What do you think?"

"We'll be doing it again." Hayes ran his fingers through his beard. Several small pieces of chopped wheat stalk and chaff fell across the headlight beams like snowflakes beneath a lamppost.

"How long will that take to prepare?"

"Sometime next week. Monday. Maybe Tuesday. The crews will have it down by then."

Nate looked off toward the other combines combing across the gentle slopes of grain.

"You know, Colonel," said Hayes, "I hope to hell we get something out of this strike." Nate turned to face him. "If we don't get that extra dollar per bushel, there's no way all this truck driving is worth it."

"Yeah," said Nate, "we talked at Mahan's about building some simple shelters closer to the fields. It's a good idea, but time is a problem."

Hayes nodded. "Not as much as gasoline."

They stood there a moment in the harsh streak of halide light. Something of the vast size of their task and the odds against them suspended in the surrounding night. Something else also. Without a word, the trust and personal ease that had grown between the two men had become evident to both of them—as real friendship.

Another farmer came out of the darkness. He was one of the drivers and was wearing a blue paisley bandana over his face like a western outlaw. He pushed the makeshift dust mask down around his neck. "This truck available?" he asked.

"Yes," said Hayes. "Pull it up alongside this combine. I'll get the dump auger set up."

The man started to climb into the cab. Nate held up his hand. "Just a minute there," he called out. "My pickup's in the back of that rig. Let me get it out before you bury it in wheat."

Hayes laughed. Nate looked at him. "Hey, man, that's my ride home." Then he joined in, laughing heartily with Hayes, blowing out the last residues of tension that existed between them.

CHAPTER 57

Unable to sleep, Atossa climbed out of bed in the wee hours of the morning and wrapped her silk robe around herself. Full of anxiety, she began to pace back and forth across her room, fretting about the field burning. She stood beneath the wide skylight and stared up into the stars. She did not like all this uncertainty in her world. She wanted to forget about the farmers and the grain market and concentrate on the healing of her face, then move on to more important things like mending her relationship with her daughter Alise—and seeing Derek Davis. This brought her to a halt. If there were no further complications with her new face, she thought, roiling her left hand at her side, she would call Derek the next day. The thought of it immediately caused a new wave of angst to wash over her.

Atossa strode over to her divining table and picked up her Tarot cards. She chopped the deck into itself several times then pushed the buzzer at the edge of the table. Moments later, the tall black man, whom of late had become her favorite, entered the room wearing black silk briefs. The man stood beside her. She didn't look into his face. She pushed his briefs down to his knees and anxiously sought the soothing comfort of his warm scrotum. While the fingers of her left hand rolled and tumbled distractedly, she continued shuffling the cards with her right hand. When she felt the man's arousal, she raised her hand to his penis.

At the moment of his climax, which she believed gave more import to the moment, she cut the cards. Although the object of her divination was Derek Davis, the face of Nathaniel Cromwell, centered in a television screen, appeared in her mind's eye. The intrusion infuriated her, but when she lifted the card off the top of the deck, it featured the image of a skeleton carrying a sickle, and a fierce grin flickered across her transplanted face.

CHAPTER 58

Tired and stressed from three long hot days on the road, Nathaniel Cromwell arrived at his Kansas farm just before two Wednesday morning. All was quiet as he entered the house through the kitchen door. The house was beginning to cool slightly after a day in the triple digits. Although he did his best not to make a sound, his mother called out to him as he rummaged through the refrigerator for a snack.

"That you, Nate?" She was in his bedroom, not wanting to miss his return.

"Yes, Mary," he said softly, going down the hallway, munching on an apple. The reading light was on, and his mother was lying on the bed with an open book face down beside her. She wore her flannel nightgown and had obviously been asleep until Nate entered the house. He knelt beside the bed and noticed the age in his mother's tired eyes.

Mary reached out and touched him on the cheek. "They replayed your video again tonight on the news."

He took a bite of his apple. "Was it any better the second time?"

"Next time, could you please take the ball cap off?"

Nate chuckled as he chewed. "Sure, Ma."

"And you got about thirty phone calls from journalists today before I took it off the hook."

Nate grimaced. "Yeah, what'd you say to them?"

"Wrong number."

"Good. By tomorrow they'll probably be at the door with cameras and microphones. Oh boy," he said, looking at the ceiling and taking a breath. "Now that I'm back, Ma, and there's nothing to worry about, why don't you just crawl under the covers. I'm kind of keyed up from driving. I'm going to have a little glass of brandy. I'll use your bedroom whenever I think I can fall asleep. We can talk in the morning."

"Okay," she said sleepily. He helped her with the blankets, turned out the light, and finished off his apple as headed back down the hall.

Nate went directly to the kitchen cabinet over the refrigerator and pulled out a mostly empty bottle of Korbel brandy. He wasn't much of a drinker, but on occasion he'd have a little glass of brandy to relax. He poured about two ounces into a water glass. He breathed in the sharp fragrance of the strong liquor then took a tiny meditative sip. Things were going as well as could be expected, he thought to himself. Maybe it would take another burn before they would get the attention they deserved, but the unity of the farmers was strong and secure.

Glass in hand, he walked back outside into the yard. He stood out in the open air and stared up into the sky. It was a beautiful cloudless night, and the stars sparkled like the jewels of the universe that they were. He took another little sip, thinking back across the expanse of his life. The years on the farm as a kid. His time at West Point. The first tour in Afghanistan. He wished he could still feel as good about his country as he did then. The second tour in Afghanistan had changed him. The Medal of Honor meant little to him that day he received it. He'd trade it all back for the old innocence when good was good and bad was bad. Nowadays nothing was particularly clear. Even the strike. He took another sip. Oh, it was the right thing to do. But risky. They were taking on some mighty big folks. And it might not get them what they wanted.

Nate wandered across the yard to the machinery barn. He pushed the big sliding door open just enough to slip in. He entered without turning on the light and felt his way past the still partly dismantled combine to the little office at the back. Peg came tail-wagging out before he reached the door. He patted her on the head, and she followed him in. He flicked on the light and dropped down in the beat-up armchair. Another thoughtful sip of brandy and he gradually began to let the road and all the strike bullshit ease out of him. Peg came over and laid her head on his lap. He scratched her behind her left ear. Damn, it felt good to be home. *Next time*, he thought with a smile, *don't wear the ball cap*. He said it aloud to himself then took the cap off his head and looked at it. *Caterpillar*. Why the fuck was he advertising for them? Wasn't he leading a fight against big agriculture? Shit, all he really wanted to do was get back to work. And that combine out there? When would he get a chance to work on that? Would he even need it this year?

He put the cap back on his head and took another sip of brandy. As his hand came to rest on the arm of the chair, he heard a crash of glass, the gunning of a car engine and squealing tires. Before he was out of the little office, there was an explosion—and he was stumbling as fast as he could through the debris all over the barn floor. He pushed out the sliding door, and his heart leapt into his throat. Flames flared from the window of his bedroom. A horrible shriek came from inside. He raced across the lot and blasted through the kitchen door. Will was standing in the kitchen half dressed, half asleep. "Dad? What's happening?"

"Get outside, Will, quick. It's the back of the house." There was another agonizing scream. He pushed past Will. "Get a hose going quick. Mary's in my room." Two steps down the hallway, he was confronted by a wall of fire. He turned into the bathroom, grabbed every towel he could, and turned on the shower to get them wet. With the screaming now nonstop, he wrapped himself in the towels and ran headlong into the flames. Mary's nightgown and hair were on fire. She was shrieking, twisting around on the floor surrounded by flames. He scooped up the fiery ball that was his mother, leapt out the nearest window, hit the ground, and rolled over and over away from the building, his mother screaming in his arms.

Will came running up with the hose. He doused them both. Nate screamed at him, "Use the phone in the barn. Get an ambulance quick." He was crying, crawling away from the house, trying to get Mary some air. But she wasn't screaming anymore. It was him screaming, tears pouring down his face. He pulled her into his arms. He couldn't let her go. He couldn't let her go.

It took two paramedics and a firewoman to get Mary's lifeless body out of Nate's arms. All of them knew him. All of them knew his mother. They could barely look him in the eye for the grief and horror that stared back at them from his shock scorched eyes. He just stood there, helpless, staring off in no direction, while the fire department fought to save the house. He was also badly burned. He didn't even know it.

Will tried to approach him. Nate pushed him away. "Dad, please, Dad?" begged Will.

Nate staggered away from everyone, out past the barn into the rows and rows of corn, to hide and bury his anguish. Will started to run after his father, but one of the paramedics caught him by the arm. He was a few years older than Will and had known him in high school. "Let him be, Will," he said.

Will stared into the young man's face, tears now running down his cheeks. "I'm scared," he said. "I'm scared what this will do to him."

CHAPTER 59

While the firefighters put out the fire at the back of the house and the young paramedic waited with Will, Nathaniel Cromwell, badly burned and fighting shock, wandered in the dark rows of corn. As his mind forced its way out of the paralysis of the tragedy, he tore at himself with blame for his mother's death. Why hadn't he just said no to Forest Mahan? Hadn't he known his involvement in the strike would eventually come back to his family? Hadn't he done enough for this schizophrenic country? He should have stayed clear of politics. All of his past experiences told him, over and over again, there was no winning against these people. There was no winning.

As he pushed his way aimlessly through the stalks of corn, ripping at himself and the strike movement, just before dawn, he entered an unexpected opening in the corn. An eight-foot-wide path had been cut in the middle of the field. In his tattered emotional state, it confused him at first. Knowing he hadn't done this, he wondered if it might have been something Will had done. He traced down the path about twenty yards where it abruptly turned left. He knelt down and, in the increasing light, tried to determine how the swath had been made. It wasn't a tractor. The corn stalks had been pushed down or trampled flat, all in one direction like in a crop circle.

Nate followed the path another twenty yards, and he came to an intersection. Two like paths branched out at right angles from where he stood. A third went straight ahead. He took the path to his right. It was the same as the last. Trampled flat. Twenty yards later, it turned right. Twenty yards farther it was a dead end. The puzzle was pulling him from his attack on himself.

He reversed directions returning to the intersection. He took the path to his left. Again twenty yards and a right angle. From there it was another twenty yards to a dead end. He retraced his steps gradually understanding that a huge pattern had been cut in his cornfield.

Something cut recently. That night. Before the firebombing. And the design, it sickened him to realize, was a swastika. A huge ugly swastika. The firebomber's signature.

Nate's first thought was his confrontation with the young man in camo that night of the first big grange meeting. Could this be an act of revenge by that youth? As he stood there alone at the break of dawn, pondering the firebombing and the symbol of hate cut in his fields, his building anger began to draw him out of his state of shock—until suddenly he remembered shoving Will away and blasting blindly into the corn field. He gathered his bearings from the rising sun and began pushing through the corn stalks again, as fast as he could, back toward the house, ignoring his burned arms and face, desperate to see his son.

Will was sitting with two paramedics at the back end of the ambulance when Nate emerged from the field. The fire trucks were gone. A third of the house was a heap of wet, smoldering char. Will and the two men stood as the burnt and tattered colonel turned farmer stumbled across the yard to the ambulance. When he reached Will, he immediately hugged him, but the ripe burns on his forearms cut the hug short. The father's and son's eyes met full of horror and sadness. Tears began running from Will's eyes. Nate put his hands on his son's shoulders. "I'm sorry, Will," he said. "I'm sorry I pushed you away. I was just so angry." Tears ran in streaks down his soot covered face.

"It's okay, Dad. Mike Hanson, the paramedic." He motioned to the younger of the two men standing beside them. "He said you might have gone into shock."

Nate nodded. "In all my battlefield experience, I never broke from reason as I did tonight. I'm sorry, Will." He turned to the paramedics. "Thank you for staying."

Mike Hanson stepped forward. "We couldn't leave, sir. We still need to attend to you. Maybe you should get into the ambulance."

"Where's her body?" asked Nate, looking around the farmyard, taking in the damage and debris.

"A second ambulance came shortly after we got here. Your mother's body will be at the hospital when we get there."

The second paramedic stepped up. "Colonel Cromwell, I'm noticing those burns on your arms. We better get you some medical attention right away."

Nate didn't fight it. He climbed gingerly into the ambulance with the paramedics and was rushed off to the emergency room. Will followed in his father's Power Wagon.

CHAPTER 60

The phone rang. Linda Bennett struggled out of sleep to answer it. "Hello?"

"What? You're not out of bed yet, Bennett?"

Linda looked at the clock. "Christ, Bob, it's six-thirty."

"Is someone there with you?"

"Yeah, sure, Nathaniel Cromwell. I bedded him last night."

Richards' hesitation was loaded.

"What are you jealous, Bob?" she snickered.

"No." His tone dead sober. "Cromwell's in the Wichita hospital."

"What?"

"His house was firebombed in the middle of the night. He was burned, but not critically. It's his state of mind that I'm concerned about."

"What do you mean?"

"His mother was in the house asleep at the time of the bombing. She was killed in the fire."

"No! Who did the bombing?"

"I take it you haven't seen the news this morning."

"I haven't even seen a cup of coffee. What's going on?"

"They've put the Homeland Guard on standby."

"What?" After her talk with the President the day before this made no sense at all.

"Houseman made the call. They don't want any more field burning. He's calling it domestic terrorism—and a federal crime."

"No attempt at bargaining? No dialogue?"

"Cromwell's video got a much better response than anyone expected. Nearly forty percent of the people polled felt the farmers' demands were valid. And with that firebombing last night, there's a lot of nervousness in Washington right now."

"What's the President saying?"

"He hasn't shown the courage to say anything. I just wanted to give you the heads-up on Cromwell. He might be a tricky one to catch up with now. No one has the slightest clue what he's going to do next."

Linda asked again. "Who's responsible for the firebombing?"

Richards took a moment to answer. "Too early to know."

"Who put those goons on me yesterday?"

"Haven't a clue."

"Bull!"

"I've got to go, Bennett."

"If it happens again, I'm done!"

He'd already hung up. Linda held the receiver out in front of her and gave it the finger.

CHAPTER 61

Cameron Phillips hurried down the hallway from his office into the White House lobby. "Where's the President?" All he got were blank faces. "We've got security on crisis alert, and nobody knows where the President is? He's not in the Oval Office. I just called up to his bedroom. Where is he?"

There was a moment of confusion and accusation. One of the secretaries said that the First Lady had left last night. This was all Phillips needed to hear. He was about to sound the building alarm, when a secret service man entered the reception area from the mansion.

"He's in the Map Room, Mr. Phillips. I think he slept there last night."

Phillips gasped in relief. "Thank you."

James Kenaghy was stretched out sound asleep on the long Victorian couch in the first floor Map Room, where Franklin Roosevelt had spent so many nights studying maps during World War II. Marjorie had departed with two secret service women for her mother's home in Boston right after dinner. The President had taken a bottle of Jack Daniel's into the Map Room and gotten out a map of the continental United States. He sat in there all night, sipping whiskey, counting electoral votes in his head, and thinking about the poll results he'd gotten earlier in the day, one on the farmers' strike and one on TES. Sometime in the wee hours of the morning, he fell asleep on the couch. Only the two secret service men outside the door knew where he was. And apparently no one cared until seven-forty-five Wednesday morning when Phillips blew out of his office looking for him.

"Jim, wake up!" Cameron Phillips banged through the door into the Map Room. The smell of perspired alcohol filled the room.

Kenaghy roused and squinted with his whole face. "What is it?"

"Houseman began putting out calls to the Homeland Guard at four this morning. They're on alert in twenty-five states right now!"

"What?" Kenaghy struggled into an upright position and groggily asked, "How can he do that?"

"Someone firebombed Nathaniel Cromwell's farm last night. His mother was killed in the fire. Houseman's been calling state governors ever since. Urging them to ready the guard."

Kenaghy turned his head to one extreme then the other, working out the kinks from an uncomfortable night on the couch. "Damn, what time is it?"

"Almost eight, sir."

The President ran a hand through his thick hair. "Christ, didn't I fire that madman two days ago?"

"You should have," muttered Phillips at a loss. "What should we do?"

Kenaghy grimaced at the taste in his mouth. "Stop Houseman. Get his office on the phone. The Homeland Guard! This is exactly what I didn't want to happen. Goddamn it!" he slammed, gradually waking to the insanity of it all. "Start calling the governors' offices. Aggrrhhhh. And…and I need some coffee." He took a step and kicked over the half-empty whiskey bottle beside the couch. He picked it up and handed it to Phillips on his way out of the Map Room.

By the time the President reached the West Wing, staff people were out in the hall, wondering what was going on. "All of you get back to work," he demanded, his anger at Houseman growing with every moment. "Where's the Presidential Counsel? Where's Sam Wedemeier?"

He stomped down the hallway in the direction of the Oval Office with Phillips behind, gripping the whiskey bottle by its neck and motioning for everyone to go back to their offices. Everything was fine.

"One other thing," said Phillips as they entered the Oval Office.

"What's that?" Kenaghy was hung over and badly out of sorts.

"The revised version of TES cleared Congress yesterday. A copy was delivered to your office bright and early this morning."

"CHRIST! I never even read the draft."

Phillips' eyes lifted to the ceiling.

Kenaghy glanced at the thick document on his desk and sneered. "To hell with them."

CHAPTER 62

Linda Bennett went right to the coffee maker then to the television after Richards' call. When she saw a sound bite of Paul Houseman wearing an American flag tie, calling the striking farmers traitors, and announcing that any further field burning would be considered an act of treason, she nearly gagged and turned off the tube.

Linda got the phone number of a small local airport out of the yellow pages and hired a pilot and a plane for the day. She already had several satellite photos she'd gotten from NASA, but she wanted to see what the fire damage looked like from a few thousand feet or lower.

Linda was in the air by eight-thirty, heading southwest toward Oklahoma. The accuracy of the burn was impressive. Black rectangles and squares were patchworked over a two-hundred-mile-wide swath. FUCK THE GOVERNMENT, spelled out in giant letters, was burnt like a brand in the center of one huge field. The physical sense of four hundred thousand acres was diminished considerably when viewed from a plane. Much more of the land was not burned than burned. Often the fields were small. Fifty acres or less. That the fires were well contained was clear. Yes, there were a handful of instances where the fire jumped the breaks. But in general, community awareness and support prevented any serious problems. Overall, Linda was impressed by the farmers' meticulous control.

Over east Oklahoma, the density of burns was very high. Linda asked the pilot to find a place to land, and he set them down in Tulsa. While the pilot waited, Linda rented a car and headed out to talk to the first farmer she could find who had taken part in the burning. At eleven-fifteen, escorted by a couple of barking farm dogs, she drove up the driveway to the home of George McNary, getting his name and phone number simply by asking around at a local market.

George McNary was standing in front of his barn, looking quite a bit like a Norman Rockwell painting with his straw cowboy hat and pitchfork. Behind the barn as far as you could see were blackened fields. The dogs continued barking as Linda climbed out of the air-conditioned car into the midday heat. NcNary hardly made a move or uttered a word as the dogs circled and jumped around her. She forced a smile through the ruckus and walked over to the tall middle-aged farmer. "I'm hoping you're George McNary," she said, extending a hand. "I'm Linda Bennett, the journalist that just called and asked to talk to you about the field burning."

McNary made her go through it all before he took her hand. "Yeah, I'm George," he said with the dogs barking nonstop. He had long arms and big hands, dark bushy eyebrows, and a gaunt drawn up look to his mouth and cheeks. He looked Linda up and down, making her feel overdressed in her tailored khaki slacks and white linen blouse. "Git outta here, dogs," he finally barked. One ran off. "Git," he hollered again, and the other one did too.

"Thank you," she smiled. "This is no intrusion, I hope, Mr. McNary."

"Well, I don't know yet," he drawled, still looking her over.

"I have a tape recorder. Is that all right? It makes things easier, you know." She couldn't believe how awkward she felt.

McNary put a hand to his chin and rubbed at two days of stubble. "It's fine, I suppose. Maybe we should go in the house. Meet the missus and all."

"Yes, please."

The front door of the little box of a house opened, and the other half of Norman Rockwell's painting stepped out on the porch—dime store glasses, graying hair up in a bun, and as overweight as her husband was thin. "George, I just heard it on the news. The President's put out a call to the Homeland Guard." Mrs. McNary paused, noticing Linda. Her once-over being even more invasive than George's. "Now who's this here?"

"It's that reporter who called a while ago, Dora. What'd you say about the National Guard?"

"Hello, Mrs. McNary. My name is Linda Bennett." She went up to the front porch, hand extended.

The woman took Linda's hand with a cautious reluctance. "You from New York, you say?"

"No, Washington, D.C. I work there for *The New York Financial Times.*"

"Sounds like Wall Street?"

"Well, yes…"

"George, you hear that? *The New York Financial Times.*"

"Yeah, I told you that when she called. What was that about the National Guard?"

"I wasn't expectin' such a young, pretty one as you, darlin," said Dora, ignoring George entirely. "I'll bet you're smart too. Come on in. Care for some coffee?"

"That would be great."

"Dora, what'd you say about the National Guard?"

She gave George a look like he was interrupting. "Homeland Guard, George. They've put the country on Orange or Yellow Alert or some such thing and told the Homeland Guard to prepare for deployment."

"That can't be good," he mumbled, staring bleakly out at his charred fields.

Five minutes later, Linda was sitting at a pine slab table in what passed for the dining room in the McNary's little home that seemed even smaller for all the things they had crammed into it. The furniture was all but stacked one piece on top of the other. Family photos and mementos covered every flat surface. Pans were hung on hooks from the ceiling in the adjoining cubbyhole kitchen. A nine-inch, pink plastic television tuned to CNN at low volume whispered from between stacks of dishes on the counter. A tiny fan spun on top of the refrigerator—while out the two north side windows, the expanse of burnt wheat stretched off to the horizon—the epitome of wide-open space. It was pretty much the exact opposite of Linda's sparsely furnished apartment in wall-to-wall Georgetown.

Dora brought a fresh brewed pot of coffee to the table. George pushed an old computer and keyboard off to the side to make room. Dora filled three cups and passed them around.

"Here you go, darlin'." Dora moved George's straw hat to reveal the cream and sugar.

"Thank you." Linda poured a little cream into her coffee and took a sip. "Just what I needed."

Linda turned on the recorder and adjusted the recording levels. There was a stiff moment of silence, George staring at her, then turning to the tiny pocket tape recorder and its blinking red light. Linda looked at Dora, then George, and began. "How long have you been a farmer, Mr. McNary?"

George stared down at his coffee. "All my life. This place was Dora's family's." Then looking up. "Almost thirty years, I suppose." He glanced at his wife and kind of grinned at the idea of being interviewed.

"How's the farming been?"

"Goin' back through Dora's family." He paused to pull a can of smokeless tobacco from the back pocket of his jeans and place it on the table. "This farm's produced as good a crop of wheat as any in the area." His brow furrowed. "The last five, six years, though, we've had a drop off in production. That is, bushels per acre." He turned his head to stare soberly out the window at the blacken fields. "This land is suffering. Some say we've been farmin' it too hard."

"How's that?"

George took a deep breath. He clearly wasn't comfortable talking like this. He reached for his can of snoose. "Just workin' it too hard. Too much fertilizer. Pushin' year in year out to get maximum yield. The land's worn out."

"How are the finances?"

"Dora does the books." He looked down and used his thumb nail to pry the lid off the green and white tin of Skoal.

"We do all right," said Dora with some defensive pride. George pinched a load of snoose between brown stained finger tips and pressed it into the gums behind his lower lip. He closed up the tin as though his part of the interview was over and got up from the table to check the news on TV.

"George sometimes takes work from other farmers to help out," said Dora, touching her chin self-consciously where a few long gray hairs hinted of the change of life. "I've been workin' a part-time job at Penny's in Tulsa for ten years. Otherwise, we couldn't make it." She took a glance at George in the kitchen. "A lot of farm families got someone working somewheres else." She stared at Linda, knowing she had no idea what life was like out there. In her makeup and Fifth Avenue clothes, Linda looked like a different species than Dora. "We done some shufflin' of mortgages and stretch out our dollars as far as we can. But we got all we need." Dora talked to the tape recorder as though she was telling her life story.

"How difficult a decision was it to burn your fields, George?"

George, a few feet away in the kitchen, staring at the tube, turned his head so he was looking at Dora with sad, troubled eyes. Neither of them said anything for a few moments. They were uneasy with the attention. Finally, George spoke, "Easy as lightin' a match." His tone belied the words.

"You worried at all?"

George didn't respond to that one. Dora filled in the blank. "No more than usual."

"What happens, Mr. McNary, if the strike doesn't get what you want?"

George looked straight at Linda. "I guess we lose the farm." He looked down at the floor.

"Then what?"

"Depends on how much we get paid back by the union for our losses."

"What if that's nothing?"

"Move to Tulsa." George drifted over to the sink and opened the window a little wider.

"You don't think it will work, Miss Bennett," said Dora. It sounded more like an accusation than a question.

"I don't know," Linda replied, feeling the fear behind Dora's slow Oklahoma drawl. "Getting your story and other farmers' stories out to the American public might help. Not too many people living in the city understand. I think that works against you."

"Why would you care?"

"I think government farm policy is wrong and has been for a long time. It might be too late to fix it. But I admire what you folks are trying to do. It's a David and Goliath story. That's how I see it. It's the little guys against the big guys."

Dora's eyes hardened. "Is this just a story to you? An opportunity to get some attention as a writer?"

"Well, of course, to some extent. But not entirely. I've been writing about this since the market upheaval in the spring, and the more I've written the more it's meant to me. I think the farmers need some good PR."

"PR?"

"Public relations. Someone telling their side of the story."

George picked a cup out of the sink. He drooled a little wet snoose into it.

Reluctance stilled the room. Linda pressed on. "How'd you get involved in the strike?"

"Forest Mahan," said Dora.

"I think she's interviewing me, Dora." George came back over to the table, sat down, and began fumbling with his can of snoose again.

Linda noticed there were several red sores on the back of George's hands. "Is that right, George? The idea for a strike began with Forest Mahan."

"Yeah, but I don't think it would have happened without Colonel Cromwell."

"How's that?"

"You'd have to meet him, Miss Bennett. He's just got that good solid feel to him. The whole thing seemed kind of fanciful to me until I saw him stand up in front of the group there in Pratt, not more than ten, eleven days ago. When he said *strike,* it felt like we were doin' somethin' right away." George nodded twice for emphasis and proof of what he was saying.

"But it was Mahan who started it. Ever since he's been President of the National Grange, he's been workin' on us."

"How's that, Dora?"

"The grange used to be like a souped-up square dance club until Forest took over. He's a real smart man. I hope you get a chance to interview him. He's the guy to talk to. He got us all computerized and emailed up."

"Dora, we've had the computers all along."

"Well, Forest got everybody usin' em."

"And he's running the strike now?"

"Along with Colonel Cromwell," said George. "Mahan is the brains, but Cromwell, he's the heart and soul of this strike. That's who you should interview. He'd make a good story."

"I hope I get a chance to talk to both men." Linda took a sip of coffee, recalling the moment the President had passed the note to her. "What do you think of this announcement to ready the Homeland Guard, Mr. McNary?"

"Pretty much figured it'd come to that. Ain't good though. Don't much like being called a terrorist."

"It don't matter what that damn President Kenaghy says," added Dora. "We'll do what we gotta do."

"You don't like President Kenaghy?"

"Can't trust any of those people in Washington," sneered Dora. Linda lowered her eyes knowing she'd just said she was from Washington. "They don't care about us. They don't know nothing about farm life. And Kenaghy's just more of the same."

"Hard to tell what a man like that's thinking," finished George. "One day he's one way. Next day he's another way. Don't much like'm."

"George, are those burns on your hands from the fire?"

George looked down at his hands on the table. He held the tin of snoose in a loop of forefingers and thumbs. "No."

"Chemical burns, Miss Bennett. Damn cancer is what it is. Handling all them pesticides when he oughta be wearin' gloves."

George put his hands beneath the table. "Dora, it ain't cancer."

Dora shook her head. "Don't believe a word of it, missy."

George's eyes suddenly widened. "Dora, turn it up." Nathaniel Cromwell's face was on the TV screen. "They're talking about Cromwell."

Dora didn't have to get up. She extended one of her pendulous arms to the edge of the kitchen counter, turned up the volume, then twisted the little black and white TV around so all could see. The screen was split. A reporter was standing before a partly burned farmhouse, while the newscaster in Atlanta was asking the reporter questions about the firebombing. There was an overhead shot of the house and another of three swastikas cut in the cornfields. Then the reporter spoke of Mary Cromwell's death.

"Goddamn," cursed George. He got up in his agitation and paced out into the living room, then came back as the newscaster rhetorically asked, "Who could have done this horrible thing?"

"Chicken-shit CIA, that's who. Or the FBI." George grumbled and stomped out of the room to light up a cigarette.

Dora turned to Linda. "Is something like that really possible, Miss Bennett? The CIA, I mean. With the swastikas and all? Or is that just us paranoid farmers?"

Linda thought of the two men trailing her at the airport. "Mrs. McNary, I'm not really sure—but it's something I'll certainly be looking into."

Out in the living room, George McNary cursed again. "Damn them government men."

CHAPTER 63

Atossa Andreas sat on the edge of her bed in her white silk dressing gown, staring at the telephone in her left hand. The fingers of her right hand played up and down the edges of her deck of Tarot cards stacked on the table beside the bed. It was Wednesday, eleven days since her gala party and her introduction to Derek Davis. A piece of paper with his phone number written on it lay on her lap. The patch of skin on her cheek had healed considerably in the last two days, and she felt good enough about herself to venture a call to the basketball player.

Most of Atossa's phone conversations were conducted through the sound system in her room. But her bedside phone was secure and reserved for personal calls. With her right hand still on the Tarot cards, she punched in Davis' phone number with her left thumb. Her heart was beating so rapidly she could feel it in her ears. She held the phone out in front of her, listening to it ring at the other end. After the third ring, she brought the receiver up close to her ear. The phone rang one more time before a recording came on. She listened long enough to hear the recorded voice and assure herself that it was indeed Davis, then hung up.

Atossa sat there with her heart pounding in her chest like a bass drum, waiting for her anxiety to pass, then put the phone aside and stood up. She walked halfway across the room and faced her mirror from a distance. She stared at the young woman in the mirror. It really was a miracle. She'd been given back twenty-five years on the outside, but there was no denying she was still the same fifty-seven-year-old woman on the inside, and the contradiction of the "in" and the "out" was unsettling in subtle ways, especially to a woman as obsessive as Atossa. There had been chilling moments in the last few days when she felt certain she was sharing her room with another woman.

In his plush office high above Wall Street, Frank Nelson, just back from Phoenix, and John McClay, up from Washington, had the audience of the Vice President of the United States, Stephen Pentecoste. Pentecoste looked Wall Street. His white hair, parted and neatly combed, was so thin you could see through it. He wore rimless glasses and looked stiff and formal in his black suit. At sixty years old, the veteran senator from Georgia was the forgotten man in the Kenaghy administration.

Frank sat behind his desk, mission control as he often referred to it. McClay lay back in a soft black leather armchair to the left of Frank's desk. Pentecoste was on the right in a matching black chair. He sat with his legs crossed and his hands folded across the knee of the uplifted leg, the foot flicking with uneasiness.

"Kenaghy got TES today," said Frank, looking at Pentecoste. "Any chance he'll sign it?"

"Not from what I've heard."

"How do you feel about that, Stephen?" asked McClay.

"Par for the course," answered the Vice-President. He knew the situation and that Frank and John had him up there for a reason, but he wasn't quite sure what it was. "What's next from your side?"

"Perhaps an override or we wait for Congress to reconvene at the end of the summer." McClay wore a dark brown suit, a pink and white striped shirt with a white collar, and a red rep tie.

"And push for a motion to impeach," added Frank.

Pentecoste was a smart man, perhaps a little too polished and a little too upper class, but he knew this was being talked about. "On what grounds?"

"National security," said Frank. "There was another hit on the Eurasian pipeline yesterday. And here's our President deliberately dragging his feet on the most important bill of his term. It's irresponsible. The entire Congress is with us. Everyone in his cabinet is as well. And he's in there holed up on his own."

"I was under the impression you were prepared to wait until January, Frank."

"The early polls show Carlson ahead of our wonderful President—forty-three, forty-one, with many undecided. A slow unfolding of the impeachment process through September and October will push those numbers farther apart." Frank grinned in spite of his real angst. "Every little bit helps."

Pentecoste sat back. "Why are you telling me this?"

McClay answered. "If the impeachment process goes through more quickly than expected, we want to know who we're putting in office no matter how short a period of time it is."

Pentecoste didn't like the sound of this, but he was angry at Kenaghy like many others in the administration. "This last year has been the most embarrassing of my entire political career," he said. "And this morning, I witnessed Kenaghy staggering through the White House halls with a bottle of whiskey in his hand. It's a disgrace to be his Vice-President. Maybe six weeks as President would take some of the bad taste out of my mouth. What's in it for me?"

"An ambassadorship anywhere you'd like with the new administration," said McClay.

Several hours had passed. Atossa had not left her room. Her entire day had been consumed by the prospect of talking to Derek Davis. It had taken all of this time to compose herself after her first attempt. As before, she sat on the edge of her bed, the phone in her lap, cutting her Tarot deck—until the two of cups appeared. Her heartbeat suddenly doubled. Her body washed over with a warm flush. Her bowels felt fluid.

Still holding the cards in her right hand, Atossa picked up the phone with her left hand and punched in the numbers with her thumb. Beside herself with anxiety in anticipation of speaking to Davis, she listened to the phone ring. Once, twice, three, four times. The recorded voice came on. She hung up the phone, deeply committed to not leaving a message and not leaving her number. Because in no way did she want him calling her at random. She could not be waiting for him to call. That would be too much.

CHAPTER 64

Upon release from the hospital on Wednesday afternoon, Nate and Will, against all hospital protocol, and with absolutely no resistance, put Mary's body, enclosed in a body bag, in their pickup and returned to the farm. After briefly assessing the damage to the house, the father and son adjourned to the big barn to build a coffin for her. Nate, his burned arms bandaged for protection from infection, said absolutely nothing while he and Will went about the carpentry.

When they were done and had placed her in the wooden box, Will asked, "Dad, we can't bury her without some further preparation of the body, can we?"

"For an ordinary burial there would be an embalming process, but your grandmother wanted to be cremated and have her ashes mixed in with the soil of our farm." Nate paused, thinking about it. "Tomorrow morning that's what we'll do."

Will had a few more things he wanted to ask his father, but the pain he saw in him was harder to take than what he felt for the loss of his grandmother, and he decided to let his questions go for the time being. He followed Nate outside to the silo beside the big barn, and the two of them climbed the fifty-foot ladder to the top.

The afternoon wind was up, as it hadn't been in many days, and though there was little chance of rain, the usually blank blue sky was moving with enormous, billowy thunderheads, gliding in out of the west and stacking up over the prairie like great airy freighters of forgetfulness. Perched atop the silo, the father and son could see many tens of miles in all directions, looking out at what had once been boundless grassland grazed by giant herds of buffalo and antelope, but was now cultivated in twenty-acre tracts. As from the masthead of an imaginary prairie schooner, sailing frothless waves of gently rolling fields of wheat and corn, the grieving pair took in the overwhelming view, saying nothing, allowing the meaning of the deed they had just completed to conjoin with the wide open.

After a while, Nate broke the silence, pointing out the swastika he'd found cut in the corn and two more he hadn't known about in the fields to the south.

"What do those swastikas mean, Dad?" asked Will. "I know the history, but why are they here in our fields?"

Nate adjusted himself on the ladder so he could sit. "I suppose they're meant as calling cards, Will. When we accepted the militia into the strike, we took on quite a few extremists—people who are looking for more than a strike."

"But why would anyone want to leave a clue to their identity? And why would the militia target us?"

"I might not be radical enough for some of them. They want secession. They want civil war." He paused and looked out upon the profound expanse of farmland. "But there's also a chance those swastikas," continued Nate, still gazing off into the distance, "were meant to mislead us or create a split in the union." Will watched his father's face as he spoke. "Whoever it was, they were waiting for me last night." He sighed, thinking of his mother. "Instead, they got Mary."

Will looked down at his hands, gripping the silo's ladder.

Nate turned back into Will's silence. He put a bandaged hand on his son's shoulder. "Should I get out of this damn strike, Will?" He let the question hold for a moment, studying his son's eyes. "There's every chance you could lose me. Or I could lose you. Or it could somehow screw up your chance to go to Stanford. Is it really worth it?" He paused again, poignantly. "Maybe you should stay with your mother in Milwaukee until this is over."

Will looked up with watering eyes and pursed his lips trying to contain his emotions. With the wind blowing in his face, lifting his brown hair off his forehead, he looked even younger than his eighteen years. "I was there, Dad," he said. "I heard you talking with Grandma that day after you came back from Missouri. She said you were clearly the best man to lead the strike." He wiped away the tears mounting in the corners of his eyes. "We're all farmers out here, Dad. Granddad was and so was his family. Maybe I'd rather go to college, be a lawyer or something other than a farmer, but I know the life. And I understand the situation enough to know it's not fair. It's not the way it's supposed to be." He tried to grin and muster some bravado. "We can't be frightened by this. These people are our people." His young eyes spiked with his new pain and anger. "And I know for sure Grandma wouldn't want you to quit for her. Same for me, Dad. Even if I have to put off going to school a year or two, I'm with you."

Nate needed to hear this. All morning he'd felt like hiding, running away from the craziness. He'd seen a lot of death in his time. A lot of mutilated and burned bodies. But seeing that same kind of ugly death happen to his mother—on their property—*instead of him!*—had taken him to the edge. As badly as he felt, and despite all the emotion he felt coming from his son and welling up in him, he pushed it aside. "Yeah, I think you're right about Grandma." He turned his gaze out on the Great Plains. "I guess we both need to get a little tougher for this one." He turned back to look into his son's face. He saw his mother's eyes in Will's. "Can you do it, Will?"

Will had run through this one already. "I'm the son of a famous war hero, Dad. I don't believe I have a choice."

James Peabody's pickup came wheeling into the yard as Will and Nate were coming down off the silo. Peabody climbed from his truck slowly and approached the colonel and his son with deliberate tentativeness. No one said anything at first. Not even a *howdy* until Peabody broke the uneasy spell. "Got the bad news from Eddie the fireman, Nate."

Nate nodded.

"Sue scooted me over here. Thought you boys might need a good meal tonight."

"Yeah, probably, James. Our kitchen's quite a mess." All three of them turned to the charred half of the house.

"Not to mention the cook," said Peabody, hanging his head, his voice catching in his throat, awkwardly reaching out to hug his friend. "I'm very sorry, Nate, Will. I'm very sorry about this."

"Yeah." Nate kicked at the dirt with his work boot. Will had to look away and wipe his eyes.

There was another long spell of silence. Nate spoke first this time. "They tell you I also got a couple three swastikas cut in my field last night."

"Yeah. That got out too, Nate. I guess a television crew flew over while you were still at the hospital. How are you? The burns and all?"

"I'll be okay." Along with the burns on his arms, there were two on his face—a wide diagonal streak on his left cheek and a round blister on his forehead. They were slick with ointment.

"Who'd ya think did it?"

Again, Nate immediately thought of the young man at the grange hall. "I don't know. My head's still kind of screwed up. I was thinking of digging around in the burn and those swastikas to see if I could find some kind of clue. Might be some help. I don't know." His mood was somber and detached.

"Hear about the Homeland Guard?"

"Oh, kinda, James. I need to get ahold of Forest. I just…you know…"

"Yeah, I know. I called him after I found out. He sends his regrets."

Nate nodded a thanks. "I'll call him as soon as I get an angle on this stuff here."

"You thinking of giving up the strike, Nate? No one would blame you."

Nate scratched the back of his head, so his cap lifted up from behind and the brim dipped over his eyes. "Don't think Mary will let me out of this now."

Peabody nodded this time. "Well, I ain't gonna bother you anymore. Come on over whenever you want. Sue'll have something good."

Nate turned a forlorn smile to his son. "Hungry, Will?"

"Not so much, Dad."

"We better have something."

Will stared at the ground.

"We'll be there in a bit, James."

"Whenever, Nate." Peabody walked away and climbed into his truck.

Nate and Will walked through the burned-out portion of their house wordlessly, kicking through the wet char, looking for remnants of the firebomb, hoping for any kind of hint as to who might have done it. After an hour, Nate couldn't stand being there any longer. The thought of his mother caught in the fire, the image of her rolling on the floor in flames was too much for him. He and Will climbed into the Power Wagon and drove over to Peabody's farm.

Sue Peabody served a big chicken dinner with dumplings and white gravy, corn on the cob, and fresh tomato slices in vinegar and oil. Nate ate heavily. Will kind of picked at his plate. Jenny Foster was there too.

She'd been staying at the Peabody's since Tom's death. This second tragedy hit her as hard as anyone. She took only the smallest portions of food. For all the energy she'd put into the meal, Sue didn't eat much either. Her eyes were red with the crying she'd done while cooking. All was silent except for the little fan on the sideboard and the clink of the silverware on the plates.

James pulled out a bottle of Dickel Brothers sour mash after the table was cleared and poured a shot all around, even gave Will a shot over a couple ice cubes. They retired to the den to check out the six o'clock news and see what the rest of the nation was thinking about the farmers' strike.

They mentioned two more pipeline bombings in Kazakhstan, but the focus was on the strike. The big news being the Homeland Guard announcement. They had long shots of Homeland Guard posts, followed by close-ups of young men in olive drab, readying gear, cleaning rifles, stuffing backpacks. Then Paul Houseman speaking: "This grain is more than just the foundation of the American economy. It's our national security. Destroying it is tantamount to an act of war." Cromwell stood up and left the room.

When he returned, the Reverend Billy Grant was being interviewed. "We all feel for the plight of the farmer. Times are hard. But burning the fields is not the answer," he proclaimed with a Bible in his left hand. "Tilling the land is God's work and a noble and honorable profession. But to waste the fruit of the garden is immoral and a sin. All of you farmers out there, trust the Lord. He will look out for you, but not if you turn away from His Word."

The respected newscaster Harold Hoerner, somber and authoritative, came next: "The Agriculture Department has just released a survey of U.S. commercial grain reserves. They are confident that no one but the farmers will feel the effects of their strike."

Jenny turned to James. "That isn't true, is it?"

He shook his head no. "Be sure they know we're watching, Jenny. Doing their best to make us think we have no chance at all."

"Well, they're doing a good job on me," she replied, turning back to the television and the face of a woman reporter standing out front of the Cromwell farm. The image caused her to look at Nate. For all their mutual pain, neither one had been able to say word one to the other all evening. "I'm sorry, Nate," said Jenny softly. Nate communicated what he could through the expression in his eyes. It matched hers.

"Early this morning," began the TV reporter, "a firebomb struck the home of Colonel Nathaniel Cromwell, leader of the Nonpartisan Farmers' Alliance." A close-up showed the back of the house, followed by an aerial view of the farm and the three swastikas cut in the fields. "Police here locally are pointing to the radical right and the militia, people who were initially aligned with the Farmers' Alliance. Many suspect that there is a rift in the movement and trouble ahead for the strikers. People close to the movement say Cromwell will pull out."

"Christ-all-fucking-mighty." Nate got up and walked out of the room for a second time. James followed him into the kitchen. Nate was standing at the sink, staring northward over Peabody's soybean crop toward his farm.

"What are we going to do, Nate? They aren't going to give us a chance."

Nate spoke without turning around. "It was a setup, James." Then he faced his neighbor. "It might not do much good, but if I get nothing else out of this strike," he slammed his fist on the counter. "I'm going to find out who bombed my house and killed Mary. So help me, God."

After a moment, Nate pulled one of the throwaway phones from his pocket and punched in Mahan's number.

"Forest. This is Cromwell."

"Been hoping you'd call. I'm so sorry to hear about your mother. How are you?"

"I'll make it. Just watched the six o'clock news with Peabody. I want you to know that I have no intention of pulling out of this thing. If anything, my resolve is firmer set."

"I'd heard reports, but figured the straight poop could only come from you."

"Yeah, well, it's a bitch. Especially with this terrorist, act of war crap. Hell of a way to treat a labor strike."

"Not to mention calling out the Homeland Guard."

"No kidding. What have you heard from Hayes?"

"I spoke with him early this morning. Right after word of the firebombing got out. You can guess what he's saying."

"Yeah. Any communication with the government?"

"Nothing worth mentioning."

"Look, Forest, I'm assuming someone wants me out of this strike real bad. So I gotta go underground. I'll be in touch, but I won't be easy to find. I'll contact Hayes as soon as I can."

"What are you going to tell him?"

"Continue as planned." Nate heard Mahan sigh on the other end. "Forest, they aren't even talking to us. What other choice do we have?"

"I know."

"I'll call again tomorrow."

The Peabodys offered Nate and Will a bedroom in their house for the night, but Nate turned them down. He felt it was important to be at his place. "No thanks, James, Sue, we can't give in to this. Will and I can sleep out in the big barn. Might have to trade off guard duty. But we'll be okay."

And that's what they did. They got bedding out of the house and made two bunks in the office at the back of the barn. Nate dug into the barn's loft and retrieved a couple M-14's he stashed there years ago. The two of them sat up for two hours, cleaning and oiling the guns. About ten, he sent Will to bed. That began a short night of three-hour shifts, sleeping and standing watch. About a quarter to eleven, Nate stood out in the center of the yard and punched a few numbers into another of his disposable cell phones. He looked up into the sky while it rang—as though he might see a reconnaissance satellite.

"Yeah? Who is it?" asked the sleepy voice at the other end.

"That you, Rusty?" The air was filled with the bittersweet smell of wet, burned wood and ripening corn.

"Fuck, Boss. I heard it on the news tonight. I tried to call."

"I ain't easy to reach. Now get your ass down here."

There was a pause at the other end. "Give me twenty-four hours."

"Can you make it by morning?"

There was another pause. "I'll start packing now. You okay?"

"No."

"How about the kid?"

"As you would expect. We'll talk in person."

"Yeah."

Cromwell turned off the phone and threw it as far as he could into the corn fields, then pulled out another of his ten dollar specials. He punched in the number of Lena Davenport. She lived in California, was married, and had two children. It wasn't quite nine there. She answered the phone.

"Lena. This is Nate."

"Sorry, Colonel. I saw the news."

"Yeah. I have *one simple message.*" It was code for what he'd described in the letter he sent her. She was to connect with Paul Priestly in St. Louis.

"Got it."

"I'll be in touch."

"Yes, sir."

Nate had just initiated the last thing in the world he'd wanted to do. A fail-safe plan that no one would know about but Priestly and Davenport. They were going to plant cell phone activated explosives in fifteen grain elevators along the length of the Mississippi. He couldn't believe it had come to this. Hopefully he wouldn't have to use them. He threw the phone the opposite direction he'd thrown the other one. Then he just stared up at the moon, not sure if he wanted to cry or howl.

CHAPTER 65

Bob Richards entered the Secretary of Defense's office in the Old Executive Building late Wednesday night and closed the door behind him. He had a large manila envelope in his hand. Lawrence Fitzgerald sat in his wheelchair at his desk reading a report. The blackout shades were pulled behind him. A desk lamp provided the only light in the otherwise dark office. Fitzgerald didn't look up. Richards took the empty chair in front of the desk.

"We got lucky with this kid Mayfield, Fitz. The Development Bank of Asia has hired him as a consultant."

Fitzgerald lifted his eyes slowly from the report. His look was grim and brooding. "First they kidnap him then they hire him. What's that mean?"

"I think they realized how talented this kid is."

"And how does it help us?"

"We couldn't have done better with a plant. I had one of our agents seed him with the names of the Teochui Kongsi. If he's as sharp as he is gullible, he'll be knee deep into their records before another week is out. But if he makes a wrong move, if they discover what he's doing." Richards' eyes squeezed into narrow slits. "They'll kill him in a heartbeat."

Fitzgerald leaned forward so his forearms laid flat on his desk. "I wonder what inspired him to work for DBA?"

"Beats me, Larry. He's a freakin' kid with rings through his eyebrow for Christ sake. Either they made him an incredible offer and he's legitimately with them. Or he's on his own trying to decipher the Asian commodities market. Or shit who knows what? In any case we can use him."

"Is this a laundering operation, Bob?"

"That's the working assumption. We clogged some of the DBA's outlets during the winter, hoping to give a little advantage to our friends in Central Asia. Everyone's looking for new ways to launder their drug profits." Richards gave Fitz a smart-ass smile. "The commodities market makes sense."

"Any advantage for us?"

"The worst of times are the best of times."

"What do you know about those recent pipeline bombings?"

"We brought our guy back to the states a couple of weeks ago, so I guess that means the extremists are on their own now."

"Could they become a problem?"

"Is there still an Islamic Jihad?" said Richards with a cynical chuckle. "Yeah, they're dangerous. But we know who they are and where they live. They are perfectly expendable cutouts."

Fitzgerald nodded and looked down at the work on his desk.

"How's the TES business going?" asked Richards.

"Kenaghy got the bill this morning. I'm sure he'll make it a waiting game. We need more leverage in Kazakhstan."

"With a little luck, Mayfield's our ticket to the inside workings of a big daddy kongsi. And what doesn't come out of the Golden Triangle comes out of Central Asia."

"What's your read on Mendelev's inner circle?"

"Russian mafia through and through. Might be the most corrupt region in the entire world."

"Worse than Beijing?"

"Worse than Washington, D.C., Fitz." Richards grinned ugly. He put the ten by thirteen manila envelope on Fitzgerald's desk. The Hamilton Heavy Construction trademark was stamped in the upper left-hand corner. "We have several ways to grease that pipeline complex in Eurasia. Stock options don't require a transaction record. The Kazakhs could use some grain." He paused as a way to prompt Fitzgerald.

"And?"

"Mendelev wants a nuclear device."

Anger swelled behind Fitzgerald's eyes. Why would Richards even mention this? Instead of exploding, he pushed on. "What's the relationship between the Russian mafia and the Teochui syndicate?"

"That's the Mayfield option I mentioned." Richards gnashed his teeth saying the words. "There's a lot of overlapping turf. Where we determine the swing."

Fitzgerald stared at this man he'd never liked. Richards' generation was different, arrogant and self-centered. His was a nobler cause.

Richards grinned into Fitzgerald's stare, then stood. "It's all in the report, Fitz."

"One more thing, Bob." The N-bomb was still boiling in his gut.

"Yeah?" Richards' hand was on the doorknob to go out.

"Who firebombed Cromwell's farm?"

Richards' arrogance washed away. "Haven't a clue, sir."

Fitzgerald suddenly realized how little he trusted this man. "Horrible mistake."

Richards pulled open the door. "That they did it? Or that they missed the target?"

Fitzgerald frowned.

Richards gave him a mock salute and walked out.

Fitzgerald hated this kind of attitude. But he knew the world was corrupt. The drugs, the money laundering, the banking schemes. Just as there must be a public world of statesmanship and diplomacy, there must also be an underworld. One could not facilitate the workings of *realpolitik* in the public world if one didn't also participate with facility in the underworld. Heroin and cocaine had become inseparable from covert action. Black money was grease for intelligence operations. He may not like it, but he was a realist. Crime was a way to political and economic advantage, a dark means to a justified end in a difficult world. He'd breathe a lot easier when the U.S. military had a solid presence in Central Asia.

CHAPTER 66

It was late Thursday night in Singapore. Jonathan Mayfield sat at the bar in the Hilton lounge looking out on the luxurious three-story lobby. His hands rested on either side of a fresh pint of Guinness capped with half an inch of thick malt froth. It was his third. *The New York Financial Times* lay folded on the seat to his left. The Filipino Supremes were off to his right, again the night's entertainment, singing, at this moment, the ancient Shangri-La hit *Leader of the Pack*.

Jonathan, in his own brilliant, piecemeal way, had envisioned the entire grain scheme. Like painting by numbers, one color at a time, the little, irregular dabs of data were creating depth and perspective. He'd spent the evening running scenarios on his laptop, reading internet news updates, and tracking the markets. Due to the field burnings, wheat was up a dollar ninety a bushel since Monday. Corn, soybeans, and rice were up but not as much. World grain reserves were desperately below the sixty-day security mark, and American farmers were holding a lit match to a critical portion of the world's exportable grain. To a speculator, this was an incredibly interesting predicament.

As best Jonathan could determine, without having access to Linton's wonderful mainframe and his array of programs, the grain market was headed for a standoff in the United States. If you included soybeans, the world grain harvest peaked at two billion tons in the 1990s and had varied little since. About three-quarters of that went to market where it was grown. The remaining 500 million tons was split between security reserves and export.

Due to the Asian shortfall, this year's world harvest was likely to top out at 1.7 billion tons. Meaning no overstock and something like two to three hundred million tons of grain for export. The Teochui syndicate owned approximately half of that grain—stored in elevators around the Pacific Rim or in yet to be redeemed futures contracts. Andreas Grain's position was almost as strong. Even after the huge reserve stock dump in the spring, Andreas still held maybe forty million tons of last year's grain in elevators along the Mississippi and another hundred million tons in futures. All other distributors, figured Jonathan, owned less than ten million tons in elevators and perhaps fifty million tons of grain as futures.

Nearly all those two hundred and fifty million tons of wheat, corn, and soybeans held by the Teochui, Andreas, and other distributors as futures were in the ground, nearing harvest, in the United States. Half of that was owned by industrial farms managed by agribusiness or the distributors themselves. The remaining one hundred twenty-five million tons needed to fill those contracts grew on family farms.

So, what did it really mean for the American farmers to hold out for a better cut? A lot. They controlled something like a third of all the available grain!

There was no real precedent for this situation. In the mid-1970s, amid the Great Russian Grain Robbery, as it was called, the world faced severe grain shortages, but they paled in comparison to what was going on now. Should the American farmers decide to burn their entire crop, many distributors would fail, but even worse, large portions of Africa and the Subcontinent would face extended famine conditions. It was possible no one in the world understood this situation on the sixteenth day of July better than the twenty-six-year-old computer freak sitting at the bar in the Singapore Hilton, clutching his pint of Guinness like he held the international market place together with his bare hands.

As Jonathan lifted this pint and sucked some of the pale brown froth off the black beer, grain market numbers swirling in his head, he noticed through the mirror a cluster of four well-dressed Asian men entering the lobby, headed to the restaurant. He turned slightly in his seat, keeping the glass to his mouth, and affirmed, his heart suddenly pounding, that one of the men was indeed the silver-haired Teochui kingpin Zhao He.

Sipping his Guinness and observing through the mirror, Jonathan watched the four men get immediate attention from the maître d' and be seated at the same table Zhao He had been at the night Dan the Hippie had pointed him out. Jonathan stayed at the bar, slowly working on what he'd determined would be his last Guinness of the night, thinking and watching Zhao He.

As Jonathan tipped his Guinness for its last swill, a thin clean-shaven man in a business suit, perhaps an electronics salesman, took the stool to his right. Jonathan's attention was in the mirror, and he took little notice of this man until he heard the word *tah-kee-la* and the snap of a shot glass on the bar beside him. He immediately turned.

"Evening Jonathan," said the man beside him.

"Do I know you?"

The man smiled and nodded ever so slightly.

"I don't recall our meeting."

"No?" The man pushed aside his tie, undid two buttons in the center of his dress shirt, and opened it just enough to reveal a red t-shirt with the words *American Holocaust* inscribed across it.

"Dan?"

The American smiled. "You didn't happen to find a computer disk I dropped here last week, did you?"

"You got my message."

"That's right."

"But your beard? Your hair? What's going on?"

Dan gave a glance to the restaurant across the lobby. "Things necessitated a change."

The three pints of Guinness had loosened Jonathan's usual reserve. "I looked at that disk, Dan."

Dan's eyebrows bobbed once. "What'd you find?"

"Well, many of the names on your list—including Zhao He's—appear in the DBA's account records."

"That's no surprise. You're working for one of the largest money laundering operations in the world. DBA is Teochui owned—as is this hotel."

Jonathan looked through the mirror at the restaurant across the lobby, then back to Dan. Dan nodded.

"When I got your phone message, Jonathan," continued Dan, "I decided not to get back to you for fear of dragging you into this. There was a threat against my life, and I had a little scrambling to do." He took a quick glance over his shoulder. "Then I began to wonder if maybe your curiosity might get the better of you."

"It did," said Jonathan. He told Dan about the Teochui connection to the grain buy and the story he'd been waiting several days to tell someone.

"Damn," said Dan. "I wonder if they were using the commodities market as a way to launder their drug profits. What a scoop that would be," he said excitedly.

Jonathan understood immediately that Dan's surmise hit the nail square on the head.

Dan leaned over a little closer to him. "What chance do I have of getting a little peek into DBA's financial records?"

Jonathan's eyes went big.

"Forget it, Jonathan. Forget all of this. It's dangerous."

But the well lubricated Jonathan was tempted. "What would you do with that kind of information?" Despite the beer, he clearly remembered being hauled off the streets of London and stuck in an eight-by-ten room for three months. A little revenge was surely justified. "What would it do for your story?"

"Everything." Dan took a drink from his beer chaser. "But I would only use the most general interpretation of the information in my writing—nothing that could give you away. I just want to get the way they work out in public—and show some of the details to my publisher to back my story. Who knows, I might even be able to get back to you with some information about the relationship between the money laundering and the grain."

Jonathan didn't know what to say. It would be dangerous. But helping Dan was also a way of fighting black market drugs. "I need to think about this."

"I hear you. These guys are no fun." Dan again lifted his beer and took a long confident swallow, his eyes in the mirror watching the men in the restaurant.

"How long are you going to be in Singapore, Dan?"

"That depends on you."

Jonathan took a deep breath. "How do I know who you are? And that this isn't a setup of some kind? DBA testing my loyalty?"

Dan laughed. "Like an American hippie journalist is going to be working for the Teochui? Give me a break, man." Dan leaned over a little closer to Jonathan. His eyes grew serious. "Don't worry about me. You know what I'm doing is a good thing. You're on the right side. Besides, none of what I'll write will reach the public for six months at the earliest. And the way I'll write the story, it won't even be evident that I got into their records. It's cool." He took another glance over his shoulder, then faced Jonathan again, eyes agleam. "Look. Think it over for a couple of days. If you're into it, go to the Night Safari on Mandai Lake Road Saturday night. It opens at seven-thirty. Get there after dark, say nine, and take the tram. Don't look for me. I'll find you."

"I'm not sure about this, Dan. I'm not."

"Then I'll do the safari alone. No biggie." Dan looked up and suddenly stilled. Jonathan followed his eyes to the mirror. Zhao He's foursome was getting up from their table. "I better get out of here before someone thinks I know you," said Dan, throwing down the last of his beer.

"What do you need from the bank?"

Dan suppressed his grin. "Full access. Computer codes. Passwords. Account numbers. The works." In the mirror he watched Zhao He's group walking through the lobby to the front doors. "Catch you at the Night Safari."

Dan placed fifteen Singapore dollars on the bar and meandered out.

CHAPTER 67

Nathaniel Cromwell had the watch in the hours before sunrise Thursday morning. He sat on a stool inside the big barn with the sliding door cracked open. He had an electric coffeepot plugged in on the floor beside him, a cup of coffee in his hand, and an M-14 on his lap. When two headlights turned off the highway and came bouncing down the driveway toward him, he stood up and leveled his M-14 at the windshield.

A red Volkswagen van with a white camper lift-up roof motored into the unlit yard and stopped. The door opened. Cromwell's rifle followed the action. Jerry Rust climbed out. In the dim light, Cromwell didn't recognize him at first and stepped into the open, rifle at the ready.

"Hold it right there."

"Easy, Boss. It's Rust."

Nate lowered the rifle and went out to greet his old Army buddy.

"Thanks for coming. I'm sorry about the gun. I'm getting a little edgy."

Rust gave him a hug then pushed him back to view him at an angle in the dim light. "Nice burns on the face." He turned and looked at the black silhouette of the house. "Whoa."

Nate took a deep breath. "Yeah."

"You know who did it?"

"Just a hunch or two. When the sun comes up, you and I and Will are going to walk through the swastikas they cut in the corn fields and see what we can find. A footprint. A scrap of torn clothing. I don't know." Deeper emotions swam behind the words.

They walked into the barn. "Do I smell coffee?"

"Yeah, right here on the floor. You can use Will's cup."

"*Gracias.*"

"Let's get some breakfast. Sun's coming up. I really do want to comb those fields—for a while anyway." He watched Jerry pour the hot coffee into Will's tin cup. "Then we're getting out of here. They might have missed me this time, but one thing I know for sure—a moving target is a lot harder to hit."

"I'm with ya, Boss. Let's eat."

Will came straggling out of the darkness with Peg trailing after him. "Hey? Who's that, Dad? Who are you talking to?"

Nate smiled fully for the first time in twenty-four hours. "Rusty. This is my son, Will. And Will, this is my old buddy. Lieutenant Colonel Jerry Rust."

Will wore jeans, no socks, no shirt. Kind of a skinny kid. He grinned sticking out his hand. "Proud to meet you, Colonel Rust. I know who you are."

Jerry shook his hand. "None of that military stuff, please. Jerry or just plain Rust is the best way to get my attention."

An hour later, a breakfast in their bellies, the three of them were walking abreast through the second of the three swastikas. They'd walk each leg as a group. Then break up and do each leg and the vicinity individually. There were some footprints, but they were vague in the crushed corn and dry dirt. It appeared that there might have been more than one of them trampling the symbols into the field.

"What are we going to do after this, Dad?"

Nate stopped walking. Rust and Will faced him. Six-foot stalks of young corn surrounded them. An early morning blue sky was overhead. A crow squawked in the distance. "We're getting in Rusty's VW and getting out of here." He gave his son half a grin. "We're going to live on the road, Will. And at every farmhouse we stop, we'll be welcomed and fed. We won't stay anywhere more than overnight. After what's happened, I have to figure somebody wants me dead—and I don't want them getting you by accident—or on purpose."

No one said anything.

"I'll stay abreast of the strike by phone. We'll go to Mahan's tomorrow or the next day and do another video. But we stay nowhere long. Move, move, move. Can you do that, Will? Live on the road with me?"

"Of course, it'd be great."

"How about you, Rusty? You with me?"

Rust nodded. "That's why I'm here."

"Hey, Dad, look at this?" Will bent down and picked something from the mat of corn stalks. "It's the heel to a shoe." He handed it to his father.

"A man's shoe. What'd ya make of this, Rusty?" He handed him the black rubber heel.

Rust lifted his own foot and compared the heel to his own shoe. "Bigger than an eleven. Almost new. Could be government issue."

"Yeah?" Nate looked at the brand name stamped into the center of the heel. "You're right. It could be." He put it in his pocket, and they resumed their search.

They didn't find anything more, and after three hours they'd had enough. When they returned to the yard, James Peabody was there, driving the tractor out of the big barn. "You almost done, Jim?" called Nate as the others pushed out of the corn behind him.

"Yeah, livestock's safe at my place. This is the last piece of machinery you own." Peabody and Horace Thompson had been moving equipment and animals all morning. "Now, you sure, this is what you want to do?"

"It's a statement, James."

Peabody nodded a reluctant agreement and drove the tractor out the driveway.

Nate led Will and Rust into the big barn to Mary's coffin. Together they carried it out of the barn and some distance into the corn fields where they had prepared a pyre. Nate leaned over the pine coffin and, using a black felt pen, wrote his mother's name on the lid in big block letters. Beneath her name, he wrote the date of her birth and the date of her death. Below that, her epitaph: *Politics and farming don't mix.*

With little ceremony, Nate said a quiet, "I'm sorry it had to be this way, Mom," and lit the stack of wood. They watched the flames rise up and encompass the coffin. Nate had to walk away overcome with emotion. Rust patted young Will on the back. But there was no stopping for grief now. The crew of three immediately began a systematic torching of the house, the barns, and the fields, burning the whole damn farm as a parting gesture and graphic statement of what was going on inside Nathaniel Cromwell.

There was a quick transfer of Nate's citizen band radio into Jerry's van, then the three of them climbed into the red VW and headed north on Route 6. They stopped on the side of the road not far from the farm and watched the flames leap up against the sky like that first morning

Cromwell had been awakened by the fire at Foster's place. While they observed the burn, Nate put in a call to Mahan.

He told him the story. "I'm sitting here watching the place burn, Forest. When Foster did his, I thought it was crazy. Now it's no more than a big barbecue."

"I hope not, Nate," said Mahan.

"We'll see," muttered Cromwell.

"When will I see you?"

"I have no plan. It has to be that way. But I'll be by soon. Little or no warning. I want to video another statement. In the meantime, I'll be talking to the farmers and keeping in contact with you and Hayes any way I can. Anything from Washington?"

"I talked to one of Missouri's senators. He told me to hold off on any more burning until Congress convenes in September. I told him that was impossible. Got nothing from agriculture or labor. The distributors are pushing out credit threats."

"Okay. Then it's one day at a time, Forest. Let's see how this Homeland Guard thing plays out. There's a good chance half of them are country boys and might struggle a bit with their orders."

"True enough. Hayes called me this morning. He thinks we have more going for us than the media's letting on. Said he heard last night that the populace is pretty much split—urban and rural. The newspapers are still stuck giving us the deep six." He paused. "But our friend Linda Bennett has a real nice piece in today's *Kansan.* Interviews with a couple farmers in Oklahoma. You might look at it."

"I'll try. Hey, get me some numbers on willing farmers and I'll talk to you later today."

"Sorry about what's come down for you, Nate."

"They will be too." He tossed the phone out into the burning fields, and Jerry pulled back onto the highway headed north.

CHAPTER 68

Linda Bennett tapped lightly on the door to Elizabeth White's office on Thursday afternoon, then pushed the door open a crack. "Ms. White, do you have a moment?"

White sat at her desk reading copy off her computer. "Yes, come in, Ms. Bennett." There wasn't the least bit of warmth in her voice.

Linda stepped into the office and closed the door. "I wanted to thank you for putting my first piece in the paper this morning."

White sat back and crossed her arms. "There's no need for thanks. It was a good piece."

"Well, all along as I wrote it, I was thinking of what you said to me my first day, and I wanted you to like what I was doing."

She gave Linda one of those over-the-top-of-her-reading-glasses looks. "They were good objective interviews. You let the farmers' words carry the story. And you refrained from pushing your own views."

Linda felt like she was being spoken to like a first year journalism student, but let it go. "Thank you."

"I got an email from Frederick this morning. *The Times* will be running it tomorrow. He said he was glad you cut out the rhetoric."

Rhetoric! Manning did not say that, Linda thought angrily, but again contained herself. "I'm hoping to get an interview with the President of the National Grange as soon as I can."

White nodded. "He has some curious ideas."

"He seems quite sharp to me. I'd like to have it for Sunday."

White looked at Linda without blinking. "I'll keep that in mind."

"Please. And thank you again."

White reached over to the left side of her desk to a stack of photos. "You might be interested in this." She picked up a ten by twelve black and white photograph and handed it to Linda

It was an aerial view of a farm. A burning farm. Fields and buildings. "What's this?"

"Nathaniel Cromwell's farm."

She took a second look. "Who did this?"

"He did. It's still burning at this moment. I got this picture a few minutes ago." She paused. "There's speculation he took his life in the fire. His truck is there. You can see it near the building. It's a burned out shell."

"That's not proof."

White shrugged. "Maybe not, but it's what people are saying. You might like to check it out."

Linda went straight from Elizabeth White's office to her rental car in the basement of *The Kansan* building. She didn't believe Cromwell would have taken his life. But things were changing fast, and she felt it was imperative to be there at his farm when the investigation began.

The news of it was just breaking on the local radio stations as Linda drove out of the city—in lock step with the Kansas Homeland Guard. With word of Cromwell's burning his farm, Homeland Security Director Houseman had pushed the terror alert up another notch to red—Severe. The Homeland Guard was being deployed in twenty-five states. Long convoys of personnel carriers, ten, twenty in a row, slowed traffic on the back roads. By the time Linda reached the outskirts of Wichita, individual men with rifles on their shoulders were posted along the edges of the wheat fields, guarding the crops from their owners.

Linda's stomach tightened at the sight of Cromwell's farm as she approached from the south on Route 6. Most of the farm had already burned. Only the distant fields were still in flames. The remains of the house and barns smoldered. Two fire trucks were in the yard. Several cars with news service logos and two television vans were parked at the top of the driveway. The KVTV helicopter circled overhead.

Linda pulled off the highway into the cluster of vehicles. Homeland Guardsmen blocked onlookers and the press from going any further than twenty yards down the drive. She showed the guard captain her press card, and he told her to stay back with the others. She turned it up a notch and demanded to see his superior and got a flat refusal. "Have they found any evidence that Nathaniel Cromwell took his life in the fire?" she asked with building irritation.

"That's classified information, Ms. Bennett."

Linda turned away brusquely and headed back to her rental car. An older, slightly overweight, spectacled farmer, with a scraggly ponytail and a red ball cap, approached her. A three-legged Border Collie trailed behind him.

"Maybe I can help you, miss," said the farmer. "I heard that guardsman refer to you as Ms. Bennett. That the Linda Bennett who wrote the article in today's *Kansan*?"

"That's me," replied Linda half-heartedly.

"My name's James Peabody. I'm one of the neighbors. I enjoyed that piece quite a bit." He extended his hand and smiled.

Linda pushed through her frustration, forced a smile, and took his hand. "Thank you."

"No thanks needed. I'm honored. Us farmers are having a hard time getting our view out to the public, and your article did exactly that."

"That's why it was there." The dog nosed up to her. She patted it on the head "What do you know about this fire?"

"A lot," he said. "I heard your question. Nate didn't take his life. Don't worry about that. But I think he's plenty angry. With every right—if you know what I mean?"

"I do know what you mean. But he's alive?"

"You can count on that."

"Where's he gone?"

Peabody screwed up a grin. "Can't tell you much about that. I think it's a good bet he's gone underground. As a matter of fact, I just heard on the radio that there's an all-points bulletin out calling for his arrest."

"Really?"

"The Homeland Security Director has deemed field burning a federal offense. They're calling him a terrorist."

"Unbelievable," muttered Linda, wondering why there had been no public statement from Kenaghy.

"I'm the county grange rep, Ms. Bennett. If you're gonna do any more writing on the strike, maybe I can help."

Mahan's name immediately popped into her head. "I can use all the help I can get, Mr. Peabody. Maybe we could get together and talk a bit." Linda gave the old boy her best smile. "The sooner the better."

"Well, they're not gonna let us get any closer to the farm, and it's nothing but ashes anyway." He looked out toward the smoldering buildings and the fires on the horizon. Peg was doing the same. "Follow me over to my place and we could talk right now."

"That would be great."

CHAPTER 69

Late that night, James Kenaghy sat on the bed in his bedroom on the second floor of the White House residence, watching the news and sipping whiskey out of a water glass. Marjorie had been gone two full days now and hadn't called.

The President had given a press conference that afternoon to make his first public statement on the grain strike. They printed the time wrong on the President's daily schedule, so he was at the podium ready to speak an hour before the press arrived. It only got worse from there. Nothing went smoothly. People coming in late. Others missing the conference all together. He spent the evening watching the news to see what parts of the conference escaped to the national audience. From what he'd seen and heard in assembled video clips and sound bites, it was impossible to tell what his views of the strike were—pro or con.

As he sat there, stewing about this, he heard the sound of footsteps coming down the hallway. He expected no one. For the way he felt, he hoped it might be an assassin. Suddenly the bedroom's double doors burst open. Marjorie stood in the doorway like a fire on the sun, anger spiking out in all directions like solar flares. She assessed the situation in a nanosecond. The partial bottle of whiskey. The glass in his hand. The TV tuned to CNN. His disturbing body language—barely reacting at all to her sudden appearance.

Marjorie came into the room within a few feet of the bed and surveyed the scene with obvious derision. "Why'd you let that madman Houseman out of his cage?"

Kenaghy looked up at her with palpable indifference.

She shook her head at him. "Severe Alert! Christ, Jim, he's taken this country right out of your hands. What's wrong with you? Have you finally just given up?" That he didn't immediately defend himself incensed her further.

"What was it you were trying to say in that press conference today? You came across like a nitwit as usual. I don't even know what your position is on this stupid field burning stunt. That damn press secretary of yours Wayne what's-his-name is doing one hell of a job for you. You'd think he was working for the Republicans."

A short clip of the President flashed across the TV screen to their left. Kenaghy turned to see himself say, entirely out of context, *We cannot allow ourselves to be blackmailed by the threat of field burning.*

"What exactly did that mean?"

His next line, which was not included, had been *We would be better off answering the farmers' demands than allowing this standoff to continue.* He raised his glass to take another demoralized sip, doing his best to ignore this latest firestorm.

Marjorie stepped forward and slapped the glass out of his hand, sending the glass and the whisky splashing across the bed sheets. "Don't ignore me. What's going on, James? Have you lost it completely?"

Kenaghy looked up at his wife. She was wearing a dress he'd never seen before. She must have gone on a shopping binge in Boston to relieve her angst. "So, what brings you back to the White House?" he asked with a pronounced alcoholic slur.

She glared at him. "That's a damn good question, now that I'm here." His eyes diverted to the fleeting images on the TV screen. She grabbed the remote and quickly snapped off the set, then stuck her face into his. "My mother said I might not want to be the first First Lady to be divorced from an incumbent President." Her voice was full of disdain. "I was thinking historically."

"Maybe that becomes a moot point if I'm impeached," he said with a sideways grin.

The whole scene fell in on Marjorie at this point. She dropped down beside the bed crying. "What's become of our Camelot? What's become of what we had that was so good and so wonderful?"

Kenaghy looked over at her, sitting on her hips, knees together, her new dress pushed up awkwardly over her panty hose, her cheeks running with tears and mascara. She looked awful.

"You won't really be impeached, will you?" She continued to cry. "James, James, speak to me, say something."

"Would you like a drink?"

Her tearing eyes spiked, then let go. "Yes. Please."

He took the bottle off the bedside table and handed it to her. She took it by the neck and turned it up over her head, taking in a startling amount of whiskey. Then she handed it back to him. He took a more modest swallow.

"Christ, Jim," she whined. "Do you believe it took fifteen minutes to pass through security tonight to get into my own home?"

The President gave his wife a sloppy grin and offered her the bottle again. "Yeah, with all those rifles and swat vehicles, I can't tell if they've sealed me *off* or sealed me *in*." His sarcasm was so thick it sounded like paranoia.

"No kidding," said Marjorie. She took another healthy slug from the bottle and handed it back. "Didn't you fire Houseman the other day? Didn't you tell me that? He's running the Homeland Guard like his own private army!"

Kenaghy gave an exaggerated sigh. "Houseman's like J. Edgar Hoover was sixty years ago. He's more than the President. He's an institution—entirely antithetical to the Constitution and the health of the country. I asked him to send me his resignation. And he effectively gave me the finger. This whole damn city has turned against me. That news conference today was a joke." He paused to take another swig from the bottle. "But it's not over yet," he said with a fierceness that Marjorie had forgotten he had. "These farmers have a solid backing. And it's a constituency completely separate from mine." His eyes narrowed. "If I can gather them into my camp, somehow reach their leadership without the media getting involved and screwing it up, there just might be some surprises in this town."

Marjorie didn't quite understand. "What?"

He turned and gave her a look that made her insides quiver. "It ain't over till it's over."

CHAPTER 70

Near noon on Friday, Atossa sat at her divining table alone in her bedroom. She wore a purple silk robe with a matching sash. The yarrow sticks were arranged in piles of threes and fours before her. Her copy of the *I Ching* was open on her lap to the twenty-first hexagram. The upper trigram was *Li*, the clinging fire. The lower trigram, *Chen,* the arousing thunder. These combined to form the hexagram called *Shih Ho* or "biting through." The image was that of a mouth held open by a stick. The first line of commentary told all for Atossa: *When an obstacle to union arises, energetic biting through brings success.*

Atossa stared across the room to her phone by the bed. She had been thinking all morning about the phone. Either hoping it would ring and be Alise or prodding herself to pick it up and try another call to Derek Davis. She faced the mirror on the other side of the room. At a distance of twenty feet, she could barely see the spidery red blemish on her cheek.

She stood from the table and strode to the phone. She had already memorized Davis' number, and she punched it in. The phone rang at the other end four times, her heart beating faster with each ring.

Derek Davis owned a huge mansion in a gated community in South Hampton on Long Island with three hundred feet of beachfront property. A concrete apron stretched the length of the back of the house with a heated pool, two tennis courts, a single basketball hoop, a cabana, and a bar. Davis had made more money in basketball and endorsements than any other athlete in history.

Professional basketball players are some of the best athletes in the world. Speed, grace, agility, and strength. Davis was all of these. He embodied sports royalty and was recognized everywhere he went. He was handsome, witty, and profound. He'd been married twice, had three children, and was now happily one of America's most eligible bachelors.

Beyond his physical attributes, Davis was best known for his competitiveness and the powerful focus of his mind, willing games into victories by sheer determination. The ultimate money player, Davis was at his best against the odds and under pressure. He lived for the heat of battle. Three years retired, he missed that now and spent much of his time on the golf course or challenging old NBA friends to pick-up games in the gym at the east end of his home or playing cards. He loved to gamble. He would bet on anything to heighten the thrill of the action.

This afternoon was no different. Two of his old teammates and a young college sensation from Davis' alma mater, all brothers, were trash-talking a little two-on-two at his place. His three thousand dollar Rolex sat on two one hundred dollar bills at midcourt. The young player, Tony McMillan, and Davis were matched up against his ex-teammates—Derek's watch against their cash. And thanks to Davis' sweet stroke that day, he and McMillan were kicking butt and enjoying the hell out of it—when his cell phone rang.

"Hey man, let it go," shouted Perry Green his one-time backcourt partner. But Davis dashed off the court to the phone sitting with his sweats along the sideline.

"Dude," jawed Jim Baines, a seven-foot pivot man. "What's the panic? I thought you were retired?"

"Ain't that a secretary's job, Davis?" chimed in Green.

Davis laughed them off and retrieved the phone from the pile of sweats. "It's my personal phone," he grinned, hinting of evil, and answered the phone. "Yeah, baby," was his opening with a wink to his buddies.

Atossa didn't recognize the voice. "I'd like to speak to Derek Davis."

"Who's this?"

"Atossa Andreas."

The grin all his buddies were watching washed away. This was not any woman. And he knew it. For a moment, impossibly, he didn't know what to say.

Baines tried to grab the phone from him. "We got a game goin'. Put that woman down."

Davis pushed him away and waved at the others to get lost. "Speak to me, darlin'," he said into the phone, walking away from his friends, out the gym side door to the deck and the ocean.

"I'd like to see you again."

"Took you two weeks to figure that out? What's a man to think?"

"Where can we meet?"

Davis held the phone out in front of him, stared at it, and shook his head. "Woman, you got a plan, don't ya?"

"Derek," she said, cool, calm. "We are both immeasurably wealthy. We can go anywhere in the world. We can do whatever we like. Would you like to have dinner together in Manhattan? Saturday, perhaps?"

"Baby, you be somethin'." He couldn't believe how hard she was coming at him.

"We were something dancing Saturday night. Want to enjoy some time alone together?"

"Love to." And he meant it. She had him with her sensual voice, clear intelligence, and all this aggressive talk, thick with a confidence he wasn't used to in a white woman. "Where baby?"

"No one calls me, baby, Derek." She paused and took a breath. "But I like the way you say it."

Davis laughed out loud. "How about tonight then?"

"Saturday is best for me, Derek. St. George's on Third Avenue. Let's say, seven."

"You be it, baby," he said. "St. George's at seven. Tonight!"

"Saturday!" she said with just enough life to let him know she had some humor. "Ask for the Nelson's table."

Davis hung up the phone and stared out at the ocean. The Atlantic breeze blew inland. He breathed in the sea air. Wow, he thought to himself. Saturday night! He did a little celebratory two-step. Then strolled back into the gym with all the cool he could exaggerate for his friends. The ball came flying at him out of nowhere. He had to drop the phone to catch it.

CHAPTER 71

Nathaniel Cromwell, Will, and Jerry Rust had been on the go for three days. Jerry's VW van only had a front seat so he drove, Nate rode shotgun, and Will sat on an empty tool chest in the back with the camping equipment. Although the radio continued to repeat the alert for Nate's arrest, they had yet to have any problems. The Homeland Guard had set up roadblocks on nearly every main road across the Midwest, but with the assistance of the farmers' tight knit network and their just-under-the-radar CB radio communication system, the outlaw trio had stuck to the back roads and neatly dodged the federal authorities.

After spending two nights with friendly farmers and experiencing goodwill throughout the rural areas, they wound through the country byways like Robin Hood and his merry men headed to Mahan Farms. Unfortunately, no one in the group was particularly merry. Above and beyond the likelihood of access to Mahan's home being blocked, the death of Mary Cromwell weighed heavily on Nate and Will. And Jerry Rust, despite all surface appearances, had his own set of personal conflicts.

Jerry, as tended to be his way, was playing both ends against the middle. He had been called back to the United States from Kazakhstan by Bob Richards because of his connection to Cromwell. Richards had correctly predicted that Cromwell would call Rust if he took a leadership role in the farmers' movement. And Jerry really was honored to act as Cromwell's body guard, but being a natural-born mercenary, he was also happy to collect a sizeable check from the CIA for his efforts, feeling he could provide Richards with what amounted to mole services while also remaining true to his friend.

So as double-triple-quadruple secret agent Jerry Rust drove the back roads of Missouri, he was also sorting out or denying his own inner turmoil and doing his best, because he did have a compassionate side, to lighten the mood of his traveling companions.

"Hey, Boss," asked Jerry after a long dwelling silence had taken over in the van. "You ever think about that Sherpa we knew back in the day, Tenzing Jast?"

"Hard to forget a man who saved our lives." For Nate, however, the day Jast died was even harder to forget. "Kind of funny you asked though. This guy we're going to meet today, Forest Mahan, reminds me of Jast. Not that he looks like him so much, but he has that twinkle in his eyes and the smile."

"Ever tell Will about meeting that little leprechaun?" asked Rust, easing through a curve.

"He never talks to me about his days in the military, Jerry." Will scooted the tool chest up toward the front, eager to be drawn into the conversation.

"Shit, Cromwell, you never told your boy about Tenzing Jast?"

"No, I guess I didn't." Nate turned to look out the window.

"Who is this leprechaun guy?"

Rust's eyes lit up and caught Will with a grin through the rearview mirror. "He was our good luck charm, Will. After Pakistan, your courageous dad wouldn't go anywhere without him."

"Really? Dad, I never thought of you as superstitious."

"There's a time and place for everything," said Nate, staring out the window at a wide open pasture and thirty or forty head of dairy cows. He knew Jerry was trying to pick things up with the banter, but he was having a hard time joining in.

"Me and Sergeant Rock, here," continued Rust, bringing the van out of the curve, "were up in the Hindu Kush Mountain Range, almost in China, looking for damn Bin Laden several years before 9/11, and we got lost. Big time. Middle of a snowstorm. We had no business being up there that time of year anyway."

Cromwell had to chuckle at this. "Man, it was late June. And just a freak we got that snow."

"Your dad and I and about six of these guys from the Pakistani ISI were following this bum lead about a terrorist hangout." Rust turned an eye to his friend. "You know, I never said this then, but I figured we were dead that last night. All of us buried in a snow cave, like eight dogs in a burrow, huddled all together keeping each other warm."

Will leaned up closer to listen. "And what about this guy Jast?"

"Hang on, give me a chance to tell the story."

Nate turned to Rust. "We *were* damn lucky to be alive that next morning."

"Shit, a couple of those guys weren't! And when we pushed out of that hole in the snow and saw nothing but gray skies and more snow, I wished I was one of them. Your damn dad, Will, he's a horse's ass when it comes to pushing on—when you'd just as soon die. We trudged along all day. No idea where we were going."

Will grinned at Rust's reference to his father. "You must have had a radio and a GPS?"

"We didn't. One of the ISI guys dropped the radio. Broke the shit out of it. The Colonel here had the GPS and lost it. That was a first," laughed Rust. "And a last."

"Dad, you lost the GPS? How?"

Nate was staring out the side window again. "Digging in the snow I suppose. I don't know. It was so friggin' cold it felt like your brain was frozen." They passed a little country store with an old fashion red and white Coca-Cola sign in the window and a big red ice chest for pop on the porch.

"It was so damn bleak, you couldn't see the sun by day or the stars at night. Just fucking white. Snow blind is what they call it. And we were." Rust eased through another curve, leaning right, then back left. "And we'd been at this blind march for eight days."

"Five days," said Nate.

"A week by my memory," grinned Rust into Will's reflection in the rearview. "Sleeping with these crazy Pakistanis at night in a hole in the snow. Eating GI rations until we're down to sucking on the wrappers. Man, look at this hand." He held up his right hand so Will could see it. The little finger and part of the meat of the palm below were wrinkly and scarred. "Frost bite, dude. You should see my toes."

"What about you, Dad?"

Nate just shook his head like it was all an exaggeration.

"This last morning, we dig out. Like I said, two of the Pakistanis are dead. I'd been using this dead dude's belly as a pillow all night. Thought I'd puke when I woke up to that. Figured we were all counting our final hours. Then the snow stopped midday, and the sky opened up. But we were still lost, short on food, and too far from anywhere for hope of any kind, when this little Sherpa appears in this silly wool cap with red tassels. Just pops up over the ridge in front of us like one of Santa's helpers, grinning like he knows everything."

"I'll never forget that one. Tenzing Jast, man of the moment," added Nate, trying to join in for Will's sake, trying to push aside the sinking feeling in his chest and the image of his mother rolling on the floor of his bedroom with her hair on fire.

"What was he doing out there?"

"Never did find that out, Will," replied Rust. "He was too intent on getting us food and warmth. As were we."

"The Tibetan Leprechaun," mused Nate. "There really is something of him in Mahan."

"And he led you back to civilization?" asked Will.

"Civilization? Right, little Cromwell. He had some dried goat meat, some nuts and oats, and a stash of dry wood. He gave us all a meal then led us into a cave. I don't know where it was. He got a fire going and warmed us up. We stayed there one whole day, just resting, letting the panic ease out of us. After another day of hiking, he brings us to a little Sherpa dental clinic some American had built there forty years earlier. And that was it. We'd made it."

"Man, Rusty, I guess I'd pushed some of that out of my mind completely. But that's about as tough a time as I can remember," said Nate.

"Worse than fighting in Afghanistan, Dad?"

"I'd say so. A firefight you might catch a bullet—you might not. Against the weather. Everybody loses."

"Heads up, guys!" said Rust suddenly. "I think we've got a tail."

Nate peered into the rearview on his side. Will turned around and looked out the back window. A Springfield police cruiser had just pulled from the side of the road and was gaining on them.

"Don't think we can out run'm in this roller skate, Boss."

"Yeah, let's play it out. We've been lucky with the cops so far."

"But that was Kansas. This is Missouri."

"Then I'm into the box." Nate scrambled into the back, changing places with Will. He squeezed into the empty tool chest—there for that reason—while Will settled into the front passenger's seat.

The squad car followed at a distance for five minutes, then pulled up close and put on the revolving lights without the siren. "He's pulling us over, Boss. Prepare yourself," said Rust as he eased off the road, and the police car pulled up behind.

A big sheriff ambled up to the van's driver's side window, wearing a wide-brimmed hat, aviator sunglasses with mirror lenses, a gun on his hip, and an ugly look on his face. Rust had his registration and license all ready for him, but he ignored Jerry's papers.

"Got a rumor floating around out here," drawled the overweight cop, "that this boy Cromwell is traveling in a red Volkswagen van."

"Oh, yeah?" said Jerry, casual as could be.

"Yeah." The sheriff peered into the van, sizing up Will and all the camping gear in the back. "Now, I'm sure, you all don't have nothin' to hide." He stared right at the big tool chest and rubbed his jaw. "But you might like to know there's a federal roadblock up ahead, and, well," he looked down the road from where they'd been, "if I was headed to Forest Mahan's farm, it wouldn't hurt knowing that every road from here on in is being watched."

"Really," said Jerry, looking over at Will.

"Us local boys don't want to interfere with the feds, but if you were interested in seeing Mahan." He used his right hand to lower his sunglasses and give Jerry a good bare-eyed look, then stared at the big tool chest again. "You might consider leaving this van here and taking a ride in my cruiser."

Rust looked over his shoulder. "You hear that, Colonel?"

The lid to the tool chest lifted. "I did." Cromwell unfolded himself from inside the box. "We'd be mighty obliged, Sheriff."

"Yes, sir." The sheriff grinned at the famous jack-in-the-box. "Let's find a safe place to park this van. Then the three of you can get in my rig."

CHAPTER 72

Linda Bennett's chance meeting with James Peabody had opened the door for an interview with Forest Mahan. She was with him now in the living room of his home in Springfield, Missouri. It was almost noon on Saturday, the eighteenth of July. The forecast was for temperatures topping one hundred, and the shades were drawn to keep the house as cool as possible.

Forest was on the couch wearing gray slacks and a short-sleeved checked shirt. Linda sat across from him in a sleeveless madras blouse and designer blue jeans with her shoulder length hair pulled back in a ponytail. Her tape recorder was on the coffee table between them, its red recording light blinking. Her briefcase was on the floor beside her, the letter from President Kenaghy inside, metaphorically ticking like a timebomb. If all went well, she intended to show it to Mahan after the interview.

"Forest, considering the industry's reaction to the first burn, the recent deployment of the Homeland Guard, and the warrant out for the arrest of Nathaniel Cromwell, does the Nonpartisan Farmers' Alliance still plan to burn more fields if their strike demands aren't met?"

"I hope it doesn't come down to that, Linda," replied Mahan. The Grange President and Linda had hit it off from the moment she'd walked through the door. He told her how much he liked her column, and they'd immediately begun talking on a first name basis. "We're trying to negotiate a labor settlement. We want a dialogue, and as of this moment, no direct communication has come from anyone except our creditors. My calls are not returned. Our strike statement is ignored. And the Director of Homeland Security has gone on record calling us traitors and terrorists. The people in power are in effect calling our bluff. So the answer to your question is—if necessary, we will burn again."

"How do you reconcile burning your grain when it could lead to food shortages in many parts of the Third World?"

Forest looked down at the floor. "I can't," he said, eyes still downward. "I dreamt two nights ago that I was burning my corn, and as the husks peeled back in the heat, there were people inside the husks not ears of corn. There were Asians and Africans, people of all colors and creeds, but also many were farmers with faces I recognized." He looked up at Linda. His eyes troubled. "What we're trying to do is change the way we farm and possibly prevent even greater and more damaging shortages in the years to come. In my mind, we're wagering the long-term stability of the harvest against this one season."

"Can this strike work, Forest?"

Forest put his right fist to his mouth in thought. He looked out toward the kitchen where Louise was preparing lunch. "The odds are against us," he said, turning to Linda.

"And if it fails?"

"The smaller farms have already begun to disappear as it is, Linda. It will only happen more quickly if the strike doesn't work out."

"Does petroleum usage play into your strike?"

Forest lifted his head thoughtfully. "Absolutely. Most of the corn we grow, the low grade stuff for feed and processed food additives, is little more than petrochemicals pumped through dead soil. We might as well be drinking the stuff. But it's not just the fertilizers. It's pesticides and herbicides. It's diesel for the tractors and combines. Plastic packaging and energy for the processing plants. It's fuel for transportation from the field to the distributors to the store to your house. Unless you grow it yourself, the various portions of food on your plate travel an average of fifteen hundred miles just to get to your table. We've got to change that. Relocalizing our local food systems is what I emphasize. A fifth of the cost of food today is from petroleum products—and that will climb as oil reserves decline."

"Then heedlessly burning fossil fuels as if there's no tomorrow is really no different than burning the crops?"

"Well, that's not a comparison I would ever make. But I know folks who'd say growing corn to make ethanol is the same as burning it." As Forest said this, the sound of gravel popping in the driveway and a throbbing V-8 caused him to turn in his seat and lift the window shade behind him. A Springfield police car rolled up in front of the house.

Forest turned back to Linda. "Looks like we have some unannounced visitors."

Linda glanced out the window and saw the squad car beside her white rental car. A police officer slid out on the driver's side then opened the rear door. A tall dark-haired man wearing a guinea shirt, faded jeans, dusty brown leather boots, and handcuffs stepped out. The officer removed the handcuffs, and the tall man used both hands to place a straw cowboy hat on his head. The officer went around to the back of the car and opened the trunk. A youth climbed out, followed by Nathaniel Cromwell wearing a faded K-state sweatshirt, jeans, and a green Caterpillar cap.

At this point, Forest stood up and turned anxiously to Linda. Their eyes met momentarily, then he called out to his wife. "Louise, we've got a few more guests for lunch." His eyes darted uneasily back to Linda's. "Sorry for the interruption."

"Should I leave?" she asked, knowing the stakes on the letter in her briefcase had just doubled.

Forest looked out the window again. The police officer shook hands with Cromwell and climbed back into the squad car. The others were coming down the walk. "I don't think it's necessary. I'd better get the door." He hurried out of the room. Linda glanced down at the tape recorder. It was still running. She heard the front door open and Cromwell's voice, then Mahan stepping out on the front porch and shutting the door. She reached over and cut off the tape recorder. She wanted no suggestion whatsoever that she might be eavesdropping.

"Quite the escort," said Forest, shaking Nate's hand and nodding toward the squad car now parked at the far end of the driveway.

"Wouldn't have made it without him."

"Should we invite the sheriff in?"

"No, he's going to sit out there and monitor the radio—just in case someone decides to make us an unexpected visit."

Forest nodded. "Who's this with you?"

Nate introduced Jerry and Will. Hands were shaken, pleasantries exchanged, then Forest turned serious. "I have company, Nate," he said, lowering his voice. "A journalist. Linda Bennett from *The New York Financial Times*. We've spoken of her material before. You might have seen her recent piece in *The Kansan* three days ago. She's here to interview me."

"Did she notice our arrival?"

Forest nodded. "Would you like to meet her? Or should I ask her to leave?"

One thing Nate knew for certain was that the farmers needed mainstream publicity. Popular support among the masses was critical. He looked over at Rust. Jerry shrugged like it was no big deal. Nate turned back to Mahan. "It's probably safest to have her stay until I'm long gone."

"I trust her, Nate. I just spent the last hour with her. She's sharp and she understands it all."

"Fine, but we need to talk in private at some point, Forest. I want to make another videotape—folks have to know I'm still at it. Then it's back on the road."

Inside Linda suddenly found herself very self-conscious. She looked at herself in a decorative mirror hanging on the wall. She pushed a few stray hairs out of her face, straightened her blouse, and checked the lay of her jeans. Then she heard the door open and the men coming in. She took two deep breaths, started to sit down, then decided to remain standing.

Jerry Rust came in first. He looked Linda up and down and gave her a sideways grin she didn't appreciate and tried to ignore. Mahan came in next, followed by Cromwell and Will. Linda's eyes went right to Nate. Even with the two large burns on his face he was a handsome man. She gave him an open smile, hoping her incredible self-consciousness didn't show, and Nate touched the brim of his hat.

"I'm sorry, Linda, it seems that suddenly I'm in demand," said Forest, turning to his guests. "As you seem to recognize, this is Colonel Nathaniel Cromwell."

Their eyes met full on—and held just a little too long. Cromwell diffused it by taking off his hat. Linda extended her hand. There was just something so fresh and authentically masculine in his face, especially compared to the stiff suits she knew in Washington, she couldn't resist peering into his eyes again as she took his hand. "I am honored, Colonel," she said.

"Nate's just fine," he said easy as could be.

"This is Jerry Rust," continued Forest. Linda shook his hand. Will edged into the room behind them. "And this is the Colonel's son, Will."

"Hello, Will," she said, as he acknowledged her with a nod.

For a moment, they all stood there in a hovering silence. Linda knew the men were there to talk and her presence was hugely awkward, but she also knew she might never get the chance to present the President's letter to both men at the same time.

She noticed Cromwell looking at the tape recorder on the table. "Oh, I turned it off," she said, giving him a shy smile. Then looking around uncomfortably. "Am I in the way here?"

"Not at all, Linda," said Louise Mahan coming in from the kitchen, smiling and breaking all the stiffness. "Too many men here, not enough women. I want you to stay for lunch and it's ready now."

Forest agreed. "Please, Linda, stay for lunch. Colonel Cromwell will not be here long. We can continue the interview after he leaves." He paused, looking to Nate. "That all right with everyone?"

"That's fine," said Nate.

"It'd be our loss if she didn't stay," added Rust, his eyes up and down her again.

"Come on, everyone," pushed Louise. "Into the dining room and take a seat."

Louise and Forest were at the ends of the rectangular table. Will sat beside his father on one side, and Rust sat next to Linda on the other. On the table were a bowl of mashed potatoes, a plate layered with slices of country ham, a clear glass pitcher of sun-brewed tea, bobbing with ice cubes and slices of lemon, a basket of whole wheat bread, filling the room with the smell of fresh-from-the-oven, and a stack of corn on the cob.

The first few minutes of the meal were all *please* and *thank you*, passing food around, clinking plates, ice tea rattling into glasses, then just plain chowing down, everyone looking relaxed and hungry, except Linda—still feeling the situation out and wondering how best to get to the topic of the President's letter.

"Now Linda," said Louise, sensing Linda's awkwardness, "did I hear you say to Forest you're from Washington D.C? Working for *The New York Financial Times,* is that right?"

Linda looked up from her plate and peeked down past Rust to Louise. "My column is based there, yes, Louise. But I'm staying in Kansas City now, hoping to get the farmers' side of the strike."

"So, what do you think so far?"

"She's with us, Louise," said Forest with a glow of pride. "Linda was the first bigtime east coast reporter to give us any ink."

Linda tried to play it down and smiled graciously at Forest.

"*Financial Times,*" repeated Rust. "Seems unlikely the farmers would be getting any support from the Street."

Nate held an ear of corn with two hands and bit into the center of it, as though he wasn't paying much attention.

"My expertise is the commodities market, Mr. Rust."

"Jerry, please."

"I've followed grain for years. I know the farmers' situation is a difficult one, especially when it comes to hedging in the market. I'm not sure what the answer is, but I do believe in the farmers' right to strike and try to make things better." As Linda said this, her eyes met Nate's peering up at her from his ear of corn. There was intelligence and warmth, and something deeper—grief from his mother's death. She felt this as powerfully as if he'd said it aloud. "It's a position that isn't very popular with my managing editor."

"But they print it."

"I have a national following. I write what I want."

"Do you believe the farmers have the right to burn their fields in protest?" Nate addressed Linda directly for the first time.

Will was staring at her. She smiled at him before answering. "I believe you have the right to protest. But I don't like seeing the fields burned." She looked at Forest, doing her best to pull the whole group into the discussion. "I'm truly hoping you can get an honest dialogue with the government and the grain dealers before the question of burning comes up again."

"Do you think we will?"

"Yes, Colonel." Linda could hear the timebomb in her briefcase ticking. "That's why I'm writing about your strike. I hope to facilitate the exchange of ideas between both sides while also getting the public up to speed. Democracy works best when the voters are informed."

Rust laughed. "As though voting mattered."

"I do what I can."

"Stop ganging up on this woman," snapped Louise. "As far as I can tell, she's here for us."

"It's all right, Louise," said Linda, looking at her then the others. "I understand how difficult it's become to trust the media anymore. Big money interests play a huge part, but there's a lot of good journalists out there."

"And you're one?" asked Rust.

"I have my principles." An image of Bob Richards sitting smugly at his desk passed through her mind. "I try to get it right."

Forest spoke up. "Linda, how does a commodities analyst interpret the grain buy last month?"

Linda tried to lighten up, but her heart was pounding. Although Forest was surely with her, she couldn't quite read Cromwell. "I think it's just what they said it was. The warm winter and dry spring in Asia hit the grain crop hard." She paused to take a sip of tea. Her hand wanted to shake but she controlled it. "It was a lot like what happened with the Russians in the seventies. Asian buyers moved on it before the information got out—cramping the rest of the international market."

Forest nodded. "And that makes what we have in the field all the more valuable for bargaining."

"If the government doesn't take over your fields and harvest them for you."

"I hope it doesn't come to that, Linda," said Forest. "We don't want a fight. We're just trying to look out for the health of the land. That's what I want you to get out to the American people."

"It seems like the health of the land would be such an obvious necessity," said Will, looking across the table at Linda and causing his father to pause in his eating.

"It does seem that way, Will. But there are other forces at play all the time. Whatever attracts the money is what gets done. Economics rules." Linda could feel Cromwell watching her, measuring her, as she addressed his son.

Rust nudged Linda with his elbow. "Hey, ain't you gonna eat what you put on your plate?" She was too on edge to eat and had taken all of two bites so far.

"You've been quizzing her right and left," said Louise. "Let her alone so she can eat."

Linda lifted her ear of corn by both ends and gave a wide smile to everyone at the table. "Don't mind me." Then went at it like a typewriter. All of them but Nate laughed. He opened up a genuine smile. Linda's eyes met his while still at the corn. Something palpable passed between them—just the vaguest sense of connection—the tiny crack in his defenses she was looking for.

Linda put the corn down and looked directly at Nate, now scooping his plate clean of mashed potatoes with a piece of bread. "Colonel, what is your estimation of President Kenaghy?"

Nate looked up. "I'm not sure I understand him." He put down the piece of bread. "I think the call to the Homeland Guard was chicken shit."

Linda nodded a little surprised at the language. "Forest, how about you?"

"I feel much the same way. I'm disappointed Kenaghy hasn't come out with a definitive statement, but presidents often allow labor disputes to simmer a bit before they make a stand. I just want him to give us his ear."

Linda held silent one moment, then eyes firmly on Nate, spoke. "I'm not certain how much the public understands what's been happening to the President. He's gotten some bad press lately for fighting what I think is a wasteful piece of legislation, and he deserves more credit than he's getting."

No one said anything. Then Rust asked, "So what are you telling us?"

"Don't dismiss Kenaghy entirely. Despite his foreign policy problems, he still has some domestic influence." She glanced around the table. It might be better to reveal the letter in private with Cromwell and Mahan, but this group had to be as close to the core as it got. She threw caution to the wind. "And I've spoken to him specifically about your position." Linda looked at Nate, then Forest. "He wants a chance to talk to you."

"Truly," exclaimed Forest.

Nate and Rust exchanged a glance.

"I have a letter from him with me."

Everyone at the table froze except Rust. "Then who are you really working for?"

Louise made a sour face at his accusatory tone, but Linda played right through it. "I'm a syndicated columnist, Jerry. I work for myself." She stood and went to the sideboard where she'd put her briefcase. She opened the briefcase and withdrew the handwritten note. "Like Forest, the President has been reading my columns, and he's indicated to me in private that he supports the strike. I believe he's your one chance at settling this thing." She handed the letter to Forest.

His eyes widened as he read through the one-page note. "This is fantastic, Linda. But I don't understand. Why hasn't he said something before?" Forest handed the letter to Nate.

"I think it's just like he says in the letter. He wants it out of the news until he's had the opportunity to exchange ideas with you. He's taking a big chance. He doesn't want to misstep with all the country watching."

Nate looked at Linda, appraising her, then handed the note across the table to Jerry. "What do you think, Mr. Rust?"

Jerry held the letter up against the light and stared into the detail of the President's letterhead. "Looks authentic to me."

"Well, I knew this girl was our lucky star as soon as she walked in," said Louise.

"I don't know how lucky," said Jerry. "Kenaghy's help might not be worth a whole lot. He says as much in this letter."

Linda took a deep breath. "I realize I'm asking you to trust me and a President who's on the ropes. But the truth is, you're up against some stiff opposition, and from what I've gathered, this is the first door to open for you."

"But if the President's on the way out," asked Nate, "couldn't this become a negative for us?"

"As it could be for him as well." Linda looked around the table. "There are no guarantees with this proposal. The note says it all. The President is offering to sit down and talk with you."

"Then why was the Homeland Guard deployed?"

"I have no idea, Colonel. I only spoke with the President about this once—in the Oval Office before I flew to Kansas City five days ago—before you burned your farm. That might have changed things. I don't know. I've given you this letter. It's for you to make the next move. I'd say you've got nothing to lose."

Again, there was silence and an exchange of looks. Forest spoke. "How do you propose we go about setting up a meeting?"

"Because of the warrant out on Colonel Cromwell, I suggest you go to Washington, Forest, as soon as possible. And I think it's in everyone's best interest to avoid any more field burning. I'll arrange the meeting. From there, you're on your own."

"I'm ready, Linda. What do you say, Nate?"

Nate stared across the table at Linda, still appraising. "I'm not certain. Would you be going with him to Washington?"

"It's up to Forest. It would be an honor."

"We don't know that they won't arrest Forest as soon as he arrives in Washington," said Rust turning to Linda. "I say we keep the journalist with us as collateral for Forest."

Nate turned to Forest then to Linda. "What do you say to that, Ms. Bennett?"

"All I'm trying to do is facilitate the meeting. I'll do whatever is necessary to make it happen. My bureau chief, Frederick Manning, can meet Forest at the airport."

"Forest, what do you think?"

"I trust this woman, Nate. I don't like the idea of holding her as a hostage."

"There's nothing wrong with an insurance policy, Forest."

"I agree with Jerry," said Nate. "But we definitely can't stay here. We're gonna be on the move—that complicates things."

Linda glanced around the table. "If this happens as it should, Colonel, I can have a meeting set up by tonight. Forest could be talking to the President as soon as tomorrow—the next day at the latest. That's two and a half days, max." She ran through the various scenarios in her head. "I could travel with you. It would be a great opportunity for me, and the best publicity you could ever get."

Cromwell's look was uncertainty. Mahan spoke. "She's right, Nate. This is our chance. Maybe our only chance. Meet with Kenaghy. Take advantage of her syndicated column. I'm for it. You know I don't want any more burning."

Rust gave Linda a look that completely puzzled her. "I like it too, Boss."

"Okay," said Nate. "But I want to make a video while we're here. Ms. Bennett can get on the phone and start setting this up right away. Will and Rusty can monitor her calls, while I work with Forest. If everything looks good by the time we're ready to leave, it's a go. If there are any foul-ups or second thoughts by anyone, we cancel."

Forest nodded. "Perfect."

"Fine, Colonel. I'll do whatever it takes to make this work," said Linda, sounding much more confident than she really was.

CHAPTER 73

Saturday night, after a late dinner, Jonathan Mayfield had the Hilton concierge call him a cab. Thirty minutes later, through the usual heavy Singapore traffic, Jonathan stepped out of the taxi in the entrance plaza to Singapore's Night Safari Zoo. It was a popular theme park, and it was crowded.

Jonathan had a four-gigabyte thumb drive in his trousers' pocket. It contained all the information that the American freelance writer Dan had requested. Yet even as Jonathan strolled across the plaza to buy a ticket for the safari tram, he was thinking about turning back. He'd struggled badly for two days with the decision to assist the writer. Then Friday afternoon, as he sorted through the huge DBA database, he convinced himself he had no real allegiance to Parker Chen, less than that—the Teochui had kidnapped him and imprisoned him for three months. He did some quick downloading and left work that evening with the thumb drive.

Now, a day later, on a hot and humid Singapore night, standing in line for the tram, anxiously looking over his shoulder one way then the other, he wasn't sure—and the damn little drive in his pocket, literally no bigger than his thumb, was feeling more and more like a steamer trunk.

With all the little grass shack concessions stands, postcard racks, and international tourist goo-gaws, Jonathan could have been at any one of the wildlife safari theme parks throughout the world. But Singapore's Night Safari was unique. Many jungle animals are nocturnal, and it wasn't until after dark that they came out of their lairs. Here you could actually witness that. And once Jonathan was seated at the back of the little open-air tram, amid kids and parents and elderly American tourists, his angst began to lessen. He gradually fell into the enchantment of the tropical zoo—listening to the call of the night birds, peering through the trees and shadowy jungle undergrowth, following the tour guide's directions to spot a family of the funny looking tapirs or a red dhole or a bearded pig. Except for the monstrous thumb drive in his pocket and the guide's repeated endangerment refrain—*there are but twenty-three of these creatures left on the planet—four of them right here at the night safari—half the primates in the world are endangered—four of the species here are protected, in fact, in one case, the only ones in existence are right here*—he might have enjoyed the slow moving trip through the dank, fetid tropical forest. Instead, poor Jonathan kept wondering if he weren't the last of the Mayfield species cozying up to the edge of extinction.

The longer the tram ride lasted without his encountering the American writer, the more Jonathan began to ease from his hyper-nervous state into mere anxiety. Maybe Dan would never arrive. Maybe the Teochui had caught up with him, and Jonathan would never really have to make the decision his being there belied.

The tram had completed a loop through an artificially created Burmese Hillside, a South American Pampas, and an Asian Riverine Forest, when it came to a stop and the guide spoke over the loudspeaker.

"In addition to this tram, there are walking trails throughout the night safari. One such trail begins here. You may get off now, if you like, and follow the trail to another tram stop, or you are welcome to stay on board and simply sit back and enjoy the scenery."

Jonathan watched several of the passengers climb off the little yellow and red train and disappear down the trail into the jungle. He remained on the tram with about half the original riders, and a moment later they were on the move again. *Still no Dan.* His anxiety dropped another level.

After passing through Equatorial Africa and the Indian Subcontinent, the tram came to a stop at the entrance to the Nepalese River Valley. Seven walkers climbed onto the tram. One of them, an older white woman, teetered down the aisle and sat beside Jonathan. The tram started up again and proceeded into what Jonathan judged, by the little map that came with his ticket, to be the last leg of the forty-five-minute excursion.

There were two more trail stops before the ride ended, and as the tram slowed for the first of these, the woman beside him turned to him and winked. For an instant, Jonathan didn't know what was more frightening the Bengal tiger or this aggressive old woman, until she whispered into his consternation, "Follow me off the tram, Jonathan."

As he watched Dan rise from his seat and work his way to the tram exit, Jonathan realized in a rush of humid sweat that this was his last chance to bail. If he stayed on the tram, he could finish the ride and hustle off to a taxi. The old woman Dan turned back and caught his eye. The scene of his being hijacked off the streets of London by another man in woman's clothing flashed before Jonathan like a nightmare. Dan intervened. He came back and took Jonathan's hand, leading him from his seat like a reluctant child off the tram and into the dark jungle.

With Dan struggling along in women's shoes, towing Jonathan, the two of them quickly fell behind the others on the trail and were soon alone.

"Quite a spot isn't it, Jonathan?" said Dan with a lipstick smile.

Jonathan nodded, catching sight of a huge lime green tree snake looped over a branch just off the trail. "Can't imagine coming to Singapore without a stop here," said Jonathan dryly.

"I'm just glad you found the time." As Dan spoke, he slid his right hand into the black patent leather purse hanging off his shoulder. He withdrew a thick envelope and pushed it into Jonathan's hand. "This might help with your uncertainties."

Jonathan glanced down at the envelope in his left hand and pried it open with his thumb. It was stuffed with American currency—hundred dollar bills. "I can't take this," he said, trying to hand it back to Dan. "You must need this more than I do."

Dan ignored him and just grinned at Jonathan. "Forget it. Got to take something for risking your life."

Not knowing what else to do, Jonathan jammed the envelope into his hip pocket. "Where did you get this kind of cash?"

"Don't worry about the little stuff, Jonathan. What have you got for me?"

Jonathan took a deep breath. He reached into his trousers and withdrew the ten-ton thumb drive. "Here," he said slipping it directly into Dan's purse. "Any decent hacker can use this to access their entire system."

"*Gracias, senor*," said Dan with a thick mascara wink.

"I'll only be here another two and half weeks," said Jonathan quickly. "Then I'm leaving." He took a look over his shoulder as an elderly Chinese couple came down the trail from the other direction. "Please don't do anything with this until I'm gone."

"*No problemo*," grinned Dan. "You go on to the next trail head. I'll turn back the way we came."

Jonathan hesitated a moment, waiting for the couple to pass on the narrow trail. "Will I see you again?"

Dan didn't answer. He just tottered off, never looking back. Jonathan took a second long, deep breath, turned a wary eye to the bright green snake in the tree, and strode off—knowing not what he had done.

CHAPTER 74

Although Linda Bennett was essentially being held as a minimum-security hostage, she could not have imagined a more timely or profound journalistic opportunity than what was now unfolding. After the big lunch Saturday, she made the necessary calls to Frederick Manning and the President's press secretary Wayne Stevens, setting up a meeting between James Kenaghy and Forest Mahan. Mahan would fly into Washington Sunday evening and be met at the airport by Manning. Manning would then deliver Mahan to Wayne Stevens at the White House. Throughout, it was understood that this should be treated with utmost discretion—and get no media play until the President chose to set it in motion.

After completing the arrangements, Linda sat down with Forest to finish the interview. An hour later, Jerry Rust was re-handcuffed and put in the back seat of the squad car. Nate and Will climbed into the trunk, and Linda sat in the front seat with the sheriff. He drove through two Homeland Guard checkpoints with nothing more than a salute and dropped his riders off at the red van. By two that afternoon, the group of four was on the road.

The first few hours in the van were awkward. Jerry and Nate rode up front, while Linda sat in the back with Will and tapped at her laptop preparing the interview for the Sunday morning edition of *The Kansan.* Although it was obvious they were headed northwest, Linda was told nothing and had no clue what this trip was about or where they were headed. Aside from Rust's CB banter and his discussion of back road routes with Nate, there was very little conversation. And in that close quiet of mixed agendas, an uneasy tension began to build in the vehicle.

Despite Linda's attention to her writing, periodically using her earphones to listen to portions of the interview, she noticed that Jerry was keeping a close eye on her through the rearview mirror. Also on several occasions, she happened to look up as Nate turned to look at her. The situation was very unsettling for Linda. She didn't feel trusted, and it made her self-conscious.

Otherwise, the drive was remarkably uneventful. Off and on, Linda tried to interpret what was being said on the CB radio, but she couldn't. They were using trucker slang and clearly saying as little as possible. It was impressive how well they disguised their purpose and still managed to chart safe efficient routes around Homeland Guard roadblocks.

About nine o'clock that evening, they stopped in Nebraska to fill the gas tank. Because Jerry had removed the wireless communication application from her laptop as a precaution and taken her cell phone, she was given an opportunity to use the service station's internet connection to file her interview with *The Kansan.* For security purposes, Nate read the interview and did the upload. Then it was back on the road with the CB barking instructions.

The red van meandered through the back roads of eastern Nebraska for another hour or so. Then well after dark, outside the town of Lincoln, Rust turned into the crowded driveway of Henry and Judith Campbell's white two-story farmhouse. The enthusiastic and heartfelt greeting of nine farmers and their families, something which had become commonplace to the boys, was the first of several eye openers for Linda.

As had become the tradition, the war hero's sudden arrival climaxed with a crowd of hungry farm folk around a big table and a huge dinner. Chicken fried steaks with white gravy, stacks of corn on the cob, oven baked bread, fresh churned butter, and home brew. Even for Linda the outsider, it was quite fun. High times in Farm Country, USA.

Linda did her best to settle into the background of the affair and said almost nothing but *please pass this* or *please pass that* through the entire meal. Mostly she watched Nate and how he handled himself. Knowing the story of his career in the military, she was impressed by his ease and humility.

While Linda watched Nate, however, she couldn't help noticing that Rust—also an outsider—was watching her. She interpreted this as a sexual thing. And she did her best to brush it aside. Other than his time in the Special Forces with Cromwell, she knew nothing of Rust's background or what he might know about her.

After dinner and an hour or so of strike talk and bullshitting, Judith Campbell offered Linda the extra bed in her daughter's room—which she graciously accepted. Before long, all the locals were gone, and the farmhouse settled in for the night. Nate and Will climbed into sleeping bags in the van. Jerry pitched a tent in the yard. And Linda took one of the twin beds in nine-year-old Becky Campbell's bedroom.

With all the excitement, Linda had a hard time getting to sleep. She tossed and turned for quite some time before finally giving in to her restlessness. She quietly got dressed and slipped out the farmhouse's back door. The backyard was small and bordered on two sides by tall stalks of ready to harvest winter wheat, whispering ancient secrets in the light breeze.

For the first time all day, it was almost cool. The moon was full and the sky clear. In an effort to relax, she breathed in the humid air, thick with farm smells, and tried to get perspective on the strike that was opening before her. She hadn't believed this kind of broad, grass roots politics really existed. It held the human potential that she had lost faith in. Being in the middle of it now was exhilarating, both intellectually and emotionally.

Foremost in her mind, however, was strike leader Nathaniel Cromwell. She'd spent almost the entire day with him, and yet they'd hardly spoken at all. In spite of this, she felt that she'd made some slight connection with him through the silence, and she was dying to interview him. It was funny though. All the questions she thought to ask him had no relevance to politics or the strike.

This upset her more than she wanted to admit, and she wandered away from the house, along the edge of the wheat fields, down toward the Campbell's two barns, just wanting to walk and relax enough to fall asleep. As she turned back toward the house, she saw the back hatch of the van open.

Much to her confusion, Nathaniel Cromwell climbed out and stretched his arms over his head and stared up at the moon. Then he turned and looked right at her—though apparently not seeing her right away in the dim light.

Linda's heart began to beat so loud she thought she'd wake up the whole state of Nebraska. She wanted to duck into the shadows and slip back into the house. But something held her. And she stood there watching the man, breathlessly, until she knew, despite the dark, that they were looking at each other through the moonlight. For a minute, maybe more, neither of them moved or said a word. Then Nate gave a little wave of recognition and started walking across the lawn.

When Nate got close enough to speak at a low volume, he removed his hat and scratched his head. "Looks like you're having a little trouble sleeping too?"

"It's exciting being out here on the road with you, Colonel Cromwell."

"Nate's just fine, Linda," he said politely, then the moment held, neither of them knowing what to say next.

Linda broke the spell. "I didn't know what was going on out here with the people. I was writing from Washington and abstracting the politics. Tonight around the table, yesterday at Forest's place, I experienced it—I felt it. You've really got something happening. It's important, Nate." *There she'd said it. His name aloud.* "This strike of yours just might work."

Nate smiled easily. "I don't know if this strike is going to achieve what we want or not, Linda. There is something going on though. I'm sure of that. But it's not something of mine. It's something that's come about on its own."

"What about Mahan?"

"If it's anyone's, you're right, it's his. Forest is at the heart of it, but as you saw tonight, and as I'm seeing everywhere I go, the people are ready. Farming must change."

"Mahan's an environmentalist. Is that part of it, too?"

Nate looked off into the night and took a breath. "Yes," he exhaled, "I think it is." He turned back to her and was suddenly struck by her beauty. The gloss of her hair. The softness of her cheek. Things he hadn't noticed in a woman for so long it unsettled him. He pushed through the nuance of the moment. "It seems so obvious when you think about it. We have to be careful with all this large-scale agriculture and industry. The water, the chemicals, the genetics. I couldn't have said that three months ago. Forest got my attention."

There was a sound back by the van. Nate turned around as Jerry Rust stood up out of his tent. He wasn't wearing any clothing and just kind of looked across the yard at Nate and Linda, then leaned back and without using his hands let go with a long stream of urine. "She got her recorder going yet, Boss?" he called out as he peed.

Nate brushed it off with a laugh. "Let's have a little decency out here, Rusty. Get your naked butt back in that tent."

Finished with his business, Rust put a hand to his crotch and gave his hips a little pump. "Don't do nothing I wouldn't do?" he jabbed and disappeared into his tent.

"Sorry, Linda," said Nate, looking at the ground.

"It's fine," said Linda, unsettled by the display, but not so much by Rust's crudeness as the tension she sensed building in the dynamics between the three of them, knowing they would be in close quarters at least another day or two

"Maybe I should try to get back to sleep," said Nate. "We've got a long day tomorrow." But he didn't move. And for a lengthening moment they both stood there.

"You lost your mother, Nate," said Linda suddenly, as though she'd been holding it in ever since she'd first met the man. "You have to be hurting."

This caught him off-guard. He turned away. Because he did hurt. And he didn't know what to do with the pain.

"Oh, Nate," said Linda in a hush, then, all professionalism blown away like star dust, she reached out to him. He accepted her embrace, awkwardly at first, then pulling her in, powerfully, as of necessity.

Linda laid her head on his shoulder, needing his embrace as much as he needed hers. The night stilled. Something deep within them both relaxed. After a minute or less, they let go of each other—equally startled and confused. "I'd better go," he whispered, then lightly touched Linda's hand and walked away.

Tears formed in Linda's eyes as she watched him amble back to the van. She was in love, and she knew it. Even more powerfully she'd seen it in Nate's eyes too—or maybe it was the grief in him reaching out. "God," she gasped, then hurried back into the house.

Linda didn't go straight to bed. Instead, she rewrote the introduction to her next column—not really certain if she could get it filed in time.

Sunday, July 19 The Kansas City Kansan

THE GLOBAL REPORT
By Linda Bennett

It is generally forgotten that ninety-five percent of the United States, by area, is rural or just wide-open spaces. Deserts. Rugged wilderness. Boundless prairie. And out there on the ranches and farms, life is blue jeans and boots and guns and four-wheel drives to a lot of people. These are the rough and tumble Americans who will forever be known as cowboys—and cowgirls to be sure.

When the farmers' strike began, it caught a lot of people by surprise. But the non-farming rural population rose to it quickly. In the days after the first field burning, they joined in with the farmers like family—pretty much throughout the nation. It might not be a huge portion of the population. The majority of Americans live in the city. But these rural folk own or manage quite a bit of the land. And they know how to live in the country. By habit, they are survivalists. It's a lot like the old Hank Williams Junior song...*we can skin a buck, we can run a trotline...country folks can survive!*

Outside the urban ghettos, these country folks are also America's poorest people, and you can bet the farm, they are prepared to rally around their swashbuckling union leader Nathaniel Cromwell. No matter how thoroughly the federal government might think they can contain the farmers' strike, if it gets down and dirty, the rural police forces, the volunteer firemen, the small town grocers, the local people will be at one with the farmers—and strike control will not be easy.

CHAPTER 75

For the first time in many years, probably going back to game seven of his last NBA Championship, Derek Davis had butterflies. It was Saturday night, and his chauffeur had just let him out on the corner of Third and Broadway at St. Michael's Restaurant in downtown Manhattan. He wore a black Armani suit, black patent leather loafers, and a black silk shirt—no tie. He made a quick assessment of his reflection in the window, gave himself a wink, and sauntered into the posh restaurant.

The maître d' confronted him with a look that made the hair stand up on Davis' shaved head.

"Could you direct me to the Nelson's private table?" asked Davis with all the restraint he owned.

"You will need a necktie, sir," said the maître d'.

Davis leveled a stare at the man as though he was a rookie assigned to guard him for the first time. "I don't believe you know who I am?" he bristled.

"In any case, you will need a necktie, sir."

Davis' eyes widened. His fists clenched and unclenched at his side with such intensity the restaurant floor manager standing across the room felt it.

"Ah, Mr. Davis, we've been told to expect you," said the manager, delicately stepping into the discussion. "John, *please*, take Mr. Davis to the Nelson Room."

"Of course," said the maître d'. "Follow me, sir."

Davis gave a little nod to the manager and trailed after the maître d' with a smug grin and a fiery focus in his eyes. When they reached the rear of the restaurant, the young maître d' stopped before the door to the Nelson room, opened it, and stood aside for Davis. Davis graced the young man with a little look that said, *Sonny, I think you've just blown the biggest tip of your short life,* and entered the cozy dining chamber expecting Atossa to be waiting.

The small private room held a table set for two with a white linen tablecloth, a basket of bread, and a single lit candle, but no Atossa. Davis took this in stride and wandered around the dark paneled chamber, checking out the black and white photographs of turn of the century oil rigs, spouting black gushers, and roustabouts.

Atossa waited in a private lounge and restroom. A knock on the door informed her that Mr. Davis had arrived. She took one last look in the mirror. She wore her hair, dyed a shocking henna-red, parted in the middle and held back over her shoulders in a long, loose braid that hung down to her waist. Her mid-length dress was made of form-fitting vermillion silk, with a single asymmetric strap, cut at a diagonal across her breasts so that one was revealed. With her new face and the pert, sculpted breast out there for all to see like a youthful drop of dew, Atossa could barely believe she was the stunning thing in the mirror.

She moved up close to the reflecting surface. The red star on her cheek had become very faint. She had resisted the temptation to cover it with something more than sterile powder and wore only eyeliner, mascara, and a light lip gloss—all within the guidelines Nina Colleen had given her.

Atossa felt good about her looks but was more than a little anxious about the later stages of the evening. As a bit of final preparation, she reached into her purse and withdrew a syringe filled with a clear fluid. She lifted her dress, tapped a vein on the inside of her thigh, inserted the needle, and plunged a special testosterone blend directly into her blood stream.

Davis' own anxiety threatened to turn to irritation when the door to the private room finally opened. The restaurant floor manager, who had come to the rescue earlier, stood off to one side and announced, "Ms. Atossa Andreas." Atossa appeared in the doorway with a white sweater draped over her bare shoulders and took two steps in. The door closed behind her.

Davis strode forward looking her in the eyes. Atossa extended her hand. He took her hand in both of his—Atossa lowered her eyes—and with the slightest bow he kissed the back of her hand.

Davis led her to her seat. He let go of her hand and pulled out the chair. Atossa stepped in front of her chair, then, before sitting down, said, "Please take my sweater, Derek." Davis gently lifted the sweater off her shoulders from behind and placed it on the back of her chair. "Thank you, Derek," she said softly, and he pushed the chair in as she sat. Davis circled the table to his seat, and, pulling out his own chair, suddenly noticed the cut of her dress. His beautiful smile said it all. He was absolutely thrilled by her audaciousness.

Davis had never performed this formal date ritual before in his life and couldn't believe he was doing it now. But he had learned more about Atossa since the masquerade ball. She was at least ten years older than he was and one of the most wealthy and powerful women in the world. Add her boldness—the night of the dance, on the phone, and tonight. It all turned him on even more. He wanted her tonight. Right here in this room, he promised himself, as he sat down and faced Atossa across the table with the long white candle burning between them.

A waiter entered the room with a bottle of pinot noir. He showed the bottle to both of them and poured them a taste. They lifted their glasses and, with their eyes on each other the entire time, allowed the wine to trickle past their lips. Both lowered their glasses and nodded acceptance to the waiter. He filled their glasses and exited from the room.

Atossa raised her glass to Derek. He reached across the table and touched his to hers. "To the devil," he said.

"To the devil," repeated Atossa, looking deeply into his gleaming brown eyes, with no disguise of her intention.

They both took a second sip.

"You're very handsome in a suit, Derek. I am quite pleased that we could meet tonight, thank you for coming."

Her poise. Her calm strength. Atossa was like no woman Davis had ever known. "Atossa, you also look fabulous. The pleasure is mine." He smiled with all his natural radiance.

"I noticed your hands at the party," said Atossa. Her voice was soft and relaxed, as though they were already an intimate couple. "May I look at your right hand?"

Davis laid his right arm down across the table, opening his palm where her plate would be. "Can you read my fortune?" he asked, not knowing of her predilection for the arts. "Perhaps you can tell me what my chances are tonight?"

Atossa bit her lower lip and allowed a thin evil smile. "One hundred percent, Derek," she said, taking his huge hand in both of hers, gripping his long middle finger in her fist, and drawing her hand out along its length. "For what other reason are we here," she said slyly. "But I might be able to tell you a little more than that." She looked up at him with such lurid appeal that he was instantly aroused.

Davis licked his lips and squinched up his nose with his own nasty little look. "Tell me what you see, baby."

Atossa became serious and moved the candle so that its light was directly over Davis' palm. She leaned forward and ran a finger down his lifeline. Then looked up at him, cold and severe. "It says we should make love before we have our meal."

Davis swallowed. Caught entirely in Atossa's spell, he reached out with his left hand so all four of their hands were intertwined as one, then leaned toward her until their faces were a foot apart. He needed to ask one question. "This ain't no setup is it, bitch?"

Atossa didn't flinch. "How did you guess?" she grinned, letting go of his hands. She stood and took three steps to the door. She put a key in the lock, then faced him. "Undress for me."

Davis laughed with delight. "You first, you little witch!"

She stalked over to him and kissed him on the lips. He stood up and she hugged him, because he was so tall, around the waist. He stroked down her back with his right hand and cupped her left buttock. She leaned back and unbuckled his belt. Davis let his trousers drop to his ankles—he wore nothing underneath—and, with his hands on her waist, eased her back toward the table. Using one hand to move the candle and the bottle of wine, he laid her back on the tablecloth. She lifted her legs up around his waist, and her dress fell around her hips. She also wore nothing beneath and was shaved clean. When Davis looked in her eyes, she grinned with such ferocity, even the proud basketball star wondered who in fact was fucking who tonight.

CHAPTER 76

Linda Bennett didn't sleep at all Saturday night and lay in bed wide awake until she heard others moving around in the house. It was just past dawn, and the temperature was already pushing eighty. She put on khaki shorts and a gauzy, white short-sleeved cotton top with a dark blue sports bra beneath, then wandered into the kitchen and found Judith Campbell in the early stages of preparing breakfast. Linda offered to help, but Judith said she had it all in hand and poured her a cup of coffee instead. They made small talk for a while, then Linda drifted outside to sip coffee and take in the July morning before it got any hotter.

The farm looked entirely different by day. The extent that the wheat fields dominated the setting had not been obvious to Linda the night before. Not another house or even a tree was visible as far as she could see. A string of telephone poles stretched out into infinity along the road that delineated one edge of the Campbell's property, and a few corrugated steel silos poked up in the distance like primitive rocket ships forgotten to be launched. Otherwise, from horizon to horizon, it was nothing but languorous fields of wheat, bleaching from green to amber in the early morning sun.

A weathered redwood picnic table with a single bench sat between the house and the barns—about twenty yards from the red van and Jerry's tent. Doing her best not to think about the encounter with Nathaniel Cromwell the night before, Linda settled down at the table with her cup of coffee and stared off one hundred and eighty degrees from the direction of the van.

After a few minutes, she heard some sounds behind her and glanced over her shoulder to see Jerry Rust exit from his tent. Like the night before, he wore nothing and without paying the least heed to Linda slipped into his jeans and the same guinea shirt he wore the day before. She pretended not to notice him until he walked right up to her from behind. She turned at his approach and caught something in his eyes she couldn't quite decipher—a reflection of the distaste she felt for him or some kind of sexual bullshit.

"Good morning, Jerry," she said, trying to push through the negative.

"Any more caffeine?"

"Should be plenty inside. Mrs. Campbell's in there putting together breakfast right now."

Rust gave her his now standard sly grin and meandered on by. Soon afterward, Nate climbed from the back of the van. Linda knew it was him without looking. He ambled up to the picnic table. It took her a moment to gather the nerve to look up at him. The reluctance in both of them was palpable. Nate kicked absently at the ground, hunting for something to say. "Get any sleep last night?"

Linda felt herself blushing, feeling like she was about fifteen and he was the high school football hero. "No. How about you?"

"I don't need much," he said, thinking how beautiful this woman looked in the sunlight. Her skin so fresh and soft. Her hair glistening auburn in the low angles of the morning sun. What had been so subtle in the moonlight the night before overwhelmed him now. He wanted to reach out and touch her face and stroke her hair, but the situation, of course, denied it. And sure enough, talk between them hung up again. Nate peered around absently at the farm he'd never seen before and scratched at the back of his head like he always did, making his Caterpillar cap bob up and down. "Pretty big place."

Linda almost laughed at the foolishness they had been reduced to. He had to be thinking the same thing she was. *This can't happen now.* "There's coffee inside."

"Sounds good," said Nate, as Rust stepped out on the Campbell's front porch, tugging at the brim of his cowboy hat.

"Better get that boy Will up, Boss," called out Rust. "Breakfast is being served. If he misses it now, he'll be begging us to stop later."

"Got it, Rusty." Nate looked at Linda with a sad little *wrong-time-wrong-place* smile, then wandered back to the van to get his son.

After breakfast, Linda asked Nate to read the column she'd written in the middle of the night, and, if it passed muster, to resend it from the Campbell's computer. While he did this, Rust and Will took everything out of the red van and loaded it into a 1998 GMC pickup with a beat-up, over-sized canopy on the back. The vehicle change was merely a precaution, with the added benefit of the camper having a false floor with a storage space below. One person could fit into it with relative ease, two if necessary.

About eight-thirty, the two-tone blue and white pickup rolled out of the Campbell Farm driveway. Like the day before, Rust drove and worked the CB, Nate acted as navigator, and Will and Linda sat behind in the camper on shallow built-in benches. A sliding window, which was left open, connected the cab and the camper. Again, there was no explicit mention of where they were headed or why, though by looking out the camper windows, Linda could see that their route was almost directly west.

Except for the squawking on the CB and Jerry's hip-hop return, the first few hours of the drive were quiet. Nate consulted maps. Linda pecked at her laptop, and Will contented himself by looking out the window. Whatever it was that existed between Linda and Nate was clearly on pause. This was difficult for Linda on several levels. Foremost she didn't really know what Nate was thinking. She had an idea, but nothing for certain. What occurred spontaneously the night before might have been entirely different for him than it had been for her. *It was only a hug!* But it had been a long time since she had been involved with a man. She had focused on her column the last few years, pushing men aside to pursue a career. As she had said to her mother many times, life is simpler alone, but for the first time in three years, she had to wonder if that was wrong. Which led to yet another complication—honesty. When did she tell Nate who her father was? And what about Bob Richards? Get with it, girl, she thought to herself. This whole situation was a screaming dead end. And with no success, she did everything she could to suppress what she was feeling.

Early on in the drive, it was apparent from the diminishing CB chatter that things were not quite as closely knit on the great northern plain as they were back in Kansas and Missouri. The farmers and the local police were probably just as likely to support the strike, but there weren't as many people out there, and Nate and his crew would go for long stretches with nothing coming in. Things didn't feel quite as secure as they had the day before, and everyone was feeling the tension. Superficially the country road, cowboy mood persisted in the truck—Rust's obscene CB chatter assured that—but beneath the surface, something about where they were headed was causing Nate to periodically shut the window between the cab and the camper.

For the most part, they drove back roads paralleling Interstate 80, and toward the middle of the day, wide open Nebraska became Wyoming's high plains. Despite the lack of communication, they encountered no trouble whatsoever as their route turned north toward Montana, and the dark fringe on the western horizon steadily grew into the purple profile of the Rocky Mountains. Mile by mile, the grand mountain range that stretched from New Mexico to Canada staged up into the Big Sky until the snowcapped peaks were looking down on the canopied pickup like giant bald eagles lined up against the heavens. This was it. The hard physical western edge of the Heartland.

Late in the afternoon, amid a long CB silence, winding along a secondary road of no apparent importance, they came out of a series of curves right into a Homeland Guard roadblock. A hundred yards ahead, ten soldiers with MP-5s, a jeep, and a personnel carrier were checking all vehicles going in either direction. With two cars behind them and three cars and a truck ahead, there was no turning around or getting away in the old GMC tortoise. Rust braked to a stop behind the vehicle ahead of them and turned to Nate. "What's fair here?"

"Total restraint."

Linda stood up and peered into the cab through the window. "Use me as a hostage if you have to."

Will got up also. "Dad, they could arrest us right here, couldn't they?"

"Could be, son. But instead of worrying about that, let me slip back there and get into that crawl space. You and Linda should climb up here in the cab."

Rust sat back in his seat, eyes ahead on the roadblock, eased out the clutch, and moved up another car length. "Don't worry, Will." He spit out the window. "They only want your dad."

Nate grinned amid the pinch of squeezing his body through the sliding window. "Don't count on that," he said as he twisted his shoulders through.

"I ain't even a farmer," Jerry cackled, giving Will a pull, helping him into the front seat while the truck two cars ahead went through inspection. "But hell, this might screw up your boy's admission to Stanford."

Will was too frightened to laugh. Jerry pulled up another car length as Linda squeezed her hips through the opening and settled into the front seat next to the window. Behind, Nate fought to get the piece of false flooring in place over top of him. They were second in line and running out of time.

As Jerry pulled up one last car length to the blockade, Linda glanced over her shoulder and saw that Nate was still struggling to get the false floor to settle down properly. She quickly slipped off her sports bra without removing her cotton top. Nate was still poking and prodding at the false floor when two guardsmen approached the pickup from either side. Knowing even a few seconds might help, Linda opened the pickup door and stepped out.

"Stop right there, lady!" ordered the guardsman on the driver's side. Eight MP-5's suddenly rose up and leveled at the truck. With the sports bra off, Linda's gauzy white top left little to the imagination about the size and shape of her breasts. The young guardsmen immediately lost focus on everything but the dark silhouettes of her nipples.

"Been in this pig too damn long, Captain," Linda protested, doing a deep knee bend with just enough action to give her breasts a sway. "Had to stretch my legs a bit." She lifted her arms up over her head, causing three mouths to fall open on the back line.

The captain waved for the men to lower their guns. "Sorry, miss. But please step away from the vehicle now that you're out." He moved up to Jerry's window. "What's your business ahead, mister?"

"Off to visit some old friends outside Spokane," said Jerry as cool as the other side of the pillow.

By this time, the second officer, a sergeant, was peering in the passenger's side of the pickup. "We'll need some ID from all of you," he said.

The captain followed with, "And I'll need to take a look inside your camper."

"Go ahead, it's open, Captain," said Jerry like it was nothing, handing the man his driver's license.

As the sergeant checked Linda's ID, the captain returned Jerry's license and circled around to the rear. He opened the camper door, stepped in, looked around, and stepped out. By this time, Will was pulling his wallet out of his jeans. He handed the sergeant a fake ID that he used to get into Wichita bars. The sergeant didn't have a clue about the ID, but all of a sudden, he stopped cold and looked at Will a second time. He motioned to the guardsman closest to the personnel carrier. "Get the photos, Private."

The private laid his rifle against the personnel carrier, opened the door, withdrew a folder, and came forward. By this time, the captain was back at the front of the pickup.

"Let me see those, Private," said the sergeant. The private opened the folder and handed the officer several pictures of Nate, his ex-wife, and Will. He took an extra-long look at the one of Will.

"We got something here, Captain," exclaimed the sergeant excitedly. He pulled out his side arm. "All of you out of the cab and away from the truck."

Behind him, the other eight guardsmen snapped to attention, raising their rifles.

The captain came up alongside the sergeant as Will climbed out and Rust opened the driver's side door.

"Looks a lot like Cromwell's son."

With this announcement all eyes turned to Will, and Rust took the shift in attention to retrieve his 9mm Beretta from behind the front seat.

"Let's see your wallet, son," said the captain.

Flustered by the predicament, Will wasn't sure what to do. As he hesitated, Rust stepped out of the cab, eyes on the other armed guardsmen, knowing that from behind the truck door and with the Beretta's fifteen rounds, he could take down all ten of these inexperienced guardsmen before they knew what hit them.

"Your wallet, son. Now!" commanded the captain again.

Will still hesitated, but before the captain could issue another word, Nate stepped from behind the camper with his hands up. "That's alright, Captain," he said. "We don't want any trouble. I'm who you're looking for."

They knew who he was immediately. A hush fell over the entire cluster of people, and eight rifles swung in the direction of Cromwell.

"I'm going to have to take you in, Colonel Cromwell. There's a warrant out for your arrest." The captain turned to the sergeant. "I think we'd better take them all in."

The guardsmen shifted in place anxiously, rifles aimed at Cromwell.

Rust eased the safety off his Beretta and visualized the order of the kill.

"I don't think so," said one of guardsmen suddenly swinging his rifle in Jerry's direction with the captain in between—freezing Jerry an instant before he would have opened fire.

The captain snapped at the soldier. "What did you say, Private?"

"Step back, Captain," said the private. "And Sergeant, put your sidearm away. There's no way we're taking these folks in."

"You're way out of line, Private," barked the captain, his hand going to his sidearm.

"Remove that sidearm, sir, at the risk of your life."

"WHAT!"

The sergeant turned his pistol on the guardsman.

"Put that gun down, Sergeant," demanded the private. "Or the captain's history." The private's eyes swung briefly to the men beside him, moving around uneasily in their ranks. "This man before us is one of the greatest soldiers to ever fight for this country. It would be a humiliating dishonor to me and this country to allow him to be arrested."

Will and Linda exchanged a glance. Nate was watching Jerry.

The captain glared at his sergeant. "Shoot him!"

Three of the guardsmen turned their MP-5s in the direction of the captain. Four others turned theirs on the sergeant.

The sergeant lowered his sidearm. "I'm with the men, sir."

The captain looked around, anger blistering from his eyes. Then all of a sudden, understanding all too well what was going on, he let it go and lifted his hand from his holster clasp. "Fine."

Instantly everything relaxed. The rifles lowered, and several of the guardsmen broke into smiles. The captain extended his hand to Cromwell. "I'm sorry, Colonel, these men are right. I'm the one that's out of line."

Nate took his hand, then all the soldiers crowded in and wanted to shake his hand too. Three farmers and an older woman from the rigs behind got out and introduced themselves. All saying hello and thanks and hoping to shake Nate's hand in respect.

This moment triggered Linda's final epiphany. All along she had believed the strike was correct but hopelessly futile. After two days traveling with Colonel Cromwell and witnessing the incredibly positive spirit of the farming community, she had begun to rethink that position. But now, with this sudden reversal, eight Homeland Guardsmen turning their rifles on their commanding officer, she understood that because of one man, Nathaniel Cromwell, a truly humble and courageous man, the strike had a real chance for success. But it was even more than that. Above and beyond the politics, Nate was melting her heart from the inside out.

CHAPTER 77

At Frank Nelson's request, John McClay set up a four-way video-conference on secure lines originating from his law offices in Washington, D.C. Lawrence Fitzgerald at the Old Executive Building across town was on one line. Frank Nelson in his office on Wall Street was on another line, and Rosalind Davis was on a video-phone in a private room at the *Les Ambassadeurs* restaurant in London.

"We've gotten some further updates on Lake Balkhash," said Frank, unusually stiff and serious. "We're looking at what could be the world's largest as yet untapped field."

"But we already knew it had incredible potential, Frank," said Rosalind. "Are you saying this is something more?"

"Yes. Lyman called me today from the site. Hamilton's top geoengineer has verified the upper estimate."

"That's a hundred billion barrels," said Fitzgerald.

"Exactly," continued Frank, watching the other three faces in separate windows on his video monitor. "And as wonderful as this is, it's causing me more anxiety about pipeline security. So Rosalind, I think it's necessary to throw a little more money at Mendelev."

"The concern, Rosalind," added McClay, "is getting Mendelev totally on board."

"I thought he was."

"Even more so," said Frank. "And we want this to happen as soon as possible. Once we get our troops in, there will be no good way out for Mendelev."

"What's Texocal saying?" asked Rosalind.

"We're the ones with the money, Rosalind," said Frank. "They'll do whatever we want."

"That's right," confirmed McClay. "I attended a meeting of the board of directors last week. They understand as well as anyone that

Russia is a critical piece in the petroleum endgame. This is all about keeping Mendelev in and Moscow out."

"So, we want to do some favors for Mendelev in the meantime," chimed in Fitzgerald. "We need to arrange for some stock sales and account transfers." It wasn't an accident that Fitzgerald was part of the conversation. This last request was the underlying purpose of the call. Even more than the announcement of the size of the field, black market money laundering was the big bait for Mendelev until the oil actually started flowing at its full potential.

Rosalind understood all of this without being told. "Fine," she said, reaffirming the most powerful link in global economics—Anglo-American banking interests. "But I have a question for you, Frank."

"What's that, Rosalind?"

"What's going on with your farmers' strike?"

Frank laughed. "It's overplayed," he said. "The money is loose change compared to what we have going in Kazakhstan. We could pay the farmers the extra dollar and still do quite well. We just don't want this union thing to get any momentum."

"Well, I knew that, Frank. But what's going on with this Homeland Security fellow, Houseman?"

Frank frowned in the video-screen. "The man's out of control."

"He's making a push for the privatization of the Homeland Guard," said McClay. "He's got the Justice Department and the FBI wound up on this domestic terrorist threat. By sensationalizing the farmers' strike, he thinks he'll be verifying the need for a stronger, highly-paid domestic anti-terrorism force."

"An American Gestapo?" quizzed Rosalind.

Frank grimaced for the mini-cam. "Please, Rosalind."

McClay intervened. "Let's stick to the business at hand. Rosalind, if you can move some money without anyone knowing, we want to do it now. Get past Kenaghy and push on with TES post-haste."

"So is Kenaghy going to sign it or not?" asked Rosalind.

"That's the other side of this," said Frank. "TES didn't get to him fast enough. Congress adjourns at the end of the week for the election year break. That's only nine days after he got the bill. If he doesn't sign it by then, he enacts a pocket veto. Which we can't override. Everything will be on hold until Congress reconvenes in the fall."

"And Mendelev is our sole source of pressure on Congress," interjected McClay. "We're setting the stage for Kenaghy's impeachment."

"If we don't get him out, we'll certainly ruin any chance of his winning the election," said Frank.

"That's some hardball," said Rosalind.

"It has to be," said Frank. Scared to death the size of the Lake Balkhash field would be leaked to Mendelev, he wanted an American military presence there yesterday.

CHAPTER 78

When everything finally settled down at the check point and Linda had put her sports bra back on—to a chorus of boos from the guardsmen—Nate took some time to speak to the Homeland Guard Captain, whose attitude had changed radically since he'd asked for Jerry's driver's license. The first thing Nate asked was why they had decided to blockade this particular rural route.

The captain's answer was simple. The federal authorities had information that General Hayes had returned to Montana after the first set of fires. And because of his notoriety and his power in Montana, it was thought best to make it as hard as possible for him or his militia to leave the state. The Homeland Guard was ordered to watch as many roads in and out of Montana as manpower allowed—which meant every main road and a high percentage of the lesser roads.

Finally, he said, looking Nate directly in the eye, "I don't know where you're headed, Colonel, but Hayes' ranch up north is heavily watched. I wouldn't go there if I were you." He paused, turning to Linda and Jerry. "And please understand, you cannot assume that this road will be guarded by these same men next week or even tomorrow. If you go into Montana, it won't be easy to get out by conventional means."

Jerry spoke up. "Captain, are you going to tell your superiors about this encounter?"

The captain looked at his men. "No, but I think it's safe to say that as the duties of this group of men changes, and they mix with other guardsmen, it will get out. Also there's these folks in line behind you. They will brag about shaking the Colonel's hand. Leaks will occur. Give it a day or two, and my guess is the authorities will know you've entered Montana."

After the captain walked away, Rust turned to Nate. "I don't like it, Boss."

Nate seemed unperturbed. "Me neither, but we're going in anyway. I've got some business to attend to, and it's got to be done face to face with Hayes—no two ways about it."

"What about the reporter?" asked Jerry. "Maybe we leave her behind."

Nate looked at Linda.

"I thought you needed a hostage," she said, staring right at Jerry. "Where's your insurance for Forest if I'm gone?"

Rust looked at Nate.

"She's with us," said Nate. He climbed into the GMC and that was that.

Five minutes after leaving the roadblock behind, Nate turned to Rust. "Rusty, did you have your Beretta out back there?"

Looking straight ahead, Rust's eyes lit up with a wide smile. "Damn right, Boss. Those guys handled that search so badly I knew they weren't taking us anywhere. I was a split second from some serious action."

Nate nodded. "Yeah, I thought so."

Rust laughed. Linda overheard this in the back and envisioned ten guardsmen shot in cold blood. It would have been a horrible error of judgment. For the first time, she realized that the situation shc had so willingly accepted the day before was a lot more dangerous than she'd first assumed.

Just out of Billings, Jerry picked up a CB message that would set the tone for the rest of the day.

"This is Yellowtail. Hawk on the wing. Holding. Over."

"That's our boy," said Nate, remembering the codeword Hayes had mentioned that afternoon in Forest's office.

"Gotcha Yellowtail," said Jerry, looking at Nate as he spoke. "This is Apollo 13. Looking for mission control. Over."

"Copy, Apollo. All around the mulberry bush. Keep your ears on. Four-five-niner is good when last checked. Over."

Nate nodded to Jerry.

"Copy, Yellowtail. Ears on. Over and out."

Nate turned around in the cab to face the back. "Linda, we're headed into a secure location to meet with General Hayes of the Montana militia." His eyes met hers with more than what was in his voice. "I'd like you to wear a blindfold the rest of the way. It might not be necessary, but it's a precaution I think General Hayes would appreciate."

"I'm fine with that, Nate." As soon as she said it, Linda realized it was the first time she'd used his first name in front of Will and Rust. It seemed important to her, but no one else seemed to notice.

"Thanks. You have something you can use?"

She nodded.

He closed the window and turned forward. Linda gave Will the madras blouse she'd worn the day before. He folded it over twice and tied it in a loose knot around her head and over her eyes.

Two uneasy hours passed with Linda sitting there blindfolded, her arms stretched out across the interior of the camper to stabilize herself as the rig bounced through some rather rough uphill roads and abrupt turns. Off and on, she thought about her father. To reassure herself, she imagined his presence there in the camper with her. With this, however, came a dark reminder; both her father's history and her connection with Richards would eventually have to come out.

Linda heard the window slide open. Nate spoke. "Okay, Linda, you can remove the blindfold."

She lifted the folded blouse from her eyes. They were deep amid a thick coniferous forest, winding slowly up on a long, narrow dirt road toward the top of a minor peak in the foothills of the Montana Rockies. It was dusk and the woods were dark and gloomy. No one said a word. Nate and Jerry were peering out ahead trying to read each bend and bump in the road. Will and Linda were alternately looking forward through the connecting window or out the side windows into the shadowy forest.

"Look over there to the right, Dad," said Will pointing.

All of them followed the direction of Will's outstretched forefinger. A man, painted completely in camouflage and draped with bits of plants and branches, stood up from behind a blind to watch them pass. He held a high-power crossbow and had a full quiver of arrows on his back.

"I think we're there, folks," said Nate.

Another camouflaged man, similarly invisible until he moved, lifted up out of the undergrowth on the forest floor. He held an automatic rifle. One by one, another three, four, five men, then a woman appeared out of nowhere as they proceeded up the uneven road. All of them were armed, all of them with painted faces and hands. It was creepy as hell—

as though the forest was suddenly coming alive with them. Impossibly a tense situation was growing more so.

Even the veteran Rust was impressed. "These guys are hardcore, Boss. Who is this guy, Hayes?"

"A man I wasn't too sure about at first but have grown to trust—even respect. I'll be interested in your take on the man, Rusty."

"General Hayes? I don't know, Boss. I think I've been a civilian too long to get excited about playing soldier again."

"I sure hope they know who we are, Dad."

"If they aren't shooting yet, Will, I'd say we're okay. They should be expecting us."

On cue, two more soldiers rose up out of a thicket and saluted, as though they did, in fact, know who rode in the cab of the old Jimmy.

The road leveled out and broke into the open. A perimeter of cleared ground, maybe fifty yards wide, surrounded a large log cabin nestled in a grove of tall Douglas firs. The GMC continued up the dirt road to a small gravel parking area and came to a stop. As Nate and the others climbed out of the rig, Hayes, in a soft olive-green cap and matching fatigues, came out of the cabin. He had a large pistol on his hip and a small silver Christian cross on his lapel. He saluted Nate. Nate returned the salute, and Jerry muttered something to Will about white men playing army.

Nate introduced everyone to General Vincent Hayes. Even with his thick red beard masking his expression, he was obviously upset when Linda's connection to *The New York Financial Times* was mentioned. She was just as disturbed. This right-wing patriotic stuff had always made her sick to her stomach whenever she heard about it or saw video clips of it on television. Now here she was stuck in the center of redneck fantasy land, perhaps the most bizarre of all America's outer fringe.

"Quite a place you've got here, General," said Nate, glancing around.

"Last outpost of the sane," pronounced Hayes with pride. Rust rolled his eyes. "Let's go inside. I'm sure you're hungry and could use a break from the road. Any trouble finding this place, Colonel?" he asked over his shoulder as the foursome followed him up the gravel walk to the log cabin.

"It wasn't easy, but I don't suppose it's meant to be."

"As close kept a secret as possible."

They entered a huge main room that looked a lot like a hunting lodge, with a ceiling that peaked into the roofline and over-sized furniture made of rough cut logs. An elk head was mounted high on one wall. A stuffed grizzly on another. It was a real log cabin made of massive hand-hewn logs and thick chinking, perhaps three thousand square feet in total area, with pine flooring and woven Native American rugs throughout.

"The running water in the kitchen comes from a well and needs to be hand pumped. Showers and latrines out back work the same way," said Hayes with a wary eye on Linda. "All our electricity is generated right here. Photovoltaic cells and a bank of RV batteries."

Hayes pointed to a plank table as they moved into the adjoining kitchen. A plate of sandwiches, a bowl of fruit, and a pot of coffee were arranged on the table. "Take whatever you like."

Will immediately snagged a sandwich and an orange. Rust wasn't far behind. Nate stood there a moment, clearly taken by the rustic feel of the place, the simple fir cabinets and cutting board counters, then reached over and poured himself a cup of coffee. He emptied a package of powdered cream into it and gave it a stir as Linda stepped up next to him and poured herself a cup as well. Nate passed her the powdered cream, and their eyes met momentarily with a subtle acknowledgement. The situation could not have been more awkward or, for Linda, more exciting.

"I'm impressed, General," said Nate taking his first sip of coffee.

Hayes' eyes lit with Cromwell's approval.

"And this place is entirely secure?"

"Absolutely, Colonel. Totally off the grid. No telephone lines. No internet. We have a TV and a radio and some huge antennas up in the trees. But no direct lines. A cell phone will work, but don't use them." He looked right at Linda. "Don't even turn them on."

"Don't worry, General," she said. "I'm a hostage for Mahan. They've stripped me of communication devices."

This made no impression on Hayes, and as he turned away, Linda noticed through the kitchen doorway that the rug in the center of the main room was moving. Suddenly a large trap door pushed open from underneath. A thin, old man with wire-rimmed glasses, a long gray beard, and two long gray braids climbed up into the room, wearing suspenders for his busted out jeans and moccasins on his feet. "What's all this noise?" he said, padding into the kitchen, just as orncry and cranky as he looked. "Where'd these strangers come from?"

Hayes smiled. "This here's my communications operator, Twist Hanratty. Twist, this is Colonel Cromwell, his son, and a couple of his friends."

Twist sneered at the guests as though their arrival was an inconvenience. "Don't mind me," he growled. "I just need some coffee." He refilled the big mug in his hand, then just as suddenly as he appeared, turned and disappeared into his hole, the trap door closing slowly over him.

"What's down there?" asked Rust.

Hayes took yet another appraising look at Linda. "Computers, communication gear, stores of food." He paused. "And weapons enough to stand off a small army."

"Computers, but no internet connection?"

"Had that for a while, but Twist forced me to tear it out along with the phone line. He won't allow any direct connection to his computers. Anything he needs he has other folks download out in the conventional world and pack in here by hand."

"And you have your militia information here?" asked Nate, some clear interest behind his question.

"This is it, Colonel. This is the heart and soul of our operation. My ranch in eastern Montana acts as decoy. I've got about fifty men there right now. Plus a look-a-like for me. As far as the Homeland Guard knows, they're watching every move I make, prepared to arrest me at the first sign of any kind of strike action."

"How do you communicate out here?"

"All low-energy stuff, Colonel. We use walkie-talkies with those people you saw out in the woods. Prearranged citizen band relays for longer distances. Nothing that will give an electric signature to a satellite. It might be a little slow, might not be foolproof, but it's the best we can do for anything close to secure."

"What do you know about Mahan's trip to Washington?"

"I got a message from Forest last night through the relay."

"Why not the pony express?" quipped Rust. Hayes found no humor in the comment. Nate continued with business.

"I don't know what to expect from Kenaghy, General, but it's our first real contact with the power brokers—if we grant that Kenaghy has any power to broker. I think it will set the stage for what we can expect down the line with the strike. We should be prepared for both good news and bad."

Hayes nodded that he understood the implications.

"How much wheat do we have ready to burn at this point?"

"Over a million acres, Colonel. So widely distributed over the center of country there's no way it can all be guarded."

"How long would it take to get it going with your relay system?"

"Well, if it needs to happen fast, I have a different plan." Again, Hayes looked right at Linda. "We'll get into that when necessary. Just take my word for it. We could have a Post Toasties barbecue started in thirty minutes."

Nate nodded. "Any thoughts?"

"I don't trust Kenaghy."

"Yeah, I figured. But Forest's got his hopes up. So, I guess we'll have to wait and see on that one. He was going to call me on one of these disposal phones tomorrow morning, but if I can't turn it on, can he get a hold of you here?"

"He's got a phone number to call in Billings. It's six CB relays to here. Again, it could be better, but it'll work—and he said he'd call."

"You know the Homeland Guard is checking traffic in and out of Montana, General?"

"We started to get word of that this afternoon. You have any trouble?"

"We got surprised by a road block on a tiny back road. But half these guardsmen are country boys, once they recognized me, they let us by. Funny thing, General, everyone that can handle a rifle in this country is on our side." Hayes let the hint of a smile flash in his eyes. "Or almost everyone." Nate dug the heel Will found in the cornfield out of his hip pocket. "Take a look at this." He handed it to Hayes.

Hayes turned it over in his hand. "Looks like government issue. What is it?"

"Any of your boys wear this kind of boot?"

Hayes frowned, lifted his right foot, checking his own combat boots. "Not quite the same as mine. But, yeah, these kind are all over."

"Found this at my place the day after my house was firebombed."

"I'm sorry about your mother, Colonel."

"Yeah, they wanted me." His tone denied his deeper sorrow, but not the anger. "They also stomped three swastikas into my cornfields."

"I heard."

"I'm not accusing anyone of anything, General. But I want you to be on the lookout. I'm concerned about infiltration. FBI. CIA. I don't know." Linda's ears burned with this. "In any case, it was set up to look like right-wing radicals did the job. If it wasn't white supremacists, someone's trying to drive a wedge into the strike alliance. We might never find these people. But keep an eye out. I got a score to settle."

Hayes nodded and Cromwell pressed on.

"Can Twist run ID checks through your computer system?"

"We have some capability."

"Remember that kid I decked in the grange that night? Any way to find him?" From the tone in Nate's voice, it was clear this was one of the reasons he'd come to Montana.

"It will take over night, but I can run it through the system and the relays. There's a chance somebody knows him."

"It's a long shot, but I got a funny feeling about that kid that night. He came up to me afterward and handed me a newsletter called *The New Patriot*—neo-Nazi stuff. Seemed like too much—you know what I mean."

"I've seen *The New Patriot*, Colonel. It's a bunch of crap. I've been told it's put out by the FBI to discredit the militia."

"Strange world we got going here."

"Yeah, we might be the most misunderstood minority in this nation."

"I'm not sure I understand you either, General, but maybe by the end of this thing, I will. In the meantime, we wait for some feedback from Mahan. Then I'm outta here. You and I being together is bad juju."

CHAPTER 79

James Kenaghy strode briskly down the hall of the West Wing of the White House headed to the Oval Office late Sunday evening. There was a certain confidence in his gait. Almost a smile on his face and a sure new sense of hope in his eyes. Compared to the last few months of doom and gloom in the White House, the last twenty-four hours hinted of the energy and excitement of the President's first six months in office. Staffers and clerks met his eye, and he would nod. Sometimes with a snappy wink. The talk was that it was Marjorie's return Thursday night that had brightened 1600 Pennsylvania Avenue. "He must have finally gotten laid," quipped one secretary to another. "I think it's that Congress adjourns next week," suggested one of his speechwriters. "Maybe, Houseman resigned," cackled one of the aides.

But it was none of the above. It was the message Kenaghy had received the day before through his press secretary Wayne Stevens from *The New York Financial Times'* Washington Bureau Chief Frederick Manning. Linda Bennett had made contact with Forest Mahan. He was quietly being ushered into Washington, landing at Reagan Airport that night. Kenaghy would be meeting with the National Grange President within an hour or two. It was a meeting Kenaghy believed held great potential, and yet, he was more than a little apprehensive about how things would go with the strike leader. The President was entirely aware that his farm record was less than mediocre, and his environmental report card was only slightly better. Nothing was assured. In any case, he'd been excited to receive the message from Manning and was even more excited to shake the hand of Forest Mahan.

The intercom buzzed as Kenaghy entered the historic office. He hurried across the blue carpet and hit the button. "I have the Presidential Counsel Sam Wedemeier on the phone, sir," said his secretary, "Can you speak to him?"

"Of course. Put him on."

There was a pause, then the President's constitutional lawyer spoke. "Mr. President, I wanted to get back to you on those questions you asked me."

"Hope you've got some good news, Tom."

"Sir, like most legal matters, there's some good and some bad."

"Let's hear the good."

"Well, concerning the use of executive orders, precedent says, you have almost no limit to what you can do—short of declaring war or revoking the presidential term limits. Congress can intervene, but it's been a rarity."

"Can I override Houseman's Severe Terror Alert?"

"That's the bad news. The Patriot Act, as amended a few years back, is filled with a variety of special Red Alert powers and actions reserved for the Homeland Security Director, which only Congress can revoke or change. These amendments were deliberately designed to allow Homeland Security to circumvent the executive branch in what are referred to as *terror emergencies*, which Houseman has already set in motion."

"That's insane."

"As you might recall, these amendments were tacked on to the Patriot Act shortly after the bombing at the Raiders-Ravens playoff game a few years back. Houseman screamed about how his hands were tied for over an hour because of delays in the executive branch response due to Washington area communication lines going down. Truth is, much like the 9/11, panic caused Congress to put some things into law that cooler heads should have prevented. Houseman's had an iron grip on domestic terrorism ever since."

"But once the terror alert is reduced, my options get better?"

"That's right."

"Can I override deployment of the Homeland Guard?"

"With the Red Alert, sir, the checks and balances become a maze."

"What about intervening in the farmers' strike negotiations?"

"That's a little easier, Mr. President. Taft-Hartley is on your side there."

The door to the Oval Office cracked open. Cameron Phillips stuck his head in. "Mr. President, excuse me, something's come up."

"Hold on a moment, Tom." Kenaghy put the phone down.

Phillips came all the way into the office.

"The FBI took Forest Mahan into custody the moment he deplaned at Reagan Airport."

"WHAT? On whose orders?"

"The Attorney General's, sir," winced Phillips.

"DAMN IT!" Kenaghy began to pace behind the desk. "How did FBI even know of his arrival?"

"There must have been a leak, sir."

"But no one knew. Only Stevens and Manning." Kenaghy's eyes narrowed. "Where's Stevens now?"

"I don't know. I got the call about Mahan from a friend in Justice, sir, only moments ago. They also seized his home in Missouri, confiscated his computer and all his records."

Kenaghy stared momentarily at the floor then lifted his head. "Where's Mahan now?"

"The holding tank at FBI headquarters."

Kenaghy wandered over to the windows behind his desk and peered out at the armed guards securing the grounds. He turned back to Phillips. "With the kind of support I've got in this town right now, it'll take a damn presidential pardon to get him out of confinement."

"And maybe two or three days, sir."

Kenaghy hit the intercom. "Amy, get Attorney General Sullivan on the line."

"According to my friend, Sullivan's preparing to make a statement in the morning," said Phillips.

Kenaghy gave him an exasperated look.

Phillips continued with the bad news. "He's going to call Mahan an enemy of the state."

The intercom light flashed. Kenaghy pushed the button. "Yes?"

"The Attorney General is not in his office, sir. You know it is Sunday night?"

"Yes, yes. Try MacFarlane at FBI." Kenaghy returned to the window and stared out into the dank, humid Washington evening. Neither he nor Phillips said a word until the intercom buzzed again.

Kenaghy turned away from the window as if coming out of a deep daydream. He punched the button. "Yes, Amy."

"MacFarlane's not there either, sir."

"Try him at home." His anger spiked. "Sullivan too."

There was a pause at the other end. "Sir?"

"Yes, Amy."

"Tom Wedemeier is still on the line."

"Right, put him back on."

"Mr. President."

"Tom, how do I get past the FBI?"

CHAPTER 80

No one stayed up late that night at Hayes' hideout except those on watch in the forest perimeter. Linda took an open bed in one of the log cabin's back rooms that was set aside for women. Will slept in the camper. Rust pitched his tent beside the rig. Nate started out in the camper but decided instead to unroll his sleeping bag on the ground behind the log cabin and sleep beneath the wide Montana sky.

Nate lay back with his hands behind his head and stared up into the night. The stars were so thick and bright it looked like he could reach up and stir the Milky Way with his finger. He tried to relax and pick out constellations but found himself assessing the strike situation and planning for the days ahead instead. Everything seemed to hinge on Mahan's trip to Washington. And yet solving the strike through negotiations seemed highly unlikely when the only government reaction they'd gotten so far was deployment of the Homeland Guard. He thought about the prospect of more fires, and it filled him with a tired sadness. Complications and logistics spread out in his mind then dispersed and reformed into images of his mother's death, followed by thick waves of grief and guilt, and finally a deep trembling remorse. After a while, this sadness transposed into a vivid memory of the encounter he'd had with Linda Bennett the night before. Nate smiled to himself. Yes, he was drawn to her. More than he wanted to admit. He hardly knew her. Hadn't really talked to her about anything but the strike. Still, she was swelling into the emptiness he had denied for so long. He felt this every time he saw her. There was an immediacy to it, an emotional relief, a physical thrilling—but it only complicated the already difficult task before him now. *Forget it, forget it,* he repeated to himself, over and over again until he fell asleep.

Linda was exhausted from a long tense day and had fallen asleep as soon as she hit the bed. But she woke in the middle of the night and couldn't get back to sleep, her mind deciding on its own to rerun the events of the day. The incident at the Montana border had been bad enough at the time and worse after she learned how close they'd come to gunfire. But the evening's encounter with Hayes and his militia mentality bothered her even more. She knew Hayes' history as a secessionist, hated his attitude, and cared even less for the weapons that everyone there was carrying. She was a beltway reporter, not an embedded war correspondent, and this militia craziness scared her in a fundamental way. The farmers' strike had already escalated into more than your ordinary labor standoff; now she began to worry that even greater levels of violence were in the offing. God, she hoped the meeting she'd arranged for Kenaghy and Mahan had gone well.

Linda tossed and turned with these thoughts for some time before finally giving in to the need to use a bathroom. She got out of bed and headed to the outside latrine. She was wearing an over-sized t-shirt to sleep in and tiptoed barefoot through the dew laden grass to the outhouses behind the cabin. When she opened the door and caught a whiff of what was inside, she decided she didn't want to go in barefoot, so she slipped into the shadows by the trees, lifted the long t-shirt, and squatted.

Nate woke to the sound of a soft hiss in the grass. He turned in his sleeping bag seeing only the white of bare buttocks—maybe thirty feet away. In the dim shadowy light, he had to roll over to decipher what he was looking at.

Linda had no idea Nate was there until she heard the rustling of his sleeping bag.

She quickly stood. "Oh my God! Nate!" She veritably glowed in the dark for the intensity of her blush. "I'm so embarrassed. I beg your pardon. I didn't know anyone was out here."

"You must have gone to finishing school with Jerry."

"His was an overt display. I, I…," she stammered.

"Don't worry, Linda. I barely noticed."

Linda stood there at a distance, embarrassed, wanting to talk, but not knowing what to say, starting to get a chill in the light shirt.

Nate sat up in his bedroll. "Come over here, Linda. It's fine." His voice was easy and reassuring.

Linda approached slowly. She tucked the long shirt around her legs and knelt beside Nate's bedroll. "God, I mooned you. I don't know what you must think."

"I think you have a mighty pretty bottom."

Again, she blushed like a floodlight.

"I never got a chance to thank you, Linda, for your quick thinking at the road block."

"It didn't help much. You were the difference. Those guardsmen knew the real thing when they saw it." She was visibly shivering in the cool mountain air.

"You're cold," he said. "Take my sweat shirt. It's right over there."

Linda reached over and slipped it over her head, covering herself in his scent and stimulating a pulse of pheromones, followed by an involuntary quiver.

"Hey, you're really cold."

Linda's eyes met his in the gray moonlight with a deep mutual recognition. There was a hesitant, awkward moment of *wrong time, wrong place*, but it was all chemistry and hormones now. Nate opened his sleeping bag. Linda slid in beside him, sighing softly at the relief of his warmth. Her t-shirt had ridden up above her belly, and he wore no t-shirt, only boxer briefs. Irresistibly they snuggled into each other—and all the rationale that might have kept them apart melted away.

CHAPTER 81

When Nate woke with the first hint of dawn, he was alone in his sleeping bag. He sat up wondering if he might have dreamed Linda's late night visit. Then he noticed his briefs lying in the wet grass and a trail of footprints in the dew leading back to the cabin. He lay back down and closed his eyes, allowing himself a moment to savor the memory. But the clock was running and all of today's actions hinged on word from Mahan. He stood up out of his sleeping bag and slipped on his t-shirt and jeans.

Jerry Rust was already up. He strode across the strip of lawn between the cabin and the gravel parking lot in the dim gray of pre-morning.

"Morning, Boss."

Nate nodded, eyes down, buckling his belt.

"What's next?"

"Check on word from Mahan. Maybe some coffee first."

Rust looked off toward the cabin and noticed the dew soaked briefs and the trail of footprints in the grass. His eyes swung back and met his friend's. There was no hiding it. Nate expected a snide remark. Instead, Rust uncharacteristically let it go. "Yeah, coffee would be good."

General Hayes came up from the basement as soon as he heard footsteps overhead. Jerry and Nate were at the kitchen table filling their cups with coffee. It was a few minutes after six. The first broken rays of sunlight streamed in the east facing windows. Hayes didn't bother with *good morning*. "Got some information for you, Colonel."

Nate looked up from his first sip of coffee. "Mahan?"

"No. Feedback on that young white supremacist you asked about last night." This woke Nate faster than the coffee. "He's from a militia battalion in Oklahoma. Twist printed out what he's got in our files." He laid a sheet of paper on the table. "Name's John Finnegan. Not too popular in his unit and has two ATF arrests for attempts to purchase firearms with false ID."

Nate picked up the paper and read through the information. Nate hadn't said much about his investigation into his mother's death, but the submerged intensity behind it was obvious now. He soberly folded up the paper and stuck it in his hip pocket. "Thanks, General."

Hayes nodded and headed back down to the basement.

Nate turned to Jerry. "As soon as we get word on Mahan, we're headed south."

Jerry gave him an appraising look. "Don't let this personal stuff get in the way of your bigger purpose, Boss." The double meaning struck them both as soon as he said it.

When Linda came out of the back bedroom, she heard the men's voices. She crossed through the main room, past the trap door that was all the way open, and entered the kitchen. Jerry and Nate were sitting at the table. She immediately felt the awkwardness of the moment—either it was her or something that was going on between them. Nate's eyes gave away nothing as he looked up at her.

Jerry stood as Linda approached the table. "I'm going to check things out in the basement." He gave her a drop dead look and walked out.

Linda sat down across the table from Nate amid a swarm of emotions and difficult circumstances. She lifted her eyes to his. "Any word from Forest?"

"No, not yet." He smiled easily though clearly other things were on his mind. "Hayes is down in the basement with that old boy Twist. I guess they're checking the news and monitoring their citizen band radio for relayed messages. I'm not really sure what we should expect."

"Too bad Forest can't just call you instead of all this relay stuff."

Nate took a sip of his coffee. "Might be easier, Linda, but no one knows where we are. That's especially important right now." Their eyes met again. Neither of them said anything. But the awkwardness that had plagued them before wasn't there, and the good of what they'd shared during the night communicated between them in the silence.

They heard someone coming up from the basement. Hayes surfaced from the trap door and came directly to the kitchen doorway. "You need to see something downstairs, Colonel." It was clear from the tone of his voice that this invitation did not include Linda.

Nate stood up with his cup of coffee and followed Hayes out of the room. He touched Linda lightly on the shoulder as he walked by. She looked down at her cup of coffee, full of unspeakable bliss and worry. A moment later, she got up from the table with her coffee and went to the bedroom she'd slept in to type some notes into her computer.

Nate descended the steep stairway into the log cabin's vast basement. It was the same size as the ground floor of the log cabin with several rooms and storage chambers off a large central area. "Below this," said Hayes, pointing to yet another trap door, "is a two room sub-basement of double-reinforced concrete for protection from forest fires—or artillery attack."

"Artillery attack? Do you really think that's a concern?"

"Hold that thought," said Hayes, leading Nate into one of the basement's side rooms. It was filled with electronic equipment—two televisions, several radios, and three computer terminals. Twist Hanratty pecked at one of the computer keyboards with his gray braids dangling over the keys. Jerry Rust stood beside him, his eyes on the screen. When Nate entered, Jerry looked up, his eyes cold and unyielding.

"What's going on?" asked Nate.

"Mahan was just on the news," said Hayes. "You can see it for yourself. Rerun the CNN piece, Twist."

The communications operator swiveled in his chair, so he faced one of the televisions. He turned on the television then hit some buttons on the recording device beside it.

"This was recorded just minutes ago," said Hayes solemnly.

The monitor flickered into a moving picture. And there it was—Mahan getting a personal FBI escort off the airplane at Reagan Airport, followed by a five-second sound bite from Attorney General Sullivan: "We want it known that we will not accept field burning as a legitimate labor strike tactic. It is an act of domestic terrorism and a federal offense."

Nate's face darkened.

"We also got word through the CB network that the FBI moved in on my cattle ranch several hours before dawn this morning. It must have been quite a surprise because we got no direct word from my people at the time. I think it would be wise to assume that they know the guy they captured isn't me."

Nate's eyes seemed to focus on something about a foot in front of him.

"Unfortunately, there's more bad news," added Hayes.

Rust spoke up. "It's our babe, Boss."

The short focus in Nate's eyes dropped away as he turned to his friend.

"I thought I recognized Linda Bennett's name, but I couldn't pin it down," Rust continued. "I came down here a few minutes ago to see what kind of identification capacity Twist had here in his files. That's when the CNN thing came on."

"And?" said Nate.

"Linda Bennett is Linda Bennett Rivenhouse. Her father is the late Arthur Rivenhouse."

Nate knew the name.

"She's been known to leak information for the CIA."

"*New York Financial Times,* Colonel," followed Hayes. "I was wondering why she's been giving us all this good ink."

"Her whole line must have been a setup, Boss. The stories in the paper. The letter from Kenaghy. Arranging Mahan's trip to Washington." He paused leaving the obvious unsaid.

Nate stared at the concrete floor. When he lifted his eyes, they were lit like a wolf's. "Let's see your fast communication system, General. We've got some grain to burn."

Twist looked up from his chair at Hayes. "Do it," said Hayes.

Twist turned his chair so he faced his largest radio. He flipped it on and started adjusting dials.

"That a ham radio?" asked Rust.

Twist looked over his shoulder. "Hell of a lot faster than 900 CB relays."

Hayes nodded. "It's our emergency system. We already have an established code. One quick signal and it's out there. Unless they're already clued into this location, I guarantee nobody in the intelligence community will figure this one out until sometime next week."

CHAPTER 82

In an unprecedented move, at almost the same time Monday morning that Cromwell gave Hayes the order to set the second big burn in motion, though two hours later on the clock due to Eastern Time, the presidential limousine and a secret service escort took President Kenaghy and Cameron Phillips the ten blocks from the White House to FBI headquarters. Presidential Counsel Sam Wedemeier, carrying an executive order for the release of Forest Mahan in his briefcase, met them on the front steps of the J. Edgar Hoover Building. Kenaghy, Phillips, and Wedemeier, surrounded by a phalanx of secret service men, marched up the stairs into the main lobby and demanded to see FBI Director Bernie MacFarlane, then, without stopping for formalities at the reception desk, continued into an elevator and up to the fifth floor to MacFarlane's office. There amid the timid protests of scurrying FBI administrators, the secret service agents barged through MacFarlane's outer office door, startling MacFarlane's secretary, followed by the President, Phillips, and Wedemeier. The entire group continued directly into MacFarlane's office, where he was seated at his desk.

McFarlane blustered, "What is this?" Then he recognized the President and immediately stood into the storm.

Wedemeier slapped the papers on MacFarlane's desk, and Kenaghy stepped forward to confront the short, fat FBI director. "Who gave the order to arrest Mahan?" he demanded. "I want him released," he continued without waiting for an answer. "And I want him released now!"

MacFarlane didn't have the top FBI position for no reason. He could be a pushy, bullying individual in his own right, but the towering presence of the President of the United States overwhelmed the beady-eyed bureaucrat. "Well, yes, sir. The order came to me from Attorney General Sullivan, and, if I'm not mistaken, he was following a directive from the Homeland Security Office."

"HOUSEMAN BE DAMNED!" screamed Kenaghy, slamming MacFarlane's desk with his fist. "He's been fired. He has no power at all." Wedemeier and Phillips exchanged a glance. "Have Mahan in the lobby to meet me in five minutes or it will be your head too."

McFarlane glanced at the papers on his desk, saw the words *Executive Order* stamped across the cover sheet, and punched a button on his desk communications system. "Ford, get Forest Mahan out of lockdown and in the lobby—immediately."

"Mahan, sir?" came back over the speaker.

"FOREST MAHAN. RIGHT AWAY!" screamed back MacFarlane literally shaking with emotion.

Kenaghy spun on his heels and stomped out of the office followed by his entourage.

Five minutes later, two armed FBI agents escorted Forest Mahan into the lobby carrying a plastic bag with his confiscated belongings. He had no idea what was going on until Cameron Phillips stepped forward and introduced him to President Kenaghy.

"Mr. President, sir, it's an honor," said Forest, looking around at the secret service men, then taking Kenaghy's hand.

"The honor is mine, Mr. Mahan," said Kenaghy, his anger now converted to open warmth. "If I'm not mistaken, we had a meeting scheduled for last night."

"Yes, sir, that's what I thought."

"Please accept my apologies for the mistake. Would you be open to a conversation over breakfast at Camp David instead?"

"Absolutely, Mr. President," Forest smiled. "Absolutely."

"Excellent. We'll take my limousine to the White House and a helicopter from there." He turned to Phillips and the surrounding secret service men. "Let's get going." And the whole bunch moved as a group out the doors of the J. Edgar Hoover Building.

Halfway down the steps, Forest abruptly stopped and addressed Kenaghy. "Is it out that I was arrested, Mr. President?"

Phillips answered. "It was on the news this morning."

Mahan reached into the plastic bag for one of his disposable phones. "Might be smart to let my people know I'm out," he said, turning on the phone.

Kenaghy stopped him. "Use the phone in my car. It's secure."

And he did. But Nate's disposable phone didn't respond, so Mahan tried the Billings number that relayed messages via CB to Hayes. His message was simple. *I've been freed. Have the ear of the President right now. Call me immediately at this secure line.*

CHAPTER 83

Glowing from the inside out, confused, elated, anxiety filled, Linda sat on the edge of her bed with her computer open on her lap. She had planned to write but found that her concentration wasn't there and decided to distract herself for the time being by reading more of her father's email chronology. She hadn't made much progress with this since beginning her series of interviews, so she ran a global search with the word *die-off* and got right into the material she was most interested in.

Linda's father had spent almost thirty years in the *intelligence* branch of the CIA. *Operations*, the covert arm of the Agency, was like the hand in the glove of *intelligence*, but periodically renegade cliques of agents stretched the limits of propriety and *operations* needed to be reined in. As an upper-level officer, Arthur Rivenhouse felt a responsibility to monitor *operations* for just these kinds of situations. And more and more, as Linda's reading approached the time of his heart attack, it became clear he was yanking at the bridle of the Terrorist Finance Division of *operations*. Specifically, he did not like the way money laundering methods were being used, and on several occasions, he mentioned Bob Richards' department by name.

Early into her reading, she found an email written to Richards' division chief by her father and dated three weeks before his death. It put a second and third exclamation point on the material she'd discovered earlier regarding population recession or the so-called "die-off" scenario:

> *I have reached the point of genuine alarm. There is increasing evidence that branches of our agency are using black money management to facilitate, even advance, economic and military positioning for this so-called "die-off" counter-culture that is surfacing in the right wing of the foreign policy establishment. At*

> *first, I wrote this off. You will always have radicals at either end of the political spectrum. Now, however, it is clear that rather than using intelligence community influence to avoid the perils of large-scale economic collapse based on environmental degradation and strategic resource depletion, agency assets are furthering the positions of transnational elites to the point of accelerating the collapse. This is unacceptable. If you cannot prove to me that I am wrong, I will take this to the Senate Intelligence Committee.*

This was incredible. It brought back the conversation she'd had with Charlie Patio before leaving for Kansas City—and rekindled concerns that her father's death had not been from natural causes. Linda closed up the laptop and fell back on the bed overwhelmed. She closed her eyes, and her entire worldview swam around her. Things she'd believed in all her life were suddenly suspect—*and there was a man in her life!* Such was her state of intellectual and emotional disarray, she didn't notice the door to the bedroom slowly swing open.

Linda sat up and saw Nate standing in the doorway. From the look in his eyes, she knew something was wrong. "What is it?"

"The FBI met Mahan at the airport last night."

"What?"

"He's been arrested for conspiracy to commit acts of terrorism."

Linda stood slowly, reading the deeper negative in Nate's thoughts. Irresistibly she reached out to him. He caught her at arm's length.

"Nate! What? What!"

"Does the name Rivenhouse, Arthur Rivenhouse, mean anything to you?"

Linda backed away in gathering dismay. "You think I sent Forest into a trap?"

"Who exactly are you working for, Linda?"

The distrust felt like a chainsaw ripping down the center of her chest. She fought to control her emotions. She absolutely knew Nathaniel Cromwell was a good man. And even as committed as she was to him and his cause, she knew how bad her convoluted story was going to sound. "Nate, please, I don't know what happened at the airport. You have to trust me on that. Haven't I given myself up as a hostage? Couldn't I have slipped away yesterday when you gave me the chance at the Montana border?" She battled against a rush of tears. "Wasn't that a perfect opportunity to escape if I knew Forest was going to be arrested?"

"I don't know what's going on, Linda. But tell me, right now—what is your relationship with the CIA?"

Although it was barely 48 hours, Linda felt like she already knew this man, heart and soul. She sensed he felt the same way about her. He had to. She steeled herself. "My father, as you must know by now, was a deputy director with the Agency until he died sixteen months ago. And yes, this did connect me to the intelligence community. On some occasions, I even used my column to promulgate leaks for the CIA. And," she bit at her lip, "I wrote my first few columns on the grain market as a result of documents I received from someone I still know there."

The muscles in Nate's jaws stood out taut. His eyes flashed with anger. "Are you a mole?"

"They may think so," she said, squeezing her eyes shut, knowing how horrible all this had to sound. "But I'm a free agent. Working on my own." Linda felt the fire in Nate's eyes flare out at her. "Everything I have said or written or done comes from me and me alone."

Linda reached for Nate again, feeling as though everything was slipping away. He caught her again at arm's length, his hands gripping her arms too tightly. Their eyes locked—his swimming with confusion, hers with anguish and loss—their time together during the night running counterpoint to all that was happening now.

"It just got so complicated when I was called to the White House the day I flew to Kansas City. Kenaghy passed me that note. You saw it. He trusted me because of my father. My father was a good man. A good man in a CIA that is horribly imperfect. But a good man. And I know you aren't like that militia general who believes everything in the government is corrupt. My father was a good man," she gasped. "That's why Kenaghy called me in the first place."

Nate glared at her, fighting the thought that her lovemaking had also been part of an undercover act.

"You must believe me," she said, tears running down her cheeks. "There was something going on at the Agency just before my father's death. He was trying to force an investigation that some people didn't want. Look at these emails." She turned away from him and went to the laptop lying on the bed.

At that moment, Rust appeared in the doorway. "Got this bitch straight yet, Boss?"

Nate spun around angrily. "Get lost," he said. "I'm taking care of this."

Rust gave Linda an ugly look, "Fine," and walked away.

Linda felt it. Nate hadn't quite given up on her. She popped open the laptop and began hitting the keys. "Read this." One by one, she led him through five of the most damning emails. Nate knew all too well how things worked in Washington. Linda's interpretation of the material was entirely credible. After the fifth email, he looked at her, measuring, wanting to trust her.

"This is what Kenaghy is fighting in the White House, Nate. This is why he's having so much trouble. Why he keeps blocking TES."

Nate glanced at the floor, then back to Linda. "I believe you," he said. "But no one else will."

They stood three feet apart. Linda wanted to reach out to him again but didn't. It had to be him this time. It had to be him reaching for her.

Nate's face tightened through the cheeks and mouth. "For the sake of the strike. For the sake of unity here and now, I'm going to put you under house arrest. You will not be able to leave this room until everything gets completely straightened out."

Linda looked at him, wanting so badly for him to take her in his arms. "Okay."

Nate took a deep breath. "I wish you'd told me this stuff in the beginning."

"I couldn't have."

Nate thought a moment then looked off.

"What about Forest?" she asked. "What are you going to do?"

Nate turned back grim and serious. "We had no choice. We've initiated another burn."

"Oh, Nate! No! That's the worst possible response."

"It's already been set in motion. Fires will be burning within the hour."

CHAPTER 84

Unfortunately for the farmers, they were up against Paul Houseman. The Homeland Security Director had taken the game of power as far as it could go in Washington. Wearing National Security like a badge, he manipulated the system by politicizing "The War on Terror" the way J. Edgar Hoover had communism. At the top of Homeland Security, Houseman also had an iron grip on the Justice Department and controlled about half of America's intelligence data. He kept personal records on every important person in the nation's capital; so that after eleven years at the directorship, it took an act of Congress to fire him, and there wasn't a majority of senators or congresspersons who had the nerve to vote against him for fear of personal attack.

In the months prior to the farm movement, Houseman had been angling for yet another marker on the board with his push to privatize the Homeland Guard. He wanted a permanent mercenary security force to replace the collection of reservists that existed now, a force that would always be on the ready—and run by a clan of Houseman's business partners from his days in the private sector of enforcement. He hadn't been making much progress with this effort and was on the verge of giving it up when the farmers' strike kicked off with its initial burn. Houseman saw this as the perfect opportunity to renew his privatization push and showcase the need for a new domestic security philosophy. He was just getting this going when Cromwell burned his farm. The Homeland Security Director could not have planned a better progression of events. Cromwell's actions gave him the leverage he needed to lift the terror alert to red, making his powers essentially equal to the President's and giving him the freedom to deploy security assets in any way he pleased.

Things really got rolling when Houseman learned from one of his moles in CIA that the President planned to meet with Forest Mahan Sunday night. Concerned all his wonderful plans for the Homeland

Guard would be ruined by the President making foolish concessions to the farm union, Houseman started pushing buttons right away, beginning with Mahan's arrest. This was followed by seizure of Mahan's house and filling it with FBI investigators to scour the place for evidence of conspiracy between Mahan, Cromwell, and Hayes to burn more fields.

Six hours later, in the middle of the night, Houseman unleashed a raid on Hayes' ranch in Montana. No one expected this kind of preemptive action, and the operation went perfectly. Not a single firearm was discharged by either side. But when word reached Houseman that Hayes was not there, he all but exploded, ordering double-time on the search of the ranch and Mahan's home for clues to the whereabouts of Hayes—and they got lucky. One of the fingerprint experts at Mahan's dusted every hard gloss surface in the house, including the glass covering the map on Mahan's office wall. Hayes' forefinger had left a print on the location he had pointed out to Cromwell and Mahan ten days earlier. This location fit so well with all the other pieces of information already gathered that Houseman decided to run with it. By daybreak Monday, when Cromwell was climbing from his sleeping bag, Homeland Guard units were already funneling in from all over the region to a twenty-square-mile area in the foothills of the Rockies south of Bozeman.

At the same time, NSA satellites were focused on the same area, scanning for any kind of electronic signal. So despite all Hayes' precautions, the moment Twist launched the burn by ham radio, though the content of the message gave nothing away, the location of this one short broadcast became the Homeland Guard's primary target. Within thirty minutes, unbeknownst to Hayes or Cromwell, six Homeland Guard units and four helicopter and drone assisted FBI swat teams were assembling on the east and south slopes of Tumble Mountain.

CHAPTER 85

"Mr. Mahan, I think we're in a position to help each other out," said James Kenaghy, looking the Grange President directly in the eye across a coffee table and a full coffee service.

Kenaghy, Cameron Phillips, and Forest Mahan sat before the fireplace in the den at the Camp David complex in Maryland's Catoctin Mountains outside Washington, D.C. It was a quarter to ten Monday morning. Breakfast was over, and the pleasantries of the President of the United States getting to know the President of the National Grange and vice versa had been completed. It was time to move on to the brass tacks of the meeting.

"As is well-known," continued Kenaghy, "there are forces in Washington that are dead set against me. I have taken a stand against what I will call, for lack of a better term, the military industrial complex, though it's really much more than that—and it's costing me my political career." Kenaghy turned his eyes to Phillips. "And perhaps the careers of anyone associated with me."

Mahan nodded, still uncertain where the President was headed.

"For my part," Kenaghy went on, "I'm very concerned about the direction of this country. And, if I'm not mistaken, so are you. But our issues are different. Yours being agriculture and the environment. Mine being the ideology driving our foreign policy and runaway defense spending. I've asked you here to find a middle ground—where our purposes overlap and we can help each other."

The President picked his coffee cup off the table and took a deliberating sip. "But that can't happen if there's any more field burning."

Mahan nodded. "Of course."

Cameron Phillips watched his boss closely as he spoke. He had not been briefed prior to this meeting, and like Mahan, the Chief of Staff was gradually being pulled to the edge of his seat by the President's piece by piece delivery.

"The people that you represent, Mr. Mahan, the farming community, for the most part voted as Sunbelt Republicans in the last presidential election. They're not my constituency. From polls I've recently received from my own people, we're talking about a block of some fourteen million rural voters. This is close to ten percent of the voting populace."

Mahan nodded. "Yes, that sounds about right."

"If you include that your strike has also enlisted a significant portion of the Green Party, who also did not vote for me, that number climbs to twelve percent."

Phillips nodded this time.

"My constituency of eastern centrists and western liberals, at least the ones who haven't given up on me," continued Kenaghy, "has been hovering in the vicinity of thirty-seven, thirty-nine percent the last few months. Suggesting to most pollsters that I have absolutely no chance of winning the next election."

Kenaghy took a breath and another sip of his coffee, then smiled—or maybe it was a sly grin. "I want to cut you a deal, Mr. Mahan."

"I'm listening."

Kenaghy leaned forward and lowered his voice. "Promise me the entire block of your people in the next election and that there will be no more field burning, and I'll get you, through executive order or whatever it takes, your extra dollar or two per bushel of grain—strictly as a government subsidy because I don't believe I can get the industry to move on this. And I'll do it as soon as I possibly can."

Mahan chewed on this for a moment, took a sip of coffee, and replied, "That's our first demand. What of the second—which I consider even more important than the first?"

Kenaghy looked from Mahan to Phillips then back to Mahan. "With your people and my people, I could very well take the next election—as a huge upset. Should this actually happen, I would name you Secretary of Agriculture and assist you in any way I could to push your vision through Congress in the ensuing four years. That's the best I can do." The President sat back in his seat and watched the wheels turning in Mahan's head. "What do you think?"

Mahan took a breath. "Can you really get that extra dollar with an executive order?"

Kenaghy looked at his chief of staff.

Phillips played it straight. "There are no guarantees, sir. But with Congress going home in four days, we should be able to come up with something."

Kenaghy's eyes swung back to Mahan.

"Okay," said Mahan. "I'll take this to my people. I need their approval before I can say another word. You are no favorite in the Heartland, Mr. President. But they might listen to me if I can get something positive out of the strike right away."

The three men were silent for almost a minute. It was as though the weight of the matter were slowly settling down on them—when there was a knock at the door.

"Yes," said Kenaghy.

An aide opened the door to the den. "I'm sorry to disturb you, Mr. President, but I just got word. The field burning has begun again—on a larger scale than before."

Mahan jumped to his feet. "It's because I was arrested, Mr. President. My message must not have gotten through in time."

Kenaghy fell back in his chair like a beaten fighter in his corner. "Christ, this could scuttle everything."

The aide in the door added more bad news. "Mr. President, there are also reports of gun fire between the farmers and the Homeland Guard."

"GOD DAMN IT!" shouted Kenaghy standing.

"They just don't know I've been released, Mr. President."

"Try calling them again," said Phillips, handing Mahan the secure phone.

Mahan shook his head. "I can't believe this is happening."

"Call them," impelled Kenaghy, now pacing frantically. "Public opinion is slipping every second the burning is televised."

CHAPTER 86

The second field burning did not get underway with the precision and timing of the first. Some fires were started as early as nine-thirty eastern time. Then, sporadically over the next hour, fields were torched in no particular pattern across the Midwest. By ten, it was on the news, and very soon after that, Homeland Guard units in eleven states were actively engaged in putting out fires as well as trying to stop new ones from being started. But the farmers' methods had sophisticated since the first burn. With even tighter coordination between neighboring farmers, the grange community, and the rural populace in general, the anti-strike force had no chance. The troops just couldn't move as fast as word between the locals. By the time the Homeland Guard arrived on the scene, either the fire had already burned out or it was too big to put out.

And who were they to arrest anyway? In blue jeans and t-shirts, the militia blended in with the locals. It was impossible to tell who was responsible for each fire or which fields were attached to which farms. There were a few ugly clashes between the guard and striking farmers—a handful of fist fights and three armed skirmishes, leaving four wounded and two dead—which of course got magnified with the arrival of TV cameras. But for all Paul Houseman's preemptive efforts to disable the strike leaders, the Homeland Guard simply could not do a damn thing to control the real energy of the strike—the farmers themselves and the fires they were setting.

This was what confronted Atossa Andreas when she returned from her weekend in New York with Derek Davis. She climbed aboard the Merit Oil jet in a joyous high. What a fantastic two nights she'd had! And Davis felt the same. They would meet again. Soon. Again and again. But upon deplaning at the Newport airport, she saw the fires on a television in one of the lounges and hurried home in a snit.

Atossa entered her bedchamber and reluctantly turned on her television, wondering why she even wanted to know. But there it was. Her wheat burning across the land—and through the eye of television cameras, it looked worse than it was, like civil war in the Heartland of the United States. Brigades of guardsmen running through small towns. Farmers with torches and shotguns. Dropping stock valuations. Climbing grain prices. It caused her skin to crawl. Her face to itch. And a warming in the center of the spidery red blemish on her right cheek. She clenched her fists, trying to fight what screamed out from inside her. She clapped her hands and the TV screen ascended into the ceiling.

"Nancy," she called out to the room. "Get Frank on the line."

She paced across the room. Stood before her mirror and stared at herself.

"Ms. Andreas. I have Frank Nelson."

"Frank!" she called, spinning away from the mirror. "Have you spoken with LaPalme?"

"Yes, Atossa, just now. He's at the Andreas Grain offices in Lower Manhattan. He says it's overblown. Relax."

"DON'T TELL ME TO RELAX!"

"It looks much worse on television than it really is, Atossa. A million acres. A million and a half. Two percent of the crop—maybe less."

"But why is this going on? Why can't we simply crush these people?"

"It's a reaction to the arrest of the Grange President."

"So? Isn't he the man behind the burning? He deserves to be arrested."

"Perhaps, but he's out now. Kenaghy stormed FBI headquarters and demanded Mahan be released. Then the two of them disappeared. Apparently to Camp David where they're having some kind of secret meeting. Who knows what lunacy Kenaghy will do next?"

Atossa cursed. "How did we ever let that man get into office? Why haven't we done something about it?"

"We have, Atossa. We've already arranged for a motion to impeach the fool in the fall session of Congress."

"Meanwhile our fields are burning. Thank God for Paul Houseman and the Homeland Guard!"

"I don't know if Houseman's making things better or worse, Atossa. But please, understand, this is all secondary to our work in Eurasia."

"Damn it, Frank, I don't care about that crap," Atossa screamed. "I want you and LaPalme here in Newport as soon as possible. Good-bye."

Atossa stood in the center of her room, her face burning and itching. "NO ONE WILL RUIN THIS MOMENT FOR ME," she bellowed to the heavens. "NO ONE FUCKS WITH ME AND GETS AWAY WITH IT!"

CHAPTER 87

In the basement of the log cabin on Tumble Mountain, Hayes, Cromwell, and Rust were hunkered down around the citizen band radio with Twist and a pot of lukewarm coffee, listening to reports squawking in on the CB and plotting a strategy for Cromwell's departure. The TV up high in one corner of the cramped communications room was turned to CNN's coverage of the fires, and it was clear the second burn was going as well as could be expected.

Then in rapid fire, three separate reports of Homeland Guard deployments in southern Montana came through the relay network on the east side of the mountain. A fourth report said that several of the CB relays around Billings had shut down due to the number of Homeland Guard vehicles moving through the area and fears of being overheard.

Rust voiced his opinion right away. "No sense staying here any longer, Boss. You, me, and the kid, let's hit the road."

"Just because they're close doesn't mean they'll find us," said Hayes. "And if they do, this is a superb piece of ground to defend. I have two thousand men hidden out there in the forest like Indians. There's no way anyone's getting in here without a good fight."

"I appreciate your confidence, General, but I think I'd like to avoid the second coming of Ruby Ridge—especially with Nate's boy sleeping out there in the camper."

"Rusty's right, General. Nothing's keeping me here. Besides, there's someone in Oklahoma I need to talk to." Rust slid a dissenting look at his friend.

"If these reports are right, it might be too late for that already," said Hayes. "With all the roads in and out of Montana blocked—I think you're pushing it, Colonel."

Before Nate could respond, the room filled with deafening static, forcing everyone to cover their ears. Twist quickly threw off his headphones, cursed in four different languages, and flipped off the TV and the Citizen Band radio. "Something's interfering with our antennas." He stood up angrily and bolted from the room.

The others followed Twist up from the basement and out of the cabin. Five of Hayes' men were already out in the yard pointing to the drone disappearing in the west. It had flown through like an alien spacecraft and shot the tops off the trees that held the antennas.

The two walkie-talkies on Hayes' belt yakked. Men on the southern perimeter had seem a small fleet of black helicopters sweeping in over the hills. In the east, Homeland Guard patrols were moving up the mountain on old logging roads.

"So much for our little trip to Oklahoma," deadpanned Rust.

"No way are they forcing us out of here," said Hayes defiantly.

Rust laughed. "You mean short of bombing us out, General? At least we've got the turncoat reporter as a hostage."

Nate took a deep breath. "No. No way we're getting into any kind of firefight up here. I'd rather surrender than jeopardize my son."

Hayes' brow thickened at the mention of surrender. "Which means the strike is over, Colonel. Is that it? All of it for nothing." He shook his head. "Damn it, how could they have found this place so quickly?" His eyes lit angrily. "Must have been that reporter you brought in here." It was the first time Hayes had been critical of Cromwell. "Anyone think of checking her for a tracking device?"

"I did," lied Cromwell for reasons he couldn't explain—even to himself. Neither of the other men liked his answer. Nate didn't budge. "We've got more pressing problems than her, General. If I'm stuck here, I want the media on hand. I want whatever comes down on TV, so we don't get slaughtered with our hands up. With this nut Houseman that's all too possible." Nate's eyes swung around the group suddenly thinking of the grain elevators on the Mississippi and Lena Davenport hanging onto a disposal cell phone. "How long will it take the Homeland Guard to get up here?"

"Days—if at all." Hayes was still bristling about being found and talk of surrender. He turned abruptly away from the group and answered one of his walkie-talkies.

"Four hours," said Rust, "if they don't bomb us out first."

Hayes cut off the walkie-talkie. "They're setting up a perimeter, trying to surround us."

Nate looked at Twist. "Any way we can get a message out of here?"

Rust pulled a cell phone from his pocket. "Maybe we should try these? No need to worry about giving away our location anymore." He punched the *on* button and the little device began to fire up.

Nate stepped up alongside Rust as the phone futilely scanned for a viable cell. "Ain't happening," said Rust. "The relay towers must be blocked."

Twist looked up at the broken tree tops behind the cabin, then at Hayes. "What'd you do with that underground landline you dug in here ten years ago, Vincent? The one I told you to tear out."

Something like a grin appeared behind Hayes' beard. "It's still in. I even got someone to hook the back end of it into the system on the sly. The loose end and fifty feet of telephone line are buried behind the cabin." He paused. "But I doubt we have a phone to plug it into."

"Get that line dug up, Vincent," said Twist. "I've got enough odds and ends down there in the basement to rig up something. I'm with the Colonel. I want some TV cameras around before I start flying a white flag."

CHAPTER 88

Forest Mahan tried Cromwell's cell phone from Camp David several times without luck, so he called the number in Billings again. The contact there told him about the FBI raid and that the CB relays were down for now, but that they were doing everything they could to get his earlier message through to Hayes. He added that local reports said the Homeland Guard was building up a position in the foothills south of Bozeman.

This was news to Kenaghy. He called MacFarlane at FBI and learned that the Homeland Guard and the FBI were, in fact, closing in on Hayes' hideout. The President's next call went to Homeland Security. He demanded a halt to the operation in Montana.

Houseman went ballistic. "With fires raging across the Midwest and the terrorists that started them surrounded, you've got to be crazy."

"But those fires were started because you stepped in and arrested Mahan!" screamed back Kenaghy.

"Good luck pushing that through committee, Mr. President," slammed Houseman. "We're taking them down now! It's what has to be done!" Then he hung up.

Kenaghy put in a call to Sam Wedemeier. The lawyer explained there was nothing the President could do short of storming into Congress and demanding an emergency session. And that would be difficult to get going in the timeframe available—for the same reason Houseman had already mentioned—the fires actively burning across the Heartland.

Kenaghy hung up lost in thought, knowing that everything he'd been putting into place the last few days was coming apart. One thing was certain—he was fed up with fighting through the red tape and trying to impress his urgency through the mouthpiece of a telephone. Time may be running out, but he was going back to Washington to make sure some people in high places felt his purple wrath face to face. Things could only get done—like when he'd freed Mahan—if he showed up and took charge. Then it struck him.

Cameron Phillips and Forest Mahan had been silent observers to the President's three futile phone calls. They'd seen the growing anger and frustration in his face. But now his expression was gradually lighting from the inside out.

"What is, sir?"

"I'm going to Montana."

"What?"

"When there's an emergency, when there's a disaster, a real leader goes directly into the center of it. I might not be able to battle through the bureaucracy in Washington, but I guarantee no matter who's giving orders out there in Montana, they're going to jump if I show up in person."

"Sir, I'm not so sure that's a good idea."

"What have I got to lose, Cameron? Not a thing. Not a damn thing. And if it works—and the strike is settled on TV—what better photo op for a failing campaign!"

"But it's nearly a four-hour trip, sir. It could be all over by then."

"We can do far better than that in Air Force One, but we're wasting time talking about it. Cameron, I'm sending you to Washington to hold the fort—and don't tell anyone what's going on. Forest, you and I are taking a little airplane ride."

CHAPTER 89

Jerry Rust went to the bedroom where Linda Bennett was waiting and with no explanation escorted her to what Hayes referred to as the bomb shelter, a chamber below Twist's communication room with ten-inch steel plates imbedded in the walls and ceiling. Will was already there reading a book when Linda entered. After Rust rudely closed the door, Will looked up from his book with a baleful smile. Linda forced a little smile in return. Then Will told her all that he knew, ending with the effort to contact the media for security should they be forced to surrender.

Discouraged by how poorly things were going and disappointed that it had been Rust not Nate who had delivered her to the bomb shelter, Linda returned to reading her father's email chronology for distraction. She began by running a global search for references to Bob Richards. She got several hits, including an email exchange between her father and Richards in the week before his heart attack:

> *Mr. Richards. I've been looking into your work with the Terrorist Finance Division and have been greatly disturbed by what appears to be active money laundering assistance to a variety of questionable sources. I'm aware that operations has closely monitored money trails to these sources for many years. I also understand that there is much intelligence to be gained from allowing these otherwise illegal financial operations to continue under the "know thy enemy" premise. However, I sense that what is involved here is more than silent compliance. I see an active hand in the laundering of what must be black market drug profits. I hope I'm wrong. But I want full disclosure on this. Give me reason to believe what you are doing is necessary. AR*

> *Mr. Rivenhouse. If I'm not mistaken, you're in the intelligence branch of the Agency. There is no reason for you to be nosing into*

operations and, quite possibly, compromising the work done by the Terrorist Finance Division. As to disclosure, your seniority means nothing to me. Until you can bring counsel to your accusations, you have no need to know. BR.

Mr. Richards. I'm only asking you to comply with agency policy. I already have enough evidence of a breach, gained through ordinary intelligence channels, to bring you and your division before the Policy Review Panel. Please do not force me to do this. Simply justify your actions. AR.

Mr. Rivenhouse. You are overstepping your jurisdiction. You have absolutely no idea what you are asking for or about. I suggest you quickly forget this situation. I repeat. I suggest you quickly forget this situation. BR

Mr. Richards. I consider your last email an ill-timed threat. I will see you at the Review Panel. AR

Linda's heart was beating at twice its ordinary rate as she read these last two emails. If she ever got out of this basement in Montana, she had to get back to Washington, D.C. and talk to Charlie Patio. It was time to reopen investigation into the cause of her father's death.

CHAPTER 90

General Hayes and Nathaniel Cromwell sat at the cabin's kitchen table with a map and four intermittently squawking walkie-talkies, waiting for Twist to come up with a makeshift telephone. They were gradually assembling the reports coming in from the perimeter on the Homeland Guard/FBI position, trying to get an idea what they were up against and what might be possible—other than surrender.

One of the walkie-talkies buzzed. Hayes took the report. FBI swat team leaders were using bullhorns to communicate with Hayes' men. They were giving Hayes one hour to stop the field burning and surrender or they were coming in with force.

"How the hell do they expect us to stop the fires if they've cut all our means of communication?"

Nate looked Hayes in the eye. "Maybe it's time to rethink this, General."

Then one right after another, three deafening explosions shook the cabin and blew in two windows. Cromwell and Hayes jumped up and ran out the front door. The open area around the cabin was thick with smoke and debris. Three steaming mortar craters bracketed the log cabin. A man was shrieking in pain. Rust came out of the cabin as Hayes and Nate hurried to the injured man lying on the ground. It was one of Hayes' long time recruits—a veritable son to the general. He'd been thrown against a tree by the blast. Stoic Hayes knelt beside him. The man choked and sputtered, trying to talk. He mentioned something about his mother and his brother. Then his eyes closed and his breathing stopped.

Hayes bowed his head and spoke a few words of prayer. Nate and Rust picked up the dead man and carried him into one of the cabin's back bedrooms. They laid the man's body on a bed and put a sheet over him. Neither said a word until they were exiting the room. Rust gave his combat buddy a grim look. "I think they just wanted us to know how close a focus they've got on us—pin point," he said, exaggerating the p-sounds.

Nate shook his head. "Pretty fucking heavy handed. And a bullshit move for this kind of operation. How's progress on the phone?"

Twist answered before Rust had a chance. "Got it right here, Colonel," said the old man stumbling up the basement stairs, carrying a handful of cannibalized electronics parts and a small box speaker. "Let me hook her up, and we'll see if I know what I'm doing." He headed to the corner of the kitchen where the loose phone line came in through the window.

Hayes was across the cabin, staring out one of the broken windows at the mortar damage. He turned and faced Nate. "Still thinking of surrender, Colonel?"

Nate was just as angry as Hayes at what had happened but didn't answer right away. He was thinking about Will's safety—and Lena Davenport. Rust made his own assessment. "And the other choice is what, General?"

Hayes hadn't liked Jerry's attitude from the beginning. But now as things were pinching in on Tumble Mountain, it was getting to him. Hayes lasered a glare across the room that Jerry met with his cool assassin's eyes and a challenging curl in his upper lip.

Twist called out from the kitchen. "Dial tone, boys!"

Nate went straight to the kitchen. Hayes and Rust remained faced off for a moment before Hayes turned and left Rust in the front room. Twist laid his jumble of electronics out on the kitchen table. Hayes looked at Nate. "This line could be cut as soon as we use it, Colonel. Where do we go first? Stop the fires or call the media." His tone was coarse and sardonic—he'd just as soon hunker down and shoot it out.

"Call the damn media," said Twist.

Nate's eyes darted with thought. He had one card to play he hadn't told anyone about, but he wasn't sure he wanted to blow up anything just yet. That was terrorism in his book and a totally different way of thinking. He closed his eyes and saw his mother rolling on the floor of his bedroom with her hair on fire. He saw his farm burning by his own hand. He saw the man's corpse lying on the bed in the back room. And finally, he saw Will's determined expression that day up on the silo. "How secure is that bunker below the basement, General?" he asked as Rust ambled into the room like nothing was going on.

"It can handle those mortars."

"You're sure."

"Much more than that," said Twist.

Nate gave Hayes a look then Jerry. "Ready for one last gamble?"

Rust didn't answer. His eyes said *no.* Behind him, Twist shook his head.

"You know I am," said Hayes.

Nate nodded ever so slightly. "Early on into this thing, I had a good number of grain elevators on the Mississippi loaded with explosives, and someone's out there now prepared to set them off by remote control. With one call I can set that in motion. One elevator every half-hour until they pull back on the siege. They do that, we stop the fires. Our strike statement for the day already made—in aces."

Hayes opened up with one of his rare, genuine smiles. His eyes were wide and gleaming. "I like it, Colonel."

Twist stared at Nate as though he couldn't believe he could have prepared such a thing. Rust wasn't surprised. "I should have known, Boss. You wouldn't have gotten us into a situation like this without something in your back pocket." He paused. "But it means we get something more powerful than mortars falling out of the sky."

"Maybe in Afghanistan, but not out here in a national forest," said Hayes.

"Well, that's our gamble," said Nate. "Either take a chance with retaliation or get word out to the media and surrender."

The men exchanged glances.

"Your call, Colonel," said Hayes. "You've got a son here. I respect that. But you know exactly what I'm thinking."

Nate read reluctance in his combat buddy. "This thing's nothing to you, Rusty. If you want, you can get out of here on your own—anytime you want."

Rust offered a sideways grin. "I signed on as a body guard. No sense taking off just as things get exciting."

Nate took a deep breath, paused, then gave Twist Lena Davenport's phone number. Twist made the connection and handed a microphone to Nate. The phone rang three times before Lena answered. "I'm here," came out of the little speaker in the center of the kitchen table.

Cromwell didn't waste a word. "We're pinned in about fifty miles south, southeast of Bozeman, Montana—on top of Tumble Mountain. Get us some media coverage as soon as possible. TV cameras for sure. We've got three simple demands. Back off Tumble Mountain. Return communications. Release Mahan. And we'll stop the field burning. Then proceed with option one in thirty minutes unless you hear from me first."

"Can I get back to you?"

Twist shook his head no, mouthing the words *one-way line.*

"No, this line is likely to be cut. Use your judgment until you hear from me. If we get our demands, I'll have a phone—and you'll be the first person I call. If we don't…"

"I hear you."

"Over and out."

Twist cut the connection.

"Davenport?" asked Rust.

Nate nodded.

There was a period of extended silence, then Nate said he needed to talk to his son and walked out of the room.

Linda was sitting in a folding chair too upset about what she'd just read to think of anything else, and Will was lying on one of the two cots with his head stuck in a copy of Robert Penn Warren's *All the King's Men.* They both looked up at the sound of someone coming down the ladder into the bomb shelter. A moment later the door opened. Nate stood in the doorway. His eyes met Linda's briefly. Questions overlaid questions.

"How are you doing, Will?" asked Nate, sitting down on the cot beside his son.

"I'm fine, Dad. What were those explosions?"

"Mortars. We're surrounded and they're trying to scare us out." He looked at both Linda and Will, making sure they understood the implications.

"Did you get a phone line working?"

"Yes," Nate nodded, looking fondly at his son. "That's why I'm down here. I wanted to let you and Linda know what's going on." He turned to glance briefly at Linda. "We got a call through to the outside and with a little luck our situation will soon be news—that helps." He paused measuring his words. "But we've also taken a dangerous chance."

His seriousness was obvious, and Will's smile eased away.

"We used the phone to deliver a message to the government, through a second party. We have planted explosives in several grain elevators along the Mississippi River." Nate gave Linda another glance, a little longer than the last, full knowing she would find this very disturbing. But she was already so upset by what she'd read in her father's emails, she didn't react.

"If the Homeland Guard doesn't back off, we'll start exploding those elevators one by one until they do." He said this very slowly and deliberately. "This is a risky move and could result in worse things for us than already exist. Like many more mortars." He looked right at Will and took a breath. "Our lives are at risk. Do you understand what I'm saying?" He said this to Will, but once again he let his eyes impress that same message on Linda.

Will said a soft, "Yeah."

"Can you deal with this?"

Will nodded. "Yes, Dad."

Nate turned fully to Linda. "I know this is unsettling news to you, Linda, but this is what we're doing. I'm sorry that you're in this thing at all, but for now, you're still considered a risk."

Linda nearly burst into tears but held on. "I understand."

Nate paused, still looking at her. "Linda, are you wearing or carrying any kind of GPS device?"

"No. Why?"

Nate continued. "We don't know how our location was discovered. Someone or something gave us away. It's what put us in this situation and forced this all or nothing gamble."

"And you want to know if it was me?" It was all she could do to keep the defensiveness from her voice.

"Yes."

"Nate, please understand. I believe in you and what you're doing. Whether you believe me or not, I did nothing to reveal this location and would not have." She closed her eyes to get a grip on herself. "I have a few more emails I want you to read. They'll prove to you exactly what my position in this is."

"Not now. I've got to go back upstairs. I just wanted both of you to know what's going on."

As Nate left the room, Linda hung her head, still not really knowing if he trusted her or not.

CHAPTER 91

Atossa Andreas was obsessing on the television coverage of the field burning when she got a call from Frank. His helicopter had just touched down on the east side of the property. He was on his way in. LaPalme had taken the Andreas corporate jet and would be there shortly by limo from the Newport airport.

An angst-filled Atossa descended to the living room to receive Frank. She sat on her throne, dressed in black, sipping herbal tea behind a veil, when Frank burst through the double doors, a drink in one hand. "Christ, every time these jerks light a match, the damn Dow drops a thousand points," he stormed, stomping into the room.

"To hell with the stock market, Frank. I've called you here for reassurance about my grain. My stomach knots up every time I think about it. I get acid reflux whenever I see it on television." She didn't mention the itching it caused on her cheek. "What's going on anyway? I thought the Homeland Guard could put a cap on this thing. Instead, they're running around out there like the Keystone Cops."

Frank flopped down on the sofa across from Atossa, more exasperated than he usually showed. "It's that damn Houseman who's screwing things up, Atossa. He's spun this labor strike into a revolt. These accusations of terrorism were uncalled for. We could've quashed this thing much more civilly. Now we're verging on all out warfare!"

"And why not?" growled Atossa. "They have no right to be burning our grain."

Frank drained his drink. "Houseman's an ass, Atossa. Continued pressure on the farmers will only result in sympathy for the strike and more grain losses."

"I thought it didn't matter, Frank."

"That was before the reports I received last week from Kazakhstan. They need wheat and corn."

"As if I care."

The double doors opened again. A steward appeared in the doorway. "Mr. LaPalme," he announced. Curtis, dapper as usual in a double-breasted, navy-blue blazer with a crimson tie and a matching handkerchief in his breast pocket, strode in. "Ms. Andreas, Frank," he said hurriedly. "Did you hear? They've got that militia general surrounded in Montana."

"It's about time," snapped Atossa.

"I saw it on my phone in the limo," continued LaPalme. "They say they're preparing to arrest him."

"I told you, Frank," said Atossa. "I knew Houseman had the right idea."

"I'm still not convinced. What do you think, Curtis?"

"I could use a drink."

Atossa hit the intercom button on the arm of her chair. "Two more whiskies." Then she turned to LaPalme. "What about these fires, Curtis?"

"It's like before, Ms. Andreas. Even with all the flames and violence on television, we're still only talking two percent of the harvest—and the climbing grain prices will probably more than offset anything we lose to the fires."

A steward came in with two drinks on a tray. He handed one to LaPalme and the other to Frank. "That's for me, damn it." Atossa snatched the drink from Frank's hand.

LaPalme took a sip of his drink and watched the startled steward scurry from the room. "I think the outcome of the standoff in Montana is critical."

"We just can't give in to labor," stated Frank like it was one of the natural laws of the universe.

"Labor, hell," snarled Atossa. "We can't be blackmailed by terrorists burning our fields."

The double doors opened halfway. Nancy Waters stuck her head in. "Excuse me for interrupting, Ms. Andreas," she said, coming a few steps into the room. "We've gotten word that there are bombs planted in the grain elevators along the Mississippi—with a threat to explode an elevator every half-hour until they stop the siege in Montana."

"SON OF A BITCH!" Frank stood up and cursed in absolute frustration. "I knew it! Houseman is underestimating this man Cromwell."

CHAPTER 92

High over Illinois in Air Force One, President Kenaghy was equally upset. He had just gotten word about the bomb threat and the demands that had arrived at the Department of Agriculture. While the President ranted and raved up and down the expansive cabin of Air Force One, Forest Mahan slumped deeper into his chair, a man of tremendous positive energy, vastly depressed by the turn of events and with no way to contact his comrades.

Kenaghy gathered his anger and called Cameron Phillips at the White House. Still maintaining the secrecy of the flight west, Phillips routed Kenaghy through the White House to FBI Director Bernie MacFarlane. The President commanded him to pull back the swat teams in Montana and open the phone lines. MacFarlane said it was out of his hands. Homeland Security was running the operation. For the second time that day, Kenaghy threatened to fire him. This time he quit. Kenaghy fumed even more, then got patched through to the Attorney General Louis Sullivan.

"I want to comply with the request we just got at Agriculture," Kenaghy seethed into the phone. Sullivan started hemming and hawing about Houseman, the elevator threat, and all the fires burning across the Heartland. "I'm the damn President," screamed Kenaghy into the phone. "I've got a man sitting beside me who can stop the burning and the bombing, if we can just get a phone line into that militia camp. Get on this now or you're done in Washington—forever! And get back to me as soon as possible." Kenaghy slammed down the phone, fit to be tied.

CHAPTER 93

Fifty minutes had passed since the initial surrender demand. Twenty-five since the call to Lena Davenport. Hayes, Rust, Nate, and Twist were in the kitchen. Twist had resurrected a small AM/FM radio and spliced together enough antenna to get weak reception from Billings. They were listening to a radio news report about the Homeland Guard operation in southern Montana, when the cabin's front door burst open. Two of Hayes' men came through the door, all but carrying a third man, who looked like he'd been running a marathon through a thicket of thorns. Hayes met the men in the main room. "What's happened? Who's this?" Cromwell was right behind him.

The bedraggled and scratched up man dropped into a chair. "I'm part of the citizen band relay network, General. We've been trying all morning to get a message in from the outside. When all efforts to use the citizen band and the ham radio failed, I decided to motorcycle in—the last few miles I've been on foot because of the Homeland Guard. They're all over the fucking place."

"Yes, we know that," said Hayes. "What's the message?"

The man gasped for breath, looked at Hayes then Cromwell. "It's for you, General, from Forest Mahan. It came in several hours ago. He's been released. He's with the President." He pulled a small piece of paper from his hip pocket. He handed it to Hayes "This is a secure phone number where you can reach him."

Hayes turned to Cromwell. "How do we know this isn't just another setup?"

"The way the Homeland Guard is closing in on us, General," said Rust. "I don't think it makes any difference."

Nate agreed. "There's no time to waste, General. You call. They don't seem to know I'm here."

CHAPTER 94

Houseman's man in Montana was standing beside the FBI swat team leader with an active phone line to Houseman when Attorney General Sullivan called the swat team leader with orders from the President. Houseman all but lifted the dome off the Capitol Building upon hearing this at his end of the line. A heated argument in Washington, D.C. took place in Montana over two phones located in the nation's capital, ending with Houseman denying the President's orders, screaming, "Standard operating procedure! No negotiating with terrorists!"

In Air Force One, Kenaghy came unglued when Phillips called with the news from Sullivan. Mahan was beside himself. Everything he'd worked on for so long seemed to be blowing away like chaff in the wind. Then the secure phone rang. One of the President's young aides picked it up cautiously. "White House staff."

"This is General Hayes in Montana. I'd like to talk to Forest Mahan." The aide gave a thumbs-up signal and handed the phone to Mahan. "It's Hayes."

"General, this is Forest. You got my message."

"Just now."

"General, you've got to stop the fires and the bombings. We've still got a chance to settle the strike, but not with this violence going on."

"Forest, we have the Homeland Guard and the FBI pressing in all around us. We are not stopping anything until they back off."

"Listen, Vincent, I'm in Air Force One right now with the President. We're headed to Montana with a proposal. Can you get a hold of Cromwell?"

"There a chance," said Hayes looking right at him.

"We could be there working through a settlement in something like two hours, maybe two and a half."

Everyone in the kitchen could hear Mahan's voice coming through the speaker. "That's not soon enough," said Hayes. "We've got less than ten minutes before they're going to start forcing things. Can't the President just shut this down?"

"The President is trying," said Mahan.

Kenaghy took the phone. "General Hayes. This is the President. I'm doing everything I can to stop the siege, but the Red Alert protocols are making it difficult. Trust me. I'll be on site in two hours. Just use the line you're on to stop the fires and violence now, and I'll have something to work with."

Then the line went dead.

Hayes laid the microphone on the kitchen table. "We've been cut off." He stared at Cromwell.

"Then either we surrender or hold out until the President arrives."

As Nate said this, two more mortars exploded in the yard, blowing in another window and sending everyone to the floor as a third hit the back corner of the cabin where Linda had slept the night before. Smoke and debris plumed into the central room.

Rust lifted his head from the floor. "I don't know about you revolutionaries, but if you guys don't plan to surrender, I'm headed to the bomb shelter."

CHAPTER 95

"Maybe they're bluffing," said Atossa, kneading her left hand in the air. "How's this possible anyway? Don't we have our elevators guarded? Can't we find the explosives somehow?"

"Atossa, it's a difficult and dangerous task," said LaPalme. "We've got more than thirty elevators with the Andreas logo on them along the Mississippi, containing three-quarters of our reserves—and any hope of making a profit off the strike. If this bomb threat is real, it's time we start talking with International and Carlyle and make the farmers an offer."

There was a knock on the living room doors. Nancy Waters stuck her head in. "An elevator just blew at our storage facility outside Dubuque. They've got it on CNN right now."

LaPalme looked at his watch. "It's been exactly thirty minutes."

"Fuck these farmers," hissed Atossa.

"They've got us, Frank," said LaPalme.

"Maybe I should call McClay? See if he can call off Houseman."

"Hell with that, Frank. Fuck the money! Bomb those militia freaks in Montana!" screamed Atossa, suddenly getting up and stalking out of the room.

Frank looked at LaPalme.

"We can't lose that grain, Frank."

CHAPTER 96

Linda Bennett was sitting in the same chair she'd been in for over an hour when Nathaniel Cromwell entered the bomb shelter with Jerry Rust and Twist Hanratty behind him. Nate sat on the cot with Will and faced Linda. Twist sat in a chair in the corner, and Rust stretched out on the other cot and closed his eyes like he was going to take a nap.

"We just spoke with Forest." Nate said this with no emotional embellishment.

"Nate, really? Is he all right?"

"He's in Air Force One with the President right now, flying this way to make a deal—meaning his arrest had nothing to do with the President." Nate's eye met Linda's with the underlying meaning of what he'd said.

"Oh, Nate!" It was all she could do to express her relief. "That's great news."

Nate took a breath and let it out. "Except that he's asked us to stop the fires, and we've lost our telephone line. We can't stop the fires or the elevator detonations." He looked at his watch and bit at his lip. "The first one should have just blown." He paused, looking to Will. "And the Homeland Guard is pressing in on our perimeter. We've gotten reports of gunfire and some casualties."

"Are you going to surrender?" asked Linda.

"Not without having it televised. We're holed up in here hoping the President can stop this thing before it gets any worse or the TV cameras arrive."

"The President can't stop this?"

"Not with fires raging and elevators blowing up—and Paul Houseman commandeering the Homeland Guard. I don't totally get it, but Kenaghy thinks only by his being here in person can he get control."

"In other words," said Rust without opening his eyes or lifting his head, "our lives are banked on that fool in the White House."

Those in the little reinforced concrete room held silent for a lengthening minute.

"Am I still on house arrest, Nate?"

Nate swung his head from side to side. "No."

Linda couldn't stop herself. She reached out and hugged him. Over Nate's shoulder, she saw Jerry's eyes crease open and slide to hers. Self-consciously she let go of Nate. "Sorry about that," she said.

Nate smiled in a way that let her know there was nothing to be sorry about. "Alright, I just wanted to give you all an update." He patted Will on the head. "Sit tight and pray this bunker can take some hits." He stood and looked at Jerry. "Come on, Rusty, we've got to see what we can do on the perimeter."

CHAPTER 97

Air Force One was passing over Nebraska at thirty thousand feet when Kenagy got word of the bombing in Dubuque from Phillips at the White House. This news was met with various presidential curses and increasing depression inside the regulated atmosphere of Air Force One. They were still an hour from Billings and another twenty minutes by helicopter to the FBI base east of Tumble Mountain. And things were rapidly rocketing out of control.

For the third time, the President had Phillips connect him through to Sullivan. He demanded to be patched in directly to the FBI command center at the siege site. Sullivan fought none of it. But it was too late. Houseman, prompted by the elevator bombing, was now running the siege operation from his office in Washington via videophone. When Kenaghy's call came in, it had to pass through Houseman's people in Washington before going on to Montana, and Houseman simply canceled it—like it had never happened. Suddenly Air Force One was feeling more like an isolation chamber than a means to a solution.

On the slopes of Tumble Mountain, Hayes' militia, defending steep ground in a dense forest, had the advantage. The Homeland Guard could make no advance at all, falling prey to an invisible army with crossbows and AR-15s, guided on the east by Hayes and on the west by Cromwell. But when the elevator blew, Houseman commanded another salvo of mortars on the log cabin, including two direct hits.

Cromwell got news of this immediately. He gave up walkie-talkie command to one of Hayes' men and, with Jerry at his side, raced back to the broken and smoldering cabin. His heart sank at first sight of the collapsed building. The front room had been blown back toward the rear, leaving the floor space wide open and the basement hatch twisted off to one side.

Nate and Jerry grappled with the heavy timber blocking the way down to the basement, then quickly dropped down to the floor below. The concrete walls were broken in several places, and again the two men had to move away planking and shattered concrete to access the trapdoor to the bomb shelter.

Sweating, cursing, driven by the worst of all fears, Nate climbed through the opening to the chamber below. Jerry followed. The door to the shelter was intact. There were no cracks in the supporting walls. Nate banged on the door with his fist. He heard the latch click. He leaned on the door and pushed it open.

Twist, Will, and Linda were standing inside, frightened, but safe.

"Jesus Christ, this bunker is solid," muttered Nate, taking Will in his arms and looking over his son's shoulder at Linda. "I guess Hayes knows what he's talking about."

"Hayes! Hell," exclaimed Twist. "I'm the one who designed this place. Now quick, close that door before they hit us again."

"What's happening out there, Nate?"

Nate released Will then took Linda in his arms with no concern for the others. "We're holding our own," he said, letting go of her and addressing everyone. "This building is their only clear target—but apparently," he scanned the ceiling and walls, "this lower portion is taking it quite well."

"When do you expect the President's arrival, Dad?"

Nate looked at his watch. "It's thirty or forty minutes before they'll reach Billings. Then a bit longer to get here."

"Are we going to make it, Nate?"

"I don't know, Linda. It's going to be close."

Two CNN helicopters had been circling the siege area for thirty minutes, but with the airspace directly over Tumble Mountain closed off, the coverage was limited. With news of the elevator explosion, and then seeing the avenging hits on the log cabin from a distance, one of the helicopter pilots swung in from the north, challenging the edge of the airspace and allowing his camera man some impressive video of the bombed-out building through a telescopic lens. This instantly went nationwide and changed the whole sense of what was going on for the stunned television audience.

One of CNN's commentators compared it to the ATF attack on the Branch Davidians in the 1990s. This rapidly filtered back to Houseman in his office in D.C. The Homeland Security Director might not give a damn about the President, but he did have a tactical respect for the power of the media and sense enough to protect himself against bad or misplayed publicity. Not knowing Kenaghy was less than an hour from the siege site, Houseman decided to pull back on the use of mortars for the moment, telling his men to simply maintain steady pressure on the perimeter, while he waited for a few more elevators to blow to build drama and justification for a final all out helicopter and mortar assault. Just as Cromwell had understood that the field burning was in part theater, so did Paul Houseman intend to play the day's violence into a feature length ad for his privatization push.

CHAPTER 98

Air Force One settled down in Billings five minutes after the third elevator went down. Ten minutes later, the President's chopper was visible from the FBI command center as a silhouette coming in out of the east. At this point, Kenaghy connected directly to the FBI swat team's leader from the helicopter—and things started to move. Kenaghy told the FBI official he was using an executive order—which was a lie—to override Houseman and any of Houseman's men there at the operation. Then he said he had a promise from Hayes that if the siege was immediately canceled and cell communication returned, the bombings and fires would be halted as soon as possible. "So do it now. Every second counts!"

With Houseman's man screaming *no* at him, the swat team's leader answered with a taut, "Yes, sir, Mr. President."

"I'll be there in ten minutes. Prepare for me."

CHAPTER 99

When Paul Houseman got word of the President's arrival in Billings and his use of the executive order, he screamed so loudly over the phone that his man in Montana didn't need to relay the message to the lead FBI agent. "All-out attack on the top of Tumble Mountain. Burn them out if you need to!" Fortunately, the team leader would not budge from his promise to the President. Houseman cursed him to hell, then stormed across town from his office into the Senate chambers yelling about violations of the Patriot Act, improper use of an executive order, and demanding immediate impeachment proceedings.

By then, however, the FBI had communicated with the militia perimeter. Word of halting the siege and the President's arrival was quickly relayed to Cromwell and Hayes by walkie-talkie. When cell service opened minutes later, Cromwell called Lena, reaching her only moments before the fourth elevator was set to explode. Hayes followed with orders to curtail the burning. By the time Cromwell was talking to Mahan via cell phone, setting up a meeting with the President, the farmers had joined in with the Homeland Guard putting out fires. The emergency was winding down just as smoothly as it had started, and a bellicose Houseman was escorted from Capitol Hill by the D.C. police. From there, the President's secret trip to Montana was steadily leaked all over town. Another skip and a jump, and CNN was at the command center with cameras. Soon afterward, the entire country was sitting before their televisions poised on the drama of President Kenaghy's "excellent adventure," as the skeptics were calling it.

The huge olive-green military helicopter settled down in the FBI command center at the base of Tumble Mountain at four that afternoon. To the thrill of the camera men and reporters, President James Kenaghy and National Grange President Forest Mahan walked down the Chinook gangway side by side. They went directly to an awaiting armored Humvee and were escorted with five other Humvees up a logging road to the top of Tumble Mountain and what remained of Hayes' log cabin.

When the six Humvees motored in single file out of the woods into the open area around the cabin, Hayes' camouflaged troops peered from the surrounding forest like painted aborigines, watching the motorcade as it rolled to a stop in the cratered gravel parking lot. Circling overhead were three news helicopters relaying live videotape back to the three largest news networks in the United States.

A phalanx of secret service men exited from the three lead Humvees and met Linda Bennett, Vincent Hayes, and Nathaniel Cromwell in front of the collapsed log cabin. The secret service men searched all three of them, then escorted them to the President's Humvee. The President and Mahan stepped out, introductions were made, and then, after the President had brushed aside any need for further security, they climbed inside the spacious Humvee and found places around a meeting table that lifted up out of the vehicle's floor. Cromwell, Hayes, and Mahan sat on one side. The President and Linda sat opposite them.

From the various appearances of the individuals—Nate in dirty jeans and a faded sweatshirt—Hayes in camo with an unlit cigar poking out of his red beard—Kenaghy in a tailored blue suit and tie—Forest in pale green slacks and a checked shirt—and Linda in the white blouse and shorts she'd worn for two days—they were an unusual group, pressure-packed inside a Humvee with tinted windows and ringed twice around by secret service men, then encircled again by two thousand onlooking Montana militia in the forest periphery.

James Kenaghy was under the most pressure of all, and it showed in his eyes as strain. He had initiated talks with a seemingly hostile farm union just as their strike tactics had reached the extreme. He was effectively answering to blackmail perpetrated by a group some people considered terrorists. To set this up, he had broken several laws connected to the Patriot Act and the use of executive orders. If he didn't gain something quite substantial for his efforts, it was grounds for impeachment. Plenty of people in Washington were already drooling over this prospect. In no exaggeration of the facts, Kenaghy was pinning the historical meaning of his presidency, his reputation as a politician, and the next election on nothing less than a high-stakes gamble—and he'd just pushed all his chips into the center of the table.

Nathaniel Cromwell's situation was hardly less perilous. He was the face of the most violent labor strike in the history the United States, in which 1.4 million acres of wheat had been burned, fifty-one people had lost their lives, and countless others had been wounded. He had also burned his farm in complete disregard of a government warning against it and planned and ordered the bombing of three private grain elevators. If things went badly, he would be facing some serious jail time.

Stiff and visibly uncomfortable, Vincent Hayes could scarcely have felt any better than Cromwell. His secret sanctuary in the Rocky Mountains was now at the center of a huge media happening, and he, like Cromwell, was part of the "outlaw" strike leadership. If this discussion went poorly, he was the type who would have preferred going out in a blaze of glory than submitting himself to any kind of legal jurisprudence. Clothed in grim displeasure, he participated in this meeting with evident skepticism, countered by a vast amount of respect for Nathaniel Cromwell.

For Forest Mahan, this was his life's work coming to a head. Concerns for legal persecution paled in comparison to the potential this meeting held for American agriculture. With his greatest dream on the line, Mahan was the man in the middle—the individual who had already agreed to the President's proposal and needed to sell it to Cromwell and the more obstinate Hayes.

For Linda, this was a journalistic opportunity of a lifetime set in a situation that was as tense with impending violence as it was critical to the survival of the American farming community. Although she would never be judged to be part of the strike, she was not an objective observer. The outcome of this meeting held vast meaning for her personally. More than just a career opportunity, she knew closure with her father's death/murder was essential to the way she would live the rest of her life. Add what she felt for Nathaniel Cromwell, and the emotional element of the situation was almost more than she could bear. Yet, in comparison to the prospects for the others at the table, who represented many hundreds of thousands of people and the direction of a nation, her wants and needs seemed nothing.

Knowing resolution was the only acceptable outcome, Forest opened the discussion by getting the others up to speed on what had taken place at Camp David.

"So here we are," concluded Forest, "the President will use an executive order to grant the first of our strike demands in exchange for the entire block of our union voting for him in the next election. If he wins the election, he will nominate me for the position of Secretary of Agriculture and use his influence to help me push through the farming changes that are part of our second strike demand." Forest paused to let this sink in. "What do you think?"

Hayes looked at Cromwell, giving him the first chance to respond, but Nate deferred. Hayes took the cigar from his mouth. "What if that executive order is somehow blocked, Forest?" His tone was all resistance. "The President, who is already fighting Congress tooth and nail, would never get them to loosen the purse strings for us." Hayes turned his eyes to Kenaghy. "We could agree now, give up our wheat, and then be told after harvest, the money's not there. The proposal sounds good enough, but we don't have any guarantees. We need something more."

Kenaghy pressed his fist against his lips. Mahan had warned him this meeting would not be easy. The men he needed to convince, Cromwell and Hayes, would not be intimidated by his high office and would judge him entirely by the substance of his being and the way he held himself.

"General Hayes," said the President, "I understand your concerns. On Forest's suggestion, I checked out your Montana Militia website during the flight from Washington and have read your criticism of me. It's clear that neither you nor the American public understand why I've been having so much trouble in Washington. The media have repeatedly garbled or misstated my position. They have been as unfair to me as they have been to you—and the Colonel here. Although I am certainly not anti-government, many of the criticisms you express in your essays are what I am fighting against right now. Particularly the influence of defense contractors and the oil industry on government policy. I am very much with you on that."

"But what guarantees can you give us? As far as I can tell, none," pushed Hayes. "We need something solid right now."

"As you mentioned, General, my position in Washington is tenuous. However, I'm not entirely without influence. In fact, I've got one card to play that might get the first part of this strike settlement approved by the end of the week without an executive order. All could hold steady until then. Leave your militia in place. Don't harvest another bushel.

Wait no more than four days, and I will either succeed or fail." He paused and met the eyes of each of the three men seated across from him.

"I'm going to offer to sign the Trans-Eurasian Security Act—it's on my desk right now—as a compromise to the majority party for a strike settlement. It's a piece of legislation I was planning to use a pocket veto to stop. Even should they override that veto in the next session of Congress, it would cost my opponents a very valuable two or three months. They want this legislation very badly and they want it now. It has much greater priority in Washington than the price of grain. Maybe this isn't the guarantee you want, General, but it's an extremely attractive compromise to my toughest political opponents."

Of those present, only Linda, and to some extent Hayes, who did pay attention to what he considered the nonsense of Congress, understood the potential of this idea. "That could work," said Linda. "I've been following this legislative battle for months. It would be a tremendously daring move by the President."

"So, he appeases the petroleum industry, one of the military industrial complex's biggest players, to help us," said Hayes without the slightest give in attitude.

"That's right, and it's not something I do lightly or without grave fears," said Kenaghy. "But I'm hoping our coalition can change the dynamics of the next election. With a second term, I can return to my efforts to constrain what I see as the most dangerous elements in the nation's governance."

"But it won't be the industry paying the extra dollar on the bushel. It will be the government—and the taxpayers," countered Cromwell.

"That's the best I can do without more time."

Hayes put on a stone face and bit into his cigar.

Cromwell continued. "What about these charges of terrorism that have been leveled against the alliance? We'll need those dropped immediately."

"The field burning, in my opinion, was a legitimate labor strike tactic, not terrorism. What's going on now is only happening because of Paul Houseman. He raised the terror alert to severe and invoked a set of special executive overrides. I'm trying to get past those overrides by being here now. But the elevator bombings, Colonel," leveled Kenaghy. "They're something else entirely. It will take some kind of general amnesty or a presidential pardon to free you from that."

Cromwell nodded. He understood the risk he'd taken. "Perhaps, as Linda Bennett says, Mr. President, you have a real chance with this compromise on TES. But tell me, what chance do you have for a second term in the White House? All that really matters, it seems, depends on that."

Hayes sat back, cigar poking out of his beard, and nodded twice.

Kenaghy took a deep breath. "No one can make guarantees about the election, Colonel. They're already maneuvering in Congress to implement the articles of impeachment against me if I don't sign TES. I'm scrambling for a foothold in this game just as desperately as the family farmer." He pursed his lips and looked Cromwell in the eye, measuring the moment. "But I have one more card to play, Colonel, and I have deliberately held off with that until I could speak with you face to face." He paused, knowing this was another long shot. "In the end, as you say, everything we're talking about will be riding on the next presidential election. *I have to win.*" He paused again to look hard, directly at Cromwell. "Will you be my Vice-President? With you as my running mate, it would be a lock."

Cromwell wasn't ready for this. Just like when Mahan spoke to him prior to the big grange hall meeting, he wanted nothing to do with politics. He looked down at the table then lifted his eyes to the President's. "The honor is recognized, sir, but I don't believe I could ever go back to Washington."

"All I want you to do is campaign for me, Colonel. Your being on the ticket is a clear winner. Presidents for years have been obsessed with polls. I'm no different and I've already run through the numbers. We hit fifty percent with farm coalition backing. But with you as VP, it's over fifty-five pushing sixty. We can pull a real upset. Your rural coalition added to the Democratic Party's longstanding alliance with labor, and we would give the middle class a position like it's never seen before in this country."

Cromwell didn't have the slightest interest in being on the ticket—less than that—but something told him what Kenaghy was saying was true—and not to be easily dismissed. So once again, his name was essential to unification. His eyes turned briefly to Linda's then back to the President's. "My first impulse is to say *no*, Mr. President. But I want to see how things evolve this week before I respond definitively."

"That's a fair answer, Colonel. The next few days will determine quite a bit."

"Everything," grumbled Hayes.

Mahan spoke. "General Hayes, I still hear suspicion in your voice. You have been instrumental in all that we have done so far. You have made important compromises and held the party line. Say what's on your mind."

Hayes took the cigar from his mouth, leaned forward, and stretched his hands out flat on the table. "I don't believe we have a chance in hell." His eyes fastened on the President. "I don't believe we can achieve anything but temporary restraint on a government out of control. We might receive some cash and the sense of a victory. But like that cash, it will be short-lived. It's nothing to me. Even should you win another term, Mr. President, I'm not convinced you can do anything lasting to help us."

The cynicism was directed at the President, but Nate answered it. "General, for me, you have been the most surprising and important element in this strike. I scoffed at the militia movement my entire life. All I saw was frustrated white men wanting to play army. But in the last few weeks, you have embodied all that I felt was important in the military. The discipline. The character. The dedication to duty. You have been straight with me and right with your authority. We would be home on our farms proceeding with harvest if not for your diligence.

"I also have many of the same doubts you have about what might happen in the next few months. You know my history. You know my battles with the CIA and the Army. I know the corruption of big money and covert politics. But like Forest said, you made the most important compromise of all that first night at the grange hall. Even should you bow out of this and reject the President's offer, and the rest of us accept, you have my respect."

This meant something to Hayes. Cromwell had already proven he was the man of the myth, and the two men's eyes locked with the conviction of a battle-won friendship.

"General," continued Cromwell, "hold on to your cynicism. Maintain the current militia position and keep a close eye on things. I have yet to accept the President's offer, and for that reason, I want you to remain vigilant, but at the same time, open to the possibility that we might do something good for this country. Give the President his four days to deal with Congress. Let's see what happens. All bets are off until then."

Hayes made no visible reaction to Cromwell's request. But he didn't speak out negatively. The moment held with an understood sense of agreement in the group—if tentative and qualified—then Kenaghy spoke. "Are we on the same page or not?"

Cromwell read stoic Hayes' eyes one more time and nodded. "Yes."

"We're short on time. If we're going to make any of this happen, I need be back in Washington as soon as possible. And I would like to take Forest with me. I want him to testify before Congress. And perhaps, Colonel, you and your son would like a ride out of here as well. It might take another day or two to get the Homeland Guard back in its cage, but you can go with me to Billings in the helicopter or all the way to Washington in Air Force One."

"I can go to Washington, Mr. President. I'd be honored," said Mahan.

Linda looked at Nate. "I need to get back also," she began, but Nate cut her short.

"Why don't you drop my son and me, and maybe Linda here, in Billings. Get us off the mountain for the sake of safety but give us a day or two. I've got some business of my own to take care of. We'll proceed from there depending on what goes down in Washington in the next four days."

Linda blushed at the implications that maybe no one else fully understood.

Kenaghy nodded. "All right."

"Hayes?" asked Cromwell. "You good?"

"Holding vigil, sir."

CHAPTER 100

Although a tentative agreement had been reached and the sense of urgency eased, there was still quite a lot of work to do before the farm movement could really say anything had been achieved—and much of it hinged on how things went between the President and Congress. No one seemed to understand this more clearly than General Hayes.

After the meeting broke up, Hayes remained on Tumble Mountain, while the rest of the group left with the President's entourage of secret service protection. Forest Mahan and Nathaniel Cromwell rode in one vehicle with the President, continuing to talk and plan for the week ahead. Linda Bennett rode in a second vehicle with Jerry Rust, Will, and four secret service men. As she sat there in silence, bouncing down the rough logging road, still buzzing with leftover adrenaline and anxiety, trying to assemble a perspective on what had just happened, she thought quite a bit about Vincent Hayes. None of this would change him. Even with a complete strike victory, he would surely remain a Montana outcast, pushing year after year for secession.

Curiously, these thoughts did not come to Linda with the revulsion they used to generate. Hayes and his stand against a badly corrupt government had gained a measure of her respect, and she reluctantly admitted that maybe a nation needed hardheaded iconoclasts like him just to keep everyone else honest and thinking. In admitting this to herself, Linda also understood that she had changed. Something in her life-long faith in American governance had been altered—or broken. It made her think of her father, and it made her sad.

Linda flew back to Billings that evening in the President's helicopter with the rest of the group. It was busy and hectic. She got no chance to talk to Nate. Their eyes met a few times, hers with unabashed longing. Tired and perhaps hopeful, she read the same in his. But the situation still dictated higher priorities for Nate, and he talked at length with Mahan and the President the entire trip, while she sat by herself in the back of the helicopter making notes for the column she wanted to send to Frederick Manning the next day.

When they landed in Billings, Nate was whisked off to the privacy of Air Force One to finalize a schedule for the coming week. Jerry waited outside the plane for this last meeting to end. And Linda, beginning to feel the depth of her exhaustion, volunteered to take an also very tired Will to the Holiday Inn beside the airport and arrange for three rooms.

After doing the necessary hotel paperwork, Linda went right to her room and slipped into the tub. When she finally gathered the energy to climb out, she put on a hotel-provided, white terrycloth robe, made a cup of tea, and sat on her bed with her laptop, poised to write. But her mind wasn't there. She turned on the television and tuned in the news. It focused on the events in Montana. She watched for less than five minutes and turned it off. As important as the strike story was, as much as she wanted to write about it, her thoughts belligerently centered on Nathaniel Cromwell.

Linda had hoped she might get a few minutes to talk with him that night, but it didn't look as though that would happen. She sat on the edge of her bed, wondering if she would ever be able to push all this strike business out of the way and really get to know the man.

It was only nine o'clock, and Linda was too unsettled to go to sleep. She did what she never did. Nothing. After three hours sitting in a bomb shelter, more frightened than she'd ever been in her life, and then experiencing the high tension of the meeting in the Humvee, she struggled with the crushing anticlimax of these moments alone.

Just after ten, Linda heard two light knocks on her door. She held her breath and went to the door. She didn't look out the peephole. She didn't latch the chain as a precaution. She just opened the door knowing Nate was there.

He held a white paper bag in each hand and gave her a heart melting, sheepish smile. "I know I owe you an apology, Linda, for all that we've put you through." Nate lifted the bags as an offering. "How about dinner for a start? Mexican okay?"

One thing was certain. Nate was a very genuine, down-to-earth, take-nothing-for-granted man. It was the real life effect of having grown up on a farm, leaving for a sixteen-year career in the military, and then returning to work the land. To a woman who had lived in Washington,

D.C., doing the high heels, makeup, and fancy clothes career thing, this man's natural-born humility was like the elixir of life. Despite Linda's being tired and emotionally drained, the sight of Nate filled her entire being with warmth and energy—like the rest of the world and its troubles had been washed away

Linda and Nate didn't make it to the burritos. All that they'd felt for each other, and contained for the last three days, burst open like a fever. She never even thanked him for coming to her room or said *yes* to Mexican. They were kissing before he'd closed the door. Nate kicked the door shut and laid Linda down on the bed so easily their lips never parted. Her robe fell away as he unbuckled his belt and pushed down his jeans. She accepted his embrace and spread her legs with such anxious surrender she knew she'd never known what love was before…

PART VI

CROSSFIRE

"No Caspian Sea explorations, no drilling in the South China Sea, no SUV replacements, no renewable energy projects can be brought on at a sufficient rate to avoid a bidding war for the remaining oil. At least, let's hope that the war is waged with cash instead of with nuclear warheads."

-Richard Heinberg, *The Party's Over.*

CHAPTER 101

Jonathan Mayfield was grateful for the weekend. After the tense exchange at the Night Safari, he drank himself into oblivion Saturday and Sunday night. Monday morning came too soon and with great foreboding for a man going into work knowing he'd just given away the corporate jewels.

Jonathan sat paralyzed at his desk all Monday morning waiting for the thugs to come get him. But they didn't come. Filled with grave misgivings about "selling" the bank's security codes to Dan, he sweated through the rest of the day. His contract ran for two more weeks. As he exited the DBA office building that evening, he wasn't sure he could last that long. He drank in excess again that night.

Tuesday morning began with a hangover and the same foreboding. Twenty minutes after the wakeup call from the hotel desk, Jonathan struggled out of bed, stumbled over to the phone, and dialed room service for a pot of coffee. Once he'd gotten a little caffeine into his system, he opened the copy of *The Singapore Times* that was at his door each morning. Blazing red headlines delivered the news: US FARMERS BURN FIELDS AGAIN! He shook his head in disbelief then went straight to the financial pages. The Dow had taken another huge tumble which rippled like falling dominos through the other world markets. Commodity exchanges went the opposite way. Grains of all kinds were pushing at record highs. The news ruined his appetite. He skipped breakfast, dressed quickly, and took the short walk from the Hilton to the DBA Building.

The morning began uneventfully, and Jonathan even began to relax a bit—until just after lunch, when he was called to the executive suite on the top floor of the DBA Building. He rode the elevator up with growing trepidation, but Parker Chen greeted Jonathan with a smile and a nod when he entered the office high above city center Singapore.

"You're doing good work, Jonathan," said Chen from behind his desk that was a thick slab of glass. "Please, sit down."

Behind Chen were two walls of floor to ceiling windows. The floor was polished black marble. The view offered a marvelous perspective on the port of Singapore, looking out on the South China Sea to the north, Sumatra to the south, and an azure sky above an ocean of deep blue to the east. Walking across the floor, Jonathan felt like he was walking on air—both for the view and the depth of his paranoia.

Two glass chairs were arranged before Chen's desk. Jonathan took the one on the left.

"I'm glad that it's working out, Mr. Chen," said Jonathan, trying to gather himself.

"Yes. Even more, I like you, Jonathan," said Chen. Then his smile washed away. "But I'm very sorry you were so easily set up."

Jonathan went cold.

"Is this really such a surprise?" Chen leaned forward and handed Jonathan a photograph. It was the snapshot the old woman in Dan's apartment building had taken of him through the door. Then another of him at the Hilton bar with Dan as a hippie. Then another of him sitting next to the old woman Dan on the tram at the Night Safari. "You have a friend, Jonathan. Who goes by the name of Dan Stephenson." Chen's presence had completely transformed. The warmth in his voice was gone and his eyes had sharpened like a cat's.

Jonathan felt like a child before him, helpless and frightened.

Chen continued. "The eavesdroppers of the National Security Agency of the United States found you first, Jonathan. They knew you had spotted something an hour after you spoke to Louis Hampton that Friday three months ago. We learned of you through our connections in U.S. intelligence. Once we had you, everyone—on both sides—even your Mr. Hampton—felt it was best you were taken out of the loop."

"I figured Louis Hampton went to Andreas Grain, but..."

"The intelligence community already had us tabbed as a money-laundering operation but didn't understand the grain implications until they stumbled upon your work." Chen frowned. "Once we had our grain secured, we didn't care what happened to the market. We only wanted to ensure that you didn't come up with any more cute ideas before we were done—thus the kidnapping. When Andreas Grain followed the lead you gave Hampton, it made our game a little more expensive, but it was brilliant business for them."

"So, you're saying I was set up by Andreas Grain?"

"Only because the NSA was already tapped into them. Dan Stephenson was working for the Terrorist Finance Division of the CIA. He's an intelligence operative. He deliberately fed you that information about the Teochui. He didn't accidentally find you that night. He didn't accidentally drop that disk. You were being used, Jonathan."

Jonathan felt like the black marble floor had vanished from beneath him. "Dan set me up?"

The door behind him opened, and the thugs he'd seen during his imprisonment entered the room. Chen lifted his head disdainfully. "Yes. Then we used our knowledge of him to use you. Once the NSA marked you, you became a wonderful asset for all of us. The thumb drive you sold to your friend Stephenson was exchanged by a pickpocket less than five minutes after you gave it to him Saturday night. He will be feeding the CIA an entirely different set of Swiss bank accounts." Chen paused to smile. "You see, Jonathan, we really did want to hire you, but not for what you thought. Thank you."

Jonathan was dumbfounded. He felt heavy hands on his shoulders. He looked around anxiously, "Mr. Chen, please."

"I'm sorry, Jonathan."

Four hands lifted Jonathan bodily from his seat. "But there are still many improvements I can make in your system."

"No, I don't think so."

CHAPTER 102

Tuesday, the day after the meeting in Montana, was a busy day in Washington for James Kenaghy. Enthused about his work for the first time in months, he and Cameron Phillips manned the Oval Office phones. The top priority was Houseman. Using the provisions of the Taft-Hartley Labor Management Relations Act, combined with the threat of an executive order, he convinced Congress to drop the Terror Alert level from red to orange, thus stripping an enraged Paul Houseman of his draconian powers and beginning the process that would end his directorship.

The second order of business was the strike settlement. Instead of using an executive order, Kenaghy pushed for a straight up, government subsidy to cover the farmers' first demand. The senior Senator from Missouri Harold Wilson and the junior Congressman from Kansas John Conlin took joint sponsorship of the legislation and by noon that day had assembled a committee to write the bill. Forest Mahan, who had known and worked off and on for years with Wilson, was assigned to the committee to ensure that it fulfilled the President's promise.

More important than writing of the bill, however, was building coalitions of senators and congresspersons to lobby for its passage—under the added pressure that Congress adjourned Friday for six weeks. Fortunately, Kenaghy still had some influence in the Democratic Party, but crossing the aisle to the Republicans would be a challenge, especially since the settlement requested almost two billion dollars from the government to cover the grain subsidy.

One time through his rolodex for favors, Kenaghy could not come up with the numbers in either the House or the Senate. This necessitated Kenaghy's last resort—a compromise on the TES Bill and a meeting with the powerful Washington lawyer John A. McClay.

Late Tuesday afternoon, McClay entered the Oval Office all too aware of the meeting that had occurred in Montana the day before and all the backroom scuffling that had been going on in Washington since sunrise that morning. Kenaghy and McClay hadn't spoken since their confrontation the day the CIA Service Star was awarded posthumously to Arthur Rivenhouse, and a stiff, icy formality chilled the Oval Office as the immaculately dressed McClay took the sofa opposite Kenaghy in front of the fireplace. Cameron Phillips stood off to one side—a draft of the farm legislation in his left hand. The TES Bill sat unsigned across the room on the President's desk.

"Thank you for coming here on such short notice, John," said Kenaghy, trying to force some warmth into his voice for this man he disliked intensely.

"You are the President, sir," said McClay full of condescension.

Kenaghy nodded. "And you are a busy and influential man."

"Not to the extent you are."

"Perhaps."

Things stilled. Both men clinging to their separate agendas like reluctant lovers. Then Kenaghy offered his roses. "The last time we spoke, John, I said I would do whatever it took to block TES. And you advised heavily against that position."

McClay nodded.

"Congress adjourns in three days for a six-week district work period. I could easily sit on TES, enact a pocket veto, and temporarily sidestep a very likely override."

"That's what we've anticipated, Mr. President," replied McClay without emotion.

"Then when Congress reconvenes, there will be a motion for my impeachment from New York's junior congressman," said Kenaghy. "Or so the winds of Washington say."

McClay made no response.

"So," continued Kenaghy, "it seems I'm doomed in my stand against TES. No matter what I do, it will pass sometime later this fall." Kenaghy looked over to Phillips standing attentively to his left, then back to McClay. "I thought to offer you a compromise before I walk the plank—that is, if implementing pipeline security two or so months sooner is of any value to your people."

McClay turned away and looked at the unlit fireplace. Then to the portrait of Jefferson over the mantle that Kenaghy had exchanged for the one of Washington earlier that morning.

"I want an immediate settlement of the farmers' first strike demand," said Kenaghy. "The junior congressman from Kansas will bring the legislation to the floor of the House tomorrow. If that farm legislation could find its way through both the House and the Senate by Friday evening, I could get TES back to Congress signed before adjournment."

Phillips stepped forward and handed the bill to McClay. "This is an early draft, sir."

McClay accepted the sheaf of paper but made no attempt to read it.

"My guess, John, is that you can facilitate this kind of speedy action—that is, if time is at all important to the security of the pipeline." Kenaghy knew it was, and he watched the lawyer run through the various trade-offs in his head.

McClay looked down briefly at the papers in his hand then faced Kenaghy. "And what of the impeachment process, Mr. President?"

This was an incredibly insulting thing for McClay to ask at this moment. If not for the anger and tension between these two men, Kenaghy might have smiled at the absurdity of it. "I can't believe that would be necessary if the pipeline was protected."

McClay remained cold as stone. "Is that what this is about, Mr. President—evading the embarrassment of impeachment?"

Yet another jab! And Kenaghy felt it. But it was a jab he would gladly take as he put the pieces together for his knockout punch. "It would be a relief, yes."

"Included as part of this compromise?"

"As a gentleman's agreement." Kenaghy didn't really feel the impeachment would fly if things proceeded as he thought they would with the strike settlement. But he also didn't mind giving the opposite impression to McClay.

McClay smiled with his eyes only. "And what is this strike to you, Mr. President?"

Kenaghy grimaced. "I've seen too many fires on television. Too many gunshots between American citizens. And too much Paul Houseman."

There he and McClay actually agreed. McClay nodded. "I will read this," he raised the papers in his hand. "And get back to you."

"That's all I can ask," said Kenaghy, standing at the same time as McClay and shaking his hand.

After McClay left the office, Phillips looked at his boss. "Well, that was ugly enough. How do you read it?"

Kenaghy grinned and put both thumbs up, then looking around at whatever devices might be listening, whispered softly, "Hook, line, and sinker."

CHAPTER 103

It was midday in Montana. Linda lay next to Nate in her room's king-size bed wearing only a sheet. Sunlight filtered into the room through drawn curtains. Nate had put Will on a commercial air flight that morning, sending him back to his mother's home in Milwaukee so he could start getting ready for school in the fall. Nate and Linda would fly to Washington, D.C. at the end of the week. Jerry, who would fly with them, was down the hall in his hotel room. For once, the new couple had some extended time alone.

"Nathaniel," asked Linda softly, turning on her side to face him, "dare we talk about what is going on between us?"

"No," said Nate staring at the ceiling with a lazy grin. "Let's not take any chances."

"You know nothing about me, Nate." Linda rose up on one elbow. "What I know about you I read as a result of an internet search." For the first time in several years, she was not thinking about tomorrow or deadlines. The who, what, when, where, and why of everything she needed to know was right here and now.

"Maybe it's better that way, Linda. What we know about each other is what's apparent. I don't need to know anything more than I already do. I think I knew that three days ago at lunch in Forest's dining room."

"Love at first sight?"

Nate turned on his side, facing her. "I think that's the way it always happens." He put his hand on her thigh and slid it up over her hip.

"Really?" Linda turned onto her back, drawing Nate's hand across her belly. "Then I fell for you that first night you spoke on television." His hand thrilled a little lower. "I remember moving up close to the TV and thinking this is the man I'm supposed to find and interview. Lucky, lucky me."

"Even with my cap on, huh?"

"That's what did it, the hat," she said with a crooked little smile, then closed her eyes as his hand slid a little lower.

Nate leaned over and kissed her on the cheek. She drew him in, pulling him over her. "God," he hushed, kissing up her neck, whispering in her ear. "For how long have I missed this?"

They rolled half a turn, so that Linda was now on top, looking down. "I don't believe I've ever quite known *this*," she murmured.

"Maybe it's just the physical need?"

"You think so, Nate?"

"Yes," he smiled, putting his hands on her hips, positioning her onto him.

"Hmmmmm," she gasped as things suddenly got much more intimate. "Maybe you're right," she gasped again as the words melted away…

They were lying side by side again, enjoying and needing the lazy afternoon, using the intimacy to strip away the stress of weeks, months, maybe years.

"Seems like we've known each other more than three days," said Linda. "Seems much longer than that."

"Wait until the end of the week," Nate chuckled. "It'll seem like a lifetime."

She rolled over to face him. "Are you making fun of me?"

"Not really."

She stared into his face. Relishing every pore, every irregularity, even the faint red remains of the burns on his cheek and forehead. "Nate, I never really thought we would break through the situation and the politics. Right up to the moment we climbed into that Humvee, I figured the timing was all wrong for us."

Nate turned toward her and smiled. "If you only knew, Linda, how many times I told myself to forget what I was feeling. That I just couldn't allow you to interfere with my duties to the union and the strike. But I knew it was all over when I saw your bare bottom." He reached over and gave her a love pat. "It's funny how strong the physical forces can be, even to a determined man." He brushed a few loose hairs off her forehead. "Then when I heard that your father was Arthur Rivenhouse, I became so confused and so angry—because I knew what we had was real. And yet." He shook his head.

"But I knew that too, Nate. I did. Even during our roughest moments yesterday, I knew you trusted me in spite of the circumstances."

Nate leaned over and kissed her on the lips, then lifted his head thoughtfully, "Yeah, my good buddy Jerry Rust put me in a very difficult spot with Twist's research. Got to talk to that boy."

"Yeah, I'm afraid he's not my favorite, Nate."

"I know."

Linda pushed herself up on one elbow and looked down at him, now on his back, his hands behind his head. "I have a serious question."

"Oh, no. Not the M-word."

"Fuck you, you jerk."

They both burst into laughter, and Linda fell onto her back, so that they were both looking up at the ceiling, laughing. "Not the M-word, Nate. The VP-word," she said, suddenly serious. "What do you think?"

Nate continued to stare upward. "I don't know. Seems like a worthless position to me."

Linda sat all the way up. "No doubt about that, Nate. But it could make all the difference in the world. Literally—if all goes well in Washington the next few days. That would be the frosting on the cake. Getting Kenaghy another term and Forest right there in Washington, working for the farmers and the land. That was the whole point of this thing."

"Is that what it was?" he said. "I thought it was about me meeting you."

"Maybe you're right," she said, smiling right into the center of his soldier's heart.

Nate lifted one of his hands and began counting his fingers, "One, two, three…"

Linda watched him with a childish curiosity. "What are you doing?"

"I'm counting my lucky stars," he said.

"Yeah? What for?"

"That the CIA should send such a woman as you to me."

CHAPTER 104

Atossa sat on her bed and listened to the phone ring at the other end of the line. After four rings, a recorded message came on. When it was over, Atossa spoke into the phone. "Derek, I'm sorry, but I have to cancel for tonight." This was the last thing in the world she wanted to do, but it was necessary. She would be leaving for Atlanta in an hour to see *that god damn Nina Colleen*. She hung up the phone and stared at the floor feeling her nerve ends sputter and spark.

After a moment, she stood up and strode across her bedroom to the mirror. She hadn't dressed yet for the trip and wore a black silk gown. The second field burning had been too much for her. Despite reassurances from Frank and Curtis that the strike would have little real impact on Andreas Grain, she had spent most of Monday watching news of the field burning, then the Homeland Guard standoff in Montana, and finally the arrival of the President's helicopter.

The stress and strain of the strike ate at her the entire time and through a sleepless night. When she awoke Tuesday morning, the spidery little star on her cheek had become a galaxy. She immediately put in a call to Dr. Colleen and arranged for a trip to Atlanta that afternoon. Hours of angst and deliberation later, she'd placed the cancelation call to Derek Davis.

Davis found the message on his recorder only minutes after Atossa left it. He'd found Atossa an incredible woman both sexually and in presence. It had been a long time since he'd been so captivated by a woman. Her message struck him hard. He called her back immediately and was told Atossa was unavailable to anyone. He took this as a horrible snub. After a rush of anger and a determined effort to brush it off as nothing more than the actions of a crazy woman, he realized in a slump of depression that he really wanted this woman—and he couldn't get that first time they made love on the restaurant table out of his mind. He'd told a friend it was the best "first sex" he'd ever had with a woman.

At five o'clock Tuesday afternoon, Atossa entered Dr. Colleen's office in Atlanta, wearing a black veil to match her black jacket and skirt. Nina rose from her desk.

Atossa stood in the center of the office and lifted her veil. "Look at this, Doctor. Look at this. Fix it," she demanded. "Or you will never perform cosmetic surgery again."

Nina felt no intimidation at all. "Have you put something on your skin again?"

"No. I followed your every order. It's something you did."

Nina came up close to Atossa and inspected her face and skin. She ran a finger over the red blemish that covered almost all of Atossa's right cheek. She stepped back and stood there thinking to herself.

"Well, what is it? What can you do?"

Nina glared at this woman she'd grown to hate. "It's a complication from that one night you used cover-up on your face."

"It can't be."

"I suggest we perform the complete transplant again."

Atossa stared at the woman, clenching and unclenching her left hand at her side. "But then I will look entirely different. There must be some other way?"

"You can leave it as it is. If the disturbed area stabilizes, you could use makeup to cover it."

Atossa could feel her ire rising, increasing her stress and working, she was certain of it, to further enlarge the blemish. She crumpled to her knees and began to cry.

CHAPTER 105

On the first leg of his flight to Milwaukee, Will Cromwell thought long and hard about spending the rest of the summer with his mother. During the two-hour layover in Denver, he decided to change his travel plans. He called his mother and told her that he was staying with his father a few days longer. Then he exchanged his ticket from Denver to Milwaukee for a flight to Oklahoma City. An hour later, he boarded that flight. Just after five that evening, he entered a car rental agency at the Oklahoma City airport and used the credit card his father had given him for emergencies to rent a car.

Jerry Rust had told Will about John Finnegan, the youth his father had punched at the grange hall meeting in Pratt. Before the settlement, Jerry had said that they were driving from Montana to Oklahoma City to see if Finnegan had anything to do with the firebombing of their farm. Inspired by the war stories and camaraderie of Jerry and his father, Will decided in the Denver airport that because the settlement had changed his father's plans, he would track down John Finnegan on his own.

Will stayed Tuesday night in a cheap little motel in Oklahoma City, then got up early the next morning and drove to the Oklahoma City militia headquarters. He walked into the office and introduced himself as the person on his fake ID.

"Yeah," he said to the older man at the desk. "I'm looking for a buddy of mine from high school, John Finnegan. He told me about this outfit, and I was thinking of joining. I'd kind of like to catch up with him and jaw it over first. Got any idea where he is?"

"Well, I reckon I might," said the man in olive drab with a corporal's stripes on his shoulders. "We've gotten word of a possible strike settlement, but we're still on standby here in Oklahoma." He thumbed through some papers in his desk drawer. "Finnegan. If I'm not mistaken, this isn't my favorite recruit." He looked up at Will and gave him a glance. "But it isn't my place to be telling anyone who to have as a friend." He paused, still trying to appraise the youth before him. "You're not one of those extremists, are you?"

Will shook his head no.

"We're trying to get away from the Nazi stuff that's infected some militia units. And that Finnegan was a bit edgy for me and quite a few others here."

Will nodded. "Wasn't like that in high school."

"You don't have any tattoos, do you?"

"Not me. Don't much like needles," drawled Will, putting on his best country boy act.

The corporal pulled a single sheet from the desk drawer. "Let's see, I've got Finnegan over there in Enid with our third battalion. I could call and verify that, but you know these boys are spread butter thin along the crop lines, and it's hard for the battalion leaders to know where each and every one of their people are—if you know what I mean?"

"I think so," nodded Will. "But I'd appreciate it if you could give the battalion leader a call. Maybe see if Johnny's really out there at all."

"Yeah," said the man. "I guess I could do that."

It took a while for the corporal to get around to it, but eventually, he found the right phone number and placed the call. The answer to the question was a negative. No, Finnegan was no longer with the battalion. As soon as he'd heard about the plans for a settlement, he'd taken off.

"Have a phone number or an address for John?" asked Will after the corporal hung up the phone.

"This information isn't for the public, young man. As a friend, it seems like you should already know his phone number."

"John moves around like a stray cat, sir. He's got one home after another. I've got a couple of phone numbers for him here in my pocket, but I tried both of them before I got here. Come on. He's just a dumb kid like me. What's his address?"

The corporal thought it over, gave Will the once-over a third time, and retrieved the needed information. Finnegan had no phone number on file, but there was an address on the west side of town.

Will left the militia office and went straight to a gas station with the address. He got directions from the attendant and headed west across the mid-size city. On the way, he stopped in a grocery store and bought two six-packs of beer.

Will found the street he was looking for in a slummy, sun parched neighborhood. He traced the street numbers to a small bungalow with an overgrown lawn of weeds. An upside-down American flag was nailed across the front window so you couldn't see in.

Not knowing what to expect, Will parked one house away and quickly scratched a swastika on the back of his hand with a ballpoint pen, ripped the sleeves off his t-shirt, and messed up his hair.

Carrying the beer in a brown paper bag, Will sauntered up to the house and knocked heavily on the front door, prepared for the worst. The door opened immediately. A young man, maybe two or three years older than Will, with a muscular build, his head shaved, and wearing a leather jacket, despite the Oklahoma heat, glared out at Will. "What d'ya want?"

Because the youth wore the jacket, Will couldn't tell if there was a swastika tattoo on his forearm. Was this Finnegan or not? He took a chance. "John here?" he asked.

"John?" the skinhead sneered. "Who the hell is John?"

"Finnegan," continued Will. "A mutual friend told me I need to meet him. This is the address he used. Said he had some interesting stuff going on."

The youth laughed derisively. "Finnegan. You mean Zombie." He laughed again. "What could you want with that dickhead?"

"I heard he was in a militia unit. I wanted to check it out."

"Man, what a waste, dude. The guy's a total deadbeat."

Will peered past the youth into the house. The place was a mess—beer cans, ashtrays filled with cigarette butts, wrappers from fast food restaurants. A TV on a three-legged table jabbered in the far corner. Another slacker slouched at one end of a dirty, pea green sofa. "You mean he does drugs?" asked Will.

"Zombie don't need drugs to be a zombie. He's in a permanent daze. What the fuck do you want, dude?"

"I'm just looking for the guy. Is he here?"

The surly youth stepped back and turned to the other skinhead. "Where's the fucking zombie?"

"Dude took off this morning. Early. Jerk woke me up banging around."

Will leaned in the doorway, trying to engage the other young man. "Know when he might be back?"

"I could give a shit?" came back from the youth on the sofa.

"What is this, the FBI? Get lost, dude," said the youth at the door.

"Yeah, outta here, asshole," added the kid on the sofa.

"Christ, man," said Will. "Lighten up. I bought this beer to tilt with John. If he ain't here now, maybe you guys could help me drink it, and I could hang out for a while until he gets back."

The youth at the door turned to his buddy, grinning. "Bobby, we wouldn't be interested in drinking beer, would we?"

"Fuck yes, we would!" bellowed Bobby from the couch.

"My name is Tim," said Will, coming into the living room, wincing at the thick stench of cigarette smoke and mildewed. "I guess that's Bobby."

"I go by Slip. Like slippery." The youth gave Will a crooked grin, revealing a broken front tooth. "Let's take this stuff into the kitchen and get it in the fridge."

Will followed Slip through the living room to the kitchen. If the living room was the barn, this cramped little kitchen was the pigsty. The sink was piled with dirty dishes. More dirty dishes covered the counter. Two open pizza boxes were spread out on a Formica table pushed up against the wall. The refrigerator looked like it had been painted with catsup. Pictures of pin-up girls were taped here and there on the door, highlighted with magnetic skulls, swastikas, and all sorts of other stupid shit. Will lifted the six-packs of Budweiser from the paper bag, pulled three cans from the packaging, and handed Slip the rest. Slip jammed them into the ongoing chemistry experiment in the fridge and took one of the loose cans from Will.

Will trailed Slip back to the living room, where he handed a beer to Bobby. Slip dropped onto the couch and Will sat on the floor. For the next hour, he sipped his beer and watched cartoons on TV, while Bobby and Slip downed one can of beer after another. When he figured his two companions were appropriately lubricated, Will returned to the topic of John Finnegan.

"I heard that Finnegan knew how to make bombs," said Will out of the blue.

Slip gazed at Will through alcohol-laden eyes. "Yeah, maybe. What's it to ya?"

"Not much," said Will. "I'm kind of interested in knowing what it'd take to firebomb a building. Nothing too serious," he grinned.

This gathered Bobby's attention. "Zombie didn't know shit about real explosives. But I watched him mix up a couple Molotov cocktails."

"Yeah? Did he ever use them?"

"I kept hoping he'd blow his ass up," sneered Slip, getting up off the couch for another beer.

"Did he, Bobby?"

"He said he did. But he's so full of shit you never know what's bull and what's not."

"He told me he blew up a farmhouse somewhere," probed Will.

Slip came back into the room, using the back of his hand to wipe beer from his chin. "Oh, yeah. Zombie our little *agent provocateur.*"

"What do you mean?"

Slip laughed out loud. "*Agent provocateur.* That's a guy who keeps radicals stirred up. Prompts them into action. That freak Zombie told me once that was his job. To keep the flame burning."

"Really?"

"Fuck! What do you mean, really? I don't fucking know what was real about that goon."

Just then a third youth came into the front room from the kitchen. He was well over six-feet with long greasy blonde hair hanging in a face of acne. He looked like he'd just gotten out of bed and had one of Will's Budweisers in his hand for breakfast. "Did I hear right? Somebody out here looking for Zombie?"

"Yeah, I was. Know when he might be back?"

"None too soon," mumbled the kid, slumping down on the sofa between Slip and Bobby.

"You mean, I shouldn't be here waiting for him?"

The youth yawned and shook his head no.

"Yeah?"

"He was up all night drinking beer and zinging diet pills," said the longhair. "He was in a terrible mood. Got this call in the afternoon yesterday. Got real weird. Said he had a score to settle in D.C."

"Zombie, real weird? How could you tell?" laughed Bobby.

"You think he went to Washington, D.C.?"

"Damn, I'm getting sick of your questions, dude."

"Shit, I don't know," said the longhair. "Said something about wanting to shit on the White House lawn. Doubt that rat-trap Nova of his would make it that far. But that's all I know. If he ain't here now, he must be on the road."

Will nodded his head. "What's the color and year of his car?"

"Flat black. Sprayed with rattle cans. Looks like homemade shit," chuckled Bobby. "I don't know the year. Old is what I'd say. It's got a red German Cross hand-painted on the driver's side door. Can't miss something that ugly."

"Does he know anyone back there he'd be seeing?"

"Yeah. Toby." The longhair laughed. "Remember Toby Ostrow, you guys?"

The others joined in laughing until Will asked. "Got a phone number?"

"Fuck the questions, dude," demanded Slip. "I'm sick of it."

"An address?"

"Hey, don't give this freak any more information. We don't know who he is."

"Uh, what difference does it make," continued the longhair.

"The difference is *I don't like it!*"

"Know anything else?" pushed Will despite the building tension.

"NO," said Slip, getting up off the couch and moving toward Will menacingly.

"Fine, guys. Sorry for the inconvenience." Will got to his feet, not certain what creature the beer might have unleashed in Slip. "Hope you enjoyed the free beer. Keep the rest."

Slip just glared at him. The other two youths were focused on the TV. Will backed away toward the door. "Sure you don't have a phone number for Toby?"

"Man, what kind of trouble you lookin' for?" Slip kept coming at him. Will reached for the doorknob.

"I think he wanted to kill the President," yelled the longhair on the sofa. All three of the youths burst into laughter. Will did his best to join in, then quickly stepped outside. The door slammed heavily behind him.

Will hurried back to his car thinking about what he'd just learned. Kill the President? Should he call the police? No, those guys were more than likely fucking with him. What about D.C.? He climbed into the rental car and dug a map out of the glove compartment. There was only one way to get to Washington from Oklahoma. Route 44 to St. Louis, then Interstate 70 east. What did he have to lose? His dad would likely be in D.C. by the time he got there. He laid the map on the passenger's seat and started the car.

CHAPTER 106

Wednesday afternoon, John McClay stood with Frank Nelson in the halls of the Capitol Building, just outside the doors to the House of Representatives. A moment later, Frank's cousin Robert Nelson III, a Republican Senator from New York, and the Republican Congressman Levon Wright of Utah, the House Majority Leader, came out of the House chambers.

The two men approached John and Frank. "So, here's the deal, Levon," said Robert Nelson, who had gone into the House to drag Wright out for this little chat. "Kenaghy says he'll sign TES Friday, if we come up with $1.9 billion to answer the farmers' first demand." Robert looked to be an older, heavier version of Frank. "Is that right, John?"

McClay nodded.

"I don't like it," said the congressman from Utah. "It gives labor the entirely wrong message about these kinds of strike methods. And why in the hell is the government offering to pay this instead of asking the industry to do it?" Wright was none too happy about being pressured into such difficult legislation on the third to last day of the summer session of Congress.

"I don't like it either," said Frank, looking over his shoulder at the security guards outside the doors to the House. "There must be some advantage in it for Kenaghy. Has anyone figured out what he's got going with these farmers?"

"My guess is he's trying to save face on the way out of town, Frank," said his cousin. "He makes this compromise with TES and, as John says, gets a gentleman's agreement that we forego impeachment. That alone makes sense to me."

Frank rumpled his nose. "He'll get a lot of credit for breaking this strike. I know the public hated those fires on television. Maybe it's an election move."

"If it is, it's too little, too late," sneered Wright. "The man couldn't win with the Virgin Mary as his running mate."

"Well, I'd feel a whole lot better if the public were going to the polls in November with his impeachment underway," said Frank.

"If we don't get this settled pretty damn soon, boys," said Wright, getting edgy, "I won't have time to get in there and make it happen. What do you want to do? Yes or no?"

"I like it," said Senator Nelson. "Let's get TES signed."

"Then it's up to you, Frank," said McClay. "How important are three months to the pipeline project? That's what it boils down to. In my mind, this little labor flare up and Kenaghy's noble exit from office are nothing compared to securing the pipeline."

Frank took a deep breath. Only one thing really mattered—securing the Lake Balkhash oil field as soon as possible. All else was secondary. "I want the three months." Even as he said it, he felt a rush of second thoughts, but there were always second thoughts in this kind of business. "Go for it."

CHAPTER 107

Parker Chen followed a servant through the stark halls of a thousand-year-old Taoist monastery in the foothills of the Himalayas not far from the mouth of the Yangtze River. Chen had traveled from Singapore to southern China to sign off on the Teochui grain buy of the past spring. It was in part a celebratory dinner, because the buy had gone so well, and in part his annual progress report to the Teochui overlord Zhao He, who had converted the monastery into a home and personal retreat.

The servant stopped at the doorway to a large room with a bare stone floor. Chen watched as another servant worked his way around the perimeter of the room lighting some twenty candles set in recesses cut into the walls. Gradually the room became illuminated. The ceiling was vaulted into a peak and supported by thick black wooden beams. The walls were unpainted limestone and contained no artwork. A long teak table sat in the middle of the room. The servant finished with the wall candles and lit three tall white candles evenly spaced down the length of the table. Four places were set. Zhao He sat perfectly still at the head of the table. His hands were clasped in front of him and his eyes were down. He wore a simple coarse white cotton shirt and matching trousers. The servant led Chen, who in contrast wore a well-tailored, silver sharkskin suit, to the chair at the opposite end of the teak table. When the servant exited the room, Zhao slowly lifted his eyes.

Chen offered his host an abbreviated bow.

"It's good to see you, Parker," said Zhao. His long hair was pulled into a queue at the back of his head in the ancient Chinese fashion. "Please be seated."

"It's an honor, Zhao." Chen pulled out the chair and sat down.

"Thank you for coming, Parker, and thank you for giving me the chance to talk to the English commodities analyst."

"Did you get the information you desired from Mr. Mayfield?"

"We learned some things."

"And you are done with him?"

"Yes," answered Zhao with a morbid finality.

"He was a talented young man."

"But naïve—and extremely foolish."

Chen nodded gravely. He had liked Jonathan.

"I hear you have seeded the American intelligence community with the proper Swiss bank account numbers."

Chen almost smiled. "Yes. I think the snake is about to bite its own tail."

Zhao nodded, also clearly pleased. "I think our friend Nursultan Mendelev will be surprised how perfectly clean his American friends have laundered his money."

"In the end, however," said Chen, "the Americans will know the source of this embarrassment. It cannot be avoided."

Zhao waved his hand. "No difference. They're the ones of the first insult."

"The Americans might understand that, but I'm not so sure Nursultan will see it that way. He's a brutal one."

"So are we."

Chen nodded. "You have received the grain contracts?"

"Xian arrived with them just a few days ago. I must thank you for the excellent work. I consider the grain buy one of the greatest successes in Teochui history."

"Not to mention the profit and the great quantities of laundered money. It was a stunning idea, Zhao."

"And our late friend Mayfield almost tripped us up. You deserve credit for turning that around."

"All the credit is yours, Zhao. I merely follow the Teochui directives."

Zhao's pleasure showed in his eyes. "Are you hungry, Parker? Do you mind if Xian and a house guest join us?"

"A house guest?"

Zhao grinned showing his teeth. "He is an engineer at the Three Gorges Dam. A German by the name of Fruehauf."

Chen tilted his head

"I see I have roused your curiosity." Zhao clapped his hands. A servant with a round Mongolian face appeared in the entry. "We are ready for the meal, Guo." The servant nodded and turned away down the hall.

"Is that a new man?" asked Chen.

"Yes, less than a year. I like him. He's unusually cold hearted."

"A Mongolian?"

Before Zhao could answer, a young Caucasian in rimless glasses came to the doorway and stepped into the room. His presence ended all talk of business, and the evening proceeded on into dinner.

CHAPTER 108

It was four-thirty on Friday the twenty-fourth of July. President James Kenaghy sat at his desk in the Oval Office with a box of ballpoint pens and the Trans-Eurasian Security Bill on his desk, containing a rider that secured $1.7 billion to answer the Nonpartisan Farmers' Alliance's first strike demand. Before him were several members of the press and a television camera crew. Behind him stood the principals, Secretary of Defense Lawrence Fitzgerald, Kazakh banker Viktor Ivanov, General Austin Sinclair, New York Senator Robert Nelson III, Utah Congressman Levon Wright, Missouri Senator Harold Wilson, Kansas Congressman John Conlin, and Grange President Forest Mahan. As Kenaghy signed the legislation on each of the prescribed dotted lines, a camera would flash, and he'd hand the pen to one of the men behind him.

Frank Nelson watched the ceremony with mixed feelings on C-SPAN in his Wall Street office. On the suggestion of Curtis LaPalme, Andreas Grain made a last-minute contribution of $200 million to the government's subsidy plan to diminish some of the pro-Kenaghy impact and create good public relations for Andreas.

With no emotion at all, John A. McClay watched the event on a small television tucked in a cabinet in his law office on "K" Street.

The signing ceremony was coming to an end. Forest Mahan received the last of the historic pens, and as Kenaghy stood to shake hands with the National Grange President, the doors to the Oval Office blew open. Paul Houseman burst into the room with two secret service men trying to contain him and two others behind, apparently not knowing what to do with a man known to be one of the most powerful in Washington.

"What the hell are you doing, Kenaghy?" Houseman shouted, shedding the two secret service men like a tight fitting jacket. "You've just rewarded a band of blackmailing terrorists."

Knowing the C-SPAN cameras were rolling, Kenaghy maintained his calm. "Please, Mr. Houseman, you no longer have a government position and have no right to be here."

Houseman's eyes enlarged, and he glared at the others present. "I'm still the Director of Homeland Security," he bellowed. "And I want this man impeached." Two more secret service men appeared in the Oval Office doorway. The four already there stood back, uncertain how to proceed.

"Get this man out of here," said Kenaghy.

As soon as the security men moved in on Houseman, he rushed at Kenaghy. The honored guests were already backing away, but Kenaghy held his ground. In a whirlwind of action reminiscent of a Mike Tyson weigh-in tussle, Houseman pulled free of the secret service agents and threw a wild left at Kenaghy, who deftly blocked it with his forearm, then ducked a following right—as four agents swarmed over Houseman, forcing him to the floor. His arms were pulled behind his back, and he was handcuffed lying flat on his stomach. Twisting to his side, the ex-Homeland Security Director spit out a parting shot, "Impeach this fool!"

Kenaghy nonchalantly stepped away from the hissing, kicking Houseman and nodded to the lead secret service agent. "Get him out of here. I think he missed his meds."

Although the camera work was unsure, most of this was televised live. In his office, John McClay simply shook his head in disgust.

Frank Nelson thought it took some of the glow from the signing ceremony and would minimize Kenaghy's poll numbers. But he was wrong. When the C-SPAN videotape was cut for network television, the President actually looked quite nifty, holding his ground and protecting himself from the raging bull Houseman. It was probably worth an extra percentage point in the polls.

CHAPTER 109

Nate and Linda flew to Washington with Jerry Rust Friday morning. They landed at six that evening at Dulles Airport and took a taxi to Linda's apartment in Georgetown. Linda's top priority was talking to Charlie Patio. She had tried to call him several times from Billings and from the airport with no success. Upon entering her apartment, she went straight to her office to dig out the phone numbers of other Agency people who might help her get a hold of him.

While Linda did this, Nate turned on the television in the living room, found CNN, and dropped onto the sofa. Jerry sat beside him in a matching armchair. The news featured coverage of the passage of TES and the rider covering the farmers' first strike demand. Nate and Jerry were laughing it up, watching Paul Houseman's explosive entrance into the signing ceremony, when Linda got word over the phone.

She walked up behind the couch and touched Nate on the shoulder. He turned to look at her over his shoulder.

She blurted it out. "Charlie's dead."

Nate stood up and caught her in his arms as she came around the couch. Linda began to cry and talk at the same time.

"Easy, Linda. Take your time."

She fought to gather herself and leaned back in Nate's arms, tears running down her face. "He shot himself in his home two nights ago."

CHAPTER 110

Saturday morning, the day following the TES signing, Linda Bennett and Nathaniel Cromwell went to the White House with Forest Mahan to attend a small private brunch with the President and the First Lady. The setting was a bit stiff and formal, but talk was light and positive with several champagne toasts to settling the first strike demand and the various players who made it happen. Despite the overwhelmingly positive mood of the morning, it was all Linda could do to mask how deeply she had been affected by Charlie Patio's suicide. Having Nate there for support Friday night was all that got her through the initial impact and allowed her to raise a champagne glass now with what passed for a genuine smile.

After the meal, the First Lady was hurried off to a Cystic Fibrosis fundraiser at the National Art Gallery. The President asked his three guests to take a walk with him through the Rose Garden, which Nate interpreted as further pressuring to accept the number two spot on the presidential ticket. Cameron Phillips joined them as they walked through the West Wing on their way out of the building.

The extra security that had been put in place during the strike had been reduced by half but was still very visible on the periphery of the grounds as the group strolled on the immaculate White House lawn. The President stopped to admire one particularly large yellow rose blossom at the edge of the garden. He leaned over to sample its fragrance then pinched it off and offered it to Linda. "You know, Ms. Bennett, I was very worried that day I slipped you the note in my office. I had no idea what would come of it. Thank you, truly, for trusting me and facilitating what's happened."

Linda accepted the rose with a muted smile, a current of grief for Charlie ran behind everything she thought or said. "I think the real trust came from these two men, Mr. President." She deferred to Forest and Nate. "For trusting me."

"But none of this would have come about without you," said the President. "It took more than ordinary courage."

"Absolutely," agreed Forest. "And she took a lot of undeserved heat when the pressure was at its greatest."

Linda bowed her head in a mix of emotions. Nate touched her gently on the arm, knowing she was struggling badly, despite the compliments.

The President's easy mood abruptly became serious. He glanced around the grounds, his paranoia for eavesdropping still quite apparent, then gave a nod to Cameron Phillips, signaling the beginning of what all of them knew was coming. Phillips stepped forward.

"We had some polls taken early this morning to measure the effect of the passage of TES and the settlement on the farmers' strike. The results were encouraging. The President made up substantial ground on Carlton, but not as much as had been forecast earlier in the week. The numbers don't predict a Kenaghy victory."

"If I don't win," segued Kenaghy, "I can't get Forest in position to advance the second strike demand. The farmers will get their cash from the subsidy, but it will go no further than that." He looked directly at Cromwell. "However, according to my people, I can pick up another six or seven percent points if the ticket reads Kenaghy-Cromwell. That would mean a win."

Cromwell didn't bat an eye. "I have no desire to be here in Washington, Mr. President. I'm sorry. I'm going back to Kansas to rebuild my farm."

Kenaghy wouldn't let it go. "Colonel, it's more than the success of the farm movement that's at stake." He moved in closer and lowered his voice. "As a politician I came to Washington perfectly willing to be drawn to the center. I had some idealistic notions, some hopes and dreams for what I might do for the people of the United States, but those quickly faded when I discovered what was going on behind the scenes.

"More than just powerful lobbying groups and big money pressure, there's a far-right wing of the corporate community that is hell bent on what, to me, is a very disturbing global agenda. I spent the entire last year fighting these people with my futile stand against the bill I just signed to enable the strike settlement. These incredibly influential people are using a powerful combination of economic leverage and military positioning to corner the world's most important natural resources. Oil is the obvious one. We've been watching that happen in the Middle East for the last thirty years, and now the march is on in Eurasia. But it's more than oil. It's water rights and forest products and every critical metal you can imagine. It's a push for control of the world's natural resources. Superficially it looks like business as usual, but as far as I'm concerned, this is nothing less than an economic cold war on the world's less fortunate. It might be too late, but if we have any chance to slow these people down, it hangs on the election. And you, Colonel Cromwell, are the key."

Cromwell met the President's intensity with unmoving silence. But the President's words struck Linda dead center. "Please reconsider, Nate," she said with more emotion than she intended. "I've been reading and writing about the depletion of petroleum resources for the last few years, and everything the President says rings true—and is furthered in my father's email chronology. I've shown you some of it, and unfortunately, what my father saw is even graver and more disturbing than what President Kenaghy has described. A syndicate of transnational elites are jockeying for position in a population rollback associated with resource depletion, environmental degradation, and climate change. I don't know what the President has seen, but instead of using the influence and power of the United States to assist the world into a new age, beyond petroleum and beyond war—with ideas like Forest's reengineering of agriculture—there's a movement to maximize profits as natural resources get more dear—and somehow it's being passed off as good business sense." Her voice brimmed with the feelings she'd been holding back the last few hours. "This sounds crazy, but it's real. Maybe it's too late like General Hayes believes. Maybe it can't be stopped. But maybe it can, and right now, Nate, James Kenaghy represents our only hope—and his only hope is you." Linda took a breath and brushed away the tears in her eyes. "I would just as soon forget Washington. I would just as soon go with you to Kansas and learn a new way of life. But I don't believe our Kansas paradise would last very long. The bigger picture will dominate. I don't think we have a choice. We can't walk out on this man."

Forest felt the same way. "I don't know anything about right-wing syndicates or plans to use corporate positioning to take control of strategic resources, but I do know about the environment, and we're at the edge of a deep and horrible precipice. I would hate to guess what twenty more years of neglect will bring. As critical as you were to our strike, Nate, you're even more critical now. I'm with Linda. I'm with the President. Please reconsider."

Nate stared down at the lawn. It didn't take a great leap of faith for him to believe what he was being told. His whole life since the day he left Afghanistan had involved a difficult adjustment to the ugly reality that unchecked greed was a major driving force in American policy. He also accepted that his name probably did have the power to garner votes and even win a second term for James Kenaghy. But he didn't want any part of politics or Washington or its media circus. He simply wanted to go back to Kansas. Then that damn sense of honor thing and his dedication to duty rose up in him. This was the real fiber of who he was—and he had no answer for it.

Nate lifted his eyes to Linda's, then took her hand. His eyes held a moment before turning to President Kenaghy. "Okay" was all he said.

CHAPTER 111

Will Cromwell left Oklahoma City Wednesday afternoon. He should have been able to make the trip to Washington, D.C. in two long days of driving, perhaps arriving late Friday sometime. Unfortunately, his rental car developed electrical problems Thursday night. Having no phone and little experience with car repair, Will lost most of a day broken down on Interstate 70—much of it standing on the side of the road in the middle of the night trying to get assistance—followed by several hours at the car rental getting a replacement car. He lost another half-day on Sunday morning when Thursday night's breakdown and related lack of sleep caught up with him, and he overslept at a motel outside Wheeling, West Virginia. Will didn't arrive in Washington, D.C. until late Sunday afternoon.

During his ordeal of driving, Will had built what he had learned about John Finnegan into something much larger than the information warranted. He convinced himself that there would, in fact, be an attempt on the President's life and that he was the only one who could stop it. He also understood, however, that what little he knew was not enough to take directly to the police, so he decided to concentrate on finding his father and going from there.

After his roadside problem Thursday, Will bought himself a ten dollar cell phone. As soon as he was inside the Capital Beltway, the freeway that circuited the District of Columbia, he tried to call his father. The cell number he had didn't work. The only other person he could call was Linda, but her number was unlisted. He knew that she worked for *The New York Financial Times,* so he called the Washington office. She wasn't there, and they wouldn't give him her home phone number, so he left a message on her voice mail.

His only viable lead was *Toby Ostrow*, supposedly John Finnegan's contact in Washington, so he went to the phone book. There was only one Toby Ostrow listed. His phone number and address were included.

Ostrow lived in Falls Church, Virginia, one of the Washington area suburbs. Will bought a map, talked to a service station attendant, and set off to find 2420 Lancaster Court.

CHAPTER 112

Derek Davis spent Sunday afternoon alone at his place on Long Island, pounding the hardwood of his gymnasium with a basketball, absently tossing the ball at the hoop, and hitting redial on his cell phone and sending text after text. Over and over, he got the recorder on Atossa's personal phone and nothing from his texts. He hadn't slept well since Tuesday when Atossa canceled their date and hadn't eaten yet that day. He was feeling unusually frustrated about being *dissed* by the woman he'd had such a sensational time with the previous week. Mostly, however, no woman blew him off—black, white, yellow, red, or brown. And this was getting to him in a way he didn't like. A little after three, he gave into his frustration and chartered a jet to Newport.

Atossa had secluded herself in her bedchamber all Sunday. Wearing her black silk dressing gown, she paced back and forth, shuffling her deck of Tarot cards, trying to make a decision about the blemish on her face, now slightly upraised and covering almost half her cheek. Although there seemed no way around it, she did not want to go through the ordeal of a second face transplant and adjustment to what would be a completely new appearance. At the very least, it would destroy her relationship with Derek Davis—a relationship that had no chance of lasting, but that was exhilarating and exciting while it did. *And she knew he was trying to get ahold of her.* She had monitored his repeated phone messages and read every pleading text—and it tore at her not to answer.

Nancy Waters' voice came over the sound system. "Frank Nelson is on the line, Ms. Andreas."

Atossa cursed to herself. She didn't want to talk to Frank, but she wanted an update on the farmers' strike. She'd been very much against the settlement, but Frank had convinced her that if spun properly they could turn it to their advantage. "Put him on," she said.

"Atossa," said Frank through the sound system.

"Yes, Frank. What's the good news?" she asked, continuing to pace and chop at the deck of cards.

"Kenaghy has changed his ticket."

"And what could that matter?" she sneered to the air.

"At a Democratic fundraiser tonight, not long from now, he will name the military hero Nathaniel Cromwell as his running mate."

"So what?"

"Atossa. It's everything. Some quick polling suggests it will put him ahead of Carlson."

"WHAT? How's that possible?"

"The grain settlement and the signing of TES have increased his public credibility. We knew it would. We also knew it wouldn't be enough to change the election—but Cromwell's name does."

"You fool, Frank. How could you have let this happen?"

"No one could have forecast that Cromwell would accept a place on the ticket. I can barely believe it now, and I know it's happening."

"FIX IT," Atossa commanded. "I don't care what you do. Kenaghy is untrustworthy and must be out. Good-bye."

Atossa squeezed her Tarot cards with both hands and a shiver of anxiety rippled through her body, immediately causing her face to tingle and itch. She stared upward through the skylight, seething with anger and frustration.

Nancy Waters' voice came through the sound system again. "Ms. Andreas, we're having a security problem at the front gate. Derek Davis is there, demanding to be let in. He says he won't leave until he sees you. The guard is confused about what to do."

Atossa didn't know what to do either. She rushed to the mirror and took one look at her face and hissed out a long, low curse.

"What was that, Ms. Andreas?"

Conflicting thoughts ran in all directions through Atossa's mind. Foremost, she did not want to be bothered at this moment. But after all his unanswered calls, that Davis should come here without advanced notice to see her, did mean something. His desire for her was as great as her desire for him. But what of her face? She'd bought some new low-impact, water-based makeup. Maybe she should take a chance with this makeup, see him now, and worry about a long-term fix later.

"Pardon me, Ms. Andreas. Should I tell the guard to call the police?"

Atossa squeezed her eyes shut and pulled a single card from the middle of her Tarot deck. She opened her eyes. It was the two of swords.

"Blocked emotions," she whispered to herself. "Let Mr. Davis in," she called out to the room.

"Yes, Ms. Andreas."

"Have him wait in the entry hall. I will be down as soon as possible."

The guard at the front gate had recognized Davis as soon as he stepped out of his taxi. But no one got through the gate without advanced notice. Davis got indignant, prompting the call to the house.

Wearing a black suit with a black turtleneck, Davis stalked back and forth in the Nelson Mansion's sumptuous entry hall, torn between anger at the way he was being treated and thick waves of emotional urgency to see Atossa.

He was all set to start searching the house room by room and had ventured into the grand hall, when Atossa appeared at the top of the staircase. She wore her black silk dressing gown with a sash at the waist. Her hair was pulled back into a long, thick brunette braid, and her face was freshly made-up. She looked ravishing. Their eyes met with fire. Davis bound up the stairs in four long strides, stopping two steps short of the top.

"Why wouldn't you answer my calls?" He nearly finished the line with *bitch,* but such was Atossa's effect on this brash man he held back on his usual trash.

Atossa advanced into his arms. "I'm sorry, Derek. I'm sorry. I wanted to see you. Oh, how I did. But this horrible field burning has been tearing at me, and I didn't want you to see me so distraught. Please, please forgive me," she said, reaching out to touch his face and gaze into his eyes.

Such was Davis' state of mind, any excuse would have worked. He smiled and pulled her into his arms. "You know I forgive you. I just couldn't bear not seeing you. I had to come here." His hands reached around behind her and glided down the silken gown.

Atossa pressed her belly into his groin and kissed up his neck, whispering, "Come to my bedchamber—where we can have the privacy this heat deserves."

Atossa had prepared the room before she'd left to greet Derek. The thick crimson wall curtains were pulled over the windows. The skylight blind was drawn. Seven tall candles spaced around the room provided the only light. The bed was open, and the Tarot cards sat in a neat stack on the divining table. Davis took this in with a huge smile. Atossa led him to the divining table and helped him slip off his jacket. He pulled at her sash and her gown fell open. She wore nothing beneath. He lifted the gown off her shoulders and dropped it to the floor. He kissed down between her breasts to her navel, but Atossa stopped him short of his target, putting her hands on his shoulders and drawing him up.

"One thing first," she said with a sly grin, reaching out to him and pulling his shirt out of his trousers.

"Something special, baby?" Davis pulled off his turtleneck as Atossa worked at his trousers.

"I believe there's something magic in sex," she said, dropping his pants to his ankles. He wore nothing but a hard-on.

"So do I," he grinned, kicking clear of his pants.

"At the moment of orgasm there is an opening in the cosmic vault of time."

"Really," he said, watching her open the drawer in her divining table and withdraw a small jar of lubricant. "Really," he said again, starting to guess at what was coming.

"Really," replied Atossa. She turned the lid off the jar and dipped two fingers into the clear jell. "And in that mystic opening, we are given an opportunity to see into the future." She placed a gob of jell on the head of his penis and with both hands spread it down its length.

"Yeah, baby," he said, as she stroked him several times up and down.

"Will it bother you, Derek" she said, continuing to stroke him, "if during the height of the act, I draw a card from my Tarot deck."

"Whatever turns you on," he cooed to her touch. "Whatever turns you on."

She turned her back to him and leaned over the table.

"I can get behind that," he chuckled, moving up to her, positioning himself to enter her.

"Easy," she cautioned leaning over the table, as he held her by the waist and slid inside.

As he put his hips into slow undulation, Atossa cut her deck of Tarot cards into three piles spaced evenly on the table. Then spread her legs as wide as she could, gripped the table with both hands, and centered her thoughts on the face of James Kenaghy and the outcome of the November election.

Gradually Davis' thrusting quickened, then became robotic. Using the motion of her hips, Atossa milked him once while drawing a card off the top of the first pile of cards. Then took a card from the top of the second pile with his next ejaculatory pulse, and finally a card from the last pile with his third pulse.

That was it. Three thick squirts and he was done. She put the three cards face down on the table separate from the rest of the deck. Davis continued to ease in and out of her until she pushed herself up with her arms and he backed out of her.

Atossa turned to face him. He had a dreamy, just climaxed look in his eyes. "Was that good for you, baby?"

"Well," she said with a wink, "that one was for you. I'm counting on you recovering as quickly as you did the other night, and this next one will be for me."

Davis grinned as she led him over to the bed and laid him down on his back. He relaxed into the pillows and watched her clean him off with a towel. "What about those cards you selected?"

"I'll get to those. First things first." Atossa leaned over him and used her hands and her mouth to revive his interests. It didn't take long, and she greased him again. Then with him still on his back, Atossa straddled his waist and eased herself down on him. Starting slowly at first, she began to rock. He closed his eyes as she built up speed, working her hips, faster and faster, trying to bring herself to orgasm. He pushed back with equal fury, intent on doing for her what she had already done for him. Harder, faster, furiously. Him gripping her hips. Her holding her breasts, gritting her teeth, eyes tightly shut, concentrating as hard as she could, working up a lather—to the point that little drops of perspiration began to bead at her hairline.

But her orgasm didn't come, and the effort turned to work. Davis opened his eyes to watch Atossa driving herself at him like a woman on a mechanical bull. The sweat on her forehead was now running down her face in rivulets, streaking her makeup so that the red, spidery blemish on her cheek began to show. The wet threads of makeup and red web behind combined in a hideous way—as though one side of her face had been stripped of its skin. Davis' interest became mixed, horrified, then lost. Without achieving his or her goal, he drooped out of her.

Atossa opened her eyes, saw the consternation in his face, then gasped out loud when, wiping a finger down her cheek, she realized what had happened. All of a sudden everything stopped. They were staring at each other, an ugly awakening occurring in them both. His of distaste. Hers of anger.

Davis sat up and with his big hands and muscled arms laid her down sideways on the bed as he slid out. Atossa read all what was running through his mind.

"Get out of here," she spat at him with palpable venom.

Davis didn't say a word. He walked across the room to his clothes. With Atossa's stare lasered at his back, he dressed hurriedly and walked out. Atossa turned over in the bed and began to cry.

Atossa found the strength to climb out of bed an hour later. Naked, her face streaked and spotted, she stumbled over to her divining table where the three Tarot cards lay apart from the rest of the deck. With hatred in her heart and anger in her mind, she turned over the three cards one by one. All were major arcana.

The first was the Fool. "Kenaghy," she hissed in a whisper.

The second was the Hangman—*reversal!* Hadn't that just happened?

The third was—"Christ," she hushed under her breath—the King of Terrors, the skeleton with a scythe.

CHAPTER 113

"What do you mean they've been goddamn frozen?" cursed Nursultan Mendelev. He used both arms to push his 350-pound bulk up out of his chair.

"I've been calling the bank in Geneva all morning, sir." His personal secretary Nita Panfilov, full figured and attractive in the rough style of the Kazakh Russians, had just entered his office with the bad news. "All the numbered accounts are inaccessible."

"That is impossible," Mendelev bellowed, slamming his fist on his brand-new desk, in his brand-new office, in his brand-new office building in Astana. "Call again. Tell them who these accounts belong to." Mendelev lumbered menacingly across the room toward his secretary.

Nita backed away toward the door. "I've called several times already, President Mendelev. They say the same thing every time. Some kind of hold has been put on those accounts."

Mendelev stopped his advance in the middle of his vast office, his eyes glazed with the thoughts behind. "Call Mr. Richards in Langley, Virginia," he said suddenly.

Nita hesitated. "But it's Sunday night in the United States, Mr. President."

"Then call his home. Now. I want to speak to him immediately."

"Yes, sir." Nita retreated to her office to make a call halfway around the world.

Bob Richards was dressed in running gear, two steps from the front door of his suburban Virginia home, prepared to jog around the neighborhood, when the phone rang. He hustled down the hall and into his office. "Richards, here," he said, noting the ID of the phone number at the same time he answered.

Mendelev had taken the line as soon as the phone had begun to ring. "What's going on in Geneva, Richards? The accounts you set up for me have been frozen."

"President Mendelev." Richards' head was swimming. "The Geneva accounts? Frozen?"

"Don't play stupid with me," accused Mendelev with volume, smashing his fist again on his desk, hard enough for Richards to feel it twelve thousand miles away. "All my private funds are suddenly unavailable to me!"

Richards held the phone away from his ear. "It must be a mistake, President Mendelev." As he said this, he remembered that the Terrorist Finance Division had recently frozen several accounts in Swiss banks due to information coming out of Singapore.

"Mistake, my ass," came echoing back with a one-second delay. "Give me money, then take it away? Someone will pay for this!"

"No one took your money, President Mendelev," urged Richards. "It's probably just a bureaucratic mistake. Let me check into this."

"Let you check into it! By God, Richards, you better check into it. I want to know today what is going on in Geneva."

"Yes, yes, fine."

"And I want a nuclear weapon!" Mendelev demanded.

"Please, President Mendelev. Hold on. I'll call you back," he glanced at his watch—seven-fifteen. "In an hour." The phone slammed down at the other end.

CHAPTER 114

It was seven twenty-five when Will Cromwell pulled into a little neighborhood off of Lee Highway in Northern Virginia. It had been a circus of missed turns and bad directions since he'd set out to find the home of Toby Ostrow. Now, with building anxiety, following instructions he'd received at a convenience store five blocks away, Will wound through the suburban housing complex until he reached the intersection of Venice Road and Lancaster Court. He took a right into the cul-de-sac. He spotted the flat black Chevy Nova before he had a chance to fasten on the street numbers.

Will continued into the cul-de-sac and verified that there was a red German Cross hand-painted on the driver's side of the old Nova, also that it had a flat rear tire. He followed the cul-de-sac around and out, taking a right back onto Venice Road. Two blocks down, he parked his car and walked back to where he'd just been.

The house of interest was a split level, set back from the street, with thick, overgrown laurel bushes planted all around it. His heart pounding, Will surveyed the area for neighbors—then dashed to the front of the house and forced his way through the laurels up against the house. Hidden by the shrubbery, he worked his way from window to window along the front of the house, hoping for a view inside.

The shades were drawn on all three ground level windows across the front of the house. He could not see inside at all. The same was true for the first window along the east side of the house. The shade in the next window, however, contained a small horizontal rip. Through that little tear on the left edge, he could see into an empty laundry room. The next window was on the back of the house and had no shade at all. It was another view into the laundry room. At that point, he had to pass across the back patio to reach the protection of more shrubbery beyond.

Having seen or heard nothing inside as yet, Will boldly approached the patio door and tried it. It was unlocked. Again peering over his shoulder for nosey neighbors, he opened the door and peeked inside. It was a small, messy kitchen, empty except for many unwashed plastic plates and several sections of newspaper spread across the counter.

Emboldened by adrenaline, Will stepped into the house and listened. Nothing but silence. He advanced into the adjoining dining room. Again, no sign of people. The house remained hauntingly quiet.

Will continued on, one room at a time. The first floor, then to the second. He climbed the stairs slowly to a short hallway. The first door on the left was open. The bed inside was unmade. Clothes were scattered on the floor. Farther down the hall were two closed doors. As he reached out to open the door on the right, he noticed dark red stains on the brass plated doorknob. Trying not to touch the stains, he used his fingers to turn the knob and push the door open. Crimson flashed in thick splatters across the pink tile work. The shower curtain was torn off the stall and lying over a body, half in and half out of the tub—lifeless enough to be dead.

Will turned away and backed down the hall. He immediately punched nine and one into his cell phone. Then hung up. He reluctantly approached the bathroom again. Fighting revulsion, he knelt beside the bloody body and, using his foot to move the arms, checked for a schoolyard swastika tattoo. There wasn't one.

Will's stomach suddenly heaved. He spun from the body and emptied his stomach on the bathroom rug.

Will gathered himself, used the back of his hand to wipe his mouth, then pulled out his phone. He punched in the three emergency numbers and went back down the stairs, waiting for the phone to pick up at the other end. When a voice came on the line, he told the female police officer that he'd found a dead body. He gave the woman his name and the address where he was. The woman told him a patrol car was nearby and would be there in a few minutes. He assured her he would wait.

Will put away his phone and began to pace nervously around the house, swarmed by a confusion of thoughts and worries. He wandered back to the kitchen and rinsed his mouth out with a glass of water. A section of *The Washington Post* was on the counter beside the sink. He absently turned a few pages. A sentence in the upper corner of page six was underlined in red: *President Kenaghy will be hosting a black tie fundraiser for his campaign tonight at seven o'clock in the Arlington Sheraton.* Will looked at the clock on the kitchen stove. It was seven fifty-five.

CHAPTER 115

"I know by now you've heard enough of politics. You're tired of campaign promises to be broken. And you're sick of me begging for money to get this campaign rolling. So let's get to the real reason I'm so excited to be here tonight and what I think is going to get all of you and the rest of the country excited too."

James Kenaghy stood at the podium in the huge ballroom at the Sheraton Hotel across Key Bridge in Arlington, Virginia. The wall behind him displayed a huge American flag. To the President's left and right were rectangular tables strung with red, white, and blue bunting. The other speakers and honored guests sat at these tables facing the audience, and included Forest Mahan, Marjorie Kenaghy, Missouri Senator Harold Wilson, Kansas Congressman John Conlin, Linda Bennett, and Nathaniel Cromwell—in a tuxedo. Behind, stood six discreetly indiscreet secret service men and Jerry Rust.

Filling out the rest of the Sheraton ballroom were two hundred round tables with white tablecloths, seating some fifteen hundred wealthy Democrats there for the $1000-a-plate, black-tie campaign contribution dinner. Farther back in the crowd and off to the side were six television cameras and scores of press photographers and journalists. It was seven-fifty-six, Sunday night, July 26th. And for the first time in almost a year, there was real optimism for the reelection of James Kenaghy. Because everyone knew what tonight's announcement would be and what its impact would be on the election.

"There is no education like the presidency," announced Kenaghy, lifting the volume of his voice. He knew this was the beginning of the campaign homestretch, and he wanted to reaffirm his political convictions while his audience held on edge waiting for the introduction of Colonel Cromwell. "My three and a half years in the White House have given me a unique view into what goes on behind the scenes in this town and how much big money interests figure in the workings of our government. From the privileged perspective of the Oval Office, I have seen what very, very few have ever see—and it frightens me.

"Since the beginning of the century, there has been a terrible misdirection of American policy and substance. Over and over again, a good old boy Congress has chosen corporate expansion over environmental repair. Over and over again, our governing system has chosen a gluttonous military dominance over domestic needs. Over and over again, a high-paid brotherhood of lobbyists has pushed for new weapons contracts and corporate tax breaks, when our schools, our elderly, and our disparaged minorities have been left behind. Something is terribly wrong when a democracy is guided by the few at the cost of the many—and it frightens me."

The President leaned forward on the podium and lowered his voice. "We have a challenge before us today like none we have ever known. Our world enters upon a new era. An era when the debts of a hundred years of unchecked consumption and waste are coming due. And I don't mean *fiscal* debts with an *f*. I mean *physical* debts with a *p*. For reasons I struggle to fathom, our present course is set on deepening these debts—not addressing them. Instead of conservation, instead of reasoned management, global economic interests will continue to reap Earth's natural resources like there is no tomorrow—with only one concern—the bottom line. And these same interests will laugh all the way to the bank, saying it's for the good of the United States. That it's patriotic. And that it's the only way to protect our way of life—that is, to protect more consumption and waste. This is nonsense—and it frightens me.

"If there is such a thing as real patriotism, if the American Revolution was a stand for government by the people and for the people, if the United States stands for something more than avarice and consumption, it must use its power and strength for the good of the world, the good of the land, and the good of humanity—not for wanton material gain. I want the chance to change the direction of this country. I want the chance to make America a world leader, not the world's leading consumer."

There was some light applause from the audience.

"To make that change, we'll need the kind of unity and strength of conviction that we have just witnessed from the farmers of this nation. Some might say that the farm movement was but a glimmer of what it will take to right the listing ship of this democracy. But it was a start—and to keep that momentum rolling, I've decided upon a new running mate for the upcoming election. And the man I have chosen was a big part of that courageous farm movement."

James Kenaghy turned to Nathaniel Cromwell. His presence there could not have been more pronounced if he'd been George Washington in a powdered wig. Ever the politician, Kenaghy clung to the moment. "The man I'm going to introduce is arguably the greatest American of our time. A man who has shown valor on the field of battle, winning our nation's highest medal for bravery in combat. Then in the face of utter ignominy, he returned that medal to speak out against American military compliance in drug trafficking. When shunned as a turncoat for this selfless moral stand, he withdrew from the public eye to enter into the life of a humble farmer." Cromwell bowed his head lower and lower with accolade. "Only to rise again in the past month to stand up against the inequities of the grain industry and to lead a valiant and important labor strike for the people who toil day to day to keep America and the world fed."

Linda sat next to Nate. She wore a flowing, full-length sage green evening dress with a gathered chiffon halter neckline. Linda was an attractive woman no matter how she dressed, but tonight she was stunning, absolutely radiant in her looks and her emotional being. She reached beneath the table and squeezed Nate's hand. He turned his head to catch her eyes, shake his head at what a knockout she was, and grimace a little embarrassed grin at the words spoken on his behalf.

Kenaghy theatrically pulled a little red, white, and blue campaign button from his jacket pocket. He held it up to the audience and ran his finger beneath the inscription—KENAGHY/CROMWELL. A twenty-foot banner reading the same dropped down behind him. "Meet my new running mate," he called out. "Colonel…Nathaniel…Cromwell."

The audience stood as one and erupted with thunderous applause.

Staring at the campaign dinner announcement underlined in red, Will again punches 9-1-1 into his phone. When the same woman's voice comes on the phone, he immediately blurts out, "I think there's going to be an attempt on the President's life tonight at the Sheraton!"

"Who is this?"

"Will Cromwell. I called a minute ago about the dead body at 2420 Lancaster Court." He walks toward the front of the house as he talks. "There is evidence here to suggest an assassination attempt tonight."

"What kind of evidence?" comes back suspiciously.

"I trailed a young militia member here from Oklahoma," he begins, realizing as he speaks how ridiculous he sounds, then notices through the living room window that a black sedan is pulling up out front. "Never mind," he says to the woman. "The patrol car is here."

At the same time, not ten miles away in Langley, Virginia, Bob Richards is entering his office at CIA headquarters. During the drive from his home, a horrible fear has been rattling around in his brain. He goes directly to his computer and begins punching in access codes. The Terrorist Finance Department entry page appears on his computer screen. He types in the password.

With the beckoning of the President, Nate stood from his seat. Amid increasing applause and cheers, Kenaghy ceremoniously pinned the little campaign button on Nate's lapel. Then he took Nate's right hand in his left and lifted their hands high in the air—to yet another burst of applause and scattered shouts of approval.

Gradually the applause diminished, and the President stepped aside, leaving the farmer/soldier alone in front of the microphone. The ballroom became absolutely quiet.

Nate looked over the black-tie crowd. "I hate to say this," he began, putting a finger in his collar and giving it a tug, "but I feel about as comfortable up here in front of this microphone as I do in this monkey suit." There was scattered laughter.

"But before I forget," he said, giving a little glance to Forest on his left. "I want to make sure everyone knows, that though I did play a part in the Nonpartisan Farmers' Alliance, the real credit for organizing the union and running the strike goes to the National Grange President Forest Mahan." He extended his hand toward Forest. Forest stood up briefly and quickly sat down to polite applause.

"Now politics isn't my strong suit," began Nate again, "especially talking at one of these fancy-dan, campaign fundraisers. But there are a couple of things I would like to say while I've got the chance." He looked to his right at the President. "First, I am honored to be chosen as President James Kenaghy's running mate. My experiences as a military officer and as a farmer very much verify the political, economic, and environmental concerns he has just addressed.

"Second," he continued, "it's obvious, as I look at you, that this audience is not exactly a blue collar gathering. And I imagine that when we farmers started burning our fields, it was a terribly unsettling sight for all of you. But it's important to understand that what happened these past few weeks in the farming community would have been a lot more disturbing if it had been an all-encompassing labor strike. The farmers are not the only group in the workforce with grievances, and for you who are more fortunate, it's absolutely essential to understand this and to back legislation for the working class people of this country, because for quite a while they have been forgotten—and without them, this nation is nothing.

"That said, I should add that I have never been a politician, and the campaign trail will be unfamiliar to me. When I speak, I will always state my beliefs with candor. There might even be times when I fall out of step with the President. This is not a warning nor a threat, just a fact of who I am.

"Fortunately," he smiled openly, "for all of you who are ready to go home, I'm more a man of duty than words. And I've said all I feel compelled to say tonight. So, in closing, I would like to thank the President again." He turned for a second time and acknowledged Kenaghy. "He has displayed tremendous courage in putting together a settlement for our farmers' strike and calling for critical changes in the way this country operates. Thank you for being here tonight and thank you for supporting our cause."

Cromwell looked around awkwardly then returned to his seat. At which point, the entire crowd stood up to applaud. Linda leaned over and wrapped her arms around his neck and kissed him. Kenaghy stood up and, stepping over to Nate, took his hand and lifted it again, pulling him up out of his seat, as the final political gesture of the night.

Will runs out into the front yard to meet the two men in dark suits exiting from the unmarked car. He jabbers about the body upstairs and the threat to the President. One of the men takes him by the arm and forces him into the back seat of the black car with government plates. "FBI," he says, flashing open his wallet, showing his badge. The other man is already on his way into the house.

"We're wasting time," pleads Will. "The guy who owns that Nova over there is crazy. He tried to kill my father. Inside there's an article in the newspaper. It's marked in red!"

"Please, son, settle down."

"No. Call the Sheraton now. Alert them! Even if I'm wrong, it's better to alert them than not!"

The other FBI agent comes running out of the house and back to the car. "There's a body in there alright, Dennis. What's with this guy?"

"Listen to me!" screams Will at the second man. "There's going to be an attempt on the President's life. Forget all this stuff here. Call the Sheraton."

The man inside the car grabs Will by the shoulders and throws him back against the car seat. "Settle down, asshole! For all we know, you killed that man in there!"

Bob Richards is suddenly feeling very sick. Before him on the screen is the list of bank account numbers that had been received from an undercover agent in Singapore a week earlier. They are listed as accounts belonging to the Teochui Kongsi and were frozen by the Justice Department on the CIA's request Friday afternoon. Richards had been informed of this action. He had been extremely pleased that it was happening and had assumed—how he hated that word now—that this was the first step in facilitating one money laundering operation and stopping another. Unfortunately, as he looks down the list of numbers, he understands someone has thrown them a big roundhouse curve.

Richards pulls a slip of paper from his jogging pants pocket. It's a list of the private numbered accounts that he created for transferring stock market sales proceeds to his connection in Kazakhstan—that is, Nursultan Mendelev. All of those account numbers are listed on the Teochui list and more. "Fuck," mutters Richards. "Those goddamn chinks." Now it's him slamming his fist on the desk. "I won't be able to unfreeze these accounts until this whole thing goes through the oversight review board."

CHAPTER 116

As the campaign event draws to a close, many of those in attendance come forward for hand shaking and congratulations. But very soon, it's time for the President to be escorted out of the building. The security team has already organized a plan to whisk Kenaghy and his party, including Forest Mahan, Nathaniel Cromwell, and Linda Bennett, through the service doors, into the kitchen, and out the back exit to an awaiting caravan of limos. Standard security procedure.

Six secret service men encircle Kenaghy and his wife and move as a phalanx across the ballroom. Nate, Forest, and Linda follow just behind with Jerry Rust bringing up the rear. The two lead agents push open the kitchen's double doors and survey the interior. Five kitchen help in white shirts and dirty aprons drop back against the ovens on the far wall, and the group of twelve is escorted into the kitchen.

As the doors close behind Rust and the whole group is in the kitchen, Nate's eyes fasten on a ballpoint-pen-blue swastika tattooed on the inside forearm of one of the kitchen workers. The forearm moves forward extending a small caliber pistol as the worker rushes at Kenaghy. Nate and Rust simultaneously dive into action. Nate reaches out with his left hand to strike at the firearm. Jerry draws his pistol and pushes the President out of the line of fire. Gun shots ring out—one—Nate's hand hits the barrel of the pistol—two, three, four—as he slams into the kitchen worker with his body. One of the secret service men staggers backwards into a sink of dirty dishes, clutching his face with hands full of blood. A gun skitters across the linoleum as Rust pushes Kenaghy to the floor. Blood begins to puddle beside the President's head. Marjorie drops down next to her husband, then looking up from her knees, screams, "My husband's been shot. Help! Anyone! Please!"

"The President's down," calls out Rust as he climbs to his feet.

Two agents gather protectively around Kenaghy and Marjorie while Nate pins the assassin to the floor. Two agents come to his aid and yank John Finnegan to his feet and throw him—spitting curses at the President and the government—up against the freezer doors. Nate struggles to his knees. He looks around until his eyes meet Linda's. Blood burps from his mouth, and he tumbles sideways to the floor. Linda takes one step toward him and trips over her dress.

People rush around hysterically, amid screams, squawking radios, and sounding alarms. Absolute chaos surrounds Linda as she crawls in a heap of sage chiffon through the mayhem across the floor to Nate. A secret service agent leaps over her. Another steps on her hand. When she reaches Nate, she sees two visible wounds, one in his palm, one in his forearm. She lifts him into her lap and notices blood staining his shirt below his rib cage. His eyes open momentarily. "Is the President all right?" Another pulse of blood burps from his mouth and his eyes close.

Crying and fighting her emotions, Linda feels for his pulse. It's strong. "Get an ambulance!" She shouts it out amid the frenzy—then again. "Get an ambulance now!"

Will sits handcuffed in the backseat of the black sedan when the two-way radio blurts out, "Alert. All agents. President Kenaghy's been shot. Repeat. The President's been shot." FBI agent Dennis Williams turns around from the front seat and stares at Will. "Doesn't look good for you, son," he says. Will drops his head into his shackled hands as a police patrol car arrives on the scene.

Richards listens to the phone ring twelve thousand miles away. He is not looking forward to this conversation. Nita Panfilov answers the phone. She transfers it to President Mendelev's office.

"Richards. Tell me you have solved my problem."

"President Mendelev, there's been a little mistake."

"But it's fixed now!"

Richards explains what happened. The rival drug cartel's involvement infuriates Mendelev. "And worst of all," says Richards, "the Justice Department is involved. It could be months before we can go through the paperwork to unfreeze your money."

There is silence so loud at the other end of the phone that Richards can hear the gears turning in Mendelev's head. Richards dares to interrupt. "I believe the Teochui consider this a very funny joke."

More loud silence.

"Perhaps we can turn this joke around on them, President Mendelev."

"No, Mr. Richards, you Amerikans have no real sense of humor. Leave the last laugh to me," says Mendelev finally, humorlessly. "I think my friend Zhao He should receive my personal compliments for the cleverness of his wit. You know the saying, what goes around comes around?"

"No. Don't do anything, President Mendelev. It's better if you leave this to me. It could make things worse on my end. This is strictly CIA business."

Mendelev looks at the phone with an evil smile and places it back in its cradle. "No," he says to himself, "this is strictly my business."

Linda rides in the ambulance with Nate on the way across town to the Walter Reed Medical Center in Bethesda, Maryland. A paramedic kneels on one side of Nate's stretcher, attending to the two bullet wounds in his left arm. Linda is across from him, holding Nate's right hand in both of hers. A second ambulance is many blocks ahead of them with the President.

Nate passes in and out of consciousness several times during the trip. On one occasion, his eyes flash to the paramedic then to Linda. Despite Linda's protest, he tries to talk. "I don't get it," he says with great difficulty. "I don't get it."

"Shsssh," Linda hushes. It's not really clear how badly he is injured. At least one bullet shard has pierced his torso. "No need to talk now, Nate. Save your strength."

"It was Jerry. Did you see that?" continues Nate, clearly troubled by something he's seen.

"Jerry's fine, Nate. Don't worry. Not a scratch. Shsssh." She puts a finger to his lips for silence.

"No, no, that's not what I mean," pushes Nate, a little drool of blood runs from the side of his mouth.

As the paramedic wipes the blood away, he shakes his head. "We need to get there soon. His lung may have been punctured."

Nate watches the exchange then mutters, "Jerry shot him."

Linda shakes her head no. "Don't talk."

"Jerry shot Kenaghy," he says. "I saw it."

"No, no, it was a kitchen worker, Nate." New streams of tears run down her cheeks every time he tries to talk.

"I saw Jerry put his gun up to Kenaghy's neck as he pushed him out of the way. I don't get it."

Linda looks for help from the paramedic. He shrugs his shoulders. Nate burps up more blood. She squeezes her eyes shut as the paramedic wipes it away.

"I've had this funny feeling about Jerry the last few days—that he revealed your identity to Hayes before he told me was the giveaway," continues Nate, against all Linda's pleading. "From that point on, I didn't confide in him again."

"Stop, Nate. Stop. You don't have the strength."

"That young man Finnegan was a decoy. I know it."

They pull into the emergency entrance at Walter Reed. Nate's stretcher is taken from the ambulance, placed on a hospital gurney, and whisked into the building. Linda follows him all the way to the emergency room doors. She has one last moment with him.

Nate's eyes are closed. She can't tell if he's still conscious. Fighting her worst fears, she strokes Nate's forehead and whispers, "Please, Nate, don't die. Don't die." As she says these words, every day she's ever known pours in upon this moment.

Nate's eyes flutter open. Linda tries to smile through wet eyes. Nate looks up at her and smiles. "What'd I say?" he says as though he's read her mind. "By the end of the week, it'll seem like we've known each other our entire lives."

Linda can't tell if he's trying to be funny or if he's sensing how critical his condition is. "I love you, Nate," she whispers as a surgery nurse arrives and pushes his gurney into the emergency room.

CHAPTER 117

John McClay got the news right away. The President had been hit by two bullets. One in the thigh and one in the neck below the left ear. The one in the thigh shattered his tibia. The other was lodged in the left hemisphere of his brain. He was in the operating room at Walter Reed Medical Center now, having the bullet removed. His condition was critical, but it was a miracle he wasn't already dead. Incredibly, the surgeons were optimistic about keeping him alive if there were no further complications.

For all his difficulties with Kenaghy, McClay took it hard. The idea of a President being shot rang of anarchy. To him, it was the worst of all worlds. He called Frank Nelson immediately. Frank was a little more stoic than the shaken McClay.

"Did they get the assassin?" asked Frank.

"Yes, he's in the custody of the FBI," said McClay, a slight tremor in his voice.

"Any profile?"

"Seems to be a disgruntled militia type. Shaved head. White supremacist tattoos. Admits doing it. Was ranting against the government. Clearly emotionally disturbed," sighed McClay.

"And you say Colonel Cromwell was also shot?" It was ugly enough to Frank, but it was good news from where he sat.

"They say he saw the assassin coming at the President and tried to stop him. Apparently, he's in worse shape than the President."

"Think Kenaghy will be able to run for office?"

McClay didn't like the question and hung up.

Atossa got the news from Frank right after he'd spoken to McClay. She'd been in an awful mood since Davis left and accepted the call from Frank with the greatest reluctance. "Serves them both right," she snapped. "Let me know if there's a death. Good-bye." She couldn't have cared less one way or another about Cromwell or Kenaghy. All her thoughts were focused on Derek Davis—spiraling in on the look he'd given her their last moment in bed together.

CHAPTER 118

Linda paced outside the operating room while two Army surgeons worked on Nate. After an hour, she got word from a nurse that the bullet that hit his forearm had broken into as many as eight pieces and entered his torso. Two pieces punctured his left lung. One piece nicked his heart. One piece grazed his kidney on its way out below his ribs. But the organs were not the problem. The surgical team was in a frantic battle to stop the internal bleeding that was everywhere. Nate's life hung in the balance.

In a state hovering between nausea and nervous breakdown, Linda alternately paced and sat in the waiting room through the night, never once thinking of sleep. Shortly after sunrise, fighting for something to hold on to, she called *The Times* and cried on the phone to Frederick Manning. She tried to explain what happened and describe Nate's medical state, but she couldn't get through it without breaking down. After her initial gush of emotion had subsided, Manning told her the FBI had called looking for her. They were holding a young man who claimed to be Nathaniel Cromwell's son.

This pulled Linda from her trauma. "Will's supposed to be in Milwaukee."

"If the young man is who he says he is," replied Manning. "He's in D.C."

Linda quickly called the number the FBI had left with Manning. It took a few minutes before she was connected to the agent in charge. The agent described Will to a tee, and she verified that he was Cromwell's son. She asked the agent to put Will in a taxi and send him immediately to Walter Reed Medical Center. But the agent would not release Will without her identifying him in person. Impossibly she contained her anger. Absolutely exhausted, a disheveled wreck of wrinkled and blood-stained chiffon, she caught a taxi and sped across town to the FBI building.

After identifying Will through a one-way mirror, answering several questions, and finally signing him into her custody, Linda was led to the lobby to wait for his release. Several minutes later, Will entered the lobby flanked by two FBI agents, looking tired and confused. The sleeves were ripped off his t-shirt, and there was a streaked and faded swastika drawn on the back of his hand. Linda ignored what she didn't understand and ran across the lobby, pulling Will into her arms, tears streaming down her face.

Will's first words said it all. "Where's my father?"

Linda gathered herself as much as she could, glared at the FBI agents, and led Will outside.

"Something's happened," Will said, looking into Linda's wrung out eyes.

She took a deep breath and wiped the tears from her face. "Your dad's in the hospital, Will. He was struck by a bullet trying to protect the President."

Will paled. "How bad?"

"Very bad. He's in surgery right now." She heaved involuntarily. "Fighting for his life."

Will froze up. Linda hugged him, but he was stiff and distant. "He'll be all right," she said. "He has to be."

Linda waved down a taxi and prodded Will into the back seat. He sat motionless beside her all the way to Bethesda. As distraught as she was, having someone to care for helped. Twenty minutes later, they were in the hospital waiting room. The head surgeon found them very soon after that.

"We've done all we can for now," said the doctor after Linda introduced Will. "He's in a coma." He looked at Linda. Will was staring at the floor. "The odds are long."

The surgeon took them to the Intensive Care Unit to see him. Nate's face was as white as the bed sheets. Tubes and wires ran from his arms and chest. His deep inner strength had been reduced to a weak trail of electronic blips on a monitor and critically low blood pressure readings. Linda gazed into Nate's motionless face as long as she could bear, then watched Will staring at his father. She maintained only by reminding herself it was harder on him than it was on her.

On exiting ICU, Will burst into tears. Linda held him and stared at the floor in shared grief.

At the doctor's suggestion, Linda took Will back to her apartment. She put him to bed and dragged herself into the bathroom. She stripped off her ruined evening dress like a horrible memory and climbed into the shower. After a minute, she simply sank down and sat in the stream of hot water, agonizing.

Linda eventually crawled out of the shower and put on a robe. She dropped down on the couch and stared into space for nearly a quarter of an hour. The sound of the mail being delivered broke the spell. She retrieved it in a daze and absently dropped it in a heap on the dining room table. She was about to turn away when she noticed a real letter mixed in among the pile of catalogues and junk mail. She picked up the letter and opened it robotically. It was a hand-written, half-page:

> *Linda,*
>
> *Guess I really screwed up. They discovered I hacked into your father's email. I'm not sure where this puts me, but nowhere good. I've also uncovered something you need to know and might not get the chance to communicate to you except in this letter. Cromwell's friend Jerry Rust is working for Richards. Be very careful!*
>
> *Catch you when I can.*
>
> *Charlie.*

Linda looked at the postmark. The way her hand shook she could barely read it. It was dated the day before Charlie's death—that this letter suggested wasn't a suicide. She dropped the letter on the table and began to pace around the apartment. With growing anger, she tried to reconstruct the events that led to the bloodshed in the Sheraton kitchen. Her thoughts raced back to the meeting with Kenaghy, back through the things she'd uncovered reading her father's email, her interactions with Bob Richards, the words Nate had spoken in the ambulance about Jerry Rust, and finally Charlie's death and this letter. Everything seemed to spin around Bob Richards. Resolving into a single, crushing and infuriating deduction: *Richards had her father murdered.*

Linda stood in the kitchen, lost to thought, staring at the floor, when the phone rang. She caught it after two rings, hoping it wouldn't wake Will. She recognized the doctor's voice immediately. His tone revealed the message before he said the words. Something broke inside her. She mumbled a few words of disconsolate thanks to the doctor, said she was coming to the hospital, and hung up.

Linda crossed the apartment to the bedroom and peeked in the door. Will was sound asleep. She wasn't sure if she should wake him. She lingered in the doorway, gazing at his face, thinking how much he looked like Nate and how tough this was going to be on him —until the flow of tears turned to sobs and she had to close the door. She returned to the kitchen to gather herself. Her insides felt fragile and shattered. Every thought hurt like broken glass. Every thought brought back images of Nate and the entire course of their eight-day romance.

In a numb trance, Linda slipped into the bedroom, took another long sad look at Nate's sleeping son, and selected a short-sleeved, navy-blue dress from her closet. She put on the dress in the living room, wrote a short note to Will, slipped on some sandals without socks or pantyhose, and headed for the hospital.

Linda remembered nothing of the drive. All of a sudden, she heard herself asking a hospital receptionist where she might view the body of Nathaniel Cromwell. She didn't recognize the sound of her own voice. It all seemed part of some bad and distant dream.

His body had been moved out of ICU to a room on the third floor. When she exited from the elevator, Jerry Rust was sitting in a chair outside Nate's room. Her heart immediately began to race. Her first inclination was to get right back in the elevator, but Rust saw her and stood. For a moment, they faced each other at fifteen feet. Linda fought to compose herself. Rust spoke first.

"*Ms. Rivenhouse*," he said, "some pretty tough news."

She nodded and tried to pretend she didn't know what she knew. She advanced to Jerry and hugged him like she really meant it. She began to cry and shake from grief and absolute fear of this man. Jerry held her until she gradually backed away.

"Do you want me to go in with you?" he asked.

Linda took a deep breath. "No, no…I'll be okay."

Rust opened the door and Linda entered. She heard the door clasp behind her. The lights were out in the room. Daylight filtered in through the curtains just as it had that afternoon at the Holiday Inn. There were two beds. Only one was occupied. The sheets were drawn up over the body. She approached the bed with hesitance.

Linda stood beside the bed a long time looking down at Nate's shroud, holding the reality at arm's length. She reached out and drew back the white sheet. There were no injuries to Nate's face. He looked calm and peaceful. But hopelessly lifeless. She stared at him so long she thought she saw his lips move. She gasped momentarily, refocused her eyes, then the tears began to splash on his face and the shroud. She closed her eyes and backed away.

After a moment, Linda approached the body again and took one last look at his face. It seemed impossible she'd only known him a week. She touched his cheek and stroked his hair, then leaned over and laid her head on his chest, holding on to him. At last, she kissed him on the forehead and covered his face.

Jerry Rust had slipped from her mind until she exited the room. He stood in front of her as she walked out.

"He was the best soldier I've ever known," said Jerry.

Linda only nodded and looked at the floor. Jerry reached out to hug her again. She involuntarily recoiled with the real revulsion she felt for him. When their eyes met, all that they really thought of each other screamed back and forth between them.

"You know you were as much a part of his death as anyone," said Rust bitterly.

He might as well have punched Linda in the stomach. "You were his fucking body guard," she spat back at him reflexively. He slapped her hard across the face, and she fell against the wall next to the elevator. She reached for the down button but didn't wait and ran to the stairwell, then dashed down the stairs as fast as she could. She didn't slow down until she'd reached her car. She unlocked the door, climbed in, and hurriedly tried to start the car. She cranked it one, two, three times. It wouldn't turn over. She looked over her shoulder across the parking lot, certain she would see Jerry coming after her. But there was no one.

Her heart banging, she tried the car again. It started. She put the car into reverse and stalled it backing up. She started it again with another look over her shoulder. Then she pulled out onto the street, wheeling into an immediate right, driving five blocks before stopping at a traffic light. Again, she looked over her shoulder. *No sign of Jerry.*

As Linda tried to gather herself, the sight of Nate's corpse returned with layers and layers of sadness and pain. But welling up beneath her grief was a vicious anger, stinging like Jerry's handprint still red on her cheek. It wasn't Jerry where the anger focused, however, it was Bob Richards. She could see him sitting smugly at his desk right now. The big operator, wheeling and dealing with the lives of people she had known and loved. Fuck him, she thought. Fuck him.

A car behind her honked. The light was green. Linda pulled into a parking place. She retrieved her cell phone from her purse and rang the switchboard at CIA headquarters in Langley. When a voice answered, she asked for Rita Thayer. A moment later, Rita came on the line.

"This is Thayer." Rita had worked many years in the same division with Linda's father. She was the highest ranking woman in the Agency.

"Rita, Linda Bennett."

"Are you all right, Linda? I heard you were there at the Sheraton last night."

Linda saw the whole thing again in the cinema of her mind. She felt more tears coming. "Yes, I'm fine," she choked out, then steadied herself. "I have a request for you. I want you to run a check on a name for me."

"Is this related to last night?"

"Not really," she lied. "Check the name, Jerry Rust, retired Army. I'm on my way to Langley now. We can talk about the results of your research when I get there. I don't mean to be so pushy, but it's urgent."

"Well, sure. I'm a little busy, but I can do that for you. I'll send your name out to the gate."

"Thanks. I'll be there within the hour."

CHAPTER 119

Atossa sat alone at her divining table, kneading the air with her left hand. She had not left her bedroom nor eaten since the incident with Derek Davis. She hadn't spoken on the phone to anyone since her brother-in-law Frank called Sunday night to tell her about the assassination attempt. She had Nancy Waters put in a call to Dr. Colleen early that morning, but as yet the doctor had not called back. Her face, without the streaked makeup from the day before, looked perfect on one side and absolutely horrid on the other. Her state of mind mirrored the shattered looking glass across the room and the shredded deck of Tarot cards scattered on the floor.

There was a light knock on her bedroom door. Atossa ignored it. When the knock sounded again, she said, "Please go away," with the voice of a broken and lost individual.

"Mother, please, it's me." Nancy Waters had called Alise and told her she was extremely worried about her mother. Alise had driven from Boston immediately.

On hearing her daughter's voice, Atossa underwent an initial surge of elation, followed by a chasm of uncertainty. It had been three weeks since they had spoken.

"Mother, may I come in?"

When there was no answer, Alise tried the door. To her surprise, it was unlocked. She pushed the door open slowly and entered the room. The curtains were pulled over the windows, and the only light in the room shone through the skylight as a bright rectangular solid in the center of the otherwise shadowy chamber. Alise saw the broken mirror and the torn Tarot cards, but no sign of her mother.

"Mother?" said Alise softly, scanning the room.

Still there was no answer. Then Alise saw her. Or just her bare feet, peeking out at the bottom of the curtains on the far side of the room.

With a heavy heart, Alise crossed the room to the place in the curtains where Atossa hid. She stood before the bump in the curtains and heard her mother quietly sobbing. "It's all right, Mother," said Alise gently. "I love you." She slowly pulled aside the thick wall drapes. Atossa stood with her back pressed against the wall and her hands covering her face. Alise reached out and took her mother in her arms, drawing her away from the wall.

Alise walked her mother, still covering her face, over to the bed and helped her in. Alise gently lifted her mother's hands away from her face and pulled the covers up to her shoulders.

Even in the dim light, Alise could see how bad her mother looked and the depth of fear in her eyes. Alise leaned over and kissed Atossa on the forehead. "It's okay, Mother. I'm here."

CHAPTER 120

It took Linda thirty-five minutes to drive to CIA headquarters in Langley. She was waved through the gate with a flash of her ID. She parked in the visitor's section and crossed the lot to the huge intelligence complex. Rita Thayer was waiting for her at the security check.

Rita watched Linda pass through the metal detectors then led her through a maze of long corridors to her office. Linda entered the office first. Rita followed, shutting the door behind her.

Rita gave her a hug. "I guess you heard about Charlie?"

"Yes." Linda hovered on the edge of emotional breakdown. Her hair was still damp from the shower and hung in matted strands around her face.

"We've begun an in-house investigation," said Rita taking the chair at her desk.

Unsure if Rita was referring to the suicide or Charlie's hacking job, Linda merely nodded and took the chair beside Rita's desk. "Get a chance to check that name?"

"I did," said Rita cautiously, drawing a piece of paper from a file beside her desk.

"All I know is the guy was Special Forces—maybe fifteen years back."

"What's this for, Linda?"

Linda felt reluctance. "Research."

Rita took a breath. "What's your clearance?"

Linda opened her purse and got out her wallet. She pulled a card from the wallet and handed it to Rita.

Rita looked at the card and handed it back. "You don't rate on this stuff, Linda."

On the verge of falling completely apart, swirling with memories of her last moments with Nate, Linda nodded calmly. "What about just leaving that piece paper on your desk and taking a walk to the ladies' room?"

Rita drummed her fingers on the desk. "I can't do that," she said, laying the single sheet of paper on the desk.

"Sorry, I asked."

Rita got up and left the office, closing the door behind her. Linda stood and went around to the other side of the desk. She quickly read the full-page of single-spaced print. Jerry Rust was a CIA operative and had been since the year he got out of the Army. He had worked in close contact with Hamilton Heavy Construction, a CIA proprietary, and earlier this year had been transferred to Kazakhstan from Colombia, then in the last month was brought back to the United States *to work under the direction of Bob Richards.*

Linda digested this with substantiated rage. She looked around the office then opened the bottom drawer of Rita's desk. Beneath two file folders was the same CIA issue, pancake twenty-two and holster she'd borrowed a month ago from Rita. She took them both from the drawer, checked to see if the gun was loaded, and hurriedly strapped the holster and gun to her thigh. She returned to the other side of the desk seconds before Rita came in.

Rita took the seat behind her desk. "Sorry, I couldn't help you, Linda," she said, taking the piece of paper from her desk and running it through the shredder to her left.

Linda nodded, shaking with anxiety.

"I'll need to escort you out," said Rita. "Are you all right?"

"Yes," she said against the obvious. "After last night, I'm a little edgy. Let me use the restroom before we go. It feels like someone's playing football in my intestines."

"I'll wait here," said Rita with a soft smile.

Linda exited Rita's office and walked down the corridor past the women's restroom. She took a left and continued down another long corridor to Bob Richards' office. The door was open, and she walked in. Richards looked up as Linda closed the door.

"My, Linda Bennett, what a pleasant surprise," said Richards with a cautious smile. "What can I do for you?"

Linda took two steps toward Richards' desk without answering his question. Her whole body quivered from lack of sleep and emotional strain. She could see Richards reading her unsteady body language.

"Ugly scene last night," he said, trying to gather an angle on her.

She nodded.

"Are you all right, Linda?" For the first time there was sincerity in his voice.

"I'm fine, Bob. I've got a couple of questions I'd like you to answer."

"Really?" he said, still appraising her.

"Does the name Jerry Rust mean anything to you?"

"No."

"You didn't put him onto Nathaniel Cromwell?"

Richards laughed. "What are you talking about?"

Linda stared into his lying eyes, thinking about the holster strapped to her thigh. "Was Jerry Rust working for you?"

"I don't even know who Jerry Rust is."

"Bullshit. I've seen his file."

Richards shook his head, as though he cared. "Someone might be in trouble for that."

Linda lifted the volume and intensity of her voice. "What was Jerry Rust doing for you?"

"Have I ever told you how sexy you are when you're angry?"

God! Is he actually taunting me? "What was Rust doing?"

Richards sat back in his chair and grinned. "If you must know, he was protecting you."

Linda took a deep breath, trying to hold on. "Bullshit."

"FBI was after Cromwell. Houseman set up the firebombing of his farm house. He was trying to incite things. You were in danger."

"Then why did Rust shoot Kenaghy?"

This caught Richards off guard, but he smiled, shining with evil. "Once your boy accepted the VP position—all bets were off."

Linda visualized shooting Richards right then and there. "Who killed Charlie Patio?"

"Suicide usually means self-inflicted, Linda."

"Who killed Charlie?"

"Whoever requested your father's email file," sneered Richards, finally getting fed up with the inquisition.

Linda just stared at him, imagining him dead.

"Get out of here, Linda. I'm sick of these accusations."

She continued to stare at him. Her eyes wide and crazy.

Richards shifted uneasily in his chair. "Get out of my office now."

"It's about time I gave you what you've been begging for all along." She sort of smiled.

"What's that, your pussy?"

"How'd you guess?" She lifted her dress up to her navel. Bob's mouth fell open. She wore nothing beneath but the holster and the twenty-two. She drew the pistol as Bob rose to his feet. She leveled it at him.

"Put that damn thing away," he demanded.

"SIT DOWN," she commanded at twice the volume.

"You're out of your mind," said Richards falling back into his chair.

"No, you are."

"Put the gun down. I'm tired of this journalist-gone-loco shit."

"What about my father? It wasn't a heart attack, was it?"

Richards reached for the security alarm on the side of his desk. Linda knew exactly what he was doing. At the moment the alarm went off, she extended the gun and shot him in the temple.

"Go to hell, bastard," she muttered, as he fell from his chair to the floor. She wiped the gun off with the hem of her dress. Then, using the dress to hold the gun, placed the twenty-two in Richards' hand. She took a quick look around and walked out of the office. The alarm was still ringing. Several security guards ran past as she strode the other way down the corridor with tears streaming from her eyes.

All exits from the building went into lockdown when Richards triggered the alarm. Because of her father, some of the guards had known her twenty years or more. Rather than being stopped, even visibly shaking, she was hurried through the check points for her safety. She walked out of the building to the parking lot and her car. She started the car with shaking hands. She motored up to the security gate and pulled to a stop. She'd been waved through by this guard a hundred times before. He stepped out of the guard booth and came up to her car window.

"Sorry to stop you, Linda," said the man. "But I never got a chance to tell you how sorry I was to hear about your father's death. He was one of the nicest men here."

"I appreciate your saying that." Linda smiled and lowered her eyes. The guard waved her through.

CHAPTER 121

Linda Bennett drove directly from Langley to her apartment in Georgetown as though blind. She was so frazzled and anxiety stricken, she hardly knew what she was doing. All she could focus on was concern for Will. Above and beyond anything else, her safety, her being pursued by the police, she owed it to Nate to be the one who told Will the bad news. Then she needed to get him home to his mother.

Will was still in bed when Linda entered the apartment, but he was awake and heard her come in. He called out to her, and she went into the bedroom. Will was sitting up. She took a seat at the end of the bed, trying to be calm, though still lit up like a security alarm from her encounter with Richards. It was immediately clear to Will that something was wrong. He couldn't ask the obvious question because he already knew the answer. His eyes darted around, looking momentarily at Linda, then away again. She couldn't say it. All of a sudden, the tears began spilling from her eyes, and she reached out to Will and took him in her arms.

"He's dead isn't he," muttered Will over her shoulder, holding on to her for dear life.

"Yes."

They held each other for several minutes. Linda might actually have needed it more than Will. She had just killed a man in cold blood and was in a state verging on shock. When the embrace ended, they sat on the bed facing each other.

"He was a great man, Will," she said from the eye of quiet within her hysteria.

Will took a breath and heaved. "He wanted to pull out of the strike after Grandmother died. I wouldn't let him."

Linda nodded. "I pushed him into running with Kenaghy. If we'd just skipped the Vice President thing…" her words trailed off into a sigh.

"How is President Kenaghy?" asked Will. "Does this ruin any chance of fulfilling the strike demands?"

Linda's head swam with images of the last twenty-four hours. "The President had brain surgery last night. He's in stable condition but the long range prognosis is unknown. All the farmers' hopes ride with him."

Will stared straight down.

Linda gave him a few moments then stood. "Maybe you should get up, Will. How does a cup of tea sound?"

He looked up sadly. "It sounds good."

Will took a shower and put on his same dirty clothes. He stumbled out of the bathroom, looking at his feet. Linda was sitting on the sofa with a cup of tea. Another cup was on the coffee table for Will.

Will sat down in the chair that matched the sofa and took a sip of tea.

After a long period of silence, Linda spoke. "You need to talk to your mother, Will. You can use my phone to call her. We could get you on a plane to Milwaukee this evening."

"What are you going to do?"

She swallowed uneasily. "I need to get out of town. I think I'm going to take a long drive to nowhere." *If the police don't show up first,* she finished to herself, very much at a loss about everything, absolutely everything.

"Can I go with you?"

The obvious answer was no, but Linda realized right away that being with Will helped her. And as crazy as it seemed to her in retrospect, the answer she gave made perfect sense at the time. "How about if I drive you to Milwaukee?"

"I would like that. I need some time before I see my mother. I need to think some things out."

"Then let's get going. I can't stay here any longer."

Fifteen minutes later, they walked out of the apartment and down to the garage. Linda drove north to the Pennsylvania Turnpike and aimed west to Interstate 70. The first hour of the drive was funeral quiet. Then they slowly started to talk. About anything and everything. It was good, a bit sad at times, but they were coping with the very worst of outcomes. Late that night, then on Interstate 80, they stopped at a motel in Des Moines. Will slept. Linda tossed and turned all night.

They got up early the next morning, had breakfast, and got back on Interstate 80 headed for Wisconsin. Barely ten minutes into the drive, Will, who had been looking at the map, made a request. "Linda, up here at the next exit, would you mind if we took Highway 35 south?"

Linda barely diverted her eyes from the road. "But that won't get us to Milwaukee?"

"I don't want to go to Milwaukee." He had called his mother the day before. She was expecting him to arrive that night. "I've changed my mind about some things."

She turned to look at him. "Yeah?"

"I thought about this all through the drive yesterday and in bed last night. I want to be a farmer."

"What about Stanford, Will? That's such a great opportunity."

Will looked out the window and spoke to the passing roadside. "Mr. Peabody has all our farm equipment stored at his place. I want to continue what my father and grandfather started in Kansas. I want to fix up the farm. Maybe give no-till a try." He turned back to Linda. "The burning of the fields might even be good for the soil." His eyes lit briefly as he said it.

"No Stanford?"

Will shrugged. "If things don't work out, I'm sure I can get into another college." He paused. "It's just that right now, I think I need the kind of work that goes with farming—not books."

Linda knew exactly what he meant. "But you have to let your mother know."

Will nodded. "Yeah, I know."

They drove down the driveway to Peabody's farm late Tuesday evening. It was a bittersweet return. There was a big meal and subdued talk. Linda stayed the night and got up bright and early to have breakfast with James Peabody. Will joined them midway through the meal. They talked about having Nate's body brought back to the farm. As the man who saved the President's life, there would be plans for a big funeral in Washington, D.C. and a burial in Arlington Cemetery. Will didn't think his father would have wanted all the attention. James and Linda agreed. As the closest relative, Will called Walter Reed Hospital after breakfast. Four calls later he had arranged for Forest Mahan to fly the body back to Kansas.

Linda stayed at Peabody's until Mahan arrived on Saturday with the pine box. There was no announcement of the ceremony. Will prepared the pyre Saturday evening. Sunday morning there was a small gathering in the center of a hundred acres of scorched corn. Forest Mahan, James and Sue Peabody, Jenny Foster, Horace Thompson and his wife Sarah, Will, Peg the dog, and Linda stood in a circle around the pyre, blanketed by the infinite Kansas sky. There was a moment of quiet with all heads down. Such was the sadness of the moment and the profound sentiments of those present, it almost seemed a sin to break the silence out there in the open, open plain. And it hung. Until James Peabody, speaking very quietly, said a few lines.

"We would waste our words trying to describe the man we say good-bye to today. He was no less than the heart and soul of this country. Let us gather strength knowing that a new farm will rise from these ashes. God bless Nathaniel Cromwell."

"Amen," said Linda with all the others. Forest put an arm around her shoulder. Will lit a torch of pitch and set the fire going. They watched for an hour without saying another word as the fire flared up then gradually diminished to a pile of smoldering embers.

EPILOGUE

After the ceremony and the little cluster of mourners had walked back to Peabody's house, Linda Bennett said a teary good-bye and got into her car headed west on Interstate 70. She never said a word to anyone about Richards. She figured the law was after her, but the authorities never came—maybe because she knew too much. In fact, there was never any effort to connect her with the death of Bob Richards. There was never any public statement about his death at all. The CIA wanted none of his story told or investigated. Richards' death was recorded as a suicide in Virginia police records.

After a few days, Linda contacted *The New York Financial Times* to say she was terminating her employment with the newspaper and was taking a leave of absence from writing her column. Six weeks later, she wrote the following letter to her friend and colleague, Frederick Manning:

> *Dear Frederick,*
>
> *Please accept my apologies for leaving without talking to you. I can only imagine what you might have inferred from my disappearance after the events of July 26*[th]*. My excuse is too long and painful to recount at this time. I hope to put the entire story together as a book under an assumed name in a year or two. My father's murder will be part of it. It will probably be considered a piece of fiction! But right now, even thinking about what happened is difficult.*
>
> *I am currently living in a cabin on the Montana-Idaho border, trying to heal myself enough to return to writing—this letter is almost more than I can do. Hopefully writing, if and when it begins, will help me take on deeper wounds. As you surely noticed when I returned from my trip to the Heartland, I had fallen for Nathaniel*

Cromwell. Impossibly this only touches the surface of my heartbreak and disarray.

Beyond my own personal anguish, the death of Nathaniel Cromwell has caused vast turmoil and distrust in the collective mind of the populace. They are sure the government was behind it. And I was there! I know that they are right!

Oh God, Frederick, it's impossible to overstate how much is riding on President Kenaghy's recovery and the outcome of the election in November. I fear the populace just doesn't know what's at stake if he doesn't win. The fires we saw in July were only a glimmer of the kind of unrest we could see ahead. If this isn't obvious in Washington already, please, please, please, do everything you can to make it so. Business as usual cannot be tolerated any longer.

Sincerely,
Linda

ACKNOWLEDGMENTS

This book was written stop and go over a period of ten years. It would not exist at all except for the love and support of my wife Judith. She more than anyone else inspired me to complete and publish this book. My thanks to her is forever.

I was also greatly aided by the feedback of a small army of volunteer readers. I thank Heidi, Chris, Monte, Kay, Tim, Ed, Kenny, Terri, Peter, Steve, David, Bob, Tom, Bill, Pat, Charles, Jim, Leah, and Lauren for taking the time to help me make this book better. My neighbor Katherine must be added to the list. She designed the perfect book cover.

The initial spark for this book came from my friend Sam when he gave me a copy of Dan Morgan's *Merchants of Grain* and demanded I read it.

The title comes from Robert L. Morlan's little known book, *Political Prairie Fire*, the story of A.C. Townley and the Nonpartisan League of North Dakota, perhaps the most successful organization of farmers in American history.

Special thanks goes to Charles E. Little whose wonderful book, *Green Fields Forever,* provided me with much needed information on conservation tillage and who took the time to correspond at length with me through email.

Lester R. Brown, President of the Worldwatch Institute for twenty-six years and founder of the Earth Policy Institute, must be credited as well. His book, *Who Will Feed China,* provided the theoretical basis for Jonathan Mayfield's grain market projections.

I should also mention Jim Hightower, the noted author, radio personality, and farmers' friend. Though I have never met him, his talk to the Oregon Chapter of the League of Women Voters in 1992 inspired the language and ideas behind the speech given by the character Forest Mahan "at the big grange hall in Pratt, Kansas."

Lastly, I owe a tremendous debt of insight and inspiration to my friend and fellow author William H. Kötke. His environmental classic, *The Final Empire,* made me realize that as humans our first concern is maintaining the garden of this planet. Without it, we have no home.

THE AUTHOR

Dan Armstrong is the editor and owner of Mud City Press, a small publishing company and online magazine operating out of Eugene, Oregon. He has written extensively in both fiction and non-fiction. Access to his books, short stories, political commentary, humor, and environmental studies is available at mudcitypress.com.

Made in the USA
Middletown, DE
19 August 2025

11679246R00319